CASSIE

THANKS TON AL[...]

DO FOR OUR IDEAL ORG[...]

$5/100

23 FEB '08

MANUELA

Gregory Kauffman

RLN & Company
Seattle

Published by RLN & Company

For information, please contact:
RLN & Company
P. O. Box 61219
Seattle, Washington 98141

www.rlnonline.com

ISBN: 0-9704250-0-7

Printed in the United States of America

Historical Personae
Names associated with the South American wars of independence.

Abascal, Don Fernando de: Thirty-eighth viceroy of Lima. In power during the revolution in Quito in 1809.

Amat, Manuel: Son of **Viceroy Amat** and Micaela Villegas (see **La Perricholi**).

Amat, Don Manuel y Juniet: Thirty-first viceroy of Lima. He loved Micaela Villegas, the woman known as **La Perricholi**.

Bolívar, Simón: (Simón José Antonio de la Santisima Trinidad Bolívar y Palacios) Military leader who liberated the countries now known as Colombia, Venezuela, Ecuador, Perú, and Bolivia. He was called **The Liberator** and considered by most to be the greatest leader in South American history.

Bonaparte, Joseph: **Napoleon**'s brother, who sat on the throne of Spain after the defeat of Madrid.

Bonaparte, Napoleon: Conqueror of Europe in the early 1800s.

Campusano, Rosita: Revolutionary leader in Lima. She was the lover of **San Martín**.

Canterac, General: Leader of the royalist forces in Perú in 1824 under Viceroy **La Serna**.

Casariego, Colonel: Spanish officer imprisoned in Callao who persuaded **Moyano** and **Oliva** to defect and turn the fortress of Callao over to the Spanish.

Charles IV: King of Spain between 1788 and 1808.

Cochrane, Lord Thomas: Admiral of the Chilean navy. Born in Britain. Attacked Spanish shipping in the Pacific, thus allowing **San Martín** to conquer Lima.

Córdoba, General José María: A brave hero of the revolution who fought under **Bolívar**. He was made general at the age of twenty-three.

Fernando VII: King of Spain after his father abdicated in his favor. Almost immediately, **Joseph Bonaparte** took the throne and held it from 1808 to 1813, delaying Fernando's rule of Spain.

Flores, General Juan José: One of **Bolívar**'s generals, who later became the first President of Ecuador.

Godoy, Manuel de: Minister of **Charles IV** who carried on an almost open affair with the queen. Hated by the Spanish subjects.

Harrison, William Henry: United States visitor to Colombia in 1830, later elected President of the United States.

Humboldt, Baron Alexander von: German scientist whose explorations of South America stimulated the study of the earth sciences.

La Mar, Mariscal José de: Peruvian leader who fought with the Colombian army for the liberation of Perú but later turned against **Bolívar**.

La Perricholi: Micaela (Miquita) Villegas. Lover of **Viceroy Amat** who captured the hearts of the citizens of Lima. Her life epitomized life under the rule of the viceroys. She died just prior to the end of the viceregal era.

Lara, General Jacinto: One of **Bolívar**'s most important generals.

La Serna, Viceroy: The man who forced the last true viceroy, **Pezuela**, to resign. He lost Lima to **San Martín** but held out against the revolutionaries for a few more years. La Serna illegally replaced **Pezuela** in order to defend the viceroyalty against the revolutionaries himself. His government was always on the move, however, and he never did have the political or social power of a viceroy.

Lautaro Lodge: Secret revolutionary organization started by **Miranda**. Its membership included nearly all of South America's intellectual and military revolutionary leaders.

Liberator: Informal title of **Simón Bolívar** with which he was first hailed in 1813 after freeing Caracas from Spanish rule. Of all his titles, it was the one of which he was most proud.

Miranda, Francisco de: The first man to make serious efforts to start a revolution in South America. He was known as The Precursor.

Monroe, James: Fifth President of the United States (1817-1825), whose administration was marked by the acquisition of Florida (1819), the Missouri Compromise (1820), and the profession of the Monroe Doctrine (1823), which declared U.S. opposition to European interference in the Americas.

Monteagudo, Bernardo: Head of the **Lautaro Lodge**. His intellectual leadership helped move the revolution forward, but he was cruel and believed in terror as a means to political ends.

Montúfar, Carlos: Early revolutionary leader in Quito.

Morales, Manuel: Early revolutionary leader in Quito.

Mosquera, Joaquín: President of Gran Colombia for a short time after **Bolívar**'s exile.

Moyano: One of the two leaders, with **Oliva**, of the Argentineans who mutinied and turned over the Callao fortress to the Spanish. This caused the loss of Lima to the Spanish and the long campaign in the Andes that followed.

Murat, Field Marshal: **Napoleon**'s field marshal who attacked Madrid and caused **Ferdinand VII** to leave Spain.

Nariño, Antonio: Printed the first Spanish translation of Thomas Paine's *The Rights of Man*.

Numancia Battalion: The finest unit in the Spanish military. Defected to the revolutionaries during the liberation of Lima, ensuring success of the revolutionary cause in that area.

O'Higgins, Bernardo: Bastard son of a viceroy of Perú. When he was sent to study in Europe, he became involved with South American revolutionary intellectuals. Later he marched with **San Martín** in the liberation of Chile and was that republic's first President.

O'Higgins, Don Ambrosio: A merchant in Perú who ascended to the office of viceroy in the 18th century. Father of **Bernardo O'Higgins**.

O'Leary, Daniel Florencio: Aide-de-camp of **Bolívar** from the Irish contingent and one of **Bolívar**'s first biographers.

Oliva: See **Moyano**.

Osorio, General: Leader of the first expedition sent by viceroy **Pezuela** to quell the rebellion in Chile. He failed, and Chile was independent thereafter.

Padilla, Admiral: A minion of **Santander**; a traitor of Gran Colombia in the late 1820s.

Palacios, José: **Bolívar**'s trusted retainer who was with the **Liberator** since his boyhood.

Pando, José María: The delegate sent to the first Pan American Congress in history. Bolívar had organized the congress in Panamá, and though it was not entirely successful, it was the precursor to the OAS.

Pezuela, Viceroy Don Joaquín de la: The last official viceroy to sit in Lima.

Pizarro, Francisco: Conqueror of the Incas in the 16th century, and the first viceroy of Perú.

Páez, José Antonio: First President of Venezuela after breaking off his territory from Gran Colombia. He fought alongside **Bolívar** for the liberation of Venezuela in the early years, but his ambition overcame his loyalty on many occasions.

Quiroga: Early revolutionary leader in Quito.

Riva Agüero, José de la: Early revolutionary leader in Perú. Later he was President, but he broke with the revolutionary leadership and was captured and exiled.

Robinson, Samuel: Alias used by **Simón Rodríguez**.

Rocafuerte, Vicente: One of the first leaders of independent Ecuador. He was in power for only a short time, losing to his rival **Flores**.

Rodil, General José Ramón: Spanish General who would not give up the fortress at Callao for almost a year after the fighting for independence was over.

Rodríguez, Simón: **Bolívar**'s tutor as a young man, and a friend throughout his life.

Ruíz, Count: President of Quito when the abortive revolution of 1809 broke out.

Sandes, Arthur: A member of the Irish contingent who became one of **Bolívar**'s generals.

San Martín, José de: Liberator of Lima, in command of the Liberating Army of the Andes from Argentina. He and **Bolívar** have nearly equal stature in history as one of the two liberators of the American colonies from Spain.

Santander, Francisco de Paula: **Bolívar**'s vice-president when Gran Colombia was formed. Later a bitter political rival and ultimately President of the republic after **Bolívar**'s death.

Sucre, General Antonio José de: Bolívar's most able general and the first President of Bolivia. He liberated Quito, and later won the final battle at Ayacucho that broke the Americas away from Spain.

Sáenz, José María: Half-brother of **Manuela Sáenz**. He helped in the liberation of Lima when the **Numancia Battalion** defected from Spain and joined the revolutionaries. Later he was a member of **Bolívar**'s staff. He died in Ecuador, a martyr to the cause of unification.

Sáenz, Manuela: **Bolívar**'s lover and most intimate advisor. She was the great love of his life, who joined him during the Peruvian campaign and later saved his life.

Torre Tagle, Marqués José de: Important Liman citizen who helped in the liberation of Trujillo, but later was a traitor to the cause by helping the Spanish retake Lima.

Urdaneta, General Rafael: Political and military leader in Bogotá who remained loyal to **Bolívar** to the end.

Villegas, Micaela: See **La Perricholi**.

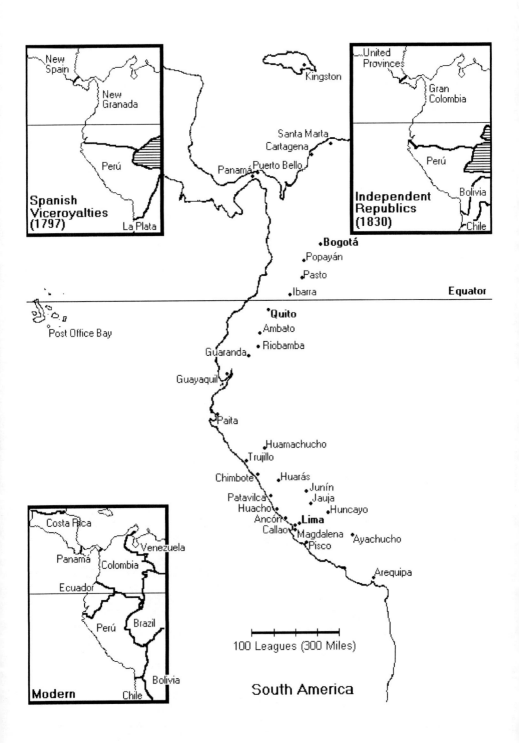

Spanish Viceroyalties (1797)
- New Spain
- New Granada
- Perú
- La Plata

Independent Republics (1830)
- United Provinces
- Gran Colombia
- Perú
- Bolivia
- Chile

Modern
- Costa Rica
- Panamá
- Venezuela
- Colombia
- Ecuador
- Perú
- Brazil
- Bolivia
- Chile

Kingston

Santa Marta
Cartagena
Panamá
Puerto Bello

Bogotá
Popayán
Pasto
Ibarra

Equator

Quito
Ambato
Riobamba
Guaranda

Post Office Bay

Guayaquil

Paita

Huamachucho
Trujillo
Chimbote
Huarás
Junín
Jauja
Patavilca
Huacho
Huncayo
Ancón
Lima
Callao
Magdalena
Ayachucho
Pisco

Arequipa

100 Leagues (300 Miles)

South America

MANUELA

MANUELA

May 13, 1857

Herman Melville, Esq.
c/o Harper and Brothers, Publishers
New York, New York

Dear Mr. Melville,

I do hope, after all this time, that you remember me and that this missive, addressed in care of your publisher, finds you in good health. I have heard that Harper and Brothers suffered a tremendous fire a year or so ago but I am optimistic that the confusion of such a calamity will not cause the loss of what I am herewith sending to you.

We met almost 17 years ago in a tiny town called Paita, on the shores of Perú. You had landed along with the rest of the ship's company from the whaler *Acushnet*. I was the United States Consul there at the time.

You and other members of the crew came to me to report that the captain had been excessive in the administration of discipline aboard his ship. The ship's captain, I believe his name was Pease, was admittedly a rough sort. He also came to see me, a few days later, demanding protection for the ship's cargo, claiming that his crew was mutinous. There was reason for concern as the crew had been brawling on the shore for the last two days.

When the local authorities demanded depositions be taken, I enlisted the aid of a dear friend, a local woman who had been married to an Englishman, to help with the translations from English to Spanish. You met my friend that afternoon. Her married name was Manuela Thorne, but she went by, and everyone knew her as, Manuela Sáenz.

When you met this lady, she was in the most profound penury, only barely surviving on the occasional sale of tobacco and such to the sailors that stopped in Paita to victual. A dusty termite-ridden house several doors down the street from where we took the depositions provided shelter for her and her adopted family.

Yet, despite the picture she may have made when you met her, those who loved her called her *La Libertadora*, The Liberatress. She had once been the most powerful woman on the South American continent—and the companion of The Liberator, Simón Bolívar.

Fortune had taken away nearly everything she ever owned. Most of the people she loved were, or were quickly becoming, victims of betrayal in the ever-changing political landscape. She was alone, in exile, and far removed from her days of glory. Nevertheless, as the years went by, her serenity rarely left her. She was a friend to all, generous to those in need (even though her own needs may have surpassed those she tried to help) and an inspiration to her friends.

Manuela is my reason for attempting to contact you after these many years. It is to ask you a favor in her name. Recently, Manuela died of diphtheria; and I am writing to implore you for help in fulfilling her last request to me before I left Perú. I learned of her demise from General Antonio de la Guerrera, a friend of Manuela's, who wrote to tell me of her last days. You will find a translation of his letter, and something else he sent along, in this package.

However, I call your attention to the main document enclosed herein. It is a personal history that I assisted Manuela in setting down. The reason she wrote her story, in English, was due to certain injustices she felt posterity was about to deliver upon her. These inequities are explained quite well by Señora Sáenz in her narrative. However, I will tell you that she was being systematically written out of history by her political enemies. She did not know what to do about it, and I could tell that it upset her.

I suggested she write the truth herself, but she rejected the idea. She claimed, correctly, that a book written by her would never be published. Then she remembered the sailor and storyteller who had entertained us one hot afternoon with whaling stories many years before.

We had heard about your publication of *Typee* and *Moby Dick* and she decided to write her story in English—if I would help her—and send it to you. She wanted to ask you to speak to your publishers that it might be published in the United States. Then, Manuela supposed, when it was translated back into Spanish and published in South America, no one would be able to deny it. She hoped that you had not forgotten your stay in Paita and that you would help her.

I could indeed assist my friend in the writing, as it was 1855 and the whaling industry had diminished so much that there was very little for me to do. Several months later, I was recalled from my position as Consul in Paita because whaling had become so poor. I left Perú, and my friend Manuela Sáenz, but not before we had finished her story. I carried the manuscript with me on my return to the United States, and you will find it included in this package.

I admit this manuscript has been in my possession for quite a while and I am only now impelled to send it to you due to the recent news of Manuela's death. I would beg forgiveness of my friend, if she were alive, for holding it this last year or so while I settled again into North American living. It has been ready all this time, and I have been remiss in fulfilling my promise to her.

However, I must make a confession to you. Prior to my departure, we both worked very hard at setting down her story. Manuela would dictate, as her arthritis had almost completely disabled her hands. I, in addition to doing much of the actual writing, assisted by occasionally correcting her English or providing an idiom to help the readability. I sometimes added my own translation, in parentheses, of Spanish words or phrases she used. But there were other ways I helped as well; although, whether it was help or hindrance will have to be decided by the reader.

You see, she would often desist from dictation and change subjects, being wary of becoming too personal or revealing too much about herself or her friends. I would then have to coax her to tell the truth exactly as it happened, instead of retelling an incident in a way that would not make her, or some loved one, look bad. I encouraged her to reveal her private thoughts and emotions, and to say what she had told no one before. She resisted the revealing of intimate details so frequently that only through great diligence was I able to have any success in this matter.

If it had not been for me, I do not believe she would have told so much of what she knew. I know it was especially difficult for her to speak of very personal moments, such as the utterances or actions that only lovers would know. But I urged her to tell what she, as a true lady, would not otherwise discuss in polite company. This she did, and I worry that such revelations will be only another means to attack her memory by those small-minded, "moral," narrow people who are so fond of denigrating greatness.

However, the result is a personal statement that I hope will reveal the true Manuela Sáenz. I believe, through my persuasion, she has told us everything she could tell, and it will fall on me for my foolish persistence if posterity decides to "judge" her for revealing too much.

The document enclosed is the life story of a great woman. I ask you, if you respected this lady and if you have any influence with your publishers, to help her publish it. I hope that you remember my friend. If so, I am confident that you will help her.

Sincerely thankful,
Alexander Ruden
Former U. S. Consul to Perú

MANUELA

My Life and My Involvement in the Revolution of the South American People for Independence and Freedom

Manuela Sáenz

As I look out from the Port of Paita, I realize that my life is but a drop in the ocean of time. I hold it dear, having traveled far and seen much, but that single drop of my life would never be part of an ocean whose name is "Pacific."

I lived in a time of revolution, when the countries of the world fought for independence, when Napoleon nearly crushed Europe, and when war marched across the world. It has only been in these recent years that I have at last found any peace. Yet there is still one thing that will not let me rest: lies.

Having heard about many recent distortions, or neglect, of historical fact concerning the revolution of the South American people against Spanish rule—some even published by those who were there and know better—I began to feel I should write an account that would tell the truth. Later, when I heard about the actual suppression of published true accounts, such as that written by my friend General O'Leary, I felt that I could no longer let my pen remain idle.

Today, as I write this, Simón Bolívar is being accepted in his rightful place in history, as a hero. This has not always been so. In the years following his death in 1830, he was ignored or lied about at the orders of his political enemies. At least now, 25 years later, he is being remembered as a hero.

His enemies should have known they could not long suppress his greatness. However, now they have decided to tell different lies. Now, wishing to align themselves with this greatness, Bolívar is being transformed into an icon, a mere picture, a shallow myth that serves only political ends.

Like every other man, Simón Bolívar was not an ideal, nor a myth, nor a romantic figure who always did right; he was a man of turbulent energy and living contradictions. I don't know whether I dislike it more that he is now being painted without depth or, as before, not at all. I am also disturbed that the same vilification, or neglect, once directed at him in death, is now being directed at our love affair.

I, who was there to provide comfort and support for my friend and lover through the years of some of his greatest hardships; I, who saved his life; I, who loved him completely and unconditionally, am seen by those writing history today as a blemish on his "perfect" life.

Our relationship has been called illicit because it was sanctified by no other religion than pure love, and so it could not be mentioned. I have been called a "public woman" because I dared to love and allow the fact that I loved to be known. My contributions to the revolution have been called exhibitionistic because I was flamboyant in my methods and uncaring of whom the truth might expose. My involvement with the making of a new world was called negligible because I am "only a woman." These injustices are the reasons I was first compelled to begin work on my account of history.

I originally intended to tell only of my years with Bolívar. However, the act of telling this story has become an act of meditation, which, if nothing else, has brought me a greater peace—and I have wanted peace for so long. As I looked back on the panorama of time, I discovered a deeper understanding of the last half century than the rush of life allowed me while living it. The early part of my life provided much of the meaning for the later part. I found myself less and less interested in striking a blow to my enemies and their disregard for the truth, and more intrigued with the expression of the beauty I found in my memories. So this history is of my life entire.

I hope, dear reader, that you too can find a little beauty in a life lived during a time of war, when the world changed forever.

Manuela Sáenz

Part I

Wherein I tell of my early years before meeting The Liberator, Simón Bolívar

MANUELA

Chapter 1

It was early on the fourth of February, in the year 1797, that the city known as San Francisco de Quito was about to change. Once called *Quitu* by the Incan princes that lived in the area before the conquest, this was the city where I was soon to be born. Like the rest of South America, this city was quickly approaching a threshold in its history.

An overcast sky glowed faintly as volcanic giants surrounding the city became illuminated by the advancing daylight. The mist enfolding the night-cloaked Andes still clung to the crags of Cotopaxi, the tall, cone-shaped mountain that commands the horizon to the south, far across the plain of Anaquito. Low clouds hid the silent crater of Pichincha that dominated the western edge of the city. The urban paths winding up its side disappeared into the pre-dawn darkness. All was still and as it should be that morning for the people of Quito. Neither their priests nor their king could have warned them of what was about to transpire.

Over two and a half centuries earlier, Cortés had conquered Mexico. With its new world colonies established, Spain had grown to become the richest and mightiest empire ever known. The king's dominion was a worldwide monarchy so powerful and so far reaching that sub-kingdoms had to be created, with authority delegated to vice-kings. With the help of these *virreys* (viceroys), who collected gold and silver and other goods for their sovereign, the mighty Spanish empire appeared to be eternal. Yet on that day in 1797, the city of my birth—the capital city of the Presidency of Quito as part of the Viceroyalty of New Granada—stood on many thresholds.

The portal between day and night was not the only frontier through which Quito was about to pass that morning. Sitting on the girdle of the world known as the Equator, hanging between land and sky, almost a league above the Pacific Ocean, balancing on the sharp hemispheric spine of the jagged Andes, Quito faced another threshold. The inhabitants of this important city and surrounding countryside did not realize that in the next quarter of a century their home and the rest of the world would change forever.

In a few years, a new century would emerge and new modern inventions and ideas would shut the door to the old. This was expected. What the people of South America did not know was that they were soon to face a revolution. It would be many years before the first revolutionary whisperings would be heard in the city of Quito, but some minor twists in the path of history—of no interest to the inhabitants of the city that day—would be reverberations of events about to transpire in the next two hours.

On that particularly chilly morning, on a very narrow street, there was a poor living space fitted in among somewhat larger houses. All were of the same *adobe* bricks, and timbers, all protected with the same white mud that covered the walls, called *tapia*.

As a child, I hated those walls. To me, their purpose never seemed to be shelter. They appeared to exist only to keep me from entering the dwelling beyond. Despite the wealth of my parents, I was born illegitimate and have been an outcast for most my life. From my earliest remembrance I was made to believe that I was, and always would be,

nothing. The cold and lonely mountain tops of the Andes often seemed to hold more of the warmth of human kindness than the people of my city. I would peer through doorways and windows, set in those same walls, to find happy scenes of mothers, fathers and children eating, playing or laughing. I would imagine, if it were not for the walls that kept me out, that I could eat or play with them. As I reflect from my years, I see that all I ever wanted from Quito was to tear down those walls that I might escape my isolation. The few people who did love and care for me often made me feel worse, because it was so clear that their numbers were few. As I grew, I longed to be accepted, respected and loved by people around me, just once.

Yet it was not to be. My course was set on this February morning before I was even born. My mother told me the story of these events at different times—as did my father, later on. The only reason I go back this far in my tale is that I truly believe that what came to pass that morning made me and shaped me and, in many ways, shaped the world in which I was to live.

On that gray morning, inside a humble dwelling, a sleeping girl of 18 rested her head in her arms and grappled with a terrible dream. Joaquina Aispuru was this young girl's name, and she was to be my mother.

She had been up all night giving comfort to her closest friend, Juanita, who lived in the little house. My mother came from a wealthy family, but my mother's companion, also about 18, was very poor.

There were many differences between the two young girls. Joaquina lived with her mother and sisters and her brother Carlos, my uncle. He owned and worked one of the largest estates in the countryside. The family was wealthy, but unhappy because they were still grieving for my grandfather who had died a few years before. Juanita, on the other hand, had only an aging, infirm mother to care for, and no money at all.

My mother had befriended Juanita and her aging mother in the beautiful Church of the Fathers of Mercy, where they attended Mass. Apparently, this was her first true friend and she loved the blithe young girl who never seemed to tire of reminding Joaquina that their names had the same initial. My mother talked about her companion for years. That night, a debilitating fever had been ravaging Juanita. My mother, fearing that her friend might die, had been up for many hours taking care of her.

At last, my mother had fallen asleep, only to be troubled by her frightening dream. Sleeping in a chair, with her head and arms resting on Juanita's tall bed, my mother was seeing images that I believe were prophecy. At first my mother also believed it to be so, but later denied there was any prediction in the dream. However, as I am now over 50 years old and can see into time where my mother could not, I do hold the dream to be at least partly prophetic.

She saw a scene of desolation, a dark wasteland of destruction filled with smoke, flame, and chaos everywhere she looked. The bodies of men and women were lying all about. Through the confusion came a cart with many dead bodies inside. She could hear terrified voices and saw figures rush by her, holding their wounds, calling for help, and praying.

Then she saw a dark figure riding a white horse through the confusion. He seemed to be the victor of the chaos around him. Not a destroyer, but a savior. Wherever he rode, his very presence brought order, and at that moment there was peace all around him.

Suddenly his horse faltered; and the savior, whose face she could not make out, seemed to grow weak. Then, next to the man there appeared a beautiful woman, who looked very much like Joaquina herself, riding a black mare.

She rode up and kissed the man and he became strong again. The couple rode on, at peace. But the chaos, and my mother's own fear, grew as they rode away. Somewhere in the confusion was a fire on gray sand filling the atmosphere with thick black smoke.

Joaquina woke with a start. She did not know where she was at first. Shivering in the chill of the morning, she pulled her shawl around her. Still shaking from the terror of her nightmare, she went to the window to see if it was dawn.

The sky was a canopy of faint gray light. The lamp by the bed had nearly gone out, and she pulled the curtain back farther to look at Juanita's face. She heard her labored breathing, and saw the tiny drops of perspiration on Juanita's forehead reflecting the light like small precious stones. Had Juanita been well, my mother would have told her what she had dreamed. Their favorite games were interpreting dreams, and deriving prophecies. The memory of their happy moments together brought the thought, and the fear, that Juanita might not recover from her illness.

Picking up an earthen jug, as Joaquina turned toward the door to go after some water for her friend, the moment took on a strange intensity for her. She felt more afraid. She perceived with an unfamiliar acuteness the rough red clay of the vessel in her hand. With a strange clarity, she heard Juanita's mother let out a sigh as the old woman turned over in her bed across the room. She saw a single drop of perspiration stand out from its fellows on Juanita's temple.

"There is nothing to fear," Joaquina told herself. "I've been frightened by a dream, that's all. It's over." She forced herself to be calm and she opened the door.

Stepping over the threshold, she experienced a feeling of unnatural stillness. Nothing seemed to be moving. The street was very narrow, with little contrast between the gray cobblestones, the ashen sky, and the white walls. An Indian woman walked up the street, a block away, yet silence and stillness pervaded everything. Why could she not shake her fear? Calming her breathing, she turned towards the square.

The sky seemed to be much lighter as she entered the plaza. It was a very wide open space with a fountain in the center that had been built, in the days of the conquest, by enforced Indian labor. There were two or three women at the fountain, but their presence and their movements did not break the sense of stillness hanging over the city.

She could see the Renaissance steeple of the Church of the Fathers of Mercy, the tallest in the city, standing like a sentinel in the calm. This church, known as "Los Padres," was a short distance down the street that led into the far side of the square. Farther on, towards the center of town, were the slightly shorter towers of The Cathedral of Quito, the Church of San Francisco, and the many other beautiful churches that dotted the already elaborate architecture of what was known to be one of the most beautiful cities in the new world.

Just then, the heavy silence was broken by the sound of hooves on cobblestones echoing loudly down the street. At that moment, riding past "Los Padres," sending the noise of irregular clacks from the feet of his skittish horse past the doorways and shop fronts, was a man she had seen at the family estate many times. She had never met him, but she knew who he was. Everyone knew him. He was well known and well liked, despite being the Collector of Decimal Tithes for the crown. He was Don Simón Sáenz y Verega—a man in his forties, destined to be my father.

My mother was surprised at the behavior of the horse, an old dark bay she recognized that was long past her prime. Joaquina wondered at the nervousness of this ordinarily languid animal, but she watched for only a second and then turned to cross the square toward the fountain.

She never made it.

Dogs howled. The sounds of barking and wailing arose all over the city. She stopped and looked around.

Wings flapped violently. Birds, nesting on rooftops and under eves around the square, took to the air.

Then she felt it.

Movement beneath her feet.

A low rumble.

The women at the well looked up in fright. Water trickling from fountain spouts moved back and forth in a macabre dance. Earthen jars shattered on the ground, shaken out of frightened hands.

The fear my mother had felt since awakening turned to terror. Images of destruction from the dream returned to her mind. The shaking grew worse. In the same dreadful instant, as the rumble became deafening, mud walls began to crack. Facades of buildings tumbled from their framework with a horrifying noise.

Instinct took over. Terrified, she ran from the sight toward her church. The earth shook more violently. Buildings trembled. She fell—cutting her hands and knees.

As she rose, a two-story building at the square's perimeter collapsed. Small sections of the wall fell toward her with a deafening crash. A flying timber almost hit her. She was nearly hidden by a cloud of dust that swept over the plaza. She turned, not knowing where to go. Unable to see through the dust, she took a step, twisted her ankle, and fell.

She struggled to stand, but the pain was too great. Then, a sudden wind cleared the dust a little and she saw, through stinging eyes, how foolish she would have been to leave the square. The streets were already filled with people crying prayers to heaven. Many rushed out of buildings only to fall under rubble raining down on them from above. Hundreds of desperate men and women were trying to open the doors of the church of "Los Padres" to seek safety and prayer.

Through the dust, Joaquina saw Simón Sáenz fight to control his mare. He dug his spurs into the horse's side, trying to race to open space, but his mount was too frightened. Standing on its hind legs, the old horse twisted around and fell, throwing Simón to the stones. Before Simón could stand, the horse jumped to her feet and galloped back up the street toward home.

At that moment, the erratic convulsions of the steeple of Los Padres shook it apart. Bricks and little stone flowers fell from elaborate renaissance decorations. Then, the entire structure came down with a noise that filled the entire valley. A sickening collapse of stones on flesh crushed perhaps a hundred people in an instant. The mare, that had tried so desperately to escape, also died under the falling steeple.

Simón, already racing toward the square and open space through the immense cloud of dust raised by the falling tower, could not keep his balance as the earth shifted beneath him. He fell and cut his forehead. Masonry scattered in front of him as he scrambled to his feet and ran on. All about him were fallen bodies, crushed and bleeding.

He made it over the rubble blocking the entrance to the street. My mother was still struggling to stand when Simón came running past her. "Help me, Señor!" she implored over the deafening rumble of shifting earth beneath them.

He rushed by her at first. Then, recognizing her, and seeing the look of terror in her eyes from which rivulets of tears stained the dust on her cheeks, he came back. He took her in his arms and carried her to the center of the square where they huddled together with a few other souls lucky enough to reach merciful open space. They held each other desperately while the ground continued to shake with terrifying fury.

Chapter 2

That day changed my mother's life. Everyone's life changed. In other parts of the country, people saw their world destroyed before their frightened eyes. They watched the earth split open, spewing forth mud, water, or lava in destructive waves that drowned their land, their homes, their loved ones, and their dreams. Cotopaxi, inactive for years, erupted. Barely hidden behind the low clouds that glowed red as the molten rock poured forth, Cotopaxi's fire reflected a terrifying pall of crimson over the faces of the people praying in the streets.

Among them were the two people who were destined to be my parents, thrown together by the violence of the earth. That violence has been my birthright. In my half-century, I have known almost nothing but violence: either that of the earth or of the men who walk upon it. I have had to embrace violence, or succumb.

It had been nearly 50 years since South America's last big earthquake, but the quake of 1797 was the worst in history. Had my mother been able to proceed up the street to her church, she would have suffered the same fate as 40,000 other people who perished that day. Most of them died trying to find a place to pray.

When the shaking died down, it left the sound of wailing up and down the Andes for over 300 leagues. My mother was crying also. She trembled in Simón Sáenz's arms, clinging desperately to him as he tried to comfort her in the stillness following the quake.

"All is well. It's over now," he said, holding her close. He wiped the blood from his forehead, and asked, "Are you all right?"

She turned and looked at the man who had saved her as he brushed the hair off her forehead. Suddenly she remembered. "Juanita, I must go see Juanita!" she said. She tried to stand on her swollen foot. Her hands shook as she reached out for support. Simón did not understand at first. Tears made wider paths in the dust on her face as she tried to persuade him to help her. "I must see if my friend is all right."

"No, we must stay in the open for a while. The earthquake may start again," he said.

"Please, Don Sáenz, I must go to her. I need to take care of her. I must know if she is all right or help her."

Reluctantly, he assisted while she hobbled up the street. Although limping, the act of making her way through the disaster in order to save her friend seemed to take away the pain in her ankle and the fear in her heart.

The little street that had been still and silent so many long moments before was now littered with debris and grief. A man wandered in a daze, blood flowing from half an arm. A woman knelt over her husband, a bloody piece of masonry next to him. As she wailed, she dashed her head on the stones on which his life flowed away. Two-story buildings had been reduced to piles of rubble. Bodies lay everywhere. Those who were still alive were frantically lifting stones and timbers, searching through rubble in a vain attempt to uncover members of their families.

Joaquina's heart leapt for joy when she saw the little house was still standing. She avoided the horror all around her as she single-mindedly climbed over shifting stone, wood and plaster. Only one wall of the little house, common with an adjacent fallen building, was gone. The door was completely blocked by rubble from the building across the street.

They climbed over stones and timbers to reach the partially blocked opening of the fallen wall. When they crawled inside, my mother realized instantly that Juanita and her mother had left, seeking safety. Safety that they probably never found. She never saw Juanita again.

Tears came to her eyes. She was about to sit down in despair when the first after-shock struck. With it came a loud crack as the ceiling timbers broke.

Simón quickly sought safety under the tall bed on which my mother had rested her head so recently while she dreamed. He pulled her in after him and held her close.

The roof crashed open. Into the room came the rainwater that had accumulated on the flat roof in the preceding days. The two survivors were splashed by the mud that rolled across the earthen floor. The shock lasted only a moment and then stopped.

When my mother told me the story, she said that after the last shock had died, my father took her home. Years later, I overheard her tell a priest, in a confession, a different account. As I reflected on that story from adulthood, it made more sense.

This is the way I now understand it: the after-shock was over in an instant, but they stayed in each other's arms, grasping for life from each other for a long time. It was almost half an hour before they left. In that time they made a silent bond. I have been close to death many times and I know what it can do to desire, and I know how she felt.

She desperately wanted to feel his hands touch her skin, yet she knew it was wrong and held back. Then, as she told the priest, the chaos of the morning made her mind re-create the images of her dream: a man on a horse who first brought chaos and then peace, and the woman who rode beside him.

Next to my father, my mother felt both safe and exhilarated. He had been her rescuer. Perhaps her dream was prophecy. That was why God had made her dream so frightening a dream. She told herself that she dreamt of her own savior. God knew she would be saved by this man and wanted her with him. She looked into his eyes and then they pressed their lips together. Their yearning pushed away all else.

The horror of the day was too much for them to comprehend. No one that day could know how complete was the devastation caused by the "great earthquake of 1797." The shaking is said to have lasted almost a quarter of an hour, and it would be 40 years before the damage done to the property in and around Quito was completely repaired.

Throughout the Andes, people lost their lives and their hope as the cities and towns they had built crumbled and fell about them. Not only Quito suffered. The towns of Cotocollao, Nano, Pomasqui, San Antonio and many others, in an area that stretched for many leagues on either side of the Equator, sustained almost complete destruction. One of the largest mountains in the Andes, Chimborazo, erupted with such heat that the ice cap partially melted, flooding the lands at its feet, while it rained down fire on the towns of Ambato, Riobamba and Guaranda.

Along with the damage to property, the effects on the people's souls would take years to restore as well. Though Quito was all but destroyed, the ground was not all that was transformed. The human "terrain" changed as well. In the few years just prior to the earthquake, Quito had been gaining a reputation for being a somewhat licentious city. Finding a way to ensure guilt, the merciless priests would not let the poor people of Quito forget the earthquake. "It was your punishment," the priests declaimed from the pulpit. This, of course, did nothing but add to the misery of those who had lost their loved ones and homes, and who were already insane with grief. The priests saw to it that the spirit of the land stayed a dismal color for years.

The effects of such persecution on my mother were devastating. She had lost a dear friend in the earthquake and she had reached out to one who could help her. Nothing could be more natural, but in the end, she would be made to pay for that "crime." If I had seen nothing else, the sight of my mother in the following years would have been enough to make me abhor the church. I know I should not say this, but I am too old to dissemble now.

Every aspect of colonial life was affected by the quake—politics in particular. Only a few months before, Spain had entered a war with Britain. The blockade of Spanish shipping at Cádiz by the British during 1797, which would have brought much needed supplies to the colonies, forced the people of the Andes to seek help elsewhere. For nearly 300 years, all trading done by the colonies was, by law, done with Seville or Cádiz. Suddenly, with the war blocking Spanish shipping and the urgent need for medical supplies and building materials, the colonies had to, and did, find new trading partners. Thus Spain's grip on the colonies lost some of its power. The interruption of the supply of gold to Spain due to the earthquake weakened the Spanish monarchy as well.

The *criollos* (aristocrats born in South America, or "Creoles") were already beginning to wonder about their attachment to Spain. Three years earlier, Antonio Nariño had published the first Spanish translation of *The Rights of Man,* in the city of Santa Fe de Bogotá. It was in this document, written by Thomas Paine in 1791, that Nariño and other South American patriots found inspiration for their own search for liberty.

Intellectual inspirations aside, the *criollos* were already vexed at injustices imposed upon them by the high-minded *peninsulares* (the aristocrats born in Spain). Those born on the Iberian peninsula, who always had the choicest positions in government or business, never tired of reminding their South American born cousins of their unlucky birth. When the king of Spain sent a little money to repair the ruins of the earthquake, he did something else that exacerbated an old problem with the *criollos*—he also sent Spanish-born administrators to further crowd the American born from office and work. Thus did the earthquake push the American born *quiteños* (citizens of Quito) closer to the idea insurgency. It would be long after Simón Bolívar had liberated the continent that I would really understand what happened politically in my city, but I see now that the earthquake of 1797 was a small turning point that had driven forward the coming revolution.

On that day, hiding under a bed in a small house, oblivious to past or future, were two souls who were also being changed forever. My father was not the kind of man who was in the habit of indulging in such improper behavior. He was well known in Quito as a wealthy importer of Spanish goods, an office holder, and a solid citizen. He was also known for his propriety. Concubinage was practiced by nearly all men of position, but my father was conservative, sometimes to his detriment, and he would not ordinarily have become involved with young Joaquina Aispuru. In addition to his successful business affairs and his civil appointment as tax collector, he was also head of the King's Militia, a not unimportant position. A few years before, he had married a wealthy noblewoman, Juana María del Campo, and they had three children, but their marriage was not a happy one. Nevertheless, my father, if anything, was very staid and would not have indulged himself thus without the force of the cataclysm impelling him onward.

This pretty young woman he was kissing, and who seemed to be of supreme importance to him in those moments following the earthquake, did not fit into his life at all. The thought of my proper father in that compromising position makes me laugh to this day. My father always resisted change, yet he was constantly being pushed and pulled by forces beyond his control.

As they hid in the darkness, exploring each other's bodies with their lips and hands, exchanging their first words of love, the outside world slowly began to intrude. Though their desire was great, they refrained from making the final act of love that day. It would not have been emotionally possible for them, despite their need. After the last shock died away, the cries of men and women began drifting in from street. They heard shouts calling to each other, as families searched vainly through the rubble, trying to reclaim their loved ones and friends—shouts full of grief and terror. As the outside world invaded Simón's and Joaquina's hiding place, creating such conflicting feelings in them, they were able to muster enough moral self-discipline to stop themselves.

My father decided to take Joaquina to a nearby home—friends of the Aispurus. He would leave her there, at the Larrea mansion, until her ankle healed enough for her to travel back to her own house, which was in an outlying part of town.

They weaved through the dusty, sorrowful streets and were still brushing dirt off their clothing as they approached the rubble that had been "Los Padres." As they looked up, they shuddered at the scene of horror before them.

A middle aged priest stood on the debris, his thin frame balancing on shifting masonry. Where his left eye should have been was a gaping wound, from which blood flowed into his beard and onto his frock. Beneath his feet, Simón and Joaquina and the other *quiteños* who were witness to the scene, could see limbs and bodies sticking out from beneath the fallen stones of the once great church.

Over his head, the priest held a rosary. In his remaining eye was the punishing fire of God as he cursed those who stood about. "Repent of your misdeeds, oh evil city. God's wrath has fallen on you. Drop to your knees and ask forgiveness for having forgotten God and king. Christ is your only savior."

Already, many were on their knees. Others did the same upon hearing his judgment. Simón and Joaquina walked as far around him as possible. As they turned the corner they heard the priest shout after them, "You shall not escape judgment!" To their emotions and their desire for each other was added the fear of God that covered them in a cloak of guilt.

Soon they were at Juan de Larrea's heavy wooden door. It was open. As they entered, Joaquina looked around and marveled that this grand house, on one of the most important boulevards in Quito, had somehow suffered very little damage. The fountain, a sculptured cherub with its arms around a swan, was still pouring forth water in a peaceful trickle, ignoring the horror all around.

The Aispurus were close friends with this very wealthy family, and Joaquina and Simón were recognized immediately. A servant called to Doña Larrea from across the courtyard.

She rushed up to them and said, "Don Sáenz, are you all right? Joaquina, oh I'm so glad you are safe. Juan is out trying to help the poor victims." Tears sprang to her eyes. "I wish he would return. I don't like it when he is gone." Then she noticed my mother limping. "Oh, Joaquina, you're hurt. Sit down."

She guided them into the courtyard where members of the household, and some others who had been brought back to the house by the generous Juan de Larrea, were lying in pain waiting for medical attention. For some of those, a doctor would do no good.

Joaquina could no longer stand and she was lowered to the ground and propped up against the wall. Simón was explaining his presence: "I came across her and she asked me to bring her here. I must rush home now." At that moment, Doña Larrea was called away.

The confession I overheard later told the story of two people destined to break the commandments after all. Once Simón had seen to Joaquina's comfort, he went to the massive door, still open to the street, and looked at the confusion beyond. Then he came back, knelt down, took her hands in his, and looked into her eyes.

"I must go," he said, softly but urgently. "If I see your brother, I will let him know where you are." Then he leaned over and whispered, "I *will* see you again. Take care of yourself until then."

He looked quickly around to be sure he wasn't being watched and then he kissed her passionately. She closed her eyes as she returned his kiss and swore to herself that she would wait for him. She felt him pull away before she opened her eyes. Simón was gone.

She raised herself to watch him walk down the scattered street. Touching her lips, she felt the exhilaration of a new love move through her body. At that moment, the sun broke through the overcast sky.

Then she saw something that brought her quickly back to her broken world. The priests had already organized a procession. Indians and poor Spanish, carrying the Virgin of Earthquakes, moved arduously through the rubble-strewn streets past the Larrea mansion, where another procession, a most important procession, would pass one day. They moved on to the main square in the center of the city. Over houses fallen on the dead of Quito, they marched, chanting of death and penance.

Joaquina took her trembling fingers away from her lips and averted her eyes. The remembrance of all the morning's events took hold of her. Slowly, she sank back to the ground. Her body shook as sobs overtook her. A mournful wail came to her throat but the penitent chanting, passing the open front door, drowned out the sound of her weeping.

Chapter 3

In the weeks that followed, my mother was happy for the first time in her life. Living first under the domination of her religious father and then her brother, of even more stern moral convictions, she had little of life that she could call her own. When she lost her first real friend and then found that relationship replaced by a deeper and more intimate one, she quickly fell in love.

She tried to ignore her feelings of guilt that the priests, in their zeal to disseminate shame to their followers, often made her feel. "The earthquake was God's punishment for the sins of Quito," she would hear almost daily. The priest who had lost his eye in the quake was one of the city's most vocal accusers and he could be seen preaching in the streets for weeks. He was so zealous that some people began to call him "mad." She felt mortified whenever she saw him even though he could not have known that she was guilty of the sins for which he condemned the city.

In the next two months, regardless of her guilty feelings, my mother was unable to keep away from the object of her love, or he from her. She tried to resist her feelings. Sometimes, when she knew she had to leave for an appointed rendezvous, she would tell herself that it was wrong and that she would not go. But she could not stay away from the joy that Simón brought her when they were together. They secretly saw each other every few days. Sometimes many days would go by before they could escape their families and meet for brief moments. Yet, any longer than a day or two apart filled her with anticipation and distraction.

At first, the site of their trysts was most often a makeshift hospital. The Church of the Fathers of Mercy, roof no longer intact, its interior exposed to the sky, was deemed unsuitable for prayer. The numerous injured and sick were tended there, under tents to keep out the rain, by overworked doctors and young volunteers like Joaquina.

Simón would enter on some pretext, and they would secretly meet in a small room in the back where broken statues were stored. There, with God and terra cotta saints looking on, they enjoyed stolen moments, moments that were filled with kisses, or the smell of each other's hair, and the touch of each other's skin. Their ardor for each other grew until, one afternoon, they met in a field outside the city and, at last, consummated their love.

For the next month, they were able to see each other almost every day, and their meetings were filled with passionate lovemaking. Then, he stopped seeing her. I have deduced that his wife became suspicious, and perhaps it is all understandable, but the effects on my mother were disastrous. Feeling happily in love one day and deserted the next naturally brought her great anxiety. No reminders of her prophetic dream on the day of the earthquake gave her any peace. No fantasizing about the future gave any hope.

She did not see him again for six weeks. Six weeks of longing and grief, and in the meantime Joaquina's monthly time came and went. Each day without her flow, and each sermon reminding the populace of the earthquake, brought her more worry and grief.

One day, she saw Simón for a moment in the market. She walked toward him through the crowd in the street, but before she could tell him of her trouble, he spoke softly and quickly. "I am sorry, but Juana is with child. It has become impossible for me to get away. Shhh. She's coming. Later. Later."

"Simón, please . . . ," she called after him, but he was gone. Joaquina was left with his name on her lips, his child in her belly, and the realization that she had been fooled by the treacherous dream she had on the morning of the great earthquake.

The weeks passed. Almost before she could think about it, she was so big that her hoop skirts were no longer able to hide her condition. Every important family in Quito, except the kindhearted Larreas, began a campaign of whispers behind her back.

Most of the things that were said about her were lies. Some of it was the truth because the servants in Simón's house heard the quarrels with his wife and spoke to the servants in other houses. The story spread quickly about the sinful Joaquina and the father of the bastard she was carrying. Everyone, especially the church fathers, turned against my mother; the vehemence of the clergy kept her from even walking through a church door in her condition. Even though my father was equally guilty, and everyone knew it, he was never chastised.

My uncle Carlos, ashamed to have her in the same house with the rest of the family, admonished her violently for the humiliation she had brought to the Aispuru name. He had been the head of the household since the death of their father and when he discovered his youngest sister's condition, he packed her up and housed her in a little hut just outside of town. He told her very explicitly that she was to stay there with her Indian servant until she was past her condition. "You will bear a bastard, a child who will be no more than a drain on public charity. I hope you're proud of yourself," he swore at her as he left her in her dismal surroundings. Food was brought from the Aispuru household by servants, but Joaquina received little from her family to nourish her soul.

Then my vengeful uncle spoke maliciously to important men in the *cabildo* (town council) and soon Simón was removed as head of the militia. The militia was disbanded sometime after that and the King's Infantry was formed. An officer named Salinas was appointed to lead it.

My father hated Captain Salinas. He was known to have a loose tongue. He was known to be foolish. Yet he was given an important position of authority. The irony in this is that because it was Salinas and not my father who was in charge of that aspect of the military in Quito, its history would be quite different, as you will see.

Meanwhile, the course of my family's history had been set. Carlos, by isolating my mother and attacking my father, only impeded Simón from giving any kind of support to her. My mother thus became resentful of him. I know my father did try to help my mother despite such impediments, but Carlos tried even harder to keep him away from her. He succeeded too well.

Some men have concubines, and the church and society merely wink at them. But my uncle Carlos was intensely angry with Simón and my mother. As time went on and the strife between my two families worsened, Carlos threatened to kill my father if he spoke to, or even looked at, Joaquina again. All of Quito knew of the scandal and the hatred between my families. Many took sides, but most agreed that Joaquina was a whore. A wedge of immense proportions was driven between the two unhappy lovers who were my parents. This strife lasted for years.

Like the city in which I was born, my life lay on a threshold: a violent frontier between my two families. It was not enough that I should be born both from both Spanish and American stock, in poverty from aristocratic parents, a colonial destined to be a revolutionary, but that my two families should always be at war kept me ever divided.

It was in the last hours of a cold day, on the 29th of December, in the year of the big earthquake, that my mother's servant made her way through the darkness carrying a small bundle. It was cloudless that night even though it was the rainy season in the high Andes. The moon, three-quarters full, glistened in the puddles between the stones in the street. This watchful orb was the poor Indian woman's only light. Her hands could not carry a lantern because they bore a more delicate burden. In her arms slept a newborn baby girl wrapped in a shawl that was far too exquisite for an Indian servant to own. My nurse—whom my mother always called Juanita in memory of her friend though I do not think that was her name—carried me through the moonlight to the rectory of a nearby church. She held me close and knocked on the door.

I did not sleep through the baptism. I am told that I began crying almost as soon as the priest's scraggly features approached to peer down on me in myopic scrutiny. No doubt I was already mad at priests.

In addition to the fact that the priest was getting ready for bed, he showed obvious distaste for babies and rushed through the ceremony. Afterwards he wrote in a large book:

> . . . the 29th of December, 1797, solemnly baptized Manuela . . . born
> two days previously, a spurious child whose parents are not named . . . .

A few days before my humble ceremony, this unnamed father attended the baptism of his youngest son, my half-brother, José María Sáenz, in one of the rebuilt churches in the center of Quito. It would be days before my father would know I was born.

Chapter 4

The course of my life was set by the events preceding my birth. Had I not been born illegitimate, who knows what I might have become? Who knows how differently my influence on those around me might have changed history, and in what way? Who knows what would have happened if I had not been born into a world already set for conflict?

My parents families were in constant strife. Yet, in spite of Carlos's efforts to keep him away, my father came to see Joaquina and me a few months after my birth. If he intended the reunion to be a happy one, the journey was wasted.

Joaquina had bowed to the priests' sense of morality and had been living a life of contrition. She refused to return home after my birth, relying rather on her humble surroundings to serve as proper penance. My mother stayed in our little house as much as possible, with only Juanita to attend to our needs. None of the Aispurus ever came to visit, despite our house being on the path they had to travel to go to town. My mother played with me, and prayed, and did little else.

Since no one came to visit, she was surprised to find my father at her door one day. Painful memories returned, and though she invited him in out of social habit, she could not bear to see my father pick me up without feeling resentment. An argument ensued shortly after, and Simón left. "She took you from my arms so soon," my father said while telling me this story, a rare look of sadness darkening his face. This was the same look I saw on my mother's face at times.

Throughout the land there was discontent and hardship. My parents were not alone in their unhappiness. The *criollos* were constantly talking of the need for change. Change was in the air. As for my mother and father, they were in conflict and most unhappy, and things stayed as they were for more than six years.

During that period, my mother became more religious, and every day she withdrew further from any interaction with other people. Carlos could have made her come home after my birth, but he was content to leave her where she was. The earliest image I can recall of my uncle is him saying angrily, "I wash my hands of you!" My maternal grandmother died without ever seeing her only grandchild, and this caused Joaquina to withdraw even more into her own world. As the years advanced, she became increasingly reclusive and finally never left our little house again.

During those first years, my father visited me every now and then, but he was never made to feel welcome. Despite that, I liked him. He always brought me a little nosegay of sweet smelling flowers, or some fruit, or a *dulce* (sweetmeat). He was nice to me, but his visits were rare. I hardly saw any member of my family except my mother.

A kindhearted priest, by the name of Father Ramón, took pity on us. He came to take confession from Joaquina and to instruct me in reading and writing. He was always meticulously clean, boyish, and friendly, with a shock of thick black hair that would forever fall in his eyes. He seemed confident about everything, yet a serious look never left his face. He was kind to me, and many times he went out of his way to take me into the city to see the Larreas.

They were the only family in Quito that even tried to maintain a friendship with my mother. "Joaquina, you and Manuela must come to dinner," Doña Larrea would write in a note delivered by a barefoot servant wearing satin breeches. My mother would never go, but she would send me with Father Ramón.

It was Juan Larrea who taught me to ride. I was terrified the first time Señor Larrea picked me up and set me down on the bare withers of a dark brown gelding. I cried in fear and clutched at the mane, but he smiled and soothed me in some knowing way. The next time he asked me if I wanted to ride, I was only a little afraid.

"Horses love people," he used to say. He was a great teacher, and I was riding by myself before I was five years old. Everyone agreed I had a knack for it.

However, I might not have become the accomplished horsewoman that I became if it had not been for Señor Larrea's kindly manner. The first time I fell off a horse, I almost stopped riding.

Don Larrea picked me up and said, "Don't cry, Manuela. You are not hurt. Simply ride again."

"I don't want to ride anymore," I whimpered.

"You're only saying that because you're frightened. You must face what frightens you. You must ride again. You must refuse to feel afraid."

"No, Señor, please."

"Now I am going to set you on that mare again. Be brave. Just say to yourself, 'I refuse to feel afraid.'"

"No, Señor, no."

"Please, Manuela, try. For me. Please."

I did. I said the words, "I refuse to feel afraid," and Señor Larrea put me back on the same horse. It was hard at first, but I conquered my fear. I was never afraid of a horse again, and the words he taught me often helped me later in life.

I learned more than riding from the Larreas. Except for the Larreas, people all around me made me believe I was nothing, nothing but a bastard. Certainly I believed that I would never mingle with such people of the upper classes. But the Larreas were different. They accepted me, and I learned many things from them. I learned what it was like to be well situated. This would have been my birthright had my wealthy parents been married, or my mother not in disgrace.

I learned to act like a lady at the Larrea mansion. If I was eating dinner at their table, I would watch the meticulous Doña Larrea delicately handle her knife and fork. I observed how to hold long-stemmed crystal. I learned the proper way to sit at a table with a fine linen covering. I also learned the things I was not supposed to do. "Manuela, we must not rest on the cloth with our elbows," she would say, gently. I learned proper manners and what was expected of society's "best."

Despite the kindly attention of the Larreas, most of the families in Quito's high society were cruel to me and my mother. These were the families of counts, marquises, and other Spanish nobility of great altitude. They all knew my mother and my father. They were merciless in their abuse of us.

I also had to endure the jibes of children, who could be most cruel. If some of the kinder children tried to include me in their games, an older one would very often see that I was ridiculed. "Do you want to play, Manuela?" one would say. "She won't be able to get permission from her parents. They live too far apart," said another. Everyone would laugh.

When I would act distant and ignore such a group in order not to be hurt by their taunts, I heard, "Too good for us Manuela? I didn't know it was so important to have no family."

When I became angry enough to hurl insults in return, to attack my attackers, I almost always heard, "Just what you'd expect from a bastard."

I never admitted to anyone that I was hurt profoundly by their taunting, but I almost always converted the pain to anger and the anger to bloody noses. Not even the boys were safe when I was antagonized into a fight. I was constantly being scolded by the parents of defeated children and sent home where I would let down my barriers and cry. "You little bastard, you're nothing but vermin on society," or some similar remark would ring in my ears while my mother comforted me.

Any vulnerability that my youth might have given me was slowly replaced by thick skin and deep resentment. As I grew, I added sarcasm, laughter, and stubbornness to my defensive arsenal, but I was never as good at making fun of my enemies as I was at fighting. I took pride in the fact that I was called formidable by those who knew me later in my adolescent years. Now that I no longer have to fight, I find it only amusing. But when I was young, it seemed I ended each day with a mixture of grief and anger.

Such was my life until I was seven, when events altered my future completely. My life may not have been the best up until then, but it was the only life I knew. I would have been content to go on living just the way I was. But catastrophic changes were about to occur. They began when my uncle came to our house to demand that my mother sign some papers.

I heard my mother say, "No, Carlos, the land belongs to all of us. I should have a say in how it is—"

"Damn you. You have given up your rights when you embarrassed us. The Aispuru name—"

"But, Carlos—"

"I have already deeded over this parcel you live on. Now you must relinquish—"

Then my mother noticed I was watching and listening and sent me outside. I heard them argue for a long time.

The conflict lasted for a week. Carlos came over every day until my mother became very ill. When Carlos came the next day, she was too weak to talk to him.

For two nights I could not sleep with my mother as I always did. I had to sleep in a chair with my head in my arms, resting on her sick bed. Then, on the third day, her fever worsened. I became frightened, as did Juanita. She ran to the Aispuru estate to find help.

I remember shivering in the doorway and calling out, "Hurry, Juanita, hurry!" I watched her disappear down the road. The sky was a deep gray with fast moving clouds. Heavy rain drops began to fall as I stood there.

When I closed the door, my mother roused herself weakly. "Manuela, bring me some paper and a pen." She spoke in such a feeble voice, that I barely heard her.

As I set them in her lap, she said, "Manuela, I am going to write my will. I want you to have something of mine—something very important—after I die."

"No. No, Mama," I said, terrified.

"Shhh, my child, listen to me. I won't be around to make it happen. Your aunts and uncle will try to take my gift from you. But you must make sure that you obtain my share of the family estate. You are a fighter, my love. Keep your spirit. Do not lose your will to fight for what is yours. My share of the estate was left to me by my father, and I give it to you. You must have it. Promise me that you will fight until you have it."

"Yes, Mama," I said, though I really didn't understand.

She had been half delirious all day, but her eyes were clear then and she spoke passionately. "It is mine to sell or give away." Her voice was raspy and strands of black hair stuck to her damp forehead. "I cannot go back to my home. There is nothing for me there. But you, you will own a house some day. You will sell what you receive from me and buy a house of your own. You will sleep in a fine bed. If I could know that you would have all that, I would be happy as I die. That is why I give you my gift." Her voice quavered in grief and her eyes filled with tears.

"No, Mama, no. Please don't cry—"

She waved her hand, indicating that she wanted to write. I silently prepared the ink and paper and set them before her. Her pen scratched the rough paper as the evening gloom filled the house.

I looked at the tattered covers on her bed. I never noticed the patches and rips before. I looked around the room. Mostly the house was made of cane and thatch with a framework and flooring made of lumber, and a stone wainscoting. In one corner was a narrow cot for Juanita. In the other corner was a tiny stone kitchen that seemed to have been added to the little house as an afterthought. The kitchen had *adobe* walls with a stone floor, a small table, and a stone hearth. This one little room and small kitchen was home to me.

I ran my hand across the blankets. It was my one true comfort to climb into bed with my mother every night. I did not really understand death, but my mother's words made me know that I might lose her. Fear filled me as I waited for her to finish writing.

The sound of wind and rain hitting the roof overcame the sound of the quill. Darkness took over the room, and I lit what few candles we had. When I was finished, Joaquina was folding the paper. She reached out to hand it to me, but there was a knock on the door.

I admitted Father Ramón. "How is she, my child?" he whispered, as he wiped the rain off his face with his sleeve.

"I don't know, Father." Tears welled up in my eyes.

"Shhh, everything will be all right." He crossed the room and sat down next to her bed. "Joaquina, I saw Juanita and she told me you were worse."

"I am dying, Father," she said so weakly that it scared me.

"Now, of course you're not," he said, though his brows knit in worry. "I gave Juanita my mule and she will have alerted your brother very soon. Carlos will bring a doctor."

The flames of the candles sputtered in the draft. Rain and wind penetrated the cracks in the walls, and the thatch on the roof rustled loudly. Near the corner next to the kitchen, the roof always leaked. I heard drops of water hitting the floorboards as I stepped behind the tattered curtain that closed off the kitchen. When I tried to light our only lamp, I heard my mother begin to confess to the priest.

"I know I have sinned, Father, because my life has been sad, because I have lived as an outcast here without a husband."

"Now then, rest easy, Joaquina."

Father Ramón was proof that all priests are not bad. His way was to pay attention to what people really needed, rather than "church business." His befriending of friendless people like my mother, who were not in the good graces of the church leadership, got him into more than a little trouble, I think.

"I sinned on the day of the earthquake, Father."

"Shhh. Calm yourself, Joaquina. I understand." He did not rattle off the usual responses to a confession. I think he believed she would be all right, and I know he had heard of the earthquake and her feelings of guilt before. "Do not speak just now. Try to rest." He was not listening as a priest, but as a friend, and he was right. She did not die that night. My mother may not have died at all, if subsequent events had not occurred.

She pressed on. "Father, listen to me. When I was carrying my Manuela, I was not allowed to go to church because of my sin. My family and most of my friends turned against me. Now I am dying and I have suffered for seven years. Seven years is long enough and I must have your help. Promise me you will help me."

"Of course, Joaquina. What do you want?"

"I want my share of our family estate to go to Manuela when I die."

"You will not die, Joaquina, if you can get some rest and—"

"Father, please help me," she interrupted. "Here is my will. Take it and help my little girl. She can sell her interest in the family property. When she has money, people won't be cruel to her anymore. Father, promise me that you will be my witness. Promise

28

me that my inheritance will go to my Manuela. I want her to have it. You can't punish me anymore."

"Joaquina, it is I, Ramón, who is before you. I do not wish to punish you. I will see that your wishes are carried out."

Suddenly, Joaquina began to cough violently. When she recovered, she said, "I am sorry, Father, but because of that dream, I thought Simón was sent to save me. Now I know that Christ is my only savior. But please help my child, Father."

"Of course I will, but you will be all right if you get some care and have a chance to rest without suffering. Try to calm yourself. It won't do any good to—"

Before he could finish, the door opened, admitting the storm. Carlos Aispuru stood on the threshold a moment, shedding water onto the dusty floor. He slowly looked around the dark room.

I peeked through a hole in the curtain, terrified, and saw an angry look on his face. Every time I had seen him before, he had left my mother in tears and me shaking with fear. He was tall and had to stoop a bit to enter the room. His face was long and furrowed, though he was only about 35. There was no gray in his straight black hair, and his aspect could only be described as stern and unmoving. He was my uncle, but I loathed him even at my young age.

He brushed the rain from his clothes. Father Ramón met him at the door and began to speak softly to him. Carlos cut him off with a curt, "Where's the child?"

My heart froze. Carlos cast his eyes around the room and ignored my mother. I could hear, and partly see, the rest of their conversation. Father Ramón looked at him as if he couldn't believe his ears. He said softly, "She's around her somewhere. But where is the doctor? I thought you would bring a doctor."

Carlos turned back to him and then looked at Joaquina, "I couldn't find him. Does she need him urgently?" Then, raising his voice and turning toward the doorway, he called out harshly, "Manuela, come here."

The priest lost his temper. He grabbed Carlos by the arm and turned him around. Whispering, he said, "Of course she needs him urgently. She might die if she doesn't get some help." He brushed the hair out of his eyes and said, "She can be saved, but her condition is very serious."

Carlos looked at the dread on Joaquina's face and said quietly, "You're wrong, priest. She is going to die whether she gets help or not. Look at her."

"Well?" the priest challenged, grabbing him tighter.

"In which case, she doesn't need a doctor," he hissed. He shook off the priest's grip and called toward the kitchen, "Manuela?!"

Father Ramón was livid. "How can you—" he started, but Carlos ignored him and walked over to the kitchen. I quickly hid behind a large water jug in the corner. I looked back and saw their silhouettes on the curtain. Before Carlos could enter, Father Ramón spun him around, saying, "How can you be so heartless? And why is it so important to find the child?"

"I'm taking her to a convent until Joaquina recovers, *Father*." His voice was full of venom as he pronounced "Father." I tried to make myself smaller behind the jar. Then Carlos noticed the will in the priest's hand and snatched it from him. "What's this?"

"*That* is Joaquina's will, *Señor*." He pronounced "Señor" with the same rancor that Carlos had just used.

Carlos read it quickly and then exploded, "Never!" I heard him thunder over to Joaquina. His shadow loomed larger on the curtain, and I saw him crumple the will. He said, "Your bastard will never have any part of our estate. Do you hear me? *Never!*"

"Carlos, please . . . ," she said feebly. But my uncle threw the paper down and came back to the kitchen.

"Manuela, where are you?" His tone was more angry than ever as he threw back the curtain. I cowered behind the jar and hid my face. His heavy footsteps approached, and then I felt him grip my wrist so hard that it hurt as he stood me up angrily.

As he started to drag me to the door, Father Ramón rushed in to protest. I screamed and overturned the table in an effort to grab onto something, spilling the oil lamp on the floor. Father Ramón stopped to extinguish the fire while Carlos dragged me across the hut to the door.

"Have mercy, Carlos, please! Why? Please, no! Why?" my mother implored as he pushed me outside.

Carlos stopped in the doorway. "I'm taking Manuela to the convent of Santa Catalina for her education. I would rather not, but I have a civic and familial responsibility to educate her." He looked at me with loathing. "Even though I can tell she will amount to nothing."

"Carlos, please—" my mother wailed.

"If you had any decency, you would have entered the cloister yourself. When I have seen to this last responsibility of mine, that's the last I'll have anything to do with you or your bastard. You have shamed our family long enough." He stormed out of the door, dragging me cruelly behind him.

I kicked at him, bit him, and screamed as he dragged me through the rain to waiting mules, farther and farther away from my mother. Finally, he stopped and shook me, shouting at me over the downpour, "Stop it! Stop it! Do you hear? Stop it! Now!" At last, I stood still. "I'm taking you to the convent, and it'll only go worse for you if you fight."

With that, he picked me up and placed me on the sopping back of a mule in front of an old Indian servant. The old man who held me understood my fear. He said, "Do not worry. Everything will be well. Do not struggle anymore. You will only make it worse for your mother."

I looked back through the door, veiled by the rain, where I saw my mother crying out for me. I wanted to cry out also, but I was so afraid for her that I could only sit shivering in the rain that covered my tears. I saw her try to stand, in order to follow, but she was so weak that she collapsed on the floor. Father Ramón impotently tried to comfort her as Carlos mounted his own mule, and we rode off.

I wanted to run back and hold my mother. I wanted to say good-bye. I wanted to tell her everything would be all right. I wanted to stay and help her, but nothing could turn me back that night. Carlos led me, cold and drenched with rain, through the streets of Quito until we came to the main door of the Convent of Santa Catalina. We entered, and after hurriedly handing me over to the sisters he turned to me and said, "Try to behave." A look of disgust crossed his face, and he walked out.

I shrank from the strange surroundings. Before I even understood where I was, I was taken to the school area in the back and given some blankets and a linen nightshirt. I did not protest at all. The words of the old Indian servant, warning me that I would make it worse for my mother, were still in my mind.

I did not speak, even when asked something directly. "You will live here now, Manuela, and learn to read and write. Would you like that?" asked a nun, while two others removed my wet clothes, and dried me.

I resented them touching me, and being part of taking me away from my mother. I wanted to yell insults at them, but I was too numb. They ignored my silence, as they efficiently washed me, dressed me in a nightshirt, fed me, and made me go to bed in a small, cold room. I never had so many people attend me, yet I never felt so alone.

As I lay there in the dark, listening to the wind and rain outside the window, I became afraid for my mother. I lay trembling for a long time.

The next thing I knew the sun was up. I could see that it had been up for an hour or so. The storm was over, but not in my heart. I felt I had to get back to my mother. I was afraid for her.

I began to look for my clothes so I could steal out of the convent and return home. As I was about to open the door, two sisters brought in a little habit similar to the white Dominican style habit that was worn by the nuns. "I don't want to wear that," I said, when they told me to get dressed.

"Manuela, everyone wears this kind of dress here," one of them began.

A very short argument ensued, and then they started dressing me. It took them almost an hour and both of them were half undressed by the time they were finished engaging in battle with me. I kicked and fought until they had to call in two others to pin me down. Immobilized as I was, I was still able to talk. I let out a steady stream of obscenities and curses, but it made no difference.

When I was dressed, two of these angry nuns dragged me back in the direction of the main door of the convent to take me to the chapel to "pray for forgiveness." I fought them, I dug in my heels, I went limp, I tried everything to resist them but they were too strong for me. Then as we went through the main entrance hall, I saw a wonderful thing. My father was there.

Apparently he had come to my mother's house that morning when he heard she was ill. Juanita had seen him and told him of her condition. Father Ramón was still attending Joaquina that morning, and he told my father what Carlos had done. My ordinarily reserved father was furious and rode immediately to the convent.

He was arguing with the *portera* (the doorkeeper) when I was taken through the entrance hall. When he saw me, he called out, "Manuela!"

His shout made the nuns escorting me stop. I was thrilled to see him. He pushed right past the *portera*, who began calling for help. My captors were distracted enough for me to break free, and I ran into his arms.

"Papa! Papa, help me!" I sobbed.

"It is all right Manuela. All will be well. They have no right to take you away from your mother."

Then he was accosted by several angry nuns. He brushed them aside and carried me out to his horse. They almost successfully blocked his way at the entrance, and there was a great deal of shoving before he pushed through. The nuns followed him all the way outside, still trying to stop him. A stream of protests came from them. "Set her down!" "Criminal!" "Abductor!"

As he put me on his horse and began to mount, they again tried to block his way. Some tried to stop him from getting on and some tried to pull me off the frightened animal. One of them slipped and fell full length, in her white habit, face first, into the mire. Despite my fear, I laughed.

He finally mounted and spurred his horse. As he rode off, hooves splattered mud all over the faces and clothes of several nuns who were trying to recover me. I watched them chase after us in powerless frustration as we galloped down the street.

Often my father was weak and lacked decisiveness, but on occasions, like that morning, he could be an conflagration of strength. So it was that I was able to say good-bye to my dying mother. Also, my determination was strengthened somewhat by his example so that I was better able to survive the next years. Having seen him only a few times in my life, and feeling the bitterness my mother felt for him, I was uncertain about him, though I naturally felt kinship with him. That day I learned to love him.

By the time I returned to our house, my mother was much worse and not aware of her surroundings. Father Ramón was not there. She was all alone with Juanita. My father asked after Joaquina, and then he left. I stayed with my mother two days and watched her die.

A doctor was there most of that time, but he could not seem to help her. My father was not there because he knew he was in trouble for taking me from the convent grounds. Neither was Juanita there when my mother died. She left to get me some food and did not return until after my mother was gone.

Father Ramón did not come until the very end. My mother asked for him, but we did not know where he was. Later I found out that Carlos had insinuated improper behavior between the kind priest and my mother, and he was in trouble with the church authorities.

In the afternoon of the last day, there was a knock at the door. The doctor went over and opened it wide. A dark apparition stood in the doorway silhouetted against a sky that glowed with the last rays of the setting sun. The doctor greeted the figure who entered solemnly. I saw it was a tall angular priest, bearded and carrying a book. When he turned to look at me, I was frightened. A beam of light illuminated his face and I saw that his left eye was only a deep socket, with a gash instead of an eyelid. The cavity watered as though he were crying. However, the rest of his features belied tears. His face was cruel and angry.

He looked at me for a moment out of his one angry eye and then walked over to my mother. I became frightened and I threw myself in front of her. She was weak and could not even raise her hand to touch my head. I was making such a fuss that the doctor took me outside.

I saw Father Ramón approaching and ran up to him, saying, "Father, I'm so afraid."

"I'm sorry, but I was called away. How is she?"

"I don't know. There is a priest in there. Come!" I began to lead him to the door.

He looked at the doctor and then said softly, "Not just now. The priest is giving her extreme unction. Let us wait a minute."

When the priest with one eye came out of the house, he walked briskly back toward the center of town. He stopped for a moment when he saw Father Ramón, gave him a strange look and then he walked on. Father Ramón looked after him and said, "Father?" The older priest ignored him and kept walking.

Father Ramón slowly turned back toward the house. I could see there was a tear falling from one of his eyes. "Come," he said.

By the time we walked back inside the house, my mother was gone. I walked over to her bedside and slowly rested my head on her hand. I wanted to stay there forever. Time stopped for me.

After the doctor left, Father Ramón said, "Come. Help me. We must dress her."

First we emptied the entire room. The two little mirrors we owned were the first to go; then all the candles but four; then the chair, the little table, Juanita's cot, and everything else that was in the room, were moved outside, or to the kitchen.

As we started to dismantle the bed, Father Ramón found my mother's will where Carlos had thrown it on the floor. He uncrumpled it, looked at it a moment, then folded it, and put it in his frock. "Family," he muttered. He turned to me and said, "You and I are much alike." He looked sadder than I had ever seen him.

I appreciated his words, knowing that someone was there to take care of me; however, I did not acknowledge him. I walked around in a daze, doing as I was bidden by my kindly friend. After the room was laid bare, a straw mat was placed on the floor with a sheet on it. My mother's body was placed on the sheet and one of the four candles was set at each corner.

Usually, a friend or relative will buy a habit or monk's robe for the deceased, but there were no friends, and no money. Unlike the usual tradition of dressing the dead, she was merely wrapped in another sheet.

Juanita came back, just as we finished. Realizing she was too late, my nurse burst into tears and held me in her arms. "Your uncle kept me all afternoon," she cried.

My mother was to remain thus for a day, and I was prepared to sit with her; but it was not to be. An army officer, the one who now had my father's military position, Captain Salinas, came to the house a little later with orders to take me back to the convent.

I was too overwhelmed to resist. After receiving assurances from Juanita and Father Ramón that they would see me the next day, I left with Captain Salinas. He seemed oblivious to my feelings and determined to carry out his orders. I cried softly as we walked back to Santa Catalina. He also talked incessantly. "My mother was a good woman." "How old are you?" "Everything will be all right when you are in the convent." "My mother died only five years ago." On and on he went, as we walked through the dark, oblivious as to whether I was listening or responding. I wished he would have kept silent.

The nuns received me and dressed me in a habit. I did not resist. I was given some solitude in the chapel, in deference to my loss, before being made to sleep in a dormitory with the other students. It was quite late when I was put to bed. All the other girls were asleep.

I was awakened early the next day and taken to the chapel. I stayed there all day, and early the next morning Joaquina Aispuru was buried. Again, the nuns roused me early and took me to the chapel to pray, and later they took me to the funeral. Father Ramón, who had been the only friend my mother knew at the end, was not there, nor was Juanita. As I stood at the edge of my mother's grave, I watched my uncle look straight ahead in icy coldness while my aunts sniffled. I surrendered to a feeling of intense hatred.

I decided to beat my uncle. Of course, I was only seven years old and had no idea how to have any effect on him. Neither did I really understand yet what it was I was supposed to get from him. All I knew was that I was going to get what was mine and make him pay for my mother's suffering.

The nuns who had taken me to the funeral tried to usher me back to the convent as soon as the service was over. Before we had taken three steps, I snatched my hand free and ran over to Carlos, who was standing stiffly next to his crying sisters. "I hate you!" I screamed at him, "I hate you!"

I tried to spit in his face, but he was too tall and the spittle sprayed all over his surtout. Before I could see his reaction, I turned to flee.

I ran straight into the arms of the nuns, who scolded me and dragged me off to the convent, and a beating, and ten years of "imprisonment." I fought them all the way.

Chapter 5

"You have upset this community more in one day than anyone has in the last twenty years." I had just had a switch administered to me for my disobedience at the funeral before being turned over to this stern woman in charge of the convent students. When she tried to take me in hand, I cursed her and I was punished a second time. I was learning what was in my future.

"We have rules here. How to dress. How to eat. How to sleep. How to talk. You will live like a consecrated nun and you will especially learn to keep your filthy mouth clean." She paused and took a deep breath. Somewhat calmer, she said, "These rules are for all citizens of this community of women. You will obey them!"

I stood rigid, tears running down my face, murder in my heart, listening to my introduction into convent life. Only one thought was in my mind: "I will never obey!"

When my disciplinarian was through with her lecture, I was immediately put to work cleaning the greasy kitchen floors. I was at that job for three days, until my "jailers" deemed me rehabilitated.

I was given only porridge to eat, twice a day. Each evening, before being put to bed, dirty, in a small room where I could be watched, I would be given a choice. "Manuela, if you will promise to behave, you can attend school tomorrow. If not, you will continue with the chores we've given you."

The first two nights I answered in an insolent manner, seasoned with foul language, for which I was punished and put to bed. Thus did I spend my first days in the convent of Santa Catalina, days that would stretch out to a decade.

I hated those years. I was in turmoil the entire time because I never agreed with my situation. I never accepted that I had to be there. Always disobedient, I fought with my surroundings constantly.

Santa Catalina was one of the *conventos grandes* of Quito. It was only 100 years earlier when large cities like Lima, Quito or Santa Fe de Bogotá had convents whose populations grew to as many as 1000 women. By 1805, when I arrived, the populations were not as large, but these convents were still little cities within cities, with their own governments and social systems, composed entirely of women.

The conventual governments were controlled by the nuns of the black veil, the highest order of nun. These women were the only ones who had the right to vote on convent concerns. They controlled the convent. Their only other responsibility was singing in the choir.

Sisters of the white veil were "brides of Christ," just as their senior sisters, but they were not of the same earthly social class and they did not have the same political or social rights in the convent. These were most often the gardeners, bakers, doorkeepers, or the supervisors of the *donadas*, maids, and slaves.

Beneath the nuns of the white veil, in this stratification, were the novices. These were often young women, with their entire lives in front of them, who had decided to forsake everything for convent life. I never understood them.

Below these were the *donadas*, who were merely workers that were allowed to live in the nunnery and imitate the nuns in dress. They wore a nun's habit and had certain community rights, but they were little more than maids living as though they were consecrated nuns.

Other women in the community were secular ladies in retirement or in seclusion, schoolgirls, occasional illegitimate babies left for the convent to raise, and a large population of servants, maids, and slaves.

The convent grounds in most *conventos grandes* were completely walled and took up multiple city blocks. Each area of the convent was designated for a specific kind of work. Most business done with the outside world was done in the *porteria* (the main entrance hall) and in the adjoining *locutorios* (parlors and offices). The entrance hall itself is where merchants would deliver their goods and those wishing to see a member of the community would wait. In the *locutorios* could be seen judges or royal officers on official business, family members visiting with their daughters or cousins, female friends come to show off the latest fashions or to gossip, priests giving confession, or even a dandy who had brought flowers to a favorite nun whom he "loved from afar."

The rest of the convent was divided into the *seglarado* (where the schoolgirls stayed and studied), the kitchen, the laundry rooms, the bakery, the sewing rooms, the dormitories, and various other areas where convent work was done. In the center of the convent was a little "*pueblo*" of "cells," as they were known, which were the living quarters of the nuns of the black veil. Each nun of the black veil, or her family, had to buy or build a cell in which she would live. Into these cells, with their little gardens and porches, they might invite a nun of the white veil, *donadas*, servants, or others to live with them.

If one of these lower class women were not lucky enough to have such an invitation, she had to sleep in the communal quarters. Those who were chosen lived with their benefactors as elegantly as women in high society. These large convents were very well organized, opulent and clean, and they all had beautiful grounds. To some women, especially nuns of the black veil, convent life was freedom, freedom from a world ruled by men.

For me it was a prison, and despite the large number of women, I was lonely most of the time. In the ten years I stayed in that convent, never did any of the Aispurus come to visit me. I know Carlos came to the convent—at least every few months—to give the usual fixed donation and to pay other fees. I saw him on occasion. But he never did ask to see me. Not that I wanted to see him either.

I suppose I should have been grateful that he was paying for my education. The fees were not inexpensive. It cost 50 pesos a year "just to stand on the ground of the nunnery," as it was phrased. In addition, the families of the convent students had to pay up to 200 pesos a year for room and board. They also had to pay for clothing, medicines, doctor's visits, supplies, and other necessities. Regardless, I was not grateful.

Neither was I grateful to the sisters for the good education I received, because I knew, to them, I was merely a means of supporting the nunnery. Occasionally the convent management would take certain parents before ecclesiastical judges for permission to expel their daughters because their families had not paid the fees. These girls would often be good students and faithful members of the convent community, yet, because their families might have missed only one expense payment, they would choose not to keep the child so that someone else could enter and pay. This, in spite of the fact that it was well known that the *conventos grandes* were very wealthy.

Carlos paid some of my expenses (I know both my father and the Larreas paid for part of my upkeep in the convent as well), but he never provided one other thing that I might need. In fact, my father is the only member of my family who ever came to visit me. He would come every two or three months, and I was always so very glad to see him.

Knowing he was in the city gave me hope and confidence. So often when I felt lonely I would think of my father possibly coming to visit me (and perhaps taking me out of the convent for good); then I would have the courage to continue. His visits kept me going, and I needed him at that young age.

Sometimes he would bring my brother, José María, to play with me, and that always made me doubly happy. I loved my brother. He was the same age as I, soft spoken, gentle, with an angelic face, and he was always friendly to me. He could usually beat me at racing or other physical activities, but with him I did not mind. He made me happy. My father, my half-brother, and the Larreas were the only people who ever rescued me from my loneliness and my grief for my mother.

As I look back through time and experience, I can see that my isolation was made more complete by my own insolence, an insolence born out of the bitterness of being reminded constantly that I was illegitimate and thus unworthy to be a part of society. Consequently, the only face I ever showed to the world was one of disrespect; sometimes it was angry, sometimes sarcastic, but always disrespectful.

There were other complications that contributed to my insolence. Most significantly, very few of the other girls befriended me. To be honest, I could inevitably do anything they could do, only better, and my attitude prompted me to make sure they were defeated in some way before I even let one of them try to be friendly to me.

Most of the girls were from wealthy families who had placed their daughters in the conventual school in preparation for the black veil or to get the fine education available. They knew they were Spanish, and therefore important. They were not used to being bested. I felt a compulsion to compete with these girls, girls who had families, and win. They, in turn, in order to regain some self-importance, would remind me of my low birth, which then led me to attack them with words or fists.

Some did not need any help from me in order for there to be conflict. Some girls were unequivocally mean. One student, my age, taller than most of us, named Antonia, was there when I arrived. She was of aristocratic Spanish blood, with strong beautiful features. Like others of the most noble families, her family considered itself of such ancient lineage and so important that they began their prayers, "Mother of God, our cousin . . . ."

Even before I showed her up or beat her in games, Antonia abused me. On my first night in the convent, as soon as the *donadas* were not looking, she yanked on my hair so hard I fell down. All the girls standing around laughed. She continued to abuse me from that day on.

No matter how many times I was disciplined by the nuns, the switch they used on me never subdued me, but rather seemed to instill in me an even greater resolve to be free of them. Contrary to their intentions, I became less and less tractable. Not even the convent jail with its awful loneliness, in which I spent a few nights from time to time when I became an adolescent, affected my behavior one bit.

Although I was the charge of the sisters of Santa Catalina, I seemed to be in the city far more than the other little girls being educated in the convent who, for the most part, were never allowed out. The rich ones usually had sisters, or aunts, who were nuns of the black veil. These powerful members of the convent community, having their own spacious cells, would invite their young relatives to dinner, to sing songs in the evening, or to live with them. Consequently, many wealthy young students had most of the benefits of a complete home life. On the other hand, a few of the girls had parents who were poor, or no parents, and were there as a result of arrangements made by charity-minded citizens. They, especially, had nowhere to go outside the convent.

A woman could spend her entire life in a convent. She might be placed in the *torno* (a revolving box used to pass food and other supplies through the cloistered convent walls) as an illegitimate newborn. She would be raised by the nuns, grow up in the convent school, and finally (and it is little wonder that such women would do so, never having known any other home) ask to take the veil. If such a girl could sing well, or could provide some other important asset to the convent, she might be taken in without even a dowry, which was a requirement. Such women, inevitably, would be obedient to convent and school rules and would never leave.

On the other hand, I, while carrying the stigma of bastard, did have a rich father who was not totally inattentive to me. I also had the Larreas, one of the wealthiest families in Quito, who really liked me, and they would invite me now and then to their home. If I had any real friends, other than my father and brother, it was Don and Doña Larrea who got me out of there every week or so.

Convent rules were usually very strict, but the very large convents in most cities were difficult to control and Santa Catalina had perhaps the worst reputation for lax discipline of any in Quito. Nuns themselves were even known to leave the convent and spend days with their families during the holidays. So when the Larreas asked to take me out for a few hours, to have me sit at their elegant table and eat fine food or to go to the theatre or to let me play in their home, the convent agreed. They did not want to antagonize such wealthy patrons as the Larreas, and I don't think they really cared that much about the rules.

Whenever these wonderful friends of mine invited me out, to the market or the theatre, they seemed oblivious to the whispers behind their backs that they had brought along that Sáenz/Aispuru bastard. The Larreas were too rich or too kind-hearted to let it bother them, if they heard. I, being overly sensitive to such whisperings, imagined that I heard every word.

Perhaps that is why I loved the theatre so. There I would become spellbound by the actors' accomplishments on the stage and be transported from the hostility I believed I felt around me. I have loved all things theatrical ever since those early convent years when I saw my first performances from private Larrea chairs.

When I was at the Larrea mansion, I would usually be allowed to play with the servants' children and I would have some normal social contact. On special occasions, I might be invited to sit at the dinner table with Don and Doña Larrea. Usually, however, I would spend most of my time in the stables and eat with the servants. The stable-hands would let me sit on a horse or ride it around the immediate area, giving me instructions in the finer points of horsemanship.

In addition to my visits with the Larreas and outings with my father, I could always find a way out of the convent on my own when I wanted to do so. I was almost always reported on such occasions, by the "good people" of the town, and was punished. I was not always caught and punished, but I was most often. But punished or not, while I was out, I would inevitably cause mischief; and when I was disciplined, I would resolve to escape again.

On such occasions, when I escaped, I might be seen purposefully impeding servants carrying chaise chairs that conveyed one of the city's matrons who disliked me most. Or, I might snatch parcels out of hands in a surprise ambush that would scatter the contents all over the ground. I might steal from vendors on the street. I would purposefully raise mischief all over the city, but my victims were mostly the "good" women and men of the city who knew who I was, those who were most vocal about their dislike for me and the "shameless" Joaquina.

Naturally, my antics did nothing to change their opinion of me, and when I went out, I would always hear expressions like, "Just what you would expect from a bastard." I have heard that so many times in my life, it has become a hymn to my unkillability. As the years went on, it would only take my presence in the squares or streets to provoke a shaking of heads, a snarl on the lips, and a pronouncement of the derogatory name I had been given by these people, "La Sáenz." I later used that name like a title that demanded respect.

Even as a young child, I realized that these people (such as my uncle) who controlled the city with their "moral," hypocritical ways and who were most responsible for the mistreatment of my mother and me, were distinguished only in their personal mediocrity. Mostly they produced little, and they controlled much that they did not produce.

It enraged me that my life should so often be dominated by the likes of such people. I realize now my impotent mischievous behavior was my own childish way of trying to bring them down. At other times, however, I admit I was equally enraged, or morose, that I could not be like them or to even be accepted by them. Sometimes I regretted deeply my low birth, which prevented me from being part of the Aispuru household. If I was an accepted member of such a family, I knew I too would then have that same ability to have power over other peoples lives (and more importantly, my own).

There was a constant war within me, not unlike some of the middle class of Quito, who were also trapped on the thresholds of their own births. Even though my veins pumped the aristocratic blood of pure Spanish stock, my life was actually like that of the *cholo* (half-breed Indian), who did most of the work that supported the city.

These people made up the majority of the population and were soldiers, priests, craftsmen, and the like. They were descended from the offspring of the conquistadors and the native Indians. Many Incan princesses were the mothers of some of the great families in Lima and Quito. It was Doña Inés, Pizarro's ex-concubine, granddaughter of Manco Capac, who, by marrying the nephew of St. Ignatius, Ones de Loyola, founded the noble family of Oropesa, which is universally respected throughout South America.

In the intervening centuries, the social standing of those first half-breeds had degraded considerably. They were excluded from high administrative office, even though they had shown their indispensability to society and ostensibly had the same rights as the Spaniards, by law, just like me. But also like me, they were constantly being excluded from the enjoyment of those privileges when not actually being persecuted by the "whites."

Whenever I looked into their eyes—when I saw them on the street or at the market—I recognized the same battle that was raging in my own heart. They, too, hated their "masters," and yet, they wished that they could be them. They, too, suffered in their souls as they tried to reconcile their ancient aristocratic past with their subservience. The only difference was that my youth kept the fires burning so hot that I *never* agreed with my condition and thus I never moved into the well-known docility of the *cholo*.

Because I so identified with the *cholo*, whenever anyone questioned me about my ancestral heritage or asked about my lineage, I would always proudly say that I was "American"—not one race, but all races.

So my life as a child was fraught with loneliness and abuse, and I see now that there were only two things that kept me from running away and never returning. First, I had never known any other existence than what I had and, therefore, everything outside of Quito was unknown and unreal to me. Second, I desperately needed the little bit of love that I did receive from the Larreas, and especially my father and brother. I needed to know they were nearby and that I could see them now and then.

Regardless, throughout those first years in the convent, I looked for an opportunity to escape from my position when I was awake and I dreamed about it at night. All I really wanted then, or now, was to be who I am and to be free from the shackles of those who have tried to control me. The small-minded who have tried to keep me in "my place," as a child or as a woman, have always been my real enemies.

I knew, even when I first entered the convent, that these were my enemies. I tried to fight them those first two days. I stoically washed that kitchen floor, wanting to show them I could take anything they gave me, but I knew I could not take it for long. When I was asked again that third night to comply with their rules, I decided that school would be a much better situation than cleaning that floor forever.

I stood up and lowered my eyes. "All right," I said softly, looking at the floor I'd just cleaned. There was a great deal of noise in the kitchen. Workers were coming and going, talking, moving knives or pottery around, and one slave was scrubbing a large brass pot.

"I cannot hear you, Manuela."

I kept my eyes on the floor and said again, loudly enough to be heard over the din, "All right!"

Having not heard me curse when I opened my mouth for the first time, the sister decided that I could "join" the community. "Very well, you may have a bath and tomorrow you will attend school and eat with the other girls. You had better have learned your lesson. Now, put these things away and go to the dormitory."

My eyes still lowered, I uttered, "Yes, Señora."

"That's better," she said as she left the kitchen.

I meekly picked up the jug and rag, rinsed them out, and put them where they belonged. Then I slowly made my way through the confusion in the kitchen. As I was crossing the threshold of the kitchen doorway, I turned to see if anyone was looking.

"I will never obey," I whispered and I spit on the floor.

Chapter 6

In August of the year my mother died, an event occurred far away from Quito as I lay in my dormitory bed: an event that would someday have great meaning for me. I had been in the convent only a few weeks. My surroundings made me feel suffocated, alone, and sorrowful. I missed my mother and felt unable to control anything at all in my life and impotent to make any effect on the world around me. I was ill that day.

I lay in my sick bed, utterly miserable, staring through the doorway to where nuns walked back and forth in the hallway like a wall of soldiers determined to keep me in prison. I sobbed in desperation and wanted to give up and die. I was sure that my captors were right about me: I would never be able to do, or be, anything at all. I was certain that I would never know love, such as I had shared with my mother, again.

My illness lasted for many days. Thus, I know that one of those days was August 15, 1805. Ironically, as I cried to myself that early morning, I did not know something was happening, at that moment, which would eventually change my life. I did not know this because this event was happening so far away that it was already a sunny afternoon in Rome where two men walked through the dusty streets toward the Monte Sacro.

One man was older than the other by ten years or so, being in his middle thirties at that time, though his thinning, unkempt hair and small, barrel chest made him look more aged. In any event, he never would divulge his years. He had eyes that looked through dwarf spectacles with intellectual fire and challenge.

Perhaps it was the way the older man wore his clothes, or the clothes themselves, but it seemed that his attire was meant to scandalize those around him rather than cover him, although to describe them one could only say "rags." On that afternoon he used a staff that he was still breaking in, to keep pace with his feet, a staff he had recently picked up on the road from France.

He had been a priest when young, for a very short time, but had been defrocked due to unwise encounters with his female parishioners and because of his refusal to know the right time or place to spout his affection for the revolution-inspiring words of Rousseau. His name was Simón Rodríguez, but he went by the name of Samuel Robinson.

The other, younger man was Simón Bolívar, perhaps the wealthiest aristocrat in the new world, though only 22 years old. He dressed in the latest fashions when attending the salons of Paris, or Madrid, or when visiting the Pope, as he had done a few days earlier at the behest of the Spanish ambassador. This afternoon he wore a very simple, but stylish, walking outfit of a matching brown coat and trousers. His visage was long and angular, with thick black eyebrows that arched over piercing dark eyes. A sparse beard had recently grown on the young face, but it was perfectly trimmed. His black hair, tied with a ribbon in back, was longer than it normally was since he had spent the last few weeks walking through Europe with Rodríguez. Years before, in Venezuela, Rodríguez had been the young man's tutor.

If I were made to say so, I would have to state that Bolívar was not really handsome. His dark skin was slightly blemished and his patrician nose was too prominent. Taller than his companion, but still a little shorter than average, he was quite slender, with quick, high-strung movements. Despite all that, he had a quality of virility, a likable intensity, and a true sensitivity that more women than I found irresistible.

Eight years prior to his walk up the Monte Sacro, while Quito was still feeling the effects of the great earthquake and I was busy being conceived, Rodríguez had to leave Venezuela abruptly. Balding and stooped even then, though only in his twenties, he had been implicated in a revolutionary plot. He left Venezuela on an English ship, under the name of Samuel Robinson. Because he was without his tutor, young Bolívar asked his guardians (both his parents had died a few years before) if he might go to Europe to study.

It would be two more years before Bolívar would leave for Spain, arriving in the spring of 1799. He was no more than 15 years old. There, coming from a wealthy family, he had taken up with the high society of Madrid, rooming with a *criollo* relative who was supposed to be having an affair with the Queen. He moved in the highest social circles and quickly learned the ways of the world.

The truth is, the man with whom Bolívar lived, Mallo, truly was one of the men with whom the Queen shared her attentions, along with the infamous Godoy. Bolívar told me about her coming to their apartment one evening, disguised, to have dinner with them, nearly causing a fight later between the two colonials as her affections appeared to be turning towards Bolívar.

Later, when Bolívar became famous and his history was being told, the rumor was that Bolívar himself had an affair with her, but he had not. He was just then learning his way with the ladies (and learning that he had a way with them) when he met María Theresa, his soon-to-be wife.

I am told that she was a delicate, beautiful girl, with whom he fell instantly in love. After a long ordeal, Simón finally gained her father's favor. It was May of 1802, at only 18 (when I was 4), that he married and began the journey to return to his country estate in Venezuela.

There he intended to live in idyllic happiness with his new wife. Considering the beautiful countryside, his inherited wealth (now that he was married), and his deep love for his bride, he might have succeeded except that six months later María Theresa died of yellow fever. Her memory continued to haunt him all his life.

By the time he was walking down the streets of Rome, angrily arguing with Rodríguez, Bolívar had spent most of the intervening three years, since his bride's death, in Europe. He was apathetic and grieving at some times or, so I'm told, living the life of a wastrel at others. Rodríguez was in France, still going by the name of Robinson, when fate dictated that they should meet.

The tutor saw that his student of long ago was wasting away in Paris and enticed him into a walking tour of Europe. Bolívar agreed and their journey took them to the south of France, through Milan, where they witnessed Napoleon being crowned Emperor of Italy, then on to Padua, Florence, and finally Rome.

They arrived in the Eternal City in late June and took an apartment in Rome's *Piazza di Spagna*. It had not been their plan to stay long, but Bolívar, true to his character, had met a Spanish noblewoman, living in Italy with her husband, and the two were whispered about as his stay turned into weeks.

Rodríguez has told me this story more often than anyone. As the two of them walked through the streets of Rome that day, their conversation was animated, spurred on by events earlier that week. Bolívar was still fuming because of the treatment he had received at the Vatican a few days before.

The Spanish ambassador had sent a messenger to rouse him early that morning. The Pope had learned that a colonial nobleman was staying in the city and had asked the Spanish ambassador to bring him to discuss life in the colonies. In the *Piazza di Spagna* were many Spanish nobles, but Bolívar was the first colonial to live in Rome for many years.

Neither the ambassador nor Bolívar was in an amiable mood as their carriage drove through the streets toward the Vatican. The ambassador, whom Bolívar described to me as a thin, wiry little man, did not enjoy having his daily routine disturbed so that this colonial, of loose morals he had been told, could be made more important by meeting the Pope. Bolívar was sour because in addition to being aroused early by a surly messenger, the note from the ambassador had been quite rude in demanding that Bolívar meet him at his palace immediately.

Bolívar had experienced this kind of treatment before, in Spain. The total disregard that the Spanish authorities had for colonials made him angrier each time he experienced it. Bolívar, in addition to having a proud temperament and a keen mind that could see the truth of things, had been raised on Rousseau and other inflammatory writings placed before him by Rodríguez and others. In his heart, he was already a budding revolutionary.

His trip to the Vatican was a moment of crystallization after a lifetime of preparation. It is said that the entire time they waited in the Pope's crowded antechamber, the arrogant ambassador lectured Simón on proper etiquette in the presence of his Holiness. Simón, as was so typical of him, ignored the man.

Finally, the two were asked to enter. Bolívar walked up to the Pope, stood very proudly, and gave a little nod of his head in respect to the pontiff. The ambassador quickly gave him a sign, and Bolívar, following the instructions he had just received, reluctantly dropped to his knees in supplication. Inwardly, as he lowered himself to the floor, Bolívar became angry. He had had enough of princes, be they holy or otherwise, degrading him.

The ambassador, after a moment, whispered urgently, "Now you must kiss the cross on his Holiness's slipper."

Bolívar did not move. The ambassador urged him again, "Kiss the cross on the slipper."

"No!" Bolívar whispered back angrily, "I will not."

"You must kiss the cross on the slipper."

Bolívar looked straight ahead while the ambassador gestured to the pontiff's foot.

Finally, the Pope saved the situation by smiling and saying quietly, "Let the young man from the Indies do as he pleases."

The ambassador stood up angrily and forced a smile at the Pope, while the pontiff went ahead and asked Simón several questions about his homeland. When they returned to the antechamber, after about three quarters of an hour, the ambassador upbraided Bolívar for being so rude.

Bolívar finally exploded in his defense, "The Holy Father must have little respect for the symbol of his own religion if he carries it on his foot! Even the proudest kings of Europe wear it on their crowns!" He walked off, returning to his apartment without benefit of the ambassador's carriage.

A few days later, an argument ensued in their apartment as he and Rodríguez discussed his audience with the Pope. Bolívar realized that the ambassador would make life less pleasant for them in Rome. He was, therefore, more determined to stay. On the other hand, Rodríguez, already feeling the need to keep traveling, made pleas to depart.

Bolívar was stubborn and said he had not seen enough of Rome's history. Rodríguez knew he was posturing and suggested a walk up the Monte Sacro, to challenge Bolívar's argument. Bolívar angrily accepted the challenge, immediately, and walked out the door, forcing Rodríguez to run to catch up.

Rodríguez retold me this story—it was his favorite—not too long ago, just weeks before he died. It was never quite the same story but the important parts were always there. He told me that the Aventine or "Holy Hill," on the edge of Rome, was the place where, two millennia ago, the people of Rome had confronted the ruling class to demand their lawful rights.

As the pair reached the foot of the hill and made their way along the path, Bolívar was still talking about the disdainful way he had been treated by the ambassador merely because he was from the colonies.

Rodríguez was actually more insurgent than Bolívar at the time, but he was older and he wanted Bolívar to calm down. "But, Simón," said Rodríguez soothingly, "it wasn't personal. That is the way the ambassador was reared—"

"Yes, like all *peninsulares*," he said cutting off the older man, "he has been taught that only they have any rights. It needs to change, do you not see?"

"Yes, but . . ."

"I wish a leader such as Napoleon had been born in Venezuela. We need someone like him to drive out the Spanish leeches."

"Napoleon is as bad."

"Yes, it disgusts me how he has declared himself emperor. I refused to go to his coronation when I was in Paris."

"Then why did you insist on attending his coronation in Milan?"

"Because . . . even though I loath his abuse of power, I respect him." As Bolívar went on to explain his logic, so he would not appear to be contradicting himself, Rodríguez knew what his student felt: youthful admiration for the conqueror of Europe. "Think, Rodríguez—"

"Robinson. Remember, it is Robinson."

"Of course. But think how much he has accomplished. He has commanded so many men and conquered so much territory."

"Yes, Simón, but—"

"I am only saying that I wish someone of his abilities had been born in our homeland. Do you know, when I was in Paris, I spoke to Alexander von Humboldt and he said, 'Spanish America is ready to be free, but has no man of stature to lead them.'"

"So you think that if Napoleon—"

"No, Rodríguez," Bolívar said angrily. "I'm saying that if a man *like* Napoleon could lead us, we could be free of these indignities and chart our own destiny."

"Yes, but . . ."

"The man we really need is someone like George Washington. He set his country free. That is what we lack, a man who can lead a revolutionary army and establish a new republic such as the United States of America."

By now, they were halfway up the Monte Sacro, and the sun was about to set. Rodríguez said nothing, knowing it was pointless to argue with Bolívar when he was aroused. They climbed the hill in silence. When they reached the top, the heat was oppressive. They sat on a slab of marble in the shade.

The two friends sat there for some time, silently contemplating the domes and towers of the world's great city. Finally, Bolívar motioned to the expanse before them and said, "So, this is the city of twelve Caesars. This is the great city with its history that goes back to before Christ."

Rodríguez said, offhand, "Yes, decadent now."

"Rodríguez," Bolívar went on, "this city has contributed something to everything: being a republic, depraved emperors, catacombs for Christians . . . ." He laughed at his own description. "Orators, poets, statesmen, philosophers, historians, naturalists, warriors . . . ." Then he spoke more seriously. "Contributions to every cause but the cause of the people. Nowhere is there something the colonies can use to fight their masters."

The legend, spread mostly by Rodríguez, is famous now. How Bolívar grew silent, and then, tears brimming in his eyes, he lifted himself and, shaking his fist, said, "I swear before you, by the God of my fathers and the honor of my country: I will not rest, not in body or soul, until I have broken the chains of Spain."

Bolívar told me what he actually said that day: "We should kick their Spanish asses back to Spain. And we shouldn't rest until we do it."

The two friends laughed and descended the hill, their argument seeming to have vanished. Despite the lack of romantic allure that the true story had, they both knew, without speaking about it, that a kind of commitment had been made.

Shortly thereafter, they resumed their tour and wandered around Italy for a short time, but a restlessness had taken over Bolívar. He had begun to consider the possibilities of a revolution in the new world. Finally he left Rodríguez to his own travels and returned to France.

After taking almost two years to put his affairs in order, during which time he joined the Masons in Paris and the Lautaro Lodge in London (of which I will speak more), he left Europe. He took a long voyage. First he went to New York, where he stayed for some time. From the people and institutions of the United States he sharpened some of his own ideas about revolutionary governments. Finally, he left for Venezuela. In July of 1807, he was back in Caracas.

I hold that day in Rome to be sacred, because it brought him to me. The young man named Bolívar, later called "El Libertador," kept his commitment. He freed South America from Spain, liberating an area far greater in size than Napoleon ever controlled. His battles one day took him to the city of my birth. That day in Rome marked the beginning of his journey to me.

While he walked on the Monte Sacro, I lay in bed and felt like nothing in life would ever happen right for me. I was wrong. Only a few years later our paths would begin to cross, sparked by the abortive revolution of 1809 in Quito. The story of my own life as a revolutionary would begin in 1808, when I was ten, with certain events preceding that tragedy.

Chapter 7

Because I was able to free myself of the convent walls so often, I had an encounter in 1808 that shaped me far more than I realized at the time. My experience that day also foreshadowed the unfortunate insurrection that was about to transpire.

Two months before my eleventh birthday, a new president of the Royal Audiencia arrived in Quito. Preparations for his arrival had kept the city in disorder for a week. Everywhere he stopped on his route from Guayaquil there had been a celebration. I knew something was happening, but I was too young to care or know what it was.

As part of the welcoming ceremonies in Quito, a theatrical evening had been arranged. I happened to meet the two men who were primarily responsible for choosing and preparing the entertainment. Later these two would have a much deeper significance to me and the land of my birth. They should have been commemorated and glorified in the annals of my country for being its first revolutionaries, but like me, they may not even be remembered.

I met them on the eve of the theatrical presentation for the new president, Count Ruíz. I was at the Larrea mansion that afternoon, where I had been playing all afternoon. Three other children and I were playing a game of tag running in and out of the stables. It was one of the few times that I was truly having fun, and in youthful glee I ran through the stable doors and right into a man just walking in to get his horse. I hit him so hard I fell back down in the dirt.

I became paralyzed at the thought that I had offended some visitor of Don Larrea's. The other children vanished, but I could only sit there on the dusty ground in the doorway to the stable while my eyes rose from shiny boots to a handsome face. Not yet approaching middle age, he had a smile that completely captivated me. This smile turned to laughter as he looked down at a young girl, frozen, mouth open, covered with a layer of stable dust.

As he reached down and took my hands to help me up, Don Larrea said, "This is Manuela Sáenz. Manuela, say hello to Señor Morales and Señor Quiroga." When he spoke my name, I saw recognition on the handsome face of Morales, and he turned his head sharply toward Don Larrea. I did not understand how he knew me. Don Larrea gave an indication to Morales that he should not say whatever was on his mind.

I stood with my mouth open while Don Larrea brushed the dust from my back and said, "Manuela, say hello to my friends."

I put on my very best adult manners and attempted a curtsy. "I am very pleased to meet you."

Morales smiled at me and said, "Well, I am pleased to meet you, Manuela. How did you get this straw all over you?" He reached down and took a long piece of dried grass out of my braid.

I felt the blood rush to my face. But he was so disarming with his smile, I found myself smiling back and replying, "Oh, just playing." When I said that, I felt childish and self-conscious.

Morales chuckled and took his handkerchief from his pocket and wiped a bit of dirt from my forehead. He said, "We have the same name. My name is Manuel and yours is Manuela." Then he handed me his handkerchief, saying, "Here, why don't you keep this. It has your initial on it." I looked at the embroidered blue "M" in one corner next to the dirt that had just been wiped from my forehead. Morales smiled at me and turned toward the stable to get his horse.

I took a deep whiff of the heavy cologne on the handkerchief and I think I fell in love for the first time. I wandered aimlessly around the corner of the stable. Then, I overheard Don Larrea saying quietly, apparently to an inquiry from Morales, "It's his little girl. She's illegitimate and lives at the convent of Santa Catalina. But, as I told you before, he should not be contacted. He's loyal to the crown and always will be. Take his name off that list."

"Very well, Don Larrea," Morales replied.

Don Larrea went on, while walking out of the stable with the two men and their horses, "Please consider my opinion again, Señors. As I said, I will not be a party to a violent coup."

"We understand," said Morales.

"Your theatrical presentation tomorrow is a fine idea, but I doubt it will have any effect on the Count Ruíz. I know His Excellency and he is as unchanging as the mountains." He lifted his hand toward Pichincha overlooking the city.

"Your reticence is understandable," said the other man, Quiroga, "but things will not stay as they are forever. The *peninsulares* pass on only official reports of the events in Europe, but we Americans hear the truth from our relatives. We must do something to stir up feelings for political change. Anyway, we thank you for your hospitality, and we look forward to seeing you tomorrow night at the university."

I paid little attention to all of this. It was only later that I thought about what was said, trying to understand what had happened. Mostly what I was thinking about was the intoxicating smell on the handkerchief. I did hear the words "theatrical presentation," and I wanted to go. As I watched them walk out of the stable, wondering if I dare ask if I could go to the theatre, I saw Morales fold something—which looked like a register of names—and tuck it in his coat. As they walked to the center of the street, unnoticed by Morales, the folded paper fell to the ground.

How would things have been different if I had let it lie? However, I saw an opportunity to prolong my encounter with the handsome Morales. Perhaps he would invite me to go to the theatre.

"Señor Morales! Señor Morales, you dropped something." I rushed to where it lay, picked it up, and carried it over to him."

"Oh, thank you, Manuela. I must not lose this."

Without thinking, I said, "Are you going to the theatre?" with a distinct plea in my voice.

Don Larrea smiled patiently at me, and Morales and Quiroga laughed. Morales said, "Do you like the theatre, Manuela?"

"Oh, yes," I said, "It's wonderful."

"Do you get to go often?"

My face became dejected as I said, "No." Then, I began to feel embarrassed by my obvious childishness.

Don Larrea saw my discomfort and said in a kindly way, "We take Manuela to the theatre once in a while, don't we, Manuela?" He patted my shoulder.

"Yes, Don Larrea," I said, smiling happily at him.

Morales, miraculously said, "Well, why don't you come tomorrow night? I'll bring a stool and you can sit in my box."

I felt like heaven had opened up and I turned to look at Don Larrea saying, "Oh, yes! Please?"

He smiled and said, "We'll see."

"Oh, please, Don Larrea, please. Please."

"Now, Manuela, I said we would see. Don't be rude."

I withdrew. I was embarrassed and worried that I might have offended Don Larrea. I backed up. Good-byes were said, while the handsome Morales and tall, thin Quiroga mounted their horses. I stood silently watching them ride down the cobblestone street into the evening gloom.

Then, Don Larrea, who had been standing in stern silence, put his hand on my back to direct me and said curtly, "It's getting dark. I had better see that you get back to the convent."

I knew I must have offended him. I cursed myself for being so stupid. I had so wanted to go to the theatre, but it seemed I had only made my friend angry with me.

As I walked back to the convent, alongside a Larrea servant, I was feeling conflicting emotions. First I would smell the cologne and the faint musk of masculinity on the handkerchief and feel exhilarated in a way that was subtle and indefinable; then I would think about how I had been so silly and had perhaps upset Don Larrea, and I would become melancholy.

My emotions shifted between these two extremes all the way to the convent. By the time we reached the portals, I had realistically decided I would probably never see Señor Morales again. Nevertheless, I said to myself, "He is my friend, whether I see him again or not." I was always making such pronouncements to myself, deciding who would, and who would not, be allowed to be my friend. I saw my world divided into "friends" and "enemies" and I made quick decisions about the category into which each person was to be placed. As for Don Larrea, I hoped I hadn't offended him and that he still liked me.

Later, I put the handkerchief under my pillow without knowing it belonged to a man who might have one day been regarded on the equator as one of its heroes. Barely remembered by the end of the revolution forming all over the continent, he and Quiroga were two of its first leaders.

Morales was a native of Mariuita, which lies in the Viceroyalty of Santa Fe de Bogotá. He had been a government official in Quito a year or so prior to my meeting him, when the Baron de Carondelet had been president. Sometime during the preceding year, he had lost his employment to a cold, ambitious *peninsulare* named Señor Arrechaga.

Morales suffered the same fate as many Creoles in the Spanish colonies. The *criollos* were always being relieved of their positions so that Spanish born, newly arrived on the continent, could take their jobs. A bitter feud between Morales and Arrechaga began when Morales lost his position.

He was feeling thus abused when he met Señor Quiroga, a native of Arequipa who was married to a *quiteña* (lady of Quito) and who had been practicing as an advocate. In Quiroga, Morales found someone of a like mind. Quiroga was a very opinionated speaker who had, in the year preceding these events so offended the leaders of the *audiencia* (local governing body) that he had been disbarred.

These two had been openly discussing the wrongs of the government throughout the city, in the salons of prominent members of society, at the time I met them. They had undeniably hinted at revolution, which was why my father, a devout Royalist, should never have been on Morales's list of potential supporters. Juan Larrea had been right in urging that the name of Simón Sáenz be removed from it. Would that the plea had been heeded.

I understood nothing of what was happening in the world at that time, sheltered as I was by the convent and my age, but the time was indeed ripe for discussions of revolution among the aristocracy. The "events in Europe," of which Señor Quiroga had spoken, had begun exactly one year earlier than my meeting with the two men.

In October of 1807, the conqueror, Napoleon, had made a treaty with Spain at Fontainebleau. In this treaty, he secured the right to march through Spain in order to attack Portugal (which at that time was still trading with the British). He was also allowed to set up garrisons on Spanish soil. This was Napoleon's first step in conquering the Iberian Peninsula. Ferdinand VII, the heir apparent, actively opposed the treaty, knowing Spain would eventually suffer.

At this time, Charles IV was King of Spain. However, he was scorned by the Spanish for his weakness. He was already in low esteem because he did nothing to stop Queen Luisa's almost open affair with their minister, Godoy, whom the populace hated. Making a treaty with Napoleon was the final act of weakness. He was forced to abdicate in favor of his son, Ferdinand VII.

The Spanish rejoiced, but it was short lived. Napoleon, after successfully conquering Portugal—sending the Royal Family fleeing to Brazil—ordered his field marshal, Murat, to attack Madrid. This was done ostensibly "to protect the Spanish coast from the English."

By June of 1808, Ferdinand VII had been replaced with Napoleon's own brother, Joseph. The effect on the colonies was turmoil.

The official Spanish government, administered by the Spanish-born in the colonies, was really not Spanish anymore, but French. Yet the positions and income of the colonials depended on the good graces of those government officials. Due to the long-standing disregard with which the *peninsulares* held the *criollos*, the American-born began talking more fervently of their rights.

The general atmosphere of the times was liberal—the United States had just shocked the world by prohibiting the further importation of African slaves. Everyone was talking about how the new century would finally affirm the rights of man. On the day I met Morales and Quiroga, even at my young age, I knew something was happening. I did not understand how but I knew my world was about to change.

Chapter 8

On the day after I met Morales and Quiroga, the day of the theatrical presentation, I was feeling listless. I still worried that I had offended Juan Larrea the night before. In the middle of the afternoon, a *donada* came up to me and said, "Get cleaned up. Señor Larrea is taking you out this evening."

I was ecstatic. I hoped it was to go to the theatre. Never did I get ready to go somewhere as fast.

When I arrived in the *porteria*, Don Larrea was there himself instead of one of his servants. He was a short man and wore the dress of a courtier, complete with powdered wig and white stockings. He had a boyish face, though to me he looked very old.

When I came up to him, he said, "I don't know if you will really enjoy yourself tonight, but you wanted to go to the theatre so badly that I decided to take you."

I giggled with excitement and said, "Oh, thank you. Thank you, Don Larrea."

"Do you promise not to fidget and to act like a lady?"

I assured him that I would sit very still and be very good. As we walked into the street, I said, "I thought you were angry with me last night. I'm sorry I was rude."

He laughed, "Not at all. Last night I was disturbed by the conversation with my friends and worried about the future. No, I wasn't angry. Come, we must go."

I followed Don Larrea to the theatre, squeezing the folded handkerchief I was secretly carrying, with the blue "M" on it. I looked forward to sitting next to the handsome Morales at the theatre.

As we approached the building where the plays were to be presented, there was a large painted board out front that said:

TONIGHT

Señor Morales and Señor Quiroga
(with the help of the collegians of San Fernando)
as part of the welcoming celebrations for the arrival of
his Excellency the Count Ruíz de Castilla
will present

Cato

Andromacha

Zoraida

and

Auraucana

When we went inside, I was a little disappointed because I sat in the Larrea's box and not with Morales. Before the first play started, Morales himself went to the stage to give a welcoming address. I had heard Don Larrea speaking about it the night before, but I did not really understand that it was Morales himself who had seen to the rehearsing and staging of the plays.

I do not remember exactly what he said because I did not understand it, and I was too busy basking in my surroundings. I could see the new President of Quito from where I sat. I remember feeling proud of Morales, but I also remember that tension was in the air.

Now that I am grown, I understand why the room was so tense. Every play presented that evening had inflammatory themes, considering the times. At the end of each play, the applause was enthusiastic from some members of the audience and pronounced in its silence from most of the rest. Some people even left between shows.

I was completely enthralled with the performances, which I did not comprehend at all. To me they were wonderful, and I still remember nearly every gesture and costume. I was captivated by the theatrical experience itself. However, I could tell that some people hated what was happening on the stage. I worried for Morales that things were not going well for him.

When the final play was over, a handful of the people who were still left stood and applauded, but most sat in stony silence. I felt sympathetic for my friend, Don Morales. I wanted to leave quickly so that I would not have to see him upset, but the Larreas made it clear that they were going to meet Morales and Quiroga outside.

A little later, when we walked into the night air, I saw Morales and Quiroga again and I met Señor Quiroga's wife, who was nice to me. I was confused, however, because they all seemed to be delighted with the evening.

Don Larrea said, "You were certainly adventurous in your choice of plays. Almost dangerous."

I heard Señor Quiroga say with laughter in his voice, "Yes. I think we will see a president a little more aware of popular feeling than was the Baron de Carondelet."

Morales said, "Yes, I thought the actors did very well indeed. He could not help but get our message. It was more of an un-welcome-ing ceremony." Laughter and general agreement followed.

At that moment, the President himself came out of the hall, followed by a few men and women. He was rather round and jolly looking. Upon seeing Morales and Quiroga, he came over to greet them while expostulating about how good the performances were. I was delighted that my friends had so favorably impressed the President. When he left, everyone looked after him in gloomy silence.

Finally, Morales said, "He either didn't understand or he is a great actor himself. Isn't that like the arrogant Spanish?!" Then they all turned to make their way to their homes.

I understood later that their intention had been to use the presentation to have a political effect on the Count Ruíz and the rest of the government. By choosing plays with a consistent theme of freedom, they were intending to imbue the viewers with a sense of liberty and to provoke the Count. These plays were supposed to be a modest act of defiance directed towards the new representative of Spain. It had apparently been a wasted effort because nothing at all happened; in fact, the new president liked the show.

They were frustrated I know, but I also know that Señor Quiroga and Morales continued their intrigues. Perhaps even more steadfastly since the notoriety of having produced the plays. However, nothing happened for a few months. Then, in February of 1809, things changed dramatically for Morales and Quiroga due to the loose mouth of a person from my past.

In the preceding months, they had been able to bring the captain of the infantry into their plans. This was necessary if they were going to have a revolution, but unfortunately he was not the right man for any discretionary conspiracy. It was Salinas, who had taken me back to the convent after my mother died and who had replaced my father as military leader in Quito. He was, of course, sworn to secrecy, but he told two priests, a Father Polo and another, in a conspiratorial way, that there was a plan afoot to depose the Spanish authorities.

Even as a seven-year-old child, I thought Salinas was the childish one as he took me back to the convent that night. He kept babbling about my mother and death and other insensitive topics the whole way. My father had even told me, when mentioning him once, that Salinas talked too much. I do not think anybody ever really trusted him, but he held sway over the only military body in the area. Thus he had to be brought into Morales's and Quiroga's confidence.

Because Salinas had been so improvident, Thomas Arrechaga, who now held the office that Morales was trying to recover, was informed by the priests of what Salinas had said. Arrechaga and Morales had been at each other's throats since Arrechaga's arrival in Quito. Arrechaga, eager to strike a blow to his rival, immediately reported the affair to His Excellency, the Count Ruíz.

The government proceeded against Morales, Quiroga, Salinas and a parish priest by the name of Riofrio, but the evidence gathered against them was mysteriously stolen and the conspirators were eventually set free.

I now confess, for the first time, that I believe I was the one whose actions freed Morales and the others from incarceration, perhaps even changing history. I have never told anyone before because it is all supposition on my part, but here is the story.

As was often the case with prisoners whose offenses were political, they were held in a monastery. At the time, I didn't know that they had been arrested. I was out without permission one day and I happened to see Señor Quiroga's wife and their two small children walking along the street. As she made her way through the busy streets, I followed closely, trying to decide whether I should greet her or not. Before I could make up my mind, she went in to the *porteria* of a monastery.

This was the same monastery that always kept a bowl of fruit in the entrance hall, and it was one of my favorite escapades to run in when no one was looking and steal some. The idea crossed my mind for a moment, but then I wondered if it would not be best to wait until Señor Quiroga's wife had gone. I very carefully walked up to the door and stood right outside, watching. She spoke to the *portero* and then sat down on a bench with her children. She appeared to be waiting for something, or someone.

She was very pretty and thin with high cheekbones that gave an almost aristocratic air to her movement. She spoke rapidly to her children and she carried a look of worry. The children were absolutely beautiful. They were younger than I, perhaps five and six years, and they were dressed very smartly. Both were quiet, but they smiled at each other as though they shared some secret. It seemed to me they loved each other. As I looked at their companionship, and the love they all shared, I really wanted to be part of them. I stood outside watching them with envy.

From where I stood I saw the tempting bowl and I decided that I would steal some fruit after all. I waited a short time for an opportunity. When the few people that were in the hall were distracted, I quickly crept inside the doorway and hid in a little cavity deep in shadows. My usual actions at this point were to immediately dart from where I was to the fruit bowl and then out the door before anyone saw me, but I lingered a moment because I suddenly thought that perhaps I should wait until Señor Quiroga's wife left after all. I didn't want her thinking me a bad person.

Just then, a man with a very red face, who looked very official, came out of one of the rooms directly off the hall. When he saw Señor Quiroga's wife, he approached her in a very genteel and courteous manner. "Ah, Señora Quiroga, a pleasure to see you. I regret your husband is being most uncooperative. Perhaps you could persuade him that it would go better for him if he would be more talkative." His big crimson nose was shiny, and he was short, well dressed, and carrying a leather pouch and fine hat.

"Señor Muños, my husband is not known for being taciturn. Perhaps he is offended at being kept in prison."

"Hardly a prison, Señora, just a place where a few questions can be answered without interruption."

"Thank you, Señor Muños, I will tell my husband when I see him that he is not in prison and that he can return home at any time."

The man's red face turned purple. "I am in a hurry, Señora," he said very curtly and put his hat on his head. "Please excuse me. Good day." The man turned and left by the front door and walked down the street towards the center of town. His manner was decidedly angry.

Just then I saw monks take Morales, Quiroga, Salinas, and the priest Riofrio from the *locutorios* and head for the inner part of the monastery. They were in shackles and I instantly loathed the man, Muños. It was obvious that he was an enemy of my friends (though I was confused because Salinas, who I didn't like, was also with my friends).

I was pondering all this when suddenly I saw a monk coming at me with a furious look on his face. I had never been in this position before. I had always snatched the fruit and was well outside before one of the brothers saw me. I froze with fear.

The monk was tall and plump. His round face was ugly, made uglier by a look of malice. As he was about to grab me, I kicked over a bench that was close by and ran. The bench hit his shins and he let out a distinctly un-holy curse.

I raced around him, made a quick decision and grabbed an apple from the bowl in the center of the room, and then I ran for the door.

The monk was on his feet, but I ducked as he grabbed for me, darted out the door, and sped down the street. I knew I was being chased by the corpulent monk, but I hoped he could not run as fast as I.

I could hear his voice, shouting at me, "You stay away from here you little wretch!"

Shortly, I turned around and saw that I was at a safe distance. I started waving at him, smiling, and making rude gestures. He started to run after me again, but I ducked quickly down a side street.

When I was sure I was safe, I began leisurely walking through the streets of town while I ate my apple. I felt proud of myself for the way I had been able to get past the monk. As I was throwing away the core, I saw that same man again, Muños. He was just then entering a *botica* (apothecary shop). I think it might have been to purchase inebriating spirits.

I wiped my hands on my dress and decided to satisfy my curiosity about this man who was keeping my friends in prison. I slowly peeked in the door, but the front area of the shop was empty. I heard voices in the back.

I crept inside and looked at all of the clay jars on the wall containing potions to cure diseases. I read the words scratched on the sides with charcoal: llama fetuses, lizard excrement, powdered dried earthworms, bezoar stones, snake skin, mercury, and others. I had never seen so many different sizes of bottles and jars. I was about to look inside one when I thought I heard the voices in back getting closer, as though the men were returning.

I ran for the door. Then I saw something that I deemed very meaningful to me at the moment. The pouch the man had been carrying was leaning against his hat on a table. It had a large "Q" cut into the leather. Believing that Muños and my friends were adversaries and, seeing the "Q" embossed on the pouch, I stupidly assumed that it belonged to, and had been stolen from, Señor Quiroga.

I grabbed it, ran through the door, and raced back to the monastery to return it to my friends. I laugh at myself now, because inside me there was a tiny spark of selfishness in my motives. While returning to the monastery, I began imagining that Quiroga and Morales would be so impressed with me for returning their pouch that they would rescue me from my life in the convent. I made up all sorts of "modest" responses to their gratitude. "You're welcome, Señor Quiroga." "It was nothing, Señor Morales"

As I approached the monastery, I saw Señor Quiroga's wife just leaving. I ran up to her and gave her the pouch. "I found this," I said. She looked at me and then at the pouch. "I thought it belonged to Señor Quiroga," I went on. I was becoming flustered. Then her children began talking about my stealing the apple; and before she could thank me or say "aren't you . . . ?" or anything else, I ran away.

A few blocks away, as I walked back to Santa Catalina, I told myself how stupid I was. What if she didn't recognize me from the theatre? What if she did and then told Don Larrea about my theft of the apple? Why didn't I ask her to ask her husband and Morales to help me get out of the convent? I was walking along asking myself all sorts of questions, not paying attention to anything, wondering about the whole affair: What were my friends doing in the monastery, under guard? Who was the man from whom I had taken the pouch? What was in that pouch of Señor Quiroga's? I was thinking so hard about these things that I did not see the fat monk come up behind me.

Without any warning, I felt his big hand grab my wrist. "La Sáenz! Just what I expected. What are you doing out of the convent? I'll teach you to steal apples." He dragged me roughly back to the convent, where I received a harsh punishment.

My capture was so unexpected, and I got into such trouble, that I forgot all about the events of the day until much later. The next thing I heard was that the prisoners had been released, and Muños had been relieved of his position.

I heard that the official transcripts of the legal proceedings against the prisoners had been stolen. I do not know what made me realize it, but slowly I came to believe the "Q" cut into the leather on the pouch of Señor Muños did not stand for Quiroga. I now believe the pouch was full of the stolen official papers of the investigation commanded by the authorities of *Quito*.

My friends had been held in the monastery for two months. No one was supposed to know they were there. I didn't until I stumbled upon them, but I suspect that everyone who cared did know. They had been questioned throughout the period of their imprisonment and perhaps something found was apparently embarrassing to the investigators. This is all supposition on my part, of course. I don't know what happened for sure or even if the pouch I snatched from that table contained the missing documents, but for whatever reason, the loss of the evidence prompted their release.

I worried for weeks that soldiers would come and arrest me for my theft. Then, when nothing happened, I entertained the thought that perhaps, out of gratitude, Morales would come and thank me and try to repay me. Weeks went by, nothing happened, and I gradually forgot about the whole incident.

The "evidence," that I believe I stole, was in fact later found in Quiroga's household. He, with Morales, had probably disseminated the contents to the Creole leaders of the town. Apparently there were indeed articles compromising to the government, because Quiroga and Morales gained many, many supporters after that.

The story of these papers was not over. Later, when finally found in Señor Quiroga's house, the papers helped put him in jail. Among his effects was the original list of potential conspirators, which I had picked out of the dust that day in order to "bribe" Morales into taking me to the theatre—the list from which my father's name had never been crossed off. Although my father had never been contacted by Morales, the fact his name was on that list altered the course of my life.

Chapter 9

The Church and its ministers were mostly loyal to the Spanish crown and were never friends of any South American revolutionaries; that is, until July of 1809. In that month, Napoleon annexed the papal states and arrested the Pope. When the colonies were informed of this sacrilegious act, about six weeks later, the Bishop of Quito was induced to join a conspiratorial meeting in one of the city's fine Creole households. His very presence at that meeting seemed to give the conspirators courage.

I was unaware of the next significant event in this political drama. Inside the convent, many incidents seemed to pass me by. A lot of blood was about to be spilled, and yet I knew little about what brought it all to the point of violence until years later. As I became more aware of the political situation and began to side with the revolutionaries, more out of defiance of authority than anything else at my young age, I met many people who knew what happened on that pivotal August day in 1809. This is the way it was told to me by Don Larrea and others.

The temperature was a bit cooler than usual as the sun was about to break over the mountains from a clear sky. It was Thursday, August 10, 1809. Two men, by the names of Ante and Aguire, walked through quiet streets that were illuminated by the coming dawn. When they arrived at their destination, they knocked on the heavy door of the palace of the President.

An elderly servant, already dressed in his black frock, opened the door and demanded to know who was calling so early. They stood in the doorway and informed the servant that they had a letter for the Count. The servant refused it and ordered them away, saying he would not deliver any message or disturb his Excellency until the proper hour.

Ante politely, but urgently, insisted. He made reference to a *junta soberna* (sovereign junta). The servant did not know what to make of it, but with the many changes in the Spanish government and its offices of late, he felt that he should perhaps deliver the letter. He did so, making sure that he repeated the same words to the President, lest he be chastened outright for disturbing his Excellency.

The President sat up without saying anything and opened the neatly penned letter:

FROM THE SOVEREIGN JUNTA TO THE
COUNT RUÍZ, EX-PRESIDENT OF QUITO.

The present unsettled state of Spain, the total annihilation of the lawfully constituted authorities, and the dangers of the crown of the beloved Ferdinand VII and his domains falling into the hands of the tyrant of Europe, have impelled our transatlantic brothers to form provincial governments for their personal security, as well against the machinations of some of their traitorous countrymen, unworthy of the name of Spaniards, as against the arms of the common enemy: the loyal inhabitants of Quito, resolved to secure to their legitimate King and Master this part of his kingdom, have established a sovereign junta in this city of San Francisco de Quito, of which, and by the command of his Serene Highness the President and the vocal members, I have the honor to inform your lordship, and to announce to you, that the functions of the members of the old government have ceased: God preserve your lordship many years.

HALL OF THE JUNTA IN QUITO, AUGUST 10th, 1809,
MANUEL MORALES, SECRETARY OF THE INTERIOR

The President dressed quickly when he finished reading the proclamation. He proceeded to the door where Aguire inquired politely if the note had been read. When the Count answered affirmatively, the two messengers bowed and left. The Count attempted to follow, but a sentry had already been posted at the door who would not let him pass.

Immediately, a salute was fired and people began to assemble in the square in front of the palace. A military band arrived and began playing music of a national and patriotic character for the next couple of hours.

At nine in the morning, the new government was able to assemble in the government offices. At the meeting, the Marqués de Selva Alegre was elected president. His son, Don Carlos Montúfar (a young patriot destined to be a casualty of the revolution), was there as well. Also in attendance were the Marqués de Solanda (whose daughter, about my age at the time, would one day change the lives of my friends), the Marqués de Orellana, the Count de Casa Guerrero, the Marqués de Miraflores, Don Manuel Zambrano, Don Manuel Mateus, as well as Manuel Morales and Señor Quiroga. The names of new government officers were then published.

The Bishop of Quito had informed the same body, in a private house a few days before, that he rejected their plans and would not co-operate. Despite this, he was elected vice president.

When the Bishop had walked away, several nights earlier, saying that he would not take part in any coup, all seemed to be lost. A few men, Selva Alegre and others, had nervously followed the Bishop when he left the meeting. Others were discouraged. But Morales, over the next few days, tirelessly persuaded other members of the group to go along with his plans. In the middle of the night, he, along with Quiroga, convened the decisive meeting.

Morales communicated his feeling that the country was in danger because they must now acknowledge Napoleon as their sovereign. He stressed that the only way they could avoid the shackles of France was to set up a provincial government in the name of Ferdinand VII. He and Señor Quiroga earnestly pressed their ideas, and finally agreement became general. As soon as all in the meeting had agreed, Morales assigned Salinas to advise the soldiers.

This he did by informing them that their beloved king was a prisoner of France and that the existing government was determined to deliver up Quito to the tyrant. Then, in an emotional call, he demanded to know whether they would defend their king or become slaves to Bonaparte. The soldiers immediately shouted, *"Viva Fernando Septimo! Viva Quito!"*

When this had been accomplished, guards were stationed at the doors of all of the current members of the government who might prove to be a problem. Then an urgent message was sent to the Marqués de Selva Alegre reporting all that had happened and requesting him to come and take supreme command of the new government. Thus had Morales accomplished a bloodless coup in one night.

Morales's revolution was officially about safeguarding Ferdinand VII's domains for him. However, he knew that once the *criollos* were in control of the government, they would be able to gain some satisfaction for the way the Spanish born had treated them.

A few days later, on the thirteenth of the month, I found myself in the midst of a cheering crowd as the new government paraded from the church of Carmen Alto, having just attended their own coronation. I did not know what to make of it at the time, but I did recognize the handsome Morales, whom I "loved" from afar, and I was caught up in the excitement of the moment.

In the days and nights that followed, I was filled with happiness, or rather a giddiness that was born out of the atmosphere of change. My life would be better now, I thought. I had fantasies that the revolution would alter everything and I would not have to stay in the convent anymore. I imagined that Morales would become powerful in the government and he would find me, demanding that the nuns give me up to him. Then he would take me away to live in his house. Foolish, childish imaginings.

I was only 11 years old and could be forgiven for having daydreams. But even if the revolution would have helped my situation, which I now know it would not have, the changes were not over. Soon the wheel would come full circle, and grown men would be disabused of their fantasies, fantasies not much more mature than mine.

The revolution of 1809 was a failure before it began. Almost immediately after the new government was in place, it began to lose control. Armies from the cities of Guayaquil, Lima and Santa Fe de Bogotá were said to be on the march to quell the "rebellion." The populace worried, and Quiroga and Morales had difficulty keeping order.

The council they had created was not really motivated by revolutionary zeal. All those counts and marquises being appointed to new revolutionary offices could only bring disaster. They were not interested in changing anything, only in maintaining their positions and money.

Selva Alegre was an even bigger problem. He was said to be altogether unfit for the job of president. All who knew him described the man as shy and conservative to a fault. When I met him years later, I saw these selfsame traits. Though he espoused liberal ideas, he is said to have wavered at every decision and brought a courtier's temperament to governing where the existing situation required force. Morales must have figured that Selva Alegre's appointment was politic and that he could be controlled. This was, no doubt, a mistake.

The city, already in turmoil from the abrupt change of government, came to a new crisis. Salt, procured from Guayaquil, began to grow scarce. The people panicked.

Selva Alegre could not maintain his power. The Count Ruíz, who had retired to a house in the country, was asked to resume the reigns of government by members of the revolutionary council. An agreement was made that everything should return to the way it was before the tenth of August. No action was to be taken against the conspirators.

Ruíz was a forgiving man. Having agreed to reconstitute his government, he tried to return everyone to their former positions. All papers documenting the "rebellion" were given, by Count Ruíz, to his minister, Arrechaga, to be burned.

On December 2, a cruel, self-important military leader by the name of Colonel Arredonda arrived from Guayaquil with 500 infantry and 50 artillery men to put down the "rebellion." It was a gray day and I remember feeling cold when I saw the soldiers in their clean blue uniforms come riding swiftly through the streets. The men of Quito still assumed that their agreement with the Count Ruíz was in place. Having no fear that they would be prosecuted, they surprised the Royalist soldiers by putting on a welcoming demonstration.

It was clear, just by looking at the man, that Arredonda loved bloodshed. His face was cold and impassive. His eyes were mere slits in his face. At first Arredonda didn't know what to do. That first week, his frustration was evident by the way he whipped his horse just to make her move across the street.

However, Arrechaga, instead of obeying his orders, had secretly concealed the documents he was supposed to burn. A day or so later, he presented the hidden papers to Arredonda.

When Arredonda had the papers in his hands, he began his campaign of revenge. He immediately disbanded the local troops, led by Salinas, in order to put off any opposition. In the next three weeks, 50 of the most respected members of the city were dragged from their beds, or off the streets, and placed in a barracks. They were to be imprisoned there while trials could be arranged. It was at this point that Señor Quiroga's house was searched. Among the papers found was a list containing the names of other conspirators to arrest, including Simón Sáenz.

Important citizens of Quito were arrested and held for trial. Even those, such as the Bishop, who had not stood up strongly enough against the coup were arrested, especially if, like the Bishop, these people were American born. It was fortunate that my father still had friends on the *cabildo* who were able to warn him that he was to be detained.

I was angry at the soldiers for destroying "the revolution," although I understood nothing of the forces or ideas involved. But this one important event during my ten years at the convent, the revolution, soon precipitated another, even more important to me at the time. This second event devastated me. It was the departure of my father.

My relationship with my father had always been ambivalent. I felt betrayed by him at times, due to his absence, even though he was kind to me when I did see him. I was prepared to be isolated and alone, yet I found myself responding with joy when he came to see me. I would never have admitted it then, but I needed him. The only reason I had any feelings of belonging at all was because I knew my father was out there and he would come to see me soon.

Arredonda's campaign to punish the revolution was in full swing when my father made his way out of the city one stormy night. He carried some of his gold, in two leather bags that hung over his horse's withers, unearthed that night from the garden at his house, but he had left the bulk of his fortune behind.

I was lying awake, listening to the rain fall in heavy drops against the roof, when the *portera* entered the dormitory and told me to follow her. It was December 27, my twelfth birthday, and I was agitated. My father always came a few days late to give me birthday greetings. In his whole life, he never remembered my birthday. I knew he would not be there that day, but I had hoped desperately, as I did every year, that he would come. Every birthday, it was the same. I waited for him to come, and by the time I climbed into bed, I was upset. I had been full of anticipation all that day despite the gloom that the rain had brought to the city. When the light began to leave the sky, I felt sad. By the time everyone else was asleep, I was still awake and fighting off tears.

I was pretending to sleep when the doorkeeper, who came quietly into the dormitory carrying a candle, shook my shoulder. She was very short with me. "Come with me. Right now."

I followed her down the hall obediently. As we walked, I said, "Am I in trouble?"

"No, but I will be if you don't keep quiet. I don't know why I'm doing this." She nervously shifted her candle from one hand to another.

"Where am I going?"

"To see your father. He's here."

I stifled a squeal of delight. He had not forgotten, after all. He must have been very insistent to get her to come get me after the doors had been closed. When I entered the *porteria* it was empty and dark, lit only by one candle, and it was cold. Still, I was excited to see my father and ran to him.

He crossed the room and reached out to take me in his arms but thought better of it since he was wet, and his clothes and hands were muddy. Instead, he wiped his hands off with his handkerchief and then held mine in his. He said emotionally, "Manuela, how are you my child?"

I realized that something was wrong and said only, "Papa?"

"Manuela, I have to go away." His voice was tight and agitated.

I sensed the full implications of his statement. Something was wrong. I stifled my own emotions.

"It is because of the revolution. My name is on a list of men to be arrested, along with many other innocent people, for taking part in the 'rebellion.' I am going away, but I wanted to see you before I go."

I asked stoically, "Where are you going?"

58

"To the Isthmus, to Panamá. I want to take you with me, but my family . . . well, it is impossible right now. They will follow me in a few days. I will send for you, too, when I can."

At the time, I had no idea how really dangerous it was to be traveling to Guayaquil, at night, that time of year. I realized these things later, when I made the same journey in more hospitable weather. With the lateness of the hour and Arredonda's soldiers looking for him, he was wasting valuable time stopping at the convent.

"Would you like to live in Panamá, Manuela?"

"I don't know, Papa. I . . . ." My voice started choking up.

He said, "Don't worry, you and I will be together again someday soon."

Then I understood what he had said. The rest of his family would follow him in a few days. "José María! He is not going too, Papa?"

"Yes—"

"No, Papa, no!"

The Larreas had left the city to stay at a country estate soon after the revolution. It scared me to think of my father and brother leaving too. Despite my resolve not to feel any emotion, tears came to my eyes.

"I'm sorry, Manuela."

"Papa, I hate it here and everyone hates me. Please take me with you. Please, Papa." By the time I finished speaking I was sobbing. I felt as though my heart were breaking. "Papa, please don't leave me."

"No, everyone doesn't hate you. You'll be all right," he said softly as he took me in his arms and held me, in spite of his wet and muddy clothes. "Don't cry, darling. Everything will be all right."

He took the handkerchief he still had in his hand, found a clean corner and wiped the tears from my eyes, in much the same way that Manuel Morales had once wiped dirt from my face.

"You'll see," he said. "When I can, I'll send for you." He folded his handkerchief and put it in his pocket.

"Papa, please, don't leave me. Take me with you." I could taste salty tears on my lips.

"I'm sorry, Manuela, I can't. You are a big girl now. Be brave. We'll see each other soon."

I went cold and stony. Stepping backward, I stopped crying and stiffened. He was not going to help me. I was alone. I told myself I had been acting like a child. An adult loneliness overtook me.

He started to hug me again and, again, I stepped away from him. He looked at me in a sad way and said, "I'm sorry, but I have to go." He kissed me quickly on the cheek and left hurriedly, saying only, "Good-bye!"

I followed him to the outer door, gritting my teeth, trying to make myself feel angry, so that I would not feel lonely. I watched in silence as he left. The *portera* closed the door behind him and then turned to pick up the candle. I turned away.

Then the door flew back open almost as soon as she closed it and a cold wind blew across the room. I watched in the dim light as my father mounted his horse and rode into the darkness towards the trail that led down the Andes to Guayaquil. I was shivering by the time the nun locked the door. Then I followed her back to my bed, where I lay awake but did not cry.

For years after that, I continued making trouble in the streets as I always did, but I would be wearing a handkerchief around my arm that had a blue letter "M" on it. People assumed the "M" stood for Manuela, but it had belonged to Manuel Morales. I had, in my heart, taken up the revolutionary banner. This handkerchief was my secret flag.

Later, when the handsome man who had been kind to me, and had given me his handkerchief became a martyr to the revolution, I wore it in remembrance of him. I still keep it among my effects to this day.

I pestered the fine upstanding citizens of Quito unmercifully, especially those who had been born on Spanish soil. People clucked their tongues and spoke disdainfully of "La Sáenz" and my antics throughout those years. I had been abandoned. I had no care as to what I did. As the years went on, I became an absolute hellion. But to me, my acts were acts of insurgency.

When my father left, the atrocities of the Royalists had not yet begun. I was really made a revolutionary, and a Royalist hater, by the Royalists themselves in the months that followed.

On the night my father left, political affairs were still in a state of change. The future was uncertain. But I was not thinking about the revolution that night. All I could think of, as I lay awake, feeling alone, was that my father was gone and he had not remembered my birthday.

Chapter 10

The day after my father left, Arredonda's soldiers did indeed slosh through the mud towards the Sáenz household, only to find the family packing, big holes in the garden where my father had dug up his gold, and Simón Sáenz gone. After questioning Simón's wife, they left the family in peace and rode on.

When, weeks later, 84 citizens had been imprisoned in the barracks, along with all of the local soldiers that had been under Salinas's command, Arredonda sentenced them to death. Even the Bishop, who could not legally be tried except in Castile, was sentenced.

Carlos Montúfar and all of the Marqués de Selva Alegre's family had been spared imprisonment. The Marqués had probably used his great wealth to bribe Arredonda. He and his son quarreled. Carlos was infuriated at the injustice, that so many of Quito's important citizens had been sentenced to death. He left the city the day he found out about Arredonda's verdict.

Count Ruíz deplored the fact that his agreement with Morales and the other insurgents had been usurped by Arredonda's zeal. He was still hoping to keep his bargain. He temporized by insisting that permission for execution be obtained from the viceroy, at Santa Fe de Bogotá, whose authority regulated the affairs of the Presidency of Quito. Arredonda was frustrated because he had to wait for the wheels of the government to turn before he could continue with his revenge. He grew more impatient by the day.

The Count Ruíz was able to delay months before a messenger was even sent to the viceroy.

In the meantime, two factions had developed in the city. Arredonda, his soldiers, and the Spanish-born of the city leaders who supported him were on one side. On the other side were the prisoners, their families, and the rest of the city leaders. The tension between them increased almost to the point of violence.

The prisoners were abused and ill fed, and their families clamored for their release. Despite the outcry, Arredonda did nothing for the prisoners. He even seemed to increase the harsh treatment. The more reasonable members of the city proposed many compromises, but Arredonda was adamant about wanting the blood of the conspirators. When the messenger, whom Count Ruíz had tried to detain through legal maneuverings, finally departed, talk was that the viceroy's decision would not be favorable. Nearly eight months of contention between the two factions had gone by, and in all that time there had never been one day of hope that Arredonda would relent in his plans.

Soon after the messenger's departure, on August 2 of 1810, almost a year since Morales's coup, the imprisoned soldiers broke from their cells and began to reclaim the city. The Spanish troops quickly put down the uprising, but then they went on a killing spree—taking revenge on everyone they could find, without regard to age or sex.

The violence overran the prison and out into the city streets, where many innocent people died. The soldiers guarding the prisoners actually began killing their charges while they were still shackled in their cells.

Tragically, an African slave girl had brought Señor Quiroga's two small children to visit him that day. These were the same children I had envied the day I had taken the pouch. They had been there only a short time when the hostilities began. Señor Quiroga watched his children hacked to pieces, before they mercifully killed him.

The bloodshed in Quito that day was horrible. The man who later told me about Señor Quiroga escaped death by lying still among piles of bloody corpses, pretending to be dead. He had to lie completely still, even when he and the other bodies were stabbed several times with bayonets.

Nearly all the revolutionaries, plus over 300 innocent civilians, died. Among those who lost their lives was my friend Morales—as well as Quiroga, Riofrio, Salinas and others of the revolutionary council—without hearing the news that in April of that same year, the city of Caracas had fallen to determined revolutionaries. Among the leadership of the Caracas victory was Simón Bolívar, under the supreme leadership of Francisco de Miranda. Miranda is known as "The Precursor" by those who speak of the South American liberation now. However, the first revolution on the continent was led by Morales in Quito, in August of 1809. The real precursors, in my opinion, died in Quito a year later—all but forgotten—without ever knowing that their deaths were not entirely in vain. That day is bleak in my memory and in the memory of all *quiteños* who were in the city then.

The populace was outraged by the massacre. Nearly all of those who had supported Arredonda withdrew their support. A meeting was called of all government officials. Despite his authority, Arredonda was told unanimously to take his soldiers and leave. Having had his thirst for blood satisfied, he left that hour.

Shortly thereafter, the messenger who had traveled to Bogotá returned with the news that a revolution, much like the one in Quito, had taken place in that city just prior to his arrival there.

Upon hearing this news, there was deep frustration throughout the city. This only increased the outrage that the people felt over the recent conduct of Arredonda's men. There was talk in every household to the effect that Quito should follow the examples of Caracas and Bogotá after all.

During this time, Carlos Montúfar had banded together some men from the surrounding countryside. In September he entered Quito with these troops and a dispatch from a "Central Junta" of the resistance in Spain giving him authority to establish a provisional government in Quito.

In Spain, the resistance to Napoleon had set up a *cortes* (parliament) to see to the legitimizing of their power while the king was in exile. The Cortes of Cádiz had made many liberal reforms to Spanish society. The populace of Quito was behind these reforms, and Montúfar, with few exceptions.

However, the viceroy in Lima, Don Abascal, refused to recognize the new provisional government in Quito. Again troops were sent to quell the "rebellion." Although Montúfar was young, he successfully defended Quito from the onslaught of more Royalist soldiers. He was victorious in many small skirmishes near towns to the south of the city.

In the city itself, people prepared for battle should the Royalists reach the city walls. Old church bells were confiscated and melted down to make bullets. Gunpowder was in production day and night. The women of the city sold their jewels to pay for arms, and the men worked around the clock in preparation to repulse any attack. All worked for the defense of Quito, except a few *peninsulares* who stayed in their homes. The church, of course, sided with the Royalists.

My own contribution was somewhat dangerous. Twice I stole money, which had been left as an offering to the convent, and deposited it in the barrel where military collections were made. The third time I was caught and severely beaten.

I didn't care. I saw in Montúfar someone who had taken up where Morales had left off. I was 13, indestructible, and determined to do something to help him. Since my father had left, it seemed I cared about nothing but the revolution.

Montúfar had great success in keeping the Spanish troops out of the city. Then a letter came from Spain, saying that the "Central Junta" had been disbanded. Montúfar no longer had his authority and he put down his arms as any civilized and disciplined soldier would. He wrote to the viceroy and explained the situation. Then, relying on the decency of the viceroy, whom he personally knew, he retired to Quito to wait for the arrival of Royalist troops.

He was foolish to have trusted the Spanish. When the viceroy's troops finally arrived, in the middle of 1811, under the leadership of a General Montes, they began to implement their plans to, once and for all, dissuade Quito of revolution. The result was the worst blood bath in Quito's and perhaps all of South America's history.

Montes immediately arrested Montúfar. He arrested every man he could find who had followed him. He sentenced them all to die in a public execution.

The families of the condemned were ordered to attend the execution—to witness the "folly of revolution." There would not be another revolution in Quito for more than ten years.

The church was one of the most enthusiastic celebrants on the day that the revolutionary council and soldiers were executed. Convents all over the city had sewn banners for the event.

The girls from the convent school of Santa Catalina were to be taken by the sisters to watch the gruesome sight of dying revolutionaries. We arrived late because I had managed to annoy and stall everyone with my lack of cooperation. I didn't want to go, but the sisters insisted that I attend.

"If no one else goes, you will go, Manuela," one of the sisters said. "It will be good for you to watch these 'revolutionaries' meet their end. Perhaps you will be educated from your intractable ways."

Since my father had left, I had been impossible. It seemed I fought anyone with whom I came in contact. That day, I was at my worse. I was upset about Montes entering the city. I was upset by the arrest of Don Montúfar, whom I admired. I hated the Royalists and anyone who had any authority over me. I did not want to see the execution of brave revolutionary soldiers. Even though I knew I would have to go in the end, I argued with everyone about it all morning. I dallied while everyone dressed in their finest. I procrastinated when we were being lined up in orderly columns for the march to the center of town. The whole procession was delayed while I was scolded for picking a flower during the walk to the city. When I answered disrespectfully, I had my face slapped.

"Manuela, you will find yourself cleaning animal stalls from morning until night for the next year and you will be sleeping in the punishment cell if you don't stop this behavior."

I defiantly concealed the flower behind my back. I said nothing and was pushed back into line. We continued walking. I smelled the flower dreamily as we marched, hoping to upset the sisters some more, but they didn't notice.

When we arrived in the great square, it was crowded and noisy, and there was a sickening sweet smell in the air that overcame the scent of my flower. It was the smell of blood along with something boiling in a cauldron.

I could see the gibbet from the back of the crowd. To one side I could see Montúfar standing on a platform, newly built for the execution. Along with him were the other chief rebel officers. It tore my heart to see Montúfar, so young and handsome, hands shackled in front of him, helpless, about to die. He and the other officers were being made to watch the deaths of all of their men before their own executions.

A rebel warrior with a noose around his neck stood stoically, looking ahead, seeming to pay no attention to the charges being read. Someone stepped in front of me, blocking my view. I heard the sound of the gallows door open and the rope snap taught. When I could see again, the soldier had dropped out of sight. Then I heard him choking, before the Spaniards in the crowed roared their approval.

I was angry when I heard cheering from the crowd. My anger turned to disgust by what transpired next. The poor soldier was cut down before he died and his head was struck from his body with an ax. Red flowed through cracks between the boards in the platform where the decapitation had taken place and filled up the places between the stones in the street in an ever widening lake of blood. As if decapitation were not enough, a knife was thrust into the chest of the headless soldier and twisted to separate the ribs. Another knife was then used to cut out his heart. The heart, still beating, was then tossed into the boiling cauldron. Meanwhile, the man's head was placed in a small iron cage that was then marched around on a pike for the crowd to see. Gore spattered on the lace and satin clothing of cheering citizens until the cage was taken from the square and hung permanently in some part of the city. These little cages, the heads inside mummified by the elements, hung on walls and under balconies throughout the city until General Sucre liberated Quito over a decade later.

The priest who had heard my mother's deathbed confession was standing in the crowd. He had acquired a reputation in Quito of being insane. However, the church authorities did not deem him crazy, since his insanity manifested itself only in zealotry. His one eye was aflame with righteousness; and as the last cheer died down, I heard him shout, "Thank you, oh Lord, for delivering our enemies into our hands." He said this with every soldier's death, becoming more fervent each time.

Not everyone in the crowd was cheering. Long lines of rebels in chains were standing waiting to mount the gallows. They and their families were silent or crying. It was the Spanish who were cheering the death of the revolution and the glorious re-establishment of Royalist rule.

I had been shoved to the front of the crowd as it parted to let a body through to a waiting cart. I watched in horror, as did Montúfar and his officers, while, one by one, his men were taken to the gibbet and made to die as I have described. I had heard that Montúfar and other higher ranking officers were to be tied hands and feet to four horses, which were then to be whipped towards the four compass points. The entire scene was one of grisly horror and it disturbed me to my core. I kept my eyes downcast so I would not have to witness any more deaths.

Though I was horrified and sickened by the morbid sights I saw that day, I was also angry. I had already taken up the mantle of the revolution in my heart. I wanted to take revenge on the Royalists. General Montes, small with a dark visage, wearing his best dress uniform, gold epaulets on small shoulders that stood in contrast to the bright red jacket, sat stiffly on a platform specially built in front of the palace where all the city leaders sat. I wanted to kill him.

Because I felt so impotent, I tried not to let anyone see how disturbed I was. All of the other girls were upset by the sights as well, but the Spanish-born girls quickly recovered, following the example of their relatives in the crowd. After a few executions, they were actually laughing and acting as though it were a party. I fought back fury and tears.

Then, Antonia came and stood beside me. I hated her. She had gone out of her way to make me suffer since the time I first arrived at the convent. When she stood so close to me I knew that she intended malice, but I ignored her. She took an apple out of her pocket and began eating it noisily. She knew how I felt and was deliberately trying to nettle me by showing disregard for what was happening.

I looked at the freshly picked but quickly withering flower I had been carrying. Tears welled up in my eyes. Antonia stood even closer to me and continued eating her apple even more noisily. I had to get away.

Unnoticed by the nun who was supposed to be in charge of us, I turned and made my way back through the crowed. To my dismay, as I walked up the empty street away from the crowd, Antonia ran up behind me and fell in step.

"Why are you leaving now?" she said, with her mouth full. "The officers are going to be pulled apart by horses and—"

I turned on her viciously, "What is the matter with you? Don't you see how they're suffering. They lost their fight and now they have to watch all of their men die in front of them."

"What's the matter with *you*? I would think you'd be happy that the revolution failed. Now your father can come back."

Her lack of understanding infuriated me. I turned away and continued walking, but she kept in step. I seethed inside and said, almost under my breath, "My father was not a revolutionary. In fact, I don't want him to come back. The crown is responsible for that massacre back there. I hate the *godos*." I used the term for Royalist meaning both "nobly born" (meant sardonically) and "rapacious conquerors."

Making sure that she stayed right in step with me, she interrupted with a voice loaded with sarcasm, "Oh my, I thought anybody who didn't have a father would want him to return."

Without thinking, I stepped back behind her, gave a swift yank on her braid, and pulled her over backwards. She screamed and landed with a thud. I jumped on top of her and punched her as hard as I could, over and over. She swung her arms and kicked her legs in defense. Soon we were rolling in the dirt: hitting, biting, and trying to scratch each other. Finally, I had her face down, straddling her.

I pulled back on her hair. She screamed loudly, but she couldn't be heard above the noisy crowd. I reached over and grabbed the dusty apple she had dropped and jammed it into her face, lodging it in her teeth.

"There, you pig," I said and let her stand, my fists still clenched in rage.

Blood was streaming from her nose. There were scratches on her face and purple bruises on her forehead where I had struck her and where she had fallen on the stones in the street. She tried to dislodge the apple as tears streamed from her eyes.

My breath was coming in short gasps. "Don't you ever talk about my father again, you bitch!" I pushed her hard so that she almost lost her balance.

She pulled the apple out of her mouth, spit out the dust, and threw the apple into the street. Wiping the blood off her face with her arm, she hissed, "You're not only the daughter of a whore, you're a traitor as well. You'll regret this." She ran away, crying, "I'm going to tell the sisters on you, you filthy, stinking bastard."

I became blind with rage and tears. I noticed that the flower that I had been carrying was lying on the stones. I picked it up and ran as fast as I could back toward the crowd, passing Antonia on the way. Pushing my way through, I ran across the opening and up the steps of the platform on which the rebel leaders stood. At the bottom of the steps leading up to the platform were two guards. I rushed right past them, up to where Montúfar was standing.

The guards were taken by surprise. They attempted to follow me, but with both men trying to gain the narrow steps at the same time, there was a moment of indecision. I ran straight for Montúfar. After I reached him, one of the guards grabbed me.

"Come here you," he shouted.

"Let me go!" I kicked the guard and broke free and ran to the edge of the platform.

I could hear the sisters from Santa Catalina yelling at me to come down. "Manuela, you come down here. Just wait until we get you."

The other guard grabbed me from below and dragged me back down to the cobblestones. "Now, little miss, you stay away from here! What do you think you're doing? Shame on you!"

Just then two nuns came over to take control of me. The guard who had me said, "Does this hellion belong to you? Ow! She bit me."

I was free. I turned and pushed a nun down. Ducking everybody's hands, I ran so fast toward the crowd that they parted for me. Some tried to snatch me as I was almost through, but I eluded them. Mostly people only looked at me in stunned silence. I heard the one-eyed priest holler out vehemently, "She is possessed by the devil."

As the crowd closed behind me, I could hear the old refrains, "Bastard," "Just like La Sáenz," and other similar comments. I felt at that moment that there was not one person in Quito who didn't know me, and hate me.

The two sisters chased me up the street for a short distance and then stopped. When I looked over my shoulder I could see that they were returning to the crowd. I ducked into a doorway and peeked back out. The sisters were back with the crowd, and I was alone.

I could see that Montúfar had followed the commotion with his eyes. He was the only one looking directly at me as I peered around the corner. I was dying inside with frustration and fear, and then I saw him slowly look down at his manacled hands and the wilting flower that I had passed to him in the confusion. He looked back at me as though he could see right into my soul. I imagined I saw thanks in his eyes.

I had felt so helpless when Antonia had run away from me. Giving him my flower was the only thing I could think to do in that moment of confusion. When he looked back at me, my heart filled with despair and I burst into tears. I had really done nothing to help the suffering man at all. It had been an impulsive act, but I knew no other way to let him know that someone cared. Montúfar looked back at the flower and continued to hold it. I turned and ran away.

I didn't know where I was going, but I was determined to run until I could run no longer. However, I was caught at the edge of town and forcibly returned to Santa Catalina.

For as long as I live, I will never forget the torture of that soul and the misery that I saw in the face of Carlos Montúfar as he looked at that wilting flower.

Chapter 11

The events surrounding the revolution and its aftermath changed me. I grew up too quickly. Any lightheartedness, and any submissivness, that I may have had prior to that time, left me. I felt alone, day and night. Feeling that I had no one who cared about my existence, I lashed out at each person around me. I believe I was on the road to being quite self-destructive. However, there were a few events still ahead that would continue to shape me.

I was punished because of my behavior at the hanging of the revolutionaries and kept incommunicado for a long time. I worked from morning till night on dirty jobs, and I was watched constantly. For many days I had to sleep in the convent jail.

When I was finally made to return to living with the other students, nothing had changed. Antonia continued her campaign of abuse more earnestly than ever, and she drew other girls into her schemes.

"Welcome back, Manuela!" she said sarcastically when I returned to the dormitory.

I ignored her, but later, when I pulled back the sheets of my bed, it was full of ashes. Everyone in the room laughed. From then on, I kept to myself of my own volition, in order to avoid either confrontation or mistreatment.

I did not have any friends. The Larreas were still at their country estate, and I did not see them for almost two years. Consequently, all I did was read.

I studied hard and occupied my mind with learning the things that interested me. Nothing happened in my life during that period, except in the books I was reading. I read histories and Spanish literature. I enjoyed learning Latin. I think the number of books I had read by the time I was seventeen was greater than the number most of my teachers had read. Books were my only way of escaping my anger.

However, not even books could interest me forever. As I became older, I wanted to do more. I could read and write and do the elementary arithmetic they taught us quite well, and I did enjoy the sewing. But as I became more certain of my point of view, I became more contemptuous of what I deemed the "stupidity" of those around me.

Of course, in this I was not alone. The other girls my age were experiencing that same certainty that everyone over the age of 20 had lost all of their wits. In my case, I had been so good at learning what the nuns had taught me in school, and I had fooled them so often in my work or duties, that I had long since lost all respect for them. The only thing they had, that I couldn't have, was control of their own lives.

One night, when I was about to turn 15, I packed my few belongings in a sheet and made for a low place in the convent wall. I had heard about the recent revolutionary victories, and a general named Bolívar who had just been proclaimed "The Liberator," in Venezuela. That was where I was going.

I hadn't thought out how I was going to get over the Andes, nor had I solved any of the other problems I would have encountered. The most important thing I failed to think about was the fact that I would not be able to help the revolution anyway. After all, I was a woman, a girl, and would simply be dismissed as unable to provide any assistance whatsoever. I ignored all such ideas and moved ahead. I wanted to change my life and was determined to leave.

It was chilly, and I was shivering as I passed between the cells of the more wealthy nuns. I whispered into the darkness, "Good-bye, you hypocrites."

I clutched my shoulder with one arm to ward of the chill. My other arm hurt from holding the sheet containing a few books and clothes that I carried on my back. I walked quietly in the cold moonlight, being careful not to make any noise.

Then, I heard footsteps behind me. Looking over my shoulder, I saw two *celadoras* (nuns whose duty it is to see to the observance of convent rules) coming after me.

"Stop!" "Come back here!" they cried.

How did they know? I couldn't stop to think about it. I raced as fast as I could for the back part of the convent grounds—the best way out. As I came to a side passage, another *celadora* came around the corner and ran into me. We both fell backwards onto the walkway, scattering my pack. My left elbow hit a large stone as I fell.

I scrambled to my feet, but the other two caught up with me before I could run off. They held onto my arms, and I screamed at the top of my lungs, "Let go of me, you ugly bitches. Let me go, damn you!"

Nuns, slaves, and servants, from the cells all around us, came out in their nightshirts to see what the disturbance was. I noticed Antonia's maid, a girl about 11 years old, in the crowd. Unlike everyone else, she was not dressed in night clothes.

We struggled there for several minutes and then I was dragged away and thrown into the cold convent jail, still screaming obscenities at my captors. It must have been almost dawn before I ceased walking up and down, rattling the door and screaming. Every once in awhile, the *carcelera* (jailer) would come up to the door, chuckle senselessly, and say, "Shut up, you stupid girl, I'm trying to get some sleep." Then she would laugh dementedly and walk off.

Finally I sat down in exhaustion. Despite my determination to stay awake, I fell asleep almost immediately. I was awakened later, very early in the morning I think, by soft laughter. Then, I recognized the voice of Antonia just outside the door, saying, "Welcome back, Manuela."

I didn't give her the satisfaction of a response. Soon, I heard her slippers shuffle on the stone floor as she walked away. I realized then why Antonia's maid had been in the crowd, dressed, when I was captured. Antonia had evidently seen me leave and had sent her maid to notify the *celadoras*. She had me where she wanted me and I could not fight. I shook with frustration.

I began pacing up and down again, occasionally hitting the wall with my fist, trying to keep myself angry. I was determined not to cry or give in. I put my hand against my mouth to stifle the tears, tasting the blood beginning to ooze from my knuckles. I walked around in that tiny space, talking to myself, bruising my knuckles on the stone wall for over an hour, stopping only once to relieve myself in the metal bowl that was in the room for that purpose.

As I paced back and forth, I filled my mind with images of what I was going to do to surprise, and get past, the next person who opened the door. I carefully planned how I would get up to ground level and over the wall, and what I would do to anyone who tried to stop me.

I sat down wearily and waited. Soon, I felt my eyelids grow heavy but I made myself wake up. I must have started to fade into sleep again because I heard a key at the door though I hadn't heard anyone approach. Confused for an instant, my heart raced. I hid in the corner and picked up the metal bowel of urine. Here was my opportunity. I made ready to surprise the *carcelera*.

The door opened slowly. Someone stepped across the threshold and I threw the contents of the bowl right in the face of a nun of the black veil.

I had intended to surprise the *carcelera*. I hoped I would be able to run past her, and up the stairs, before she caught me. Instead, I had drenched a very important nun, who stood in the doorway dripping with the noxious liquor.

The *carcelera* saw what had happened in the moment I stood in uncertainty. When I started to run through the door, past the nun, she picked up a mop leaning against the wall and struck me on the side of my face so hard I fell to the floor, banging my head against the stones.

I rolled over and lay on my back, in the doorway, dazed and moaning in pain. The *carcelera* pressed the mop to my neck so hard that I could barely breath or even move.

As I opened my eyes, I could see the sister of the black veil standing over me. She wiped her face with her sleeve, looking right at me. I said, with difficulty, "What are you looking at? I would have been gone if you hadn't gotten in the way, you—" The *carcelera* pushed the mop into my neck, forcing me to be quiet.

The nun said, "I believe you would have. Before you go, I want you to know that I came to get you out of here."

Despite my choking, I was able to ask, "Why?"

"I don't know—now." She frowned at me. "I have been with the Abbess all morning, and she has finally agreed to release you to me. Although, with your reputation it was much more of a chore than I imagined, and now, this." She looked thoroughly disgusted as she took a large ruby ring off her finger and wiped her hand on her habit. Then she stepped around me as if to leave.

The *carcelera*, seeing that I was not struggling with her, let me up. I could see the nun was being genuine with me, but I didn't understand. Still skeptical, I sat up and I asked again, "Why?"

She turned to me and said, "It *was* my intention to help you become a productive member of the convent. When I saw you dragged off last night, I felt sorry for you. I lay awake thinking about it, and I decided to see if I could help you."

"How could you help me?" I said sarcastically.

"You would have started by living in my cell, being my servant, for which I would pay you a coin or two now and then. If you could be productive at that job, I thought I might sponsor you for the veil."

I sneered and said, "Stick it up your ass."

The *carcelera* struck me again with the mop. I fell against the door and smacked my head again. "Ow!" I said. The pain had caught me off guard and tears came to my eyes.

I sat up again, slowly, holding my head with one hand. With the other, I tried to wipe away the tears without being obvious about it. I was miserable as I glared back at the nun. She looked at me a long time without speaking. Finally, slowly shaking her head, she said, "Before we talk further, I'm going to get cleaned up." Then as an afterthought, "I have not yet changed my mind, but I am beginning to regret my decision." She walked off.

The *carcelera* stood me up and laughed. "You are a foolish girl." She laughed again. "That was Doña Luisa Esclara."

I rubbed my head and said absently, "So what?"

"She wanted to help you, you dim-witted girl." She almost shook with laughter, before she went on. "She is one of the most powerful sisters in the community, and you just threw piss in her face." She laughed even more enthusiastically and said, "Now take this mop and clean up your mess, you pig." Then she walked down the hall chuckling.

As I mopped up, with a *carcelera* sitting on a bench at the end of hall watching, and laughing softly, I was baffled. I just knew I could take care of myself, if I could only get out of that convent. Something had to change for me soon, and I wasn't going to wait around for it to just happen. Now, I had been offered that change, a much better situation, but it required that I stay in the convent after all. That is, if Doña Esclara, or the Abbess, didn't change her mind after my indiscriminate method of escaping from jail.

I had never known this nun's name, but I had seen her before and knew that she was one of the wealthier nuns at Santa Catalina. She wore fine jewels with her habit, a habit that had been especially embroidered with Spanish lace. She was about forty years old and owned one of the most lavish cells in the convent. I also knew that she had two servants already, a *mulatta* and a *mestiza*, and she didn't really need another helper.

When I thought about that, I realized she had perhaps seen my suffering and truly wanted to help me. The more I considered what she had said, the more I saw how her offer might be a true act of kindness.

I regretted what I had done to her and decided that cooperating with her could be a great opportunity for me. If nothing else, it would be easier for me to escape. The more I thought about the wonderful possibilities of living with such a powerful nun, the more frantic I became. I hoped I had not ruined my chances already.

If the circumstances had been different, I would have been much too proud to be a servant, regardless of how much it might do for me. But these opportunities seemed too good to pass up. I would have to follow convent standards, if I agreed, and that bothered me. I didn't know if I was capable of such conformist behavior.

After I cleaned the hallway, I was put back in confinement. There I sat in anticipation for a long time.

Eventually, the key turned in the lock. The *carcelera* slowly pushed the door open while I sat still on the bench. When it became clear that I was not up to anything, Doña Esclara entered and stood silhouetted in the doorway. I couldn't see her face clearly, but I could tell she was impatient before she spoke.

"I won't argue with you, and I won't waste my time," she said at length. "What will you do?"

There was a moment of silence while I considered how to respond. I decided to say what I thought she wanted to hear. "I'm sorry for my behavior. I will try to do what's right."

My voice was too flat for sincere contrition and she knew it. I could tell by the long pause that followed.

She entered the little room and said, "Very well. But remember, I can put you back in here any time. I will not fail to see you punished if you are not sincere." She went on, explaining what my duties would be, forcing me to respond to her now and then and questioning my responses, until she felt I was in earnest acceptance of her offer.

Finally, she said, "Now then, if you will be obedient and apply yourself, you may come with me."

"Yes, Doña Esclara." The words, in a tone so against my nature, stuck in my throat. I forced myself to follow my benefactor through the doorway and down the hall in contrite silence. Contrition was not in my mind, however. I was planning what I was going to do to Antonia.

However, the violence in me quickly passed. My life was changing, and I knew it when we walked up to the doorstep of Doña Esclara's cell, near where I'd been captured only hours before. When I stepped inside, it was wonderful: light, airy, full of fine furniture and the aroma of good food. Knowing that this was the environment in which I would live changed me before I knew it.

I learned later that the reason my benefactor had difficulty convincing the Abbess to have me move in with her and become one of her servants was for the same reason that I had agreed. I would then be in a position where I would not only have access to all of the convent, but I might even be, officially, outside on errands for her. I intended to use such opportunities, and the Abbess had correctly foreseen it all.

However, after I began to live with my benefactor, I found that I enjoyed my situation much more than I had anticipated. For one thing, I no longer had to attend classes with the other girls. That delighted me. Also, her cell was spacious and pleasing, and the people I lived with were mostly nice to me. In fact, everything that had been bothering me about the convent before seemed either to be mitigated or disappear as soon as I spent my first night there. I was surprised at the difference.

I did housework and errands. I received, in addition to an occasional coin, much better food: fresh fruit every day and delicious stews of mutton, or rabbit, prepared right on the porch of our cell. I also received a little extra clothing of Indian cloth which, thankfully, was not like a habit and I was allowed to wear it in the cell.

I did continue my studies, but I worked and studied alone in Doña Esclara's cell instead of with the other girls. I had a much better outlook and I renewed my study of literature and history with enthusiasm. However, I did not study as often as I did prior to that, because it wasn't too long before I had other things on my mind.

Chapter 12

Sometimes I think it might have been better for me if I had succeeded in running away before Doña Luisa "saved" me. When I was running away, I knew what I wanted and who I was. I wanted to escape. I wanted to "join" the revolution. I was "La Sáenz"— bastard and revolutionary. Of course, the question of how I would have survived at that age, had I tried to leave the city, I had never answered. Still, when I was on my way to Venezuela, I knew exactly who and what I was. Living with Doña Luisa, despite its comfort, confused me.

The most seductive thing about my new quarters was that I had friends. This is something I never hoped to have in the convent and it blinded me to all else. A day or so after I arrived, I was so taken with my surroundings and so happy to have some cordial companionship, that I forgot about what I had wanted days before. I went to Doña Luisa, apologized again, and thanked her earnestly for allowing me to live with her. When she saw my genuine gratitude, she became bright and talkative. "Oh, Manuela, you're very welcome. I'm glad you're here."

She began to trust me, where before she had been watchful and quiet to see if I would run away. After that, her genuinely warm-hearted treatment, most of the time, in contrast to the way the rest of the convent treated me, was refreshing and endeared her to me.

However, she was very unpredictable. Sometimes she was straightforward and easy to talk to, at other times she was distracted, petty, and unreasonable. One day she would be bright and friendly, entertaining friends in her cell or in the *locutorios* with the vivacity of the finest society matron in the city. The next day, in sharp contrast to the day before, she would be morose and quiet, spending her hours praying and doing penance, or locked in her room. I couldn't imagine why one such as she should feel any need for penance. She was a good woman. However, there was something she felt bad about. I did not understand her until shortly before I left the convent. The only pattern I could see, of no help to me at the time, was that her unlikable *mestiza* servant, Beatríz, always appeared to be in a mood opposite to that of Doña Luisa.

Beatríz resented my intrusion into her life at first and when we were introduced she was not as polite as she could have been. She was about 24, not very pleasant to look at, or to be with, and she was as unpredictable as Doña Luisa. She was so incompetent at her duties that I wondered why Doña Luisa kept her on. I supposed that my benefactor pitied her also, like me, and had taken her in. After a few weeks, Beatríz seemed to accept me and we got on fairly well. Since she was a half-breed Indian and I already identified with such, I tried hard to make friends with her.

Doña Luisa's other servant was wonderful: friendly, funny, likable, and pretty. Though she was about 26, over 10 years my senior, I took to her in an instant. I learned that she was a quadroon *mulatta* whose grandmother had been born on a slave ship. She had many stories to tell about Africa, as the continent had been a century before. These stories had been passed down, mother to daughter, from her great-grandmother in Africa. My friend confided in me that she wanted to pass on this legacy and that she would leave Doña Luisa one day, marry, and have a daughter of her own. I did not understand how a slave could imagine she would do that, but I accepted what she said. She also knew many interesting facts about herbs and plants, her great grandmother having been a "witch," or something like that, in Africa. Her name was Carmen and she was my favorite of all the people I ever met in the convent.

My life was happy then and the only disconcerting aspect of my new situation was that I could not tell how Doña Luisa would react to anything. Despite her changeability, she was quite intelligent and helped me in many ways. The one important time when she gave me counsel, it had a lasting effect on me.

I recollect the day clearly, as well as the story she told to illustrate her point. It would have been better if I had listened to the real meaning of her advice—I could have avoided a lot of trouble—but I didn't.

It was a hot summer day and we had been waiting to eat a pot of mutton stew, one of my favorite meals, prepared with potatoes, corn, special spices, and thickened with *maíz* flour. Beatríz had started to prepare it, but Carmen took over. "She makes too many mistakes," my friend confided in me. It was true. In fact, just having Beatríz in a room could cause one or the other of us to make a mistake at our sewing, in preparing food, or whatever we might be doing.

The stew had been cooking on the porch of our cell all afternoon and the aroma was delicious. We were all having a good time, singing and joking, while we waited for it to finish cooking. I was basking in the comradeship I felt.

As we were cutting a block of cheese to make another of my favorite foods, "toasted cheese," Carmen began teasing me. "You so pretty, you'll be marryin' a fine man someday." I don't remember how that started, or exactly what else she said that upset me, but suddenly my whole mood changed.

I felt the emptiness of my life crash in on me. Something that had always been in the back of my mind unveiled itself. *Nobody will ever love me.* The words entered my mind without my control. *Love only means I will be abandoned.*

The laughter in the room seemed to cut me.

I don't belong here.

Tears sprang to my eyes. Carmen didn't notice and went on teasing me about the man I would meet some day. It seemed to me that I had been tricked into thinking these people were my friends. I lashed out at them, saying, "Stop it. I don't want any man to love me. Leave me alone." Everyone was startled into silence. They looked at me. I felt angry and stupid and I ran outside, slammed the door, and stood on the porch in the doorway fighting back tears.

I felt terrible. I didn't know what was wrong with me. I truly liked Carmen, and I had been rude to her and made everyone else think me childish. I had never felt so out of control.

Doña Luisa came out. I stayed in the doorway, insolent and silent. She stepped around me and stood facing me.

"Look at me," she said. I looked up and she wiped the tears from my eyes with her own handkerchief. She searched my face for a long time and then said softly, "Come with me."

She turned and walked away. Her command was gentle, but I slowly followed her off the porch, between the rows of cells, and into the main building. There, she sought out the *campanera* (bell ringer). With a bit of persuasion, Doña Luisa persuaded her to open up the stairs to the belfry, and we climbed to the top of the tower where we could look out over the city.

I said it was a summer day even though, in Quito, because it is on the equator, most days have all four seasons in their aspect—the morning is spring, midday and the afternoon are (a cool) summertime, evening is autumn, and the night is winter. Also, the days are the same length throughout the year, unlike north or south of the equator. On this day, the summer had been there all day and we were experiencing a hot summer afternoon, as I later learned other localities enjoy throughout the summer months.

That afternoon, the sun was about to touch the southern slope of Mt. Pichincha on its descent into night. Doña Luisa looked at the city for awhile in quiet contemplation, resting her arms on the ledge. The bleached lace on her cuffs stood out in sharp contrast to the dust on the parched, white mud covering the ledge.

Finally, still watching the shadows lengthen, she said, "I know that you are lonely and sometimes miserable. I know you believe you will never be happy. That is why I took pity on you in the first place."

I sniffled a little bit, feeling sorry for myself. She spoke truly of how I felt.

She turned toward me and said, "I also know that the reason you said downstairs that you don't want a man to love you is because you desperately need exactly that."

I began to protest, but she turned back and looked out across the city and continued. "It is not good for you to be in such need. Even though you deny it." I prepared myself for some moralizing, but I had not really understood what she meant. She went on, "It is not that love between a man and a woman is bad; what is regretful is the need."

I did not expect this. She, in a matter of one moment, had taken me inside of myself and brought me out again. At first I thought that she wanted me to see the truth— that I really wanted to be loved by a man and to accept that I was normal. Then I thought that I would hear a sermon. But it was deeper than that.

She looked at me again and said, "Out there is a world full of men, a world that you will one day walk out into because I doubt you have the temperament to take the veil, although that would be my wish for you."

She smiled at me in a knowing way and then continued, "Your need for love is not good for you. It will cause you to make decisions that you will eventually regret; though you may not know it is your need that you are acting on. Your pride, and your stated aversion to men or love, will make you do the same thing: make decisions that you will come to regret. Two such unnatural forces pulling you in diverse directions, will only pull you apart.

"The truth is that not all men will leave you, not all men will betray you; some will love you truly and some will not. But they are not important. What is important in your life is *you* and what you truly desire. Whether you decide to be with a man or not, what *you* desire should not be lost.

"You must know who you are, and it is only by having a clear mind that you can make right choices."

She looked directly at me. "Perhaps you will one day decide that you would rather live with women, as I do, or perhaps something else entirely that we cannot think of now. But whatever you are, learn to love it; learn to know and love yourself and act on your inner desires, not your needs and hungers. For, in the end, the ability to love others despite what has happened to you, is what you should aspire to."

I tried to take it all in. As I looked at her, I know I loved her all the more for caring enough to even talk to me and be concerned about me. She looked in my eyes, and said, as though I was not comprehending, "Do not, in the meantime, settle for anything less then what you actually want—in men or your work or in your life. Do without rather than settle for half-good. Give up your false pride and learn to know yourself. Accept that someday you will meet a man whom you admire and who you will want to spend your life with him. Or you will not. If you do, stay with him, but do not forget yourself. If you don't meet a man, be sure you at least learn to love, and live with, yourself and those around you."

I knew she was right. I saw myself so clearly at that moment and I was overwhelmed by her kindness and wisdom. I began to stammer, "I . . . Doña Luisa, I . . . ." She reached out and pulled off my head covering and brushed the hair from my face. She smiled and said, "And in the meantime, don't forget to accept the help of those who *do* love you."

At that moment, I felt better about myself than I had ever felt before. She spoke a truth that I think I already inwardly knew. My affection for Doña Luisa grew immensely. I stood there looking stupidly at her as I marveled at my good fortune in being her ward. She smiled and said, "The reason I brought you up here is to tell you a story."

She looked at the rusted bell, worn where the clapper had struck it over the centuries. She said, "Over a hundred years ago, a woman stood in this belfry and threatened to jump rather than be dominated by men.

"I don't know her name, but everyone who is a nun here learns the story; and it is a true story.

"You see, at that time, this convent was under the control of the Dominican order in the monastery over there." She stretched out her hand towards the Dominican building that I had walked past many times—a somber place with silent men in white robes, coming and going.

"It was election time, and the nun who was certain to be elected Abbess had already stated that she was going to petition to have juridical control shifted from the Dominicans to the bishop, thus giving this convent greater control over its own future.

"The Dominicans tried to stop her election by internal political tricks and threats. When it looked like they would be successful, almost 60 nuns of the black veil, and many lesser nuns, proposed to leave the nunnery rather than remain in the control of the Dominicans.

"They organized a march through the streets of the city to declare their opposition to Dominican control; but as they were about to leave the convent, the monks broke open the doors and began to persuade the nuns to their way of thinking—with clubs and fists.

"This is true, what I tell you. They beat several nuns very badly, and they broke into cells and destroyed personal items. They continued to riot thus for almost two hours.

"The President of the *audiencia* arrived just as one nun fought her way up here, pulled herself onto this ledge, and shouted to the crowd gathering below that she would throw herself to her death rather than be dominated by the Dominicans.

"The President had one of his men fire a pistol. The crowd quieted. He shouted up and assured her that he would look into her grievances. Then he had his men enter the convent and stop the riot.

"The situation improved for the sisters of Santa Catalina as he had promised. It took seventeen years from the time of the first mention of freedom from the Dominicans until they finally let this convent be, but it did happen."

She looked at me and smiled and said, "I brought you up here to let you know that despite the violence of the world of men down there, it is possible to achieve freedom and self-respect if you will refuse to accept, and agree with, the wrongs around you. If you have self-respect and integrity, you will be all right. But you must first know yourself."

I marveled at her wisdom. I understood perfectly. Right then, I believed I would be all right. I knew it was more often true than not that I moved and acted with my own sense of myself. I usually had nothing to lose, and so I would let my pride carry me through difficult situations. It was when I hated, or doubted, that I often felt miserable.

I determined at that moment, from then on, I would always act or speak exactly as I felt that I should. Up until that moment I had not known that such pride was a virtue. I resolved that I would never let what I might lose or gain be the deciding factor in my choices. I would be true to myself, first. I would achieve my goals. My determination would take me to Venezuela after all, and to any other place I wanted to go. I would listen to my inner self, then I would act no matter what seemed most comfortable. I spoke these promises to myself.

I was about to thank Doña Luisa when she started fluttering about, saying that our supper was getting cold and how dusty it was in the belfry and other such trivialities. She hurried me down the steps and through the "streets" of the little pueblo of cells standing in the center of the convent to our own warm cell where we ate our supper. No one seemed to mind that I had interrupted the afternoon and the whole group quickly fell again into having fun.

During supper, I felt a change in me. I reflected on Doña Luisa's story and I felt I had matured in the last half an hour. I loved these people. I wanted to be like them. I wanted to be with them. As I sat there, I forgot about Venezuela and the revolution and escaping; I thought only about how I could fit in. Ironically, it was the story and the advice of Doña Luisa that caused me to respect and like her so much, which in turn caused me to do exactly the opposite of what I had just been advised against.

I did not feel angry anymore. I was almost at peace. Because I was enjoying that feeling of "belonging" so much, having been deprived of it all of my life, I felt a compulsion to maintain that feeling at all costs. That was the first time I thought about becoming a nun.

Chapter 13

I kept my secret thoughts about becoming a nun to myself. Every day, such a possibility seemed more attractive, but I was not truly certain that was what I wanted. I was devoted to Doña Luisa as a mother. I loved Carmen as a sister. My feelings were deep, and I followed both of them around with a passion that was almost "romantic." My imaginings—of myself in Doña Luisa's position one day—were always in my mind, but I revealed such desires to no one.

It is easier to succumb to blind passion in one's youth than at any other time. It was my age that was causing me to need such intimate involvement with others. My new friends were all I cared about.

Carmen received all of my adolescent affection, which might have gone to boys, had there been any around. I relished every moment I spent with Carmen, who, unlike Doña Luisa, was always bright and happy. I sometimes called her Sister, I felt that close to her. As we went about our daily chores, she laughed with me, listened to me, hugged me, caressed me, and confided in me. I grew more fond of her each day. Whenever I imagined being in control of my own cell, like Doña Luisa, Carmen was always in such thoughts as my partner. Sometimes at night I had romantic fantasies about her.

As the months passed, Carmen would often comment on my beauty and womanliness. I loved such compliments. I needed them. She flirted with me and I did all I could to show myself off to her, without being too obvious. I would become coy with her, and she would say, "I'm jus' waitin' for you to be full grown."

She said it in such a sensual way that I wondered if she meant it the way it sounded. I knew she had a lover, a man whom she would slip out of the convent to meet every two or three weeks, so I felt certain that was not what she had in mind. However, I was so devoted to her, I would have preferred she kept all of her attention on me.

Months later, I was still wondering whether I should be a nun when something happened to make up my mind. Carmen asked me a question, one sunny day, in Doña Luisa's patio.

Doña Luisa's cell was large, even for a wealthy nun such as she. There was a small covered porch recessed into the front exterior walls. Above the two steps leading up to the porch were the words "Luisa Esclara" carved into the masonry. Inside the front door was a comfortable room furnished with beautiful chairs and tables from France and Spain. To the right was a door to a smaller room where Carmen, Beatríz, and I slept. This room also had a small table where I would study. Across the main room, from our little one, were steps against the wall that led up to Doña Luisa's room. Inside her room upstairs was a large bed made of dark hardwood. It was beautiful, with tall posts on each corner and covered with gauze curtains. Directly across from the door in the main room below was a door leading to a small enclosed patio, which had roses growing in each corner. On the day Carmen asked me her question, we were in the patio area washing clothes. Without warning, she looked at me inquisitively and said, "You hidin' somethin' from me?"

I said, "No, Carmen, why do you ask?"

"Look!" She held up a soft cotton cloth. A dark red stain, which she had been washing, was covered with soap bubbles. "We wash three of these a month, not four." She smiled. "Are you hidin' yours?"

I blushed, and said, almost under my breath, "I have never started my flow."

She said, "How old are you?"

"Fifteen."

"Turn around," she said.

I did so, and she looked me up and down. I was acutely aware of the fullness of my breasts and hips. In the right clothes and setting I could easily have been mistaken for a grown woman. It embarrassed me to have her look at me so.

I half-expected her usual compliment, but she said, "I think you should have." She returned to her washing, and I did the same. We worked in silence. Until then, I had no hint that something might be wrong with me.

I did not have long to worry. Carmen spoke to Doña Luisa about our conversation, and when the doctor came to the convent again, I was sent to see him. I was a little anxious as I walked to the *locutorio* where the doctor did his examinations. A doctor had never examined me before in so private a place.

When he stated that I was "uniquely formed" and that I would never be able to have children, my worry was replaced by a profound feeling of isolation.

It was not a new feeling, but it was stronger than I had ever known. The melancholy I suddenly felt may only have seemed intense after my new, and very deep, feelings of being part of a community. Prior to Carmen's question, everything had been going perfectly for me. I did not fully understand it then, but it was the fear of being all alone again that cast a pall over my emotions. It so terrified me, after having had some respite from this fear, that I was sullen, morose and uncommunicative for days.

A week or so later, after I had steeled myself to my condition, I again began to carry myself with that stoic rigidity that I had learned to muster so well to protect myself from the world. I had been "different" all of my life and I could be so again, I told myself.

In addition to the uncertainty the diagnosis posed to me as a person, and my sense of myself in relation to others, the meaning it had for me as a woman brought on its own mixture of feelings. If my new friends had reacted otherwise to the news, it might not have been so meaningful to me. However, sadness, and a sense of incompleteness, were given impetus by the expressions and looks of the three other women with whom I lived. I think they tried, but failed, to hide their feelings. It was never spoken, but it truly seemed that they felt sorry for me. It became clear that other women considered me "incomplete." I felt that my friends no longer considered me a real woman.

I was used to being alone. I do believe, had I been someone else, without my special experiences to prepare me for what I faced, I would have felt much worse. As a woman, although I felt loss, I also felt unencumbered. From then on, I felt no obligation to try to live up to any image that the world might have of what a woman should be—which I knew I would never be able to do anyway.

It was the mixture of these two events that helped me make my wrong-sighted decision. It was Doña Luisa advising me to be free from my need for men (though the advice had deeper implications) and my physical incapacity to live up to any man's expectations of my being a mother that made me decide firmly, after watching the power and easy life of my benefactor: I would be a nun.

In addition to the fact that I was, to some degree, trying to hold on to a feeling of belonging—in direct opposition to the advice I had received from Doña Luisa—there were other reasons that made sense to me at the time. The most important was that if I did not take the veil, there was nothing to which I could look forward in life. I was illegitimate, and no man of position would be serious about wedding me—especially with no dowry or family name. And yet I realized that without the skills even of a craftsman, and no money of my own, I knew I must live off the money of men if I left the convent. I might have to be a concubine. Perhaps I might be forced into prostitution. Every time I thought about my future, it worried me.

I watched the daily life of the convent carefully, seeing the power which Doña Luisa wielded within the community. Nuns of the black veil were, very much, living a civil life almost as rich as that of any man outside the convent walls. The only exception was that men were more openly capable of sexual satisfactions—such satisfactions being mostly denied to women, inside or outside of the convent. There were known to be cases of women slipping out, or men stealing in, to engage in unholy activities. I know of more than one nun who gave birth to the child of her confessor or some other priest. Women being with women was not unknown either. Even at that age, I personally knew that it happened on occasion.

At age 15 I felt I could conquer any sexual desires I might have in the future, or get around the restrictions on sex. One of the things that made me decide not to worry about the prohibition on male contact was an event that occurred while I was out with Carmen one day on an errand.

We were to bring back two large boxes containing a silver service. One box had a tray and the other a teapot, and they had just arrived from the coast. Doña Luisa purchased this silver from an acquaintance in Potosí, intending to use it to entertain friends in the *locutorios*.

When Carmen had prepared to go out that day, she made herself up. She put on a necklace of pretty stones, washed herself and delicately dabbed on a special scent that she had made from a formula of her mother's. She also put powders and paints on her eyes and cheeks. Later, as we walked down the streets, she turned the heads of men of all races and classes.

At one point, as we were walking back, we were stopped by a man on a horse. Carmen instructed me to continue on with the tray I was carrying to a certain point, and then wait for her. She climbed on the horse behind the man, her own box still in her hand, and they rode off.

I followed her instructions, and when I arrived at the correct street corner, I waited. After about a half an hour, I was becoming bored.

Just then, a group of soldiers came by—the King's Guard—and in amongst them was the handsomest young man I had ever seen. Of all the men in the unit, he drew my attention immediately as I watched them ride toward where I was standing. His white uniform clung tightly to his muscled thighs and hips, and though he wore a stern expression, his eyes seemed to laugh. They all looked straight ahead, but I saw him glance at me as they stopped for a moment.

As I was watching the good-looking soldier, Carmen walked around the corner. She said, "Come, Manuela. We're late. Let's go quickly."

I had my attention on the soldier and did not respond. When Carmen saw where I was looking, she said, "Oh, I seen him before—all the girls look at him." She laughed.

I felt a little embarrassed. "I don't know who you mean. I was watching the horses," I said. I picked up my box and walked toward the convent.

I knew why Carmen had gone off. I deduced that the man on the horse was her lover. It became apparent to me that Carmen could get out of the convent any time, if she wanted to do so, and her lover could take her anywhere in the city she wanted to go. Being beautiful and sexually aware gave her power. I had wondered about her absences before. Now I understood and decided that I could be like her.

Having just seen the handsome soldier, with whom I wished I could have been riding, I was a little jealous. I didn't really want sex, but I wanted an encounter, as Carmen had. I wanted excitement. I wanted more than I had.

Encouraged by this realization—that I could have what I wanted, despite my seeming to be living by convent rules—I decided for certain that I would be a nun. I had finally made up my mind.

I imagined it, off and on, for almost a year, but shrewdly, I did not tell Doña Luisa. I did not mention my thoughts to anyone at all, though Doña Luisa kept suggesting it. I knew I had plenty of time to tell her, and if I spoke too soon there would be new responsibilities and expectations. I would enjoy my life as it was for awhile.

Despite my decision to stay and take vows, if I could have found an opportunity to leave the convent, I would have. I thought it might happen when I received a letter from my father stating that his wife had recently died. At the end of the letter, he said something like, "I hope to see you soon." It seemed that he meant to bring me to Panamá. I was full of anticipation for weeks, but the next letter I received had a different tone. He did not mention my joining him, and none of his letters ever did again. With that hope gone, I decided to tell Doña Luisa about my decision. When I proposed the idea, she was delighted and proceeded to help me.

With such encouragement, I might have become a nun after all. However, a series of events that continued for the next year got in the way. These events were sparked by something that happened very soon after I mentioned my desires to Doña Luisa: I saw the soldier again—the same young man I had seen that day when I had been out with Carmen.

Two or three days after stating my intention to become a nun, there was a civic celebration to welcome a dignitary from Spain to Quito. The students from Santa Catalina were to bring a woven chain of flowers to the festivities. I did not want to go. However, I went because the celebration committee had persuaded Doña Luisa that I should be included to round out their numbers.

All of the girls my age were standing together, bored, as the afternoon wore on. The sun was bright and hot. We were talking to one another, being shushed regularly by the nuns, when the King's Guard rode by. I saw him again, the handsome soldier. The troop was riding down the street toward us. He was on his white horse, looking straight ahead.

It was impressive enough that he was a member of the King's Guard, but he was so very good looking. As the sun reflected off the gold braid on his uniform, I thought he struck a magnificent figure. His smile would make anyone want to know him. When I saw him that day, I very much wanted to have his attention. However, I could not imagine being so lucky. I noticed the other girls my age—I was about 16 at this time— looking at him too.

Antonia—who had grown to be a very beautiful young woman with long, beautiful, black hair spilling from under her lace cap—was standing near me. I overheard her say something about the soldier to another girl. ". . . his name is Fausto . . . ."

When I became aware that Antonia was paying special attention to my soldier, and that she apparently knew him, I was disgusted. I tried to think of something else, I wanted to get through the ordeal of standing there in the hot sun, with these girls that I hated, as fast as I could.

I was not prepared when, as he rode by, he looked right at me, made a special point to salute me, and smiled. His smile was radiant and endearing. I froze, and I know that I blushed. I only barely restrained myself from looking around to see if he was lavishing his attention on someone behind me. But as he continued on, he turned in his saddle to smile at me. When he had passed, I noticed Antonia glaring at me with undisguised hatred.

He was on my mind all day long. The next day, I made a point to get out of the convent, and I tried to be where I could catch his attention. I saw him once, but he did not see me. I thought about him for days and days after that. I dreamed about being with him at night. We saw each other on occasion, from afar, and we would smile at each other. He would always salute me, or stop his horse and wave at me. All of this interest in a young man was going on while Doña Luisa helped me in my preparations to be a novice.

I made a hundred plans to get to know him, but I never executed any of them. Then, one day I learned that Antonia had arranged, through her family, to have him come with them to visit her in the *locutorios*.

I was beside myself. She, after all, was not studying to become a nun; she was only a student there. She would leave one day when her education was done, and she would already be wealthy and positioned due to her family. She could have any man she wanted. She would marry someday. She would have children and all she wished for, throughout her life, just as she did in the convent. I was totally frustrated that she could see him socially, and I could not even make actual contact with him. Finally, giving it up as hopeless, I tried to stop thinking about him.

Then, one day, as I was out buying spices from the Indian vendors for one of Carmen's meals, I stopped at a street vendor on my way back to the convent. I wanted to spend one of my coins on an *hielo*—snow from Pichincha, flavored with honey and fruit.

I was digging in my pocket to pay for it when my soldier, unseen until this moment, walked up behind me and put down his own coin. His rich, masculine voice said, "Let me pay for the lady's ice."

I stammered "Thank you!" and tried to assume an attitude of composure, but I was nervous and probably looked it. I received my "ice" on a large leaf and I was happy, and relieved, when he bought one for himself. It saved me the embarrassment of having him watch me consume such a messy treat. We laughed as we saw each other wipe sticky pink rivulets of juice from our chins while trying to keep it from dripping onto our clothes.

He congratulated me on my success and I teased him about a single tiny pink glob on the toe of his immaculately shiny boot. He laughed and cleaned it off, and then we walked and talked for an hour or more. It was my first opportunity to get to know him.

I found out his name was Fausto D'Elhuyar. I had daydreamed about this encounter for a long time, and I was not disappointed. I liked him—far beyond mere "attraction."

This, of course, caused me a good deal of inconvenience. Not only did I get in trouble for being late that afternoon, but after I met him, I was even more infatuated with him. I would sneak away from my lessons to see him, almost daily. I "borrowed" Carmen's perfume and paints and dresses. I would arrange to be where I knew he would be. I would walk through town, barefoot, wearing flimsy, indecently revealing dresses, hoping to run into him.

I wanted to look comely so that I would keep his attention, but I always felt a little silly when I "tried" to look attractive. I was never convinced that I was beautiful, which is why I loved Carmen's compliments so much. Thus, when I "tried" to look beautiful, I know I tried too hard.

However, no matter what I thought of myself, whenever I saw him, Fausto seemed to like me. I was very often successful in my missions to "accidentally" meet him, and these "accidental" meetings would take us both away from our duties. It was so easy to be with him. We could talk for hours.

A big interest we had in common was a love of horses. He would let me ride his mare, which I enjoyed immensely. He was an excellent horseman and he performed several clever tricks for me. Of course, I insisted that he teach them to me. The first trick he taught me was to snatch a hat out of his hand while riding at a gallop. I learned quickly, and soon could take the hat right off his head. In the weeks that followed, I raced through the streets of Quito on his horse, scaring people and scattering animals, grabbing hats off heads I did not even know. Fausto and his fellow guardsmen cheered me on.

We very nearly got into real trouble once. He was teaching me how to use his pistol, and he challenged me to ride and fire at a target he had set up. I took up the challenge but missed the target, putting a bullet in a new hat on the head of an important member of the *audiencia*.

Despite the danger we put ourselves in, we continued to see each other. When the Larreas returned to the city, they allowed me to borrow a horse from their stable a few times, and Fausto and I spent the entire day riding together. Riding, walking, or talking, these rendezvous went on for months. I was always jumping over the wall and I was put into the convent jail twice for being incorrigible. My seventeenth birthday came and went with Doña Luisa becoming increasingly upset with me.

I could rely on Carmen as an ally, and so despite all, I was able to see Fausto quite often. I never mentioned to anyone except Carmen what was holding my interest outside the convent walls.

I saw Fausto many times, but I never let him go beyond kissing me. He was clearly interested in moving our relationship forward, which confused me. Since I did not really find myself attractive, and knowing he had a reputation with the young ladies, I worried that he might just be using me. I was afraid, if I let him have me, I would never see him again. I was afraid of the same thing, if I did not.

We would often end up in some remote area where we could hold hands or embrace. When he kissed me, I was longing to let him do more, but I became afraid when I did and either broke the mood or left.

I even picked a fight with him one day because it appeared that I would have no way to deny him any longer, and my nervousness got the better of me. A young man, dressed in a rather foppish way, presented me with a bouquet of flowers one afternoon. I had been walking down the street to meet Fausto when this dandy suddenly stepped in front of me. Many men, since I had taken to dressing in a provocative manner, had tried to get my attention, but this one had gone out of his way to buy flowers from an Indian girl and bring them to me.

"Could I offer the lady a token of my admiration," he said and bowed very low.

I noticed Fausto walking his horse down the street toward me. He could see us talking. I knew that Fausto was intending that I ride out of the city with him to "be alone." I wanted to go, and yet I was afraid.

I took the flowers and smelled them, looking beyond to see Fausto stop and stare at us. "Thank you, Señor!" I said and chatted with him for a moment.

Fausto walked up, interrupted the dandy, and said, "Excuse me Señorita, did we not have an agreement to meet farther up the street?" The dandy instantly understood the situation and excused himself.

"That was rude, Fausto," I said, when the other man had gone.

"Perhaps. I am sorry. A young lady too easily accepting a man's attentions is also in bad form."

I did not admit to him how much I enjoyed the flirtations of the men I encountered. He had spoken truthfully, but I said, "That is insulting." A small argument ensued, and I walked away.

I had not been back at the convent for an hour when I regretted it. I had been sitting on my cot. The room was small and dark, having only one small window set high in the stone. I was alone, thinking about kissing Fausto. The thought excited me, and I was suddenly filled with desire for him. *You are silly, Manuela*, I told myself. *Get over your fear. You like him. Go back and find him.*

Then it struck me that perhaps I had ruined my chances of ever being able see him again. "You are more than silly, you are a fool," I said out loud. I sprang to my feet, resolving to find him and make up with him. Before I reached the door, Doña Luisa entered.

"Where are you going?" she asked angrily.

"Nowhere," I lied.

She looked disgusted. "Yes. That is correct."

"What?"

"The Abbess has received reports from all over the city of your behavior in the last few weeks. She has had enough and has insisted that I keep you in my cell."

"Doña Luisa, I—"

"It is scandalous enough that you will not conform to convent rules," she looked me up and down, "but you insist on breaking society's rules as well Going barefoot! Despite my admonitions. And you insist on wearing skimpy Indian dresses that reveal far too much."

"Is my bosom too much for this city's hypocrites?" I challenged.

"How dare you talk to me that way?" She put her hands on her hips in disgust. "You are to stay at your desk and will not leave this room until I say." She started to exit, and then she turned back. "Another thing—you are not to bother the Abbess anymore with your rude demands. Why you want a dowry when you are so determined to throw away your future is beyond my ability to understand." She closed the door loudly, leaving me alone with my thoughts.

She was referring to the fact that, in the few months just preceding, I had rightfully demanded of the Abbess, almost daily, that she contact my uncle so that I could obtain my inheritance. I needed a dowry so that I could be a nun of the black veil. I believed my inheritance was the only money I would ever get. There was no sense in being a nun if I could not have the kind of power Doña Luisa had, and the only way that would happen was if I could pay a large dowry.

I was quite a pest about it, and I was foolish. The Abbess would never take my side with my behavior being what it was. Also, I should have seen that the Abbess would never speak to Carlos about my inheritance when he was regularly paying the convent a large sum of money for my upkeep.

I was really a very confused and headstrong young girl. I was demanding justice with Carlos from the convent management in order to get money to become a nun in a place where almost everyone hated me. A vote on my acceptance would probably never be affirmative, and what else could I expect when I was so demanding and self-centered. The only chance I had to be voted into the convent, even with a dowry, was with Doña Luisa's help, yet I was not paying attention to her or my studies, which would have shown her that I deserved her help. To make matters worse, though I wanted to be a nun, I also wanted to violate the most sacred rule of the convent.

The truth is, I did not know what I wanted. Maybe I just wanted everything. I moved ahead making enemies, left and right. The only thing I was sure about was that I would not give up Fausto. I wanted him, and I was determined to have a relationship with him one way or another.

I listened at the door after Doña Luisa had left. I could hear her pacing around the main room in agitation. I was worried because she was so upset with me, yet I was still determined to get out. I hoped I would be able to sneak out quickly, and back in again, just one time, without Doña Luisa knowing about it. I wasn't.

My afternoon confined to my cell turned into days, and the days to weeks. I was able to pass one or two letters to Fausto through Carmen's contacts in the city, but I received no answers. As time wore on, without being able to communicate to him, I became more and more frustrated and distracted. I was not studying, or working very hard on anything. All I could think about was Fausto.

Finally, what I had been dreading most, happened. I felt I must find Fausto, and I was about to leave the convent without permission, when Doña Luisa caught me. She was already there as I approached the back fence. I didn't know how she knew I had planned to sneak off, but she was there and she was angry. She marched me back to her cell in silence.

"I have reached the end of my patience," she said at last. "I am not going to continue to keep you out of trouble with the Abbess. Either you start paying serious attention to your duties and your studies, or I am going to send you back to the convent school."

She practically pushed me into my room. She left saying, "It is one or the other, young lady! Decide! This is your last week of shirking. You have seven days to make up your mind what you are going to do. In the meantime, I'll be watching you, and I had better see some improvement."

I sat down on my bed—weary. I wanted both power and love, and it appeared that I could not have either. It would not be so bad if I could just communicate with Fausto: to let him know I cared, to tell him to wait for me, to let him know I would see him again—but I was trapped.

As I was sitting there in misery, Carmen came into the room. Finding me looking so forlorn, she sat down next to me and began softly rubbing my back. "What's the matter? You look sad," she said softly.

I turned and put my arms around her, my head against her breast. I hugged her hard; a lump came to my throat. I told her all I was feeling. Finally, I asked her, "Why hasn't Fausto answered my letters?"

She said, "Don't think 'bout him. Fausto is the most desired young man in Quito. You know that." She was right. "He has taken advantage of the young girls who have desired him on more than one occasion, and he has the worst reputation in the city for breakin' promises said only in passion."

Her words hurt me. I was about to rebuke her. As I lifted my head and opened my mouth to speak, I stopped. She was right. I was a fool to expect anything from him, and his not answering my letters only proved that I had been right in not letting him go beyond kissing me.

She saw the look on my face and said, "Forget him, my sweet. You're too pretty to let it bother you." She embraced me again and rocked me back and forth. "Don't worry. He may have forgotten about you, but you can forget 'bout him too."

I agreed with her, but inside I knew I would not forget him, and I think Carmen knew it too. More important to me, at that moment, was knowing someone cared about me. I was grateful that Carmen was there.

When she got up to leave, she stopped and touched my cheek very softly, looked in my eyes for a long time and whispered, "You are a very beautiful young woman." She turned and left the room.

She often made such remarks. I had never felt the least bit pretty, let alone beautiful, except that I did like the contrast of my white skin and thick black hair. Everything else about me seemed quite unattractive. I looked at myself in the mirror and I decided that I had been a fool to think that Fausto was seriously interested in me, except as someone to seduce. Carmen did not really mean her compliment, I thought. She was merely trying to make me feel better.

Chapter 14

After Carmen consoled me, I swore to myself that I would never think about Fausto again. However, a few days later, I heard that he was in the convent visiting someone. I ran to the entrance hall as fast as I could.

It was busy that day, and I looked at all of the people in the *portería* and listened at the doors to the *locutorios*. I could not find him. I did find something else—something very interesting.

I had given up on locating Fausto and was walking back through the garden to return to Doña Luisa's cell when I noticed Antonia and Doña Luisa's servant, Beatríz, having an intense conversation. They were just ahead, but they did not see me because they were leaning close to each other and speaking in a conspiratorial way. Then I saw Antonia take a sealed piece of paper from Beatríz and walk toward her dormitory. I followed Beatríz back to our cell.

I wondered what Beatríz was doing talking to Antonia. I found my answer two days later when Carmen came up to me and said, "Your soldier caught me as I was walkin' through the *porteria*." She handed me a sealed letter, just like the one I had seen passed from Beatríz to Antonia:

Dear Manuela,

> Why have you not answered me? This letter will be the fifth I have given Doña Esclara's servants.
>
> As I have stated before, I am sorry about the way I acted when last we met. Please accept my apology. If you are being stubborn, please answer me and let me know how you are. I miss you and I long to see you.

Fausto

What a difference that letter made. I was suddenly extraordinarily happy. At the same time, I was infuriated. Antonia had been intercepting Fausto's letters to me, and she was using Beatríz to do it.

I wrote a long letter to him and had Carmen see that it was delivered. Inside were instructions that he should send his replies only through her. Then I began spying on Beatríz.

I tried to follow her around, but she had more freedom than I. I had to pretend to be taking a serious interest in my chores and studies, so I was not always successful in seeing where she went. However, I was able to learn two things. First, she was definitely following and watching me, and second, she was reporting to Antonia about what I was doing. That was the reason it was so difficult for me to sneak out of the convent.

I decided that I would win that game. I made sure that I arose before she did and retired after. Whenever Doña Luisa was around, I was certain to appear busy. Paying such close attention to Beatríz soon made me feel capable of eluding her if I wished. Doña Luisa became convinced of my sincerity in attending to my business, and shortly, I felt I could jump over the wall to see Fausto without being found out.

In the meantime, we had exchanged two more letters and I was anxious to see him again. He understood my predicament and stated his willingness to wait until I could safely see him without getting into trouble. He urged me not to take unnecessary chances. I agreed with him, but I was becoming impatient.

The only thing stopping me was Doña Luisa. Even if I could avoid Beatríz and sneak out of the convent, the dangers were much greater than they had ever been. If I was caught, I would lose my position in Doña Luisa's cell. The last thing I wanted was to return to convent school, and my battles with the girls that hated me. My fear of being excluded again exacerbated my already confused state of mind. I was looking for something. I needed something. I did not know what I was supposed to be doing. I knew I wanted to be with Fausto, at least long enough to confirm our feelings for one another, but I felt like the convent had become a labyrinth. Somewhere in all this confusion was the truth. Somewhere were my secret fears. I seemed to be going in circles, afraid to move forward but unable to stop.

All I could think to do was the one thing that was most dangerous. I had to wait for the right opportunity to sneak out and find Fausto. Then I would know about my future. While I waited, I discovered something that changed everything.

It was late and I had made myself stay awake until I was sure Beatríz was asleep. Often she would sneak out late at night to discuss something with Antonia or her maid. As I was falling into sleep that night, I heard Beatríz rise again.

It was after midnight. Her manner was definitely that of someone doing something she did not want discovered. She quietly opened the latch and slipped through the door into the big room. She left the door slightly ajar so she would not have to make noise closing it. I ran to the door as soon as she left the room. Carmen appeared to be asleep.

I looked through the door expecting to see Beatríz carefully working the latch to the outer door. Instead she was climbing the stairs to Doña Luisa's room. I slid through the door very carefully and followed. Because I was being so silent, it took me a while to get to the top of stairs. When I arrived, I looked through a crack in the door jam and could see plainly to the bed of Doña Luisa. Beatríz was leaning over her, kissing her face and neck. Luisa was breathing heavily and I saw her take down her bed covers.

I was startled. My first instinct was to turn away, but I stayed. I watched and listened. That night, I learned a great deal about the women with whom I had been living. From previous conversations, I knew that my benefactor considered what they were doing to be wrong, and I knew that she would suffer for it.

I did not feel morally superior. I did not consider what they were doing either right or wrong, nor did it upset me. But I knew Doña Luisa, and I knew that she was violating her *own* sense of morality. I knew with a certainty that night that what she was doing was what brought on her guilt and her dark moods. I was amazed at Doña Luisa, who always seemed able to have things exactly as she wanted them. She obviously wanted her relationship with Beatríz. If so, why feel guilty? If not, simply discharge her. She had all the power, it seemed, except her own power of will, in this regard. Though perhaps she was a afraid Beatríz would talk if she let her go. The sad thing is that I did not believe she really wanted Beatríz, who was so unlikable. I think she just needed to be close to someone.

When they were undressed, the sensualness of their embrace made me think of Fausto. As I watched, I became aroused. As soon as I thought of him, I knew I had seen enough of what was happening in Doña Luisa's room. Silently, I descended the stairs.

As I walked quietly back to my room, I heard Carmen whisper behind me, "Did you see them?" I turned with a start. She was standing in the shadows, almost beneath the stairs. She indicated to the room above with a smile.

I relaxed and nodded.

She came close to me and said quietly, "It's been goin' on for years. They need each other."

Then she held my eyes with hers and reached out for me. She stepped closer and gently put her arms around me. Instinctively, I embraced her in return.

She held me very near, and kissed me softly on my neck and cheek. Shivers raced through my body, and I could not move. Then she kissed me very tenderly on my mouth. My breath quickened. She kissed me harder and parted my lips with her tongue. I stood frozen with uncertainty, captured by the feelings of my body.

I loved Carmen. I knew then that I had wanted her to kiss me since I first knew her. I wanted her to continue. I was fully aware, at the same time, of the difference between my desire at the moment and even stronger inner desires.

What I "needed" just then could have easily become confused with what I truly wanted. The lesson I had just learned upstairs, taught to me by an unhappy nun and a malicious servant, made me know that this was not for me. Doña Luisa's advice, that she had told to me on that summer day, was in my mind.

"It is not good for you to be in such need. Even though you deny it." Her words came to my ears as though she were standing there speaking to me. "What is important in your life is *you*. You must know who you are, and it is only by having a clear mind that you can make right choices. Whatever you are, learn to love it; learn to know and love yourself and act on your inner desires, not your needs and hungers."

I had made up my mind in that bell tower: I would always act or speak exactly as I felt that I should. I would achieve my goals. I would go to Venezuela and help the revolution. I would listen to my inner self, then I would act, no matter what seemed most comfortable.

All these promises, which I had made to myself that afternoon, came to me as Carmen held me close. I realized that I had betrayed myself almost as soon as I had left the tower. Within the hour, I had desired to be a nun because of my need for companionship. That had drowned out all else. I forgot what I wanted: to find and help the revolution, and more importantly, to leave the convent, which stifled me. I had done neither of those things. As soon as I experienced love from Doña Luisa and Carmen, I had abandoned myself.

While these thoughts filled my mind, Carmen moved her hands over my back and my neck and then she brought them forward to touch my breasts. I stood frozen, savoring the feelings with my body, which felt so good, while my mind raced.

What do I really want? I asked myself. *Fausto. I want to be with Fausto. I want to leave this convent. If I continue, I will never leave.* It all became clear: what I wanted and who I really was. My physical feelings changed. How I was responding changed. For a brief moment, I could see myself in a clear light.

I gently pulled away. "No, my sister," I whispered. Carmen's breath was coming hard. She looked at me and frowned at first. She grabbed my arms as if to hold me, to keep me from leaving. Then she smiled and kissed me gently on the mouth and said, "I love you." Before I could answer, she turned and walked back to her bed.

I whispered, "Carmen!"

"Yes."

"I'm sorry."

"Don't worry, beautiful, I'm your friend and I will be there when you need me." She turned and walked away.

That meant so much to hear. I stood there for a long time and then followed her into our room. We did not speak. I lay awake thinking a long time about my life: my foolish decision to be a nun, loving Fausto, my determination to love myself no matter what, my feud with Carlos (the enemy who would never show himself but always kept me from what was mine). I was 17, I did not have to stay in the convent any longer if I really did not want to do so, and there was nothing keeping me there any more. I determined that night what I would do.

When morning broke, everything seemed normal. Carmen treated me as she always had. Beatríz arose from her bed in one of her happy moods. I could not resist saying, "Did you sleep well, Beatríz?"

She looked at me sharply and I saw that she realized I knew. Her look changed to hatred and she left the room.

I saw Doña Luisa once or twice throughout the day. She was in a very bad temper. Mostly she stayed in her room all day and prayed. Her moods suddenly became understandable, being clearly precipitated by guilt. I had tried to like Beatríz, though she could be quite unpleasant at times, but now I hated her. I realized that she was leading my friend, Doña Luisa, where she would rather not go. I wanted to do something to help my benefactor, but I knew there were bigger forces at work than my abilities could manage.

It was my own life that needed my abilities just then. I had decided it was I who should be ruling my life, and I was about to take steps in forming my existence into what I wanted it to be.

Early in the morning, I wrote a message to Fausto and Carmen carried it to him directly. "I want to see you tonight. You know where to meet me. Nothing will keep me away."

Chapter 15

That night, it was I who was sneaking out of my cot. As soon as I thought Beatríz was asleep, I dressed in a simple shift and proceeded to the outer door. I opened it quietly, crossed the threshold onto the moonlit porch, and silently closed the latch. I tried to re-think my plan as I walked between the silent convent cells.

I knew that I needed my inheritance. I could not just walk out of the convent and not return. How would I survive? Carlos was not about to give me my money, and I did not know what I could do to make him.

Unless I could travel about the city freely, I would never be able to have any effect on him. I needed to be free of the convent somehow to win my inheritance, but I needed my inheritance to be free. I didn't know if it took letters or a formal appeal to the *audiencia* or just what, but I knew that I needed help.

I felt sure that Fausto would help me all he could. If I asked him, I knew he would be my eyes and ears and legs outside the convent. With a member of the King's Guard as my "champion" in the governmental halls, I felt sure that I would have my money within a few weeks, and then I would be free.

I was very careful to make sure I wasn't being followed as I raced across the back courtyard to the low part of the back fence. Fausto was there to catch me as I climbed down.

We stifled our giggles as we ran around the adjacent buildings to where Fausto had left his horse. We both mounted and rode through the streets and into the fields bathed in moonlight.

When we reached a secluded spot, we climbed down and Fausto pulled a blanket from behind his saddle to wrap around our shoulders. We laughed with delight as we walked through the grass, Fausto leading his horse by the reins, the moon shedding its blue light on us.

He said, "It is so good to be with you again. I missed you."

"It is wonderful to be with you too."

"Are you sure no one will know you've left? I don't want you to get into any trouble."

"It doesn't matter," I said slyly.

He stopped. "What do you mean? Why not?"

"It's a secret," I teased.

Smiling, Fausto pulled one more blanket from behind his saddle. He was about to reply when I put a finger to my lips and said, "Come on."

It was a warm summer night for the Andes. I turned and ran. Fausto dropped the reins and followed. He caught up to me and pulled me down into the long grass. He covered us both up with the blanket and we lay there happily for awhile, hand in hand, laughing and talking, and looking at the clear night sky. His horse stood where it was, grazing lazily.

Fausto broke the silence with a chuckle, "What's the secret?"

"I don't know if I should tell you," I said coyly.

"Very well. But I have a secret too."

"What?"

Fausto smiled slyly and said, "You tell me first."

I laughed happily at our game and said, "No, you first. Tell me, Fausto." I sat up and clutched the braid on his uniform playfully.

"All right, but you promise?"

"Yes, yes. Tell me," I insisted.

"You know that my brother is fighting with Bolívar in Venezuela."

"Yes. I always wondered what you were doing here in the King's Guard. I can't see the D'Elhuyar brothers fighting each other some day."

"Oh, we won't. I'm leaving in a few days to join him."

I was stunned. I had not expected that. It took me a moment before I could speak. Fausto looked at me expectantly, but I was quiet.

Fausto's father, after whom Fausto had been named, was a scientist living and working for the king in Mexico. He and Fausto's uncle had invented a new metal called "tungsten." However, he had little time for his sons as they grew.

Fausto and his brother had become very close. Somehow they had been separated, his brother staying with his uncle and Fausto coming to Quito. Fausto's brother had been living with their uncle in New Granada, in the city of Santa Fe de Bogotá, ever since.

When Fausto learned that his brother had joined the revolution, he wanted to join him. He longed to be with his brother again. I knew the background, but I did not expect him to leave.

I said, "Oh, Fausto, that is exciting . . . ." My voice trailed off, and I felt like I looked more morose than I wanted to appear. It was not just that his departure would ruin my plan. Much more importantly, I realized I might never see him again. I was sad, but I did not want him to know it. I lay back and looked at the millions of stars sparkling in the void. They were together, but each was separate and alone. Some, those that were a part of a constellation, had "families," but each had its place. The stars were like people. What kind of a star would I have been?

"Please keep my secret, Manuela," Fausto said, breaking my thoughts. I had not known exactly how to respond.

I answered, still looking into the night sky, "You know I will."

Then he raised himself up on one elbow. "What's the matter?"

"Nothing."

"Yes there is."

"I'm only sad that you won't be here any more."

He looked into my eyes for a long time. "Why don't you come with me?"

I reached up and put my arms around him. I pulled him down to me and held him close. My eyes became teary. I made myself stop crying and said, "No. I don't mind being alone, Fausto. But I am truly grateful that you asked."

"Manuela, I want you to come with me," he whispered.

I hugged him and said, "I've been outcast all my life and you have made me happy by being with me—just by being my friend." He sat up as though searching for something to say. I went on. "I know how to be alone. And I don't want to hold you back." Then I added, "But I want you to know the affection I feel for you."

I paused and looked at him. He was about to speak, but I said quickly, "I ask you only one thing. Promise me, promise me," I said intensely as I sat up, "that you will stay my friend wherever you go, whatever you do. You know you're the only one that has made my life bearable here for the last year. I do care about you, Fausto." I reached out and held him. "Promise me."

"I promise," he said solemnly.

"I don't know when I will ever again find a friend I like so much."

He laughed. "That's a compliment, coming from you. You don't like anybody."

I was taken aback. "It's not that I dislike people," I protested.

He smiled at me.

I laughed. "All right. But such emotions are too tame. I hate my enemies and I love my friends. That's all. It is one or the other."

"I know," he said. Then he gave me a big smile.

I continued trying to explain myself. "You're a good friend. The fact is, I don't just like you—I love you."

I suddenly realized what I had said. I meant that I felt deeply about him, but the other meaning was expressed as well. He looked at me. Because of his reputation, I started to retract what I had said, but I didn't. It was the truth.

We sat there looking at each other for a moment and I wondered what he would do, and then he burst out laughing. "That is what I like about you," he said. "You never do anything halfway."

I had been unsure of his response. But his merriment, and the way he seemed to enjoy me, made my heart light. I smiled and then I started laughing too.

Finally he said, "Now you tell me your secret."

I stopped. I thought about what I would say, since I did not want to tell him my plan now. I said simply, "I have decided that I am going to leave the convent."

"What? How are you going to do that?

"I do not know, exactly."

"When?

"As soon as my uncle gives me my inheritance." He knew about my mother's will. I had told him about it, and how important it was to me, many times.

"When will he do that?" he replied.

"I don't know, but I'm going to bother him or steal from him or . . . I don't know what, but I am not giving up until he gives me my inheritance. It may take me a couple of months or more, but he is going to do it."

Fausto said, "It would probably take more than a couple of months, but why don't you take him to the law?"

"Yes, Fausto, yes. That is a wonderful idea."

Fausto fell silent and lay back in the grass. Then he said, very seriously, "Manuela, I want you to come with me."

I was moved by the sincerity in his words. I really hadn't believed him. "Why?" I found myself asking. I looked down at his moonlit face.

"Because I will miss you," he said very simply.

"Oh, Fausto," I said, brushing it off. I leaned on one elbow and put my hand on his chest.

He propped himself up and looked at me. He said, "Manuela, this is the truth. You are the most beautiful and intelligent girl in all of Quito. I will miss you. And I want to always see you in the moonlight and hear you laugh." He reached out and caressed my cheek.

He touched me more deeply than he knew. Tears came to my eyes. Then the thought struck me that he was merely trying to seduce me. No one had ever been so tender with me before.

I looked into his eyes and said softly, "Never mind, Fausto. I don't need your flattery to be here. I am here because I choose to be. I love you and that is all there is to that. There is nothing else, and I'm here by choice."

"Nevertheless, it wasn't flattery. You *are* the most beautiful girl in Quito and I do not want to lose you. I want you with me. I love you too."

Never had I felt so disarmed, so open, so intimate, with anyone. He began to speak again and I put a finger to his lips. I looked into his face for a long time. I desired him.

He took my face in his hand. He leaned forward slowly and softly placed his lips to mine.

He was very gentle as he lay me back in the grass. He continued to kiss me—slowly and tenderly. His hand moved softly under my shift, between my legs. I held him tighter and kissed him eagerly.

He pulled his hand out from under my dress and touched my neck. Then he slowly lowered the dress off my shoulders. I savored the feelings that filled the moment. His lips brushed across my breasts.

I held his head in my hands and smelled his hair and then lifted his lips to mine and kissed him, kissed him with all my heart, as I opened my soul to let him in.

Chapter 16

Fausto and I stayed in each other's arms until the cold Andean night forced us to dress and return to the convent. We kissed each other for a long time before he helped me climb back over the wall. As we embraced, I could see clouds start to cover the moon and stars and I felt the night grow colder. Though I knew I had to return before my absence was discovered, I longed to stay with him. As we shivered together, we made plans to meet in the same place in the fields on the following afternoon.

Despite being unsure if it was the right thing to do, I decided that after I made Carlos give me my inheritance, I would indeed follow Fausto to Venezuela or wherever he was. My idea of taking my uncle to litigation made me foolishly imagine that I would have my money very soon. After that, I might as well do what I originally wanted to do. The fact that Fausto would be there only made my old decision to go, to help the revolution, more attractive.

If I took Carlos to court, I imagined, I would only have to stay a couple more months in the convent to obtain my inheritance. Fausto agreed to help me all he could while he was still in Quito, though he would be gone in a few days. After he left, I would just have to carry it all through to completion myself. Once I had my money, I would go wherever he was and find some way to help him. He warned me that the courts were slow, but I didn't listen. I kept thinking it would only be two or three more months.

I kissed him good-bye one last time, feeling the desire he felt for me, making me feel an even stronger desire for him. But, I climbed the wall.

Thinking about Fausto's last kiss, feeling it still on my lips, I crept between the buildings of the convent. When I came to Doña Luisa's cell and stepped up to the doorway, I heard something that froze me with fear.

"Welcome back, Manuela."

I spun around and peered into the darkness. The all too familiar words filled me with loathing. The voice in the shadows became embodied as Antonia stepped onto the porch.

She approached me. Her aristocratic features, full of confidence and beauty, were almost frightening. She picked a piece of grass from my hair and smirked at me, saying, "I wonder if Fausto knows that the little novice he's bedding is only a bastard."

"Why don't you leave me alone?" I snarled.

She smiled. "Someone has to watch out for the honor of the convent, I don't think you care too much about it."

I clenched my teeth and whispered, "I don't think honor is what motivates you—more likely it is jealousy."

"It is you that is jealous!" she hissed. "Why would I want to be a bastard born in scandal?" Then she was gone.

I hated that girl. I could not seem to stop her. I was hurt because there was a little truth in her last words: I was jealous of her. It wasn't just that she had a powerful family. It was because, unlike me, she did have a family.

I shook off the pall that had come over my feelings. Fausto loved me. I would have my inheritance.

Doña Luisa was sure to find out that I had left the convent, but I hoped for the best. I wanted to keep my position, so I was determined to bluff my way through the accusations.

I began making up stories to explain my absence as I eased the door open and stepped inside. The thought came to my mind that I might have to threaten Doña Luisa with exposure in order to keep my position while I campaigned for my inheritance, but I was uncertain if I could do it. I did not want to hurt my benefactor, whom I still considered my friend.

As I crept across my room to my cot, I sensed someone watching me. I turned around and saw Beatríz, silently preparing for bed, smiling a knowing smile. How Beatríz communicated with Antonia, or her maid, so late at night, I never found out.

I avoided her eyes. With both Antonia and Beatríz able to speak against me in the morning, my prospects were not good. I wanted to confront her, to find out what she had been up to with Antonia, to find out her plans. If Carmen hadn't been in the room sleeping, I might have. Instead, I decided that whatever was to happen was beyond my control at that moment. I lay down with weariness, still in my clothes, and pulled a blanket over me. In my drowsiness I recaptured the feel of Fausto's body against mine, and I fell asleep.

I was awakened about dawn by two *celadoras* who dragged me from my bed. I was very groggy from my lack of sleep and offered little resistance at first. When I realized that they were taking me to the convent jail, I kicked and screamed and fought with them until I was pushed into the same dark room where Doña Luisa had first offered me a chance to work for her.

About an hour later, I was dragged, just as unceremoniously, to the office of the Abbess. It was cold that morning. I could see the sky, overcast and gray with loneliness, through the small high window above her chair. The fire had not yet been lit in the office and I shivered. I stood there alone, in front of the Abbess's desk, waiting for her to arrive.

That desk represented everything I hated about the convent. It was heavy and immovable. It must have taken many men to bring it up the long narrow stairs to this office. It was European, made out of wood from the peninsula, and intricately carved by Spanish craftsmen. It was lavish, proclaiming the power and wealth of the convent. It looked shameful when I glanced to the crucifix of the naked Jesus on the wall. I imagined it burning to ashes.

The smell of Fausto was all about me and my mind kept drifting back to the night before and I wondered what would happen. I waited for a long time, becoming impatient. I thought about leaving, but the nuns who had brought me were just outside. There was no point in fighting with them further. I knew I was in trouble and yet what I felt was exhilaration and love for Fausto more than fear of the Abbess's reprisals. My night with Fausto had given me courage and I planned what I was going to tell the Abbess, which was what I thought of her and her stinking convent. Then I would simply leave and find someplace to stay in Quito while I battled with Carlos. I felt, for the first time in my life, that I knew who I was. I was La Sáenz, the bastard, and I knew how to fight. I would not back down now.

These thoughts gave me strength, despite my predicament. With or without Fausto's help, I would take my uncle to court, obtain the inheritance that was rightfully mine. I did not think anyone could stop me, and I was in as adversarial a mood as I have ever been when the Abbess arrived.

A scowl was on her face as she entered, sat down, and looked at me. She was an older woman. She had held onto her position as Abbess through many triennial elections because she was a very powerful woman. Her features were a pale pink, coming from good Spanish aristocratic stock, with tiny threads of red and blue showing through the translucent skin of her cheeks. She was about my height, slender, and while her hair must have been white (I never actually saw it), her eyebrows were a pale brown over cold blue eyes.

I glared at her. Finally, I said, in as surly a manner as I could muster, "Well, you brought me here. Do you want to say something or not?"

She could not contain the vitriol in her voice as she coldly said the same thing that I had heard all my life, "This is exactly what one would expect from a bastard."

This infuriated me, but I controlled my anger. "Is something wrong?" I taunted.

"You have gone too far this time. Did you really think you could get away with debauchery while in my charge?"

"Are you surprised that I want to get out once in awhile instead of rotting in this bitch kennel?"

"Ever since you came here, you have been nothing but trouble. We knew then that you would never amount to anything. Sadly, you have proved us correct. You never have, and you never will." She was hurting me, making me feel low, but I was not going to give her the satisfaction of knowing it. I laughed in contempt. She said, "We have tried to civilize you, but you have obviously taken up your mother's whoring ways."

I slammed my hands down on her desk. "You leave my mother out of this, you pile of shit." She had cut me to my heart. I was beyond reason and I started to scramble over her desk to strangle her. "I didn't ask to come here, damn you!" I shouted. "I didn't ask to come here."

The old woman jumped up and retreated. Her chair fell over. She called for the *celadoras*. Two nuns and two or three *donadas* came into the room and pulled me off her desk. I was screaming and spitting and fighting with them, but they were too strong.

The Abbess said, in forced calmness, "You're through here. You've broken the rules, and I am done with you."

Breathing hard and still struggling, I said, "So what?! I am done with *you*! I'm leaving this rat hole in a few months."

She said, "You're leaving all right. Today. I'm sending you to your father in Panamá."

That stopped me completely. I ceased struggling. "The hell you are!"

She saw that I was not struggling and motioned for the others to let me go. They did not leave, however.

"I'm not leaving until I want to. Do you hear me?" I said.

"Yes, you are."

I didn't know if she could do that, and the last thing I wanted was to be expelled and then sent to my father. "My mother left me her share of her family's estate, and I want what's mine, and I am not leaving this city until I get it."

"I do not have a thing to do with the Aispuru family affairs, and you do not have anything to say about your expulsion. Whatever your uncle is doing is right as far as I'm concerned." I started to interrupt her but she stopped me by saying, "I have spoken to him already this morning, and you are leaving for Guayaquil—today."

"I am not, you whore." I made a move toward her, and the nuns grabbed me. I tried to pull free, but their hold on my wrists was firm and unyielding. "He's a thief! I am not going anywhere until my uncle gives me my inheritance," I shouted.

"Enough! For the last time, you are being informed that you are not wanted here, and you are going to Guayaquil today, to be put on a ship, to join your father in Panamá. That is all you need to know." Her icy calm had started to crack. She practically shouted her last words.

She composed herself and continued in a more normal tone, "Señor Aispuru will pay for your trip to Panamá, but he refuses to pay for you to stay here any longer. Your father has already written, months ago, to say that he can care for you there. So you're going; and that's the end of it."

"As much as I hate this town and all it's done to me and my mother, I am not going to let you throw me out. First I will get my inheritance, and then I'll go gladly, because I *want* to go. But to Venezuela, not Panamá, and then *when* I want to go, not when you decide. And believe me, you had better beware of the day that I ever return."

Her cold rigidity melted and she said angrily, as she walked across the room to the door, "You will go today and I don't want to hear any more of your arrogance." To the women holding me she said, "Now get her out of here!"

With that she threw the already open door open wider, so that it banged the wall loudly. Then I was literally dragged out of the room. As I left, I saw a *donada* come in with firewood. I heard the Abbess say hotly, "Get out of here; I don't want a fire. Bring me my breakfast." Then she slammed the door.

I screamed and fought all the way downstairs to the entrance hall. Beneath my anger, with every step, there grew an ever increasing sense of disaster and grief. It all seemed so unfair to be forced out: when I finally had a reason to stay, when my happiness seemed to depend on following the plans I had made, when I wanted so much to be with Fausto. My heart was breaking at the thought that I might not see him again. The more I felt this impending doom, the harder I fought.

As we were leaving the main door of the convent, I saw Carlos crossing the street. He had just left the convent and was about to climb onto a mule. I became even more enraged and broke away. I ran across the street and jumped on him. He fell under the impact, and I climbed on top of him, trying to pull his eyes out of their sockets.

We both rolled on the cobblestones while he defended himself. Finally, I was peeled off by a gaggle of nuns, all babbling at me. Blood ran from Carlos's cheek.

"You bastard!" he said as he stood up. "I am glad to be rid of you."

"You'll never be rid of me until you give me what's mine."

"You're leaving here with all you will ever get from me you little hellion." With that, he grabbed the rope around the mule's neck and walked toward home.

"Damn you to hell!" I shouted after him. "Damn you to hell!"

Then I noticed something. In my haste to attack Carlos, I hadn't recognized Juanita. My beloved nurse, who had cared for me in my mother's house, now a middle-aged woman, was standing nearby. She was standing next to a monk who was holding the leads to five mules ready to make the trip down the mountain to Guayaquil.

I wanted to run to her for maternal comfort but I was restrained. She came to me and put her arms around me, and then I broke down and sobbed. The nuns let me go.

Juanita held me tight and cried too, saying, "Señorita, Señorita Manuelita, how I've missed you. Oh, how I've missed you. Oh, Mother of God, thank you!"

I learned that Carlos had given Juanita to me as a companion for the trip to Panamá. I thought it odd that Carlos had thought of my traveling comfort, but later I learned from Juanita that she reminded him of my mother and he wanted to get rid of her anyway. Besides, one of my aunts had insisted that I not be made to go alone to the coast. Whatever the reason, I was glad for my old friend. I also learned that the mules Carlos had provided were to be delivered to someone in Guayaquil anyway.

I was told to get on the back of one of the mules. I was too exhausted to fight anymore, and complied. Then, the monk, Juanita, and I, and two pack animals, began to make our way through Quito towards the city gates.

Just after leaving the city, as we began to cross the plain that lies south of the city, two riders approached from behind. I recognized them as Carmen and her "friend." Without speaking, Carmen dismounted and brought over a large cloth sack full of my belongings.

The monk was fairly disinterested and didn't say anything when I climbed down and embraced her. Tears mingled on our cheeks as we held each other close. I knew I would miss her.

"I love you, pretty thing," she said.

"I love you too, Sister." We hugged again. Through my weeping I said, "Please let Fausto know what happened."

"I'll see he understands." She looked at me with tears in her eyes. "I will miss you." Her words caught in her throat. I held her tightly, and I sobbed at the thought of losing my beloved friend.

The monk started moving down the road, saying gruffly, "It's getting late!" Carmen put a peso in my hand. Then she wickedly kissed me full on the lips, too passionately, but I don't think anyone noticed. She mounted her horse and slowly rode back to the city, her friend beside her. I tied my sack to the wooden saddle of one of the pack animals, put the peso in the pocket of my shift, and climbed on my own mule.

Then I started for the first time on my travels, travels that have taken me all over the continent, that never really stopped, until I reached Paita. As the mule started slowly down the road, I turned to wave good-bye to Carmen, but she was gone.

Chapter 17

The road from Quito to Guayaquil is a dangerous one. This is especially true in the latter part of the journey when descending the mountains that lead into the valley of San Miguel. The first two-thirds of the trip are easier. One travels south along the sierra between the eastern and western cordilleras of the Andes, amidst great beauty. After that, the perilous descent begins. People have died making the journey. Parts of the trail are passable, along precarious ledges, by only one person at a time. A traveler might wait on windy precipices while teams of mules, riders on horses, or Indians on foot pass from the other direction. My travels down the mountain were no less dangerous than those before me, yet the road that was most threatening to me I passed in my first hour.

I felt as though I had been uprooted and tossed down the mountain, like some weed in the Abbess's garden. In Quito I was hated, but I had an identity. I did not know what would await me down the trail, and I felt like a ghost, passing from hell into deeper darkness.

That first morning, as our mules padded along the worn path of dirt and stones, my defeat weighed heavily on me. Images of the abbess and my uncle filled my thoughts—they, who represented all of Quito, stood as a citadel in my mind that I had not yet conquered. I did not want to leave without my inheritance. I did not want to lose Fausto. I did not want to be forced into anything that I did not desire. Yet they appeared to have won.

There were moments of great beauty on the sierra, far away from any city. The majestic alpine giants that towered over plains where rivers and streams cut through the sparse vegetation made me feel as though we were pilgrims visiting ancient shrines. The sight of so much beauty should have lifted my spirits. Every other time I have been on that plateau since, I have felt a resurgence of my inner self. But not that day. All morning long, I battled my enemies. I searched for a workable way to return and gain what I was after, but I found none.

Later, when it started to get dark, the inescapable facts of my situation crowded my thoughts. I sank further into an abyss of fear as the shadows from the mountains of the western range crept up the acclivities of the eastern cordillera. By the time the sun had set, my emotions were darker than the sky.

I am sure my melancholy was exacerbated by the fact that I had slept very little in the past two days, nor had I eaten much. Since we had left Quito that morning, the monk had barely acknowledged me or Juanita except to hand us a little bread every two or three hours. I desperately longed for a bath, a hot meal, and a soft bed.

There are no inns as such, as I am told there are in England and other parts of Europe. We carried equipment to build a fire and cook, and rolls of blankets in which to sleep in the cold. However, there are also many pockets of habitation along the road in which a traveler can find shelter. We stopped that first night at a poor hut somewhere near the foothills of Cotopaxi, not too far past Chisinchi. There, we availed ourselves of the hospitality of an aging Indian and his wife.

The monk who had led us across the sierra knew our gracious host. He and his wife were friendly and kind, but they did not have much to offer for an evening meal. I was so incredibly tired that after I ate some bread and broth, I simply dropped down on an insect infested poncho covering some straw on the earth floor. As I listened to Juanita softly say her Hail Marys, I fell into a shallow and troubled sleep almost immediately.

I awoke a little later. The night was quiet and I listened to the breathing of the others in the hut. I considered my situation while I watched gloomy shadows dance on the ceiling, cast from a tiny flame dying in the earthen stove in the corner of the room. I was without friends, except for Juanita. I was a bastard with no family ties, except my mother's, and they were hostile to me. I had nothing to which I could look forward, except living with my father in exile, which in itself held no promise. I felt certain he would be unhappy with me for having been expelled from the convent. I would be friendless in Panamá. The pain that hurt most was missing Fausto. I thought about stealing out in the middle of the night, to run back to Quito. I feared I would lose him forever, but I knew there was no practical way for me to return there.

I wept. I rolled over, again and again, fighting my battles in half-sleep. Always I came back to the one problem which if solved might help all of the others, yet it seemed the most insurmountable. I had no money, and no way to get any.

As I lay in the dark, I despaired over the unfairness of life. I realized that even if I had taken my uncle to court, I would never have been able to obtain my inheritance in only a few months. It was then that I remembered stories I had heard, but had chosen to forget in my youthful enthusiasm—was it only two days ago?—about court cases sometimes taking years. After my confrontation with him in the street that morning, I was more certain than ever that I would never be able to force my uncle to give me what was mine. I wept more deeply at the thought that he might be able to forever keep me from my mother's gift. It was a rare moment in my life. I stifled my sobs in the darkness as I became overcome with grief, feeling very lost. Finally, comforting sleep found me again.

The next morning, though I was hungrier than ever, Juanita had to coax me to rise. "Come, Manuelita," she said. "There is a large tray of fruit on a bench just outside the door. Come. Rise and take breakfast."

I was weak and weary. I rolled away from her without speaking.

"Please, Señorita," she pleaded. "Come eat with me."

It was only my beloved Juanita who could make me rise that morning. Slowly I stood up, walked to the doorway, and stood in the sunlight, rubbing my eyes.

Somehow, the old Indian and his wife had produced a great amount of fruit—sliced and ready to eat. The sun was warm as I sat down and sampled apples, pears, and delicious wild cherries (called *capulis* by the Indians) that grow in the region. As I ate, my spirits improved. Things did not look quite so bad in daylight or with a little sweet food in one's belly.

When Juanita was done, she started to pack my things. As I sat there in deep thought, the old Indian came over and talked to me. He was very interesting. He was the only person I had ever met who could interpret the braids and knots of the *quipus*. This was the ancient means of recording events and times with knots in little ropes, used by the Incas, into which great detail is said to have been woven, literally.

He told me that he was a descendant of the *Puncay*, the ancient lords of the surrounding country, and the country to the south. He brought out several *quipus*—sticks to which many dangling, multi-colored, knotted ropes had been tied—that had been handed down to him through many generations. He read them for me, his hands flying deftly over the knots and braids. He told me about the population of Indians in that area and their comings and goings throughout time. I was fascinated.

At one point, he spoke of a time shortly before the arrival of Benalcasar, the Spaniard who conquered the Indians in that area and founded Quito.

"It was before the Spaniards, in the 'year of the great heat.' Hundreds of monkeys crossed the western mountains near what is now the town of Riobamba. They invaded the countryside rapaciously, and my people lost their crops and stores. Only through persistence were we able to destroy them."

Taking some inspiration from the story, I said, "So your people fought and persevered and were thus able to survive."

"Yes, but it caused us many problems. Later, when the first Spaniards arrived, my people underestimated them. They treated the problem as another migration of destructive monkeys. They fought them, trying to prevent their ingress into the valley, but this only brought about violent reprisals from the Spaniards."

He looked wistfully across the plain. "Most of my people died, and much of the remaining population traveled east to join the tribe known as the *Maynas*."

"How sad," I said.

He laughed. "The joke was on the Spaniards!" I looked at him inquisitively. He laughed louder and stated, "There was nobody left to tell them where gold and silver mines were."

"What mines?"

"Oh, Señorita, there were many very rich mines in this area. The richest in the world, I will wager. To this day, those mines have never been found."

I think there may have been an element of truth to that story because I heard somewhere that the area we were about to ride through had sent more gold and silver for the ransom of Atahualpa, from Pizarro, than any other in the Incan empire.

"No one knows where they are?" I asked.

He looked at me and smiled slyly. "I do. I've deduced it from what is written here." He held up a *quipu*.

"But—"

He motioned me to be silent, and leaned close. He whispered, "How would I have strength to search for it, or work it, or keep it? It would only be stolen, like everything else. However, many years ago, out of curiosity, I went to the region where I found something." He pulled a small leather pouch from beneath his clothes and from inside it he produced a gold nugget about the size and shape of my thumb.

"It must be true," I said. "You have deduced where the mines are."

He chuckled.

Just then, the monk came by and rudely announced our departure. "Enough time has been wasted, girl." The old Indian hid the nugget. The monk went over to get his mule.

As I stood to leave, I gave a wistful sigh. The old Indian looked at me intently and said, "You are sad, but do not worry so much. The river of life is long, and change is constant."

I did not know that my aspect had so accurately conveyed my feelings. "I am all right," I said.

"Of course you are. That is what I'm telling you. Drift where the waters lead." He chuckled.

He made me laugh. I smiled in return and said, "That seems too easy."

"Life is very easy. It is too bad that the races of man do not understand that. Everything changes, and everything we do changes something else. Yet men continue to fight each other. In the end, what have they gained. The river flows on and all they have done is drown their fellows, and themselves, in blood."

"Perhaps, *viejo*, they wish to reach the other side of the river. Perhaps they wish to carry their brothers there. Perhaps there are other men who wish to stop them. Is it not worth the price to try to achieve something glorious?"

"Why? When one's life is over, the river rushes on. Whether one drops on a battlefield and is forgotten or one dies in one's sleep and is carried through town in a parade of affection, one is still dead. On the other hand, if you drift, you will land somewhere. Look at my beautiful wife."

She was very old and frail, walking toward us from behind the house. "She has seen many years, as have I. We drift. We are happy. We will land somewhere."

Juanita came up and indicated the monk who was looking at me angrily from where he was packing his mule. "Come, Manuelita," she said, "we must go."

I turned to the old man and said, "I appreciate your kind thoughts, Señor, and our conversation. But I know no other way than to fight the current."

"Much better to drift." He smiled.

I tried to imagine just complying with the vicissitudes of life. I couldn't. "I thank you again for your hospitality, but I will never stop fighting," I said, with new confidence.

He shook his head and made a noise with his tongue.

The monk yelled, "Stop wasting time. We leave now!"

I defiantly strolled very slowly to my mule. The monk glared at me as he walked back over to the old man and his wife standing in the doorway. He expressed his thanks quickly and dropped a coin in the old man's hand. We left them.

My spirits had improved. After eating, and after talking with the old man, I felt better. I still did not know how I would get back to Quito and defeat my enemies, but my prospects seemed somehow brighter. Perhaps the old man was right. All I could do, it seemed, was to go forward and try to return when I was able. Perhaps it was better to drift where life was leading me.

As we rode across the wide plain, I tried to set my mind to merely drifting, but I would not be content. I was losing Fausto, to whom I had given my virginity and my love, only two days before. I had made a bond with him, that I was prevented from keeping. The currents of life were tearing us farther and farther apart. I tried all day, but no matter how hard I thought about it, I did not feel like I was drifting. I was being swept away by a catastrophic flood.

The next night, we camped near the road on the southern edge of the plain of Latacunga. As we dismounted, I could see the outline of an ancient Incan fortress, called Callo I learned, on the sierra floor. As I examined it carefully, I noticed that it had been built entirely out of shiny black stones. I wondered where such rocks came from.

The stones that were native to that area were a light gray and called *piedra pómez*. They were so light that I could lift huge boulders by myself and throw them into the river. Then, amazingly, they would float. Juanita and I laughed at how funny it looked to see apparently immovable stones carried off by the current.

On the following night we stopped in the town of Ambato, which sits in the shadow of tall Mt. Chimborazo. The monk arranged for us to stay in a parish church building, and for the first time since I'd left Quito, I was warm and comfortable. I was reminded of my cozy cot in Doña Luisa's cell. When I thought of that, I grew sad. Perhaps I could be brave about my situation, but I desperately missed all the people I loved, not only Fausto, but the Larreas, Carmen, and Doña Luisa as well.

The next morning, I was able to do a little sightseeing while the monk made "arrangements." I found Ambato very pleasant, though still suffering from the cataclysm that had hit it so hard 18 years earlier. The original town had been destroyed once before in 1698 by a volcanic eruption, and then completely leveled again in 1797 by the great earthquake.

Juanita and I strolled lazily through the town in the bright morning sunlight. It was a delightful place—peaceful, home to friendly people, with magnificent beauty all around.

We purchased some bread just out of the oven. It was the best I had ever eaten: warm, soft and sweet, inside a chewy brown crust. Its aroma gave one a good feeling inside. Every time that I have been in Ambato since, I have made a point to eat some of their bread. It is more delicious there than in any other place I have traveled.

I also ate a red fruit, with many black seeds from a prickly plant. I worried when I made water a couple of hours later. It came out as red as blood. The condition turned out to be temporary, thankfully, caused by the fruit.

When we returned from our little tour of the town, I saw the monk talking to an attractive older man, who had the look of a worried merchant. Which is exactly what he proved to be.

Apparently, the monk was to take me only as far as Ambato, where Juanita and I were to be transferred to another guide for the rest of the journey. Our new escort was indeed a traveling trader, who was taking a mule train loaded with high elevation coffee beans, as well as the famous textiles of the region, to the coast.

I did not know the man's name until much later, but he seemed to know mine, and my reputation. He walked over to me, running his hand nervously through his short gray hair. He said with a European accent that I had never heard before (from the northern European countries, I found out later), "We leave in half-hour, and I won't have no trouble. You can know what I say. I say it."

He was taking himself so seriously, and he spoke with such a humorous accent, that I looked at Juanita and we both started laughing. He mumbled something else and then walked back to his mules.

The monk handed his mule over to our new escort. Then, his tonsure gleaming in the sun, he came up to me and said, "You behave yourself."

I glared at him. The injustice of it filled me. How dare he. Why could he not help me, instead of pushing me down the mountain? I spit on the ground and turned my back on him. I heard him say, "Hopeless," under his breath, as he walked back to the parish church.

The merchant came up just then and said, "We must go. Now, we go," in his funny accent. I laughed at him. I decided that here was one who would pay for my misfortune, if I could penalize no one else.

We mounted our mules and ambled out of Ambato. As we rode down the trail, I tried to get our funny guide to talk to me, so that I could make fun of him. At first he tried to ignore me. After a while he answered by speaking in a foreign language under his breath. I imagined he was saying something like, "What have I gotten myself into." Later, he did speak to me, but in short answers to direct questions. He knew what I was doing and my fun did not last long.

That evening we reached Riobamba and found more evidence of the destruction caused by the earthquake of 1797. Prior to that year, this town had nearly 20,000 people living in it. With few exceptions, the whole population had perished that day.

The town now stands on a sandy plain, but the ruins of the old town sits on either side of a nearby valley. Each half of the ruins are more than a league from each other. A native pointed two steeples out to me that had belonged to the Franciscan church. They were on one side of the valley and a portion of the body of the church was far away on the other.

The face of the country was changed permanently during that cataclysm, affirming the truth of the things my father had told me about the enormous changes in the city of Quito. After the shock, inhabitants of Riobamba who were still alive could not even tell where their homes, or their neighbor's homes, formerly stood. Mountains rose where cultivated valleys had been. Rivers disappeared or changed their course. Plains became mountains. The largest farm in the area, belonging to the family of Zamora, was lost and no one could tell which part of the land belonged to them when the last tremor stopped.

We were taken in by a friend of our guide in Riobamba, and we slept warmly again, and ate well the next morning. When we left, we followed a path around the foot of Mt. Chimborazo for the next two days, making our way through the valley of San Juan.

The first night, on the trek around Chimborazo, we camped in the cold, near a cloth manufactory. Some very beautiful cloth comes from that valley, but the plight of the Indians, who are used as workers to make the material, is so dire that I swore I would never wear that fabric. Though such Indians were the first masters of that valley, they were forced to labor there for 14 pesos a year, for which they also had to endure beatings and other injustices.

Late in the evening of the next day, we came to a *tambo* (resting house) on the southern plain of Chimborazo. We did not have to make camp that night. We spread *pajón*, the long dry grass that is a prevalent floor covering and is indigenous to the valley, in the little house to make it more comfortable.

I expected to be warm in the *tambo*, but I was too warm. During the night a candle fell over, the grass ignited, and we barely escaped with all of our possessions. We had to huddle in our ponchos next to a campfire for the rest of the night.

Later the next day, we arrived tired and hungry at the shorter, eastern slope of the first mountain we would have to cross. Up until this time we had been traveling in a roughly southern direction. Here we stopped for a meal before turning toward the west to make first an ascent and then a descent to the village on the next lower plateau.

Traveling down the mountain was hard. At the foot of the western slope, we arrived in Guaranda—which was later to be the site of a major turning point in my life. Our guide went to the house of the *corregidor*, Don Gaspar Morales, and paid his respects, and was invited in. He was only gone for a moment, and then he came back down and directed Juanita and me to where we had to sleep, with the servants, behind the fine house.

I loved that house. It was beautiful, nestled among the hills. From the outside, it looked so opulent and comfortable. I longed to sleep in it.

That evening we ate a meal of maize cakes. When salt was offered, I noticed that it was very, very fine. When I asked about it, the Indian servants explained that it was very special, manufactured in a place nearby called Tomabela. There is a spring there, which is so thick with this salt that the mere splashing causes thick deposits of white crystals to be encrusted around the edge.

Indians put the water into barrels and stir it with long pieces of wood. When crystals form on the edge of the barrel (and the sticks), it is scraped off and packaged. Then this special seasoning is sent all over the empire. It is desired because it is so very white, and it is believed to relieve ailments of the chest if one merely eats food spiced with it.

I was enthralled with Guaranda. Besides this interesting knowledge about the specialness of the salt that came from the area, I was taken with the vegetation. At this lower level, the vegetation was somewhat more plentiful than the dwarf pines and mosses that I had known all of my life. I was pleased with the lushness all about, never having known anything else, yet I learned the next day that I was still amid sparse vegetation.

The following morning, Don Morales noticed me as we prepared to mount our mules. He was short and rotund, with a large mustache. Very affable and friendly. He walked up to me and said sociably, "Did I meet you last night, Señorita?"

"No, Señor."

He turned to our guide and said, "Why did you not say you had a pretty one with you?" Our guide looked uncomfortable. "If you had introduced me to this beautiful woman last night, I surely would have invited her to supper. She is pretty, no?"

The foreigner said, his strange accent obliterating his Spanish, "*Muy linda, si.*" He looked at me and spoke sincerely.

"Señorita, if you ever come this way a second time, you must stay in my house. Do not sleep with the servants again. You will sleep in one of my spacious rooms for important guests." He smiled, and I cursed our guide under my breath for denying me the opportunity to sleep in the house. I thanked him brightly, but underneath my mood was foul. I was very angry with the foreigner.

I did not pout very long. Soon we began our frightful descent into the valley of San Miguel, and that leg of the journey took complete concentration. We would climb and then descend, climb and descend. The entire day was spent traversing the ill-kept road. Sometimes we rode on narrow trails with precipices on either side, or there was a sheer face on one side and the edge of a cliff on the other. Later in the day we went through narrow ravines with steep rock walls on either side, only wide enough to let one mule and rider pass at a time. In such places the mud was sometimes so deep that the animals were wading up to their bellies. Some parts of the trail on the western side of the mountain were nothing but long steep descents covered entirely with mud. The mules literally slid down these slippery inclines with all four feet locked hard to slow their fall. I was thankful that our animals had made this journey before.

The ride was terrifying at times. We all had to work together to get ourselves, and our animals, safely down the mountain. The foreigner was helpful, and we were all able to descend without any mishap, despite my fears. When we made it to the edge of the town of San Miguel, we set up camp for the night. We were all tired by the time our meal was eaten.

I was still exhausted the next morning. My legs were very sore from days of riding. Our guide told me, from there on, traveling was easy. "San Miguel in one end of long shallow canyon. Much profuse vegetation all about. We following well made trail to reach savanna . . . the beginning of it is here." I looked at the plant growth. He was right; it was even richer than in Guaranda.

At the end of a pleasant day, as we left the western edge of the valley of San Miguel, we arrived at our last stop before crossing a large flat expanse of grassland on the approach to Guayaquil. The town is called Bodegas de Babahoyo, but we did not have a patron there so we camped on the plain. The weather was very warm. I was comfortable camping for a change.

Our guide was becoming friendlier. Throughout the day, he seemed to want to talk, but no matter what he said or did, I laughed at him and was rude. I wanted a fight, I admit it.

That last evening, around the fire, he sat silently listening as Juanita and I reminisced about what had happened to each of us in the last ten years. Only once did he try to interject something.

"It is good to see two friends . . . the word is what? . . . yes, re-united, after long absences each from other," he said in his broken Spanish. His eyes looked wistful and his thoughts seemed far away, as if thinking about someone he missed who would not be forgotten. He smiled at Juanita and me. "Happy I am for you."

"Yes," I said sarcastically, "a reunion between *two* people is a happy affair. Too bad the circumstances are so inhospitable."

He looked a little sad. Then he lay down in his blankets and turned his back to us.

Juanita looked at me with disapproval. "Manuelita!" she whispered. But I ignored her admonition and went on with what I had been saying. He was all I had to rebel against, and I felt justified in trying to hurt him.

As we prepared for bed, Juanita said, "The foreigner is a good man. He wishes to be a friend."

"I do not want such a friend." I was clearing some rocks from under my blanket, only half-concentrating on what she was saying.

As we lay down next to each other, after wishing each other a good sleep, Juanita whispered, "I know you, Manuelita. For someone who values friends as you always have, I do not understand why you are rude to such a man."

I could say nothing. After that, neither could I sleep. I listened to Juanita say her prayers, and soon her breathing was deep and slow. Despite my weariness, I lay awake looking at the lonely stars, thinking of what she had said. The wind whistled through the grass as though hissing condemnations in my ear.

As I thought about all that had happened in the last several days, only then did I fully realize I was finally away from Quito. Of course, I knew where I was—on the road to Guayaquil. I saw, however, even though I was many leagues down the trail, I was still fighting those who had abused me all my life.

Perhaps it was the vastness of the mountains we had "conquered" which made me see things more clearly. Maybe it was being away from the cursed convent, or perhaps it was the way Juanita's comment cut to my core, but as I lay awake that night, only a few hours away from Guayaquil, I saw things from a broader point of view. I still hurt. Every day, every night, I longed for Fausto until I thought my heart might break. However, despite my longing, I saw that I had achieved some measure of my goals.

I had wanted my life to change, and I saw how much it really had, in only a few days. The changes were not what I had sought, exactly, but at least I was not being mistreated by the same people who had been my enemies for almost two decades. At least I was not trapped in a convent. At least my life contained more than a past. I had a future, uncertain though it may be. There was no reason to punish our guide, who was obviously a man of good will, or other people I might meet, for things that happened in Quito. After thinking all this through, I felt very ashamed about the way I had treated the foreigner.

I knew then, if I was going to make the best of what was happening to me, I was going to have to grow up and see things exactly as they were. I should not expect other people to give me what I wanted. My fortune was my own to make. I was 17, a grown woman. I could do anything I wanted to do, go where I wanted to go. I would survive, and I would succeed, because I willed it so. I only needed the means. The best way to get the means, under the circumstances, was to continue on to Panamá, where I had some kind of connections.

"I should be leading the way, not pouting because I cannot have what I want right now," I said out loud. Juanita rolled over in her sleep.

Then, a new sense of purpose filled me. A plan formed in my mind. I reasoned that if I could get to Panamá soon, I might be able to have my father book me a passage to Venezuela and I might be able to catch up with Fausto in Caracas.

I knew Fausto would have left Quito by the time I reached Guayaquil. Then there would be three or four weeks or more, traveling from Quito over the mountains to Bogotá and then down to Caracas, where he would try to find the location of Bolívar in order to enlist. If we hurried, I might arrive there about the same time as he.

Excitement filled me as a I laid out my future. After fighting the idea of going to Panamá so hard, now I urgently wanted to be there on the morrow. I felt light for the first time in days, and I could not arrive there fast enough.

The next morning, I was all business: up, washed, packed, and ready to go before my companions had finished their chocolate. "Come, we must be off," I said, mounting my mule.

They looked at me as if I had lost my wits.

"Come, let us go."

"There is no hurry, Señorita," said our guide, "in Guayaquil will we rest before the nightfall."

"Well, I'm going to get started," I said, and turned my mule to the road.

Juanita cried, "Wait!"

The foreigner said, "She pretty, that one, but she addled. Wait," he called out, "we go."

I stopped and looked back. They finished their packing and I sighed at both of them. "You two are so slow," I said, and turned my mule down the road. They had to hurry to catch up.

When they caught up to me, they began to tease me. It was comical, and they soon had me laughing. We rode across the plain, toward the future I had mapped out for myself. I laughed with them, but I continued to urge my mule to travel faster. I needed to be in Panamá soon.

Chapter 18

"Señor," I said, as we rode along that last day, "I would very much like to talk to you." He gave me a look as though he was preparing for sarcasm. "Do you live in Guayaquil?" I inquired.

Most of the day, the foreigner had been silent and withdrawn. I had determined to make friends with him and had ridden close to him all day and asked several questions. My questions only elicited very short responses however, and so I had told him plainly I wished to communicate with him.

"Yes, Señorita, I live in city."

"Please tell me about it."

He looked at me warily, unsure whether I was sincere or not. With seeming reticence, he said, "What you are wishing to know?"

"Anything at all," I said. "What is it like?"

"You be there soon, but I tell. Guayaquil I like. It a harbor city. Many leagues it is, 30 or so, from end of delta, on the Guyas River. The Guayas, she very large. It is wide near the city, but mouth is many, many leagues across." He stumbled over his words, often pronouncing them first in his native tongue and then in broken Spanish.

"Is the city big, too?"

"Spread out. Cover much land. Like all port cities, not so cultured, like centers of government, like Quito or Lima. But more alive."

We were just then crossing one of the many tributary streams that feed the big river. I asked, "How soon will we be there?"

"Soon, very soon. You see soon."

I was surprised, because I could see nothing but grassland ahead and some small trees. "Where?"

"Beyond those far trees, we see first houses. City divided into two separate, how you say . . . wards, connected by long wooden bridge. The bridge he is over 800 yards long. This bridge cross several—you say how?"

He described what he meant to say and I said, "Estuaries?"

"Yes—estuaries, that it. The bridge she cross many estuaries and some low ground, often flooded by river. The main part of city—we see later—she extend along river itself.

"The dock yard is at southern extremity. Main street she called the Malecón, because it makes its name from its purpose. Like a sea wall, she runs straight alongside the river."

He spoke about how many times he had made the trip from the mountains, becoming more friendly as he talked, despite how I had treated him the night before.

I listened intently and when he seemed to run out of things to say, I said, "Thank you, Señor, for your instruction." He shrugged. "I wish to apologize for my behavior last night and in the preceding days. I'm sorry."

He looked surprised and did not know what to say. I could tell he was still wary of me, but a little later he began another conversation with me. He talked about his business of selling coffee, textiles, and other goods to his connections in Europe. He was more enthusiastic as he spoke and he also asked questions and showed a real interest in me. I discovered I liked him after all. Soon he was talking incessantly, showing me this or that and telling me what sights to look for in Guayaquil.

Coming from the relatively peaceful Quito, I was in a state of intense stimulation as we rode into the main part of the city. I never saw so many things happen at once. There was more activity than I could take in—especially around the docks. It was all new and exciting.

As I followed our guide along the Malecón, I looked out on the river. There was lush green foliage on the opposite banks far away, the deep blue sky and wispy clouds making a delicate backdrop to the many weather-tossed ships resting in the muddy water. I knew from the foreigner's talk that I was looking at ships from all over the globe. Most were back from runs to Panamá or various places on the western coast of the Americas, but there were many from other exotic world ports.

"They drop anchor, unload goods from cities in Europe, Asia, Africa," our guide explained. "They stay only few days. Load cacao, timber (very good are Guayaquil's sea-resisting mangroves), tobacco too they load, and coffee, cattle, and . . ." He stammered, looking for other examples and the words for them. He finally gave up. "Then they return to far away ports."

"There are so many," I exclaimed over the sound of a team of horses just then galloping down the street.

"Some ships you see here, maybe they built in Guayaquil. Many ships built here. More ships they built here than all other places on Pacific Coast." We rode on, and I continued to marvel at all I saw.

It was late afternoon when the foreign merchant, whose name I still did not know, finally left Juanita and me on the grounds of a convent as he had been directed. He smiled and waved as he left, saying, "I hope to see you more, Señorita."

I was happy he was not angry with me and that we were friends. I did not know until much later how much of an impression I had made on him.

In the convent, Juanita and I were put into one of the tiny cells that are kept for wayward wives. The furnishings consisted of two hammocks.

This pervasive bit of cloth seems to be almost the only kind of bed (or chair) possible in this part of the world. Insects of all varieties abound in the hot climate, and hammocks not only keep a sleeping person suspended where the crawling pests cannot run all over the bed clothes, but the swaying tends to keep off the flying ones.

Having come from the high mountains where the beetles did not even have wings, I was unprepared for the large number of insects I found on the coast. They were everywhere. There seemed to be mosquitoes by the millions, and I was bitten from head to toe on my first night. Also, at night, we had to contend with the *jejen*, which is so tiny that it can pass through the bed curtains and its bite causes much more irritation than a mosquito. But it wasn't only the flying insects that I found so pestiferous. Ants seemed to be omnipresent.

In Guayaquil, it is not uncommon to open a jar of preserves, or pick up a sweetmeat and have it be already entirely devoured. While I was there, I saw a cold fowl brought to a table in an open air kitchen and, on seeing it carved, ants came out by the hundreds, running all over the table. Also, no *guayaquileño* who does not sleep in a hammock would ever think of lying down in a bed without first shaking the ants out of the bedclothes.

There were other worrisome insects that I saw for the first time in Guayaquil: the *comejen* (termite) which has been more destructive to the city's wooden houses than fire, the *nigua* (a small flea which lays its eggs in the cuticle of the foot), and the *alacrán* (scorpion), whose sting can make one very sick.

The local remedy for such a sting is to cauterize it with the lighted end of a cigar. In fact, in order to keep insects out of their homes, entire families smoke cigars, believing that the smoke will drive them away. While in Guayaquil, I was offered a cigar, but it made me cough. I thought it might make me look more adult, but after I tasted it, I decided maybe I would try it again later.

Despite the strange new insects, I was comfortable enough while in the city. At least I was able to bathe, a luxury after so many days on the road without being able to wash properly.

Instructions, money to book passage, as well as letters from the abbess in Quito about my misbehavior, were apparently left with the nuns by our escort. I believe it was

because of the letters that Juanita and I were treated rather rudely. But at least I was able to stay in my room, away from the general population of the convent, so I didn't mind. Juanita brought most of my meals to our cell.

Despite the relative comfort, I was restive. I wanted to proceed to Panamá. Everyday I was there, I paced my room until I drove Juanita nearly crazy. I pestered the *donadas*, who came to our cell for various reasons, with incessant questions. All I could think about was that I had to be on my way soon if I was ever going to catch up with Fausto. After a few days, I was filled with frustration.

One afternoon I was sitting in my hammock, having just finished some chocolate, and I was feeling energetic. I had absolutely nothing to do but gnash my teeth at the loss of time.

"Let us go out," I said to Juanita.

She gave me a look, like I had just suggested that we eat wood for lunch. "Señorita, we were told to remain in the convent until passage on a ship is obtained."

"I know, but would you not like to see the city?"

"No! And you should not think about leaving. There are rules."

"Oh, Juanita," I scoffed.

"Besides, it is not proper for a young woman to be out alone, walking the streets."

I laughed at that, having walked alone in the streets all my life. "I'm an adult and I am going to start making my own rules." I began looking through my bag of clothes for something to wear.

She came up to me and said, with a plea in her voice, "It is because you are an adult that it is not proper."

"If I shouldn't be alone, come with me."

"I do not want to sneak out of the convent like some thief."

"Very well, but I'm going," I said.

Juanita looked exasperated. While I prepared to leave, Juanita continued to try to dissuade me. "Very improper," she said several times.

After I had dressed in some conservative attire, I left the convent during the noon time busyness, when most of the day's guests are coming and going. I slipped out in a crowd of women who were just leaving as I arrived at the *porteria*.

Guayaquil is more exciting than it is beautiful. The greater part of the houses in the principal streets have an upper story where the inhabitants reside, the ground floor being occupied by shops and warehouses. The upper stories have long balconies, as wide as two arm's lengths, on which the residents can take the air under a canopy.

Almost all of the buildings of Guayaquil are built of wood, the poorer houses in the outlying sections being built of segmented cane. This, of course, makes the buildings quite susceptible to fire, which almost destroyed the city in the years 1692, 1707, and 1764.

I was unprepared for the heat, filth, and deprivation all around me. A few of the wealthy Creoles had nice houses, but most of the buildings were of poor quality. The streets were dirty and the river looked brown and opaque. I realize now that most of what is in the river is silt from far upstream, but at the time it looked filthy to me.

The marketplace was enjoyable. I enjoyed seeing the profusion of colors. Indians sat on beautiful blankets, in picturesque clothes, with piles of multicolored fruits all about: oranges, limes, lemons, *paltas* (from which the green "butter" that is my favorite delicacy can be made), mangos, guavas, coconuts and other delights to the palate.

There were also many different kinds of bananas: red, green, and yellow. The most plentiful of all, however, were plantains. I think everybody in Guayaquil ate them. I had eaten them in Quito and I never did like them very much, but in Guayaquil I had them at every meal.

I walked for awhile longer and I saw a *calesa* stop in front of a workman's shop. I had never seen a *calesa* before, because there are no wheeled conveyances of any kind in Quito. Perhaps that is because it would be so difficult to get one through the mountain passes. In Guayaquil, there were many.

A well-dressed woman stepped down from the vehicle and, after giving some instructions to the workman, walked up the street. When she was gone, the workman, who was obviously a *cholo*, began removing one of the *calesa*'s wheels. Even though a *calesa* has only two large wheels, it is still a fairly spacious carriage, with high, wide, open windows, front and sides. Some of these carriages are bigger than others. This one's wheels were almost as tall as I. The *calesa* is pulled by one or two mules, the driver sitting astride one of them.

The African driver for this *calesa* was barefoot but the rest of his clothes were nearly as fine as the woman's; a tall hat, a short green jacket with its collar open, and matching pants. He stepped down and detached his mule from the vehicle.

While the driver was feeding the mule, I startled the workman by speaking to him. "Excuse me, Señor," I said, politely, but he gave a little jump.

"What, Señorita? What do you wish?" He looked a little irritated at having been disturbed.

"I was admiring your carriage. Is it comfortable?"

He looked at me, as though he wondered why life was so unfair that he should have to be bothered by an inquisitive girl. While tugging on the wheel, he said, "This is *not* a carriage, Señorita. This is a *calesa*. Only nobility are allowed to ride in a carriage. As to this *calesa*, it is not mine; it belongs to the mistress who has gone into the shop yonder. And I have no idea whether it is comfortable or not. Only those with means are wealthy enough to own and ride in one. Do I look like I have means?"

"You work as though you own it."

He stood up straight. "I am a professional; I know all about wheeled vehicles." Then, he grabbed the wheel again and pulled.

"You must be very good," I said.

He pulled a little harder, and the wheel came off. He continued, "Of course I am." After a pause, while he retrieved something from his shop, he said, "Those of the nobility do not ride in *calesas* either." He continued his lecture while spreading a dark brown grease inside the hub of the wheel. "They ride in many-wheeled carriages which are much longer."

I said nothing, but watched him work.

After a moment, he said, as though I were lucky to be having him explain the nuances of his trade, "Of course, even the nobility will ride in a *calesa* now and then for discretionary purposes."

"I am sorry, Señor, but I do not understand."

The *cholo* sighed at one so dense as I. "Come, come, girl. Do you not see that the *calesa* has a tall flat roof?"

"Yes, to avoid the rain, or sun."

"Yes, that, of course. But on most *calesas*, curtains are installed which can be pulled down from inside for privacy. He leaned forward a little to whisper, "Perhaps to hide a lover."

I lifted my head in a knowing way. He looked happy that I finally grasped his meaning.

"These curtains," he went on, "are semitransparent, such that those inside the *calesa* can see out, but those outside cannot see in. Take a look, but do not touch." I peeked up to the roof where the curtains were tied. I marveled at the ingenuity. "Most often, however, you will not see the curtains down. Such would draw attention to what was being hidden." He was reattaching the wheel.

"Of course," I said, as though it were totally obvious. "I think it would be fun to ride in one."

He sniffed. "Well, you cannot ride in this one. It belongs to the mistress. Ah, she is leaving the shop. Be off, girl."

I left the well-informed workman and walked for awhile longer. I saw other interesting things, but after a while I became anxious to find out if any arrangements to depart for Panamá had been made yet. Perhaps passage had been booked and they were wondering where I was. When that thought struck me, I picked up my pace.

Returning from a different direction, I noticed a deserted back street. It would save me two or three blocks, so I turned into it. I found myself in an alley, short and narrow. A featureless wall was on my right, and there were only a couple of back doors to shops on my left.

Walking quickly on the wooden planks laid down to cover the mud and garbage that had been thrown out of the doors, I did not see what was happening until too late. My head was down, and I was wondering if there were some sort of harbor master from whom I might find future arrival and departure information. Immersed in my thoughts, I did not pay any attention to my surroundings. Suddenly, three young men stood up from a doorway where they had been sitting. Before I knew it, they were blocking my path.

One had a stick in his hand and he hit his leg with it as he spoke to me. "Good day, Señorita," he said in a surly manner, although what might pass for a smile curled his lips. Encouraged by his two fellows, he came very close. I could smell his drink-ridden breath and took a step back. "What is your name, Señorita?" he slurred, the stick whipping his leg.

I was silent.

"Would you like some rum?" He indicated a clay jar in his hand.

"Let me pass," I said firmly.

He put his face near mine. The revulsion I felt because of his stink was multiplied by the sight of his black teeth. "We were just saying how nice it would be if we could have some one to share our rum." His hideous smile disappeared as the stick struck his leg with a loud slap.

While he spoke, the other two moved behind me.

I was afraid. I had never been in a situation like this before. In Quito, I knew everyone and there was a sense of community, even though I was not considered part of it. In Guayaquil, the attitude was different. It was a thriving commercial center, and no one cared about anyone except their own. Apart from the fact that I was in a strange city, with Juanita as my only friend, what really frightened me was the realization that I had no escape. *Why didn't I pay more attention?*

The man with the stick used it to lift my dress as he went on, anger in his voice. "You think you're too good to share a drink with us?"

I tried to back away, but the other two prevented me.

"I just want to get to know you better." He lifted my dress to my waist.

I slapped the stick out of his hand. "Stop it, you pig."

He looked surprised and watched the stick fly across the alley and hit the wall. He turned back to me and smiled, showing me more of his dirty teeth, but venom was in his eyes. He grasped the lace around my neck and pulled me to him. I heard the seams rip in my dress as his smile turned to a snarl.

I grabbed his fingers and tried to loosen his grip. The other two seized my arms. We struggled. I yelled, "Let me go!" but one them covered my mouth with his dirty hand. The three of them pushed me into the covered doorway area where they had been sitting.

All of the fights I have been in, throughout my life, have taught me that when blows fall, the only thing to do is to use everything I have and fight hard until I win or lose. But I was not mentally prepared for this fight. I was in shock and I did not do very well, though I tried. I screamed. I punched. I kicked. I saw one of them fall, his hands on his private parts, moaning in pain. I heard my dress rip from my shoulder. I felt my hands become immobilized by the strong grasp of one of my assailants.

I fought hard, but the third man did not stay down long. He came back and struck me while uttering a stream of violent curses. I was soon on my back, my hands held tightly above my head. Two of them nearly had my flailing legs pinned down. I was fully exposed up to my waist and totally vulnerable. Their dirty fingers touched me all over.

Because I was so outnumbered, I slowed them down only a little. I might have been really hurt, and violated, if a soldier had not come by.

"You filthy dogs, let her be!" I heard from the alley. The men stopped and looked up. I could see a soldier, cocking a pistol. One of my attackers rushed over and pushed him down. As he fell, he discharged his weapon with a loud boom. The bullet flew off harmlessly in the air. Then, all three men fled down the street with the soldier in pursuit.

Without waiting for the chivalrous soldier to return, I ran around the corner to the convent. I composed myself and walked right past the *portera*, who was busy with someone. I raced down to my cell, flung open the door, and collapsed in a corner, sobbing.

Chapter 19

First Juanita sympathized, until she discovered that I was not really hurt, and then she scolded me. As she helped me take off my torn clothes, she kept repeating how foolish I was to walk without an escort. "Oh, Mother of God, forgive her. Manuelita, you must not walk in the streets alone."

The idea had never entered my mind before. It infuriated me that I was not able to walk by myself without having someone to protect me. "You are a grown woman now. You cannot just walk the streets without a friend or a man with you," she said. Juanita seemed to know exactly why I had fallen into trouble, and admonished me again and again to be with a man when I went out.

My mind told me what a woman ought to be able to expect, to walk alone unmolested; my emotions told me such expectations were wrong. "As a child, I could walk all over Quito, and now that I am grown, I have to be with a man?" I demanded, raising my voice, my fear turning to anger.

"It is because you are grown," she answered.

I wanted to scream at the injustice of it. In the end, her arguments were convincing. I began to succumb to her ideas.

In order to avoid thinking about what had happened, I kept my mind on the problem of getting to Panamá as fast as I could. Deep inside, however, there was a fear I had not conquered, which weighed me down. I was rude and annoying to the convent authorities as I asked again and again about our passage. A kind of desperation accompanied my urgency.

After I had created useless agitation for everyone around me for several days—the ships leaving for Panamá were not ready to go any faster just because I was demanding it—we were informed by a *donada* that we could get ready. Passage had been booked on a ship for Panamá that very morning.

For the first time since I knew how to do so, I chose my clothes so as not to draw attention to my femininity. The day was bright, beautiful, and warm, but I dressed to cover myself. If I could have been on the ship, without going out and walking through town, I would have.

I was very nervous as Juanita, a priest, and I walked down to the dock. I, who had learned to dress and act seductively in the past year or so, and enjoyed it, regarded the men we passed suspiciously. I imagined how I would handle it if I were trapped by them, even though there was no reason to think that these men were of the same ilk as the men who had attacked me. I made up ways to defend myself against them, despite the fact that I was in no danger.

I walked quickly, faster than Juanita or the priest. I wanted to be on the ship. I paid very little attention as introductions and arrangements were made when we arrived. I was glad when I could be alone with Juanita in our cabin.

May the winds blow us quickly to Panamá, I thought, as I sat down wearily. I told myself I could be patient while our ship made its voyage. Then I would be in Panamá, and I could prepare to travel to Venezuela. All would be well if I could just remain in my cabin until we arrived at the Isthmus.

I would have to stay a couple of weeks with my father in order to have time to convince him he should buy me passage to Caracas; but even with such wasted time, it would still be possible for me to arrive about the same time as Fausto, barely. I had not yet solved the problem of how I would find him once I was there.

These thoughts and plans filled my head as I lay down in my clothes. Beneath my thoughts, however, I was keeping my fears buried. It was an effort; and as I lay there, I suddenly felt quite tired.

In my drowsiness, I heard Juanita come and go. I drifted into a light sleep. Then I heard her come into the cabin and over to my bunk.

"You must come see, Señorita," she said while pulling on my arm.

"No, Juanita, I don't want to see anything."

"Manuelita, you are missing the sights on the river. This you must come see."

When I came on deck, I noticed the weather had changed. It was overcast and gray. "It was so hot and sunny this morning," I said, somberly.

Juanita pointed out what she had discovered, the famous rock-island called *El Amortajado* (the shrouded corpse). It looked very much like a body shrouded in the Franciscan habit: head, trunk, arms folded on the breast, and the rising of the feet all appear in perfect proportion when seen at the distance of a league or so and at the correct angle.

At any other time I would have been delighted to see such a sight, but not then. I was feeling seasick. Also, I was not used to the vastness of the expanse of water, having been raised in the mountains with high peaks all around me. Even on the river, which is very wide at the mouth, the open space all around made me feel vulnerable. I returned to my cabin.

"Only a few more days," I announced to the cabin as I closed the door. I told myself I could wait calmly, but I felt confined already. I thought about Fausto. The realization that I would soon be in Panamá, making arrangements to go to Venezuela, consoled me a little, but I still felt seasick and I was still exhausted.

Later that night, Juanita told me we were far from land. "I could still see distant lights on the shore before it started raining."

"It's raining? The weather changed quickly," I observed, to no one.

"Yes, I heard a sailor say that the rain was unexpected. This trip is very exciting, no?!"

I covered my head with my blankets and said, "Very exciting, yes." Then I moaned as another wave of nausea hit me.

I thought I could avoid throwing up, and might have done so, except that we encountered a freak and unexpected storm that night. Over what seemed like many days, we were blown in the opposite direction from where we were headed, far to the west, or southwest—far away from Panamá, Venezuela, and Fausto.

Time did not pass in an orderly fashion for me. I was walled up and disoriented, and I was nauseated. I felt at times like I would die—and believed that preferable to another minute of agony as I leaned over the chamber pot that slid back and forth on the floor. The storm outside raged on.

Juanita cared for me, cleaned up after me, held me in her arms, prayed to The Virgin for me, and gave me comfort when the fury of the storm seemed especially frightening. In my weakened state, I clung to her. Having her with me made me regret all of the time that Carlos had kept us apart. She must have regretted it, too. "Take comfort, Manuelita. I love you," she would say as she held me in her arms. I never realized how much I had missed her. She made me miss my mother less. I held her close, never wanting to leave her. It was good to have her with me, even if nothing else went right.

Eventually the weather subsided, but my nausea did not. I was feeling caged. I did not have enough strength to walk around the ship, and yet I felt like I couldn't stay in the cabin another minute. I did not know how long the storm had lasted, but I knew it would be days more before we were back on course.

Regardless, I still hoped we might be able to make up for lost time. I kept my thoughts on Fausto, and how I would make it to Venezuela. I anticipated working extra hard on my father to have him pay for my trip to Venezuela without staying with him more than a week. It looked difficult, but I had hope.

Then, the morning after the storm, I woke up and knew something was different. I was not seasick. We were not rolling anymore.

I was weak as I climbed out of bed. All those days of losing my food had made me shaky. I washed my face and, with feeble step, made my way to the open air.

The sails hung limply. They looked like tall white buildings as they dangled from the yards. The ocean was like a mirror upon which our tiny ship merely sat.

The master of the ship was standing nearby, leaning against the rail, looking down at the waterline. He was a tall, rugged man, his face swarthy and lined from years in the sun, giving the impression of seafaring competence. His beard was medium-long and mostly gray, but recently trimmed. His hair also was gray, and long enough to hang over his ears and his collar. He wore shiny boots, into which he tucked his trousers, and he had on a muslin shirt. He carried a pistol in his belt.

We had been introduced as I boarded, and I remembered that his manner was as rough as his appearance. I never did learn his name. I even asked him once, and he said, "Call me Captain." I believe his actual title was Master, but for some reason he wanted to be called Captain.

I braced myself, walked up to him, and asked, "What happened?"

"Happened? St. Christopher's ass! Nothing happened! Nothing is happening! The wind isn't blowing and we're not moving." Then, as an afterthought, he said, "This big, old, out-of-date tub is hard enough to move when the wind is blowing. Humph!"

I could feel my plans evaporate into the thin unmoving air. "How long will we be like this?" I asked, my voice quavering.

"Once every hundred years, God plays with us and sends an unexpected storm from a direction it should not come. In another thousand years, curse the elements, a calm like this will follow a such storm. Perhaps He did not think we would appreciate His first surprise and sent another, along with a girl to ask questions." He stood up and looked at the horizon. "Who knows what is in His mind? It could last days, or weeks. In the meantime, we're drifting west. Now, don't bother me, girl. I'm busy, doing nothing." He turned and walked away.

It was too much. When I did not want to leave Quito, I was forced to travel to Panamá. When I wanted to get to Panamá as fast as I could, I was forced to drift: west, away from my destination. I imagined the old Indian, on the road from Quito to Guayaquil, laughing at me. It was all so unfair.

The next day was the same as the day before, with the one exception that I felt much better with some food in me that was not doomed to come back up. I went on deck and contemplated the northern horizon, beyond which lay Panamá. The Captain was there, pacing back and forth in frustration.

Without wind we were completely unable to move. I wondered how often the ships that traveled the seas, that kept Spain supplied with gold and colonial goods, stood as still.

"Why has no one ever thought of a way to move a ship without wind?" I asked of no one in particular.

The Captain heard me and said, "The North Americans have been making steam-powered ships for five or six years. They don't need wind." He noticed my look of surprise and said, with a bit of disdain, "They are only good for coastal waters. Crossing the ocean without wind will never happen."

I thought about steam coming from kitchen pots and wondered how steam could move a ship, or why, if it could move them, they could not move on the ocean. I began to ask him about it, but he had put a glass to his eye. He seemed to know what he was talking about, so I believed him. I've lived to see him wrong.

I looked at the horizon where the Captain was looking, but I saw nothing. Abruptly, he collapsed his glass and went below.

I reckoned that if we did not have wind in two or three days, I would *never* be able to catch up to Fausto. The prospect of my having to stay in Panamá was becoming ever more real.

Just when that worrisome thought struck me, a sailor with a scar on his face sauntered towards me and sat close on the rail. He stared at me in a way that reminded me of the men in the alley in Guayaquil. His leering chilled me, and I went below.

As I was about to leave the deck, another sailor stopped me and said, confidentially, "You best stay away from him, Señorita; he likes to see people hurt. It is not good when someone gets his attention." He seemed sincere, and I was already frightened of him, so I resolved to keep his advice.

We were becalmed the next day, still drifting westward, or so Juanita informed me, since I had not been out that morning. In the afternoon, Juanita went to get us some food and water because I did not want to meet the sailor who had made me afraid. When she came back, she had only half the usual rations and only a cup of water for each of us rather than a whole pitcher. The Captain had told her that our water was low. I detested not being able to wash.

Finally, after another day of doing nothing, fighting the growing realization that I would never find Fausto again, and feeling too afraid to leave my cabin, I could stand it no longer. I went up on deck to get some fresh air.

It was dusk, and the evening was warm. Everything had a golden glow, illuminated by the setting sun. I took a deep breath and cleared my head with the rich smell of sea salt. I looked toward land, somewhere to the east. I contemplated the calm featureless water reflecting the heavens so perfectly. It seemed as though there were sky above, beneath and all around. I walked to the bow and watched the almost indefinable horizon, lost in the quiet of the moment. Then, I felt a presence behind me and turned around.

The sailor with the scar stood there smirking at me, his expression menacing. He was quite tall, and might have been handsome if it were not for an ugly scar on his face. It ran from his chin across his mouth to the corner of his left eye, causing his lips to curl in a perpetual sneer. He tried to smile at me and his face became more grotesque.

I rushed by him. I heard him make a derisive sound. I walked on and retreated to my cabin. I did not look back and I closed the door quickly when I arrived at my room. Juanita looked up from her sewing. "What is wrong, Manuelita?" she asked.

"I don't know. No. I am afraid." Tears came to my eyes, and I explained to her how the sailor with the scar was following me.

She looked worried, but she said, "Don't worry; everything will be fine when we get to Panamá. You must only stay away from him."

By the following afternoon, however, I knew I could not stay caged. By then, my emotions were boiling: fear, depression, anxiety, suffocation, restlessness and anger were all mixing into a violent brew. I was a little bit crazy.

Juanita had watched my agitation grow all day. Finally, she said, "Please, Manuelita, sit down. Calm yourself."

I ignored her. "I cannot let another person decide where I can, or cannot, go. *I* must be responsible for what happens to me."

"But Manuelita—"

"I know what is wrong. I must be *acting* like prey. That is why I am so vulnerable. That is why he pursues me. I cannot be like this-"

"Now, Manuelita—"

"I am La Sáenz," I almost shouted, feeling out of control. "I have fought all my life. Why am I hiding now?" I paced up and down in the tiny cabin, becoming angrier and angrier.

As my rage grew, my thoughts came more rapidly. I thought of the old Indian. Juanita must have thought I had lost my senses when I said to no one. "Better to drift?!? Where will I land if I do not direct myself?"

"Please, you must—"

"All right, I am drifting," I said to her. "I can do nothing about that. But I can conquer my fears. I refuse to feel afraid, Juanita. I refuse." I slammed my fist on a shelf, overturning a small bottle.

I remembered myself in the Larrea stables, at only five years old, the first time I fell off a horse. I remember Juan Larrea's words. I remembered getting back on the horse that frightened me, despite my fear. I remember how I conquered my fear and was never afraid again. "I have to confront that sailor," I said to myself.

"What?"

"I must!" I said, to the air, oblivious to Juanita.

"Manuelita, what do you mean?"

Turning to speak to Juanita, but really asking myself, I said, "What would a man do?"

"Manuelita! Please."

Then, it seemed to my confused mind that I could have prevented some of my troubles. "Juanita, that is it," I said, coming over to her. "A capable man would never have put himself in a position which was indefensible in the first place. That was my mistake in Guayaquil. Not because I was alone. I was inattentive. I do not need a man to protect me. I need to protect myself, just as a man would. It is wrong to think someone else must protect me."

"No! You are not a man. You are a woman."

"It does not take a man to pay attention or to be competent."

"Are you really not afraid? Manuelita, you are scaring me."

I stopped. "Yes, you are right. I am afraid."

She relaxed. "There, now. You see it is just better to just stay away from such—"

"No, Juanita. Men are afraid sometimes—and my fear is killing me. No, I will go watch the sunset. I will act as though nothing is wrong. If I get into trouble, I will face it."

"Manuelita, you are not a man!"

"I will be fine. I'm sure nothing will happen," I called out to her as I strode out the cabin.

Juanita came to the doorway and said, "Be careful, please! Oh, Manuelita, I never could control you. Oh, Mother of God!"

When I went up on deck, Scarface was nowhere to be seen. I relaxed. I walked up to sit on a large pile of rope on the bow. I felt confident. I contemplated the peaceful water for a long time. The storm inside of me subsided, and I became as calm as the ocean.

As I sat there in peace, I thought about my rage earlier in the cabin. I even laughed at myself. I thought, *I don't know anything at all about what I'm supposed to do if I'm attacked. How could I defend myself?* The more I thought about my vulnerable situation, the more I became more afraid. I felt foolish for acting so brave in the cabin. I certainly did not feel brave outside. *I can talk myself into a fury,* I thought, *but I certainly got into trouble in Guayaquil. Yes, I am probably right about what I said in the cabin, but who am I to know? I am only a girl. Juanita is right. I should go back to my cabin.*

Just as the last arc of the sun dipped beneath the ocean, I knew that I was too afraid to remain on deck. I could not meet Scarface. My emotions were at rest and the refreshing air had brought "reason" to me.

Then I saw him come up from the hold. I quickly looked back at the ocean, but I could still see him out of the corner of my eye.

He looked in my direction, and I thought I saw him smile. He walked toward me.

Fear gripped my heart and I turned slightly away. I heard his footsteps on the deck behind me and I started to shake.

Stop it, I told myself, hoping he would not notice. I prayed he would go away and kept my gaze on the darkening horizon. I tried to breathe slowly to make myself calm.

Then, I felt his hand at my back. I felt my hair being stroked. He took a lock of my hair and began twirling it around his finger.

Fear overtook me anew.

Until then, I still had a trace of confidence that I would be able to handle whatever happened. Now, I was in a panic.

It is one thing to be in a cabin and decide to face anything, and yet another to face it. Terror raced through me. I felt my heart beat as though it would burst. A red cloud covered my eyes, blinding me. I clenched my fists to stop my shaking. He laughed when he saw me stiffen.

I do not know what would have happened if he had not laughed. Perhaps La Sáenz, who had been the object of laughter all her life, who knew how to fight someone who was laughing at her, emerged. Something broke inside me.

I turned around quickly and slapped his hand away from my hair as I turned. He looked at me in surprise, and I stared him in the eye. My nerves were like guitar strings that are pulled so tightly they vibrate just before breaking. I was still shaking but I said very directly and hard, pronouncing each word distinctly, "Leave me alone."

He was taken aback. I think he was surprised to have a woman as young as I talk so defiantly to him. No doubt he was used to seeing fear in his victims. However, he laughed mirthlessly and said, "You're such a pretty thing. Don't you think we could get to know each other?" His face was oily with sweat, making his scar shine in the twilight.

"You have already proved yourself to be rude and arrogant. I doubt we would have anything in common," I said as haughtily as I could. Then I tried to pass him.

He put his right hand on my chest and pushed me back. His smile was gone. "It is you who is being rude, Señorita." Then, he grabbed my shoulders, pulled me close, and tried to kiss me. His breath stank of rotting teeth, his fingers bruised my shoulders, and the stubble on his chin scratched my cheek.

I spit in his face, wriggled out of his grasp, and ran back down the deck toward the stairs to my cabin. I could hear him say to someone, "Watch. I'll have her now." Then

I heard his shoes on the deck as he raced after me. One or two of the men standing about cheered him on.

As I reached the steps to go below, I ran straight into the Captain, who was just coming up. I still don't know why I did not let him take over. Perhaps because I had decided already to take care of the matter myself the thought never occurred to me to defer to authority. Instead, when I slammed into him, I grabbed the Captain's pistol that he always carried in his belt. I stepped back, turned around, pulled back the hammer, and fired.

My pursuer was close, and though I had tried to aim at his chest, I was clumsy. The ball went through his right arm close to the shoulder. The muscle and bone changed the shot's direction, and I saw it slam down into the deck behind him. At the impact, he twisted and fell to his knees with a groan of agony.

His back was to me as he started to rise. "You damn bitch," he swore almost yelling. The few cheers from the other men had turned to silence.

I had meant to kill him; but after I saw the blood fly from his arm and smelled the gunpowder, I became uncertain. He was almost to his feet.

Does he deserve to die? I wrestled with my guilt. Did I have the right to kill anyone, no matter what they've done?

He was standing.

Juanita came up from below, having heard the gunshot. "Oh, my God! Manuela," she said. My resolve wavered. Her admonitions, about proper womanly behavior, filled my mind. Why did I not let the Captain, or some other man, take over?

Scarface turned slowly toward me. His left hand held his wounded arm. Blood was spattered on his face, and it oozed from his wound onto the deck. His face was vicious—full of hatred and cruelty as he came toward me.

When I saw the look on his face, I told myself that I had defended myself exactly as a man would have done. As any competent fighter, I had to continue until my adversary was vanquished or stopped. I saw it clearly. There was no turning back. There was no other way to treat an enemy.

I pulled back on the cocking lever of the second barrel. I tried to remember all of the things Fausto had taught me about using a pistol, though the Captain's was different. Only an instant had gone by since my first shot. There was no time to think, or waver, anymore. He was approaching.

I believe I would have killed him, but I fumbled with the hammer on the second barrel, perhaps saving the sailor's life with my inexperience. Then I heard the Captain behind me.

I could sense that he was going to try to grab the pistol out of my hands. I spun around, and I leveled the gun at him, just as I succeeded in cocking it.

We both froze. We looked at each other, unmoving, with the exception of my trembling hands. I backed up a little, against the bulkhead, so that I could see both men at once. I tried to keep my hands still.

I said, as forcefully as I could, "I am keeping this pistol, unless you can guarantee that I will be treated with respect."

Silence. The Captain looked first at me and then at the sailors standing around. He said, "I think I understand what happened." He looked at Scarface and a few other men with disgust, while saying, "And for my crew, I apologize."

He came toward me. I stiffened my arm.

He stopped and then cautiously approached again. He smiled and said, "I think you have already earned more respect than I can guarantee."

Then he reached out quietly and gently disarmed me. As he took the pistol out of my hands I was unsure as to whether I had won or lost.

I decided to act as though I had won, as though I had given him the pistol. I turned and looked aristocratically at the rest of the men for a moment and then walked back to my cabin, feeling good about myself for the first time in days.

I was so unsteady, I almost fell as I descended the steps on shaky legs. Juanita followed close behind saying, "Mother of God!"

Up on deck I heard the Captain say angrily, "Take that man to the surgeon. And by God, don't let me catch anyone else acting a fool. Because after I get done with you, I'll turn you over to that Fury down there."

Chapter 20

Two days later the ship was still drifting west. It became hotter each day, while our rations continued to decrease. Since my scrape with the sailor I was feeling confident again, though I did experience a lack of vitality from so little food and water. I slept quite a bit. The crew was suffering as well.

However, I no longer saw a need to confine myself to my cabin. On the contrary, I was rather enjoying the trip. Except for the one thought that continued to darken my outlook—I was probably too late to catch up to Fausto—I felt spiritually renewed. I dressed as I pleased, and I walked where I wished. The Captain had been right. I had earned my respect. The crew either treated me courteously or left me alone.

Whenever I saw Scarface, he always gave me a menacing glare. His arm being in a sling made him look even more threatening somehow. I had made an enemy, that was certain. I felt anxious when he was around, but I tried not to let it show. I cautioned myself not to let down my guard, as I had done in that alley in Guayaquil. I told myself that all I needed to do was to pay more attention and I would be all right. I felt I had conquered my fear and him, but I had much to learn.

Except for Scarface, I was happy and spent a good part of my time topside. Consequently, I found myself increasingly in the company of, befriending, and being befriended by, the Captain.

He was very interesting, and he was quite humorous when he wanted to be, despite his gruff manner. I remember one time he really made me laugh, by making fun of the way I pronounce my words.

"You are from Quito, no?" he said, after I remarked on a school of dolphins I had been watching through his glass.

"Yes. How do you know?

He looked at me slyly. "One can always tell when someone is from Quito." He smiled. "Besides, I was told when you boarded."

"Oh, well," I scoffed, smiling back at him.

"Even if I had not been told, I would have been able to tell."

"How, Captain?

"Your 'lisp,' Señorita." He saw the puzzlement on my face. "I am sorry, it is not really a lisp. You merely pronounce your words like a Castilian. Everyone born on the equator does—especially those of the upper classes."

"I did not realize my speech was unique to Quito."

"Listen." Then he went on to imitate me. He did a very good job, and I laughed. As my giggles died down, I thought: if ever I want to fool somebody about my birthplace, I must hide my "lisp."

He showed me many interesting things, and I almost regretted it when, two or three days later, we were no longer becalmed. The evening before, I saw the sun descend behind enormous, beautiful clouds that were being irradiated with streaks of red and purple. This sunset was much different from those on previous days. I almost thought I felt a gentle breeze. The Captain, who was close by, confirmed what I could tell. "Now it changes," he said to himself. The next morning, we were under sail.

When I came on deck, it was overcast and cool. There was a strong wind blowing and the Captain was directing the ship back towards Panamá. Though I was still in a hurry to arrive there, I was also certain that I was too late. He was looking through a glass as I approached him. I tried to speak to him and he said, "Just a minute, child." I resented the epithet, but I merely turned seaward in an attempt to determine what he was looking at. I couldn't.

He put his glass down and said, with exasperation, *"Las Encantadas."*

I did not know what he meant, and he explained. "There is a strong current that originates at the South Pole and travels all along the west coast of the South American continent and then turns westward at the equator line." He pulled out a crude world map and opened it up to illustrate what he was saying.

"This current, without wind to counteract it, has taken us west of this group of islands here," he pointed to the some specks on the map. "They are sometimes known as *Las Islas Encantadas* (The Enchanted Islands), but they are named *Las Islas Galápagos.*"

He turned to the east and peered through his glass again. "We should be seeing them about now, and we are not. Which is why they are called *Las Encantadas*, because they have a reputation for seeming to appear and disappear at will."

"Oh, I see. And they are true to form, today?"

"Always," he said. "These islands have confounded sailors since the time of Pizarro."

"I understand why they are called 'enchanted,'" I said, "but why are they called '*Galápagos*'? Do they look like turtles?"

He laughed and said, "You will see."

He was busy, so after a while I went below and shared a little *charqui* (jerky) with Juanita. Then we lay down for awhile.

When I went back on deck some hours later, I was met with a magnificent sight. The sea and the sky were still gray, but birds were flying above our masts. When I looked in the direction we were heading, I saw volcanoes emerging from the sea.

Actually, it was two islands, but it looked like one enormous island, with five volcanic peaks. They were, I learned, almost one-fourth the height of the Andes. We were still some distance away, but they gave the impression of being tall and violent. One, in the middle, was actually smoking. What I was seeing was the westernmost islands of a large archipelago covering over 300 square leagues. There are 11 principal islands in the group.

These tall smoking giants were not what I expected to see at all. With a name like *Galápagos*, I imagined the islands to look slightly rounded and smooth, like a turtle's back. Once again I asked about the name, and once again the Captain only laughed and said, "You will see."

The islands were green from a distance. When I was up close, it appeared the foliage grew from dark boulders. Later, when I walked on one of the islands, I could see that most of the ground was made of volcanic rock: inky black with razor sharp ridges made by thousands of tiny craters covering the entire surface of the lava stones.

As we rounded the southern end of these volcanoes, which was actually the southern end of the largest island in the archipelago, we were within swimming distance from the shore. There, I saw the strangest birds I have ever seen. They stood up and walked like a man. They had white bellies, black heads and back feathers, and little stubby wings. They apparently could not fly; but from the way they were jumping in and out of the water, they looked like they could swim better than fish.

Later, when I told narrow-minded people about those birds, they looked at me like I had been seeing things. But whenever I spoke to a sailor who had sailed in those waters, such as the whalers I met in Paita, they would confirm my observations. Some said there were millions of these birds at the South Pole.

There were other strange birds as well. There were the big black ones with forked tails that seemed to float, wings outspread, as though hanging from some invisible ropes stretching into the clouds above. For hours they would fly thus above our masts, seemingly without moving. There were also very funny birds with blue feet that seemed to know how to fly but not how to land. When I observed them trying to land, they always fell on their faces.

We sailed all night, and by the next morning we had entered a small bay on a much smaller island than the two I had first seen, which had the big volcanoes. The day was sunny and we were all able to go ashore to stretch our legs. Men were dispatched inland to bring back fruit and kegs of water.

When Juanita and I stepped out of the little boat that had brought us to shore, along with the Captain, I noticed something very peculiar. A deteriorating barrel sat on the end of a post held up by a mound of rocks on the far side of the beach.

I started to walk toward it, but I felt odd. I had the impression the island was moving like the ship. Juanita felt the same thing. As I walked back and forth to get back my "land legs," I watched the Captain go directly to the barrel and take out several letters.

I staggered up to him and said, "What is this barrel, Captain?"

As he sorted through the small stack of letters, he said, "This is the only place in the world like this—that I know about. These islands are on an oceanic 'crossroads,' and it is customary for sailors who stop here to drop off their mail and to pick up what may have been left by others, to post in their next port."

I asked the obvious, while the Captain continued looking for those with addresses which could be facilitated by being mailed from Panamá. "What if someone were to take mail that is not his?"

He gave me a look that made me feel foolish. "Well, child," he said putting five or six letters in his belt and returning another five or six to the barrel, "they wouldn't get delivered, would they?" Then he walked off to talk to one of his officers.

No wonder he calls me "child" all the time, I thought; I ask such stupid questions.

I sat down in the cool golden sand, which was coarse and seemed not to be sand at all but tiny fragments of seashells. As I looked at the mail barrel, I felt it was a shame that we had nothing to leave, since we were only to have been on a "short" cruise up the coast to Panamá.

The Captain had finished talking to one of his officers and had come back to sit on a black, rugged stone nearby, to enter notes in his log. When he finished, I asked him if he might spare his quill and some paper.

He obliged me and I wrote:

Dear Manuela,

I am in the middle of nowhere. Hope to see you again soon.

Your best friend,
Manuela

I chuckled to myself and showed it to Juanita, who laughed as well. Then, I folded the paper, sealed it all along the free edge with pitch, and addressed it to myself in care of my father in Panamá.

I said to Juanita, "Now, let us see how long it takes to arrive."

When the men came back with full kegs, we all had long swallows of fresh water. While we were standing around drinking, I saw Scarface walk up. For the first time since our confrontation, he smiled at me in a friendly but contrite way. He stopped as if to speak to me, and he had something wrapped in cloth. His manner was humble, but I turned my back on him.

I spent several hours exploring and saw some bright orange creatures that were, in fact, crabs. Before this, I had only seen some darker, smaller crabs for sale in the market in Guayaquil. I did not know what they were called until a sailor told me.

Another strange creature was a big black lizard, hundreds of which I saw swimming in the surf or sunning on the rocks. They were quite large, almost as long as I am tall, and I am told they live only on these islands and nowhere else.

Also, I finally saw the animal that gives the islands their name. It was enormous, and looked like a huge inverted bowl, or perhaps a saddle, the size of a large table. Before this, when I thought of a turtle, I thought of something that could be held in the hand. This animal was a hundred times bigger. I watched as it plodded laboriously out from the underbrush.

He was instantly killed and gutted for meat by the sailors. The Captain counted the scales on his back and told me he was not very old, only about 30 years. These peaceful creatures are said grow to be over 90. I was sorry to see him killed. The Captain said, "They provide a lot of meat, and there are thousands of them."

All day long, men took supplies to the ship. Finally, when it began to get dark, Juanita and I climbed into the little boat and returned. Torches were lit, and for a while longer, men rowed back and forth between the beach and the ship, bringing water, fruit, meat and fish.

The next morning, after I had washed my face and put on a dress, there was a knock on the door. Juanita opened it, and there was Scarface.

I began looking around for something to use as a club. I never expected him to be stupid enough to come to my cabin. I cursed the fact that I did not have a pistol of my own.

He spoke softly to Juanita, saying, "I have come to apologize to the young señorita. I picked some delicious island fruit for her, which can be found nowhere else." He handed her a handkerchief with something wrapped in it, and he tried to smile at Juanita and me, but his scar only allowed an ugly sneer. Then, he left.

Juanita and I chuckled with relief that he had not come to hurt us. She began taking the little "apples," colored in splotches of red and green, out of the handkerchief, to place on a ledge near the window. Then Juanita asked me if I wanted some breakfast.

I was hungry enough to eat one of the little fruits whole, but at that moment, I became aware of the anchor being lifted. "No, Juanita, not now. I don't want to miss the departure. You eat without me." I grabbed one of the "apples" and ran up to the deck.

The Captain was near the wheel, looking at a map. It was a bright sunny day, and I went up and looked over his shoulder. He moved me out of his light and said, "It will not be long now." On the map he pointed out the direction in which we would be heading.

I looked up from the map, toward the little island we were leaving. I marveled that such a place existed, with its strange rocks, swimming lizards, big orange crabs, and birds with blue feet. There were so many new and interesting and unknown things about these islands, I wondered if anyone would ever know about them besides a few sailors. I looked at the strange little green and red "apple" in my hand and wondered how it tasted.

When I began to rub it on my arm, to clean off the dust, the Captain snatched it from my hand. "Where did you get this?" he demanded. Before I could stammer an answer, he said, "Do you not know these are deadly poison?" He threw it overboard.

My whole body recoiled with terror. I ran downstairs without saying anything. When I flung the door open, Juanita was lying on the floor gagging. A death "apple" lay beside her, one bite missing from its shiny surface.

Her lips were red and swollen to twice their size. She looked like she was in terrible pain and she gasped for air as though she were being choked. I did not know what to do. I grabbed the water pitcher, freshly filled, and in a vain attempt to wash her affliction from her, I poured a little water into her mouth.

I was screaming impotently, "Juanita! Juanita!" She looked at me with death in her eyes. Her throat was too swollen to speak and her hands clutched at me in terror.

The Captain came in. He swept Juanita off the floor and placed her on the bed. He put his finger in her mouth to make her gag, but her throat was too swollen. Only a tiny portion of the bite she had taken came up. He immediately poured water over his fingers and wiped them clean. I was still feebly trying to get some water into her mouth to wash her throat, but she was gasping more and more desperately for air.

The Captain took the pitcher away and shook his head.

"No!" I cried in anguish. I held her close to me. Her hands clawed at my back in desperation. "Oh, Juanita, Juanita, no! It was meant for me. Please. Please, don't go." I sat there holding her in my arms and felt her die.

I learned later that even the sap from a broken branch of this tree can burn and poison you. Apparently, a few strong men have survived a bite of this fruit, but mostly it is deadly.

Fate was merciful to Juanita in that she died quickly of suffocation without enduring days of burning pain as have some of the little "apple's" victims. There was no mercy for me. I had to watch her suffer in her innocence until she died.

Juanita was "buried" somewhere in the archipelago waters. The sailor who took her life was put in irons and later turned over to the authorities in Panamá. As for me, I grieved Juanita's death for the rest of my life.

Chapter 21

I spent the days that followed in solitude. With the exception of the Captain, I talked to no one and saw nothing but the horizon or the walls of my cabin. The funeral service at sea had been spoken eloquently by the Captain, but I blamed myself for Juanita's death and could not be uplifted in any way by the words he spoke.

As we were about to make landfall in Panamá, the Captain knocked at my cabin door. "Señorita," he called, "we will soon be arriving." We had not conversed since the funeral.

I went to the door and opened it and stood there in silence.

"Are you all right, Señorita?" he asked with concern. Water dripped from his hair and beard. Though it was raining heavily, it was quite warm and the winds were mild.

"Yes, Captain, thank you." I spoke quietly, but without emotion.

He looked at me with worry in his eyes. "Very well," he said, finally. "If you wish it, I will escort you to the customs house when we arrive. It will still be raining when we land and it may be difficult to find." He ran his hand over his head to brush off some of the water.

"Yes, Captain, thank you."

He gave me a long look and then climbed the steps.

I stood in the doorway and watched him go. "You are kind, Captain," I said to myself. "But that fact is only proof that others are not."

I had changed. With Juanita, I had lost whatever might have been left of my childhood—killed, like my innocence, by a bloodthirsty world. The vengeful sailor was not the only man I had known who had been murderous. I could see clearly that I had lived among predators, throughout my life.

Every human institution with which I had been associated, institutions that should have been havens of comfort and justice, had been peopled by nothing more than ravening beasts. Not church, nor family, nor government, nor pretense of human decency was aught but a threat of destruction to me or to those I loved.

I knew I could not claim to have been an example of goodness. Among the virtues of which I could never boast were humility, maidenly modesty, or respect to my elders, but I had never been guilty of any lapse in human kindness. Despite the fact that I had been abused, I always desired to be decent to those around me. Forgiveness was another virtue in which I was lacking, but I sought only to remove my enemies from hurting me further. Never, until the man who killed Juanita, had I wished for any serious harm to come to anyone.

I could see that such feelings were too delicate in a barbarous world. Aggression, pride, and ruthlessness were the only emotions that counted. No matter what I did, I was told I was base, and cursed with the name of "bastard." No matter how much I wanted peace, the world warred with me. I had never been loved or wanted, nor did I have any position in society, yet I had foolishly believed in society—believed that I might yet have what was rightfully mine. I had been a fool.

True, there are always good people, and there were those whom I had loved, despite many of them being taken from me. To such friends, and others I might meet in the future, who treated me with respect, I would give equal respect—only equal and no more. All others would be fair game.

No rules of decency would I follow with regard to them. From the likes of such I would take what I might; I would use them, and if they thwarted me, I would vanquish them, if I could. I stood in the doorway a long time while my heart darkened. I knew such thoughts were against my nature, but I steeled myself against any future guilty thought.

Later, with Juanita's and my few things in my hands, ready to accept whatever my new life might be, I stepped onto the soil of the Isthmus. True to his word, the Captain escorted me to the customs house and helped me through the unfamiliar process of declaration and recording of passage. When the officials were done with their business, we went outside to try to find my father.

The Captain spoke to someone he knew and found out how to get to my father's address. He arranged for my things to be held near the customs house until my father could send someone to pick them up. Then he escorted me through town.

I walked silently, my shawl covering my head, the heavy rain pouring down. Both the Captain and I were drenched after walking only two blocks. I hardly noticed.

I was deep in thought—anxious about meeting my father. I felt bad about the way I had treated him when he left Quito. When no letter had come for months after he left, I assumed he had been angry. When I finally did receive a letter, he stated his desire that I might come live with him. However, he wrote to me very seldom and made no attempt to bring me. One time, when he mentioned bringing me to live with him, he led me to believe that the reason he did not send for me was because his wife would object. I did not understand such matters at my young age, and I had decided that he truly did not want me. Also, I did not know how he had reacted to the news of my being expelled from the convent, or how he felt about the fact that I would be living with him. I knew he had already heard that I was on my way, because warships and other craft that did not carry passengers, did carry mail, and had left for Panamá from Guayaquil before I departed. Now, after eschewing human decency, I was prepared to be cruel to him if he was not kind to me. But I was worried about what would happen when we met.

"What do you think of Panamá?" the Captain said as we ran from one overhang to another along the muddy streets.

I could not see anything through the heavy rain. The buildings I passed were weather worn and mostly dirty. The crowds were smelly and hurried. Beyond that, I could see little. I wanted to see the place I would have to call home, but the rain was like a veil, hiding it from me. "I don't know. Does it always rain like this?"

"No," he said, "it rains, on and off through the middle of the year, but mostly it is hot. However, near the ocean it is pleasant."

When we arrived at the warehouse owned by my father, we had to walk across a wooden plank to the entrance—the street was flooded. The plank was at a steep angle as the doorway was set about a foot above the street. When the Captain knocked, an African slave, stripped to the waist, opened the door.

He said in Spanish, in an accent that I could barely understand, "Señor Sáenz not here. Not here," and tried to close the door.

The Captain placed his hand on the door. "This is the daughter of Señor Sáenz. I'm sure she is expected." The Captain stepped down from the high sill to a small platform on the earth floor of the warehouse. The slave did not seem to understand, but he did not try to stop us from entering.

It was evident that his native language was Portuguese. What little bit of Spanish he spoke was almost unintelligible because of his thick accent. He stated again, "Not here. Gone. Not here."

I stepped from the door sill to the small platform. The warehouse was not large, but there were other small platforms inside on which were sacks of cocoa beans. Many had wooden boxes of various other products that had ports of origin, or destination, written on their sides: United States, India, Brazil, Spain, and other countries. Like the Portuguese slave, the boxes, and me, it appeared everything in Panamá was foreign.

Other slaves were moving platforms, crates, and sacks to the wall farthest from the street. A few were digging a trench against the street side wall in order to keep the water from reaching the goods inside. The flooding outside had not yet reached the inside of the building, but precautions were being taken.

The slave who answered the door, whose name I later learned was Paulo, took us through the noise and a hint of dust to an enclosed office in the back. It was furnished with a long table and three desks. Stacks and stacks of books, papers, and small boxes sat collecting dirt in shelves about the walls. The desks were piled with papers as well. The table was absolutely clean and bare, apparently used to set out goods for inspection. Walking to a small stool at the end of the table, I took off my wet shawl and sat down.

The slave left immediately, saying, "You wait. I find. You wait."

That is what we did—waited—for almost an hour. I sat in the gray light streaming through a small dirty window, and I was extremely weary. I tried to rest my head in my arms and sleep, but I was not able. I talked a bit with the Captain, but I was not a very good conversationalist.

Twice he tried to depart. "You will be all right now," he said. Each time, I asked him to stay, and he acquiesced. I did not want to be alone.

The Captain stood up and began to announce, for a third time, that he felt he must take his leave, when my father walked in. His hair was grayer, and he was rounder than when I had last seen him, but he seemed much happier than I had ever known him. He came into the room saying, "Manuela, you're here at last! My how you've grown." To my surprise, he took me in his arms, hugged me, and kissed me on each cheek.

Such a warm welcome was totally unexpected, but it felt wonderful. He did not seem to notice my amazement and went right on speaking. "I received word of your ship's arrival this morning. But when I went to the ship, of course, I could not find you. You were already here." He laughed. "I checked with the harbor master, and he had to tell me about his new grandson and . . . . My you are so grown up; you look fit as can be. Did you have a good trip?" He went on, stopping only long enough to introduce himself to the Captain. The Portuguese slave returned from searching for my father and was immediately sent back to the customs house to get my things.

126

Finally, my father said, "I was happy to hear that you were on your way, but I was somewhat frantic when your ship did not arrive when expected. What happened?"

"I wish I could say the voyage was uneventful," said the Captain, and went on to tell my father about our mishaps. It was only then, while the Captain explained about Juanita, that my father really looked at me and saw that I was unhappy.

"I remember Joaquina's maid. Like your mother, she was a good woman. I am sorry," he said sincerely. An expression crossed his face, as though painful and long-forgotten memories had suddenly flickered in front of his eyes.

The room became quiet. All three of us were lost in our thoughts. Then the Captain walked over to me, kissed my hand, and said, "Now you will be all right, Señorita."

"Thank you for everything, Captain."

"Yes, thank you," said my father and escorted him to the door. My friend left, but not before my father invited him to visit whenever he was in Panamá, which he did on occasion.

"Well, Manuelita, perhaps we should go upstairs," said my father as we stood alone in awkward silence. He took me through a back door of the office and up a flight of stairs to the living quarters above. It was a fine place—not the finest I had ever seen, but the best I had ever been invited to call home.

He showed me around and finally said, "Here is your room. Freshen up and we will talk." Then he gave me another hug. "It is good to see you."

In my weariness, I only said, "Thank you, Papa."

As he walked away, he said, "Oh, and later, I have a surprise for you. I have to go out now, but I will be back shortly."

I crossed the threshold to my own room—something I never had before—and closed the door. I was moved that a such nice apartment had already been prepared for me. It had a window facing the ocean and it was sparsely but pleasantly furnished with a modest four-poster and a cabinet. I took off my muddy shoes and lay down on my own, comfortable bed. I felt much happier at that moment than I had in days. I was indeed wanted here. However, I was very tired, and though it was only late afternoon, I fell asleep in my clothes.

When I awoke, it was morning and I had a cold. I realized then it had been coming on the day before and was, no doubt, why I had been so tired and out of sorts. The rain had stopped, which made me glad.

When I looked from my window, I could see the harbor, ships rocking slowly in the gentle swells that came from far out to sea. Many patches of blue were scattered across a gray sky. As I looked at the scene, I wondered what my future would be like in Panamá.

I walked to the cabinet and found a mirror. Though I did not feel too bad, when I saw my red eyes and watery nose, I considered undressing and going back to bed. I might have, except I felt I should eat something. I brushed my hair and left my room.

I called, "Papa!" but no one answered. I walked through the hallways toward the dining area and found the surprise my father mentioned. My brother sat eating breakfast at the dining room table.

He looked up at me and gave me a big smile, and said, "Hello, Manuela. You're late for breakfast."

I rushed over to him and threw my arms around him. "Oh José María. It is so good to see you." I kissed him, again and again. "Why didn't Papa tell me you were here? The last I knew, you were at school in Spain."

While he continued to hug me, he said, "I've been here for months, working for father. He sent me to the eastern coast a few days ago on business. He knew I was to be back by supper, yesterday, and he wanted to surprise you. But you fell asleep." We laughed and he said, "It is good to see you too."

I had not seen José María since before the revolution in Quito, when we were both about 11 years old. He had grown to be a handsome young man with curly black hair and a slim face, unlike mine, which was more round in shape.

My other half-siblings, all being quite a lot older than José María and I, were married and off on their own: two sisters and another brother. They were either back in Quito or in Spain. I had seen one or another, once or twice, when I was young, but I had never spoken to, or met, any of them. José María, on the other hand, was a part of me.

My father was already out on business, so José María and I shared breakfast. However, during the meal I found out he was to leave soon, for Venezuela, to join the Royalist forces trying to suppress the revolution. Not only did I instantly feel the emptiness I knew I would feel when he was gone, but I was suddenly very afraid for him. He was only 17, the same age as I. When I looked at his thin frame and still boyish face, I felt cold all over at the thought of him going to war.

"Oh, José María," I said, "it is too dangerous. You are too young."

"I am *not* too young. And besides, Bolívar has fled to Jamaica. The war is almost over."

I had not known this. I regretted that the patriots were losing, but I did not think about it much, except to be thankful that José María would be out of danger. It was not until later that I thought that Fausto would be making a useless journey to Venezuela, since the fighting there appeared to be over.

If Fausto had heard the same news, I wondered what he would do and where he would go. I feared I would never find him or see him again. I was thankful, however, that he and my brother would not be fighting each other.

As we were getting up from the table, I announced, "José, *you* are going to show me around."

"Manuela, I can't. Father expects me to check arrivals today."

"José María, I have only a day or so with you, after all these years, and I want to make the best of it. I insist."

He gave me a glowing smile and said, "All right, but let's get out of here now, before Father comes back and puts me to work."

We laughed and left quickly. I made him take me everywhere that day. I learned many things about the city and had a wonderful time. We talked and talked as he showed me around. Our friendship deepened.

I told him about my years in the convent and of the events of the revolution after he left. I recounted the story of my being expelled. Though I think I shocked him, I confessed my "sin" with Fausto. When he heard about my encounter in Guayaquil, I had to listen to another lecture on being escorted by a man when I went out. This brought up Juanita and I cried in his arms as I told the story of the sailor, the islands, and Juanita's death. He was very sympathetic and helped my grieving, as I unburdened myself for the first time to one who cared enough to listen and understand.

We talked of other things, too. He talked about himself and his schooling, his stay in Spain, and the death of his mother a year earlier. Upon his return a restlessness accompanied him, and finally, he made a decision to join the military.

When I tried to convince him that the revolution was the right cause to fight for, he spoke about his comrades from Spain and how impossible that would be for him—to fight on the opposing side. It was these friends that he was to meet in Venezuela, where they would enlist together.

I saw the fierce loyalty he felt when he spoke of his friends. It was evident in his face. He was extraordinarily handsome, with an inviting sensitivity that belied the stone-hard seriousness of which he was capable when he spoke of something important to his heart. He reminded me of myself. I could not go against the feelings I had for my friends and those I loved either.

As we wandered about the city, he introduced me to his many acquaintances there. We had lunch in a fine inn, owned by one of them. When it started to become dark, we headed for the warehouse. Having avoided the docks all day because we did not want to run into Father, we decided to walk home along the wharf for a change. That is when I made a discovery.

As we strolled along, my arm in José's, the sun was setting and I watched the water slowly darken. I became aware, just then, of a strange fact. The sun was setting behind the hills.

I knew enough about the compass points to know that when on the west coast, the ocean should be to the west, where the sun sets, whereas land should be to the east, where the sun rises. That was simple, but here I was on the west coast of Panamá and the sun was setting in the "east."

I remarked on this to José María and he bent down and drew a picture of the twisting Isthmus in the dirt. All of the previous day's rainwater had dried leaving a reticulated pattern in yesterday's mud. It was so hot, it was almost as if it had been weeks since it rained. As he drew what could have been a picture of a snake, I saw why directions appeared to be reversed. Because of the turn the continent takes at that point, almost doubling back on itself, the sun rises over the ocean in the morning and sets over the hills in the evening. It is also interesting that when traveling from the west coast to the east coast, one is actually heading toward the northwest.

That evening, we followed the same path I had taken the day before, walking with the Captain. What a difference. It was complete chaos without the rain to dampen the natural activity. Dockside was the most difficult, and even dangerous, place to walk in all of Panamá, even at this time of day. Ships were being loaded and unloaded by black slaves day and night. Soldiers, or weapons, were everywhere, traveling in both directions across the Isthmus to put down revolutions directed by both San Martín in Chile and Bolívar in Venezuela—though the war in Venezuela, seemed to be almost over. The soldiers added most to the chaos: they would stand around on the city's streets in groups and fight, drink, or gamble. Any individual unit was not in town very long, but there were always soldiers about.

"We have to have soldiers if we want to have a war." My father declared. "It's good for business. However there are many more, lately."

When I asked why, I found out that the revolution was in a great state of flux. A little more than a year before, Napoleon had been exiled to Elba. Later he had escaped and was subsequently defeated at Waterloo—only a few months before I arrived in

Panamá. With all the unemployed soldiers in Europe, many had joined the revolution or the Royalists in the New World.

I was most interested in the affairs of the revolution and world events, and asked many question. My father never took my interest seriously, only seeing me as a girl and therefore not able to comprehend what was told to me.

Yet, I did learn a great deal. I learned that Fernando VII, no longer being threatened with removal from his throne, abrogated the liberal and beneficial constitution of 1812 written by the Cortes of Cádiz (the opposition government set up during Napoleon's occupation). Even I could tell that his reign was far too reactionary for there to be peace in the colonies. For example, he reinstated the inquisition, which had been suspended a few years before by the Cortes, and he withdrew certain rights that had been recognized as necessary in the colonies. Not only did he do away with much needed reforms of the constitution, he began to send more and more troops from Europe to resist the growing revolutions in his American dominions. This only caused the revolutionaries to redouble their efforts.

I believe if anyone was responsible for the bloodshed that followed, it was Fernando VII. A wise ruler would not have given the insurgents any more excuses to continue. However, no matter what Fernando might have done, the seeds of liberty had already taken root and monarchy was dying all over the world.

At the time I arrived, with revolutions in both the northern and southern regions of the continent and the constant flow of soldiers from Europe, Panamá was very busy. My father's business, which I learned had never done very well, improved a great deal during that period. In the end, however, the revolution was bad for business, but I will tell of that in its proper place.

Unfortunately, in 1815, the war was far from over, and there was still room for my brother in a fighting unit. Only days after I landed, riding mules along a well-traveled trail, my father and I accompanied José María as he rode across the Isthmus to board a ship for Caracas.

I saw the Caribbean Sea for the first time on that trip. On every occasion, then and since, when I have been near that body of water, it has been a hard time for me. On that day I was so distracted I could not even enjoy being shown around the well-named Puerto Bello.

As my brother made ready to board a ship, I fought back my tears. He embraced my father, discussed some details of his trip and then he came over to me. He gave me one of those smiles that made it impossible not to love him and said, "Manuela, you must take care of yourself. When I return, I want you to be right here, and happy."

My weeping could no longer be stilled. I embraced him and held on. He hugged me with equal intensity and kissed my cheek. "You also must take care of yourself," I said.

"Do not worry about me," he said smiling. I knew I could not follow that command. He seemed so young and vulnerable, I could not imagine him being able to survive even one battle.

As he boarded the vessel, he waved at us. Then I watched as the ship set sail, towards what I deeply feared was to be his death.

Chapter 22

"How could you let him go?" I demanded.

My father, deep in thought, unprepared, looked at me in surprise. He stopped his slow-moving mule and searched my face for the reason he should feel an accusation from me.

"If he does not die in battle, the violence of a soldier's life will surely taint him," I said.

Our mules were walking through the streets of Puerto Bello toward the trail leading back to Panamá. We had just departed from the main square in front of the customs house. Papa had left me waiting in front of the massive building—wide enough to have ten entrance arches, each as tall as three men, the building itself being over twice as tall as the arches—while he went in to discuss business with his associates. I was disturbed by something that happened while I waited.

The square was littered with refuse, painting a picture that contrasted with what I had been told about Puerto Bello's history. The town is, just after the nearly abandoned Nombre De Dios farther down the coast, the oldest settlement on the American mainland, and it has an illustrious history. The setting is beautiful, and the town itself had once been grand. When galleons arrived from Spain in the sixteenth and seventeenth centuries, bringing products from Europe and collecting tribute, a grand marketplace would be set up in the square. Tall towers of silver and gold bars would be guarded by soldiers while waiting to be loaded onto ships. Large white tents where merchants would buy and sell goods would ring the perimeter. The population of the town would double for that week. The prices of rooms and food in town would be four times what they were before the ships arrived. For days, there would be a festive market, with everyone participating in an orgy of trading. Those were days of splendor and glory, but those days were gone.

At the time of the revolution, the political and economic chaos had left its mark on Puerto Bello. The constant arrival of men and materials on the Atlantic coast, the endless mule trains to the Pacific coast, bringing men and supplies for the war, had worn the beauty of Puerto Bello thin. The houses were dilapidated, the great square was untended, and the famous customs house itself was showing bricks through the plaster. Soldiers were everywhere, many drunk on Jamaican rum, keeping alive the businesses established in that district to cater to their needs: brothels and canteens.

Having just left my brother, sailing away to join the military, I watched the soldiers to imagine what his life might be like. I tried to discern what kind of men he would be working with, and thus how he might fare. To my horror, I saw a young recruit, not much older than I, quarrel with an older soldier. They were fighting over money, the younger man being drunk and combative. While I watched, the quarrel grew violent. Soon, they both had knives in their hands and were attacking each other. I watched it all, wanting to stop it, but not knowing what to do. While I sat there, the young man died.

My father came from the customs house, a little later, and he had to pass near the spot where authorities were investigating the death of the soldier, still lying in blood. He was reading some papers in his hand and did not even notice the crowd.

When he climbed on his mule, he said, "Good news. Our profits should be up next month, considerably. Oh my, something's happened." He had finally noticed the crowd.

I could not speak and turned my mule around. I rode in silence as we left the square. He talked, but I could not pay attention, nor did I answer. Finally, he was silent for a long time. When I had fully collected myself, I had asked my question.

He thought for a minute and said quietly. "It is true; a soldier's life is violent." He grimaced and seemed to glance back in the direction we had come. "I wish it were not so, but it is, and always has been. I wish he could stay."

"Why can he not?" I asked.

"It is he who has decided to go." He prodded his mule into motion. "When his mother died, I had hoped he would become my partner, but business bores him. In a whole year, he never once remembered one important customer's name." He rode in silence for a moment, and then said, more to himself than to me, "I need a partner."

"Now you have *me*," I said.

He looked at me as though I did not know what I was saying. After a minute he said, kindly, as though to a child, "I would not burden you with my problems. Do not worry. Just enjoy your life here."

I am sure he did not mean to hurt my feelings, but he did. It was more his tone of excessive deference than what he said, but I felt like Cain. I had offered up something to serve my father; it, and I, had been rejected in favor of my brother. Unlike Cain, I was not angry at José, I was embarrassed at the rejection.

To change the subject, I said, "I had always understood it was because of your wife that you could not send for me."

"That is true."

"Then, with all respect, Papa, why did you not send for me over a year ago, after she died?"

He looked surprised. "But I did. Not two weeks after Juana passed on I sent a letter to the Reverend Mother saying that I would be pleased to take you. She replied, saying that you did not wish to leave your studies. She gave me the impression that you were very happy there. Naturally, I was shocked when I learned you had been expelled."

Fury rose in me. All of those months I had wished to be gone, and the abbess had lied to me, and my father, just to keep receiving Carlos's money. I rode on, trying to calm my anger. There was nothing to be done.

"Manuela?" my father said, questioning my silence.

"It is not true, Papa. I was most unhappy there and would have given anything to come."

"Oh, I see." He looked straight ahead.

"Now that I am here, what will I do?"

"Now you can enjoy yourself," he said brightly. After some thought, he said, "There are one or two families, with whom I am close, who will accept you. I will introduce you, and you will have some friends."

I heard what was unspoken. You are a bastard and thus inappropriate for me to introduce except to the most liberal of families.

We rode on in silence. When I did not answer, he said, "One day you will marry. When business improves, I will be able to give you a dowry. To be honest, I do not expect to have sufficient money for a dowry until after I return to Spain, sometime in the next five years. However, if you do not marry here, you will marry in Spain."

I rode in silence. My mule walked in step with my father's, without my guidance, my eyes blurred with tears. The irony was that my father had been trying to encourage me. I knew as much, but his conservative prattle had only hurt me.

He had made more clear the ever-present uncertainty of my future. I was still a bastard, still without a family of importance to overcome the social stigma attached to my birth, and still without any money of my own. I was in a new country where my prospects were still no better than when I was in Quito. Nor would they be, unless I could force Carlos to give me my inheritance, which seemed an impossibility. To make matters worse, my father was talking about going to Spain, and taking me. I believed at that time that I would have been much worse off in Spain, and the thought only made my future seem more uncertain.

In the days that followed, my father was warm with me and truly seemed to enjoy my company. Yet I could tell that he avoided discussing my arrival with others. In regards to most of society, my conservative father was ashamed of me.

As I reflected on my situation, in my more realistic moods, my future held only a few narrow probable paths: obtain my own money (which did not seem possible), marry (the prospects of which were nothing), become the concubine of some wealthy man (the most probable course from what I could see), or become a prostitute (which was not too far afield of concubinage).

With these distressing realities plaguing my thoughts and encumbered with the grief I was still feeling, I began to sink into a deep apathy almost as soon as José María left. My worries, coupled with the newness of my surroundings, reduced me to inactivity and lifelessness. It did not help that I still felt guilty about Juanita's death.

For almost a month, I sat around and did nothing and saw no one. My one activity was to do a little shopping for the household. My father never commented on my idleness, never seemed to notice my distress, nor did he make an effort to introduce me to anyone. He could be excused for that because he did work hard, day and night. However, the more I stayed idle, the less capable I felt of doing anything and the more frightened I became of my future.

I do not know how long I might have stayed like that, except that one day I met a young man, to whom I been introduced on my tour of Panamá with José María. In the end, he was not good for me, but my encounter with him on the street that day did change things for the better.

"Manuela, is that you?" I heard a voice say, as I was walking to the market.

I turned around and saw a well-dressed, handsome, dandy approaching me. He tipped his hat and said, "Aren't you Manuela, José's sister?"

"Yes, Señor."

"Ah, I thought so. We met a few weeks ago. Has José left?"

Recognition set in and I said, "Yes. Are you not Juan Romero?"

"Yes, Señorita. I see you did not recognize me at first. I could not help but remember one of such singular beauty as you. How goes your life in Panamá?"

"Quite well, thank you," I lied.

"Good, very good. I am having a few people over this evening. You must come. Do you remember how to get there?"

"Yes, I do."

"Fine. I must go now, but you should come over anytime after the evening meal. Nice to see you again."

I almost talked myself out of going. I found lots of excuses to stay home. I went through all of them: I was too busy, I was not feeling well, I was tired, and so did I go on with lies to myself. I was, of course, merely afraid. I would not admit that to myself. I had to force myself to attend the gathering, because I knew I needed to do something different.

Once I was there, I had no problem fitting in, or enjoying myself. In fact, I was very happy to meet some new people. Everyone greeted me warmly, and I began new friendships. Juan Romero was particularly attentive. I returned home, late that evening, with a much healthier outlook.

That evening, I was invited by some of these new friends to come to their salons the next day. I went, and I went the day after, and the day after that. I stayed away longer each day, and soon, I was staying away until the hours of early morning. I was still as unproductive as I had been, except that I was receiving a valuable education in the ways of the world, to which my cloistered life so far had not exposed me.

In that learning period, I discovered the pleasures of cards, wine, cigars, political discussions, social gatherings, and men. To be honest, I overindulged in all of these things. Having led a convent life for so long, I tried to experience everything. Completing my growth into womanhood on that continental nexus, where the world's cultures collide and mix like many wines being poured through a funnel into a bottle, my tastes and indulgences became quite eclectic. I mingled with people of all races and enjoyed the social gatherings of all nationalities. I learned much from each of them. The most surprising thing I learned was that people liked me.

I did not have to fight with everyone, as I had been used to doing on a daily basis in Quito. I do not think it was only physical beauty that allowed me to get close to people—women, as well as men, seemed to want my company. Something flowered deep inside me during those first few months in Panamá that attracted people to me. Consequently, with more friends and admirers than I'd ever thought possible, I became quite promiscuous in all of my gratifications.

Thus, the good became obfuscated with the bad. I was exhilarated by the new things I found in my life, and so I went too far in all I did. Who could blame me? It all suddenly became so easy. It was no battle anymore, to live, to be liked, or to be admired; therefore, I followed wherever flattery and admiration led—to the detriment of my well-being on some occasions. Before I knew it, I was riding a river of experience flowing over a broken dam. I was like a woman starving in the desert who wakes up one day amid plenty and then makes herself sick from consuming too much.

This was especially true of men. At 17 years old, just turning 18, I had developed a voluptuousness that brought a surprising amount of attention. I had learned to swing my hips seductively in Quito by copying other girls on the street, although I did not really understand the nuances and I found my beauty very flawed. But in Panamá, without trying, I began receiving so many compliments on my comeliness that, at first, it made me self-conscious. But the effect on me of such admiration was intensely beneficial. The more confident I became, the more I seemed to exhibit those traits my admirers praised.

"You captivate me, Manuela. Your beauty is magic to me," said Juan Romero one night. It was after midnight, and he was walking me home. I still did not know how to respond to such welcome words. I kept silent. I looked at him to see if he was joking with me. Then, he stopped, pulled me close to him, and gave me my first kiss since leaving Quito. I was to experience similar scenes with many men, but that night I was amazed at my ability to impel a man to do that.

However, the "magic" that I worked on men came back at me. Because I did not see the same beauty that others saw when I looked at myself, I relied on others to tell me. Thus, I found myself unable to resist the truly persistent man who desired me. I sometimes let myself become seduced when I knew better. For example, Juan Romero's foppish ways were not to my liking and I was not really attracted to him, but, like too many other men to follow, I gave him whatever he wanted.

As I reflect from these many years, I see that my lack of self-love made me do all sorts of things that I should not have done, in order to get affection from others. Not only was I promiscuous, but I took dares, put myself in danger, and did anything I could to have attention and what I deemed to be admiration.

I had to be the one to tell the funniest stories, dance the most modern and shocking dances, drink the most wine, associate with the roughest crowds, and flirt with the most dangerous men. Soon, it was expected that when I arrived at a social gathering, the fun would begin. I was told so on more than one occasion.

What others did not see was that I was compensating for my inward lack of esteem by exuding an exceptional outward self-confidence. I hid my fears, even from myself, and I made myself what I became. I believe it was this confidence that was the real attribute that seemed to captivate men. I know this was true of Juan.

"It is delightful being with you, Manuela," he said on one occasion. "You always speak just as you feel. Women are too coy. Modern times dictate that women must know what they are about."

I was happy that he seemed to like *me* and not just my "beauty." I liked my confidence, but there was a reverse side to this attribute. This same self-confidence was the basis for many arguments with members of the opposite sex.

A man, when we met, might enjoy my ability to speak with anyone, about anything, unlike delicate women who put their hands to their ears at the slightest hint of sexuality or violence in the conversation. However, later, after feeling that he had some ownership of me, such a man would complain that I was arrogant, brash, or embarrassing. Where at first a man might choose me as a lover because he said he admired my strength of character, or my tenaciousness, later he would criticize me for being "unfeminine."

What happened to Juan and me foreshadowed my relationship with other men. One of the last things Juan ever said to me, in our final argument, was, "How could I have been such a fool to think that one so haughty as you would ever know her womanly place?"

When he said that, I stopped the tears that I had almost let fall and refused to react to the discussion any further.

He saw me turn cold and he said, "You are cruel and heartless, Manuela. I would think a real woman would cry."

I reminded myself that cruelty was the way of the world, and I should not let human decency, or kindness, sway my actions. I would not react. I sat still and merely looked at him.

This angered him further and he said, "I expected at least an attempt to reconcile."

I gave him no satisfaction. Long before, when I knew I would never have children, I had decided that I would never try to live up to men's expectations of me. I said nothing. I merely stood up and left his house.

The next day, when I saw him at a friend's salon, he pulled me aside and said, "I apologize for my rough ways yesterday and my anger. However, we must end off."

I had already received the attention of other men, and I had no intention of changing things. I wanted to tell him so, but I only said, "Thank you for explaining things to me."

He bowed and left, but he was always cold to me after that. Thus did my relationship with Juan set the pattern for many men who followed.

The time I spent in Panamá was filled with arguments with men. My father was one with whom I argued. I could tell he disapproved when I was away all day, everyday, but when I had begun staying out until the next morning, we had quarrels.

"Where were you all night?" he demanded, the first time I came home while he was eating breakfast.

"Papa, I'm tired. Let's talk later." I gave him a peck on the cheek and walked toward the door.

"I want to know, Manuela," he pressed, anger coming to his voice.

I flung my words back in defiance. "I've been out, Papa, out!"

"Manuela, decency proscribes such—"

"Papa, I am a grown woman: I will do what I please." I turned to walk out of the room.

He stood up so quickly, tipping over his chair. "MANUELA!"

He had never raised his voice to me before. I turned around and waited in silence, uncertain of what was to follow.

"This is not right. You have been out all night like some trollop. Your hair is uncoiled. Your clothes smell of cigar smoke and your breath has wine on it."

"Papa, I'm tired. May I please go to bed?"

"You must be tired. I do not imagine what you were doing last night was *sleeping*."

I looked at him angrily but did not respond. I turned and went to my bedroom. He did not speak to me for days.

All of our arguments were as predictable as that one: he would express his opinion about my morality (which actually was slightly better than he imagined) and I would assert my independence. He complained about me smoking cigars, and I asserted my independence. He suggested that my friends were of a character not becoming a proper lady, and I defended them, while I asserted my independence. He was emphatic that I drank too much, and I continued to assert my independence. Always, we would end up not speaking to each other for days.

We accomplished nothing, except to build up bad feelings between us, until the discussion about gambling. I was able to effectively assert my independence on that subject only until I owed someone money that I could not pay. It wasn't much, about 80 pesos, I believe, but my father had to pay it for me. When we had our expected discussion, I did not fare so well.

"Things are going to change, Manuela." He had already paid my debt and he called me to the table where he sat with a piece of paper and a pen. "I will not discuss your immoral ways with you any further since you do not listen to my advice anyway. I do not claim any virtue, but I worry about you, and I do not know what to do for you. However, business, I know." He handed me the paper.

It read:

> I, Manuela Sáenz, owing the sum of 80 pesos to Simón Sáenz, will work for him during all daylight hours, and longer each day if necessary, until this sum is repaid.

"Oh, Papa! You can't be serious."

"I am most serious. You must pay your own debts, and this is the only way I know to have you do so. It would take too long to pay me from the allowance I give you, and besides, you would then have no money to spend while out with your "friends" anyway. You might as well stay here and do some work instead."

"Papa, why do you wish to deprive me of my friends?"

"Your friends are immoral, but to deprive you is not my wish. You simply have to pay your own gambling debts. If you cannot do it on the allowance I give you, you will have to work."

I snatched the pen from the table, signed my name with a flourish, and walked off to my room in haughty disdain, without saying anything further. Again, we did not speak for days, except to attend to business.

I made a vow to myself then: I would never gamble again. However, as I look back on those 80 pesos now, I see I was lucky to lose them. I had been on a self-destructive road which this little mishap had turned into a great opportunity. Neither my father nor I was prepared for the discovery that I could be of some actual use to him in his business.

I was quite good at the paperwork he gave me, and I was able in a single day to bring a measure of much needed organization to his affairs. Not only did it make me happy that I helped my father and that he acknowledged my contribution, but more importantly, my productivity helped me to gain some self-respect. Being competent at something proved to be more important to me than anything I had been doing before, regardless of how much I missed my friends. From those days on, I was no longer so desperate for the admiration of others.

Gradually, I became necessary to the everyday concerns of the operation. We did business with merchants, sea captains, rich dowagers, government officials, and every other kind of man or woman. It was I, more often than not, who remembered people's names unfailingly. I was diligent in seeing that my father kept his appointments. I noticed when we were being cheated. I kept track of important dates, and I did all the other things that go into being a good assistant. From the time I took on my duties, the desks and filing boxes in the room behind the warehouse, where I had waited for my father on that first day, had in me a friend who kept them neat and orderly; the dust had found an enemy.

After a month, I was earning my keep as an adult and making more of my own money then the small allowance I had been receiving. From then on I took the privileges of an adult. I spent all my evenings with my old friends—enjoying, with a great deal more moderation, some of the pleasures of which I had grown fond.

However, my involvement with men changed considerably. I stopped letting any man have me merely because he admired me. I quickly realized that what I wanted from men was what I thought I had, or did have, with Fausto. I wanted reciprocal love. I only had two short affairs after I began to be my own woman. However each one taught me more surely, that I must love the man with whom I become involved.

Still, these decisions were mine. I still did not defer to my father about my behavior. Even less so, since I was making my own money. I came and went as I pleased, and no longer even bothered to assert my independence to my father, and he no longer commented on my behavior.

He was still exasperated at my apparent lack of judgment. "These so-called friends," he would say when the subject came up, "will never do you any good."

This was not true. Having people to whom I could talk freely was very good for me. It was also good for Papa. I mingled with everyone, from an African sorceress and her clan, to the brooding intellectuals in coffeehouses, to the elite of Panamanian society.

Because I mingled with all classes, I was often privy to important information, such as pending government actions or ship arrivals, that my father had not yet found out. More than once this information proved valuable to him, although he was loath to admit it.

I was good for him and his business and he knew it. No matter how long the night before had been or where I had spent it, I would always make certain that I was to work on time to tally incoming shipments, see that deliveries were made, and otherwise fulfill my duties. After a few weeks it was clear that I was the partner my father needed.

He was criticized, I know, for allowing me to work instead of keeping me idle like most of the indolent women that lived in that city. But I was becoming too valuable for him to do anything else.

It was for this reason that he had little to say when I stayed out all night or when men came to visit me while I worked to invite me to the famous or infamous salons of the town.

"Manuela, do these 'gallants' have to visit you while you're working?" he asked disgustedly one day, but no more was said. We no longer argued. He put up with my foibles because I was doing my job. I would only let my visitors stay a few minutes anyway. I tried to keep them away entirely, but I could not always help it.

However, it was not always my friends who lavished attention on me. I would often receive unwelcome attention from men who did business with my father. I am speaking of men who were older, conservative, and not interesting to me. Some were decent and respectful, but many were crude, vulgar or suggestive. I did not like the comments they made or the way they leered at me or the way they tried to see down my dress. I received indecent advances from tradesmen almost daily. I was often successful in turning the incident into a joke, or, if that failed, I did not have too much trouble putting a man in his place. Still, I did not like to fight off unwelcome attention merely because I had work to do and was in the same room with the man.

In one case, it turned nasty, and ultimately tragic. A merchant by the name of Juan Guzmán came into the warehouse, and my father rose to greet him. I had seen his name on shipping papers before, but I had never met him. He had a thick wiry beard, and deep black curly hair that fell from his head like stones cascading off a mountain. I think he was a mixture of Indian and Spanish blood. He looked most like a *cholo*, and I was initially disposed to like him. Short and heavily muscled, his clothes were ill-fitting, but he was well-dressed enough to do business. Though his clothes were the same plain business attire that everyone wore, his long hair and the knife he wore in his belt gave him the look of a street fighter. He had the appearance of a man who was born and raised in the gutters, and had fought his way into affluence.

My father spoke to him for a few minutes and then there was an interruption. Paulo, not able to speak Spanish any better than when I arrived, ran in, saying, "Señor Sáenz, come quick. A woman outside. She saying something wrong with shipment."

Papa said, "Damn! I know who it is; please excuse me a moment, Señor," and left.

The instant he was out of the room, Guzmán came over to me and said, "You are a lovely creature. Perhaps you would like to spend some time with me this evening. I could buy us a bottle of fine wine."

He smiled, but his eyes looked vicious. He gave me the impression that even though he had a lot of money, he was always frustrated in matters of the heart. I could understand that, because he was most unappealing. I was walking back and forth putting papers from a desk into file boxes on the shelves. "I do not think so, Señor. Thank you, but I have other plans."

His smile changed to a frown. He took a step closer and said, angrily, "Perhaps another night."

I made little attempt to hide my revulsion since his manner was so aggressive. I walked away from him saying, "No, Señor. I do not wish to socialize with you."

When I turned around, there he was, blocking my path. He gave no indication that he wished to speak further, so I stepped around him to return to the desk. As I passed him, he grabbed my arm and spun me around. "You white bitches are all the same," he snarled. "You think you are queens; and if a man has some color in his skin, he is dirt to you."

I was very angry at his implication. The last thing I would ever do is let a person's color or birth or class interfere with how I actually felt about that person. I had grown up as an outcast, and I knew how such animosity felt. Because I had felt an anger similar to his before, I made myself not snap back at him. I took a breath, pulled my arm away, and said, quietly, "That is not true, Señor."

"Then why do you refuse to let me buy you some wine?"

"Because I do not wish it." I raised my voice on the last words, as my father reentered the room.

"The woman comes here every week with a complaint. You know the type, I'm sure," my father said to Guzmán as he came back in the room.

Guzmán turned to meet him affably, but my father had seen us glaring at each other. He said, "What is going on, Manuela? I am sorry, Señor Guzmán, my daughter is new to the business. Manuela, bring Señor Guzmán some tea."

I felt the blood rise in my cheeks. It was all I could do to keep from exploding.

"That is all right Don Sáenz. Just a misunderstanding." He turned to me. "No tea, thank you."

"Anyway, your prices are certainly the best I've seen," my father said, continuing where the conversation dropped before he left the room. "I think we can do business. I'll expect your shipment next month."

"Certainly, Señor." My father did not see him leer at me as they turned around and headed for the door.

From then on I kept an eye on his account. There was always something a little wrong with every shipment. I could not quite prove it; and when I pointed out the discrepancies to my father, he paid little attention. "His prices are very good," he would say.

I saw Guzmán on occasion about the city, and I asked my friends about him. Every businessman or political figure who knew him agreed that he was dishonest and each had some story to tell about his dealings with Guzmán.

When I brought these stories home, my father ignored them, because it was me reporting something that he did not find convenient to believe, from sources that he objected to.

"I'm supposed to lose money and buy from a higher vendor, simply because your 'friends' tell you stories. Humph!"

Except for his exasperating unwillingness to listen to my good advice, we got along very well once I had proven myself valuable in business. On one point, however, we were never reconciled. Whenever I would come from a gathering where the works of the revolutionary and free-thinking writers of the time were discussed, bringing such ideas home, he was extremely insulted.

When I quoted from Bolívar's celebrated Jamaica letter, copies of which were being circulated among the intellectuals, he became extraordinarily angry. One time I tried to quote him: "The revolutionary, Simón Bolívar, says, 'We are still in a position lower than slavery—'" I was not allowed to finish. Our discussion was already heated, and my father exploded.

"How dare you speak that rebel's words to me, a Spaniard? How dare you espouse insurgent writings while your brother risks his very life for Spain? Slavery, indeed . . . ." The admonishment that ensued showed me that we were to the point of causing irreversible damage to our relationship, so I learned to keep my revolutionary ideas to myself.

We had only recently heard of Bolívar's return from exile in Jamaica and of his winning control of the Magdalena River. We also heard stories of other great patriots, such as San Martín and O'Higgins, fighting for the liberation of Chile. Almost as soon as Bolívar was back from Jamaica, the revolution began interfering with trade. From then on, our business declined and my father took to brooding about the war. I, on the other hand, was delighted about patriot success, despite the fact that I was also fearful for my brother. We heard from him now and then, and he was indeed fighting hard.

Almost a year after my arrival in Panamá, my father announced that he had decided that we would return to Spain sooner than he had originally planned. I did not want to go, but he was already making arrangements, writing letters, and sending investment money to his friends and relatives in Europe.

Spain was the last place I wanted to live. I had had enough of being looked down on because I was illegitimate, which I had managed to overcome in Panamá, but to go to a place where I would be scorned just because I was from the Americas was not to be desired. The antipathy the *peninsulares* felt for native-born Americans, if anything, had become worse since the war had started. I knew enough world travelers and had seen enough of how *criollos* were treated by Spaniards in Quito and Panamá to be certain that it would be much worse in Spain.

I fought with my father a great deal over this subject. It did no good. He was financially and emotionally committed to returning before he even mentioned it to me. I would have to go with him or find some other means to survive where I was.

The best alternative was marriage. However, the trouble with marriage as a "choice" was that no matter how often I was entertained by men, I knew it was as a concubine and not as a potential wife. Many men invited me to their beds in that period, and I am bold enough to admit I too often accepted their invitations. However, there was no future for me in any of these dalliances; it was carnal and not conjugal relations that men wanted of me, due to my lack of family, dowry or noble birth.

Clearly, the only opportunities I realistically had in front of me were to either be the concubine of some well-off man or to follow my father to Spain and live the life of a second-class citizen. Any other opportunities depended on the unlikely event of somehow obtaining my inheritance.

Though I knew the business of importing and exporting nearly as well as my father, it did not do me any good. As a woman, it would be impossible for me to do business with men. Some men would deal with me, but most would not. "I do not do business with a girl. Where is your father?" I heard too often. Also, there were some aspects of the trade in which I could not even partake, when it came to importing and exporting, due to certain legal restrictions.

My father spoke often of our departure for Spain, but never was it clear just when we were leaving. Then, one afternoon about 14 months after I arrived, I received the news that Papa had finalized his plans.

I was busy matching the day's bills of lading with our orders. I had just run out of cigars and had sent the Portuguese slave, Paulo, to fetch some for me. "Don't buy the kind you bought last time," I told him. I handed him a coin across the desk.

"Sure, Señorita, sure, sure." His Spanish still poor, and I was not as sure as he was that he understood me. I thought about Juanita at that moment, who would have known exactly what I wanted.

"And, Paulo, let me know if there are any other shipments to unload today," I said, as I picked up my pen.

"Sure, sure, I tell." He left, and I returned to making my notations.

Papa walked in just then and said, enthusiastically, "Well, it's all settled."

"What, Papa?" I said, as I recorded the arrival date of an order.

"Why, I've finished making arrangements with my cousins in Spain. I can leave in about six months or so. No more than nine." I stopped writing, and a look of anger must have crossed my face. "Now, Manuela, let's not quarrel. I have to go."

I was silent.

"I know you want to stay, and I know that you cannot do so without getting married. But a lot can happen in a year. Let us just wait and see."

I was weary of the arguments about Spain myself, and I decided to talk to him about it when my work was done. "Very well, Papa," I said stiffly. "Let's talk later."

"Yes, good, we will talk at dinner."

Then, something bothered me. As he was about to walk out of the room, I said, "Papa? What do you mean 'a lot can happen in a year'? I thought you just said you were leaving in six months."

"Oh, yes, that was the other thing. I have to leave, no later than nine months from now—six would be better. However, we will not be finished with all of our commitments by then. You must stay a little longer—perhaps as long as nine months, or a year, from now."

I was already on my feet, coming around the desk. "Papa, I can't run this business alone!"

"Not to run the business. There will be very little left to do by the time I leave. However, there are certain things that I cannot move closer: commitments I am obligated to uphold. Yet, I must leave on schedule if I am to avoid losing a large amount of money."

I opened my mouth to speak.

"Now don't worry. You wanted to be my partner; this is what a partner would do. There is nothing difficult about doing what needs to be done. These concerns have to do with the selling of our property, the arrangements for which have already been made, and the transferring of expected shipments to other importers. You can do all of this with my power of attorney."

I looked at him skeptically.

"When these affairs are handled, you will follow me," he said, enthusiastically, oblivious to the fact that he had not convinced me. Then, he noticed my scowl, and said, "What's the matter? You did not want to leave your friends. Now you can spend more time with them. The work will be very easy by then. You should enjoy yourself. Who knows, you may find someone to marry before you have to leave. Business has been good enough that I have almost saved a respectable dowry. Come now, don't worry."

"All right, Papa. But I think it is a big responsibility."

"Yes, Manuelita, I know. But I think you will be fine." He kissed my forehead and turned to leave.

"Papa?"

"Yes?"

"You know, we don't have a single female servant. If I am to stay here and then travel alone to Spain, I would like you to buy me a female to attend to my needs."

"Oh, no, Manuela. I can't afford it."

"Please, Papa. I don't know what commitments you have for your money, but I do know the current accounts. Are you saying you cannot spend some of it on a slave to help me out—after deciding to leave me here all alone?"

"Manuela, the expense—"

I could see how the discussion would go, and I became impatient. "Damn the expense, Papa. You know I am right."

"Don't raise your voice to me. I do not think another slave is necessary, and I do not want to spend the money."

"All right, Papa! All right. I don't want to cause your financial ruin."

"Now, Manuela."

I walked back behind the desk, picked up my chair, and slammed it back down. "After all, what does it matter. I'm only your daughter," I said, letting my peevishness get the better of me. I sat, picked up my pen, and began to work.

Anger rose in his voice. "I'm going for a walk, and I hope you are in a better mood when I return." He picked up his hat and left.

I tried to work, but I was too distracted. I think I picked up the same piece of paper ten times. I did not want to accept that his plans were clear and irrevocable. Neither did I like the idea of making the trip to Spain alone, which is the main reason I had insisted on procuring a servant. I felt guilty that I had tried to force him to spend his money, yet I knew I had to have someone to help me out. The more I thought about it, the more angry I became at his stubbornness.

These thoughts went over and over through my mind. I did not want to go to Spain, and yet I had no way to stay. The more I considered it, the more it all reduced to the real problem. I was unable to determine for myself what I would, and would not, do. Would I ever be able to control my own life?

Chapter 23

My father had not gone very far on his walk that afternoon before he met one of our customers who was on his way to dinner: James Thorne. Don Jaime, as he was known, was a wealthy English merchant who lived in the great city of Lima. He was about forty years old, tall, and solidly built. His blue eyes and thinning brown hair, which was just starting to become gray, gave him a distinctive look. Constantly on the move throughout the colonies, he had acquired a reputation, wherever he went, of being fair, affable and prosperous. He was also somewhat of a rarity, being a devout English Catholic. I had met him a few times and did not dislike him. He always treated me with deference.

Meanwhile, I sat in the office for perhaps half an hour, unable to work, my emotions boiling inside me. My father infuriated me. He had to return to Spain! Yet he could not bear to part with a few pesos to help me, even though I was to stay and make it possible. Did he think me a child? Would I ask for something if I did not really need it? I was in this state when Paulo arrived with my cigars.

He also brought a bill of lading, informing me that one of our wagons was being loaded with a shipment of cacao down on the dock. The anger I was already feeling turned to wrath when I saw the name on the bill. As I too often did, I let my emotions drive me rather than wisdom. Letting out a low howl of frustration, I stood up and started for the door.

At the same moment, Thorne and my father were returning to the warehouse. I came through the door like a bullet, almost running them down. I had the lading papers in my hand and I am sure Thorne was not prepared for the scene he saw next.

My father, oblivious to the subtleties, as usual, started right in with a cheerful, "Oh, Manuela, Don Jaime has offered to help you with the business when I have . . ."

I waved the papers in his face and said, "Look at this. Why are you still accepting goods from that thief, Guzmán? I have told you what I have heard about him, and especially this shipment of cacao."

My father said sternly, "Now, Manuela, we have argued this out before. We don't know for sure about him, and the price after all . . . ."

"You belittle my friends, but when I bring valuable information from them, you ignore me. Well, I'm not going to be so foolish." I stormed past them and down to the docks, where the object of my ire was unloading his ship.

Before I was out of earshot, I could hear my father say, "But, Manuela— Manuela! I'm sorry, Don Jaime. MANUELA!" I kept walking, and they could only hurry after me.

I was not prepared for the encounter I was about to have, but I was too angry to show good sense. Slicing through the activity on the dock, I walked directly down to Juan Guzmán's moorage. My father and Thorne followed a several paces behind. My father continued to call out to me, but all my attention was on Guzmán.

As I arrived, sacks of cacao were being unloaded from a ship onto our wagon. Guzmán was standing on it giving orders to the slaves. As I approached, I saw him pull his knife and threaten the life of a "laggard."

My approach should have been more calculated, but I was "invincible" then, or so I thought, and my blood was up. I walked to the wagon and yelled up at him, "I'm glad you're still here, you thief. Put these sacks back on the ship and get out of here."

I saw Guzmán react inwardly with violent anger, his eyelids narrowed and his jaw clenched. He held his hostility in check, stuck the knife into the sheath on his belt, and jumped down from the wagon. He looked directly at me and said, "I do business with your father, not with you."

At that moment, Papa and James Thorne arrived. Guzmán turned to them and said, in a threatening manner, "Don Simón, I do not have to be insulted like this."

Intimidated, my father turned to me angrily and said, "Manuela, I told you we do not know anything. "

"Papa! Do not be so 'fair minded' with this criminal. Do you not remember the last time this thief did business with us?"

His face reddened. "Manuela! That's enough!" He immediately turned to Guzmán, suppressing his own anger, and said, "I am sorry, Señor; please forgive my daughter."

All I could see was a blur of red. "Papa, this man is no more than a criminal." I walked around Guzmán and spoke to the slaves on the wagon. "Get these sacks unloaded immediately," I ordered. They did not know me at all, but the force of my command was enough to make them stop and stand in confusion.

Guzmán followed me. "Back to work!" he ordered. They stood in stupid indecision, looking first at me and then at him. Guzmán became furious. He jerked me around by my shoulder. "How dare you interfere with my business?!" he said, as some spittle trickled onto his beard.

My father, seeing that Guzmán was so angry, tried to step in between us and pleaded, "Manuela, please!" He turned around and said, "Now, Don Guzmán, let's not get upset."

I spoke over him, "I happen to know that half of this shipment has already been delivered, and I know what was really in it!"

Guzmán calmed down, knowing what I could say. "Don Sáenz," he said, self-righteously, "it is only because it is you that I do not take my shipment and leave."

"Now, now, I'm sure everything will be fine."

Just then Thorne said, "Don Simón, may I speak to you for a moment?" and pulled my father aside. Guzmán and I looked at each other. Thorne whispered, "Forgive me for interfering, Don Simón, but why *are* you doing business with this scoundrel? He has the worst reputation on the seas."

My father said, "His prices are the best after all."

Both Guzmán and I overheard. He avoided my eyes and stepped toward them. I sensed that he was going to try to save his reputation. As he took a step, he purposefully knocked his shoulder against mine.

I don't know what got into me then, overconfidence no doubt, or maybe it was having performed a similar trick on the ship, but when he pushed against me, I grabbed for Guzmán's knife.

I held on to it with my right hand and started to push him away with my left, but it was not so easy this time.

144

Guzmán grabbed my hand. He looked into my eyes with hatred and started to twist my arm. "No you don't, you white bitch," he whispered.

Fear rushed through me. Instinctively, I swung at him, reacting without thinking, and smashed the heel of my left hand into his nose. He reached for his face, allowing me to step back from him with the knife still in my grasp.

My father noticed the commotion and said, "Manuela!"

Before my father, or Thorne, could come to my rescue, Guzmán recovered and came back at me violently, blood trickling from his nose into his beard.

I backed up with my weapon extended to defend myself. "Give me that knife," he snarled. We all stood there frozen for a moment, though I felt myself shaking.

My father said, "Manuela—" But he was stopped by what I did next. Without taking my eyes off Guzmán, I lifted my arm and swiftly sliced open one of the bags hanging over the end of the wagon next to me. Then, I backed away.

Some cocoa beans fell out, but mostly a rush of small pebbles cascaded to the dock. My father's expression changed to one of fury. Guzmán lunged at the bag to stop it from spilling.

I stepped back a few more steps and threw the knife at a box several feet away, hoping it would stick dramatically, but it only fell impotently on the dock. I pretended that was my intention and walked away.

Guzmán let out a roar. I heard his footsteps and I turned back around. He had reclaimed his knife, and I saw him come at me.

Thorne stepped in front of him. Thorne is quite tall and imposing. Guzmán took a step to the right to go around, but Thorne pushed Guzmán back by his shoulders. He probably gave Guzmán that look that I've seen when he has commanded other men. Guzmán stopped. Thorne, icy and threatening, said, "I think it would be bad business to stay here any longer, Don Guzmán."

Guzmán's breath was coming hard. He said, "Don Jaime, because it is you who requests it, I will respect your wishes and withdraw. I must find the scoundrel who sold me these sacks." Then he went quickly back to his ship.

As I turned around and walked into the dispersing crowd, I heard Thorne order the slaves to unload our wagon. If he and my father then started after me, I did not know it. I was soon far up the dock, and lost in the dockside throng.

I walked fast, because I did not want them to catch up with me. I did not want to hear any advice right then, which I am sure I would have. I was exhilarated and exhausted from the experience, and I walked to the salon of one of my friends, told my story, and drank some wine. I did not return home until after midnight.

When I arose, my father was already eating breakfast. He looked at me sternly and said, "You worried me yesterday. Don't do anything like that again." I regarded him silently, and then his face softened and he said, "Thank you for saving me so much money." He smiled.

I walked over and kissed his cheek. "Don't do business with him again," I chided.

"Of course, I won't." He smiled back. "I don't think many people will do business with him again."

Actually, Guzmán did manage to keep doing business, although word of the affair got around and he was hurt by it. I heard from my friends that he was still practicing the same kinds of deceptions, but he did not have as many victims as before. To get even, he lied to everyone about my father and me, and he did us quite a lot of damage on occasion. It infuriated me and I sometimes imagined ways to put him out of business permanently. That morning, I did not know what was to happen, and I merely answered my father with, "Let us hope so."

"To thank you for the money I've saved, I am prepared to purchase you a slave." He smiled.

I put my arms around his neck and hugged him. "Oh, thank you, Papa. It is not necessary to pay a large sum. As long as she is female." I hugged him harder and said, again, "Thank you, Papa."

"Yesterday, Don Jaime was very impressed with you. He talked about you all evening, and when I told him about your request for a slave, he had an idea. He knows of a man who, like me, is also leaving for Spain. Don Jaime thinks he will be selling his slaves at a good price. He even said that he would personally negotiate for us."

"Wonderful, Papa. I hope you do not have to spend too much."

"Don Jaime will come in the early afternoon and take us to meet the gentleman. That is, if you wish to go along."

"Of course, Papa."

"Very good, because Don Jaime asked me to invite you to accompany us."

That afternoon, when Thorne arrived, he was particularly solicitous; and he brought me a bouquet of yellow flowers. As I was to find out, Thorne's interest in me had become a passion.

After I arranged the flowers in a vase, we walked toward the other end of the harbor. Thorne said, "The gentleman is a neighbor of mine, in Lima. However, he has lived most of the last three years here in Panamá, and he has six female slaves he is planning to sell. Recently, he decided to leave for Spain and has sent to Lima for his furniture. His ship docked this morning and is unloading now."

As we approached the moorage, James pointed out a portly, well-dressed man. He was supervising several slaves carrying boxes, large and small, from the loading area of a recently arrived ship to waiting wagons. I don't know how the man expected all of his possessions to get to Spain without being damaged a little on their journey, or why, if he was taking his furniture, he was selling his slaves; but there he was fussing and giving directions as though his whole fortune were invested in every piece of wood and brass. He was making such a spectacle of himself that there was actually a crowd gathered around to watch the show.

Every once in a while he could not contain his worry and would actually take this piece, or that box, from one of the slaves and carry it himself across the dock. I never saw such an energetic fat man.

As we approached, he recognized Thorne and started to come over to us in greeting. At that moment, a particularly odd shaped box was dropped on the dock by two slaves. It broke with a musical sound.

"Oh, my heavens," said the man, horrified. He ran over to the box, wringing his hands and shouting ferocious curses at the slaves. He tried to peer into the broken slats. He turned to yell again at the slaves but they had already retreated back to the loading area to find something else to do. The man tried to lift it himself. When he couldn't, he stopped the closest two slaves, part of a group of females who were scurrying back and forth across the dock carrying small bundles, and told them to help him lift the box.

One was very ugly, pock-marked, with heavy locks of thick African hair almost covering her heavy dangling earrings. She was very acquiescent when she acknowledged him. The other girl was very pretty, lighter skinned, wearing a red turban; she too wore large circular earrings. She said nothing.

As soon as the man turned around to wipe his brow and pick up the box, the first girl grinned at the other and then she pretended to be a fat man carrying a box around in a circle. The pretty one covered her mouth to contain her mirth, but all around, people watching this adroit performance, including me, started laughing.

The man turned to see what was happening, but she was very quick and assumed the posture and attitude of a humble servant trying to help lift the heavy box. The other girl was also immediately at the box preparing to lift, hiding her face to keep from smiling.

As soon as the man turned around again, the mime immediately stood up and looked at her friend with the same expression with which the man had looked at her. Everyone around her chuckled, except Thorne and my father, who were perturbed at the insubordination.

I said, "I want her."

Both my father and Thorne began to protest, but we were distracted by more laughter. Everyone was watching the fat man walk across the dock, carrying the box on his back. The two slaves were marching a few feet behind in mock superiority. Having lifted and balanced the box on his back, they had let go, and the poor man had to carry it all by himself.

He looked exactly as his impersonator had portrayed him moments before. The slaves then rushed to help when he set the box down. Before the man stood up, the homely mime took an invisible handkerchief from an invisible pocket and wiped her forehead. The man took a real handkerchief from his pocket and wiped his brow, as though to imitate the slave who was pretending to be him.

By this time everyone was roaring. Even my father and Thorne could not contain their laughter. The fat man turned around, realized his slaves were up to mischief, and started after them angrily. They began to back up. I started to run between them.

I was saved from a perhaps unfortunate confrontation because, at that moment, we were all distracted by the sound of yet another box being dropped and broken by the slaves at the unloading area. The man forgot the insubordinate women, let out a yelp of dismay, and ran over to inspect his new losses.

Then, I turned to my father and insisted that I wanted the "mime."

"But, Manuela, she will not make a good servant," said my father.

"She will be better than the most expensive slave in Panamá. Please, Papa."

My father looked at me and then shrugged his shoulders. He and Thorne went over to the man and made arrangements to buy her. I found out later, it was she who talked them into buying the other girl, too. I think the overfed *peninsulare* gave my father an excellent price.

That is how I first met the mime, Jonotás, and her friend Natán, whom I have cherished since that day. No woman ever had dearer companions. No woman ever had more loyal friends. They suffered and gloried with me through nearly every important event in my life since then, and I love them from the bottom of my soul.

Chapter 24

"James Thorne has asked for your hand," my father informed me one morning when he came to breakfast. I was already up, drinking some coffee and eating some bread. As he sat down, he said, "I wonder if you could have Natán bring me some porridge."

"Thorne? Asked for my hand?"

"Yesterday evening, while you were out. He came over and politely requested my permission to marry you. Though business has fallen off a bit of late, I felt I could come up with a decent dowry. We worked out the details and it is all settled. Manuela, would you mind?" He motioned to Natán, who was cutting and arranging some freshly picked flowers in the next room.

"What do you mean 'it is all settled'? No one has talked to me."

"Now, Manuela, I know. Thorne himself insisted that he would only finalize our arrangements if you agreed. Where is the cook?" He started to rise.

"Never mind, Papa. Natán, there is some *zango de nanjú* cooking for Papa. Would you bring it up to him?" She went off, and I said, "Now, what are these arrangements?"

"Well, we have agreed on the dowry, as I said. However, he wants to wait a few months. In that time, he will try to arrange his affairs such that he need not travel as much. He earnestly wishes you to be his wife; and when business is more settled, he will take you to Lima to marry. Ah, good, I'm famished." Natán set down the porridge and my father poured some honey on it. I made a face because it is so sweet already, being made from corn flour and raisins.

"You mean he wants to take me to Lima, to live?"

"Yes, he has a large house near the center of the city there. What do you think?"

I did not know what to think. If everything else had been right about James Thorne, I was not delighted by the prospect of marriage to a man over 20 years older than I. That alone might have made me refuse. If that were not enough, there were two other big problems: I did not feel any attraction to him, and I sensed that we would never get along. Before giving it any thought, I almost flatly refused.

However, I knew I must investigate this bit of luck further. After all, what I had longed for—an opportunity to stay in the colonies—had presented itself. In fact, it was far more than I hoped. This proposal promised other advantages that I did not think I would ever have. Because James Thorne was a powerful and prosperous businessman, I would, as his wife, have both respectability and wealth. This is to say nothing about my living in the most beautiful and important city on the continent.

I told my father I would think it over, but before the day was out, I invited Thorne to dinner. When my father found out I had written a note to him, asking him to eat with us, and sent Jonotás off to deliver it, he said, "He will be upset by your forwardness. Really, Manuela!"

However, Thorne did not seem to mind and came on a Sunday evening. My suitor, my father, and I had a modest and enjoyable meal.

Our cook prepared plantains. He was from Guayaquil, so they were frequently on our dinner table. I did not know it at the time, but nearly all Europeans hate plantains. Thorne was no exception. I could tell because he poured honey all over them to kill the taste. He was very polite and endured it without so much as a grimace. Making such an effort flattered me.

After dinner, I asked, "Don Jaime, would you accompany me on a stroll? The evening is so nice." I saw my conservative father's eyes roll.

"I would be delighted, Señorita."

We ascended the sloping street outside the warehouse in silence. The glow left on the hills by the setting sun made everything look warm and golden.

The first comment my future husband made to me (in what I took to be a critical tone) was, "You realize how dangerous it was to pull a knife on a man like Guzmán, don't you?"

By this time, the incident was weeks behind and not in my thoughts. Besides being surprised at his bringing it up, I was nettled at the criticism. I wanted to dispute, but I was more interested in making friends with the man who wanted to marry me than arguing with him, so I agreed. "You are right, Don Jaime. It was dangerous."

He said, "Call me 'James.' That is my true English name. Would you like to learn to speak English someday?"

I had never thought about it, but I considered the idea and told him, truly, that I would. Then, to avoid returning to the subject of Guzmán, I asked him to tell me about England.

He said, "Ah, I miss it, especially the town where I spent my boyhood: Aylesbury, in Buckinghamshire. The countryside is beautiful. I also love London. There is no more important city in Europe."

I asked, "Is London beautiful?"

"Not really. Though London is as much the center of Europe's culture as Paris, it is not really beautiful, not like Lima. But it is full of activity: trade, art, politics, society. People are more businesslike and refined. Not like Paris or Lima."

"Oh, tell me about Lima," I said, and I began asking him many questions. He spoke about his mansion near the center of town, his servants, the impressive buildings in the center of the city, the Old Comedy Theatre, the society families that were his friends, and he told me a story or two about his life there. The more he spoke, the more I wanted to go.

We had left the houses and shops, and the road had become narrow, so we turned to go back by an alternate path. As we walked along in the gathering darkness, James grew silent. I peered at his face to see if something was wrong. I could discern nothing. A moment later, he stopped me, took my hand, and led me to the side of the road, under the branches of an old tree.

There, he said, with an urgency in his voice, "I have watched you for many months now while doing business with your father. I know you have not paid any attention to me in that time, Manuela, but I truly desire your esteem. I hold great affection for you."

He looked at me with intensity. His manner demanded a response, and it made me uncomfortable. I was not ready to give him one. We looked at each other and finally I said, "I am flattered Don Jaime—James . . ."

As I paused while forming my words, he tentatively put his arms around me. When I did not resist, he pulled me roughly to him and kissed me. I pushed him back, because I did not like his manner. It was too demanding and indelicate.

"I am sorry," he said, looking like he did not know whether to walk away in embarrassment or become angry. The corners of his mouth twitched as he stood there waiting to see what I would do. A lock of his gray hair fell in his eyes.

I did not want to hurt his feelings. I wanted to know and understand him. "Let us take it slowly," I said. Taking my time, I put my arms around his neck and pulled him to me. I kissed him softly on the lips.

I only intended to kiss him once, but he held me and kissed me again. Then he kissed me again, only for a longer time. I was not overly taken by his kisses, but it was not unpleasant. At first his kisses were tentative, almost passive, but I could feel that he had become aroused as he pressed against me. Suddenly, he stopped and pulled away.

I had the impression we had gone beyond what he considered decent behavior. He looked as though he did not know what to do. Then he pulled me to him and kissed me again, hard and rough. He brought his hand to my breast.

His manner was so unpleasant that I had to stop him again. "Please, sir. We are not yet married." He looked frustrated and confused.

"I . . . am sorry—you are so . . . impossible to resist and—"

In order to allow him to save face, I said, "I am flattered, Señor, and I am happy about your regard for me. I truly thank you. But, you must not take liberties."

He looked at me apologetically and said, "I am sorry, Señorita."

I smiled at him and it gave him courage to take my hands in his. A gentle breeze shook the leaves of the tree as he held them tightly and kissed my fingers with great feeling. The "need" in his manner unsettled me. I said, "Come, we will talk more tomorrow," and I led him back down the street to the warehouse.

We walked in silence, and as I opened the door and stepped over the high sill onto the dirt floor, James grabbed my hand. He held it as though he would not let me go.

"Manuela, I . . . please, would you make me happy by considering my proposal of marriage?"

"Señor, I—"

"Manuela, I very much admire you. Please. I must know if you consent to the marriage I have arranged with your father."

I had not expected to have to decide right then. I only wanted to get to know him better. I wanted to think about this for a long time.

He took my other hand and our arms reached over the threshold. He pressed me again. "I truly love you, Manuela."

I almost felt like I should run away, but many thoughts came to my mind: *A marriage has been offered. It is either marriage or concubinage if I want to stay in the colonies. My father has said James will accept the dowry my father has offered. There are no other offers. There are not likely to be any others. Yet, I do not love him.*

I admired him, to a certain degree, for his obvious competence in business and the respect that he was given by anyone who knew him. Yet, I could not imagine ever having a really intimate relationship with him, beyond mere physical congress.

I knew he was more conservative than my father, and I could see that we would fight, even then. *How will we live together?* Not only was it probable that I would become unhappy, but I was sure I would make him unhappy. By that time of my life, I believed that the only way to have a relationship with a man was with a heart full of love.

I cannot, I told myself. *The decent thing is to refuse, as gently as possible.* However, a picture formed in my mind's eye without my control. I could see myself as a respectable society woman, in Lima. My thoughts were beset with images wherein I was accepted and admired by people around me. I saw myself in a community where every one of importance called me "friend." In Lima, I could be everything I had not been in Quito.

Then I thought about the pledge I had made on the ship. Decency was not to be considered. I knew I should not manipulate the opportunity of his affection for me to selfish advantage; but if I was to be true to my pledge, I must use opportunities and people to my ends. I could still see the picture in my mind. I was living in Lima. I was respected. I was what I wanted to be.

Though still uncertain, I decided to accept.

I stepped back over the sill, still holding his hands. I looked at him a long time. I said, "I appreciate your affection and your words." I reached up and kissed him quickly on the lips. "I will marry you, James, and make a home for you in Lima." The words felt strange as they left my lips. I felt an inner struggle; as though something in me tried to bring back the words as I spoke them.

He hugged me passionately. "Thank you, Manuela. You have made me very happy." He smiled more at that moment, then I ever saw before or since.

It was done. I had accepted his proposal. I would have all that I had hoped for, and though I would try to make him happy, I was certain I would not be able to do it. I felt sorry for him for a minute, and then I repeated my pledge to myself, to wipe away any feeling of compassion.

He hugged me again and tried to kiss me further. Silently, I pulled away, affecting girlish modesty.

He smiled at me in generous understanding. He kissed my hand, and then I turned and entered the warehouse.

He said, "Manuela, tonight, there is no luckier man than I. I have been given the sweetest flower."

I could not help it. I felt sorry for him, for how I was using him. "Won't you come in and have some chocolate?"

He accepted. Soon we were upstairs and Natán was bringing us something to drink. He talked happily as he spoke of his plans for the future. I did not tell him that the children, of which he spoke, would not be possible.

At one point I asked Jonotás to bring me a cigar. James stopped talking about the future and said, very seriously, "I know that every woman in Panamá smokes, high born or low—I have never seen the like—but I do not like it."

I slowly took the cigar out of my mouth. I could feel my neck grow hot from the anger rising in me. That is the first time I saw that getting married might bring freedom in one way—in another, there might be bondage.

I remember thinking, *Wait until we are married, James Thorne, and then I will do as I wish.* Instead I said, "Maybe it's the insects; I noticed that everyone in Guayaquil smokes, even the children." I fought with my temper. I did not want to ruin what I had set out to have.

"Yes, perhaps," he said, and went on talking.

I did not feel sorry for him anymore, and I ended the conversation soon after, politely but abruptly. As I stood in the doorway and watched him walk away, I told myself, *I have taken this opportunity, and that is the end of it. I will no longer reproach myself. It is done.*

Had I been a man, I might have had more choices; but some form of prostitution was all I could see in my future. The only other possibility was the worse condition of all in this world of men—impoverished womanhood.

I would have stolen either affection or money at that time to keep from going to Spain and to gain adult independence. However, I never realized how far reaching, and binding, the decisions I was making in those moments were.

Perhaps it all worked out for the best. After all, the course of action I took did lead me finally into the arms of the man I truly loved. It is possible that I would have met Bolívar anyway but I, of course, had no idea of such at the time. I only thought about my desperate need to climb above my poor beginnings.

It was done. I would have what I had wanted. What I did not realize was that I had escaped my past by muddling my future. The chains I put on myself that day weighed me down for the rest of my life.

Chapter 25

Not too long after our betrothal, James left Panamá on a business trip. I went about my life as usual. I think I was avoiding the thoughts that came to my mind when I imagined married life with James.

In the mean time, my father continued to make plans to leave for Spain on schedule. I was to be left quite a lot of furniture as well as business and personal items to sell while I finished up our affairs. The proceeds, along with the money I had saved from my wages, eventually provided me with a good deal of my own money when I finally left for Perú.

There were also several items left over from my father's marriage that I inherited, such as mirrors, brushes, a small writing desk, and a few other things, which I took with me to Perú. The day he left, my father made a special point to present me with a possession of his which I had long admired—his Turkish pistols.

They were of shiny steel, ornamented with brass and set with white alabaster handles. Having true beauty in their craftsmanship, they gave a most stunning impression when their oak box, lined with red velvet, was opened.

"I know that you have long admired these. I want to give them to you—a special gift to remember me by." As he handed me the finely polished box, which he held open, I beamed with happiness.

"Oh, Papa, how wonderful of you."

He smiled and said, "You might need them."

I set them down and threw my arms around him, tears filling my eyes. I loved him despite all of our arguments and I knew I would miss him. He held me close and said, "Take care of yourself after I leave, Manuela." I held him for a long, long time and I thought I heard him sniffing back a tear.

Later, I had holsters made for my pistols, with my name inlaid in brass on both. It is noteworthy that although I was about to be married, the name I placed on these holsters was "Manuela Sáenz."

He departed for Spain about a month earlier than I had anticipated. He left at about the same time that we heard the news that Chile had been liberated by San Martín and O'Higgins, and was completely under patriot rule after the decisive battle at Chacabuco. After hearing that news, I don't think my father could depart for Spain fast enough.

Fortunately, he had finished nearly all of his business affairs before he left. It was not long after that when I finished off the last of my father's commitments in Panamá. With everything done, I could leave at any time.

A month or so later, James returned from sea. My dowry of 8,000 pesos was safely banked, and we were ready to take a ship to Lima.

Before I left Panamá, one more thing happened concerning Juan Guzmán. A few days before I left, customs officials came to my address—I was staying with friends—and told me they were about to arrest him. They were looking for confirmation of piracy to use at his trial in addition to other charges. They had reports, but nothing they could depend on.

"To tell you the truth," said one of the men, who was a large, overfed, Spanish official, the kind I despised, "his nefarious behavior is well known, but nothing is substantiated. These reports of piracy, especially, would cause him to go to the Cartagena dungeon."

"Why do you come to me?" I asked.

"We were actually looking for Simón Sáenz. Your father, no?"

"Yes."

"Yes. We are contacting everyone who knew him."

We talked awhile longer, and then I did something I should not have done. I lied to them. I told them an elaborate story, full of details, which made Guzmán a pirate. I'm sure he was, from the stories I had received from my friends, but I had no first-hand knowledge.

Since I was leaving in a day or so, I knew I could not stay around to openly accuse him, and so I wrote out a statement. I was to discover later that Guzmán went to the Cartagena dungeon. I assume it was at least in part due to my testimony. When I found out he was in Cartagena, I was more than sorry. That is what I intended, but I ended up regretting it.

If I had thought it all out the day I lied and truly imagined sending someone to prison, I would not have done it. What I thought that day was, *He should be stopped. It does not matter if I lie. The rest of the world lies, and La Sáenz will not let human goodness stand in her way.*

The officials looked happy to have my statement; they complimented me on my civic duty and left. I then put Juan Guzmán out of my mind.

In the afternoon of the eve of our departure, a letter arrived from my brother. He admonished Father and me for not writing, though we had actually written every month or more. Our letters were not finding him. The reason for this became evident as I read on. He had enlisted in the famous Numancia Battalion of the king's soldiers.

When I read the words, my heart froze. This was like a death sentence for him. Everyone had heard about these warriors. They were the hardest fighters in America. More than once they had saved a battle for the Royalist forces—defeating the most determined rebels. They were the very best of Spanish soldiery. I cursed him. Why had he been so foolish? James and I had to board a ship and depart the next morning. I had no time to write him back or ponder his fate, but I was terrified for him. Why would he decide to put himself in such danger? I did not know it then, but one day I would be glad about it.

James did not want me to take my slaves to Perú. "You will have plenty of servants in Lima. You don't need them," he explained, but I knew that was not his true reason. He had learned to hate them, from the very day he had helped to purchase them. However, by that time, Jonotás and Natán were more important to me than anyone. We were inseparable and I would not have gone anywhere without them. He was jealous of them, and that is why he hated them. However, James and I left Panamá according to schedule, along with Jonotás and Natán.

The journey to Lima was less eventful than the one I had taken to Panamá. I did become sick almost immediately, for a day, as I did on my first sea excursion. However, I recovered quickly. After I no longer felt queasy, I tried unsuccessfully to get to know my future husband.

Because James and I were yet to be married in Lima, he had one cabin, and my slaves and I had a separate one, for decency's sake. I was glad to have my companions along, as I was not willing to have my future husband's full attentions just yet. They provided me with isolation when I wanted it. Married or not, Thorne expected more intimacy than I was ready to give him. I know he would not have taken me to bed then, as his religious principles would not permit it, but he was desirous of my body up to (but not including) that restriction.

I might have shared my body more readily if I could have also shared my mind. We had been together only a few times since my betrothal and it was always a strain for me. I was not speaking freely with him and so I always felt as though we were strangers. Whenever we did converse, he rarely talked about England or himself or anything else of any actual interest to me. With James, everything was business.

Once I asked him, "James, why did you ask me to marry you?"

He smiled and said, "I have long admired your beauty, ever since the first time I saw you, almost two years ago. However, it was watching you, so strong, capable, and able to handle yourself in your encounter with that swindler Guzmán that really made me decide to ask for your hand. A perfect example of why one should demand proper letters of introduction. Often in business, one will find . . . ."

Thus would all of our conversations go. I would try to talk of him or myself or our relationship, and the conversation would become a discussion of proper business tactics. This particular conversation, I wish I had pursued. Later, when I showed the same spirit he said he admired, he found my behavior aberrant.

Unlike my voyage to Panamá, none of the sailors threatened me in any way. On the contrary, they were most pleasant to me. The only threat came from my future husband.

One particularly handsome young man addressed me with a friendly greeting one day. "Good morning, Señorita," he said as I came on deck. He was coiling a rope that he pulled out of my way as I walked to the side of the ship.

"Good morning to you. You are up early," I said, rubbing my eyes.

He smiled and said, "Oh, I've been up since dawn."

I laughed lightly and said, "You are right. *I* have arisen late."

"Manuela!" James had come up behind me.

I spun around. I could see him watch the sailor move off. "Yes? Did you want something?" His manner upset me and I knew that I was about to have a fight with my husband to be. I gritted my teeth in order to keep from saying anymore.

When he saw the sailor was gone, he smiled at me and said, "Nothing. I just wanted to say 'Good Morning.'"

I could see the blood leaving his face as he relaxed. Here was a man who could easily be jealous without cause. I had no intention to give him cause, but my innocent conversation with a sailor had obviously angered him.

I did not like it. It promised to be a problem for me later. I excused myself and returned to my cabin. If I had stayed, an unseemly argument would have occurred in front of the crew.

While we were still in Panamá, because we were not really communicating with each other, I had been in a state of worry that he would change his mind about marrying me. Once we were aboard ship and under way, I relaxed because I was sure that he would marry me after all. However, he was feeling more confident too, I think, because as soon as we were at sea, he stopped courting me the way he had in Panamá. He seemed to have lost all interest in *me* as a person and seemed interested only in a physical romance, which interest I did not share. He made an effort to communicate with me, when I insisted, but he was not attentive except in a demanding way. I think he loved me deeply, but his manner and his ideals conspired to stifle the expression of that love.

The weather was fine and warm. The scenery as we proceeded down the coast was beautiful. My female companions were delightful company. Everything was in harmony, except for the discordant notes which James and I "sang" as we attempted to communicate to each other. Neither of us was really seeing or giving up to the other's point of view.

Before I was three days on that ship, I began to ask myself (as I believe many young brides do, once they see the reality of marriage), "What have I done?"

Chapter 26

Every day throughout the trip, James tried to be alone with me and always it was impossible because of Jonotás and Natán. I had told them particularly to be around me constantly, and why. They understood, as they always have, the desires of my heart, and obliged me.

"Manuela, we are alone," James said as he came into my tiny cabin one afternoon after we had been at sea several days. The ship tacked just as I was standing up. I lost my balance and fell into his arms.

After we recovered, he held me close. "Manuela, I have longed to hold you like this." He tried to kiss me. I resisted a little, and he said, "I know, we are not married yet, but. . ."

Before he could finish, Jonotás and Natán opened the door, "Manuelita!" Jonotás said excitedly, as she entered. James stepped away from me. When Jonotás saw us, she became serious. "Oh, I am sorry, Ma'am."

"That is all right."

"We will wait outside, Ma'am," she said subserviently and closed the door.

After we were alone again, James said, "Really, Manuela, why do you allow them to address you in the diminutive? They are slaves, after all." I said nothing, but I gave him a look that I hoped would tell him I did not like the criticism. "It's disgusting. Everywhere you go, there they are. 'Manuelita! Manuelita!'" he mocked.

I was perturbed and did not hide it. "I allow it because it amuses me, Señor."

"But, Manuela, it is not right." He stopped when he saw my face become darker. "Oh, Manuela, let's not argue. We have so little time alone." He put out his arms. At that moment, we heard a howl outside the door.

Natán came in. "Ma'am, come quick, it is Jonotás."

I rushed to the door. Jonotás was sitting against the bulkhead holding her ankle. She appeared to be in terrible pain. Natán said, "She fell, Manuelita."

"Help me get her inside, James."

He let out a sigh and picked her up. As he carried her to a bed in my cabin, she said gratefully, "Oh, Señor, you are most strong."

As he set her down, he said, "I'll fetch the surgeon."

"No, Señor, thank you. I am fine. Just let me rest." She carefully stretched out her leg and laid it down. The pain appeared to be unbearable.

"Well, Manuela, perhaps we can see each other later," James said, curtly, and left. As soon he closed the door, I started to look at Jonotás's ankle. Before I took one step, she sprang to her feet, ran to the door, and peered out.

"'Oh, Señor, you are most strong,'" I scoffed. They both giggled, and I laughed too. They cleverly saved me from too much intimacy with my future husband many times during the trip. By the end of the voyage, James was thoroughly disgusted with them.

While I did not get to know my future husband much better on that journey, I did get a chance to learn about my new friends, Jonotás and Natán.

Jonotás was about five years older than I. Born on a sugar plantation in Jamaica, she and her mother had been brought to Panamá to be household maids while she was still very young. So young that she had forgotten almost all but a few words of English. There, in the same house, she met Natán, who had been born on the Isthmus and who was younger by a year. A deep friendship developed.

I was very interested in their childhood and asked many questions. "I always had a bad face," Jonotás told me when I asked about her complexion. A life-threatening illness when she was very young was the cause. "I don't remember the illness. I do remember havin' to fight with folks that didn't 'preciate my beauty." She laughed. "I was much better at makin' fun of them, than fightin' them, when I learned I could do it." I recognized a kindred soul here. Jonotás was more clever than I; instead of fighting all the time, she had learned to be a jokester to defend herself from the cruelty of other children.

She told me something else that made me feel close to her. Like me, she had lost her mother. I thought the manner of her loss was even more bitter than my own. "I remember somethin' that happened when I was near a baby," she said, in response to a question of mine. She was helping Natán, who was putting on some new earrings, but her eyes drifted toward the horizon. "I was so young I was still spendin' my days in the hut for babies. All these black infants sittin' 'round a big wood bowl, eatin' milk out of it, usin' seashells for spoons. Some old black woman was sittin' there tendin' the babies, but they was too many. I was cryin' but she didn't come over to me.

"The reason I was sad was 'cause my mama was working in the cane field. I wanted her, but I couldn't see her till after dark. I cried and cried, but my mama didn't come, and the old woman just kept holding that other little baby.

"I fretted 'bout my mama again and again when I was growin'. I missed her 'most every day she was workin'. I slept with her at night, and then I was happy. When we were sold and come to Panamá, I was with her all day long. I was so happy then. But later, the worst thing ever happened."

That was the first time I saw Jonotás look sad. She looked like she was fighting back tears. I walked over to her and took her hand.

She looked at me and said, "My mama was sold."

The horror of it made tears come to my own eyes. I put my arms around her.

Jonotás pulled away and tried to laugh as she gave a friendly shove to Natán and said, "I nearly died of grief if it wasn't for ol' Natán here."

Natán took the earring out of Jonotás's hand and patted her affectionately on the cheek.

Jonotás went on, her voice fighting off sorrow, "I never saw my mama again." By then, tears were streaming down my face and she had to comfort me. Soon we were all laughing at being so morose.

Fortunately, Natán's parents were always within a few leagues of where she was. She had been separated from them by sale also, but she saw them two or three times a week. Her stability helped Jonotás bear her grief. By some miracle, Jonotás and Natán stayed together despite being sold three times before my father bought them.

When they were adolescents, they were sold to a spinster woman. That was where Jonotás really developed her talent as a mime. The old lady had a friend who was an actress, and she invited the performer to stay with her for several months. Upon observing Jonotás's sharp wit and talent for mimicry, the actress, who had played in comedies for almost 20 years, had said, "No one can make me laugh like you." She befriended Jonotás and taught her many tricks of the art of imitation.

One time, the actress invited an English dandy, with very effeminate manners, to her room. His name was Jonathan. After he left, Jonotás began imitating him. She made the actress laugh so hard that forever after she called her Jonotás—"Jonathan" as one might say it in Spanish.

Jonotás said, "I told the lady, if I was going to be Jonathan, then my friend here would be Nathan." She laughed with delight and patted Natán on the back. Then they both laughed. I cannot tell what their real names are. They both told me they did not like what they had been called and made me promise never to reveal them.

Jonotás learned something more than imitation from the experienced artiste. It seemed the lady was something of a wanton, able to seduce any man to whom she might take a fancy. By example, Jonotás learned much about the art of love from the actress. For as long as I knew my friend, despite her ugliness, Jonotás was always able to have a man if she was feeling amorous.

Natán on the other hand was shy and reserved. She was contemplative by nature and, except when goaded on by Jonotás, she usually kept to the background. She was very beautiful, but she stayed away from men. Not only did she not seem very interested in romance, she did not even seem to attract men due to her social reticence.

"I don't want no man," she said when I asked her about her shyness. "I hate it when someone tries to use me dishonest like. I been used by my masters, even though I told 'em I was a decent girl." She lowered her eyes. "Even men that seem kind at first, when their wives don't look, they are after me. I can tell what a man is goin' to do when I first meet him." She smiled at me. "I'm glad I'm with you now."

I was glad she was with me, too. She had a piercing intelligence that was of benefit to me on more than one occasion. When it came to deducing the true heart of a person, no one was her equal. She was always quiet and calm, and I recognized in her the peaceful soul that I longed to be.

From the beginning, I think they liked me as much as I liked them. I never lied to them or treated them with less respect than I treated any of my other friends, and they knew it. They knew when to act subservient, in the presence of those to whom it might matter, and when to be themselves.

If they accompanied me when I went out, I indulged them whenever they displayed the same misbehavior I had seen the first time I saw them. Natán always dressed in a gaudy manner, and Jonotás smoked with me and would exchange banter with the street people as we passed. They annoyed everybody that had a mind to conservative social airs, like my future husband. I adored them.

When we were alone, they made my life very pleasant. Jonotás would not let anyone else bathe me or pamper me, because she took such delight in the chore. Natán kept my life and belongings organized. We were a perfect team.

Despite how much I enjoyed my female companions, James and I did not do so well. Every time we were together, it was an effort for me, due to our inability to communicate to each other. However, James did not seem to concern himself with our relationship at all. He was no more attentive to me than he would be to a business associate—except when we were alone. I think he assumed he had me—there was nothing more to worry about in regards to our relationship—and he need only mold me into the right kind of woman.

Only once did he demonstrate any deep feelings for me other than "passion," and that emotion was jealousy. He had the captain of the ship punish the sailor who talked to me after he saw the young man speak to me again. I was very angry about that, as the sailor's manner had been decent and innocent. The tone of our marriage to come was forecast on that trip to Lima.

Except for the strain between James and me, it was a delightful journey that ended one morning in a glorious way. I was awakened by a cacophony coming from the throats of hundreds of birds. I dressed, washed my face, and ran up to the deck with Jonotás and Natán behind me. The sun was just breaking over the Peruvian Andes behind the spires and domes of our destination. We had arrived before midnight, but customs laws require disembarkation to be in daylight and so we stayed at anchor in the harbor.

There I stood, the ship rocking softly amid the brilliant color, the avian "symphony," and the motion of so many seabirds in the air. I looked around the harbor of Callao. All about us graceful winged creatures were making circles over the water, gathering their breakfast: huge pelicans with their beaks full of fish, petrels flying slowly on their long wings, and gulls of many varieties. Behind us was the barren Island of San Lorenzo (barren except for a signal post to communicate with the fortress of Callao and a quarry manned by prisoners). To our right was the famous impregnable fortress that housed soldiers, called the "Royal Philip." From the angle that I was at, it looked like two large flat hats sitting next to each other, with flag poles atop each one.

There were perhaps a dozen ships in the harbor between where we were anchored and the town of Callao directly inland from the fortress. The masts of the ships between us and the shore kept shifting in the swells, and the sun was in my eyes, so I could not see the town very well. I learned later there was not much there to see.

To the left of Callao, I could see the steeples of the tallest churches of Lima standing above the rise that blocked our view of the rest of the city. Lima is inland two leagues, at the end of a road following the small Rimac River that meanders to the coast from the surrounding hills.

Beyond Lima itself, one could see the western cordillera of the Andes. On the shore, and all about the town and fortress, the barrenness of the Peruvian coast lay like a blanket.

James had told me in Panamá, "When you stop seeing trees, you're in Perú," and it was true. On the trip southward, at one particular point, all we could see was desert. From then on, the little towns we passed seemed very insignificant, there being very little to sustain life in them. Even Paita, the largest town where we stopped, was very much as it is today, only a few termite-infested houses on the beach.

It was strange to have arrived so soon at our destination because, though we had traveled twice the distance as my trip from Guayaquil to Panamá, it had taken half the time. We had made no "side trips."

Several hours after we dropped anchor, our trunks and effects being secure and waiting ashore, we were given permission to disembark. The four of us departed for land in a small boat rowed by a dark-skinned, smiling youth.

When we arrived at the shore, we pulled alongside the oddest pier I have ever seen. I said, "It looks like a shipwreck."

The youth said, "Yes, Señorita, my father told me that when they wanted to make a pier 40 years ago, they ran this old ship aground. Then they filled it with stones and sand and rubbish. Funny, no?"

I allowed that it was funny, but actually quite practical. It was protected from the sea and held in place by mangrove pilings brought from Guayaquil, and it looked like it would last 400 years at least.

When we landed, I finally had a good look at the few poor houses that make up the town of Callao, at the entrance to the castle. Callao had been a large town less than 100 years earlier, situated directly south of its present site. However, it had been swallowed up by the ocean during the earthquake of 1746.

One can still see the ruins, at times, under the water. The superstitious say the dead souls killed in that earthquake still continue on about their business in the underwater town. Some are adamant that, if you listen carefully, you can hear a cock crow at dawn from under the sea.

Further on down the coast, a league or two to the south, is the beautiful little village of Magdalena, used as a retreat by the wealthy members of Lima society. This town was later to have much meaning in my life, but it was to be some time before I actually went there.

The customs official who questioned James knew him. When he found out that the well-liked Don Jaime was bringing home his bride-to-be, the man let us pass without further ado.

"Many congratulations, Don Jaime. Many years of happiness, Señorita," he said as we walked away.

We went a short distance to a drawbridge and through an arched gateway, which was the entrance to the road to Lima. There, James's servants were waiting with a wagon in which our belongings had already been loaded. There was also a *calesa* for us to traverse the two leagues to the city. Other arriving travelers were also climbing into *calesas*; some were double-sized, being there for hire.

On the road, just outside of Callao, we passed the ruins of an ancient native village to our right. These interesting little mounds of earth, which had been huts centuries before, have never been adequately studied and I wondered at the time if they would be forgotten by future generations.

Halfway up the route is a chapel and a small cloister dedicated to the Virgin of Mount Carmel, the protectress of seamen. This is called *La Legua*, being "one league" from Lima.

The road itself is better than any other I have seen in the colonies, meticulously paved with stones. It is unfinished, however. Its completion was interrupted when the former viceroy, Abascal, whose grand design became more apparent as we approached the city, had to retire unexpectedly. The current viceroy, Pezuela, was appointed to handle the growing revolutions. This had caused Abascal, one of Lima's greatest reformers, to lose his position. Where we started, at the beach, is the most unfinished part of the road. As we approached the last third of the journey, we could begin to see beautiful gardens on either side, giving evidence of the original plan for the groves of shade trees and flowers meant to follow the entire road down to Callao.

As we approached the city, tall willows flanked both sides of the road, which itself was edged by stone walls. Benches had been built right into the stone every 100 yards or so. The shade that dappled the broad avenue and the beautiful vegetation all about gave one the impression of entering a grand and ancient city of mythical beings.

We passed through the ornately decorated main gate, which had a center door for wheeled vehicles and two side doors for pedestrians. Overhead, the city's shield, consisting of three crowns, was carved into the archway. Lima is known as "The City of Kings," having been founded on January 6, the day of the celebration of the Magi.

As I entered, I was somewhat disappointed. Humans lived in this city after all, not mythical giants. In front of us, we were faced with a long street of low houses. From these came poor citizens of all colors, and there was a profusion of beggars. This, one of the poorest quarters of the city, greets every traveler coming up from Callao.

The dust in the street was mixed with the dung of numberless mules that continually trod through the streets forever being powdered by the elements. This noxious mixture arose from the *calesas* in front of us, making the atmosphere repugnant. It did not help that a ditch carrying waste ran down the center of the street, which added greatly to the smell. All of Lima's streets were thus.

Our *calesa* and the wagon with our trunks finally made it to the center of town, where James had told the driver to go. There, we passed through the busy Plaza Mayor that held much more of the promise of the great city that Lima was. On one whole side of the plaza was the cathedral with its twin towers. All around the perimeter were the various office buildings for the Viceroyalty's government, including the viceroy's palace. The square was extremely crowded with stalls set up in long rows—many with white cloth coverings over them. In a glance I could see dandies walking their ladies, fine society women and men on expensive horses winding their way through the crowd, military officers, monks, Indians, Africans, water bearers, mules, llamas, and flowers, all in a vast milieu of motion and color.

There were also many women dressed in an unfamiliar and strange fashion. These women, I soon discovered, were called *tapadas*, which I will explain later.

Above the noise of people talking and selling their wares and urging their animals forward could be heard the calls from various street peddlers: "*¡Jazmín! ¡Jazmín! ¡Señoritas, jazmín!*" or the long cry of the cake-seller, or the woman selling tisanes for all kinds of ailments, or the man selling lottery tickets. "*¡Lotería! ¡Lotería!*"

I know I was wide eyed, and James chuckled at me. But I had cause to be excited. I had entered one of the most stimulating places in the world, which appeared at first glimpse to contain all it promised. I could hardly wait until I was settled in and could begin to explore the city further.

Having shown me the square, James had the driver turn back westward a few blocks. There, we arrived in the district called San Sebastiano. This is a wealthy neighborhood, known for its beautiful homes and their elite owners. Thorne had his own house set in among them.

Similar to the other houses on the street, there was the massive front door in James's house with the usual big iron nails set in large planks. Also, there was the usual overhanging balcony with shutters. The shutters were a turned-wood grill work, which had a Moorish quality. A little higher up was an open balcony. The walls were painted a warm ochre.

Like all large houses in South America, immediately inside the door there was an entrance way, with small rooms off to the side, beyond which was a patio. As we entered the courtyard, I was delighted by many flowers blooming there in separated squares of color (planted by the servants especially for my arrival).

After being shown around the lower floor, we returned to the sweet-smelling courtyard, there to ascend the covered steps to the second story. The bedroom was a surprise.

The bed was tall and on a dais, as usual, at one extremity of the room. However, it was under a massive arch that covered that entire end of the bedroom. This was a feature I had never seen in a house before, but I was soon to learn that it is quite common in Perú. It is built to protect the sleeper from the roof falling in during an earthquake.

The servants were friendly to me, and the entire aspect was one of comfort and livability. I was delighted with my new home. Unfortunately, it would be awhile before I could stay there.

According to church laws, I could only marry in a town where I was a resident. My father had arranged for me to stay with his friend, Don Toribio Aceval, a retired knight in the Military Order of Calatrava, while I waited for the marriage banns to be announced.

I was fortunate to have such a fine place to stay. His wife was gracious and she began to introduce me to some of the society ladies. I don't think my slaves were appreciated, however, since I refused to make them stay in the Thorne household, but insisted they stay with me in my room.

Don Aceval was a very important person. He had the finest coach in Lima (next to that of the viceroy). Many people owned *calesas*, but only the most noble of families, grandees of Spain, were allowed to have many-wheeled coaches. The way I was treated by the knight and his family made me believe that I might no longer have to face the painful exclusion that I had felt all my life. It is difficult to describe when one finally feels a sense of belonging to, and being in some small way important to, a community. It was only an impression, and it was only because of James Thorne, but I felt how it would be. I knew it was a feeling, once fully felt, which I might not be able to do without.

On the morning of the second day, James informed me that he would be taking me to our marriage interview that afternoon, with no less a person then the Archbishop of Lima. I was surprised, because the investigation to see if there are any impediments to a marriage is ordinarily managed by a parish priest. However, Lima's senior cleric was a friend of Thorne's and, as a favor, he had agreed to do the interview himself.

I remember I wore a black veil to look as respectable as possible, but I need not have bothered. Archbishop Bartolomé María de las Heras was over 76 years old, and neither his vision nor his interest in me seemed very acute. Because he was James Thorne, I think my future husband could have married anybody.

The interview was supposed to determine whether James and I were too closely related in blood, had previous marriages for which no divorce had been obtained or if there were any other such obstacles to our union. Because of the details that might come out in such an interview, I expected to find out a great deal more than I did about James Thorne. All I "discovered" was that he was "over 25," he had left England as a young man, and he had been a prisoner, in 1812, at Cádiz.

When I asked him to clear up this mystery later, he changed the subject. How he went from prisoner to a man acquainted with the archbishop, the viceroy, and the rest of Lima's elite, as well as being one of its wealthiest businessmen, in the five intervening years, I never found out. I am curious to this day.

When we left the interview, I asked him to take me for a ride. Although I had been for a couple of short walks, my hosts were very demanding of my time and very protective. I wanted to see more of the city, and James obliged me. We drove through the city and James was taciturn as usual, except when I asked him questions about the city. When we reached the city gates, we drove out into the weald as far as the roads would take us before we turned back.

I was impressed and fascinated with him after the interview, and I told him that I loved him. I don't think it was the truth, but I was letting myself (or making myself) feel something for him because I very much wanted to stay in Lima and because I wanted to make our marriage happy. When we were far outside the city, he took me in his arms and we kissed each other hungrily. I was beginning to want some intimate companionship by that time. Between kisses, I put my lips to his ear and said seductively, "Why don't you take me back to your house?"

That was a mistake. He pulled away, saying, "I do not think that is a good idea." When I gave him a puzzled looked, he frowned at me and said sternly, "We must wait." He did not speak again until he said "Good-bye" at the door to my residence.

I was frustrated and felt rejected. By the time I went to bed that night, I was fearful he was having second thoughts about me. I had felt so certain about my future earlier in the day.

As I lay awake between sheets of fine cotton and Belgian lace, I wondered what I, a bastard, was doing there. Was I ever going have the acceptance and respectability that seemed so close?

The next morning, James came by and took me for a walk. He was sullen and uncommunicative as we walked around the block of my residence. I tried to persuade him to talk to me, and he appeared to make an effort, but our conversation did not flow. I questioned him subtly about how he was feeling about me, without appearing too bold or too worried. I could not tell for certain whether he had doubts about proceeding with the marriage, or, as I suspected, it was only his religious convictions that had held him back the day before.

Guessing what was on his mind, I said, "I'm sorry about yesterday, James. You are right. We must wait."

"Yes, Manuela."

We fell into a long silence until I asked him about his business affairs. He began to tell me about his latest successes. Discussing business seemed to change his mood.

I realized I should have spent more time with him on the ship. At that moment, I regretted keeping him at such a distance. I wanted to understand him and find some way to love him. However, unable as I was to control the situation, I knew we had to spend more time together, even if we only discussed business.

When he was about to leave me at the knight's house after our walk, I said, "James, I would so love to have dinner in the house which is to be mine. Don't you think it would be possible for me to come over and eat with you tonight or tomorrow?"

He gave me a critical look and said, "People might talk if we were alone together."

"I will simply go for a walk with my slaves at promenade time and come to your house. No one need know."

He considered it for a long time and said, "Very well. Come this evening. We'll eat late."

I left for promenade early, so that my hosts would not try to accompany me. I walked directly to James's house, so that I would lessen the chances of being seen and possibly be joined by any of the knight's friends who had already been introduced to me.

We ate while the rest of Liman society was out for a walk. However, during dinner I was again faced with what seemed like only perfunctory social interaction from my future husband. He confused me more than ever. I guessed that he was only fighting his natural desire to be more intimate with me than he felt he should. However, I was not sure.

Later, as we walked in the courtyard, I could stand the mystery no longer. I threw my arms around him and kissed him, to see how he would respond. He returned my kiss. He pulled back and looked at me with painful intensity. I pressed my breast against him and held him close to me. Then he lifted me in his arms and took me up the wooden stairs to his bedroom. There, half-dressed, James Thorne and I were intimate for the first time.

James and I were as incompatible in bed as any two people can be, I think. At the time, I had hopes that things would change, but I was foolish to think so. He was too wrapped in guilt about the sexual act, and he was, by nature, conservative and inexpressive. I should have known then our relationship would never work, and perhaps I did, but I could not have done anything differently.

He was passionate, that first time, because he was in need, but he did not fulfill my desires in any way. I think he suspected that I had not been satisfied at his completion, although he did not ask. However, I made a generous show of being happy, and he relaxed with me and talked a little before falling asleep.

I was relieved that he never mentioned, at that time or any other, that I was not a virgin. I think he suspected, long before that evening and never brought it up in order to spare us both the ordeal of discussing my past.

I crept downstairs as soon as I could. I found Jonotás and Natán in the kitchen with all the servants. They were all laughing while they watched Jonotás pick an imaginary pear from an imaginary tree. I motioned to Natán, and the two of them met me outside a few minutes later.

We walked quickly back to my quarters. I wanted to return before arousing the suspicions of the people in the knight's household. By the time we arrived, the sun had set only minutes before.

The next morning, James came by quite early and asked to speak to me alone. We went for a walk in the garden, and he was quite determined as he made a point of telling me we had to wait until we were married before continuing our sexual relationship. He looked ashamed and said, "I feel I have dishonored you."

"No, James—"

"Yes. I am sorry." I didn't know what to say. In the silence he added, "We will be married soon. We must wait."

I agreed, but it was he who was kissing me, and touching me intimately, before we left the garden. That evening, he again invited me to dine, and he again took me to bed.

The next day was Saturday, and I had wanted to get out and explore the city. Before I could leave the house, one of James's servants brought me a note and a flower from his garden.

Manuela—

I will be over soon. I am going out now to make some arrangements, and then I must speak to you. It is important.

James

The urgency and obliqueness of his note unsettled me. I stayed in my room, uncertain about what he could want. He finally arrived, late in the afternoon, and asked to walk with me in the garden.

When we were alone, he said, "We are to be married tomorrow evening in the San Sebastiano church." He kissed my fingers and looked at me longingly.

"James, how can that be? I need to live in Lima longer than a few days. I cannot be considered a resident yet, can I? "

"It is all right. I spoke to the Archbishop, and he has given me special dispensation." I must have looked confused. He said, "Manuela, I cannot wait any longer. You are too seductive, and I must have you."

He took me in his arms and kissed me, hurriedly but passionately. "I will inform you of all you need to know tomorrow. My servants will bring you anything you want. Until then, my darling, I will suffer until I can legitimately have you."

He left hurriedly, his face flushed with passion. I stood alone in the garden and tried to take in the fact that what I had wanted was about to happen. Why did I feel apprehensive?

The banns require three consecutive church announcements on Sunday to see if anyone comes forward with a reason why a couple should not be married. James, however, could not wait. After only one such announcement, earlier that morning, we were married on the evening of Sunday, July 27, 1817, in a small but intimate ceremony. Only a few close friends of James Thorne were in attendance, and Don Toribio Aceval stood in for my father. I was 19 years old.

These "few close friends" were some of Lima's most formidable citizens, and I was looking forward to getting to know them all. As I left the church, I felt (for the first time in my life) that I owned something.

There was only one woman who momentarily gave me that old feeling of exclusion. She was the wife of one of James's friends, Domingo Orué. She wished me well but seemed aloof. Then, I could see that she envied me. She glanced at James with what I imagined was desire and said, "You are very lucky." She made me feel threatened.

Later her words came back to me. Was I "lucky?" Did I merely drift into what promised to be a pleasant life? No. I had made my way there full of purpose. Even then I felt apprehensive and sensed that I would eventually have to take responsibility for what I had caused to come about.

Chapter 27

Despite a wedding night that contained too much tension and too little pleasure, I awoke the next morning in a giddy excitement. No more would I have to fight for respectability. No more would I have to fight for acceptance. I was a woman now—grown and about to become a lady of Lima, a city that I felt was about to open up to me.

If I could, I would have become acquainted with all of Lima's society that very morning. I wanted to get out and enjoy the new friends I had met the night before. I wanted to see every part of my beautiful new city. I wanted to explore my new home as a free and adult woman. But it was not to be, not yet.

At breakfast I talked freely with James about the wedding ceremony, my plans to rearrange the garden, and other ideas that were on my mind.

"Manuela," he said, "I am so happy. How would you like me to take you to London?"

The thought thrilled me. The entire world was opening up to me. "Oh, James, how wonderful. Yes, please. I would love to go."

"Perhaps we will, soon."

We talked some more. I was very happy. I was enjoying myself and my husband very much. At one point, I said something about going back to the knight's house to pick up the rest of my personal items.

James looked at me strangely and said, "The servants will get them."

"I know, James, but I will enjoy the walk. Perhaps I will explore the city a bit."

Again he gave me a peculiar look. "You can't."

I put down my chocolate. He continued to watch me. "Why not?"

"You know."

"No. What?" He was silent and after a moment or two, it struck me as to what he meant. "Oh, James. You cannot be serious. No one strictly observes that custom."

"What are you saying? Of course they do."

"I am not going to do it."

"Yes, you are," he said sternly, his face flushed with anger. With our marriage not yet one full day old, the first of many arguments occurred, all having a similar theme: I expected to do as I pleased, and James expected me to follow his conservative principles. I acquiesced that day, in order to keep peace. However, James knew I was not happy.

Being newly married, James was insisting that I go into seclusion for one month, as was the custom. With the Virgin Mary being the ideal woman, the practice was no doubt started by women themselves, to avoid having to appear in public so soon after having engaged in the sexual act "for the first time" and thus admit to their humanity. Despite it being an ancient custom not strictly observed in this modern era, when it *is* enforced, it is by men, such as my husband, who wish to preserve the illusion.

While the four weeks after a wedding are spoken of as "seclusion" and a woman will not do much socializing, a new bride can be seen out now and then to take care of important affairs. I did not think it mattered much at all. However, James was quite insistent that I observe a strict seclusion. I was annoyed because he expected each element of the marriage ritual be observed to its fullest extent; but when it came to the banns, which were in his way, he was able to circumvent them.

This "seclusion" would be very difficult for me. I was enraged inside that I could not do what I wanted to do; imprisoned, as though I were back in the convent. It was worse than being in a convent, since I knew I would have to share my bed with a man I did not enjoy, every night. My deep anger was exacerbated by the realization that the same restriction would not apply to James. My marriage, once again, had proven to be a trap.

After breakfast that morning, I walked alone in the garden while my husband made ready to go out "on business." Once dressed, he came to the garden where I was standing, walked up to me from behind, and put his hands on my shoulders. His touch made me cold. He laid his cheek against my hair and said, "Oh, Manuela, I love you so deeply." He kissed my neck and whispered, "We could go upstairs before I have to leave."

I turned. I looked him in the eye and said quietly, but firmly, "I think not, Señor."

He returned my gaze for a long while. His expression changed from surprise, to hurt, to understanding. "Señora, I am sorry. I have presumed too much." His face grew stiff and he looked at his watch. "I must attend to business, but I will see you late this afternoon." He left.

I stood there fighting back tears of anger. Under my breath I said, "It is only for a month. It will work out, eventually."

For a couple of days after that, I did not do well. I became ill, and I'm sure it was due to the fact that I could not express myself freely. Ever since that evening walk with James back in Panamá, almost a year earlier, I had been holding back the things I wanted to say. Finally, I was married, an adult, and I was still not able to speak my mind.

In June, when I arrived in Lima, the sky was overcast nearly every day, which I found depressing in my solitude. To make my depression worse, I was becoming more convinced, with each passing day, that James Thorne and I were not, and never would be, right for each other. I felt I would explode with frustration trying to maintain a pleasant facade. To be also locked away was really too much.

After a few days, I apathetically pulled myself from my sick bed and tried to spend my time making a home. I found a stray puppy at the door the next morning and brought her in to feed. She was very dirty and quite ugly, even for a puppy, but I kept her because I could not bear to see a living thing abandoned. I called her "Antonia."

Having a pet did not sit well with James, but I insisted. We fought a day or so later when I took in a scrawny cat that came by. I called her "Abbess." The only interesting thing I did, which also seemed to please James, was to continue with my English lessons that I had begun back in Panamá. I even made an agreement with him that whenever practical, he and I would only speak English. I would learn faster that way. Because James seemed so pleased with my interest and progress, it was fun for me, but I continued to be otherwise bored and I was eager to get out.

However, there was conflict at night. James wished to be amorous, while I, feeling locked up, could not or would not give myself to him. He thought I was punishing him for adhering to the custom of seclusion. I was not. I simply could not experience passionate emotions while feeling trapped. My seclusion reminded me too much of my convent days, and thus was I reminded of the years of ostracism and humiliation I suffered in Quito.

From my windows, I could see the beautiful city of Lima, of which I had only a brief taste in the few days before my marriage. I desperately wanted to see more. I wanted to meet the people who were my neighbors. I could not count myself as having really achieved respectability until I could be certain that I was truly accepted by those around me.

I thought about simply leaving and enjoying the city after my husband left the house on business, but I was afraid I would run into him and cause serious damage to our relationship. I wanted to have the life of wealth and position I sought and so I did not want to displease my husband by flagrantly disobeying him.

After a few days, I decided vicarious experiences would be better than none. I sent Jonotás and Natán out one afternoon to buy some flowers and other decorations for the house. Lima was a new place for them also, and I gave them way too much money and admonished them jovially, "You are to find some exciting adventures and return with some good stories." Little did I realize how well such an investment would be repaid.

At the end of the first day I was a little disappointed. They told me of how they had discovered, in the suburb of San Lazaro across the river, many social organizations— called, in Lima, "*Las Cofradias.*"

"What kind of organizations are they?" I asked.

"For slaves," said Natán. She and Jonotás went on to explain that these are associations of the African slaves in Perú. Each group represented a different nation or tribe of the African continent. I learned that they have general meetings every Sunday and activities during the week. Jonotás and Natán had visited a number of these clubs and talked about the friends they had made there. They had spent all day with these friends and did not bring home any flowers or anything else except a big mangy dog of indefinable breed that had followed them. I kept him of course, naming him "Carlos," but I was a bit disappointed. There was not enough adventure in their stories, and I still needed some flowers.

Thus, I sent them out the next day. That evening, they came home late, with a curious excitement, a package, no flowers, and all their money spent. When I questioned them, they had no time to explain. James entered the house just then, and they motioned that I should wait.

That night as I prepared for bed, they teased me about the surprise. By the time I went to bed, I was so curious I almost burst. The following morning, after James left the house, they showed me what they had acquired—after a lengthy explanation.

They had learned something interesting the second day out. They learned that if a member of royalty of the nation represented by a *cofradia* is found living in the city, that person is called "king" or "queen" of the *cofradia* and treated with every royal respect possible by their "subjects." They had met a very old woman, the prime example of this "royalty," known as "Queen of the Mandingos."

Apparently she had been a princess in her own land. This pretense at royal airs is enjoyed by everyone, and I learned that on particular days she (like other "kings" and "queens" of these fraternities) is conducted from the house of her master, by a number of Africans, to the *cofradia*—dressed as gaudily as possible. For this purpose her young mistresses, in order to partake in the merriment, will lend her jewels to a considerable amount, to go with flowers, feathers, and other ornaments she wore. Also, her kindly master had presented her with a scepter inlaid with silver to enhance her regal stature among the other slaves. This she always had with her.

"We found her sittin' on her porch holdin' court," said Jonotás. She laughed with merriment and sat down in a chair very regally.

Natán said, "Her name is Mamma Rosa, and her subjects come to kiss her hand and receive a blessin'." Jonotás held out her hand. Natán went on. "We told her our whole story. We told of our arrival here, and the weddin', and we also told her how unhappy you are right now."

I started to protest, but Jonotás broke in. "The old woman laughed." Then she gave a regal scoff in imitation of Mama Rosa, followed by her own laughter of delight. "She pulled herself up in her chair and said, in a low voice, very serious, 'What about the solution of the *tapadas*?'"

Then, with a great deal of giggling, Jonotás and Natán quickly unwrapped their bundle and presented me with the most amazing invention for women I have ever seen— the *saya y manto*.

The *saya* is the walking dress of Lima. It is made of velvet or satin or other rich material that is pleated in tiny folds so it becomes tight fitting but stretchable. It hangs close to the body to show the shape of the wearer to the best advantage. At the bottom, near the ankles, it is decorated with lace or small flowers, or whatever the fashion might be. It is too narrow to allow the wearer to step forward freely. However, the short step adds to, rather than detracts from, a graceful look. It is usually dark, but it can be of all colors—especially when worn by members of the upper classes. Most often, it is wrapped around the dress that a woman might already be wearing.

The *manto* (mantle) is really a shawl, tied at the waist and worn over the head or around the neck. The *saya y manto* create a style that is peculiar to Lima. With the exception of evening promenades or other outings with their escorts, where the English or French costume is in fashion, no woman will go walking without it.

The "solution of the *tapadas*," as Mamma Rosa had put it, was in reference to a class of women seen walking in small groups. These women wear the *manto* in a special manner: covering all of their face—except for one eye. This fashion was undoubtedly influenced by the Moors, but nowhere else in South America will you see *tapadas* or even the *saya y manto*; and yet they are literally everywhere in Lima. It is surprising the fashion has not become popular elsewhere, because it affords women such freedom.

A *tapada* will go where no "respectable" woman would be seen, such as to certain sections of the bullfights or to cockfights. The men at such events feel no compunction to turn them away, since, with their faces hidden, their identity is unknown, and the usual rules of respectability have no meaning. They are usually seen in groups of three or four, and when so grouped, they are in complete control wherever they go. Their manner of dress, and the mystery created by hiding the face thus, seems to fascinate men and they draw attention that other women do not receive (a respectable woman being unapproachable without an introduction). Also, through skillful manipulation of the *manto*, revealing only half the face, or a shoulder and the upper part of the breast, a woman can make herself quite irresistible.

Consequently, women who are considered "respectable" take up the ways of *tapadas*. A young woman can leave her father's house dressed decently to go to market or to church, and within one block she can be transformed into a woman of the city, going where she wishes to go and doing what she wishes to do, by merely covering her head except for one eye.

Having only been in Lima a few days, I had seen *tapadas*, which are everywhere, but I did not understand their significance. I saw how easily I might fit into the picture.

I was, of course, delighted at their brilliant "solution," and I hugged and kissed Jonotás and Natán as we all giggled with joy at the implications. They had wisely decided to buy a *saya* and *manto* for each of us, all colored a dull inconspicuous brown. We pulled on the garments, Jonotás making a few adjustments for both Natán and me, having more closely observed the style, and we went out.

Our house is only a few blocks from the main square so we walked in that general direction, taking a turn now and then to look at an interesting house or building. We saw many new and delightful sights and had a grand time.

We walked through the neighborhoods to the south and east of the square. Then, as we were looking at the Church of San Pedro, I noticed a beautiful mansion close by. It was the most magnificent house I have ever seen, before or since. It was more impressive than the neighboring church.

"Who lives in this house, sir?" I asked a passerby.

"The Marqués de Torre Tagle, of course," said the man who tried to peer beneath my *manto* to see who could be so stupid.

I had never heard of him. I thought, perhaps James, who had mentioned most of Lima's great family names, must not know them. I was wrong.

As we continued our circuitous tour, we saw other churches and we visited the crypt that holds the remains of Santa Rosa de Lima. There had been many nuns, when I was at the convent, who had said Marian de Jesús from Quito should be canonized, but it has never happened. Consequently, it is Lima that has given birth to the only canonized saint from the new world.

As we walked through the streets, we saw the hall of the inquisition, which was a tiny little building with fat columns in the Greek style—very pretentious.

Finally, we came to the Plaza Mayor, with its famous brass fountain in the center and the cathedral built by Pizarro. More impressive than the architecture was its throng of people. It is in the center of the city if you include the district of San Lazaro across the bridge. On one side of the square is the palace of the viceroy with its intricately carved stonework. It looked fairly impressive on the outside, but I found out later that it was not so elaborate on the inside after all.

On the opposite edge of the square, on the south, there are private houses. It is on this side of the street where Pizarro's palace used to be and where he was murdered. Also, this is where the ex-viceroy, Don Ambrosio O'Higgins, had a shop when he was a poor merchant. This man started as a simple Irish peddler but failed in his attempts to sell his wares, so he left for Chile to make his fortune. There he became captain-general and eventually he was promoted to viceroy.

The west side of the square is similar to the south except that there are civic offices and the jail at one end. In this square the largest market in the new world is held, and it is a delight to the eye. All of Lima comes to this plaza to shop. In food stock alone, in less than a minute, I saw beef, mutton, pork, salted and dried meats, sausages, salt fish, mackerel, shrimp, poultry (both slaughtered and alive), peas, lentils, maize of several varieties, *gurbansos*, cassava root, camote, potato, yam, *okra*, grapes, peaches, apricots, nectarines, apples, pears, pomegranates, tomatoes, strawberries, melons, guavas, *guanabanas*, oranges, limes, citrons, plantains, and bananas.

Large pebbles are placed between the vendors, and between the vendors and the walking area, to make a definite division between each space. The portion of the square allocated to the flower sellers is called the "street of danger" because the women selling the flowers, with their own beauty enhanced by the beauty of their "wares," are too irresistible for a man to walk among without falling in love. The mixture of fragrances and colors in such quantity, the lovely faces of the flower girls themselves, plus the parade of beautiful women walking or riding by with their shawls and hats and colorful dress, and the handsome men attending them, all form a picture that is exquisitely pleasing to all of the senses.

As I stood up from smelling some of those flowers, I saw James walking out of the Archbishop's palace. He was walking right towards me, and he looked stern, possibly angry. I pulled my *manto* closer about my face. He meandered through the confusion in the square, still walking swiftly toward me. I stood frozen. He reached me, then walked past, and finally stopped to purchase a nosegay from a pretty flower girl. Then, he walked on. I finally breathed.

As we continued our excursion, we saw many other sights, including the home of the famous actress called La Perricholi, the woman who had captured the heart of a viceroy. She was in her seventies when I first arrived in Lima. In her younger days, this lady, although only an actress with no social position of any kind, had eventually become Lima's most powerful woman. Her house, the Quinta de la Presa, was designed by her lover, the Viceroy Amat. It was almost a palace itself, beautifully decorated, with two stories, fine large windows, and ornate balconies. I will tell her story soon.

I returned to my house happy that afternoon, for the first time in days. However, I arrived only minutes before James. When he entered the house, he still had the flowers, but they were wilted.

"I'm sorry, Manuela," he said, as he handed them to me. "I meant to bring them right home, but I found I had to attend to an urgent matter which detained me." He looked disappointed.

I was so grateful about his being detained that I took the flowers and gave him a kiss on the cheek. "They're lovely, James. That was very thoughtful." Jonotás and Natán gave me a look from across the room that said *we were lucky.*

I did not tell him that I had been out that day, and he either did not notice or chose not to remark on my renewed energy that evening. The servants, fortunately, kept quiet.

In the next couple of weeks, I was able to escape, as though from a secular convent, once or twice a week dressed as a *tapada*. Those excursions saved me from withering during my seclusion. I wanted to get out more often, but I did not want to risk being found out. My relationship with James was fragile enough.

Chapter 28

When my month of seclusion ended, custom dictated that James and I visit everyone who had attended our wedding. I considered it a great opportunity, and I urged James to introduce me to all the families with whom he was acquainted, not just those at our wedding. He agreed.

Matrimony had proved less than a blissful institution, but I had never expected happiness. I had accepted James's proposal because of my hunger for respectability. I still had hopes of making a happy marriage, but whether my union with James was pleasant or not, I was determined to use his connections to establish myself in the city that I now considered my home. Respectability was not possible without acceptance, and I was determined that a great number of people in Lima would accept me. Such would be the measure of whether I had pulled myself out from under the stigma of the illegitimacy I had left in Quito.

"Do you not have close ties with the viceroy?" I asked, while looking over his shoulder at the many names he was writing.

"Yes, Manuela, but this list should only include those who attended our wedding. I have added these others, at your request, to be seen later, because I wish to show you off," he smiled and put his arm around my waist. "I am not really close to the viceroy, only a business associate, and not a very close one at that. In fact, it is strange, I have not seen him at all since the wedding. He always seems to be too busy."

"Oh, I see." I hid my disappointment and then I noticed something. "Who are these?" I pointed to a line half-way down the second page that contained a name I recognized.

"Ah, one of the most important families in Lima. They have a beautiful mansion not far from the center of town."

"Oh, James, let's go there first," I said.

I had pointed to the names of the Marqués and Marquesa de Torre Tagle. They owned the impressive house I had seen that first day I spent as a *tapada*, near the church of San Pedro.

"Manuela, we should visit those who were at our wedding, first. We were married in such a hurry that the ceremony was small, so it will not take long before we get to these others. I do wish you to meet the Torre Tagles, but later." He looked at his watch. "Tomorrow we will start at the top of the list, but for now, I have an appointment. I will see you this evening, Manuela."

I had asked to visit the Torre Tagles first, not only because I wanted to see inside of that house, but because I had a plan. I thought most others would follow if I could gain the acceptance of the most powerful families first. I was foolish and did not think it through.

The following day, we began to visit James's friends starting with his very close friend Domingo Orué and his wife. Within an hour of our arrival at their house, I felt uneasy about his wife. There was no question that the Señora Orué wanted my husband. She seemed like a woman who could be obsessively possessive. I felt threatened, even though I believed that James's morals would not let him take up with her.

The evening was uncomfortable for me, but fortunately we left early. I deduced later that it was because the man was a *criollo*. James enjoyed the man, but the discussion turned to politics, which James did not enjoy. Our visits were interesting but short whenever we visited Creoles. Wherever we went, the talk always turned to politics. James would rush us out early in such households; Creoles being naturally interested in the revolution. He had far too many business dealings with the Spanish-born to be sympathetic with revolutionary sympathies. *Peninsulares* were also interested in the war, but their talk did not offend him.

Our next visit was to a couple whose name I do not even remember after all these years. I visited them only once. I do remember they were at the wedding and they lived in the San Sebastiano neighborhood. They were not the closest friends James had, but he put them near the top of our list because they were to leave for Spain on an extended visit in a day or so.

When we first came into their spacious drawing room, the lady of the house, who was an older woman, had a vase of flowers in her hand. She set them down, and then she splashed something on them.

"You add a scent to flowers!" I remarked, as I stepped near and breathed in. I was about to continue and say something about how unnecessary it seemed.

"Spirit of Musk," she interjected proudly, as though I had given her a compliment. By interrupting me before I could continue, I had been saved from making a social mistake.

She smiled and held up a hand to indicate I should wait a moment, and then she left the room. The man of the house asked James and me to sit down. The lady came back shortly with a potpourri of apple and lime slices, cinnamon, and cloves wrapped in a handkerchief on which she then sprinkled orange water and a little essence of jasmine from some perfume bottles sitting on a nearby table. She put the small bundle in my hands.

I did not know what to do. I almost asked her what it was for, which would have been very rude, though I did not understand this at the time. She seemed to be expecting a compliment, so I breathed in the fragrance and said, "That smells wonderful."

She smiled and seemed happy. "Place it in a large bowl when you get home; you will be delighted with how long this particular mixture stays strong," she said.

I learned that I had just adequately partaken of a ritual among the women of Lima. I was to find that the women of the city are very fond of perfumes. Often a scent would be added to flowers in a vase, and once I became used to the idea, I rather liked the result as well. The women themselves were always well perfumed, and they all experimented with mixtures of various scents. This love of perfumes extended to the social ritual of bringing new and interesting mixtures to their friends. It was not uncommon for one woman to come to another's house, without an invitation, and present her with a concoction of pleasant smells. These were always bundled in a handkerchief such as that lady had presented to me.

When I understood the convention, I decided I could use it. A day or two later I sent Natán to the house of the Marqués de Torre Tagle with a concoction of sweet smells. I told her to present the handkerchief to whomever answered the door and say that I, knowing we were to meet sometime soon, wanted to present the *marquesa* with a gift.

Two days later, James said, "Oh, by the way, Manuela, it seems we must change our schedule. José de Torre Tagle and his wife have invited us to visit tomorrow evening."

"How nice," I said, innocently.

"I will have to do a bit of rescheduling. It is really quite a bother, but they are such an important family that I cannot refuse them."

When we arrived, just as the sun was setting over the rooftops of Lima, I was again taken by the splendor of the Torre Tagle dwelling. The door itself, over twice as tall as a man, looked like it would allow two or three mounted horsemen to enter side by side. Not only is the door very large, but its decoration was most ornate and impressive. Outside the entrance there were tall, elaborately carved columns on either side, which the deepening shadows showed off in heightened relief. A coat of arms was cut into stone above the door and a large window above that was surrounded by columns and arabesques. To either side of the center window were long balconies, much higher than other houses, with wood encasements all around, carved intricately in the Moorish fashion of cedar and wood from the cinnamon tree.

Inside was a large courtyard. The *marqués* was a wealthy ship owner and, all about the patio, were many fascinating figureheads that seemed to be emerging right out of the walls. The spacious living quarters held many beautiful paintings and other objects of art. I had to remind myself to close my mouth as I walked through such palatial beauty for the first time.

The Marquesa de Torre Tagle appeared to be a very old woman with an expression frozen cold in wrinkles, though I think she was only about 45. She did not take to me at all, and despite an air of gentility, she made me uncomfortable from the first moment we met.

The *marqués* himself was tall and slightly heavy, with a very red complexion. Some might have considered him handsome. He seemed slightly younger than his wife. I found his conversation vacuous and his manner repugnant. When I complimented him on the beauty of the house, he was not gracious.

"The construction of the house was begun in 1690, and yet it was not finished until 1735 because it was such a large and expensive project," he answered, while seeming to puff out his chest. "It took Indian artisans almost two years to achieve the intricacy of those carvings," he said pointing to the ceiling. "The tiles on the floors were glazed specially for the family by the world's best craftsmen, in Seville. They are wonderful to behold, no?" I was put off by his flaunting, but I had to admit he was right.

Whether the conversation was about the paintings on the walls or the wine in our glasses, he had the best or the most or the finest. We were far beneath him in social rank, and his attempts to impress us showed an emptiness of character that I despised.

Within minutes after I met them, I started to doubt my scheme to impress the most impressive of the city. True, it would be a measure of whether I was truly accepted, but I did not like these people. Yet, there I was, trying to find favor with them. In my whole life, I had never done that. These thoughts did not come clearly to my mind until many months later. At the time, I only had a vague uneasiness that I had made an error.

At first, the men carried on a separate conversation, which left me to deal with the *marquesa*, alone. As we talked, she spoke to me as if I were a long lost friend, asking me probing questions. I tried to answer truthfully without giving away too much of my past. No matter what I said, upon hearing the response she had elicited, she looked at me in a disapproving manner. I never knew what to expect, and she made me nervous. I could see she was not to be trusted, and I rebuked myself for having forced this encounter.

The *marquesa* seemed to control her husband's actions like a puppeteer, except when he got on to a subject that allowed him to demonstrate his pedantry. Then, nothing could stop him from expounding on his theories and knowledge. Whenever she could, the *marquesa* would break in and have him do this or that little task hoping his attention would wander enough to be quiet.

During the evening, she discovered that I smoked. She immediately said, "José, offer a cigar to Señora de Thorne."

"You must call me Manuela."

"Oh, thank you," she said, her voice a mixture of acid and ice. "Offer *Manuela* a cigar."

I could see that he was reluctant, but he did so anyway, at her urging. All three of them looked at me with slight disapproval as I accepted the cigar and the help of the *marqués* to ignite it with a newly fashioned device that uses flints. I did not understand their behavior, but since I had been offered a cigar, I smoked it.

There was a moment of embarrassed silence. Then, as though he were trying too hard to make conversation, the *marqués* said, "Well, the Lautaro Lodge is not encouraged by the latest news."

Tension filled the atmosphere in the room. Both James and the *marquesa* looked at him askance. "What is the Lautaro Lodge, Señor, and to what news are you referring?" I asked.

James looked at his watch and said, "Manuela, we should—"

The *marqués* went right on, saying, "Oh, perhaps I should not have mentioned it. You being a Creole, I expected you to understand."

"I am sorry, Señor, but with all of the excitement of arriving here and the wedding, I am not quite as well informed as I would like. I would be most grateful if you could share your knowledge with—"

"Manuela, I think . . ." said James at the same time as the *marquesa* said, "José, perhaps now is not the time."

It was clear that both James and the *marquesa* would prefer him to keep quiet. However, he was too impressed with his own self-importance. I had suddenly become one to whom he could explain all he knew.

"Oh, I think it is all right, my dear," he went on. He inflated his chest and said, in the manner of a lecturer, "You are not seeing the customary personality of Liman aristocracy, my dear. The Spanish inhabitants of the city are not acting in their usual manner—which to an outsider can sometimes seem even arrogant. Before the fall of Chile to the patriots at Chacabuco, under the Generalship of José de San Martín—"

"Last February, Señor?"

"Yes, February. Before then, the Spanish-born of Lima were quite happy and verbal about their superiority to their American cousins."

"They *are* superior to most of the rabble," interjected the *marquesa*.

The *marqués* went right on, "Since that time, they seem to have become almost timid and worried." The marquesa scoffed, but I had verified this myself. Overhearing conversations as a *tapada*, I had encountered a gloomy atmosphere whenever word of the revolution came up among the *peninsulares*. The *marqués*, being a Creole, was supposedly on the side of the revolution, but I sensed that he was a shameless fence sitter, which later events proved correct.

He went on. "Viceroy Pezuela has ordered his foremost general, Osorio, to mount an expedition to reclaim Chile. This was just about the time you arrived in Lima, I believe." The *marqués* walked over and sat down in a chair, which was supposed to have belonged to French royalty. He continued, "As General Osorio's preparations have proceeded, the Spanish-born have begun to feel confident again, but there are serious problems for the viceroy."

"Excuse me—" said James, in an effort to interject something that might change the subject.

"Now, Don Jaime, I know the viceroy does business with you. I, myself, consider him a friend, but this expedition should not be financed from the fund belonging to the Commissariat of the Crusades."

"I do not think Manuela is interested, and—"

"On the contrary, I am most interested. Do go on, Señor."

"You see, this fund is supposed to be used to support a war only against Turks, Moors or Infidels. There has been so much discontent, since it was discovered that this money was to be used for the purpose of waging a war against Christians, that the viceroy has had his hands full."

"Who do you think will win, Señor?" I asked.

James and the *marquesa* went stiff. The *marqués*, who was enjoying his role, said, "I do not know." He stood up and paced the room, his hands behind his back, as though his answer would affect the course of history. "I do not see how a dilapidated group of revolutionaries can possibly succeed against the minions of a great and powerful nation like Spain," he said, frowning at the floor. "I sympathize, of course, with their cause." I heard the *marquesa* take in a deep breath.

He sat back down. "Right now, the Spanish are winning. The news to which I was just referring is that the Royalist forces holding out in Talcahuano are keeping the insurgents from securing all of Chile. No, I do not think that the revolution can succeed. Spain has too much money and power to let her colonies just slip away."

The *marquesa* said, "Of course not." The *marqués* looked thoughtful. "Still, there almost seems to be a divine intervention. "

"Señor?" I said, urging him to continue.

"Well, there almost appears to be a coordinated effort at work on the continent—between the forces of Simón Bolívar in the north and those of José de San Martín in the south—which I know for a fact has not been coordinated at all."

"How do you mean?"

"The two armies, of Bolívar and San Martín, have never communicated to each other as far as I know." He paused to think about that. "And yet the actions of these two men are working together in such a way, both heading toward Lima, that the eventual downfall of Spanish rule on this continent now seems a distinct possibility. Really, I think it is impossible to predict."

"In what way are they working together, Señor?"

"Simón Bolívar is a madman; I do believe that. I have a letter from a distant cousin who is fighting with him. Although Bolívar is a brilliant strategist and political theorist, he has had his share of mishaps. His campaign in Venezuela has been one day victorious, on another day, ignominious.

"Now my cousin tells me that while Bolívar stood in water up to his neck in the water of Casacoima Lagoon to escape a Royalist ambush, he suddenly began ranting. My cousin thought the general had gone mad as he spoke loudly, predicting all he was going to do in the next ten years. First he would liberate Angostura, then re-liberate New Granada, then he would form a new country called Gran Colombia composed of all the northern districts, then he would liberate Perú. As I say, I think the man is a madman."

"Could he do all that?"

"Manuela, we really must—" began James.

"My deluded cousin believes he will do everything he says, no matter how impossible. I do not believe it, but if he does, then San Martín will invade from the south, Bolívar from the north, and Lima will have to fall. If Lima falls, the Spanish domination of the continent is over."

"I see." I saw James stand and look at his watch. Before he could say anything, I said, "You mentioned the Lautaro Lodge. What is that?"

This was the first time the *marqués* hesitated to answer my questions. In the silence, James insisted that we must leave, and he ushered me out as quickly as he could. He complained about "those damned revolutionaries" (which he sometimes pronounced in English) all the way home.

All of the talk of revolution made me remember how much I always wanted to be a part of it. I was in the center of the continent, in its largest city, the fighting coming closer everyday, and I did not know anything I could do to help. "Is that man really a serious revolutionary?" I asked.

"He does not know what he wants. He is a Creole, so he is sympathetic, but his wife, who was born in Spain, wants things to remain the same, so as not to disturb her position. You should not have encouraged him."

I ignored that, and said, "Yes, she did not seem very friendly."

"It is worse than that. Now she has a story to tell about you."

"What do you mean?"

"Polite women in Lima, unlike Panamá, do not smoke while visiting. Alone in their home, at the theatre in their box, at the bullfights, yes, many do. But not while visiting. I know you did not know what was expected, but you should not be smoking anyway. I hate it."

We walked on in silence. I thought about the *marquesa*, and deeply regretted having been so anxious to visit her. I had hoped that meeting them would make my fitting into society life much easier. As I walked home, the more I thought about her, the more I realized that I had made a big mistake.

In the days that followed, I was proved correct. Nearly everyone we visited after that was cold to me, if we were received at all. One visit after another had to be canceled because those we were to call on sent flimsy excuses. I became discouraged, and even frightened, that I had lost all I thought was to be mine. My heart was not in the making of visits anymore. Being married to James may have brought me to a respectable situation, but I could see that Josefa de Torre Tagle was going to make life in Lima impossible for me. I had lost.

James sensed I was unhappy about something. In an effort to lift my spirits, he suggested that we go to the Old Comedy Theatre.

"I do not feel like it, James."

"Come, Manuela, do you not like the theatre?"

When he asked me that question, I knew I wanted to go. My love for the theatre overcame my social fears. Perhaps I could enter and find my seat before meeting any of the women who had snubbed me in the last few weeks.

As I rode to the theatre in a hired *calesa*, I felt sick. I was wearing a new blue gown James had bought for me, cut in the popular English fashion, and I felt quite beautiful when I looked in the mirror. Yet, as we approached the theatre, my dress became a reminder that I did not fit in. I could wear the most expensive clothes in the world, but if I was shut out of society, as I was in Quito, it would not matter. I thought I would find acceptance in Lima, and instead I had found the same ostracism I had known my whole life.

As I stood in the lobby, I encountered some of the women whose homes I had visited in the preceding weeks. A few were barely civil to me. Most snubbed me. Even though I was not being rejected because I was a bastard, merely because the Marquesa de Torre Tagle did not like me or did not want to let anyone new into her circle, the feeling still hurt. I was ready to ask James to take me home.

"James?"

"Yes, Manuela."

"I'm not feeling quite well." Just then, the *marqués* and *marquesa* walked in. She looked like she wished to avoid us, but then she put on a big smile and said, "Don Jaime—and Manuela. Did I get your name right my dear? How good to see you." I was trapped. If I left now, it would look like a retreat.

After the greetings, the *marquesa* said, "Offer Manuela a cigar, José. Don't be rude." Her voice dripped with poison.

"No, thank you," I said, smiling as broadly as I could.

"If you are offering cigars, José, I would like one," said a voice behind me.

When I turned around, there was a woman whom I thought a little less than 60 years old. She was absolutely radiant, and I learned later she was actually in her seventies. She was dressed at least as well as anyone else in the room, and she moved with exquisite grace despite being a little heavy. She had black hair that was streaked with gray, and her dark eyes gave evidence of *cholo* blood.

"Of course, Doña Villegas," said the *marqués*. He handed her a cigar and she turned to a candle next to her and lit it.

The *marquesa*'s face turned cold and ugly. "We had better hurry. The show will start soon. José!"

"Believe me, the show will start late. I know," said the older lady. "Won't you introduce me to your friends?"

The *marquesa*'s voice took on an air of polished, but false, gentility, and said, "Micaela, may I introduce you to Manuela de Thorne; Manuela, Doña Villegas. You remember Don Jaime Thorne, do you not?"

"Oh yes, of course, how are you Don Jaime?" she said, "I am truly sorry I failed to recognize you at first. It has been so very long."

"Yes, Doña Villegas, we have only met once before, quite a long time ago. How are you?"

"Very fine, thank you." Then she said to me, "I am pleased to meet you as well. You are new to Lima, are you not?"

"Yes, Señora, it has been only three months."

"Only three months? That is new. But you must call me Miquita. It was my childhood name, and I miss it. Don Jaime, your bride is lovely. Won't you come sit in my box? I assume your box is full, is that right, Josefa?"

"Not at all; I was just about to invite the Thornes to come sit with us."

"But, Manuela is not feeling well—"

"Oh, James, I feel much better. The room was stuffy earlier. There seems to be some fresh air in here now." I turned to the fascinating lady and said, "I would be delighted to join you."

"Well, *I* do not wish to be late," said the *marquesa*. "José! Let us go!" They excused themselves and left.

When they were gone, we followed Doña Villegas upstairs, in the opposite direction from that taken by the Torre Tagles. James whispered to me that we had been very honored, but I could not hear everything he said. When we came to her door, the sign on it said: *La Perricholi*.

Even before coming to Lima, I had heard of this woman. Legends about her had spread all over the continent. She had been only an actress when she was young, 50 years earlier. On the stage she had so captivated the viceroy, Don Manuel Amat, that he fell in love with her. So deeply in love that in one story about her, she was able to persuade him to feed her mules at midnight in his nightshirt. Another time, it is said, she insisted he grant a reprieve for a criminal on the morning that he was to be executed because she did not believe the man was guilty.

The viceroy, an architect in his own right, had built a secret entrance into the palace especially for her. He had also built the beautiful house in which the aging woman now lived.

In a way, her story, as I learned more of it, became an inspiration to me. If a simple actress, looked down on by the leaders of society, could captivate and move a viceroy, anything was possible.

I heard later that she was called La Perricholi because her neighbor, who was Italian, in a moment of wrath, tried to call her a half-breed bitch, "*la perra chola*," but with his accent it came out "la perri-choli," which she was called ever after. This was after she had became the lover of Viceroy Amat, which she was until he left Lima in 1776.

During the show that evening, she leaned over and whispered to me, "Why don't you come visit me tomorrow? We can have a nice chat, just the two of us, and we can get to know each other." I was very flattered and accepted her generous invitation.

As I leaned back in my chair, I happened to look across the auditorium to the Torre Tagle box. Just then, the entire audience laughed at one of the actors, except Josefa. She was glaring directly at me.

Chapter 29

When I arose the next morning, I went out and purchased the freshest fruits and flowers I could find. I took them home and made a concoction of sweet fragrances to take to my new friend. At the noon hour my *calesa* drew near one of the most famous (or infamous) houses in the city.

Despite her scandalous mis-adventures in the past, she was well loved by all *limeños*. When I questioned James the night before for more information about La Perricholi, he did not say much. He did tell me she spent most of her time and money on beneficial works in the hospitals. His attitude told more than his words. I perceived that he admired her, despite her outrageous past. I hoped the gracious lady and I would become good friends.

La Perricholi received me warmly. During the afternoon, she showed me her house, with its many beautiful rooms, elaborately decorated wooden floors, and furniture that had come from Spain or France or Portugal. I saw a large picture of Viceroy Amat dressed in rich viceregal attire and the huge bed where they had conceived their two illegitimate children: a son whom I was yet to meet and a daughter who was in Europe.

"How old are you, my dear?" she asked, as we looked at a bust of Viceroy Amat.

"Nineteen."

"No! I was just that age when I fell in love with him," she said, indicating the viceroy's image. "I was doing a senseless comedy, which required dressing in rural peasant clothes, that revealed . . . uhm, too much of my charms." She smiled gaily. "The viceroy returned for every performance, and each day his applause grew louder. It was embarrassing to see a man, not much younger than I am now, carry on thus." She laughed. "I made him wait when he asked me to come see him."

"Of course, you finally met," I said, anxious for her to continue her story.

Her eyes appeared to look far into the past, and they became a little wetter. She went on, "Oh, yes. I loved him so very much." Then she laughed—light and innocent. Something in her laughter made me love her. By the end of the afternoon, I had become as captivated by her as the rest of the city was.

"I am so grateful for last night," I told her as we sat down to have some tea.

"Not at all," she said, knowingly.

"You saved me from an embarrassing moment."

"I suspected as much. That is why I intruded."

"Why?"

"Because I could tell you were new to society, and I know how Josefa treats those who are new. Besides, you turned out to be as charming as I predicted."

We became good friends that day, and she set my mind to rest about whether I would be accepted in Lima. When I told her that Josefa de Torre Tagle was sabotaging my social standing, she said, "Do not worry. Even they have a past which they would like to keep hidden."

"Do you mean an unsavory past, Miquita?"

"Oh, yes. The Marqués de Torre Tagle's grandfather was removed as payroll master at Callao for overcharging the soldiers for their supplies. They would like to forget that incident. They are not as formidable as they seem."

I smiled, feeling better about my future.

Very wisely, she said, "You should not try to befriend those whom you do not admire."

She was right. I had been foolish in trying to measure my success in Lima by the number of people that accepted me. Besides, I had won. Being La Perricholi's friend proved far more valuable for that purpose than being Josefa de Torre Tagle's friend ever would have been.

More often than not, when she went to the theatre, La Perricholi invited me to go along, and we had many good times together. The same women who had snubbed me in that same lobby the night that I met her began going out of their way to talk to me. Coupled with my acquaintance with the merchant class, through James's connections, soon there were very few important people in Lima who did not know and accept me.

There were, however, two people who would later be important to me whom I had not yet met. La Perricholi introduced me to one of them one evening while we were watching a play.

It had a military theme, and during a pause, I offhandedly mentioned my desire to help the revolution. "Ah, my dear, I sympathize with liberty, but I will be sorry to see the old ways go," she said. The actor's voices floated up to her box, and she looked a little sad.

Then, as if a great idea had just struck her, she brightened and said, "I think I know someone you should meet."

She motioned to an Indian servant sitting behind her and whispered something in her ear while pointing to a beautiful blonde woman across the auditorium. When the intermission came, the servant left and returned with the lady, who seemed only slightly older than I. She was even more attractive up close than she had seemed when Micaela pointed her out.

"Ah, thank you for coming up here, my dear, without a proper introduction."

"Not at all, La Perricholi. I have been here less than a year and feel honored that you know who I am and have invited me to meet you."

"You are kind. But you must call me Miquita. I would like to introduce you to a friend of mine: Manuela Sáenz de Thorne. Manuela, this is Rosita Campusano—I hope I have not made an error in your name. You are both from the same part of the world, I believe."

"Oh? I am pleased to meet you. Where is it you are from?" I asked.

"I am pleased to meet you as well. I am from Guayaquil. And you? Ah, but of course, you must be from Quito—I can tell by your accent, if I may say so."

I laughed and La Perricholi said, "If it will not offend those you came with, why do you not join us here?"

"I would be most happy to do so. Thank you." She sat down, and we all talked right through the second act.

It turned out Rosita was about 27 years old, and she had arrived not too many months before I. She had moved to Lima after receiving a large inheritance. Guayaquil is no place for a very beautiful and wealthy young woman, whereas Lima was the Paris of South America. Even if I had not known a soul there, I would have done exactly the same, had I been in her circumstances. I envied her ability to come to this wonderful city on her own without the constraints of a husband.

Because we were both from the same area, she and I had much to talk about and we became friends instantly. I was invited to her salon the following week, and in the next month or so, I spent many a happy hour with Rosita.

The clever Miquita had known one thing about Rosita that I did not find out until later. I had thought she wanted me to meet someone new because she assumed we would like each other, although as I reflected on our introduction later, I remembered that she had never met Rosita. What had prompted her to have us meet was my discussing the revolution, and I soon discovered something quite interesting about my new friend.

One evening, after the weather had started to warm, I was feeling somewhat restless and took a walk with Jonotás and Natán. When I discovered that I was near Rosita's house, and seeing lights on, I decided to visit her, even though it was late. My companions decided to go back home, which was close by. I went to the door and knocked.

When a slave let me in, Rosita met me in the patio and motioned me not to say anything. She rushed me past the *principal* (main salon), where I saw many men, and into a smaller room, nicely decorated. Through the doorway, I had recognized José de Torre Tagle and other important Creoles. I thought it was a *tertulia* (a social gathering of men for the purpose of conversation), but it was more.

"We cannot go in," she said almost inaudibly, "that is the Lautaro Lodge, and the gathering is supposed to be a secret."

This was the second time I'd heard the term. "Rosita, what is that? You must tell me." Without answering, she ordered her slave to bring us some wine, and then she closed the door.

"Very well, I will tell you all I know. What have you heard already?" We walked over to a settee.

Still standing, I said, "Nothing, really. I've heard mention of it, and have gathered that it has something to do with the revolution, but . . ." I shrugged.

"Well, the Lautaro Lodge is a secret organization founded by Francisco de Miranda—you know, The Precursor of the revolution. Come let us sit down. You know of Miranda?"

"Yes, of course. Miranda, along with Simón Bolívar, made the first real revolutionary efforts in Venezuela."

"Yes, but I understand Miranda had been struggling for years for a South American rebellion before that. He traveled throughout Europe and North America, over decades, without success, trying to gain support for his plans of insurgency. The way I understand it, he began to feel he would not succeed, so he created a secret organization of like-minded men. This was back in the late 1790s, in London."

"Why did he call it the Lautaro Lodge?"

"Miranda was a Mason, and I assume that affiliation suggested the word "Lodge." "Lautaro" was inspired by the name of an early Araucan Indian rebel. Spain never succeeded in fully subduing the *araucanos*."

"So, that is the Lautaro Lodge."

"Not quite; there is more. One of Miranda's early devotees, and a member of his Lautaro Lodge, was Bernardo O'Higgins, the bastard son of the man who was viceroy of Perú at that time."

"Do you mean the man who is now the leader of Chile?"

"Yes."

"And you say he is the son of Don Ambrosio O'Higgins, the man who was viceroy?"

She sipped some wine and nodded. "Although it was not Don Ambrosio's intention, he unwittingly helped his son to where he is now. Way back when Don Ambrosio was captain-general of Chile, he had made many improvements in the road system, including rest houses along the Andean passageways that were later used by his son Bernardo and General San Martín as they crossed the Andes to attack Chile from Argentina." We both laughed at the irony.

She went on. "He unwittingly helped the revolution, in the form of his son, in other ways. You will enjoy this." She sipped her wine and smiled at me. "Having risen on his merits, Don Ambrosio finally gained the high office of viceroy. However, before he became viceroy, his illegitimate son had been secretly sent to England to study. Don Ambrosio wanted to conceal his son's existence from the Spanish Colonial Office. The soon-to-be-viceroy did not want his career ruined by scandal."

Some of the gaiety I was feeling, drinking wine with Rosita, learning something new and interesting, left me. I did not even know Bernardo O'Higgins, and yet I knew him perfectly. He was a Creole bastard, like myself. "He must have been very frustrated and lonely, a young man in Europe, knowing he would never have a role in the affairs of his father."

Rosita, smiled. "Yes, but there is justice. Due to the fact that Bernardo was in England, he met and came under the influence of Miranda. Being thus stirred, he took Miranda's oath to dedicate his life to the liberation of South America; and nearly 20 years later—it was just after I arrived in Perú—he became the leader of the new revolutionary country of Chile."

I could not help laughing in sympathetic triumph. "Oh, Rosita, there is justice."

"Also, Bernardo O'Higgins, earlier in Cádiz, was the one who recruited San Martín into Miranda's secret organization. San Martín himself is as troublesome to the Spanish as Bolívar."

"Yes, I have heard of him. Have you met him?"

"Oh, no. But he is the one that formed the Army of the Andes, crossed the perilous mountains from Argentina, and won the victory of Chacabuco—along with O'Higgins."

"I have lived in the Andes, although in the northern cordillera, and crossing them must have equaled Hannibal's famous crossing of the Alps," I said.

"Oh, I understand the General is most formidable—capable of doing anything, they say. I believe he will be the one to liberate Lima." She heard a noise outside the door and went to look. "The meeting is about to break up, but we have a few minutes."

"Tell me more about the Lautaro Lodge," I said.

"After Miranda died, it was not active for a while. But now it is a somewhat important organization. It was reformed in Buenos Aires, in 1812 by San Martín, and is now headed by a great intellectual named Bernardo Monteagudo. It has been joined (in addition to San Martín and O'Higgins) by all of the great revolutionary leaders, including

Carlos María de Alvear in Argentina, Simón Bolívar in Venezuela, and Riva Agüero in Perú."

"Who is Riva Agüero?" I asked.

"I will introduce you." She went to the door and motioned me to follow. The men in her salon were leaving quickly. All except José de la Riva Agüero, Lima's most important voice for the revolution.

He was only about 35, yet fine threads of gray were scattered through his hair. He was thin, strong, sensitive, and serious. His father was a grandee of Spain, and he had held many important posts in the service of the viceroys. He had also been secretly involved in the revolution since 1809. He was high-minded, idealistic, and proud. It did not seem to matter what was said to him, he always took a second to respond, as if he were trying to decide if there was something hidden in the meaning.

When Rosita introduced us, she merely announced our names. She was discreet, but I did not want to be left out.

"Señor," I said to him, "please call on me if there is anything the revolution needs that my humble hands and spirit can provide."

His eyes narrowed. He looked at Rosita, and then at me. Rosita looked embarrassed.

"Please do not pretend with me," I said softly. "I have already lost dear friends to the savagery of Spanish revenge. I seek only to help in our quest for liberty."

He paused a long time, as though he could discern my true intentions by looking at me, and then said, "Thank you. A brave soul is always welcome. But, there is little happening in Lima. All of the action is in Chile. Osorio is still preparing to mount his expedition in that direction. Until we see the outcome of those events, we must all wait."

"Señor, someone recently said that the armies of Bolívar and San Martín are not coordinated. Is that true?"

He looked as though he wondered why I asked, and then said, "Only by the Spirit of Liberty."

"Are they not both members of Miranda's secret organization?"

"Yes, but they are both Masons, as well. And both were friends of Miranda. It means nothing. The Lodge is a source of continental inspiration only. Local meetings such as this are for local concerns. Bolívar and San Martín have never shared their plans or strategies, as far as I know. Nor have they ever met. I do not believe they have even had more than superficial communication with each other."

"I see. What do you think will happen next."

"Right now, the last I heard, Bolívar is having his troubles. However, I am more concerned with what will happen to Lima. And I believe that will depend upon the stability of the new Republic of Chile. Here in Lima, there is no revolution. We can only wait to see what happens after Osorio leaves."

He was right. In Lima, the revolution was stagnant. However, I visited Rosita's salon often, and I became good friends with Riva Agüero, who was a constant visitor there. He was so taciturn and careful of what he revealed, that I did not pry out of Rosita that they were lovers until much later. We spent a great deal of time together and had many long talks about the shifting tides of the war.

Having someone with whom I could discuss political events made me remember that, in my soul, my true interest was the revolution. Having a large number of acquaintances was only a game I had felt compelled to play, which I never should have started. Ironically, it was my interest in the revolution that turned me again to courting people I did not admire.

Chapter 30

I had been in Lima about four months and I was enjoying my new adopted city. I was accepted, after all, in Lima's important circles, and I felt as if I had a home. In fact, I look back at much of the time I spent in Lima as being some of the happiest in my life. I had friends in high society, and I had friends who were revolutionaries; in fact I had friends or acquaintances in every social level.

Now that I had the position I always wanted, I was determined to take part in the revolution. Yet, there was no revolution in Lima. Then, one evening, my relationship with James, my social contacts, and my involvement in the revolution all became upset by one event and its ramifications.

At that time, my husband and I were pleasant to each other, but our alliance was not a happy one. Our conversations were logical and short, and our love-making the same. Everything about our life together was too staid, complacent, and businesslike for my tastes; and James, I think, was also unhappy, because he knew that I was. Regardless, without compromising my own life, I was determined to do all I could to please him.

He was in the habit of inviting a certain class of men to dinner: the English and Spanish sea captains and officers that might be anchored in Callao harbor. It was in his interest to keep good relations with men who might help his shipments of the various goods he bought and sold. Also, the intelligence they provided about political and economic affairs in other countries was invaluable to him.

One evening he had invited an especially large group of guests. James had asked that I make particular efforts toward the entertainment of our visitors that night, and I had worked hard to make an enjoyable evening for all. I had been happy that I was able to provide James with something that would please him. Apart from the pleasure I took in making James happy, the occasion itself was great fun for me because I had an opportunity to practice my English. I could almost carry on a whole conversation without help by this time.

At one point, the discussion turned to the revolution. I did not need to be coaxed to enter my opinion. "I was in Quito in 1809, and after seeing the atrocities perpetrated by the Spanish Empire, I am hoping for patriot victory," I said, in my best English.

Others took up the discussion; some agreed that the Spanish were brutes; others were more sympathetic to the crown. I noticed one English officer, a Captain Bowles, quietly translating what I had said to a gentlemen he had brought with him, a Don Domingo Torres. When he was finished, upon noticing my observing the private discussion, he said, in Spanish, "Ah . . . Señora, forgive me. We have recently anchored in Callao harbor, and Señor Torres is an emissary from General San Martín. He is here to see if certain—"

Don Torres broke in, "Shall we say, certain . . . uhm . . . negotiations are possible."

"Oh, I did not know. Welcome, Señor," I said.

"Thank you."

"Is it going well for you?"

"No, I'm afraid not. The viceroy will not see me, and I am kept incommunicado. I must stay with Captain Bowles, and I am not allowed to visit any part of the city except on official business. This fine dinner you have prepared is officially official," he laughed, "or so Captain Bowles was able to convince the authorities in Callao this evening."

I laughed, too. "Why do they restrict your movements?"

"They do not want me to discover anything about Osorio's expedition which I might then report to San Martín."

"In that case, I wish there were a few people to whom I could introduce you." I laughed mischievously.

"Manuela!" I turned around and James stood behind me. He glared at me, but said politely, "Manuela, could you have Natán bring more wine?"

James never liked revolutionary talk. I ignored his attitude and said, "Certainly. Señors, we will continue our discussion shortly." I left them. As I walked away, I overheard a man by the name of Manuel Escobar, a captain of a Spanish ship, say something to James about "impropriety," but I dismissed it.

I did not have a chance to return to Captain Bowles and his guest right away. Later, while I was opening a door to the patio to let in some air, Don Torres came up to me and asked, "Were you really in Quito in 1809?"

"Yes, Señor, but I was only a child. Still, the massacre of the brave revolutionaries was horrible, and I feel scarred by the event."

"I lost a niece in the melee," he answered. We tried to discover if we had any common friends, but we did not.

"Tell me about San Martín and O'Higgins, if it pleases you," I said, being fascinated with their heroic achievements after my discussion with Rosita.

"It pleases me very much. They are great men, who have risked much to bring freedom to the continent."

We continued to discuss the revolution in Chile for a short time. Two or three others joined our conversation. When I said, "One day I hope for the entire continent to be free," James pushed between us and closed the door.

"It's cold," he said sharply. It seemed to me that the conversation had followed a natural course, but I could tell he was angry. I assumed he was jealous without cause again. I did not want to upset him, or cause an ugly scene in front of our guests, so I changed the subject. Regardless of my good intentions, as soon as our last guest, Captain Escobar, had gone, he upbraided me.

"Manuela, I have had enough. You were far, far too bold this evening . . ." He barred the door. " . . . and talked far too much." He looked at me angrily and walked off across the patio. As he entered the salon, he ordered the servants who were cleaning to go away.

I followed him, my own anger rising. "What exactly do you mean, Sir?" I demanded, in English, as I entered the room.

He sat down and began winding his watch. He said, menacingly, without looking at me, "It is not for you to speak to British or other emissaries about the rights or wrongs of the government."

"Sir—"

He raised his voice. "And if one of our English guests is rude enough to bring a revolutionary to our house, it is foolish of you to befriend him." He held his watch to his ear and shook it violently.

I wanted to lash out, but I controlled my emotions. I moved in front of him. My voice quavered. "Sir, I will befriend whom I will."

". . . imagine a woman smoking cigars and talking politics."

"Señor!" I was too upset to continue in English. "Is my opinion any less valid than any other person's?"

"Damn it," he said, in English. He again held his watch to his ear, and shook it. He tried to wind it again. In Spanish: "Do you have no thought for my position? How can you tell a large group of men, whom you do not really know, that you are hoping for a revolutionary victory? I have seen so little of the viceroy since the wedding, I do not know if it is safe even to have these visitors to our house."

"*I* did not bring the subject up."

"No, but you made it continue." He stood up, towering over me. "You are *not* working for the revolution, or hoping for any such victory, ever. Not in my house. Whatever that means to you, you can decide to desist right now. The members of the present government are my friends."

I looked him in the eye. I kept my voice low and steady. Yet, I could not disguise the intensity of my wrath. "Señor, I *am* working for the revolution. In my heart, if in no other way. There is little else I want more, and *you* cannot make me abandon my principles."

The blood rushed to his face. He jerked his hands up, and I thought he would strike me. Instead, he hurled his watch into the corner. Pieces of glass and metal flew in all directions. He took a few steps away, and then turned back to me. I thought then that he was surely going to hit me, which angered me even further. "You are my wife and you will obey me. You are not to proceed in these affairs."

"Your wife? Of what consequence is that? Wife I am, but your slave I will not be."

"Manuela! You will obey. Your obligations as woman of this house demand—"

"Obligations? Do you expect me to be obligated to holding my tongue?"

"Your obligations as my wife—"

"I will not listen to this. Marriage obligates one to nothing."

He grabbed my shoulders and made me face him. "You vicious snip. As my wife I expect obedience and cooperation. You are nothing but a young girl, not even out of her teen years, and you know nothing of the world. This is a dangerous activity. And I will not allow you to involve yourself. I would kill the man whom you took for a lover. I will be no less lenient on politics. You will not interrupt our marriage—"

I was shaking, ready to cry, but furious. "Marriage exists for pleasure. I will not give up my soul—"

He yelled at me, "Manuela!" Then in frustration, "Damn!" in English. "You will learn your obligations. You will learn. You are my wife and you *will* obey." Then, before I could respond, he turned and walked toward our bedroom.

At the door, he said, "I am not going to discuss this with you anymore. All over this city are foolish people, believing in some future revolutionary happiness. You are to stay away from them. You are not to be involved in any revolutionary activities, or discuss it again, with anyone, *ever*." I was about to say something but he raised his voice to a new height and said, "And you are to hold your tongue!" He looked at me a moment in stormy silence. Then he turned and went to bed.

I stood there alone, with stillness all about me, my heart racing. I felt a violence I was unable to satisfy. I wanted to hurt him. I had cared for him a little before this, but now I felt at war. I paced the room, trying to calm down. At last, I pulled a cigar out of a box and sat down. I lit it and contemplated the remains of the shattered watch, and my marriage.

I sat up smoking for a long time thinking about this latest turn in our relationship. I saw once again that marriage had a second face to it. Despite the respectability, acceptance, and freedom that it had given me, I knew that I could not continue thus. This was not who I was, nor would it ever be. The longer I thought about it, the more rebellious I felt.

My blood rose until I walked into the servants' quarters and found Jonotás and Natán. I put on a *saya y manto*, an extra one that belonged to Jonotás, and presently three *tapadas* knocked at the servant's door to Rosita's house.

I was in luck. Riva Agüero was there. He and Rosita were having a discussion.

"Oh, I am so glad you are here. I am sorry to come so unexpectedly, Rosita. José, I have some news." I told him about Don Torres, and on which ship he would find him. "Perhaps, if you have anything which may help San Martín, you might want to deliver such report to his emissary."

"Manuela, you have done a great service by coming here. I do indeed know much about the expedition, which might be helpful to the Chilean forces. This is a great piece of luck." He left abruptly.

I stayed and talked with Rosita for a short time, telling her about the evening and the quarrel with my husband. She was most sympathetic.

Finally, I returned home. On the way, I prepared myself for another battle. James would surely ask me where I had been. I was almost prepared to tell him, but I did not want to endanger my friends.

However, his awareness of my presence must have been as small as his knowledge of my heart. He was asleep and did not know I had left the house, nor had he foreseen that I would defy him.

The next month was littered with similar quarrels, which grew increasingly acrimonious. I stayed away from the house as much as possible, which only caused the fights to become more bitter.

We had maintained a certain gentility before that, but the night we quarreled about the revolution seemed to have changed things permanently. In addition to my political leanings, James was daily more disgusted with my slaves, my smoking, my insolence, and my private zoo. By this time, I had acquired two dogs, six cats, a parrot, and a lizard. I constantly took in strays, and for each one there was another argument. The number of his complaints increased each day.

I think what irritated James most was that I would come and go as I pleased, invite my friends over, and exercise what I considered my own freedom with only the courtesy of informing him, not asking him, about what I was doing. He did not know how to control me when he was in Lima and, therefore, he knew there was no possibility of controlling me while he was at sea.

During one particular week, he did not speak to me for days, but at least we did not argue. Then, he utterly surprised me.

He came home one afternoon and said, "Manuela, I am sorry about our quarrels. To make it up to you, I have bought you a present." He was not smiling, and I assumed that he thought I would reject it out of hand.

I felt he was acting strangely and I asked him, "Are you really sorry?"

"Yes, Manuela, I am."

We stood there and looked at each other for a moment. Finally, not knowing where to go from there, I said, "Where is the present?"

"Come. In order to see it, you must come with me." He indicated the front door, as if the present were outside.

I went outside with him. There, he indicated I should climb into our *calesa,* which was waiting in the street. There was something strange about his actions, and I was apprehensive. What was he going to do?

"Where are we going?"

"Please, come with me, and you will see."

I was worried. I felt like I was walking into a trap. Finally, with a certain uneasiness, I pulled the *manto* over my head and climbed inside. He climbed in and called out to the driver, saying only one word, "Go!"

We rode in silence but when we approached the city gates, I asked, "James, where are we going?"

"You will see." He looked straight ahead.

I felt like jumping down and running away, but we rode on. A little more than a half an hour later, we rode into the small seaside town of Magdalena, a league or so outside Lima. I had heard about this little town, but I had not seen it yet. He had the driver stop in front of a nice looking house close to the sea.

I looked at him questioningly, and he pointed to the house. I did not know what he intended, but I was not going to go in a strange house until I understood what he was doing. Then he said, "How do you like it?"

I did not understand him at first. Then, the realization came. He had bought me a house.

I could not believe my eyes. My mouth fell open, and he said, "It is ours. I bought it, and I'm going to move the entire household here, including your animals."

I was speechless.

That house was beautiful. It was even more beautiful, though smaller, than our town residence. The village all around had such a peaceful loveliness that it seemed like heaven. Only the richest and most important people in Lima could afford second houses in this seaside village, and ours was only a few blocks from the viceroy's personal retreat.

Once he saw how enthusiastic I was about his gift, James became more animated. The house was only one story and painted a brilliant white. He escorted me through each room, sometimes giving a little bow as he showed me something new. "For you, madam," he would say, or something similar, as he opened a door to a bedroom or a porch.

I was very impressed. I loved that place, and to this day, I wish I could be in it. Only the very smallest part of my enjoyment was the prestige such a purchase brought me.

I was so taken by James's generosity and the loveliness of the dwelling that we had good times for many days after that. Only gradually, fool that I was, did I become aware that James's love for me was not the reason he had moved us to Magdalena. My premonition while riding in the *calesa* had been somewhat correct. The new house was never meant to be a present, but only an expensive jail.

Within a week or so, his behavior began to give him away. It soon became clear to me that he wanted to keep me out of the city and away from revolutionary activities or social events that he could not control. He became very strict with the household finances after the move, and he sold our *calesa*. When I spoke to him about the difficulties I had in getting into the city, he refused to buy me another. I knew he could afford it, yet I was left stranded when he took his horse to Lima. The walk was not impossible, but it was long and inconvenient.

The arguments started up again. Then, soon afterward, he left on a business trip. I had his power of attorney for emergencies, but he made it clear that he had a man in Lima watching his assets carefully. I was left alone, with limited control of my situation regarding money, and without much social interaction. The families in our neighborhood in Magdalena, with whom I was close were rarely there. A seaside resort was only a retreat for them.

I was angry for days after he left. Finally, I walked into Lima with Jonotás and Natán and bought some horses: One, a black mare I named Midnight, and two bays, one each for Jonotás and Natán. Rosita thought I was crazy to spend good money on horses for slaves, but Jonotás and Natán were friends who went nearly everywhere with me, and I did not want to be slowed down.

I paid for these horses using some of my money and some of James's credit, which nearly equaled what he obtained for the sale of the *calesa*. I knew there would be a fearful row over it, but I had not acted unfairly.

When I rode home that day, I was again aware that regardless of how secure my position seemed, if I did not have my own money I would always be under the shadow of my husband. That thought stayed with me for three days. Then, realizing what I should have known all along, that I must secure my inheritance, I started a lawsuit.

I rode into the city to see a lawyer, and I had the necessary documents filed and sent to Quito. The men in the legal office where I went were not very helpful. I did not understand legal affairs, and I never have. To this day, anything "legal" is a confusion to me. In addition to my obvious ignorance, I was only a nineteen-year-old "girl," so the men there did not have much interest in me. However, I was persistent with my questions, though I did not fully understand the answers, and I had money to pay for their services. Soon after, I was informed that the documents were on their way.

I was a happy woman as I rode home that day. I envisioned the courts compelling a chagrined Carlos to give me my share of the estate. He would, no doubt, have to sell the land to pay me, but I cared not for the Aispuru affairs any more than they cared for mine. Then, I would buy my own residence in the heart of Lima and live as Rosita did. At last I would be free!

I was not aware, until later, that to a certain extent James had won. As I began to pursue my inheritance, I became preoccupied with that and little else. Without noticing it, I became less and less interested in the revolution.

Chapter 31

Near the end of November 1817, General Osorio left Lima with his expedition to put down the revolution in Chile. I feared for the patriots as I watched his soldiers parade through the city, outfitted in their newest uniforms, carrying the most modern weapons.

The force consisted of a battalion of hussars and the Regiment of Burgos, 3,400 of the best troops that had arrived from Europe, and their destination was to be Talcahuano. There they would join the Royalist forces consisting of 1,700 men with 70 heavy guns who were holding out in a fortress described as the Chilean Gibraltar.

When they left, the entire attitude of the city changed. Delighting in the prospects of victory, Spaniards would verbally accost Creoles on the street, in the church, or wherever the opportunity arose. Some even entered into bonds with one another, putting up as much as 1000 pesos, that they would never again hire a Creole.

Viceroy Pezuela was the hero of Perú, matched only in adulation by General Osorio. As daily reports of the general's victories came up the road from Callao, there was continual rejoicing. For months we heard nothing but glorious news of Osorio's crusade. The bells of the churches hardly ever stopped ringing. Whenever the general's name came to a Spaniard's lips, it was as if he was speaking of a god.

I tried to ignore it. I had my mind on my lawsuit. I received only one letter asking me for clarification of some detail, which I answered promptly; no others came. I wrote a letter every week—sometimes two. I bothered the men who had helped me send off those first papers. My letters became increasingly angry. However, it was all for naught. I waited in frustration, with no word from Quito.

James returned from sea without any change of heart. I could tell from the moment I saw him that he was suspicious of what I had been up to.

"What have you done with your time while I was away?" he asked, as though it were offhand.

I let my emotions overcome my good sense. "Why do you want to know? Are you afraid I have led a revolutionary charge on the viceroy's palace?"

"Manuela, that was not called for. I merely asked what you've been doing."

"Nothing."

Happily for him, there was nothing to report about my revolutionary activities. The Spanish appeared to be winning, and I was preoccupied with my own concerns. During our discussion, he picked up the bill of sale for the horses. "What does this mean?"

"That, Sir, is what I bought with the proceeds of the sale of the *calesa*."

"Who told you that you could do this?"

"No one."

"'Nothing.' 'No one.' Am I going to get some answers or am I not?"

"*Not* if you yell at me, Sir."

We had quite a fight. But by the next morning, he had forgiven me. "With the exception of the horses, you have done a fine job. The house, the papers, my affairs. Everything seems quite in order. Better, in fact, than when I left them." It was true. I had brought my administrative skills to his affairs and had gone out of my way to see that everything he found on his return was exactly the way he liked it. Only when it came to legal documents, which confuse me, did I have to seek outside advice.

Seeing that no disaster had happened and that I was waiting for him dutifully when he came home, he left again, a week or so later. I do believe he expected much worse and that he was prepared to put off many future trips if his affairs, as managed by me, had not been in such good shape.

During this period when James was away, I felt conflicting emotions. Not about James, but about myself. In one way, I was content because I did not have to fight with my environment anymore; most people liked me and I was a part of a community. This was a seductive and dangerous feeling for me. The one persistent encroachment on my peace of mind was the thought that I might somehow lose what I had. I never wanted to return to the exclusion I had felt in Quito, and securing my own money was my way of holding on to the small island of contentment I had made. Thus, all my creative energies were spent simply waiting—waiting for a reply from Quito.

Without realizing it, I started to wither. I was not making anything, winning anything, or gaining anything. I was merely trying to keep from losing what I had. Nothing could provide greater evidence of my decay than the fact that, during this period, I began to pay court to the Marquesa de Torre Tagle again.

Through many discussions I had with my friends, it became clear that the only way to ensure swift justice was with bribes. Everyone agreed there was no reason whatsoever for officials in Quito to actively work for my cause, against a wealthy land owner in their own community. If I had been in Quito to see that things were done, the outcome might have been more predictable. Yet, how could I leave that which endowed me with any strength and authority I had—James and Lima?

I believed only two roads lay open to me. I either had to encourage some member of the *audiencia* in Quito with my limited funds or I had to convince officials in Lima to hear my case. In this regard, I came to believe the *marquesa* could help me. Two conversations in particular made me think so.

The first was with José de la Riva Agüero. "The Marqués de Torre Tagle no longer comes to our meetings," he said one evening. "He asks me about the next meeting agenda when he sees me on the street as though he will surely come and be fully supportive, but he doesn't arrive." His eyes moved to the cigar in his hand. "I do not tell him the truth."

"Why, José?"

"He cannot return," he said. "The Lodge would be compromised." After concentrating for a moment, he said, "Recently, I heard the viceroy has it in his mind to have the *marqués* head up the militia in Trujillo should hostilities advance this close to home. If fighting ever came to that region, he would be fighting the patriots. However, San Martín will be coming from Chile, not the north. Nevertheless, if the *marqués* is appointed to Trujillo, he will be a traitor, if he is not one already."

"Do you think he has given you and the others away?"

"I believe the *marqués* is inflated with his importance and is actually now wishing for a Royalist victory, but I do not think he would betray us. He wants to be on

both sides. His wife, of course, has never liked the revolution and is no doubt urging him to cooperate with the viceroy."

I thought about the *marqués* defending Trujillo, which is a not unimportant city controlling the whole area north of Lima. "Why would the viceroy trust a Creole?" I asked.

"A Creole he may be, but he is also a nobleman descended from important Spanish lineage. Also, he may want to remove him from Lima because he does not trust him. Also, Torre Tagle is so much a part of Spanish society in Lima, that the viceroy may have forgotten, or never learned, that he was born on this continent. Pezuela only took over from Abascal in late 1816, not even two years ago. Also, the *marquesa* is not a Creole but a loyal *peninsulare*."

Later, when I spoke of this to Miquita, she said, "The reason the viceroy is bringing José de Torre Tagle into his circle is because he doesn't trust him. He thinks if there is any treasonous Creole activity, it will be led by Torre Tagle, because he is so high born. I, personally, do not think the *marqués* really capable of such independent action."

"Neither do I," I said.

"There are also a few other Creoles who are gaining viceregal favor right now because they are friends of the *marqués*. Who would have thought it? In the streets we see solid citizens denigrated by *peninsulares* merely because they were not born on the Iberian peninsula. Yet, the viceroy invites Creoles to the palace to sup with him. Ah, I must be getting old." She laid her head back against her chair and closed her eyes. In one way, she looked as vital as ever, but as she closed her eyes she seemed almost lifeless. A chill went through me. She was older than she appeared, and I feared for her.

Her eyes still closed, she said, "My dear, I do hope you will forgive my rudeness, but suddenly I have become very tired."

"Not at all, Miquita. Is there anything I can do?" I stood up and took her hand. It was cold.

"No, my friend." She looked at me. "The world is changing and we all grow old." She smiled. "I was born when Don José Manso de Velasco, Count of Superunda, the thirtieth viceroy was in office. In my time, counting him, I have seen ten viceroys sit in Lima." She was silent for a moment, and then said, "I never imagined times would change so much. I feel quite old."

"Oh, Miquita, no! No one is as young as you!"

"You are kind. People indulge me, but unlike you, most condescend to indulge me. They know I am not a modern woman. I was born in the age of kings. I wonder if I will ever the see the line of viceroys end."

"Yes, I am sure of it. Revolution has been in the air for as long as I can remember. Eventually we will be free of Spanish rule. I think soon, very soon, a new order will be established."

She looked weary. "Perhaps you are right."

I felt stupid. After I had already spoken, I could see that my words were not consolation. If anything, my words might have made her even sadder. I left La Perricholi's house in order to let her rest. I was worried about her. What would I do without that precious lady?

As I rode back to Magdalena, I began to think about the viceroy and Torre Tagle. It seemed the only way for me to win my lawsuit, without going to Quito and fighting the battle myself, was if the viceroy in Lima would hear the case and adjudicate in my favor. If I could become close to the Torre Tagles, I might become one of those Creoles rising in the viceroy's gift.

I did not know how to renew my relationship with them. The thought of being nice to Josefa Torre Tagle made me sick to my stomach. Yet, if she liked me and worked for me, the *marqués* would follow.

I slowed my mount to a stop. "I will use the *marquesa*. She is fair game and I will use her," I told myself, trying to find my justification for going back to her. "La Sáenz does not need to have a moral reason," I said. I sat for a long time on the road to Magdalena, trying to bolster my resolve to go see her. My horse danced around impatiently, demanding to move. I paid little attention. How could I go back to that woman who had tried to undermine me? After a long time, with my horse still prancing restlessly, I found my courage. My desire for my inheritance overcame my aversion to the *marquesa*. "I will do it," I told Midnight, who only shook her head.

I pressed my ankles against her side and started forward. Then I realized, due to my horse's turning about while I contemplated my future, I was going the wrong way. Turning my horse around, I continued for home. If it were in my nature to see omens, I might have seen my horse's direction as a sign. I might have avoided a near disaster in months to come. At 20 years of age, one can be quite stupid.

The next day, I went to see my old enemy. Since I did not know how else to do it, I decided to boldly ask for her help. At least I would know what her response would be. She received me coldly at first but warmed up considerably after I told her about my lawsuit.

"Why, Manuela, why did you not come to see me sooner? Of course, I can help you. It is a bad time for Creoles, and we must stick together. I myself was born in Spain, but my husband is a Creole. When did you initiate your suit?"

I explained when I had first sent the papers to Quito and how I had received only one letter in return.

"I have a relative in Quito who is in the *audiencia*. He will help you. But first, you should meet Viceroy Pezuela. My relative will be much more likely to help you if he believes you have the viceroy's sympathy."

I was incredulous. "Can you arrange a meeting with the viceroy?"

"Of course, my dear."

She was so warm, friendly, and helpful, I forgot that I had come to use her and that I had already decided I could not trust her. As I rode home, all I could think of was my inheritance. I could see it coming into my hands very soon. She asked me to wait a week or so, and I promised I would. Then she would contact me.

The insolence of the Spaniards was at its highest in April of 1818. In that month, we heard about the defeat of San Martín and all of the patriot forces at Cancha-rayada.

I was devastated by the news. The Spaniards paraded down the streets, formed into groups, and harassed every Creole who had the misfortune of crossing their path. Osorio's wisdom and military abilities were sung from the pulpit to the street. For the next two weeks, we heard of nothing but Osorio's victories: Osorio was in Santiago; Osorio was about to cross the Andes and destroy the revolutionary government in Buenos Aires; Osorio was having this victory or that success. These depressing reports were constant.

There was still no word of my lawsuit from Quito. The only mail of interest was an invitation to a victory ball to which the viceroy had invited us. Since it was supposed to be for Spaniards, I assumed we were invited solely because James was a friend.

However, James had not returned from sea; and even though I was tempted, I did not want to go alone. Under the best of circumstances, being a Creole in the social climate of Lima at that time was hard. It would surely go badly if I attended a celebration of Spanish victories. Not having an escort and being a Creole woman, who was the same Manuela Sáenz who talked too much, according to her husband, could only bring disaster should I go to the ball.

The following day, as I was reading a letter from the men in the office in Lima, stating that I would be hearing about my case soon, Jonotás came to me. "That *marquesa* is sittin' outside waitin' to talk to you."

"What? Why?"

"I told her to come on in, but I think she is glued to her seat."

I laughed and went outside. I could see the *marquesa* sitting in her *calesa*, looking straight ahead.

I walked over to her and she said stiffly, "I have arranged for you and Don Jaime to attend the ball." A look of understanding must have crossed my face. She said, "Yes, I arranged for an invitation to be sent to you. I have a friend who is a scrivener who actually wrote them and I had him add your names to the list. I hope you are pleased."

"Yes, but . . ."

"If you make a good impression, your suit is as good as won. Are you pleased?" She smiled at me for the first time.

"What a surprise. Yes. I'm delighted."

"You will meet the viceroy, of course. Once he knows you, you will be sure to have his favor."

I was very grateful. "Marquesa, I am truly thankful. I can hardly believe my good fortune." She smiled at me. "I hope for an opportunity to repay your kindness," I said.

"That is not necessary. But do not disappoint me. Be sure you are there."

"Of course, Marquesa."

"You must call me Josefa."

"Of course, Josefa."

When I told La Perricholi about my good fortune, she looked at me a long time. I thought I saw disapproval in her eyes. Finally, she said, "I know how much your inheritance means to you, but you should not have gone to the *marquesa*."

Fear struck my heart. "Miquita, she has been most helpful," I said, to convince myself.

My friend looked at me indulgently.

"Why do you say such a thing?" I asked.

"The viceroy is not a man to help any Creole, despite his seeming to be helping Torre Tagle. He will certainly not help you."

"Are you sure?"

"No, I could be wrong, but I have been around for a long time and I am quite certain the *marquesa* does not have a relative in the *audiencia* at Quito, as you say she told you."

I worried about that conversation for days. Despite appearances, I came to believe that the *marquesa*'s true intentions were most certainly trickery. The more I thought about it, the more convinced I was of her deceit and the more foolish I felt. I was glad that James was still at sea, to provide an excuse to the *marquesa* when I did not go to the ball.

However, James returned from Guayaquil, the same day we were to attend. When he saw the invitation, he was delighted.

"What a bit of luck, eh, Manuela? He does not always invite me to such functions."

"I did not know you would return today. I could not be ready in time."

"Please try, Manuela. You will look beautiful no matter what you wear."

"I do not think I can be ready, James, and besides—"

"Please. Ever since the wedding, I have seen very little of the viceroy and he has not joined my trading ventures as he has in the past. I was worried something had upset him, but things must be all right now. I need to take this opportunity to make contact with him again."

Suddenly, I understood, and fear overcame me. James had married an American-born woman, a Creole. That was why James had seen so little of the viceroy in the last several months. Now if we showed up, when the viceroy never intended to invite us, it would certainly make things worse for James.

"I am not going, James."

"What?! Why?"

"I do not want to attend a celebration of Spanish victories," I lied. "I do not think you should go either."

"I do not understand you, Manuela. You've always wanted to meet the viceroy and to see inside the palace. Now you have a chance. And why should *I* not go?"

I did not know what to say. I went over and put my arms around him and kissed him on the lips, long enough to arouse his passion. "James, you have been gone for some time. Could we perhaps stay home?"

I could see the conflict in his eyes. He said, "Oh, I want to stay. I have longed to be with you like this." He kissed me. "Manuela, I love you." He opened his mouth as if to speak another endearment, then he stopped. His eyebrows knit and a frown crossed his face. "However," he said at last, "I must go."

I did not have to pretend anger at the rejection. I pulled away violently.

"Please try to understand, Manuela. It would be rude to neglect his invitation."

"Very well! You go, but I will not."

"Manuela, I am sorry, but you must. You have been invited. Besides, I am sure he will like you, and you him. Please. It will be good for me." I looked at him in indecision. "Then, later tonight, we will be together," he said softly, as he put his arm around my waist.

I did not respond. I stood still, thinking, trying to find a way out. Finding no rational reason I could give to him for refusing, I finally agreed, despite my reservations. I imagined that perhaps I might be able to turn this disaster to my advantage.

He rode off to Lima, on my mare, to hire a *calesa*. When he was gone, I told Natán to ride up to Callao and intercept the mail from the ship on which James had just arrived. I believed the letter I was expecting from Quito was on that ship, and I did not want to wait for a regular delivery. Sometimes, it takes as much as two days for letters to be delivered once the mail arrives in Callao. If the letter indicated that I might gain my inheritance soon, I would not feel so trapped by my circumstances.

As Jonotás bathed and dressed me, I had an uneasy feeling.

"Manuelita, you are troubled."

"I am worried, Jonotás. Once one begins in the wrong direction, it is difficult to return."

"I do not understand, Manuelita."

"I do not understand either. We will talk when I come home tonight." Then I was silent, trying to find some way to undo what I had started. It seemed I had set my own trap and was being forced to walk into it.

Chapter 32

While Jonotás was still putting little white flowers in my hair, James came into the room. "Manuela, let us leave soon."

"But, James, it is much too early. I am not ready."

"I know, but I would like to take a ride around the city first. Also, I thought we might eat a little something in Lima before the ball."

I said, "It will only be moments." However, I procrastinated, hoping Natán would return from Callao with news from Quito.

My mood was still dark, and Jonotás told me a risqué story to cheer me up. I laughed in spite of myself.

James came back into the room. "Manuela! Perhaps your play can be put off until later. I wish to depart."

I did not respond, but my worry returned.

When Jonotás was done with my hair, James escorted me to the *calesa* he had hired. Natán had still not returned.

When we arrived in the city, James had the driver take us across the San Lazaro bridge at the end of the street that runs past the main entrance to the palace. I admit that I was excited as I watched slaves running in and out of the door carrying flowers, food, and decorations. The palace guard were dressed in their finest uniforms, and there was a feeling of celebration all over the city.

It being promenade time, people were out for a walk across the bridge. As young Creole women, with straw hats held down by ribbons, passed the door to the palace, I could see the look of envy in their eyes as they watched the early arrival of a few *peninsulares*. They all wished that they could be attending the ball that evening.

James took us quite far out of town. He wanted to talk to me about what had happened while he was gone. Happily, he didn't press me about my political life at all, which did not exist, but would have caused an argument. We had a rather pleasant conversation. "I was worried, Manuela, before I went to sea that first time," he said as we rode back across the bridge.

"Why, James?"

"Because I did not feel I could control anything that happened in my house. You have done a fine job, and I'm glad to be back. Perhaps we can start over." He looked straight ahead, immobile and serious.

I knew we would never work as a couple. "It is that we are so different, James . . . ." I was going to go on, but I felt him grow tense. He did not want to hear the truth.

"Yes, perhaps we can start over," is all I could think to say. I did not want to start another fight.

We arrived back at the Plaza Mayor, and James dismissed the *calesa*. He was intending to hire another when we left the ball to take us back to Magdalena. We went into a cafe to have a little *puchero*, a popular Peruvian meal, which I had never eaten before arriving in Lima. It is composed of beef, pork, smoked mutton, cabbages, sweet potatoes, sausage meat, pig's feet, yuccas, sweet corn, bananas, quinces, black puddings and *gurbansos* all cooked in a pot for several hours with highly salted water until it becomes a jam-like mass, usually served on a *tortilla*. I can't have too much of it because it lies heavily in my stomach, but it is quick and nourishing.

When we were done with our meal, we walked across the square to the palace. Spanish aristocrats from all over the city were being brought to the entrance in chaise chairs, *calesas*, and carriages.

We ascended the few steps to the entranceway, passing a guard room and smartly dressed guards, and entered the "Hall of the Viceroys." This is a long room with full-length portraits on each of the 39 wall panels, depicting every viceroy from Pizarro to Pezuela in sequence.

I noted that there was not one spare panel left on which to hang another painting and wondered what they were going to do when the next viceroy was appointed. The problem never arose, however, because somewhat later San Martín entered Lima, making Pezuela the last real viceroy and the architect of the palace something of a fortuneteller.

My anticipation in wanting to see inside resulted in disappointment. I saw only the great hall and found what I did see not as impressive as I had imagined, including Don Joaquín de la Pezuela, the viceroy himself. He was the most unremarkable man I ever saw: neither short nor tall, not ugly and not handsome, no darker or lighter than a good Spaniard should be, and without any real personality beyond the gold braid on his uniform. I watched him from across the room. His aspect was that of a social outcast rather than an aristocrat, and without his fine clothes and the royal setting, no one would believe he was otherwise. I was sure La Perricholi was right. He would not help me.

I looked around quickly to see if I could see the Torre Tagles. By that time, I was convinced they had never been invited. I was not surprised to find that they were not there. As James talked to his associates, I saw how singular I was, a Creole, amongst this crowd of Spanish aristocracy. As near as I could tell, there was not one Creole in the room, except me.

I tried to think if there was some way I could escape and walk back to our San Sebastiano home to wait for James. However, he insisted that I greet everyone.

At the moment we were close to the viceroy he did not seem to be too crowded by those hanging on his every word. James steered me over to meet him. "Come, I can introduce you now," he said.

"I really do not wish to meet him now, James," I protested.

"We must. Come."

"James, not now—" I pulled my arm from his grasp.

"Manuela, I insist. Come." He gently took my arm again, and we walked toward the viceroy. With great trepidation, I allowed myself to be walked through the crowd to where the Viceroy Pezuela and his wife were standing.

I could see the viceroy was taken aback by my husband's presence, "Don Jaime, I am surprised to see you."

"Yes, I just returned today. Thank you for your invitation."

The viceroy gave him a look of astonishment but apparently decided not to color the occasion with questions that might gather unpleasant answers.

When James introduced me, Viceroy Pezuela barely glanced at me and immediately started discussing business with James. Two military men, standing close to the viceroy, began expostulating loudly about the revolutionary army's inability to match their betters in the recent battles. When that happened, Pezuela was distracted by their discussion and turned his back on James and me completely.

My life in Quito seemed to flash before my eyes. I was 5 years old, fighting with children in the street. I was 7, fighting with Carlos and the nuns. I was 13, being snubbed by aristocratic members of society—snubbed by the same people who had persecuted my mother so cruelly. Infuriated, I felt the blood rush to my cheeks, and I forgot I was in a room of *peninsulares* who considered *criollos* insignificant. I felt ready to fight.

The vicequeen was a woman with a sympathetic face and great beauty. She had the sensitivity to notice that I had been affected by his Excellency's rudeness.

"I am pleased to meet you," she said to me. "Don Jaime, I am glad to see you again. My husband . . ." I believe she started to say something that might have served as an apology, but could not find the words.

I was too embarrassed to speak, and excused myself. I started to turn around and walk for the door when someone backed into me and stepped on my toes. No apology came. I felt it was as though the man knew of my low birth—yet he had not even been aware of his offense. I stood there in pain and anger, collecting myself. Then, I overheard the vicequeen whisper, "Joaquín, you hardly said hello to Manuela de Thorne. She and Don Jaime are leaving—"

He interrupted her, and said quietly, "What can it possibly matter what one adolescent Creole girl thinks?" Then he started talking to someone else.

Anger flooded my thoughts, pushing out all reason. I turned to him and said, "Your Excellency!" He turned around. More quietly, directly to the viceroy, I said, "I am a woman, not a girl. I am your guest. I also delight in being a *criollo*. Please accept thanks from this unimportant person for your hospitality. Good evening."

Blood rushed to his face. James began apologizing. I curtsied and left. Fortunately, only one or two people besides the viceroy heard me. I moved quickly through the crowd of Spanish aristocrats as though I were escaping from a forest of trees sprouting poisoned flowers.

James caught up with me in the street and was extraordinarily angry. I was crying by that time, walking swiftly toward our San Sebastiano house. Feeling his words hit me as though they were fists, he upbraided me for my behavior. "Manuela, how could you? Have you no thought for my business? Do you not—"

I turned on him. "Business! Business. Why do you plague me with only your concerns? Can you not see? It is I who have been hurt. Do you never care about me?" I hurried on as tears streamed down my face.

"You? Manuela, the viceroy was livid. He left the room, followed by his wife."

The news terrified me. I quickened my pace. I was not sure what would come of what I had done, but I felt a deep foreboding, as though disaster would soon crash all about me.

James chastised me all the way home and all the way up to the bedroom. By that time, I had enough. I turned in the doorway and said, "Please, Sir, stop." I tasted the salt from the tears on my lips. "If you desire to have your wife insulted, perhaps you should have chosen one who enjoys it." I slammed the door to our bedroom and locked it and immediately collapsed on the dais, at the foot of the bed, and sobbed.

James knocked on the door for awhile, calling my name. At last, he said, loudly and angrily, "Manuela, this is too much. I am through with you. I'm going to bed, and in the morning things will change." I heard him walk down the hall to the room we keep for visiting merchants.

His words chilled me. My life in Lima was over.

What would happen to me now? I had ruined all I had gained, ruined it al beyond repair. One thought stayed in my mind without my control. *I am nothing. Only a hated bastard, trying to fit in where I do not belong.*

I had gone too far at last. Surely word would spread. After this, the *marquesa* would be merciless in excluding me from the rest of society. Since I had offended the viceroy, I wondered if even my dear friends Rosita Campusano and Micaela Villegas would think twice before associating with me. I worried about it for hours and became more and more woeful as I prepared for bed without my Jonotás and Natán to help me. My future seemed to wait, like a dark monster ready to attack, behind the curtains and furniture. I climbed under the covers a couple of hours later, leaving one lamp glowing faintly in the corner, but I could not sleep.

I wanted it all to be a dream. Yet I believed, when morning came, I would have enormous problems, problems that would surely confound my abilities. I would end up friendless, and with nothing after all.

I think I slept restlessly for a short time, but it was the kind of sleep where you feel as though you have been awake worrying. Suddenly, I was aroused by a tapping at the door. I said, "We will talk in the morning, Señor."

I heard in a whisper, "It's Jonotás."

I rose and unlocked the door. Jonotás stepped in, rubbing her arms to ward of the chill. "I was worrin' 'bout you, so I come to find you," she said shivering.

I shivered myself. "What hour is it?" I asked.

"Some time after midnight. I heard the crier. Natán wanted to come, but I left her to wait, in case you went home."

I was deeply touched. She had come all that way, at night, in the cold. Tears came to my already moist eyes and I said, "Come here. You are both silly and wonderful." I held her close, and felt her heart beat next to mine. She somehow calmed me.

While I held her, she said, "Are you all right, Manuelita?"

"I don't know. I don't know." I was not ready to talk about what had happened. I said, "Did you come here just because you were worried?"

"And to bring you this." She held out an envelope. In the dim light I could see the Quito address. I practically snatched it out of her hand and tore it open. Perhaps there was some hope after all.

Walking over to the light, I leaned over to read. The prose was lengthy but ultimately it stated that my suit was being set aside indefinitely. I recognized Carlos's manipulations.

"Damn you," I swore. My voice was hoarse. "Damn you, damn you to hell."

I sat down slowly on the floor, alternately crying in grief and swearing in anger. Jonotás came over and put her arms around me. I lay my head on her breast and sobbed. "Oh, Jonotás, what am I to do?"

She kept saying, "Don't cry, my sweet. Don't cry."

I sat there sobbing a long time. Jonotás closed and locked the door, and then she urged me to get in bed. We lay down in each others arms under the warm covers. She caressed my hair and kissed my cheek until we fell asleep.

When I woke, Jonotás was coming through the door with some chocolate. "Where is James?" I asked.

"When I was makin' the chocolate, he come in. He looked angry when he saw me, and he left the house."

I told her the details of my evening at the palace, and she sympathized with me and made jokes. She, as always, made me feel better. "This is what I think of the viceroy," she said, as she lifted her dress and turned around to show me her naked rear. I laughed for the first time.

"That is good," she said. "I don't want you sittin' 'round, cryin'"

"But, my brave Jonotás—I don't know what to do now. The only thing I have, which gives me any kind of freedom, is my marriage. Yet, it is a trap in itself. Besides, I know now for certain that James and I are through."

"But, Manuelita—"

"I know, in the eyes of the rest of the world, we will always be married. Divorce is not possible to a devout Catholic. But to me, we are not man and wife. We are friends only—if he wishes it." I could not drink my chocolate and sat the cup down. "I cannot go on as I have, and without his support I do not know what to do. Now I will only have a small amount of money that is mine and no power of my own." My words caught in my throat. "Also, the rest of the city will certainly turn against me."

I heard a knock, downstairs, on the heavy outside door. Jonotás went and looked out the window. She said, "It is that man, the one that's always bringin' us the mail." He knocked again. I gave her some coins to pay him and she ran down the stairs. When she came back, she said, "This one has done some travelin'."

I looked at the crumpled paper, stained and torn, sealed with pitch, the addresses of places in Mexico, Panamá, Guayaquil and Perú written all over it. I did not recognize it at first.

It sat in my hand, brown from weather and sea salt. The pitch that sealed it, shiny at one time, was dull and brittle; its once perfect corners and edges were frayed and ripped, yet still keeping safe its contents. It was like a ghost from the past, calling to me.

Tears slowly welled in my eyes. That day, almost three years earlier, when Juanita and I had written a letter to my father's address in Panamá from those remote volcanic islands, came back to my mind with vivid intensity. It was as though I were there. I could hear the waves crashing against sharp black stones. I could feel the rough sand beneath me. The wind brushed my hair against my cheeks. Slowly, I opened the letter, and read the words:

Dear Manuela,

I am in the middle of nowhere. Hope to see you again soon.

Your best friend,
Manuela

I cannot describe the emotions and memories that came to me in that instant. I remembered Juanita that last day I had spent with her. I remembered my mother and how much I missed her. I remembered Quito and my life there as an outcast. I recalled Doña Luisa and the story she told me about the nun who was willing to die for her integrity. I remembered the promise I had made to myself that same day I heard her story: never would I let what I might gain or lose decide for me. I would do as I desired. I would survive. Through determination, I would win.

I thought of the evening prior when I was hoping that an unexceptional man would recognize and validate me as a human being merely because he was called Excellency. I saw myself in Panamá, standing in a doorway, as I decided to marry James Thorne in order to have the life he had made because I lacked faith in myself to make my own. I thought of my life in Lima since then, devoted almost entirely to acceptance in other's eyes, as though I could only live if others were there to tell me I was a person. I thought about how poorly my marriage and my life in Lima had turned out, despite my manipulations. All of these thoughts and their attendant emotions rushed in on me in seconds.

I said to myself softly, "I am a fool." I hit my head with my fists in anger and repeated, "I am a fool. I am a fool."

If I was anywhere or nowhere, it was I who put myself there. Whatever I might have to go through in Lima, I had probably been through worse before, and I realized that of all my friends, I was absolutely and utterly the most important. My anger turned to a mixture of laughter and tears.

Jonotás stood by, silently watching me. When I looked at her, there was worry in her eyes. That letter from my past had been the hook to pull me from my fixation on Lima. No matter how important it was, the world was bigger and I had always felt that I was a citizen of the world. I knew who I was. That day, I stopped being my own enemy.

"I am La Sáenz," I said calmly.

Jonotás's look of worry turned to puzzlement. I walked across the room and picked up the other letter and read it again. Then I said, "Come, we have to go back to Magdalena and start packing."

"Packin'? What are we packin' for? Where we goin'?"

"Jonotás, my friend, we are going where the battle is. We're going to Quito."

Chapter 33

I dressed quickly and went downstairs, consumed by my own determination. Just as we left the house, James arrived in a *calesa*.

"There is no need for you to walk," he said.

"I have my horse, Sir. You rode it up here last night."

"We can get it later. Mine is here too. I wish to talk to you."

"I do not wish to fight with you, Sir," I said, looking up at him. I held my hand over my eyes to shield it from the sun.

He looked straight ahead. "I do not wish to fight either. Last night is past. I am offering you a ride."

After all the trouble I had caused, I was surprised at his conciliatory manner. I found it unexpectedly generous of him. "Jonotás, please bring our horses back to Magdalena." She went off to get them, and I climbed into the *calesa*.

He sat in stony silence for some time. I sat planning and thinking. Jonotás rode behind us, leading the horses. When we were almost there, he said, "I returned to the ball last night. To try to smooth it over with the viceroy."

"I did not hear you leave."

"When I arrived, the viceroy had returned to the room and was himself again."

"Nothing happened?"

"Apparently not, with the exception that he glowered at me when he saw me. That gave me some concern. You should not have been so bold."

I ignored that and asked, "But nothing happened?"

"No. Later, when I spoke to the vicequeen, she gave you a compliment. She said something like, 'Your wife is quite beautiful.' She was most sincere and I had the impression that she had smoothed it over for us with the viceroy."

My heart filled with admiration and gratitude for the good-hearted vicequeen. I remembered her kind face and I knew what had happened. She had calmed her husband and persuaded him to rejoin the ball. That is why he had apparently dismissed the incident. The fears I still had about reprisals from the viceroy were much assuaged. I was still not sure of the effects of what I had done, but I swore to repay her kindness one day.

What James said also explained his seeming generosity. He was risking little by reconciling with me. He could afford to do so, since my actions had evidently caused him no harm. My decision of the night before had been correct. It was over between us. I did not know how to tell him, but the decision was made and the action taken in my heart.

I knew I would always be married to James in the eyes of society—a divorce would never be granted, although that was what I would have wished. Thus, my position as his wife, and whatever endowments that afforded me, were mine. He had given me much, and I loved him in a way. I would support him, as I would any of my friends, but we were not man and wife. Whatever happened from that point on, I would not depend on James Thorne.

He sat in silence for the rest of the trip. When we arrived in Magdalena, Thorne said, "I apologize for the way I acted last night." I looked at him and he went on, "I know you were hurt and I should have realized that. I was worried. After all, a viceroy is only one step under a king."

I was gratified that he could see my point of view. I replied, "I understand, James. You have much to worry about, and so do I. I am sorry too. Let us forget it." I spoke matter-of-factly, without further commitment. Still, I know he took it as complete reconciliation.

I continued, "But I realized last night that I was failing myself in the thing I want most."

"What is that, Manuela?"

"To fulfill my mother's wish that I should have the gift she gave to me when she was dying." Then I showed him the letter from Quito.

I made sure he did not see the other letter in my hand. No one ever saw that letter again except me.

After he read the notice from Quito and clarified what it was all about, James looked distressed. "But, Manuela, you don't need the money!" "When did you first request this proceeding?" "Why didn't you tell me about it?" "You'll have to go to Quito to get it." "It's not worth it." "You'll only lose." and so he went on.

I answered him the best I could, but mostly I sat quietly and listened to him. At length, I said, "James, nothing is going to change my mind."

"Damn!" he expostulated in English. "Manuela, the money is unnecessary. We do not need it. Tell me why, of all things, you want this."

I slowly descended from the *calesa* and turned to face him. "Because it is mine." "Manuela—"

"I am packing to go to Quito. If you love me or if you want my friendship, you will help me." Then I went inside the house. After a short time, he followed and sat down at a table to write a list of things for me to take.

We packed all day. Since it would be easier, for many reasons, to depart from the San Sebastiano residence to Callao, we planned to move the entire household back there over the next few days. All day, the servants went back and forth between Lima and Magdalena, taking our clothes and household goods in a wagon.

As we were leaving Magdalena that evening, we passed the Torre Tagles on the road. They were apparently on their way to their seaside retreat. The *marqués* had the driver stop and he walked over to talk with James. I went over to the *marquesa*, who sat rigid as a stone, looking straight ahead.

The first thing she said was, "I heard the viceroy was upset last night." She was not delighted to see me.

"He did not seem so to me. I missed you, Marquesa."

"Yes, I was ill last evening." Her face looked more sour than usual.

"But I do thank you for having me invited to the ball. It was quite grand." I went on, telling her what a good time I had. She gave only perfunctory retorts. I acted perfectly innocent and carried on my discussion with her as though nothing had happened.

The *marquesa* did not know what to do; she wanted to gloat, but there was no reason she could put her finger on. As a last resort to get at me, she said, "Do come by tomorrow, we will compose a letter to my relative in Quito."

I thanked her and said, "I will be in Lima tomorrow. James wants to move the household back there. Later in the week perhaps." I went on as though we would get together, but, of course, I had no intention of ever doing so. I did not tell her anything about my plans to leave.

She left smiling. She was even amiable as she said, "Good-bye." She would have turned on me in a second, if there had been any cause, so I felt the repercussions from my outburst the night before, if any, would be few.

I met Rosita Campusano later in the evening. She had not been invited to the ball either, but she seemed to know exactly what had happened and was vociferous in her admiration of me. We had a good laugh.

"I am going to Quito; but when I return, I want to do something to help the revolution. I want us to take some action."

"What can we do?"

"I do not know, but we will find something."

Over the next few days, my household continued to prepare for our departure. I would have left within two weeks I am sure, except for something that happened a few evenings later, on the fourth of May.

I was walking home from the center of town, where I had gone with Jonotás and Natán to visit Rosita, when I saw a curious sight. A rich chaise was making its way through the nearly deserted streets. It being after ten o'clock at night, my curiosity was piqued. The chaise looked like it had come from Callao. The three of us pulled our shawls over our heads, concealed our faces except for one eye, and followed the slow moving chair.

It was not as light as usual that evening because the moon was in its dark phase. We followed the chaise through the side streets to the edge of the main square and saw it stop in front of the side door of the viceregal palace. We watched to see who would get out.

I was very surprised to see that it was General Osorio. My curiosity overcame me and I led Jonotás and Natán in his direction. I started giggling to make it appear that we were not interested in events around us but rather in our conversation. Jonotás and Natán took my cue and started to talk about some imaginary lover. We walked as close as we could without seeming to be spying, and I got a good look at Osorio as he waited for the guards to open the door. He was thin and had the unmistakable look of worry on his face.

When we arrived at the end of the block, we stayed for a while; but it was clear we would learn nothing, so we went home. On the way, Jonotás said, "Somethin' must be wrong. I never saw a general look like a sick puppy."

"Yes," I laughed. "I am extremely curious."

It was a truly dark moon for General Osorio. The next day I found out that he was there to make an ignominious report: his troops had suffered a total defeat at the battle of Maipo. It was rather a new moon for the revolution in Chile because the country was, at last, securely in patriot hands where it stayed forever after.

On the morning of the fifth, the following day, Creoles were finally allowed to pass through the streets unmolested, as the Spaniards were walking about the town with their "tails between their legs."

Osorio, who only two days before was a god, was suddenly an ignorant coward. All the Spaniards could do, besides complain about what a dolt Osorio was, was to hope for the arrival of the latest expedition that had left from Spain. Pezuela immediately sent Osorio back to Chile, even though his objective was lost. Osorio did not return to Lima until September.

On the sixth of May, the next day, James left for Panamá on urgent business, which was somehow precipitated by the news of the Royalist defeat in Chile. I do not know what particular meaning it had for him, but it seemed extraordinarily urgent. I never saw him so nervous. He asked me to stay in Lima for another month.

"Please, Manuela, it is quite important; I beg you to stay until I return. Please do not to proceed to Quito without me.

"But why, James?"

"For one thing, I think the seas will be quite dangerous; but the main reason has to do with my business. I need someone here to watch over our affairs. I would ask Captain Escobar but he will not be back for many weeks. I simply do not know what is going to happen in the next couple of months with the changing political atmosphere. Please. It will only be a month or so."

I did not want to abandon my plans, but I agreed. His request seemed so important to him, and I wanted to show him I was his friend, regardless of how our marriage turned out. I had not told him, in straightforward terms, that I considered our marriage over, but it was becoming evident.

As it developed, almost the moment he left on an English ship, all departures from Callao were canceled by viceregal edict. Perhaps that is why he left so quickly, knowing that it would be impossible for him to handle his affairs for awhile. I waited, frustrated, with no idea of when I would be able to depart.

About a week and a half later, I suffered a great loss. La Perricholi died. She passed away quietly, in her sleep, without seeing the end of the rule of viceroys.

I was one of many hundreds who mourned her. The funeral procession, the largest I ever saw, left the parish church and made its way outside the city to the Panteón—which had been built by the prior viceroy, Abascal, to ensure that the dead were not buried inside the city walls. At the head of the procession was an empty coach, led by four white mules, which were being led by a middle-aged man. He looked very morose.

I learned that the empty coach was the same famous coach that had belonged to La Perricholi—the one built for her by the Viceroy Amat, at her request. I had heard the story, of course, but I had never seen the actual coach.

It was in La Perricholi's younger years, in the late 1780s, that she asked and received a special favor from the viceroy, after much protest by him. In Lima, at the time, a *calesa* or other riding wagon was used by most people to get around town. This particular kind of coach, however, is a symbol of aristocracy. Only the *grandezas* born in Castile were allowed to ride in such a coach.

She had specifically requested of the viceroy that he build her a coach and allow her to ride it through the town. He had argued, but in the end had done as she asked. When she made her one trip through the streets of Lima in her coach, she had shocked the city. I, of course, being a town shocker myself, loved the story, and I laughed in spite of the sadness I was feeling for my friend when I saw the coach itself.

I also learned that the man leading the coach was her bastard son, Manuel Amat. I was intrigued by him because he had my name in the masculine and my history—being the bastard offspring of a Spaniard and an American. I decided to meet him.

After the nine days of mourning were up, during which I myself cried deeply for the loss of my friend, I arrived at the house of La Perricholi. Manuel Amat answered the door himself. He looked drawn, unkempt, and unsteady. He was almost as old as James, but he appeared much younger.

"Yes, what is it?"

"My name is Manuela Sáenz de Thorne. Your mother was my dearest friend, and I have come to offer my condolences."

He looked sad. His vest was undone and his shirt was hanging out. He swayed as he stood there. After a moment, he said, "Everybody loved my mother."

"Quite right. The truth is that I wanted to meet you."

"Me? Why?"

"Because, Señor, I feel a kinship with you."

He rubbed his eyes and looked me up and down. At length he invited me in. It being early in the morning, I was given some chocolate to drink. We began a conversation that lasted several hours and a friendship that did not last long enough.

During that first meeting, I became less and less enamored of Manuel. He had not had any hardships, being the son of the viceroy; in fact, it appeared to me that he had grown up quite spoiled and had wasted the many opportunities he had been given.

On the other hand, he seemed to become more fascinated with me every minute. Just before lunch, while we stood admiring a painting, he took me in his arms and kissed me. I was flattered in a way, and I was extremely aroused, not having had a man really satisfy me since Panamá, and because his kiss was very exciting.

However, I could no longer move without a whole heart in matters of love. As he kissed me on my neck, I fought back my desire to let him know that inwardly I was responding. With great self-control on my part, I gently pushed him away and told him, "I cannot." I quickly turned and walked out of the house.

Over the next few weeks, he made many vain attempts to consummate our relationship. He had the viceroy's oval face, but he was much more handsome, having La Perricholi's eyes and sensitive features. I wanted him and I would like to have had some satisfaction in love, which he appeared to be able to provide, but I did not deem it prudent. Though I would not respond to his advances, he became more interesting to me each time we met.

We did share a love of horses and we rode into the hills on occasion. During those rides, we got to know each other, and eventually, Manuel and I became good friends. Consequently, I changed him.

"Manuel, I know you are sad, but I suspect that you were sad before your mother died," I said to him one day.

We were sitting on our horses, on a hill overlooking the city. He looked at me quickly in denial, and then I had the impression that he suddenly understood something about his life. "Yes, Manuela, that is true." He looked out over the ocean. Then he asked quietly, to himself, "Why am I sad?"

I edged my horse next to his and put my hand on his arm. "My friend, I believe you have wasted your talents."

He looked at me, questioning me with his eyes.

"You do not have any idea about the political events that are going on all around you. You, the son of a viceroy."

"Political affairs bore me."

"I do not believe you. I do not believe you have ever tried. As far as I can see, you have never paid any attention to anything, except bedding young girls and gambling."

He looked sheepish, and after a moment he said, "Manuela, you strike a man hard, but it is truth."

After that day, I was able to involve him in what was happening to Perú. He soon took an active interest in the success of the approaching liberation. Once we began discussing intellectual topics, Manuel showed a sharp mind, and a profound curiosity.

He began to visit regularly to tell me of this or that revolutionary news item or merely to engage me in long philosophical discussions. This was in sharp contrast to his visits weeks before when he would come over only to continue his conquest of me in his bed, not that he ever stopped trying.

In the meantime, a month had turned into two and then three and still James had not returned, even though the traffic in and out of Callao had long since returned to normal. I began trying to find passage to Guayaquil despite my promise to stay until James's return.

Manuel tried to dissuade me. He had made many new acquaintances among the revolutionaries to whom I had introduced him, but I think I was the only close friend he had who shared his new intellectual interests. However, I told him, and everyone else, emphatically, I was leaving on the first ship on which I could book passage. Then Jonotás and Natán came home one day with news that changed everything.

She and Natán gossiped with other slaves because she liked to discover what was going on behind the closed doors of Lima's finest. I encouraged her in this, of course, because she told me everything, and sometimes she provided me with important information. Eventually, this habit of theirs would become invaluable to me.

On this particular day, they came running back from the center of town the very moment they heard this special bit of news. "Manuelita! Manuelita!" Jonotás hollered from the door downstairs.

"I'm up here," I called down to them. I was in my room packing a trunk.

They ran upstairs and Jonotás said breathlessly, "You better stop packin.'"

Natán, equally breathless, said, "That's right."

"Why? We're leaving in two days."

"Oh, I don' think you're goin' to want to go," said Jonotás.

"What are you two talking about?"

Natán giggled and said, "We know somethin' that's goin' to make you want to stay."

I smiled at them and said, "Very well, let me hear the news that would make me put off my plans."

Together they said, "The Numancia Battalion is comin' to Lima."

Chapter 34

They were right. Nothing could make me leave after hearing that news.

I will never forget the day, almost two months later, when I saw my brother ride with the famous battalion as they galloped through Lima. Their gray uniforms, with red piping, gave them a look of imposing strength. That the revolution had come to Lima was marked by the arrival of these fierce defenders of the city.

The battalion charged up the avenue that connects from Callao, turned at the main square, and rode across the San Lazaro bridge and out beyond the hill of San Cristóbal to camp. There was no ceremony—no official welcome—even though this unit of 650 soldiers was considered the flower of the Royalist forces in South America.

I saw José María as he rode through the square with the other soldiers. I waved at him, frantically, but he looked straight ahead with a disciplined military air that was frightening. He appeared ten years older, rather than three.

The reason they were so somber was because of the news that had just arrived the day before. The expedition from Spain, which was supposed to be on the way to Chile to take up where Osorio had failed, was not coming. The soldiers had murdered their officers and taken the ship, *La Trinidad*, to Buenos Aires. The looks on the faces of the Spanish-born in Lima were desperately gloomy that day.

The dust had not yet settled from the battalion's ride through the city when I sent Jonotás and Natán to the site of the Numancia encampment with a letter:

Dearest Brother,

Words cannot express my happiness at knowing you are again in the same country as your sister, who has longed for your companionship.

Please do come to see me, and return your answer, as to when that might be, with these two who have brought you this letter.

Your loving sister,
Manuela

Jonotás and Natán returned with his reply scratched on the back of my letter:

My dear Manuela—

I am beside myself with surprise and happiness. Your words are an oasis, in a wide desert, to a tired man. I have not received letters from you or father in almost two years.

These delightful messengers have instructed me as to the best way to find your house and I would be pleased to come visit you on Sunday.

My happiness is only surpassed by my excitement at seeing you soon.

José

He arrived at our door at about two o'clock the following Sunday. I threw my arms around his neck, giving a little yelp for joy.

"Oh, my sister, I'm so glad to see you," he said, still pressing his cheek to mine.

When he hugged me, I was so happy I began to cry. "José, I am glad to see you too."

I looked at him through my tears. He was as handsome as ever, but, as I said, too old for his years. There was a new scar above his left eyebrow, and he looked thin and tired.

I showed him around the house, and we played with my animals. Then we walked through the patio and settled down in the main salon. I told him all about Father's departure for Spain, of my marriage to James, and my life in Lima. I left out my involvement in the revolution, little as it was.

"Tell me about yourself," I said at last. "How does a soldier's life suit you?"

He smiled slightly. "I don't know if this is a good topic of discussion. There is not much to tell."

"Oh, José, you are not going to leave me for three years and not tell me about it. Surely you have a story or two."

He appeared thoughtful, remaining silent a long time. I regretted pressing him. "It's true; I have stories. Some I would rather forget." He smiled at me. "I have fought in many battles," he said at last.

"Do you not wish to speak about it?"

His face seemed to show anger and weariness at the same time. His eyebrows knit. He looked at me, and I thought I saw his eyes reach out to me. "I am not sure I should have left Panamá."

I thought about the day, three years earlier, when he embarked so happily on his soldiering life. I thought about the young soldier who died that day in the knife fight. I had been right. The brutality of war had changed my innocent brother. I fought back my tears. "Why, José?"

"I am a captain now." He pointed to the braid on his sleeve. "I have risen swiftly in rank." He looked at me, as though he had to decide how much to reveal. "It seems that the more rank and responsibilities I have, the closer I am to . . ."

I could not prevent a gasp of surprise and fear. I knew the word he did not speak: "death."

"It is just a feeling, of course. I feel proud of my accomplishments. I know Father would be proud." He was thoughtful for a moment.

I sat frozen, afraid to move, thinking I could stop time if I kept still. Fear for my brother filled my body. He sat looking at the floor.

At last, he said, almost jocularly to break the mood, "I do not trust the viceroy's leadership—that is the problem." When I did not respond—I was still holding back my fear—he said, "Nor do the other officers in the battalion."

"You are unsure . . . ?" I did not know how to ask him about his loyalty to the crown.

The mood would not be broken and he looked at me. His eyes were hard as he said, "Yes."

"José, why do you not change—"

"Manuela, don't."

"But, José . . ."

He said quietly, "I am a soldier in service to the king. I cannot be disloyal. But my true loyalty is to my comrades. They are all in the battalion, and I could no more leave them than cut off my arm. That is the real reason."

"José, I—"

"I know, Manuela, I know. The king may lose these colonies after all. If it were only me, I would agree with you. I *should* change sides. I cannot. Could you fight—or even leave—*your* friends?"

I lowered my eyes. I feared I might cry if I looked at him. "No, José, I could not." After a moment, I looked up. "Do you not fear the outcome? What will happen if Spain loses this war?" My voice was full of dread.

"Oh come, Manuela, it is not so bad." He smiled that broad smile of his. "I should not have spoken to you thus. I have worried you." When I did not say anything, he came over and sat beside me. He lifted my face to look at him and said, "Truly, I will be fine." His joviality could not undo my fear.

"What if Spain loses the war?" I said.

"Manuela, I insist on not talking war," he playfully chided. He stood up and walked to the door and looked out on the patio. He did not speak for a long time.

"José?"

He turned around. When he saw how persistent was my concern, he said, "If Spain loses, it will not be so bad. Only the colonies will be lost—or some of them. Despite my strange premonition, I do not believe I will die in battle." He looked confident as he spoke and he calmed me. "Spain will always be there," he continued, and laughed.

"Do you feel they will lose then?"

He stopped smiling and came back over to sit beside me. He spoke softly. "I should not be saying this. It is treason. But the war is not managed well. You are right. This is the first time I have ever believed it, but I fear there is a possibility that Spain might lose." I did not say anything, and he went on. "I have also heard that the naval war is going badly."

"Yes, we heard about *La Trinidad*."

"Other ships have been taken as well. I have not been told officially, but I am sure the seas are in grave danger for Spain. The only hope is the *María Isabel*."

"A Spanish warship?"

"Yes, a mighty warship, still in Chilean waters. It is the only ship that has the fire power—234 guns—to beat down the newly formed Chilean navy." He seemed to bolster his own spirits and said, "Despite all that, I actually believe it is possible to put down the insurgency." Then, more seriously, "However, the viceroy and the other generals will have to double their resolve."

He talked for half an hour more, filling the air with the horror of war, becoming more serious by the minute. Having started it, I tried to change the course of the discussion and, at length, had some success.

"You say you have not heard from Papa?" I interjected.

"No, we move around too much. I take it you have written to me?"

"Yes, I have written every month, with the exception of when I was preparing to depart from Panamá and just after my arrival here. I have heard from Papa just recently. I will show you his letters."

"That would be wonderful. I miss him. Since we are here to defend Lima, we will no doubt be here for awhile and I will at last be able to receive some mail."

"José, why did you join the Numancia Battalion? It is said they are the fiercest fighters in South America."

"Yes," he said with a sardonic laugh.

"Is it not true?"

"Oh, yes, it is true. We are unbeatable." He smiled. "I only wish we were allowed to fight without interference from the viceroy."

"I specifically told you to keep yourself from danger," I playfully reproached him. "What made you want to join?"

"My companions decided to do so. It was for them an act of bravado. For me it was a cleansing."

"How do you mean, José?"

"I was worried at first, and nearly refused to follow my comrades, but I had an encounter which changed my mind."

"Tell me."

"As I said, I was afraid. In fact, I had been so afraid, in every battle I had been in, up to that time, I almost felt like deserting. Then I met a soldier, an officer, at least twice my age, who had been in Quito during the great earthquake. He described the quake and how horrible it was.

"At first, he said, when his bed started to shake, early in the morning, he was frightened. He ran outside, only to be stopped by the sight of a wall falling in front of him from across the street. He stood dead still and refused to move. He did not know why he did it, but he stayed in one position and observed only what was happening in his line of vision.

"He said he was ready for the quake to take him. When he realized that, his fear went away. Since that time, he said, he has never again been afraid during an earthquake."

"Yes, but how does this—"

"Somehow, when I heard the story, I knew I had to join the battalion. I had to face my fear. My first fight with the battalion was horrible, the worst I had ever seen or imagined. But I came through it. Since then, I have been afraid, but not terrified, like my first encounters with battle."

He became quiet, and we looked into each other's eyes. The irony was frightening. If it had not been for that quake, I might not have been born. Now, that quake so long ago had put my brother in danger. He saw the look of pain on my face and said, "It is all right, Manuela. There is always a chance that one can die. I have faced my fear and conquered it. Now my problem is finding glory in the battles I have to fight."

"José, you may not be afraid, but you make me afraid. Let us talk of something else. In fact, it is almost four o'clock. Our meal is ready. We'll eat a little early, if you don't mind."

I sent Natán to find a street vendor for some *ante con ante* as a special treat. I wanted José María to taste it. It is an iced desert drink composed of wine, syrup, almonds, cinnamon and an assortment of slices of lemon and little bits of mixed fruits. I had never tasted it before living in Lima, and it is delicious.

While Natán was gone, José María enjoyed his first home-cooked meal in two years. I had personally supervised its preparation, but it was really the handiwork of one of James's servants. She had not only suggested it but had prepared it for the most part. It was a mutton dish garnished with yuccas, *camotes*, cabbages and a kind of rice preparation called *sancochado*. José María was profuse with his compliments.

As we finished the meal, we heard the door open and I remarked that the *ante con ante* had arrived. When Natán entered the room, she looked as though she had something on her mind.

"Natán, is something wrong?"

"I do not know, Manuelita, they're talkin' in the street and they're excited."

"What is it?"

"Yes," José María said, "please tell us."

"They are sayin' a ship, I think it's the *María Isabel*, has been taken."

José stood up. "When did it happen?"

"On October 29, they said."

"That is it then. The naval dominion of Spain, in the Pacific, is gone. I am sorry, but I must return to the camp."

"José, is it that serious?"

"I do not know, but I may be needed. I am sorry. I will see you soon, I hope." He kissed me on the cheek.

"Wait, José."

I tried to detain him, but despite my protests, he left soon. As it turned out, his fears were justified regarding the meaning to Spanish naval efforts. Spain never controlled the Pacific after that.

However, in Lima, absolutely nothing happened for weeks and weeks. We heard no news of San Martín and his plans, or of any movement of Spanish troops. Slowly, the

Spanish began to walk through the streets with their usual arrogance. The viceroy made a vehement proclamation that another expedition was coming from Spain and he himself was going to take personal charge of the defense of Lima.

I still had not heard from James; and after waiting a few more weeks, I began to think again about my plans to go to Quito. However, I decided to put off my plans a while longer. I wanted to see more of José María. I wanted to have a mutual birthday celebration with him; and with carnival only a couple of months after that, I thought it might be fun to share it with José.

If José María had not been in Lima, I would have left for Quito. As it turned out, there was not much of a carnival to share. What's worse, because I stayed, I could not get away when I finally wanted to do so. Since I could not get away, I became ever more involved in the revolution. I ended up staying in Peru for three more years.

Chapter 35

My plans to spend the March Carnival with José María were in vain. The usual plans were cut back so much that there was hardly any carnival at all. What should have been the first day of the celebration, February 28, 1819, was instead used by the viceroy to review the squadron in the bay of Callao. He staged a mock sea battle to keep the soldiers and sailors battle-ready.

A thick fog obscured the harbor as his Excellency, on his own launch, directed the operations. An hour or so after he arrived in the bay, the mist was broken by a strange ship entering the harbor from a direction never used. It was the *O'Higgins* (the recently captured and renamed *María Isabel*) commanded by Lord Cochrane. This famous English naval hero, who had been made admiral of the Chilean navy, was not to be trifled with. When it was found who was in the mysterious ship entering from the south of Callao, the Spanish were extremely fearful.

By arriving on the first day of the carnival, Lord Cochrane had anticipated catching Lima unprepared. As it was, a fight ensued which was indecisive, except that it utterly demoralized the *peninsulares*. I do not think they ever expected the war to come so close to home.

Also, James, being English, was now suspect and it was clear that he would not be returning until the situation changed. I decided to leave immediately, but again, normal traffic in and out of Callao was stopped.

All of Lima waited, but there were no more attacks. We heard that Cochrane was having great success in destroying Spanish shipping up and down the coast. We heard that San Martín was mounting a very large expedition to conquer Lima, which would invade from the water now that the Spanish could no longer control the seas in that latitude. We heard of skirmishes here and there for over a year. In the meantime, I was stuck in Lima.

I decided it was about time I did something to actively advance the cause of the revolution. One morning I went to see Rosita. Her salon was empty and we had a long talk alone. I confided to her that I earnestly wished to do something to help the cause.

"You *are* helping the cause," she said. "People like José," by which she meant Riva Agüero, "speak to me of how the information you are able to acquire throughout the city has more than once been helpful."

"I know, but I want to do more."

"What do you have in mind, Manuela?"

"I know that José writes the bills that appear around the city. I recognize the style. What I want to know is, who puts them up?"

"He does, or other members of the Lautaro Lodge."

I said, "There. Too dangerous. He should spend his time writing them. Why don't we put them up?"

"Us?"

"Yes, or at least I want to do it."

She said, "If it is too dangerous for him, how much more dangerous would it be for us?"

"However dangerous it is, a *tapada* would take only half the risk of a man."

She thought about it for a minute, and then she sat up and said, "You are right! Let's find José and tell him."

That is how Rosita, Jonotás, Natán and I became couriers for the seditious writings of Riva Agüero and other members of the Lautaro Lodge. Every couple of weeks, José would have a new bill to post and the four of us would take off late at night dressed as *tapadas*. We would walk through the streets, the bills hidden under our *mantos*. When we found a likely spot, some of us would keep an eye out for the authorities, while the rest posted the bill. It worked. We were ignored by other people on the street. Gradually, Rosita and I were taken more and more into Riva Agüero's confidence.

At one point I overheard him say that he needed some guns. As it happened, on the very next day, Jonotás heard from a slave that there were some rifles in the customs house in Callao, being held for transport to Trujillo. I wanted to procure them for Riva Agüero, but I did not know how to get them.

Having those guns so close yet so unobtainable preyed on my mind all day. In the afternoon, I went to La Perricholi's house to visit Manuel Amat. He was surprised but happy to see me.

I was unprepared for the feelings I encountered as I entered the house. Everything reminded me of Miquita, and I felt a profound sense of loss. "Manuel, I have something to ask of you, but being in this house has made me miss your mother terribly. Let us sit down and talk awhile."

"Yes, I would love to talk with you. I miss her, too." He sent a servant off to get us something to drink. We sat down, and he said, "I'm happy to see you."

We reminisced for awhile and drank some English tea. Then I came around to my business. I told him about the guns and tried to convince him to bribe the officials to get them.

He was uncertain. "Bribes are dangerous." His brows knit.

I could see he did not feel the need to procure those guns for Riva Agüero as keenly as I, and I was sorry I asked. I felt I might have compromised him in some way. It was curious how fond I had grown of him since La Perricholi's death. "You are right, but I have another plan. Will you at least lend me the money to make a bribe?"

"I am not going to allow you to take all the risk."

"Manuel, I should not have asked you at all. I know a way that will not expose me to risk. All I need is the money." This was a complete lie.

At length, he agreed. "I will bring you enough money to make a suitable bribe—tomorrow."

I thanked him and talked with him for another half an hour. I enjoyed his company and regretted not spending more time with him.

When I was about to leave, he surprised me. As he opened the door, he turned abruptly and took me in his arms. The moment was unexpected, but I did not resist. I looked into his eyes and he kissed me. It was the first time he had kissed me since that arousing kiss the first day we met. I found myself responding, uncontrollably, to his passion.

Since the days of my oath on the ship where I had lost Juanita, I had prided myself in my disobedience of society's, and especially the church's rules about what defined decent behavior. In Panamá especially, I had indulged my hunger for intimate satisfactions, determined to obey my own desires and nothing else.

When I arrived in Perú, there were many men whom I could have taken to my bed in James's absence, but I did not. It was my indulgences in Panamá that had made me decide, for my own sense of moral integrity, that I must love the man to whom I might become romantically attached. True, I did not love James; but when I agreed to marry him, I convinced myself that I would. Besides, he was a victim of my determination to stay in the colonies. He was a means to an even greater purpose than any romantic dalliance. James kept me from poverty and obscurity. Still, I believed that I should love a man before becoming intimate with him. I believed it even more, after I was married and after I stopped being intimate with James.

However, over the months living in Lima, I began to believe that I had been wrong to restrain myself. When I looked around at society, at the way men and women were treated so differently, I fumed at the inequity. Men could have concubines with not so much as a scowl from a priest, while women such as my mother could be driven from their home and ostracized for loving a man too much. I had seen this unfairness all my life. However, not until I became a grown woman, and could see the ways of men and women from an adult perspective did I realize just how unfair it was.

Women were expected to live up to the ideal of the Virgin Mary in public. Yet men were expected to make conquests of virgins. The day after I was married, due to this high ideal of women as virgins, I had to go into seclusion. James, on the other hand, moved about freely, coming home with energy from the interests of his day, and then expected me to be anything but a virgin in bed.

The more I thought about it, the more I sensed that the adoration of women as chaste and virtuous by the church and society's leaders was merely a way of entrapping women. If one can control what a woman desires, one can control the woman—and *I* would not be controlled.

I wanted Manuel that day. He was sensitive, interesting and generous—and he truly admired me. His reluctance to take risks and his being about the same age as James were the only blemishes in a very attractive man. I liked him very much, and wanted him.

But, I stopped him.

"I'm sorry, Manuel, but it is not right." I slowly backed away from him.

"Yes, I am sorry, too. It was unwise of me. You are married, after all."

He had misunderstood. He assumed it was fidelity that stopped me. Why would he think anything else, since my reasons were so subtle I barely understood them myself? It was not propriety or anything close to it that restrained me. I would take him as a lover if it pleased me. I would not be held back by the unfair rules and conventions of a church that has been an enemy my whole life. No, I stopped him because I did not have a heart wholly ready for him.

I did not wish to explain my reasons, which he might not understand. Instead, I said, "Do you still wish to help me?"

"Manuela, of course, please do not think badly of me."

"I don't." I kissed him lightly on the lips and said, "Do not think badly of me either." I left.

The next day he came by with a considerable amount of gold, asking me to return what I did not need. We did not speak about our moment of passion the day before.

Late that night, Jonotás and Natán and I rode down to the customs house. The only idea I had was to try to bribe the guard. If that did not work, then we would try to bribe the officials. As it turned out, a bribe was not necessary at all.

We left our horses up the road and walked into Callao. It was late, and we slipped from shadow to shadow. We could hear the waves crashing against the sides of the fortress on the other end of town, but otherwise the night was quiet. Everyone seemed to be at home. A *tapada*, outside of Lima, would have aroused interest, so we did not try to hide our faces. We did wear the *manto*, however, because I carried my pistols, in their holsters, over my shoulder.

When we found the customs house, a guard was standing in front of an open door in the back. He was in his thirties, a three-day stubble on his face, and obviously bored. He had come outside to smoke a cigar and had left the door ajar. Beyond him, in the building, we could see a lamp on a table and boxes that were very likely full of rifles, stacked against the wall.

"If he could be distracted, we could steal one of those boxes," I whispered.

"I can distract him," said Jonotás.

"How?"

She smiled a wicked smile and said, "I'll get some help from somethin' inside his trousers," and crept around the corner.

I didn't know what she was going to do, but I saw ugly Jonotás approach the man. Despite my faith in her, when I saw her walk up to him, I was frightened.

Jonotás's powers of seduction have always been a source of amazement for me. In no time, with no beauty to rely on, she had enticed the man away from his post. He followed her into the shadows, across and down the street.

In his hurry to follow her, he had made a poor attempt at closing the door. It was slightly ajar, and Natán and I stole inside without even having to unlatch it. With great difficulty, we lifted one of the heavy crates and carried it out, around the neighboring building, and some distance away. Taking the rifles out of the box, we hid them under some bushes as fast as we could.

We quickly returned and put the box back where we found it. Then we returned to where Jonotás had left us.

Natán whistled.

Shortly, Jonotás arrived, naked, pulling her shift over her head. "Quick, let's go," she said, "I told him I was going to relieve myself." We suppressed our laughter and silently crept out of town, found our horses, and then galloped back to Rosita's.

José was there. I pulled him aside and told him where Natán and I had hidden the rifles. He was incredulous. His sensitive brow curled and he looked at me for a moment to see if I was lying.

"I am telling you the truth. If you want them, you should hurry."

He called some other men to join him, and he left immediately. I was able to return all of Manuel's gold. After that I was always invited to the midnight meetings and was given a much more active role in revolutionary planning.

As I came to know Riva Agüero, it seemed to me that he should be the one to assume power when Perú was liberated. He certainly worked harder than any one else. The only thing I noticed which I did not like was that he seemed to be jealous of San Martín. It was almost as if he did not want the heroic general entering the city.

In August, we heard that San Martín had launched an expedition known as the "Liberating Army of Perú," consisting of six battalions of infantry and two regiments of cavalry (4,450 officers and men), 31 guns, 2 howitzers, 2 mortars, and spare arms and equipment for another 15,000 men (in the hope that there would be desertions from the Spanish to the patriot cause). The squadron bearing the army consisted of 8 warships with an average of 200 guns.

By September, we heard that Viceroy Pezuela was trying to negotiate with the recently landed army, in Pisco, just south of Lima. I was worried for José María's safety. Any day, he might be meeting San Martín's army in a bloody battle.

As it turned out, San Martín was not a bloodletter. I came to know him later; and although he was criticized for not moving his troops into Lima earlier, I know that he was firmly convinced that the highest victory is one achieved without fighting. He did not attack; instead he began surrounding the city, by the sea to the west and with his army to the east. Such was the state of affairs through October; and then we heard of the revolt in Guayaquil, which brought the last important seaport outside of Callao under the patriot flag.

Less than a month later, there was another naval loss for the Spanish. The fleet directly under the viceroy's control had been reduced to three frigates in the Callao harbor—the *Prueba*, the *Venganza* and the *Esmeralda*. Lord Cochrane took the finest, the *Esmeralda*—the last important warship left to the Spanish—from under the fire of 250 guns mounted at the citadel in a bloody night battle. Over 160 Spanish lives were lost.

The mood of the *peninsulares* was ugly and violent. Two days later, some men who were not part of the Lautaro Lodge were caught putting up handbills at night. The Spanish soldiers who found them were merciless, and the men were instantly slaughtered. Nighttime travel throughout the city became prohibited. The night watchmen, who in the good districts such as mine were usually on every corner, were dismissed because they were mostly American born. Instead, soldier's horses could be heard traveling the streets throughout the night.

Regardless of the danger, Rosita, Jonotás, Natán and I went out regularly and posted the bills written by Riva Agüero. Once or twice we were questioned, but our pretending to be only silly females out for fun saved us.

The only thing that diminished my resolve was thinking about my brother. I was an active revolutionary, my brother an active Royalist. I knew who I was and what I wanted, but that did not prevent me from regretting the fact that I was actually fighting my own brother.

One morning, I was awakened by a small earthquake. As I lay there, I thought of the earthquake of 1797 and how José María had joined the Numancia Battalion after hearing a story about it.

That night, when I was supposed to go out with Rosita to post bills, I feigned illness. I could not continue until the problem of my brother was solved. I could not give up the revolution. Neither could I fight against my brother.

I thought about abandoning Lima and traveling to Quito, but I knew I would only be running away from the problem. By the time the sun arose the next morning, I was sick—with worry.

All day long I fought with my dilemma; but that night, after hearing something Riva Agüero said, I had a dangerous idea. I did not know how I would accomplish what I envisioned, but I knew I had no other choice. The next day, I sent Jonotás off to bring Manuel Amat to me.

When he arrived, he said, "I regret not having helped you more in your endeavor to obtain those rifles."

"I have something more dangerous, and far more ambitious, in mind this time. I hope you will not refuse me." I paced back and forth in agitation. I needed his help, and I was prepared to do anything to get it.

"Manuela, I . . . tell me what it is."

We were alone in a small sitting room so that my plan would not be overheard by the servants. Jonotás was standing guard outside the door. In my agitation, it was hard for me to speak quietly; but I told him each step of my plan, as I strode up and down.

I was determined to do what I had in mind, with or without his help, but I very much needed him. I anticipated a long afternoon trying to persuade him to participate in my scheme, and my nerves were frayed.

"Yes, yes, I see," he said at last. He rose from his chair and came up to me. "It is impossible, of course, and I foresee how it could come out very badly. It really depends on how well you carry out your part, which is the most dangerous—very dangerous."

I was not going to be stopped. I found my breath coming fast, as though I were fighting. "Listen, Manuel, I am going—"

He smiled and put his hands on my arms. "Yes, Manuela, I know, you are going to do it with or without me. The part you ask of me is not hard. And yes, it would be better if it were one lone rider, one such as myself who has political influence in Lima."

"But it is dangerous."

"Not really. It is you I am worried about. You have chosen a role which is most unpredictable. You could hang."

"I don't want to talk about that; I need to know if you will do it." I was worked up, prepared to talk to him all afternoon. If he did not agree, I would have to find someone else—or go myself. I could feel my teeth gnaw as I clenched my jaw, ready to do battle with him.

"Of course, I will do it. Man or woman, Manuela, there has never been a braver patriot than you. I will never refuse you again."

I was suddenly overcome. So much of my energy has always come from "battle." No matter what the conflict, I draw my energy from my opposition. Occasionally, I find myself suddenly unopposed and admired. After all the worry I had been through in the last few days, I felt so suddenly relieved that I was deflated. In this case, what I had in mind was so dreadfully important to me personally that Manuel's admiration, so freely given, threw me off balance. Tears sprang to my eyes and I put my arms around his neck and held him close. "Oh, thank you, Manuel, thank you."

He held me for a long time, and then he kissed me softly, first on the cheek and then on my lips. Very softly. I found myself filled with desire. I returned his kisses. An urgent hunger took over me.

I wiped my tears and we began to undress each other. A few moments later, he pulled me to the floor and we made love. Both of us still half-dressed.

Afterward, we did not speak. I felt satisfied for the first time in a very long while. We stayed there, quiet, for almost a quarter of an hour. My head rested on his arm and at last he kissed me tenderly on the cheek. He arose and dressed.

"I will leave on your mission as soon as I make a few preparations," he whispered. He leaned over me and kissed me gently, on the lips, and said, "I am your servant, and I will come back successful."

Before he left the room, I said, "Thank you, Manuel."

"Let's wait and see what happens."

After he left, I wanted to bask in the good feelings I was enjoying, but there was no time. Instead, I bathed, dressed in the stylish French costume that was popular for the Promenade, mounted my horse, and rode out towards the site of the Numancia Battalion.

Chapter 36

What I had requested of Manuel was very dangerous, and not easy, despite his bravado. Riva Agüero had told me that San Martín was just north of the capital, and I had asked Manuel to find the general and make a petition for me.

I myself was going to attempt the impossible. Knowing that my brother's sense of loyalty was as fierce as my own, I knew he would never abandon his comrades. I also knew that I could not persuade him to desert. The only thing left for me to do was to urge not only José María but all of his fellow officers to have the entire Numancia battalion join the revolution.

While I would be safe by mentioning it to José María, what I feared was having someone in the battalion find out about it who was loyal to the crown. Not only could I be hanged for being a spy or a traitor, but José María could also suffer the same fate.

I did not take Jonotás and Natán with me that evening because we always drew attention, a white woman and two slaves on fiery horses. I did not want to be noticed.

I rode quietly and in step with the rest of the traffic that were out riding or walking. When I reached the Plaza Mayor, I turned toward the city gate and rode across the San Lazaro bridge like many other people do in the late afternoon in Lima. However, once I reached the suburb I continued down the road and up over the hill of San Cristóbal to the encampment of the Numancia.

I rode along, becoming more uncertain with each step. I had to remind myself that José María had often spoken of his fellow officer's discontent with the viceroy's leadership. I hoped that I had a true understanding of what I had been hearing. *What if I had misunderstood? I could be endangering both my life and the life my brother.*

When I arrived, it was busy. Men were scurrying back and forth—apparently making ready to decamp. *They are leaving. I have no time for my plan to work.* A chill went through me. I was too late.

The sentry would not let me pass. I cajoled him into sending word to my brother that I was waiting to see him. After some time, José María appeared, a frown on his face.

"We are preparing to leave," he said, with worry in his eyes. "San Martín is north of the city and we are to begin harassing him."

"When, José?"

"Soon. Tomorrow or the next day. I am not sure. When the city's defensive situation is secure."

There was not enough time! "José, let me talk to you alone."

We walked off where we could not be heard. Before I had a chance to begin my ill-prepared, but hopefully convincing, speech, he said, " Manuela, I know what you want, but I cannot leave my comrades. Inside I agree with you, but I will have to go ahead and fight the insurgents."

"I haven't come to ask for that."

"Oh," he said, "I thought that was why you had come. I was expecting you to try to talk me into changing sides."

"I've come to ask for much, much more."

He looked puzzled.

"My dear brother, I suspect, from many things you have told me, that you have spoken at times to the other officers in your battalion about the prospect of changing sides."

"Yes, it is true, but they all feel the same as I, and—"

"If they all feel just the same, then they all want to change sides. Now, don't speak for a minute. Let me tell you something. I can arrange for San Martín to give you all safe-conduct—and I can secure his promise for repatriation after the fighting—if you can convince the entire battalion to desert."

He snapped his head back, as though struck in the face. He gave me a long look.

I could tell what crossed his mind next. "No, José. This is not play. I am deadly serious about this."

"How can you be sure? We are marked men. The patriots would never accept us. We have done too much damage to them in the past."

"It is not important how I can be sure. I am."

He questioned me, and I was able to convince him that it was possible, through my contacts, to gain such a gift from San Martín. Although I could not imagine any officer refusing the incorporation of the Numancia into his ranks, I could see that José María believed they would never be accepted by the revolutionaries.

When I had convinced José at last, he said, "Wait here." He ran back to the encampment. While I waited, the temperature dropped as the sun lowered. The wind picked up, and the wide brim of my hat flapped as dust began to fly into my eyes. Still I waited.

Finally, José María brought out three officers, the leaders of the battalion. Fear went through me when I saw them. But my brother would not have betrayed me. I was introduced and then asked to repeat my proposal.

"Where is San Martín?" asked one.

"I cannot tell you until all is agreed," I said.

Again I was questioned and again I lied enough to convince them that it was possible.

The three officers excused themselves and talked for a moment. They returned and the leader said, "This is between us. If it is mentioned again outside of this circle, we will deny it and José María will be court-martialed for bringing a spy into our midst."

"I understand." *This was too dangerous.*

The officer said, "Very well. We are bound to depart in three days to find San Martín and harass him. If, as you say, you can bring us San Martín's assurances, in writing, that we will be taken into the patriot army, and if he will guarantee to pay us and repatriate us to Colombia when Lima falls, we will join the liberating forces. You must give us a written promise, before we leave—at dawn, three days hence."

Not knowing how I was going to do it, I assured him I would return on time. They gallantly tipped their hats while maintaining frozen and serious expressions and walked briskly back to the camp. I kissed José María and said, "José, thank you. I don't know what I would have done, if this had not worked."

He frowned. "It hasn't worked yet." He gave me a hug, said, "Take care," and walked back to the camp.

After I arrived back home, I went to sleep. I was up early the next day and all I could do was wait for Manuel to return. I paced up and down and did little else, all day. I dared not leave my house, in case he arrived. Finally, late that evening, he rode up tired and hungry.

"What happened? What did he say?" I asked, without noticing that he ached as he walked into the drawing room.

"I have brought you the news you desire," he said, as he slid into a chair.

"Oh, Manuel, thank you." I came over and kissed him. It was then that I noticed how sore he was. "But my poor man, are you all right?"

"Yes, but I am tired." He reached up and kissed my lips. Then, I poured him some brandy that he sipped while he told me about his excursion.

"It took me a while to find the patriot forces. But they were close, near Ancon." Not that close. Manuel had ridden over 16 leagues in the last 30 hours. No wonder he ached. He must not have had any sleep. "I had to elude the guards on both sides, and I was very nearly shot. However, I found his encampment and was finally able to speak to the general."

"What is he like?"

"Thin. Masculine. Quiet and thoughtful. I was impressed with him. He assured me that the Numancia Battalion would be received gladly."

"Oh, thank you, Manuel, thank you." I was so excited I could not contain myself. I hugged and kissed him.

"How did you fare?" he asked at last.

I told Manuel about my interview with the officers of the battalion. Then I sat down and quickly wrote a letter to San Martín explaining what the officers desired. I wanted Manuel to take it back immediately, but he was exhausted.

I made sure that Jonotás and Natán kept the servants busy, and I took him upstairs to bed. We spent the night together, and I ushered him out early the next morning before the servants were awake. I expected him back by the next evening easily. That would give us more than enough time to reach the battalion before they left. I was quite frightened for him, however. He would be shot if the *godos* found that letter on him.

Later that afternoon, Rosita arrived with many leaflets, which had been smuggled in from the patriot forces. They contained a proclamation, made by San Martín while at Ancon:

> Spaniards, your destiny is in your own hands; I come not to declare
> war against the fortunes and persons of individuals; the enemy of the
> liberty and independence of America alone is the object of the
> vengeance of the arms of the Patria. I promise you in the most positive
> manner, that your property and persons shall be inviolable; and that you
> shall be treated as respectable citizens, if you co-operate in the great
> cause.

Later that night, Rosita, Jonotás, Natán and I, as *tapadas*, posted the proclamation around the city. It was dangerous. Only the night before, more men were killed doing the same thing. I knew one of them.

The next day, I waited impatiently for Manuel to return. I expected him to be back by dusk, at the latest.

When night fell, I was extremely worried. Only a few hours to go and no way to regain the opportunity. If Manuel did not return, José would have to go into battle fighting a lost cause against a cause I held dear.

I was beside myself when Manuel showed up an hour or so before dawn, both he and his horse exhausted. "The general had already started for Huacho. He was quite hard to find," Manuel said, as he quietly entered my house. At first, I could not tell from his manner whether he had succeeded or not.

He had. As he sat down, exhausted, he handed me a letter from San Martín, stating that the Numancia Battalion should receive all that it desired.

"I am going to have to hurry if I am to make it to their camp by dawn."

"I will go along." He rose from where he was seated with great weariness.

"No, *tapadas* will move more freely. Go home now, and thank you. From the bottom of my soul, I thank you." I called to Jonotás and Natán and we walked out to where his horse waited.

He followed. "May I not wait for you?"

"No—the servants—I will see you tomorrow. Go now." I kissed him long and hard on the lips.

He saw that we would be walking to the encampment and said, "Perhaps you are right. As it is, my mare will have to find her own way home while I sleep." He smiled, mounted his horse, and rode away.

Jonotás and Natán and I started off for the bridge to San Lazaro. Then I remembered something. Hiding the letter under my clothes, I ran back upstairs, grabbed one of my pistols, hid it under my manto, and returned to my companions.

We walked because *tapadas* walked and because we would never have been able to leave the city walls at that hour on horseback. We would have to hurry because we would have to walk the entire distance to the encampment while finding some way to get through the city gate—in little more than an hour. I felt the cold steel of the barrel of my pistol beneath my shawl as we started down the street to the Plaza Mayor.

The streets were deserted except for small groups of soldiers who rode by. It was quite late, and to avoid being seen, and perhaps stopped, we ducked into the shadows many times. I assumed that *tapadas* would be ignored, as we had been while putting up bills, but it was very early in the morning for *tapadas* and neither did I want to take unnecessary chances.

We came to the plaza and I peeked around the corner. I did not want us to be seen in the plaza until I felt confident that we could get through the gate without being questioned too much. The square was dark and empty, and the gate next to the palace was closed. Two sentries stood against the wall, smoking and laughing. I watched them, trying to form a plan. I hoped one or the other would leave for awhile.

I whispered, "I don't think we should all try to leave the city. It would be easier if only one of us went through the gate."

"But, Manuelita, you can't go alone—"

"I'll be all right. You go back home. When I return—"

I heard a horse coming down the street behind us. I spun around. A young officer was looking at us as he urged his mount in our direction.

"Come on," I said, and walked toward him. I started laughing quietly. Jonotás and Natán joined in, as we tried to give the impression of three *tapadas* coming home from a night of fun.

The officer continued to watch us. I knew before it happened that he would stop us. When we were about to pass, he said, "Halt!"

My heart raced. I silently cocked the pistol under my shawl.

We stood frozen while he dismounted and walked over to us. "What are you doing here?" he asked.

We said nothing. Jonotás and Natán giggled a little.

"What are you doing here this time of night?" he demanded.

The letter from San Martín, which I was carrying between my breasts, crackled as I shifted my weight. In desperation to say something, I concentrated on hiding my "lisp" and said, "An adventure, Señor, of love."

Jonotás knew I was struggling with my accent and asked, "Do you wish to join us?"

He looked at us suspiciously and said, "Let me see your faces."

We didn't move. I could feel my knees start to shake. He reached up to pull back my *manto*.

With his hand almost touching my shawl, I put my pistol to his nose. My own hand shook slightly as he looked down the barrel in shock.

I kept my *manto* closed, and in a whisper so as not to give away my Quito accent, I said, "I will kill you if you don't do exactly as I say."

He took a step back in fear. I followed, my pistol right between his eyes. I whispered, "You don't want to do anything that will cause me to kill you—do you?"

He shook his head, but I could see he was beginning to recover his composure. He was looking for a way to disarm me.

I ordered him to mount. Natán held the horses reins and Jonotás held my pistol while I climbed on behind him.

She handed my weapon to me and I whispered, "Later," to Jonotás.

She nodded and Natán let go of the reins.

Then, holding my pistol to the man's neck, I said, "Ride out of the city, through San Lazaro" I said. He urged the horse forward. "If they question where you are going, let them know you intend to enjoy me up in the hills. Do it right."

He did not say anything, but touched his spurs to his horse's ribs. When we arrived at the gate, they opened it up without even speaking to him. They smiled lewdly, believing what I had hoped they would believe.

As we rode across the bridge, I saw light starting to silhouette the hills. After we were a short distance away from the light of the viceroy's palace it was too black to see the street, yet I made the soldier urge his horse faster anyway. I was frantic that my brother was already leaving.

Despite the faint outline of the sky behind the Andes, the darkness was almost perfect. We had not gone very far down the road past San Lazaro when the horse stumbled.

I felt myself flying forward, and we both fell with a dull thud in the dirt path. Pain tore at my left wrist as I landed. I lost the pistol from my right hand.

"You bitch," the soldier hissed as he rolled over on top of me. He reached for my arms, to pin them to the ground.

I could make out the pistol just out of my reach, beyond my right hand. I reached for it.

The soldier saw it. He scrambled toward it. I clawed at him to get it first. The pain in my left wrist seemed to sear my whole body.

Closer we fought toward the pistol. When it looked like I might reach it first, he pulled back and slapped me so hard I almost passed out. Feeling me go limp in his grip, he started to stand to reach over and secure the pistol.

I brought my foot up hard, to where it hurts a man most. The pain stopped him, dead still, and he sank to his knees.

I lunged forward, grabbed the barrel of the pistol, and brought the handle across his jaw. I heard his jawbone crack as he fell into the dust and lay still.

I scrambled to my feet, blood flowing from my lip.

It was lighter now. The sun would be up in minutes.

I staggered to the horse, mounted, and raced on to the encampment. The horse was favoring his right foreleg, but I pushed him faster.

When I arrived at the encampment, the soldiers were assembled to depart. José María was at the head of the path, waiting for me.

I quickly wiped the blood off my face so that he would not be worried when he saw me. I dismounted and placed the precious letter in my brother's hands.

"Manuela, you've done it," he said, reading it over quickly. I stood with my back to the approaching dawn, so that he would not see any blood or dust on me.

He kissed me on the cheek. "I must go now," he said.

"Make sure that I see you again, my brother."

He took me in his arms and held me close. He said, "Don't worry. You be careful too." He raced off.

I would worry, but I felt better.

I had no time to relish my victory. I had to hurry back to the soldier before he regained consciousness. I rode swiftly so that I would come upon him before he had time to hide when he heard the hooves on the trail, if he was awake. It was light enough to see.

I was right to hurry. He was already walking back to San Lazaro. I pointed my pistol at him and ordered him to lie on the ground, while I dismounted. He could not

speak, because his jaw was broken. He looked miserable, and I felt sorry for him, despite the pain in my wrist and the taste of blood in my mouth.

When I dismounted, I removed the horse's reins. Then I chased the animal off into the hills.

I made him stand and pushed him behind some bushes. I tied his hands and feet with the reins. It was hard to make the leather straps tight with my wrist in such bad shape.

Feeling that he would not be able to move or be seen for awhile by those coming to town to sell their wares, I left him and walked in to San Lazaro.

I went to the small plaza. Already, Indian women were coming and going at the well. Feeling a deep exhaustion, my body still aching, I waited. Soon, the plaza was temporarily unoccupied. I walked over to the well and washed my face and hands.

I tried unsuccessfully to clean the dirt from my clothes without looking too suspicious. One or two women came to the well, but I don't think they paid any attention to me.

My *saya* was ruined. Aside from being filthy, there were two large rips, one showing my underslip, the other showing bare leg. My manto was also filthy and when I pulled it up, *en tapada*, you could see blood on it.

The city gates were open, but I did not want to cross the bridge. I saw that the same two guards were still on duty, and it would be disastrous if they decided I was the same *tapada* who went out with one of their fellows who had not returned. Once in a while, one of them would walk out on to the bridge and look up the road. I assumed they wondered why the soldier had not returned. The longer I waited, the greater the chance that someone would go look for the missing officer or he would free himself and walk back to the city.

Then, I saw Jonotás and Natán crossing the bridge. They had their faces covered, but I could tell by their walk. I was annoyed, because now I had to consider them in my plans to re-enter Lima. That is if I had a plan, which I didn't.

I motioned to them, and we found a place to talk. I discussed possibly finding one of their friends from a *cofradia* to hide with for the day, but I did not want anyone to know that I had been in San Lazaro when the soldier finally got back to town and an investigation was started.

"I am weary, I said, absently. We had been up all night, and the indecision was wearing me down. I did not know whether to walk back home and risk being seen, or wait until the traffic became heavier on the bridge, where we might lose ourselves in the crowd.

"It is too bad we cannot take that *calesa*, yonder," Natán mused. "It is a long walk home."

I looked at the *calesa*, standing outside the door of a nice looking house. A mule was already hitched to it. An idea flashed in my mind. I remembered my conversation with the workman in Guayaquil, the first time I saw a *calesa*.

"Come on," I said. "Quickly before the owner or driver come out of the house."

We quietly led the *calesa* away from the house. Then I had Jonotás strip off her *saya y manto*, which I put on. She had on shirt and trousers underneath as I suspected. She had been wearing men's clothes for some time. Natán and I climbed in while Jonotás got up on the mule. With her ability as a mime, she looked masculine enough to be a real driver. I pulled down the curtains, making the *calesa* look like it contained a frail old dowager or a pair of lovers who did not wish to be seen. I had Jonotás hurry toward the bridge before the owners of the *calesa* came looking for it.

We successfully rode across the river and entered the city. Through the gauze I saw the guards standing out on the bridge looking up and down the river for the officer. We rode safely on toward our neighborhood. Before we got too close, we stopped the *calesa* and left it. We walked the final three blocks to home.

Exhausted and aching, we tip-toed into the house, being careful not to wake the servants. I knew one or two were already up but we did not see them.

Jonotás and Natán helped me undress, as my wrist was really hurting. After I wrapped it in cloth, we went to bed, all three of us together in my bed. We slept soundly, and I was happy beyond words.

Chapter 37

On the third of December, 1820, the Numancia Battalion left the administration of Spain and joined the forces of the revolution, bringing 650 of the finest soldiers on the continent to their cause. This event, because they were such a superior fighting force, triggered many other desertions from Royalist ranks. The entire military situation changed in a matter of days.

I won't claim that my contribution was any better than anyone else's, but I feel I did save my brother's life and perhaps the lives of many, many more. There never was any real fighting for the liberation of Lima.

The Marqués de Torre Tagle, who had been sent by the viceroy to defend Trujillo, took his cue and also changed sides. He heard of the various officers and military units that had gone over to San Martín after the Numancia Battalion, and on the twenty-fourth of December, he called an open *cabildo*. He advised submission to the superior force of San Martín. The bishop and a few other Spaniards stoutly opposed, but Torre Tagle merely imprisoned them and opened the gates to the city with his own hands. This gave San Martín unhindered access to the provinces of the north, all the way to Guayaquil.

On the night of the twenty-eighth of January, 1821, the Royalist General La Serna—in an outrageous exhibition of treason to the crown—told the viceroy that he had four hours to turn over the government to his control. He cited the military failures of Pezuela resulting in his inability to contain San Martín and demanded the power to fight the insurgents as he saw fit.

Viceroy Pezuela temporized, but had to give in. The man who had insulted me in the Hall of the Viceroys had to take refuge with his family in the viceregal retreat in Magdalena. With discord on the Royalist side, this might have been good news for the patriots. However, La Serna was known to be a ruthless military leader, unlike the weak Pezuela. The patriots would now have a harder time of it.

A day or so later, Jonotás, through her contacts in the city, found out that the vicequeen was requesting free passage to take herself and her children back to Spain. The Spanish had granted it, but the patriot forces refused. The squadron in Callao harbor would not let any ship pass.

I immediately wrote a letter to General San Martín, boldly reminding him of my contributions in the desertion of the Numancia Battalion, and asked him, in the name of mercy, if he would please allow the beautiful and kind vicequeen to be allowed to depart.

Receiving no answer, I made ready to travel to San Martín's encampment myself. I was determined I would repay the lady for having mitigated her husband's ire that fateful night at the victory ball. However, before I could depart, I heard that Lord Cochrane's wife, out of kindness, had petitioned to her husband on the vicequeen's behalf as well. Doña Pezuela and her family had already left. I was grateful to Lady Cochrane.

In the early months of 1821, with guerrilla action all around the city, food became scarce and the populace began to succumb to yellow fever and starvation. My household had enough money that we were not severely affected by the lack of food, but we feared the yellow fever.

It is a horrible disease. Its victims bleed inside, causing black vomit, and their skin turns yellow. I believe we might have escaped the scourge thanks to Jonotás and Natán. Mama Rosa, who had offered the solution of the *tapadas* when I first arrived in Lima, told them yellow fever is caused by mosquitoes. I did not understand how that could be, but they saw to it that we kept vigilant in our dress, put netting above our beds, and kept the doors and windows to our house closed. In any event, we did not suffer from the disease.

To try to assuage the suffering so prevalent in the city, we began working in the hospitals. At the request of Jonotás and Natán, I spent most of my time at the hospital of San Bartolomé, which is dedicated to the treatment of Africans.

While both African slaves and African freedmen seemed to have better conditions in the Spanish colonies than those of their brothers in English colonies, the conditions for the black race in South America are still shameful. After spending only one day in San Bartolomé, I did not want to help anywhere else. No other hospital seemed to need as much.

It was still months before anything decisive happened on the military front. In the meantime, a split occurred between Rosita Campusano and Riva Agüero. For months, she had been complaining of his jealousy. "I have let him use my house, all this time, for *tertulias* and political gatherings, and yet if I am more than barely civil to one of "his" guests, he accuses me of 'flirting.'"

At last, she could take it no longer and told him that his jealousy must stop. He avoided the issue, stating, "I'm too busy for this, anyway." He started holding his meetings somewhere else and avoided her after that.

Rosita was hurt when he stopped attending her, but soon, with Riva Agüero out of the picture, she had many new admirers. She is a most handsome woman. Without her fidelity to Riva Agüero constraining her, she had no problem having whom she wished. However, she did not take advantage of these opportunities. "I cannot shift my emotions so easily," she told me.

I had a somewhat different problem. Manuel Amat and I saw each other once or twice more, but I let him know that I did not feel right about our relationship. "If James were to find out," I told him, "it could be disastrous."

I did not tell him that the most serious problem was that I did not love him in that way. It was in a moment of need and weakness that I had taken him to me. In more sober moments, I regretted it. Despite all the justifications for me to take the pleasure he gave me if I chose to do so, it seemed wrong to me.

"I know you do not love him, but I respect your wishes. Perhaps when this war is over—" He kissed me. "Good-bye, Manuela." He left without my telling him that I felt it would be best if we did not resume our relationship at all.

The war gave everyone's life an uncertain future. It kept James from returning to Lima as well. I did receive letters from him on occasion. He was still away in May when a 16 month armistice was negotiated between San Martín and La Serna. On July 4, La Serna and all of the Royalist forces left the city—at which point panic struck.

Priests and loyal Spanish had painted San Martín as a "devil with horns." Despite the general's promises, the nobility of Lima was certain that the patriot army would sack the city and kill everyone. They fled to the fortress of Callao, to churches, to monasteries, and to nunneries. San Martín was not one to flaunt his authority and was nowhere near the city, yet the confusion in the streets was pathetic and frightening.

Of those that remained, a citizen's committee was formed. They sent word to San Martín asking for leniency and protection. He immediately pulled the guerrillas out of action and sent regular soldiers to the city walls with food. Still, he did not let the main body of his army approach the town. He was adamant that the Peruvian people themselves must take responsibility for their government.

On the ninth, authorities with patriot sympathies had to formally request San Martín to enter Lima. On the tenth, after dark, he quietly slipped through the gates of the city.

Jonotás and Natán and I were on our way home from San Bartolomé Hospital that evening when I saw him. I was not completely sure, but I thought I recognized the general from Manuel Amat's description. He had a frayed poncho over his uniform and was quietly making his way down the street that ran past the hospital. He had only an aide-de-camp with him, a man I would know later as General Miller.

We immediately rode over to Rosita's house. "San Martín is in the city."

"Are you sure?" she asked.

"I think so. Hurry!"

She sent a slave to inform Riva Agüero, and we all rode off to the city square to search him out. By the time we found him again, a large group had gathered around him.

We dismounted in order to walk up to him, to express our congratulations and praise; but before we got close, the commotion escalated to frenzy. Women in the crowd fell on the ground, calling him "savior," and heaped their adulations on him amidst tears and wails. They made so much noise that people came out of the houses all around, many of whom were members of the *cabildo*. Soon, the general was surrounded and he seemed quite embarrassed. His aide-de-camp hung back and laughed at his general's distress.

I wanted to speak with the man who had liberated Lima, to introduce myself, but the giddiness of the other women and the rest of the crowd, prevented us from getting close. Rosita, Jonotás, Natán and I mounted our horses again and watched the turmoil with amusement while grateful women and townspeople crowded around the handsome man.

Rosita turned to me and said sensually, "I want him." We laughed.

On the twenty-eighth, San Martín announced from the Plaza Mayor, "Perú is from this moment free and independent, by the general vote of the people, and by the justice of her cause, which God defend!"

On the third of August, 1821, the general, at the urging of the Lautaro Lodge and other patriot leaders, issued a proclamation that he had adopted the title of "Protector of Perú" and would be the head of government "until the end of the war." He also announced three ministers of state: Don Juan García del Rio, Don Bernardo Monteagudo (head of the Lautaro Lodge for the continent), and Don Hipoliot Unanaue.

San Martín took steps, which pleased me, in the following weeks. He made many, much-needed reforms, but first he created a strictly Peruvian military body so that Perú would be strong when his Argentinean, Chilean, and Colombian forces (this last sent by Bolívar) returned to their homelands. That accomplished, he began to set the groundwork for the founding of a new republic. He declared that all children born of slaves would be free citizens, with full rights from that day on. He abolished serfdom, corporal punishment in educational institutions, and forced labor. He also founded new schools and libraries.

What made me happiest was to see José María again when San Martín brought the Numancia Battalion back to the city from patrol. I believed all the years of waiting, worrying, fighting, and hoping for patriot victory in Lima were about to come to an end. La Serna was still holding the highlands, but we were so close to victory.

I had not seen Manuel Amat for weeks. When I did see him, his interest in me seemed to have waned. This was just as well, since I had felt that the carnal aspect of our relationship was ill-fated. He came by one day and said, "I wanted you to know that I still think about you. I did not want you to think that . . . what we shared . . . that you were merely a conquest for me."

"I know, Manuel, it is only that . . ."

"Yes, Manuela. I knew that first time that you did not love me that way," he said. "I am sorry. I know I am much older than you—"

"No, Manuel, that is not the reason."

"I respect your reasons, whatever they are. After all, you are married."

I did not want to discuss my marriage with him. He still did not understand that was not the reason. To simplify everything, I merely said, "Thank you, Manuel. You are a good friend."

"If your husband does not return—I mean—I want us to be—"

"Please don't, Manuel."

"You are right."

We talked for a while, and he left a little later.

I missed the pleasure he gave me when he stopped attending me, but I was more aware than ever that there was nobody whom I truly loved. There was only my poor marriage in my future, and after Manuel left that day, I felt a deep loneliness.

As the weeks came and went, Jonotás and Natán and I continued to keep busy in the San Bartolomé Hospital. Like many other women, we also tried to help the treasury by gathering donations. I was something of a leader of the circles in which I traveled. In addition to everything else I was doing, I also collected money to build ships, organized the women into war units, did a house-to-house search for material for uniforms, and anything else which was needed by the revolution and San Martín.

The only trouble I had in getting donations from the populace was because of Jonotás and Natán. Not only did Jonotás wear men's clothing, she started wearing it cut in the style of a patriot soldier's uniform. Natán followed her example. Along with this, Jonotás also wore the dark red turban and huge golden earrings which Natán was so fond of wearing. True to form, Jonotás wore her top unbuttoned too far. Their entire appearance, especially ugly Jonotás, was more than most people could bear. I enjoyed them. However, when I was accompanied by my brazen slaves, I lost a few too many people before I could even talk to them.

Yet, I persisted in my efforts to help the cause. However, I did not see my old friends Riva Agüero or Rosita much anymore. I missed the earlier times when we had been close friends before the liberation.

One day Rosita came by. I realized I hadn't seen her since the night San Martín entered the city. "Come in, come in," I said, excitedly.

"No, I'm sorry I can't. However, the reason I came by was to invite you to come to dinner."

"I would love to Rosita, but I am so busy these days."

She lowered her eyes at me and smiled. "I have a surprise for you."

Her manner made me chuckle. "You are making me very curious. What's the surprise."

"Then you'll come?"

"Of course, I will come. You don't need to coax me. What evening?"

"Next Tuesday."

"Very well. But what is the surprise?"

"The surprise? Oh, by the way, you'll have to leave the hospital earlier that evening."

"Why? I can—"

"Because you'll have to go all the way to Magdalena. Oh, and wear your best, you'll be dining at the viceroy's old retreat."

It took a moment for what she was saying to sink in. Then I laughed and hugged her as we jumped up and down like schoolgirls. She had become San Martín's lover after all.

I hadn't thought she was serious when we stood in the street watching those women mob him. She was and she had contacted San Martín soon after that. Riva Agüero was extraordinarily jealous. He and Rosita had been on speaking terms, but after this he did not speak to her again.

The following Tuesday, I met the Protector of Perú. Knowing it was only a short walk to my own home in Magdalena where I would spend the night, I was prepared to stay as late as I could.

The villa itself was sumptuous. On the outside it was simple, built of sun-dried bricks, except for its large windows and an imperious stairway that led to the entrance doors. There was, of course, a plaza in the front. It had tall fig trees to provide shade for afternoon walks. A beautiful garden in the back had fruit bearing olive trees planted randomly. The rooms were spacious, with exquisite designs inlaid into the walls and ceilings. Sienna-colored tiles covered the floors, which caused the heels of boots to click in an official way. The furniture was very expensive, in the French style, and the smell of the furniture oil was pleasant and made the rooms feel comfortable. The dinnerware was silver, embossed with the shield of Lima, bearing its three crowns. On the walls I saw art that appeared to be from every era of the last four hundred years.

I found San Martín to be a cultured man, very unaffected, quiet, and cordial. I enjoyed talking to him, and I received personal thanks that night for my work in persuading the Numancia Battalion to change sides.

As we were discussing José María and some of the other Numancia officers, Bernardo Monteagudo arrived with some news for San Martín, which the general took privately. When they emerged from an inner room after a few minutes, I was finally able to meet the famous leader of the Lautaro Lodge.

My impressions of this intellectual light of the revolution were mixed. On the one hand, I was full of admiration for him, as I was for all of the officers of San Martín who had liberated half a continent. This one especially held my esteem. He represented the group that was the spirit of Liberty in South America. On the other hand, he left me chilled.

He was a native of Upper Perú, and a bastard like myself. He had a mixture of Spanish, Indian and African blood—though he was very handsome, with refined features and an elegant style of dress. His face was slightly pock-marked, and he had an almost feline look to him—narrow and dark, with kinky hair. Never did I see any dandy dressed more exquisitely than he. There were diamonds in his many rings, and his jeweled watch had a gold chain, at the end of which dangled a gold nugget. His shirt was of the whitest silk with dainty ruffles coming almost down to his sharpened and polished fingernails. He smelled prettier than a man-hungry *limeña*. I could tell he had an extremely quick mind (having studied law), but I felt attacked, not comforted, by his intelligence. I had an impression that his aspect, wearing a mask of social cordiality, betrayed a sinister and violent soul.

After he left, San Martín, Rosita, and I returned to our conversation. We talked long into the evening. As I was about to leave, San Martín said, "I very much wish that I could do something to publicly recognize you for your contributions."

"Thank you, General, but I assure you that such a demonstration is entirely unnecessary."

Rosita said, "What about your, 'Order of the Sun'?"

San Martín said, "It is to be knights."

"Excuse me, but what are you talking about?" I asked jovially.

They laughed, and San Martín said, "I am sorry, Manuela. I have discussed with Rosita an idea of mine: 'The Order of the Sun.' The notion is to found a brotherhood, bestowing quasi nobility on 'knights' of the republic. I wish to replace the nobility of Spain, but I have not yet decided to implement it. Mostly I am undecided as to the questions of *how* and, more importantly, *who*."

Rosita placed her hand on San Martín's and said, "I still say it would be perfect, if you truly desire to make some public acknowledgment for Manuela's contribution."

"But, Rosita, you don't understand: it is to be *knights*."

"I understand perfectly. However, why will you not consider 'knightesses?'"

"Please, you are embarrassing me, Rosita. I need no thanks. The outcome is thanks enough." The subject was changed and I finished my wine before departing.

As we all stood up, I saw San Martín wince in pain and hold his stomach. As we walked slowly to the door, stopping now and then to discuss the endless trivialities people seem to talk about at the end of a social affair, I noticed that San Martín looked more and more uncomfortable. I made a remark about a painting on the wall, and when Rosita began to explain something about it, San Martín excused himself.

Rosita watched him leave with a troubled look on her face. When she turned back to me, she said, "He told me that ever since the fighting for Chile, he has had bad stomach pains." It seemed she had more to say, but she stopped and rearranged a lock of her blond hair that had fallen out of place. I waited. At length, she said, "I'm worried. He has begun taking small amounts of opium to ease the pain, but he refuses to see a doctor."

I could not offer up anything helpful, and eventually our conversation came back to the painting. We discussed the artist, and our conversation touched on the other works of art acquired by the viceroys over the centuries. Just as I was about to take my leave, San Martín returned, looking slightly better.

We continued our conversation for a moment and I departed. I felt I had made a wonderful new friend in San Martín. However, after what Rosita had told me, I worried for him also.

Later, it seemed Rosita and I had inspired San Martín to go ahead with his plans after all. On the sixteenth of December from the galleries above the shops on the Plaza Mayor adjacent to the viceregal Palace, 26 founders of his new "Order of the Sun" were named by the Protector (who constituted himself President of the order). Also, 138 of Lima's finest men were named as members and each was given a badge of honor.

Then, awards were handed out to the knightesses, of which I was one of a list that had grown in the intervening weeks to 112—including existing Spanish nobility, 32 nuns, and, of course, Rosita Campusano. Apparently, once they got around to naming me and a few others, the list grew and grew as each woman became one who "couldn't be left out." I did not mind sharing the honor as I stepped up to the corner of the gallery and had the badge placed around my neck by San Martín himself. On the contrary, I was as happy as I have ever been.

On my birthday, the twenty-seventh of December, the Protector of Perú issued a proclamation that a congress was to be formed and a suitable constitution drafted. Then he handed over his authority to Torre Tagle and Monteagudo jointly and retired to his house in Magdalena to see what would happen.

I know he wanted the Peruvians to build their own government, but that was not the reason he turned over his power. Rosita made me see that he could not stand to be the leader in Lima anymore. San Martín was quite conservative and he delighted in solutions to problems that could be entirely viewed and then attacked with mathematical precision. Lima was not like that. There was no money, no trade, and no loyalty any one could depend on. Each private faction was trying to have all the power to itself. Everyone spoke of republican virtues—it was the fashion—but not one group seemed to care at all how they came to power.

I was frightened when I learned of San Martín's actions. Of all men to whom the government might be entrusted, these two were the last I would have chosen. Torre Tagle was shallow and not to be trusted. Though San Martín did not really know him, I knew the marqués would turn his coat at the slightest danger. I did not know Monteagudo well, but I knew that very few people liked him. Most had the same cold impression I did when considering him as a leader. Why not Riva Agüero? Also, why loosen control when the *godos* were all about the city, waiting for a crack in the "fortifications?"

During the next few months, I heard that Bolívar was almost ready to attack Quito, and I worried that the war might make my returning there even more remote. Also, at that time, the Numancia Battalion expressed dissatisfaction at not being paid and they left to return to Colombia, their homeland, now under the leadership of Simón Bolívar. I was saddened to see them go, but as they were heading in the general direction to which I intended to be departing eventually, I felt certain I would see José María again.

In the middle of all of the reconstructive change, I attempted to maintain the life that I had carved out for myself in Lima. I was still dedicated to charitable hospital work and the many other activities that were of benefit to the new government. The days were short for me in those months because I was so busy. Then, after an absence of four years, James returned.

By the time he arrived, our differences were compounded beyond human ability to reconcile them. Quarrels on every subject grew more bitter every day. I am sure that matters were made much worse because I would not sleep with him. I had made that decision when I received my own letter from those far away islands; I would not be a wife to James Thorne, in that way, again. Finally, after numerous conflicts, he made an unwelcome decision.

"Manuela," he said, as we argued about my long absences from the house, "I cannot allow you to neglect your duties at home. I have no choice but to retract my power of attorney."

This would be a disaster for me. It meant that I would not be able to handle any of his affairs or take care of any business in his name. I had a little of my own money, but not enough to last for long, not that I would ever misuse James's funds.

"How do you expect me to take care of your business while you are at sea?"

"I will find someone else—whom I can *trust*—Escobar most likely."

"That, Sir, is unfair. You have always been able to trust my handling of your affairs, and you know it. No one would look out for your interests like I do. You anger me, Sir. My administration of your affairs has always been—"

"That is not the point. I do not trust you, Madam. I will find someone whom I can rely on."

"Very well. Do as you see fit. You will not chain me with your power of attorney or by any other means." I walked out of the room.

Despite my bravado, I was quite upset by this turn of affairs. I realized again a truth about my life with James: I must have my inheritance.

I decided to leave for Quito immediately. I stayed only long enough to attend the ball for members of the Order of the Sun on May 4, 1822.

I asked James to accompany me, but this time it was his turn to desist and my turn to insist. Finally he agreed, believing that he should meet members of the new government. I wanted him to attend for the irony of it.

When we finally arrived at the ball, I found it humorous that I made him meet San Martín that evening, though he did not wish it, just as he had made me meet the viceroy four years earlier. Contrary to my experience with the viceroy, San Martín was very affable and friendly toward my husband.

I had a wonderful time that evening. I was treated warmly, even by the most celebrated of patriot heroes, and respected instantly, if not by the spirit of liberality in the room, then by my membership in the Order of the Sun. It had taken 24 years, to rise from an infant bastard with nothing, to a wealthy "noblewoman" and I was very happy that night.

I had made poor James stay until the very last so it was quite late when we left the ball. On our way home I saw a curious sight. It was a harbinger of things to come that sent a chill through my soul.

A soldier came riding down the street. He was prodding an old man, dressed only in a pair of britches, down the street with his lance. I recognized the old man as one of the vociferous Spaniards who was still making trouble for San Martín's government in the city.

I called out, "Soldier!"

The lancer turned his horse around to face me after stopping the panting and shivering old man.

I said, "What is happening here? Where are you taking this old man?"

He said simply, "Monteagudo's orders," and then spurred his horse and left, prodding the old man along. I felt a cold shudder pass through me.

The worst elements that made trouble for the new government were the church and its ministers. I had applauded when the Archbishop—who had interviewed James and me when we were to be married—was deported along with several of his contemporaries, even though he was over 80. I had also wished to see other loudmouth Spaniards removed, to forgo their creating any more trouble. However, I did not like what I saw that night.

Later I found out what happened. During the ball, Monteagudo had sent parties of soldiers to the houses of Spaniards. Once there, they disturbed the infirm and elderly, as well as the able-bodied, and made them march the entire two leagues to Callao, in the cold night air, poorly dressed.

Several of these had numerous family members in Lima, some of whom were celebrating liberty and justice at the ball. There were clergymen, octogenarian civil and military officers, as well as sick and able bodied upper class Spanish from the oldest families in Perú. Without any compassion, they were seized at midnight and marched, almost naked, to be placed on a ship in the harbor.

There, they had to buy a passport for thousands of pesos if they could afford it, in order to be allowed to leave. Two old men died while waiting for these deliberations. No one was allowed to talk to their family members during this time; wives and children stood on the shore and cried in desperation.

I was disgusted. Most of those people should have been ousted, no doubt, but the indecent cruelty displayed by Monteagudo took the shine off my happiness. I did not like that man.

Over the next several days, I tried to find out what had caused Monteagudo's actions. I discovered several things about him. One such fact was that Monteagudo was always feared and hated wherever he was in power because his means included midnight assassinations, secret character defamations, and any other instrumentality to see that the revolution succeeded. This latest was only one in a long line of similar actions. Despite his intelligence and his love for the revolution, I shuddered to think of him running the government.

There was one mitigating factor to my ill feelings after the ball. James had evidently been impressed with my connections and my prestige. He decided not to retract my power of attorney after all. His business affairs were in shambles with Spanish wealth being dispersed. I think he felt that my contacts might help him. He became solicitous and even proposed to take me with him on a trip to Panamá so that I might stop in Guayaquil and thus return to Quito. I think that he felt the ship would be less likely to be harassed if it carried a member of the Order of the Sun.

A week later, on the 25th of May, we all sailed past the island of San Lorenzo on the English Brig *Deadema,* Jonotás, Natán, James, and me. As we stood on the deck and watched the island slip into our wake, I was full of anticipation and hope about the future.

Soon, I would be in Guayaquil. It would only be a week or so later when I would arrive in Quito. There, I would prevail over my uncle. At last, I would have all my mother had promised me. I was prepared for the bribes, because I had letter for a small amount of credit from Manuel Amat in addition to what little money I had myself. I was also prepared for the resistance I would encounter from Carlos's friends who might be in charge of my suit. I thought I was prepared for anything. I was full of confidence that I would soon have my inheritance.

Chapter 38

There is a strange irony that on my passage to Lima I could not share a cabin with James for appearances, and on my passage from Lima I had to share a cabin with James for appearances; and on neither trip did I let James sleep with me.

Throughout the trip, he became less and less civil. At first he couldn't understand why things could not go back to the way they were "before." I tried to point out to him that "before" did not exist.

"We have never really had a good time together," I told him. "You like to talk about business. I don't. Sometimes we talk about everyday affairs, but we have little else in common. We have different religious views, political views—we don't even agree on how to run a house."

"I did not know you were so unhappy. I can discuss anything you wish." We stood watching the Peruvian desert go by. Sailors with mops were approaching, so he took my arm and escorted me to the other side of the ship. It had been overcast all day and the sun was starting to descend through the clouds, promising a murky sunset.

I shaded my eyes and looked out to sea. "Do you not see, James? We do not enjoy each other."

Turning his back to the glare, he said, "I enjoy you."

"No, James, think about it."

"Manuela, I love you. I want you to love me."

I told him as kindly as I could, "James, we will simply not work. I do love you as a friend—"

He turned away in disgust.

"Wait, James. I am trying to say that I know you have been as fair to me as you know how. I think I even understand you. But we are not made for each other."

He stormed away from me. We did not speak for the next day, while he brooded. It upset me, but I could not do more for him than I had.

He came into our cabin the next afternoon. I was sewing, and did not look up. He put his hand on my neck and began to caress me.

I said, "James, please."

He leaned over and kissed my hair. I pulled my head away, but he stroked my neck again. I stood up, intending to walk out the door. He put his arms around me and tried to kiss me.

I pulled away.

He said, angrily, "I am your husband; I have the right." We continued to struggle.

"James, no!" I raised my voice enough that he stopped. He was afraid of being embarrassed. The ship's officers berthed close by.

After two more such scenes, our relationship disintegrated into icy silence. Whether I talked to him about essentials or nonessentials, he ignored me. This made things quite troubled, because most of the time we were forced into uncomfortable closeness due to our ship-bound situation.

The *Deadema* was a much smaller ship than the ones on which I had journeyed to Lima and to Panamá. The cabin that James and I shared was in the aft part of the ship. It had only two bunks attached to the bulkhead and barely enough room to turn around on what deck space there was. Jonotás and Natán had to sleep on straw outside our door.

When I was first informed of the smallness of the ship, back in Lima, it caused me to change some of my plans. I had it in my mind that I was going to make the trip from Guayaquil to Quito on horseback. I did not want to ride into that city in the same fashion that I left, on the back of a *burro*. I had wanted to bring my horses, but doing so was impossible. We barely had room for ourselves and our trunks. So, even before I left Lima, I knew that I would have to buy horses in Guayaquil.

Such a decision would ultimately make me shorter on funds than I had hoped. This was compounded by another situation. When I left Lima, General Sucre was advancing on Quito from the south and Bolívar was advancing from the north, but there was no sign of a victory any time soon. Therefore, I supposed that I would have to stay in Guayaquil for weeks, perhaps months, until the patriots were able to secure the mountains and Quito itself. Also, there was always the possibility that they would lose. I was worried that such eventualities might cause me to run out of money.

One of my attempts at frugality accomplished more than I hoped. I purchased some material before I left Lima, and I spent the long hours aboard ship sewing a riding habit. I made it myself to save money, rather than commissioning a seamstress to make me one.

Besides allowing me to save a little money and take up a little time on the ship, I was able to express an idea I had. I wanted to make my own clothes because I rather liked Jonotás's idea of dressing as a revolutionary soldier. I decided to do something similar with my habit.

I chose a heavy material, such as used for soldier's uniforms, colored a bright bottle-green, not quite the color of the revolutionary army, but similar, only brighter. Jonotás and Natán and I worked on this elegant riding habit during the long days on the ship. We gave it a dashing military-type cut that still showed off my bosom and hips, and I placed simple epaulettes on the shoulders to complement shiny black boots I had purchased. I was quite happy with it once I was finished, about the time we started up the Guayas river.

I took Jonotás and Natán up on deck with me that day so we might see *El Amortajado*. When we had made our original trip from Panamá, we stopped off in Guayaquil for a few hours, of course, but it was too dark when we arrived, and departed, to see the rock shaped like a shrouded corpse.

I smoked a cigar for a while as we watched the muddy river water and the islands going by. Then we started to go below to commence making arrangements to disembark. As I turned around, James was walking up, and he said, "I want to talk to you."

Jonotás and Natán slipped away. The moment we were alone, he said sternly, "I think you had better reconsider your ideas about our marriage. We are going to be separated for a few months, but when I return to Lima, I want and expect to have a wife waiting for me."

"Is that a threat?" I said angrily.

"You know what I mean, Manuela. I love you very much—when I married you it was in God's eyes, and mine, for all time. I have a right to have children issue from this marriage, and I have the right to a normal marital relationship."

I became angrier (partly because he had touched on my failure to ever tell him that we could not have children) and I started to lash back, "I don't—"

"Let me finish," he snapped. He went on, calmly, "I want to remind you of something. If you don't consent to keeping your marriage vows, it will not be impossible to persuade the church authorities, even under these God-less revolutionary governments, to have you kept in a nunnery until you see the error of your ways."

He had hit me hard. I felt terror mixing with a deep and righteous anger. My heart went cold. If the right people conspired with the right people, I could indeed be forced into a nunnery. This, after all I had been through since I had escaped from Santa Catalina, was too much.

I could find nothing to say. I looked at the muddy, brown river going by. Many thoughts rushed through my mind. I must have stood there for some time because he went on as though I was waiting for him to continue.

"I am not saying that that's what I will do. It is not what I want at all. I am only pointing out to you how inappropriate to married life your actions are." I was still silent. "I am not asking for anything abnormal or wrong. Merely to have my conjugal rights and your wifely obedience."

I stared out across the river, my anger turning to rage.

He went on, "During our separation, I hope you will come to see me as one who loves you and one who deserves some requiting of that love—if for no other reason than the fact that I am your husband."

I looked right at him, but I was still unprepared to respond. My breathing was rapid. I wanted to lash out at him, but I knew that this was a dangerous discussion and I wanted, for once, to use my head.

He said in Spanish, "*Por favor, Manuela,*" and then in English, very softly, "Please."

"Señor, I do not respond well when threatened."

"Manuela, I only want you to see that we can't go on this way. We are Catholics. We are married forever. The church authorities will see it my way and no other. I am only asking you to think on this until I see you again. That is all."

I said, "I do not wish to be a Catholic—or married."

He looked at me as one would look at a child who had just said something incredibly stupid. I, too, felt it was a stupid thing to say, stupid and impotent. "What is it that you want?" he said, in a patronizing manner.

"I want to be free to do as I deem correct."

The blood rushed to his face. "You are not free. You are mine. I will not let any other man have you. I will have my marriage and I . . ." I could tell he felt out of control. He took a deep breath.

I stared at him in defiance.

He softened somewhat and said, "I am sorry. I don't want to be angry with you. I ask that you think about what I have said."

I had nothing to say.

He continued, "There is no other way Manuela. You know that's true. I hope you come to your senses by the time we meet again." Then he left, leaving me to do exactly what he said he wanted me to do—think about it.

There was one thing I did not have to think about. I knew when he said it, that he was absolutely right. We could not go on the way I had fantasized that we might. I was married to James Thorne and it was certain that I could not maintain the form I had given to our relationship.

I was very frustrated. Because I was married, I could not determine for myself what I would be or how I would act. I could accept that I had given up choosing with whom I would sleep, but it was too much to accept that I could be forced into a convent for living the life I had chosen. I would not acknowledge a persistent thought in the back of my mind: *I brought this on myself by deciding to marry him in the first place.* I had few choices then, perhaps no other choice, but I had been the one to entrap myself.

Until my discussion with James, I had been confident that I could use my wits to get around civil, religious, or my husband's authority. Now I was becoming very aware of how dangerous that would be. I cursed myself for a fool to have taken such a simplistic, childish, cavalier attitude in my behavior. I was still too overconfident. Merely being determined and clever would not get me through everything. I had to consider hard how I was now going to counter James's "chess move."

I do not know where James went, perhaps to another cabin, but I did not see him after that. All the way up the river, and while preparing to unload, I did not see him.

When I went to find him to say good-bye, I was told by a cabin boy that he would see me again in Lima in a couple of months. His aloofness chilled me. As it turned out, it would be almost four years before I would see him again.

Chapter 39

As we approached the dock, not far from where I had first stepped on a ship seven years earlier, I was deep in thought. It took me a moment to realize what I was seeing. The Malecón was busier than the docks in Panamá had been. Almost all of the people on it were Royalist soldiers in chains, clad in dirty blue and gold uniforms, sitting or lying or standing about in somber, unsettled resignation.

When Jonotás, Natán, and I finally disembarked, I noticed a toothless old man sitting on a pile of rope nearby. He was eating a mango that dripped yellow juice on to his already dirty white shirt. A mango is so stringy and has such tough skin that I could not understand how anybody with no teeth could eat one.

I walked up to him and said, *"Viejo,* where was the battle that determined all of these *godos* should be in chains here?"

He smiled a cavernous smile, and said, "The *generalísimo* has conquered Quito."

I did not quite know what had happened except that Quito was now in patriot hands. It seemed that I would not have to endure a protracted stay in Guayaquil after all. Excitement filled me, and I was eager to know all about the battle.

"Which general is it who has conquered Quito?"

He looked at me like I was simple-minded and said, "There is only one *generalísimo*—Simón Bolívar."

So the *marqués*, with his "divine intervention," had not been too far wrong. It was almost as if there *were* a coordinated effort between Bolívar and San Martín. Without knowing each other, or what the other was doing, Bolívar had begun his revolution in Venezuela and, as history unfolded, making his own predictions come true, he had crossed the Andes into Bogotá, captured all of New Granada, formed a new state called Gran Colombia, and from there he had entered Quito. San Martín, starting in Buenos Aires, also crossed the Andes, had taken Chile, and then Lima. It seemed a coordinated effort that a mighty general, bigger than both Bolívar or San Martín, might have planned.

Bolívar had been a household name in America for almost ten years. Early in his career he had been proclaimed *"El Libertador,"* which he was still called. He was so famous that extraordinary events were attributed to him by those who didn't know better, such as the foolish old man eating the mango.

In reality, Bolívar was not yet in Quito at the time I arrived in Guayaquil. He was farther north, putting down a stiff resistance in Pasto, but one of his best generals was in the city of my birth.

Over a year before, Bolívar was fighting the same persistent Royalist strongholds in Pasto and Patia and other encampments in the mountain passes between Bogotá and Quito. The Royalist forces in that area, supplied from the Pacific, might have been able to prolong the war indefinitely, and they might possibly have retaken Bogotá. However, the revolution in Guayaquil had cut them off.

Bolívar saw that the port of Guayaquil had been necessary to the continued survival of the Royalist forces in Quito. But more importantly, if he was going to annex Quito to his newly founded republic of Gran Colombia, already composed of the old provinces of New Granada and Venezuela, he must have Guayaquil (and thus access to the Pacific Ocean). He could not permit the port city to be separated from the rest of the land known in the vernacular as *El Ecuador* (The Equator) by allowing it to perhaps join the newly independent country of Perú.

He immediately sent his most able general, Antonio José de Sucre, who was later to become a great friend of mine, to attack Quito from the south. It was Sucre who had taken Quito and all the lands between there and Guayaquil.

Sucre was born in Cumaná and had been educated in the sciences. He had served from his youth in the revolutionary battles of Venezuela and New Granada; the brightest student of warfare Bolívar ever had. It was Sucre who was chosen for Bolívar's double mission in the province of Quito and sent around by sea to Guayaquil.

First, he was to offer assistance to the new state of Guayaquil against the Royalists. Second, he was to do what was necessary to see that it joined the newly formed state of Gran Colombia.

At Popayán, Sucre collected troops that had been dispersed in prior skirmishes there and was able to attain a count of over 1000 men. He reached Guayaquil one year prior to my arrival, in May of 1821.

When he arrived, there had occurred an insignificant counterrevolution, which Sucre and his men put down immediately. He naturally became well respected for his brilliant soldiering and was commonly considered one of Guayaquil's revolutionary leaders in a very short time.

Using his new influence, he gathered some *guayaquileños* into his army and marched against the Royalist troops coming down the mountains from Quito to take back Guayaquil. In his first real campaign at Yahuachí, he defeated one of the columns of descending Royalists.

Then he climbed the slopes of Chimborazo and occupied the Plain of Ambato. Here his army was attacked and he himself was wounded. He pulled his troops back to their previous position. Finally, he was pushed all the way back to Guayaquil.

There, he was reinforced by troops sent by San Martín, and with 2,000 men he again began his heroic ascent to Quito. This time, through circuitous positioning and guerrilla attacks, he made the Royalist defenders of the passes retreat from one position after another.

On May 23, 1822, Sucre deployed his forces for a frontal attack on Quito itself. Then, during the night, he had his men climb to the rim of Pichincha, the nearby mountain I could see from my window as a child, to be ready for a flank attack. When the Spanish soldiers awoke on the morning of the twenty-fourth, they were confronted by Sucre's entire army perched high above them.

The Royalist officers sent their men up the mountain to attack. With the disadvantage of having to attack uphill, their charge was disastrous.

On the morning of May 25 (as I was leaving the port of Callao in the *Deadema*), the Royalist forces capitulated. We who had been on the ship naturally did not hear about the victory until we arrived in Guayaquil.

But it was Sucre, not Bolívar, who had conquered Quito. Bolívar at that time was still in Pasto. The last of the resistant *pastusos* would keep him busy for another month.

When I heard the old man's assertion, I did not yet know the true story. I was full of admiration for Bolívar, who I believed had accomplished what I had seen such men as Morales, Quiroga, Montúfar and others attempt so many years before. The patriot forces were winning in my country, and I was overjoyed. I turned happily to Jonotás and Natán and told them what this news meant to us as we made our way through the chained, defeated soldiers.

I decided to try to find some of Rosita Campusano's relatives to see if I could stay the night with them. Before I was across the Malecón I heard a voice, with a familiar accent, call "Señorita!"

I turned around, and a European with gray hair came running up to me. I recognized him but could not remember from where at first. Then it struck me. He was the worried merchant who had brought me to Guayaquil seven years earlier. He now wore a short beard and his hair was whiter, but he still had that same distinctive way of speaking.

We laughed with glee as we greeted each other, and he acted like I was a long lost childhood friend. This amused me because he barely spoke to me until the last day or so of our journey to Guayaquil, and I had been quite mean to him before that.

He admired my riding habit, asked me about my life, asked me about the Order of the Sun medal I was wearing, about Perú, and on and on. His command of Spanish was not any better than it was seven years before. All the while, he was telling me how glad he was to see me as we stood in the middle of the street. *Calesas*, horses, and carts were having to go around us, their angry drivers informing us how wrong we were to be taking up road space.

I answered his questions and when I told him that I was on my way to Quito, he became thoughtful and said, "Oh, it be impossible. I can no you take there." That was not what I had asked or even implied. "All commerce, she stop on the road for awhile. Patriots they bring down columns of Royalist soldiers to be . . . ahh . . . what is the word?" He gestured to the soldiers sitting all around.

"Repatriated?" I suggested.

"The very word, yes, repat-riated. Mules I must deliver to Quito, but patriots they put down a little Spanish . . . uhm . . . resistance here or there, a little in and about towns on the road—"

Just then, a troop of patriot lancers, in their green battle-worn uniforms, came trotting down the street. Like everyone else about us, we had to rush to the side of the street to avoid being trampled. As the lancers went by, the captain saluted and smiled at my "friend," who smiled back and waved.

He said, "He friend of mine. Returning, he is, to Quito, tomorrow."

I smiled and said, "Do you know where he was going just now? I want to ask him if he would consent to escort a member of the Order of the Sun to Quito."

He returned my smile, and said slyly, "No, I not know where he goes, but he come to my house tonight, have dinner." I laughed and he said, "You join us, I think."

I said, "I would be delighted. Tell me where it is and I will be over after I have made some arrangements for our lodging."

He said, "You do not have yet a place to stay? I will not think you are staying anywhere but at my home. Plenty there is room for you and servants. Since you be escorted, I'm sure, I can send my mules to Quito with you. They belongs to landowner up there."

He went on and on about how he insisted on my staying with him. I had no intention of refusing, yet he kept insisting as though I were arguing with him. He said he would send someone back for our trunks; all the while he was holding my arm and walking me toward his dwelling.

I barely had a chance to tell Jonotás and Natán to stay with our goods before he rushed me off through the city, that city I had left years before as a frightened girl. With the exception of my worry over my marriage, I was returning to my country in a most satisfactory fashion.

Chapter 40

When we arrived at the foreigner's home, which was a large apartment over a *botica* not far from the waterfront, I did two things. First I asked him his name. His name was Carlson and he was from Norway. He had been in South America for almost two decades and had slowly built up a profitable business exporting coffee, textiles, and other goods. I was very amused that after seven years, he had finally introduced himself.

After that I told him that I needed to buy some horses for my trip to Quito. He immediately sent a couple of servants off to get our trunks and then escorted me down the street to a stable area, where he introduced me to a friend of his whom he called El Árabe, a foreigner from the Levant, who sold horses.

The man liked me very much. He was tall and heavy set, with dark hair and eyes. His face was well shaved but could not hide a dark outline where a heavy beard would have been. His accent was strange, but he laughed at my jokes and more than once admired my beauty.

"The Señorita is very pretty. Perhaps she would like to take food with me," he said, looking right at me after we were introduced. His eyes twinkled with desire, and he smiled broadly.

"You are most kind, Señor, but your friend here has already asked me."

"Good, yes. That is fair, but you must make time for me later."

"Perhaps, Señor," I said, returning his smile.

Then, El Árabe showed me his stock, and I was able to buy a black and two bays, very much like the ones I had in Lima, for a good price. The bays were older and not as fine as my Lima horses, but I liked the black very much. Her name was *Espectra Negra* (Black Ghost). I got the tack at a good price too.

When we left El Árabe, he said, "Good, yes. You return, Señorita."

I laughed at him. "I'll be back tomorrow morning, to get my horses."

He laughed also, and said, "Good, yes."

When we returned to Carlson's apartment, Jonotás and Natán were there, pushing our trunks to the side of the room. He saw that we were tired and he offered us his bedroom in order to take an afternoon nap. When I would not let Jonotás and Natán be escorted to the servants quarters, he brought blankets for them to sleep on the floor. However, I remembered Guayaquil's famous insects and we all climbed into his wide bed together, behind the netting, and slept through the afternoon.

When I awoke, I heard voices in the next room and I could smell plantains being fried for dinner. I washed my face and put on a simple dress. I made a mistake and chose one that revealed my shoulders.

The captain of the Lancers whom I had seen earlier in the day was there. His name was Captain Valdéz, and he was a pleasant man with a mustache that covered his full lips. Over dinner we had an interesting discussion. He was very inquisitive about the

campaign in Lima, and asked me many questions about San Martín and the city itself. He also told me the truth about Sucre's campaign in Quito.

"So it was not Bolívar who actually liberated Quito?"

"No, it was Sucre—a great soldier—both brave and intelligent. Almost as great as the Liberator himself."

"You have fought under the Liberator as well?"

"Yes. That reminds me. I have some news. It seems the *pastusos* are about to capitulate, and Bolívar should be in Quito in three or four days." I thought how exciting that would be, to be there when the Liberator arrived. Captain Valdéz echoed my thoughts. "I would like to be there, but we will not arrive in time, even though we leave in the morning."

"Captain Valdéz, would you consent to escort me to Quito when you return?"

"I would be delighted. We are to leave early, however."

"The earlier, the better."

When dinner was over and Captain Valdéz had left, Carlson asked me more about my life since he had conducted me through the Andes. I told him a few stories. We drank wine and smoked cigars, and I slapped mosquitoes.

I have noticed that when you first arrive in a new area, the mosquitoes bite you unmercifully. After you have been there awhile, they do not bother you quite as much. Carlson seemed to be immune, but I had bites all over my shoulders and arms an hour after the sun set.

We had been talking for some time when Carlson began telling me how much I had changed and how attractive he found me. At first, I was only flattered. But he persisted with his compliments, and a strange and wonderful thing happened. I felt a feeling of release.

Since my discussion with James, I had been feeling boxed in. This delightful man enjoyed me. He found me beautiful. He desired me. It was completely unexpected, and I saw all at once that life had hundreds of possibilities. I marveled that something in what he said, or the way he said it, changed my whole outlook. I smiled at him as he continued complimenting me in the manner of an anxious lover. I saw his desire for me in his eyes and I knew he was about to kiss me.

It would have been difficult for me to resist him, even if I had not found him desirable, because of the way he made me feel so free from my circumstances. I did not avoid his advance as he moved his chair next to mine, put his arms around my waist, and pulled me close. He kissed me on the lips, a deep longing kiss.

I returned his embrace. I heard him speak. "Manuela, you are so lovely." I felt his hands come up to my breasts and sensed his fingers slip under the cloth. He kissed my neck and then began to move down. I was reminded of Manuel Amat.

Then, thankfully, reason took over. When I thought about Manuel, I remembered how uncertain I had felt after succumbing to my desires with him. Worry about my future crowded out the feelings I was experiencing. Carlson's touch on my skin ceased to be arousing. A foreboding came over me.

I was trapping myself again. If I allowed what we were doing to continue, my problems would only be compounded. What I was doing was not right, no matter how seductive the feelings. Carlson was not a man I would love forever, any more than I would Manuel Amat.

I did not know then if such a man existed. I feared I would not be so lucky, as I was with Manuel, who merely stopped making advances. In Guayaquil, neither the time nor the situation was right for a romantic encounter with a man who was not my husband.

True, there was no commitment, but actions in themselves are commitments. If James were to find out about this, it would be much worse for me. Yet, even if James were not in the picture, I knew I could not continue. I did not love him.

Carlson reached for the hem of my dress. His amorous feelings, by this time, I did not share. I gently pushed him away from me and pulled my dress to a modest level. Looking directly in his eyes, I said, "I am sorry. I cannot."

He barely looked at me and said, "Manuela, I adore you. I want you stay with me in Guayaquil."

"I cannot. I am married," I said, giving what I thought was the most understandable reason.

"You told me yourself your marriage is not happy one." When I did not respond, he said, "We could go into hiding maybe. I make more money and return to Norway with you." The discussion became even more ridiculous after that.

Finally, I stood up. He followed, held me, and began kissing my shoulders (mosquito bites and all). Then Jonotás and Natán walked in the room from the servant's area. Carlson jumped away.

I said, "I think it is time for bed."

Jonotás, seeing the look on my face, pulled Natán into Carlson's bedroom where we had slept that afternoon, to preempt Carlson from following me.

"I thank you for everything. Truly. You do not know how thankful I am. Nor how sorry I am. Good night." I reached up and kissed him softly on the cheek.

He looked like he wanted to say something, but instead he said, "Good night." I walked out of the room.

As I prepared for bed I wondered if I had done the right thing. I had been aroused, and the man obviously loved me and would try his best to protect me. No matter what arguments I gave myself, I knew I had done right. I knew that I must move with my whole heart in matters of love. I still had my husband to contend with, and I did not know if I would ever be able to break the chains of my marriage, if it were possible at all.

When I awoke, the sun was not quite up. Two hours later, after we picked up our horses and I refused El Árabe's insistent invitation to stay for a morning snack, we crossed the bridge over the estuary behind a troop of Colombian lancers. In tow were several mules, which carried our trunks, that I was to deliver in Quito for Carlson. He had been sad and distracted when I left.

About 20 minutes down the road, a galloping horseman overtook us. When we stopped and I was pointed out to him as the person he was looking for, he said, "I am a courier, hired to deliver a message, for Don Carlson." He handed me a paper folded several times.

I took it and started to unfold it.

"Don Carlson says that he forgot to give you the bill of sale which is to be given to the owner of the mules. His name and address are within." Before I could say anything, he went on, "He also said to tell you he loves you and waits for the day you return."

The lancers standing around started laughing in a stifled manner. Embarrassed and angry, I stuffed the paper into my saddle bag. "You can tell Don Carlson for me that his message was both impudent and rude. And that he had better rue the day when I return." Then, I spurred my horse forward and galloped across the savanna.

Chapter 41

The journey was more arduous going up the mountains to Quito than it had been coming down. Besides the fact that we were traveling uphill, it was not too far into our journey that the rareness of the air somewhat drained the energy of the people and animals that were used to living near the level of the ocean: myself, Jonotás, Natán, our horses, and our mules. The soldiers, having only recently come down from weeks in the mountains, were not affected as much.

Every day we would pass one or two columns of Royalist soldiers being escorted down the mountains to Guayaquil by patriot lancers. Wounded, sick, or well, they all looked miserable.

The patriot soldiers were in good spirits, though it was obvious that they were not as well equipped as their Royalist captives. The loose-fitting patriot uniforms—made of a homespun material of green and piped with red—seemed insufficient to keep out the Andean cold. Their bare feet were set in brass shoe-shaped stirrups. Spurs with large rowels were tied to their heels. It was easy to see why so many had died of exposure crossing the mountains when Bolívar attacked New Granada.

Yet these soldiers were the tough victors who had survived. They were proud as they held their lances high—lances that were nothing more than long knives tied to the ends of cane poles. Always, one of the soldiers carried a red, blue and gold gonfalon of the triple Republic of Gran Colombia, which now included the presidency of Quito (soon to be called the Department of the South).

We had to traverse such narrow ledges that when we met a descending column of defeated men, the lancers ordered the Royalists to flatten themselves against the rock face so that we could pass. Consequently, I could see into the faces of the defeated *godos*, covered with dirt and despair. The once well-fitted uniforms of blue and gold were now ragged and filthy. Spain had lost the battle for Quito and I was glad, but I felt sorry for the defeated soldiers.

Many times throughout the trip, we passed the body of a Royalist left where it had dropped. Sometimes the Indians were there burying the body. Sometimes it was being devoured by white-throated condors that flapped their great wings at us. As much as I was fascinated by the strategy and tactics of the battles I was learning about from Captain Valdéz, I was dismayed by the death and suffering that was evident throughout the land. These were not the same idyllic mountainsides I had passed on my descent. The scars of war were everywhere.

We did not stop in Guaranda, but I saw the corregidor's house as we passed. It had changed very little. I would like to have stayed there, but Captain Valdéz knew of a place farther along.

Having remembered how uncomfortable I was on my trip down to Guayaquil, I made sure that we had plenty of warm blankets. I had also packed two large pieces of heavy cloth to use for tents. I had wanted some privacy (since I did not know with whom we might be traveling) and I had hoped it would provide a bit of warmth.

I had intended to sleep in one and have Jonotás and Natán sleep in the other. However, on the first night, Jonotás made the rounds of the campfires, bantering and smoking with the soldiers. Captain Valdéz and I watched her exchanging obscenities with first one and then another, and making them all laugh with her comic gift.

Soon she found a soldier with whom she wanted to share her tent. Natán and I slept in my tent, which was probably better. Once we were in the mountains, and I felt how cold it was, I was sure I would not have been warm enough sleeping alone.

When we reached Riobamba, I dropped a letter off at the house of Carlson's friend, the same friend with whom we had stayed when I first descended the mountains. He graciously granted my request to use their water to wash my clothes, which had become muddy in the ascent to the sierra.

Captain Valdéz had ridden at the head of the column until our arrival in Riobamba. At that point, he asked me to ride next to him and he explained how Sucre had outmaneuvered the Royalist officer Lopez in the battle there. Sucre inflicted such serious losses to the Royalist forces that he rendered their cavalry no longer useful in that campaign.

I was fascinated by stories of the battles. As we rode together he frequently pointed out the various battlegrounds and what happened on them. He was a most enjoyable escort, with a wealth of information about the history that was unfolding even as we were living it.

My clothes needed washing again by the time we reached the land near Cotopaxi. I used the river, but I had to put on a dress while my riding habit dried. I felt silly in my feminine attire amongst the soldiers. It was amusing that they became more chivalrous when I looked more feminine. I had not changed, only my dress; and yet they treated me so very differently.

Next morning, June 11, I arose to the last day of our journey. When I put on my riding habit, I was much more comfortable. It felt good to get rid of the dress I had worn while waiting for my clothes to dry. A dress is a silly garment for anybody engaged in any real physical activity such as riding or camping.

Our camp was only a short distance from the little hut in which I had slept when I left Quito. I rode over in the morning to see the aging Indian and his wife. I thought I might buy some fruit. Jonotás and Natán accompanied me.

As we rode up to the hut from the rear, I let my eyes wander to the perfect peak of Cotopaxi. It was so beautiful. I realized I had missed it. I had to remind myself I was not returning to Quito because I loved it there, although there were a few people I loved (I was going to stay with the Larreas when I arrived), but rather, I was returning to get what was mine.

When we rounded the corner to the front of the hut, it was obviously deserted. The door was closed, and one of the benches was overturned. We sat for a minute looking at the scene. I wondered what had happened to the old couple.

I thought about that morning seven years earlier when I had eaten breakfast there. I thought about the people whom I had left with my sudden departure, and wondered what ever happened to Fausto and Carmen. It all seemed so long ago, and so far away.

I looked at Cotopaxi again and turned my horse around. "Come, let's return to the camp. Wait! I heard something."

I dismounted, walked to the door, and pushed it open. It was warped and only opened enough to allow me to enter by sidestepping.

The tiny windows and open door did little to illuminate the room, but since I had slept in this hut before, I knew where the fireplace was. I walked over to it. The stove was cold, a few sticks of wood beside it. I was about to dismiss the sound I'd heard as the scrambling of a rat or some other animal when I heard a weak moan from the other side of the room.

I could not distinguish what I was seeing in the gloom until I was right next to the tiny bed in which the old Indian and his wife had slept. Then I saw the whites of two eyes.

It was the wife of the old Indian. She was lying on top of the bed clothes. When I reached out to touch her, if I had not seen her eyes blink, I would have thought she was dead; she was as cold as stone.

I tried to talk with her but she would not respond. I made all of the usual inquiries: where is your husband, are you all right, why are you lying in the cold, and other questions, which gleaned no response.

While I spoke to her, I found a dirty blanket on the floor and threw it over her. Then I looked around the room for some food. There was nothing to eat, and it struck me that the woman was dying of starvation and exposure.

I quickly went outside and said, "The old woman is here. She's dying. Ride back to the camp and get some plantains and warm tea."

"Yes, Manuelita," they said, as they spurred their horses.

"And come back as quickly as possible," I shouted after them.

I returned to the old woman. I lifted her to lean against me, I rubbed her icy hands trying to give her some warmth. I again asked her what happened and where her husband was. She spoke for the first time, saying in an emotion that could be described as a mixture of fear and apathy, "Armies."

I said, "What armies? Where? When?"

She said, "Where are you?" as tears filled her eyes.

"I am here," I answered, but then I knew she was not talking to me. Her husband was gone, and she was grieving. "Don't worry, now. Everything will be all right."

She repeated, very softly, almost like death, "Where are you?"

I continued to hold her close and rub her arms as I tried to get her to continue to speak. Then I heard the clinking of Captain Valdéz's sword as he rode up. I lay the woman down and went outside. "The old woman I told you about is inside. She is not lucid and seems to be afraid. Please, do not enter just yet."

"I understand. I will stay here in case you need anything. Your slaves will be here soon."

I returned to the woman's bed and held her against me, with the blanket around us both. I tried to warm her while I again asked her where her husband was. Her cold body seemed to drain the warmth out of me. She said again, with a little whimper, "Where are you?"

Jonotás arrived carrying a jug of warm tea. Natán was carrying some plantains. Although plantains do not taste good without being cooked, they were my first thought as a source of fast nourishment. I had Natán use her fingernails to break off small pieces while Jonotás tried to get some tea through the poor woman's lips.

She did not respond. The tea ran down her chin. She seemed to become more frightened and said something I could not hear.

I put my ear next to her lips and said, "What? Tell me."

With her final breath, she whispered one word.

Then she made a low wavering sound in the back of her throat. I rubbed her arms harder, which were still as cold as when I found her. I felt her stiffen. Her eyes closed. I felt life leave her body.

Suddenly, I became quite angry. She had died a slow death that I was unable to stop because I was too late. I lay her down and put my ear against her chest in the hope that I was wrong. It was no use. The poor woman had withered away in my arms.

As I left the hut, I pulled angrily on the warped door. Its leather hinges broke and it fell. The light outside hurt my eyes. I could see a *quipu* trampled on the floor that the old Indian had shown me. The rich gold mines he told me about were now lost forever, along with the old man.

We did not know where her husband was buried, so we could not bury her next to him. Captain Valdéz had two of his men dig her grave at the side of the hut. Nothing was said as we put her in the ground. Then we all rode silently back to camp.

I was saddened and thoughtful as we began the last of our journey that morning. I barely knew the woman, but I wished that she had lived. I thought about my discussion with the old man seven years earlier. I remembered his advice to me, that I should drift through life. I hoped that she and her husband had drifted together pleasantly for awhile, and I hoped they had finally both landed on the same shore.

Still, their drifting had not been able to save their lives. For a moment, I thought they had been wrong. *Better to direct one's life.* Then, I thought of my own life, and how I had actively pursued what I wanted and trapped myself in a loveless marriage. Had I been right?

Of course, I never learned what happened to the old woman. She was one of thousands of South American women who had lost their men, and ultimately everything, since the revolution began. I did not know which army, Royalist or patriot, had been the cause of her husband's, and consequently, her own, demise. Yet, I somehow knew it was the war that had caused their deaths. Both sides were capable of violence and cruelty, and ultimately I realized that it did not matter which army she had been thinking about.

We were all responsible for the war. I knew I could be as bellicose as anyone when angered, and I had always believed in the revolution. At first, the war was a way for me to strike out in vicarious violence at the people who had wronged me. Anything that seemed unfair could cause me to fight, and when I started fighting I too could be cruel and destructive. Though the revolution was a fight against injustice, which is why I lent it my support, I questioned my beliefs that morning as we rode the trail around Cotopaxi. What greater injustice could there be than for an old woman to die all alone.

I thought about the vow I had made to myself after Juanita died, seven years earlier, and I was ashamed. True, I did not believe I had ever obeyed my vow in a way that brought any significant harm to anyone of good will, with the possible exception of James. However, I had at that moment agreed with the cruelty of the world—the same cruelty that had killed the old woman.

"La Sáenz is no predator," I told myself. I was no different from the old Indian woman, or any woman. I merely wished to survive in a brutal world. To defend myself is one thing. To live on the loss of others, as I had promised myself that I could do so long ago, was wrong. I decided that moment, as I rode along the trail in silence, that I would no longer agree with such barbarity.

Of course, my thoughts at the time did nothing to change the world. The revolution could not be stopped, and I would have to accept the reality of the way of the world. Still, it was sad, but not surprising, that the old woman whispered the one word as she died that stood for the only significant fact for all South Americans at that time: "Soldiers."

Chapter 42

All day long that old woman's voice haunted me. I was reminded of her every hour. We saw nothing but soldiers from the plain of Latacunga to the gates of the city. Our day started by seeing a column of defeated *godos* being marched to the coast by patriot lancers while we broke camp. Making our way around Cotopaxi, Captain Valdéz saluted several higher ranking officers that rode by, as squadrons of patriots galloped past us in either direction. When we passed thatched canteens, the riotous sounds of soldiers drunk on *chicha* (corn beer) could be heard from within. All about us were the signs of battle. As the day wore on, we passed condors feeding on both men and their horses. The other marks of war were more subtle: burned houses, deserted fields of potatoes left untended, scattered weapons, and homeless Indians walking the road to the city to find food. As we approached the city, we saw men doing close order drills in the fields. The nearer we came to Quito, the more crowded with soldiers was the trail and the more we had to fight for road space.

When we came over the rise, from where we could see the shallow valley of Anaquito with the city at the farther end, I was dismayed at how "threadbare" it looked from a distance. Years of war and a final violent battle seemed to have taken some of the luster from its renaissance towers.

The highway just outside the city was very busy. I noticed many people stop what they were doing to look at us. I remarked to Jonotás about this. She laughed and said, "It is not strange, Manuelita. You're distractin' all of these men with your fine uniform and fiery black horse." I laughed at her, but it made me feel good. I very much wanted to look elegant and proud when I came to this city.

It was almost evening when we arrived at the gates of Quito. I had left those same gates as an illegitimate young girl, expelled, unwanted, and with no future. I was returning as a wealthy member of Peruvian "nobility," escorted by a troop of Colombian lancers. I said good-bye to Captain Valdéz, who chivalrously kissed my hand before spurring his horse in another direction. Moments later, we were inside the gates.

There were several soldiers checking the papers of those arriving in the city. All about them were groups of men, young and old, standing around taking stock of the new arrivals and drinking *chicha*.

When I showed the soldier my passport, he looked back up at me sharply. I could tell that he recognized me. When he called a fellow over to look at my papers, I overheard him whisper the words, "La Sáenz." I could tell from their new uniforms that these men had recently joined the Colombian army. They were residents of Quito that had now joined their conquerors. They knew who I was. The way they looked at me made me believe they were impressed with my appearance. I smiled as I took back my passport and rode on towards the Larrea mansion.

Before we had gone a horse-length, a man a few years older than I grabbed my horse's reins. He was drunk.

"I remember you. Manuela, no?" He smiled at his comrades and staggered, but held onto the reins. "You were expelled from a convent for being too friendly with some young man. I'm a young man," he said ironically, as he was almost thirty. "Will you be friendly with me?" He laughed drunkenly and looked back at his friends, who smirked at him in encouragement.

"Let me pass," I said simply.

He took a long look at me. "You are fine woman, but you are not acting too 'friendly.'" He laughed at his own joke and looked at his fellows. When he looked back at me, one of my pistols was between his eyes.

"I am a most friendly woman," I said, smiling. "You will come by tonight, won't you?" I cocked the pistol.

His mouth dropped open. Terror came to his face, and he began to convulse. He was trying to stifle the *chicha* coming back up, but all other parts of him were frozen in terror. I pulled back on the reins and put my heels against the ribs of my "black ghost." She reared and stood on her hind legs, yanking the reins from the man's hand. When her hoofs hit the earth again, she began prancing excitedly.

I put my pistol back in its holster and said, "Nice to meet you!" The man was already on his hands and knees, vomiting. The other men standing around were laughing. Jonotás and Natán laughed too, and we rode on.

When we rode through the city, it still seemed worn and diminished, but I liked the fact that it was being actively repaired. People were everywhere, polishing and painting metal work. Large groups of Indians were painting the walls along the streets. Captain Valdéz had told me that General Sucre had ordered that all facades were to be freshly colored. Such colors though! I had always remembered Quito being white. Now the houses were in every color of the rainbow, with no consideration for adjoining walls. Some streets appeared to be bordered by multi-colored blankets. As we rode along, I noticed patriot soldiers taking down the little iron cages containing mummified heads that had been hung up 12 years before by the vengeful Spanish. Sucre had ordered them, at last, to be removed.

I went out of my way to show Jonotás and Natán the Santa Catalina convent, which I had told them about many times. I waited to see if there was somebody that I knew coming out of the *porteria*, but there was not.

I had Natán enter and ask after Doña Luisa and Carmen. She returned and said, "I'm sorry, Manuelita, your friends are not here. The one, Doña Luisa, she died."

My eyes became wet. "How long ago?"

"Two years." Natán mounted her horse. "One of her servants made a stew that had contaminated meat. The food was poisoned."

I knew instantly it was Beatríz. Things always went wrong when she was around.

"The nun who told me was old. She looked like she spoke honestly to me."

If Natán evaluated a person's character, I knew I could depend on it. "Oh, Natán, how sad that makes me. What happened to the servants?"

"When the old lady died, her relatives took them. They went to Potosí. The one you told us about was not one of them."

"Carmen? How do you mean?"

"These were *mestiza* servants."

"What happened to her?" I asked absently, not expecting an answer.

"The African? She ran away six or seven years ago. The nun told me she thought she was in the Indies."

She had run away soon after I left. I wondered where she was—Cuba perhaps. I would have loved to have seen Carmen, but I probably never would.

I grieved for my old benefactor as I looked up to the belfry where she had given me such good advice so many years before.

"I am truly sorry they're gone," I said, to myself more than my companions. Jonotás asked, "Why you lookin' up there, Manuelita?"

I told Jonotás and Natán the tale about the nun who had threatened to jump from the tower. When I was done, I felt better; it made me feel that Doña Luisa was still there. Jonotás and Natán were impressed with the story.

We left the convent, and I visited my mother's grave. My uncle, or aunts, had seen to it that she had a headstone that was maintained more than those around her. Most of the other graves were nothing more than mounds of earth where I knew that several bodies were stacked one on top of another. Such resting places as these, with their anonymity that would last forever, made me feel sad. We spent only a short time there, while the last of the sun dipped behind the mountains, and then we mounted our horses to go.

As we left the cemetery, a figure jumped up from the side of the street. I could tell the man was dirty and wearing a tattered priest's frock, but I did not recognize him until we took a few more steps and he spoke.

"The devils have entered our city. You shall not prevail." He was pacing back and forth, shaking his finger at us, staring at us with one eye. Suddenly he ran down the street and was gone.

Jonotás and Natán chuckled. Jonotás made a face that perfectly resembled the mad priest. Natán laughed. Jonotás started laughing, too. Through her giggles, Natán asked, "Who was that?"

"It is a mad priest," I said. I was not laughing. "He took my mother's last confession." I was still feeling sad from seeing my mother's grave and I was reminded more deeply of the pain I felt that day. I fought the tears that came to my eyes.

Jonotás and Natán stopped laughing and looked after the man. Jonotás edged her horse close to mine and stroked my shoulder. "We're sorry, Manuelita."

"Never mind," I said. "I have returned here to take what is mine. We will win, so let us begin." I smiled and they agreed with me and we rode off.

As we hurried on, I passed the many familiar spots I had known as a child. It was good to be in Quito again, despite how much it reminded me of the painful years of my youth.

At last, just as it was getting too dark to see, we rode up to the Larrea stables. Juan de Larrea was already outside waiting for me. News of my arrival had made it across town before I did. When I dismounted, he came up to me saying, "Manuelita,

Manuelita, how good to have you home." He hugged me and kissed me like he would a daughter. We both had tears in our eyes as I embraced him.

"I have a sleeping chamber all prepared for you."

"Oh, thank you, Don Larrea. Is there room for my servants?" I introduced Jonotás and Natán.

"You do not wish them to stay with the other servants?

"No, Don Larrea. Can they stay with me?

"If that is what you wish."

He ordered his servants to unload our mules and horses and put them "to bed" for the night. As we walked up the stairs, he asked, "Do you think I might be able to buy your mules?"

"My mules?" I did not understand at first that he meant the mules I was to deliver for Carlson.

"Yes, General Sucre has put out a request for a team of mules just this afternoon. I thought I might purchase them from you and donate them to the General.

"Oh. Gladly would I donate them myself, but they are not mine. I am delivering them for a friend." I still had not read the bill of sale so I did not know who was to receive them. "Perhaps their owner will consider it."

"Yes, perhaps. But now, you must come upstairs—"

"I have missed you and Doña Larrea so much. How is she?"

"She is fine. Better still, I'll warrant, when she sees you."

While we talked, he escorted me into the living quarters and had our trunks taken to my room. Then, I followed him to the dining area. Doña Larrea was there and as happy to see me as if I had been her own. I cried when I embraced her.

"Oh, Manuelita, you have returned. You have returned," she said.

They had a fine meal waiting for me, and she bade me sit down to eat. It was just as though I was sitting at their table as a child. We had a familiar dish: roast mutton and potatoes along with a special spiced cabbage. It was like home when they served me some *guayusa* tea. Only *quiteños* drink it, as it is made from plants that grow in thickets on the slopes of Pichincha. For desert they served my favorite of the ices, which I used to love when I was young, oranges and milk mixed with mountain ice and molded in a pewter mold.

I laughed when Don Larrea showed me a special mold he had made since the Battle of Pichincha. It was in the shape of South America. He said that he hoped to be able to invite the Liberator to dinner when he arrived. If so, he was going to make ices with red, blue and yellow colors where Gran Colombia was on the little ice continent.

"Then I have not missed seeing the Liberator enter the city?" I asked.

"He is still a few days from arriving," said Doña Larrea.

I was excited that I was to be there for his triumphant arrival into the city. Festivities were sure to follow, and it would be fun to be part of the celebration of the liberation of my city.

After I ate, we sat at the table and talked. The Larreas did not seem to appreciate it when Jonotás brought me a cigar. Don Larrea was smoking, but they did not want me to smoke.

I told them of my time in Panamá and how every woman smoked there. I told them a few other stories, in as condensed a form as possible, as I was very tired. Even so, we talked into the night, and at last I was escorted to my bedroom door, where we all hugged each other again. It was wonderful to see those two lovely people once more. By that time, they were almost in their sixties. I felt sad to have missed the intervening years.

Jonotás and Natán were already in our room. I had never been in this room before, but I could tell that the furniture and decorations were new. It was the finest bedroom I have ever seen. There was a magnificent wide bed at the end of a long *estrado* (dais), which was raised higher than usual. The bed coverings were of crimson velvet, lined with satin and trimmed with broad gold lace and a deep gold fringe. The velvet cover was embroidered with gold and silver designs, and the sheets and pillow covers were trimmed with fine Brussels lace. I was overwhelmed with the sumptuousness of it all.

Rolls of cotton batting had been brought in to provide a space for Jonotás and Natán to sleep, but I had them sleep with me. The bed was certainly big enough. I fell asleep that night, happy and content.

Chapter 43

When we awoke, we had hot water brought to us by the servants and we each enjoyed a luxurious bath. I did not leave my room until mid-morning. I was happy and excited at being back with my old friends, and I was looking forward to conquering Quito—and Carlos.

We had chocolate and fruit for breakfast, during which I finished some of my stories for the Larreas, and heard a few also. Later, Jonotás, Natán and I rode down to the address from which I had received my last communication regarding my litigation. I was hoping to find out the most effective way to push forward my lawsuit.

The men there were most uncooperative. The looks on their faces, when I announced myself, went from surprise to anger. One of them walked briskly over to me and tried to look down his nose as he said, "I am most sorry, Señora, but with the recent changes in government, it will be months before you will be able to continue with your suit."

I could hardly believe what I was hearing. "Why?" I asked.

"The government has changed, Señora," said the man with a superior sneer.

"Señor, I have come all the way from Lima so that I might manage my affairs here. And now you tell me I must wait."

"I'm afraid, even when the administrative difficulties with the new government are solved, you will have to start all over."

"All over? What do you mean?" I was so upset I couldn't think straight. It was like a bad dream.

"The suit was not filed correctly to begin with."

"What? Why not?"

The man's eyes were shifty and his explanations were weak. I questioned him as much as I could, given my confusion regarding legal matters, but I sensed that Carlos's money was talking louder than anything I had to say.

"I'm sorry, Señora, but there is nothing I can do. You will simply have to wait until officials from Bogotá arrive and the new government settles in. Then we will see."

I was so angry I could hardly see. We walked our horses back home, and my companions wisely kept silent so I could think. My frustration knew no bounds. I could not have said a nice thing to anyone, had I met someone I knew. The more I thought about it, the more sure I was that Carlos was paying them off and had been all these months. I fumed with rage at the injustice of it. Carlos had stopped me. The wall I faced seemed so complete that I was devastated. In my dark mood, it appeared that everything I had gained thus far was empty, empty unless I could find another means to gain my inheritance.

I had intended to show Jonotás and Natán around that day, but I could not. In addition to being upset about my lawsuit I was also worried by the realization that I would need more money to stay longer in Quito to fight for it. I could not impose on the Larrea's kindness forever. I walked back to the mansion in silent frustration.

After I arrived and composed myself a bit, I tried to see what I could accomplish to make my situation better. I was apathetic as I sent Jonotás off to fetch the bill of sale for the mules given to me by Carlson. I was not interested in the mules at that moment, but all the more reason to finish the chore of seeing that they were delivered. Once I had petty distractions out of the way, perhaps I could figure out a new strategy to fight Carlos.

Natán found the bill of sale in my saddlebag and brought it to me. She said, "Here it is, Manuelita," as she handed it to me. However I was in too dark a mood to even be civil to her.

I stood by the light from a window and opened the paper. When I read the name, I had to sit down. From my lips came a cry of joy. Then, I laughed so hard that Don Larrea came in from the other room to see what was going on. There on the bill of sale, dated some months before, in amongst the correspondence creating the trade, was the name Carlos Aispuru.

I was so delighted to have control of some of my uncle's property. The first thing I did was start calculating the money I would be able to accrue from selling the mules. Then I remembered that General Sucre needed them.

What a predicament. I knew I would need that money, but I wanted very much to supply what the victorious general needed. I was certain that some one else would provide the mules, but I wanted very much to help the cause. I did not know what to do.

In the end, I had Jonotás take them over to General Sucre. I wrote to him:

Dear General,

I am sending these mules to you because I have heard that they are needed by the revolutionary army.

My admiration for you and your soldiers is undying. These are my way of repaying you for your bravery.

What I regret most is that our brave soldiers do not have all that is needed. Nevertheless, you may count on the slender resources I possess; which, despite the fact that they are small, are always at your disposal. I shall not call this a sacrifice, knowing it to be only my duty.

Manuela Sáenz

I truly meant it, and I felt much better after I decided to donate my windfall to the cause. Jonotás must have been quite a sight in her soldier's uniform, her red turban, and her gold earrings, leading a string of mules to the offices of the General.

I also sent Natán out to the Aispuru estate with this letter:

Dear Carlos,

As I know you so well and I know you to be an unselfish patriot, I have sent your mules to General Sucre to help in the cause of liberty. It is very generous of you to help our soldiers so magnanimously.

However, since I have not yet received my inheritance from you, I have taken them as a small commendation for my patience and I have sent them to the General in the name of Manuela Sáenz, as I am sure you would wish.

Your niece,
Manuela

She handed the letter, with the bill of sale and other documents, right into his hands. She left immediately, but she said she could hear him swearing before she climbed back on her horse. I was overjoyed.

What really pleased and touched me was an unexpected personal note from the General, in his own hand:

My Gracious Lady—

The noble offer of your possessions for the defense of the state is already suggested by your generosity. Please accept the gratitude of the whole corps of the Army of Liberation, in whose name I am able to assure you that nothing gives them greater pleasure than to know that there are heroines, such as yourself, with whom they can share their glories.

Antonio José de Sucre

It felt wonderful to receive such a letter, and I decided then that I could solve my problems. I would stay in Quito, I would help the revolution, and I would win, one way or another.

Until I had a solution, I was going to enjoy myself. But I would not shirk my duty; I would begin working in the hospitals again to do my part in the making of a new world.

As it happened, Juan Larrea insisted on splitting the cost of the donation. He gave me a considerable amount of silver for half the price of the mules.

I said, "No, Señor, no. It was a gift to the revolutionary army. When the Liberator arrives, I want to be among the 'heroines,' as General Sucre has called me. I want to remain deserving of the honor of a Knightess of the Order of the Sun."

"You will be that anyway; I am only paying half. Here." He handed me the money.

"Thank you, Don Larrea."

"No need to thank me. It is not charity, except to the cause. Now, I want you to wish me luck."

"Of course. Why do you need luck?"

"I am off to speak to the revolutionary council and the *cabildo* to see if we might be able to have a victory ball for the Liberator right here in the mansion."

"In that case, let me be more eloquent." I gave him a big kiss on the cheek and said, "May fortune smile on you." We smiled at each other.

Chapter 44

The early days of liberation kept the inhabitants of Quito busy. There was a new republic to build amid the daily chores of mere survival. Along with all this, everyone was preparing for the Liberator's arrival. He was to enter the city sometime in the middle of June. There was an undercurrent of excitement that carried us through each day.

Bills were pasted on walls throughout the city announcing that Bolívar was on his way from his mountain victories in Pasto. These also carried the statement he had made to the Colombian people on the surrender of the *pastusos*:

> From the banks of the Orinoco to the Andes of Perú the liberating army, marching from one triumph to another, has covered with its protecting arms the whole of Colombia. Share with me the ocean of joy that bathes my heart, and raise in your own hearts altars to this army which has conquered for you glory, peace, and liberty.

Excitement was in the air. The fresh paint on the buildings in many pigments, the new brightly colored wicker arches over the streets the Liberator was to follow on his way to the main square, the rehearsing of bands filling the city with music, and the thousands of other things that were happening in Quito gave a cutting excitement to the most banal activities.

Two days after asking me for luck, Don Larrea gathered his entire household together. He quieted everyone down and said, "I have just spoken to the revolutionary committee. I am pleased to announce that the Liberator is to parade right past this house when he enters the city." Everyone gave a cheer and clapped their hands with delight. "Wait, please, there is more. I am also most pleased to announce that this house has been chosen as the site of the celebration ball . . ." We all shrieked in delight, excited as birds let out of their cages. Don Larrea had to shout to finish, ". . . which is to be given that same evening."

We waited with ill-contained anticipation for Bolívar's arrival. On the day that the Liberator was to come, Jonotás, Natán and I galloped north through the city gates. People turned to watch these three women dressed as men, two of them black, one of them white, riding too fast through the city. We galloped far beyond the city gates by the side of the road. Then we turned on to the road itself and headed back, weaving our way through the crowds of Indians and visitors from the outlying districts making their way into the city. We wanted to ride the route that Bolívar was to travel that afternoon, to see the decorations and sights that he would see.

Triumphal arches had been erected all along the highway, draped in the tricolor of the Republic. Some were festooned with large flowers (many of which had been procured all the way from the coast). "Let's add our own touch," I exclaimed at one point.

The three of us dismounted and walked into a nearby, untended potato field and each of us picked a dozen or two of its little purple flowers. Then we stuck them in among the other flowers on one of the arches. They were tiny, and could not really be seen, but I felt the Liberator should be welcomed by the flower that represented the countryside he was entering and its Indian population.

By the time we re-entered the city, the crowds in the streets were starting to gather. We noticed both men and women wearing either a tricolor ribbon or a cockade. Everyone had put on, and had decorated their dwellings and shops in, what they felt would make them look their very best and most patriotic. The women young enough to be interested were dressed to attract the most attention to their feminine charms. The men were dressed in their finest, whether it be a velvet three cornered hat or the cleanest and brightest poncho.

Street vendors were already pushing through the crowds beginning to line the streets, selling sausages, pastries, corn cakes, bread, wine and *chicha*. There were other vendors selling trinkets, home-made medals, cockades, sashes, and sheets of music to patriotic songs. In the center of town, the victors of the Battle of Quito, dressed in new uniforms (which I had helped supply with a little bit of my meager funds), were practicing again the close order drills for ceremonies later in the day. Every *quiteño*, of every class, was in the streets or on balconies or on overhead bridges (except on those bridges which already held little Indian girls dressed as angels ready to drop flower petals on the Liberator) or in high windows or on the tops of statues or fountains, most likely sharing whatever viewing space they had with a member of some other class.

That day, excitement filled the very air we breathed. Jonotás, Natán and I were absolutely full of giggles when we finally made our way through the crowds and rode up to the Larrea stables. It was mid-morning, and the sun was blazing. Everyone in the Larrea household agreed it was one of Quito's finest days.

Jonotás and Natán helped me to bathe and dress. Then they went down to mingle with the crowds gathering along the streets. I sat down to powder my face and had one of those rare views of myself in the mirror where I felt I looked beautiful.

I wore a brand new white dress that Doña Larrea had given to me as a present. I think she was hinting that she would rather not have me dressed as a man that day. It was made of the finest and brightest white linen, with fancy laced edges, trimmed with silver and cut as low as decency would allow. From my shoulder hung a red and white sash leading across my bosom to hold the small golden medal that signified me as a member of the Order of the Sun. My hair, which might have fallen to the middle of my back on other days, was pulled away from my face and coiled on the back of my head. I had painted my eyebrows to emphasize their arch and I put on dangling silver earrings set with three bright red stones.

In the Larrea house, like all the wealthy houses in South America, the upper floor is the living space and the lower floor is for storage and the servant's quarters. There might be day rooms on the lower floor or a grand entrance hall with a wide stairway, but the ballrooms and the dining rooms and other places where one entertained were on the same floor as the other principal rooms of the house, including the major bedrooms. So I could hear the wealthy members of the *cabildo* down the hall laughing and talking with Juan Larrea.

I knew the women would be in the next room, but I walked right in with the men. Their conversation stopped. Don Larrea took my hand and lead me to over to the men. "My friends, please meet Manuela Sáenz de Thorne." I saw some expressions change as they recognized me and my name. "Please note, gentlemen, that Señora Thorne has been awarded membership in San Martín's Order of the Sun."

One man said, "Ah, an honor. I have a relative fighting with San Martín." He gave me his name and asked if I knew him.

"I do not, Señor, but if I had known I would meet his handsome cousin, I would have made a point to meet him."

Everyone laughed. Two or three other questions were asked about the Peruvian revolution and soon we were all in a high-spirited conversation that covered many subjects: the fall of Lima, San Martín, whether San Martín or Bolívar was the foremost "liberator," how much had the English really helped the cause, and so on. I made them laugh, and I was pleased at how easily I could fit into a social gathering in Quito.

About a half-hour later, when I was describing a dance I had learned in Perú a year or so before, we heard a rocket whistle over the housetops near the entrance to the city. Everyone rushed out to the balcony. We craned our necks to see if we could make out the Liberator on the road, but all we saw and heard was a colorful profusion of rockets exploding over the city gates. Then there was a thundering of cannon being fired. The Liberator was about to enter the city.

When the cannon reports died down, we heard the peals of every bell in every church, as Indian bell ringers worked feverishly to compete in loudness with the preceding cannon fire. Then, a single horseman rode through the streets at a gallop, announcing his arrival: "*¡El Libertador! ¡El Libertador!*" Everyone cleared the street. There followed a few soldiers who rode in wide formation to push the crowd back. Way down along the route we began to hear cheering and we knew that the great general was in the city.

Servants brought up generous stacks of flowers, as well as laurel made into wreaths, that Don Larrea and his guests could throw in the path of the hero. I chose the largest wreath I thought I could throw. As I held it in my hand, feeling the tricolor ribbons woven in among the laurel, I thought about finding a smaller one. I was sure I would not be strong enough to throw it past the edge of the street. It was too large. When I turned to look for something else, everything was taken.

Then Doña Larrea said, "Manuela, he's here."

I saw him. He came around a corner and waved at the populace on either side of the street. A squadron of lancers in bright green uniforms marched in front of him and another marched to the rear. As he rode down our street, I was very impressed. This day had been exciting and I was relishing the joyous emotions, but I did not expect to be as taken with the man as I was. He made a magnificent figure on his white horse, Pastor, and I found my admiration for him riding a tidal wave.

He had a gleaming white hat with a broad brim that he held in his hand and waved at the cheering crowd. A cape of a deep blue hue, with brilliant highlights in the crests of the folds, draped over the back of his horse. His jacket was of the same material, with two rows of golden buttons making a line from waist to shoulders. He wore knee-high, military-style boots of the shiniest black. His pants were white and the trimming on his saddle blanket and collar and sleeves was intricately woven with gold designs. Sparks flew from Pastor's iron-shod feet as he pranced along the stones.

Everyone on the balcony with me was alive with excitement, but I do not believe anyone was as taken with him as I. He rode down the street as the cheering grew and grew. He lifted his hat to wave at the crowd. Everyone was throwing flowers at the feet of his mount. Some tried to rush out to touch him, but they were prevented by lancers who moved up quickly to cut them off.

As he rode past our balcony, he smiled at us. We all began throwing our flowers and wreaths. I threw my wreath very hard, trying to make it land right in front of his horse.

But a devil seemed to take hold of my ring of leaves.

It did not sail down to the street at all, but flew up on drafts of non-existent wind and then plunged right into the Liberator's forehead. He stopped, his horse prancing in impatience. The demigod looked up at me angrily.

I was aghast. Everyone on the balcony shifted their eyes back and forth between Bolívar and me. I was looking straight at him in apologetic glances. My eyes were as wide as saucers I'm sure and my hands were trying to decide whether to clutch each other or cover my open mouth.

In an instant, he saw what had happened. He gave me the handsomest smile I have ever seen. His horse danced around nervously, trampling on the offending wreath. Then he threw me a kiss and rode down the street to the main plaza where he was to be greeted by the president of the now defunct *audiencia*.

He had paused for less than the time it takes a heart to beat, and yet we seemed to spend a lifetime together in that moment.

I laughed in relief and expressed my disbelief along with everyone else on the balcony. I was positively giddy. Then the guests dispersed as everyone went home to change for the ball.

Don Larrea walked up to me and kissed me on the forehead and said, "Oh, Manuelita," and then he too walked off to get changed.

Chapter 45

Everyone wanted to wear their very best clothes on the night of the ball, and I retired to my bedroom to put on the evening dress that I had packed for special occasions. It was a light blue organdy, very modern, very English. The skirt fell in long folds from a high waistline. My satin ballet slippers could barely be seen under the hem. It was cut indecently low, half revealing my bosom, modesty being served only slightly by the sash, carrying my medallion, draped from my right shoulder. I had piled my hair in a Grecian knot and placed some dainty white flowers in amongst the braids to accent my coloration.

When I was finally done, I looked at myself. I thought, *in this city, in front of mirrors in this very house, I used to think of myself as plain.* As a child I had not looked much worse than any other awkward child my age, but I had seen myself as ugly because of the feeling of self-loathing I had buried deep under my bravado.

Now, seven years after leaving Quito, I felt able to accept my own beauty at last. I could see that it was mostly my perception of myself that had changed. It is a cruel thing to make a child feel different or "bad." Only a little more encouragement in my early years would have done me wonders. I do not know what more I would have accomplished than I did, but I would not have had so far to come or such misery to transcend. I had gained so much since my convent days in Quito and as I sat looking at myself in the mirror, I realized that I need not have suffered. I had been beautiful all that time.

Jonotás and Natán interrupted my reverie, all smiles and excitement. "Manuelita, you must listen. We found someone," said Jonotás. "Yes," said Natán, "in the plaza."

"I am listening. Was it a very handsome general on a white horse?"

They laughed. Jonotás said, "No. Someone younger." She laughed again.

Natán said, "He was standin' with the general's officers durin' the ceremonies, and he was very smartly dressed. Guess who it was—"

Jonotás could not contain herself. "It was José María!"

"Jonotás, I wanted to tell her." Natán gave her a little shove.

I gave a jump for joy and laughed. "Never mind, you two. Where is he now?"

"We caught up to him, before he entered the palace," said Natán.

"He recognized us right away," said Jonotás. Who would not recognize Jonotás anywhere? "He has to ride back to Pasto tonight to take messages to the garrison there, and he won't be attendin' the ball."

"We begged him to wait. But you must hurry." I left immediately, after pulling on my *saya y manto.*

The Liman dress customs are so sensible. I was dressed to attend a ball. In only a moment I was ready to go walking; when I returned I would merely have to remove the outer garment to be dressed again in my finest, ready to meet the Liberator.

The three of us walked the few blocks to the Plaza Mayor, and I was able to persuade the guard to bring José María out of the palace. He looked the same, except he was now a member of Bolívar's staff and wore a brand new uniform. I embraced him and held on as he spun me around.

He was happy to see me too, and kissed my cheeks. Then he took my hands and said, "How are you, my sister? It is so good to see you."

I said, "I am wonderful. Come, I want you to myself. Let's go for a walk."

He smiled, reminded of the time in Panamá when I had made him show me all over town. "All right," he said, "but let's get out of here before the general comes and puts me to work." We laughed and started off across the square. Jonotás and Natán stayed and talked with some new friends, newly freed slaves, they had made that afternoon.

We walked all over the city, strolling through bits of paper, crumpled flowers, and other trash that was covering the streets. We stopped and had a light dinner made from various snacks purchased from vendors still doing business amongst the lingering crowds. Every now and then we would tarry and talk about some sight from our childhood.

We walked past the house where José María had been born. It had long ago been sold, and we could see through the gate that the present owners had let the patio garden go to seed. We were silent as we looked at it, and I thought about how I had never even been in that house and how cheated I had felt by that fact as a child. Now I owned two houses that surpassed this one in beauty and space.

We both said, at the same time, "It looks smaller." We laughed.

It was almost sunset by the time we returned to the palace. There was still commotion everywhere in Quito, but nowhere as much as in the great plaza. We found Jonotás and Natán there, still celebrating, eating sausage and corn cakes with several Indians and Africans.

As we were saying good-bye, a huge, somber-looking Indian, but with darker skin from African blood, bright red hair, a short black cape, dark trousers, and an immaculately clean white shirt came around the corner with Pastor. Beside him walked two enormous mastiffs. The Liberator's horse was saddled and ready for riding.

As he went behind the building, José María said, in answer to my inquiring eyes, "That is José Palacios, the General's bodyguard and personal servant. He's been with him since he was a boy." Then, as an afterthought, "He must be taking the horse around to the side for the general to ride to the ball." Immediately, several other mounted officers and four lancers rode around the corner in the same direction.

"Yes, José, it is getting late."

José María said, "I must go." We hugged each other. I would miss him, as I always did, but I felt more comfortable with his leaving this time. He was a personal aide to the most powerful man on the continent, and he would be safe now that the fighting was almost over.

Jonotás and Natán and I went behind the building as soon as José was inside, but we could not find the horse or the general. He had already left.

My companions and I began to make our way back home. We did not go directly, but spent a good while wandering through the streets in order to enjoy the lingering excitement throughout the city. On every street corner we saw men and women standing around braziers, with large fires illuminating their faces. They were cooking sausage, drinking *chicha*, playing guitars, brawling, gambling, or singing. In fact, wherever we turned, there was riotous celebration. Rockets would intermittently light up the sky and little "poppers" of fire and noise would be set off by the exuberant celebrants. Everywhere there was a crowd of happy people, excitement, and activity.

After walking around a bit, soaking up the feeling of victory and the sense of new beginnings, we made our way up the street to the Larrea mansion. We could see the house clearly from the direction we approached and we enjoyed how festive it looked. Every candle in every room (as well as those in the huge overhanging candelabrum in the salon) and every storm lantern outside was lighted. Soldiers were on duty to keep the riotous populace from inviting themselves inside to partake of the new republican custom, "shaking hands," with the Liberator. In the meantime, Indian servants with powdered hair, satin waistcoats, and bare feet, were lined up and down the surrounding streets, holding torches to light the way for Quito's upper class citizens as they made their way to the ball. Some of the "finer women" of society's "best" arrived in sedan chairs. I chuckled at them as they rode by, traveling in this archaic mode to such a modern celebration.

Classic waltzes could be heard coming from the brilliantly lit ballroom above when we arrived near the entrance. We walked around to the back of the house and through the stables. I saw Pastor and I petted him and gave my own "black ghost" some hay. Then, after removing my Peruvian walking dress and giving it to Natán to take to our room, I went inside.

When I climbed the stairs to the ballroom, I noticed every fashion, from the oldest colonial costume with its tricorne hat and powdered wig, to the narrow frock coat of a generation earlier, to the most modern trousers strapped under varnished boots and complemented by high beaver hats. The women were as varied in their attire: stiff brocade, high heels, walking sticks, and quizzing glasses on the one hand; on the other were young beautiful modern women with ballet slippers on their feet, wearing bold dresses of organdy, gauze, or brocade. There were even some women at the ball who had daringly cropped their hair short to reflect the spirit of the revolutionary times.

The house was aglow with conversation and laughter as I passed through the outer room with its tables holding wines, sweetmeats, and sliced fruit. I stood at the door to the ballroom for a moment while men and women pushed past me to enter or leave the dance floor. A small orchestra of Indian musicians—only Indians can play wind instruments in the high altitude of Quito—dressed in satin uniforms and powdered wigs were playing waltzes on one side of the room. The windows were open to cool off the dancers.

Through the cigar smoke I saw Simón Bolívar standing on a low dais at the end of the room under a tricolor canopy next to Don Larrea and a member of his staff who I later learned was his aide-de-camp, Daniel O'Leary.

I had heard that Bolívar always dressed rather simply, but on this night he had on a red uniform, the jacket of which was heavily braided in gold, with large epaulets that held the three stars of a General of the Allied Armies of Liberation. His hair was combed back and his Wellington boots had very high heels and a shiny blackness to match his hair.

I watched him, fascinated by his style. He greeted everyone as though they were his very favorite people. He let his eyes linger too long on the eyes of the ladies he met, imparting intimacy and attention, while he kissed their hands. He led each woman, young or old, with his expression and the quality of his conversation, to secretly believe that he hoped he would be able to go home with her that night. He greeted the men as if they

were trusted advisors and led each man to believe, in a similar way, that he had a special place in his entourage just for him. Simón Bolívar was pure theatre.

I could be theatre, also. I would meet him and, I decided, I would make as deep an impression on him as he was used to making on his admirers. I started to cross the room to the dais. Then, to my horror, I recognized the tall, beautiful woman whom Bolívar was greeting at that moment: Antonia.

I stopped, uncertain of whether to advance or wait for a more propitious moment. After all this time, she was still in my way. She had apparently finished her convent schooling and had taken her place as an adult in her family's affairs. She was more beautiful than ever, and I could tell, even from where I was standing, that she was turning on that seductive charm at which she was so adept.

I'm sure that none of her desires were lost on Bolívar. He spent much more time with her than anyone else he had met. When he had to turn to meet someone else, he watched her walk away out of the corner of his eye. As she crossed the room, she was smiling the confident smile of a conqueror, a libidinous look in her eyes.

Why were the Fates so unkind as to place her again in my path? All the cruel things she had done to me in the convent I relived in a moment. She crossed the room, coming straight at me. When she was a few feet away, she recognized me. She stopped. We looked at each other for a few seconds. I saw the emotions cross her face: surprise, hatred, social cordiality. When she regained her composure and put on a friendly smile, she passed me. Her smile was betrayed by her venomous voice as she said, "Welcome back, Manuela."

I did not respond but let her pass. I adjusted the sash, carrying my "Order of the Sun" medallion, and said, under my breath, "Yes, Antonia, I am back."

I walked across the dance floor, weaving my way through the dancers, heading toward the dais. Before I was half-way across the room, the handsome general had his attention on me. Don Larrea, in his tailcoat and knee breeches, came off the dais and led me directly to him. Before stepping back up on the platform, he said, "Your Excellency, Señora Manuela Sáenz de Thorne."

With embarrassment, I noticed that there was a small scratch on his forehead. Then, I looked right in the eyes of the man I had thought about all day—the liberator of half a continent.

I felt his eyes move over the roundness of my breasts for an instant, as I hoped they would. Then, he returned my gaze, and the moment was a familiar one. I felt the same rush of blood as I had felt earlier that afternoon and the same sense that time stopped for an instant. He smiled at me, that friendly, welcoming smile that I had seen from him earlier. He leaned forward to kiss my hand, saying, "My lady."

I did not take my eyes off his and said, "I hope, Excellency, that you were not wounded too badly this afternoon when that foolish woman on the balcony tried to place that wreath right on your head."

He laughed and said, "I owe that woman a debt of gratitude. The blow made me see visions." His eyes twinkled in merriment.

I laughed and looked around the room, at all of the beautiful women at the ball. I noticed Antonia watching us, a look of malice on her face. I said, "There are so many beautiful visions to see here tonight."

Without taking his eyes off me, he said, "None so lovely as the one before me."

I could not contain my laughter and said, "How very gracious of you, Señor."

Then I paused just long enough to feel that he was about to respond but not so long that I could not speak first without being rude. Then I said, "But I am selfish to take up your time; important people are waiting to meet your Excellency. So I will only thank you and depart."

"Thank me? For what, Señora?"

"For freeing my country, Señor." I smiled. Then, I turned and walked back across the dance floor.

Near a table by the wall, an Indian servant gave me a glass of wine. Before I had taken two sips, I was asked to dance. I accepted. I kept an eye on the Liberator as he continued to meet the citizens of Quito. Every now and then he looked around the room, and our eyes would meet.

When he was done meeting the new arrivals, he came down to the dance floor. He danced with one woman after another, even dancing with Antonia twice. I never saw a better dancer. When he started dancing, I turned down invitations that came my way so that I might talk to his fellow soldiers and watch him. He fascinated me.

I particularly enjoyed meeting his officers and I was most pleased to finally meet General Sucre. I wanted to talk to him, but he was vying with an officer from the Irish contingent for the attention of a beautiful *quiteña*. Her name was Mariana, and she was the daughter of the Marqués de Solanda—who had been in that first revolutionary junta formed by Manuel Morales and Señor Quiroga.

I met other interesting heroes of the war: Antonio de la Guerrera, a junior officer whom I was to meet again in a few days and who would became a good friend of mine; Juan Flores, swiftly advancing in rank and reputation, later to be pivotal in my country's history; the hero José María Córdoba, whose valiant charge had turned the day, a month before, during the battle of Pichincha; and the elder veteran, Jacinto Lara, who seemed to think that women were a subhuman race. These last two would prove to be something less than friends.

I was also able to use my English that evening. I met Daniel O'Leary and the other English-speaking officers whom I would get to know so intimately in the years to come. These included blond Arthur Sandes, who competed with Sucre for the attentions of the beautiful Mariana; William Fergusson, with his long reddish blond mustache and a taste for Irish whisky; Sowerby from Bremen, who was extraordinarily friendly and handsome, and who bragged that he had come through the Napoleonic wars and the wars in South America without a scratch. I also met Duckbury from London, Captain Hallowes of Kent, O'Conner of the fighting O'Conners from Dublin, the Scottish officer, Rupert Hand, and others.

All the men from the isles of Britain loved me, then and later, because I could speak to them in their native tongue. I bantered with them, I told them risqué stories I had learned from James's sea captains, and I made them laugh. At one point, I made Fergusson laugh so hard and unexpectedly that he sprayed whiskey all over his fellow officers. Everyone roared as they brushed the liquor off their uniforms. " Ah, Lass, it's a knack you have for makin' a man laugh," he said while still trying to clean up. "If you're ever in trouble Lass, I'll be comin' to save ya." Then he laughed again. I was having a wonderful time.

As the night wore on, and the wine took what was left of the sobriety from the occasion, I took up a challenge from one of the officers to dance something more lively than a waltz. I danced by myself, the *ñapanga*. This dance has many twisting and sinuous movements in it and must be performed with one's skirts held high. The officers loved it and the women standing around obviously hated it.

As I finished and the officers applauded, I laughed and said, "I am sorry that we can't dance it together, but it is not that kind of dance."

At that point, Bolívar came over and said simply, "Would you care to dance with *me*, my lady?" His smile was broad and inviting.

I returned his smile and said, "I would love to dance with you, your Excellency."

"Then come," he said, smiling broadly, as he offered me his arm.

If Bolívar was enjoyable to watch on the dance floor, he was a marvel to dance with. He held me close enough to make the experience sensual and stimulating, and firmly enough to control me. All the while, I felt that I was floating.

The first thing he said to me was, "I insist that you call me Simón."

"Do you think that is proper?"

"You strike me as one who enjoys more the rustle of life than its proprieties."

I laughed and said, "You understand me well . . . Simón."

He smiled. "That's better."

We danced one dance after another. Neither of us danced with anyone else that night. I saw the other ladies, especially Antonia, and those of society who knew me as "La Sáenz, the bastard," glare at me through thick thunder clouds of animosity.

The more we danced and talked, the more we liked each other. We waltzed and talked to each other as though we were the only ones on the floor. He made me feel a deep desire for him, an attraction and longing beyond any I had ever known. Each movement made me want him. The custom was to hold your partner at arm's length, but he held me scandalously close. His leg stepped between mine as though it were a caress, his arms encircled me like a hunter who has caught his prey with his own hands, and his eyes never left mine.

At one point, while waiting for the musicians to tune, as we stood talking, Antonia came by and dropped her handkerchief. Bolívar picked it up and handed it to her. She said, "Thank you, your Excellency," a little too seductively while she put the handkerchief between her breasts. I wondered for a moment whether Antonia, after all these years, would best me one more time.

At that point the musicians started playing a familiar dance, and I said, "Oh, Simón, do you know this one?"

He immediately took his attention from Antonia and said to me, "It's one of my favorites."

We danced. We danced for a long, long time.

Late in the evening, he said, "Do you know what I hate about affairs such as this?"

"What, Simón?"

"Leaving! Not because I am having too much fun. Which I am. Rather, because as soon as you start for the door, everyone wants to talk to you."

"I know what you mean."

"When I was just starting my soldiering, I could leave a *fiesta* in a tenth of an hour at most. With each victory, or promotion, the time has grown. Now it is two hours. One can measure one's success by the amount of time it takes to leave a social affair." We laughed.

"Perhaps I can help you with this problem," I said after a moment.

"Do you think you could? I would be eternally grateful."

Without anybody seeing us, we stepped behind the tricolor cloth covering a door near the dais and descended the back stairs. In a few moments, we were in the stable. We laughed and joked while we had our horses saddled by the Larrea servants. Then, we rode out into the night.

I was first out of the stable. However, I was in an evening dress, and had to ride "sidesaddle," though my saddle was meant to be ridden astride. This slowed me down so much that soon Bolívar was far ahead of me.

The neighboring streets were still alive with brazier fires, brawling, drunkenness, and celebration, though it was past midnight. Everywhere I looked, there was confusion: shouting and noise came from all directions, figures darted across the streets, and those too full of spirits lay where they fell to sleep off their inebriation. Everywhere I looked, there was smoke, flame, and chaos.

Wherever he rode, Bolívar, the Liberator, brought the noisy streets to quiet. At first, some thought they recognized him. Then they would whisper to their friends or turn to one another to point him out. They could not believe their good fortune to be able to see their hero. Then, as he rode past, the people who knew him raised a cheer. The streets were constantly crowded behind him and I could not get through. At last, he took a side street and escaped to the outskirts of the city, and I followed. He rode into a field and reigned in his horse to wait for me.

As I rode up, I noticed that he seemed to slump in his saddle somewhat. I had the impression he was very tired. I slowed my horse to a walk. Not until I was right next to him did he straighten up. I turned my mount in the opposite direction of his, along side, so that we could face each other. He coughed a little. He looked at me with feverish eyes and said, "You are a fascinating woman, Manuela."

"Are you all right, Simón?" I reached out to touch his face, and he took my hand.

"Quite all right. I am merely tired. It has been a long, long day."

"Of course."

"However, looking in your eyes has renewed me. Truly."

I smiled at him and edged my horse closer.

He raised my hand to his lips, and said quietly, "Come back to my quarters with me." He kissed the inside of my fingers and said, almost in a whisper, "Come now."

Excitement coursed through me. I put my hand on his cheek, pulled him close, and kissed him lightly on the lips, saying, "I will go wherever you wish."

He put his arm around my waist, drew me to him, and kissed me on the lips, long and hard. Then, as he looked into my eyes, and stroked my hair, he said, for the first time, "Manuelita," with such tenderness it inflamed me. Never had I been so alive in the arms of a man. He held me close and then looked me in the eyes again, and said, "Come."

We turned and rode back to the presidential palace. He let me lead him through side streets and we arrived without being recognized enough to be stopped. José Palacios was waiting to take our horses, as though he knew we were coming. Both of us were tired and laughing as we dismounted and climbed the back stairs.

When we arrived in his apartment, there was only one brazier to give the room heat and, at that moment, its only light. It sent deep shadows across the room and highlighted only one side of Simón's face as he slowly pulled me to him. He kissed me again and again. I returned his welcome kisses—deeply, hungrily. I knew then, with utter certainty, that I loved this man—and I would love him forever.

He stepped back and looked me in the eyes, the left side of his face in shadows. Slowly he reached out his hands and slid the dress off my shoulders. His hands followed my gown as it slid to the floor. He touched the fullness of my breasts, and then my waist, then my hips. Each moment found me more deeply in love, wanting and needing him. I brought my hands to his coat, ignoring the cold metal of his buttons and braid. Very slowly, with growing desire as each button came free, I undressed him. In our nakedness, we stood on that little island of time, upon which no world of revolutions and trouble could intrude.

Later, with our clothes still on the floor where we had stood, we lay together, our naked bodies touching. We kissed. We loved. And I experienced fully, intimately, and completely the man who had held my thoughts all day. I loved him. I felt I was knowing real love for the very first time.

Chapter 46

When I made my way home after being shaken gently awake the next morning by José Palacios, after kissing Bolívar and exchanging a few soft words, after dressing and making my way downstairs, before the sun was up, having barely slept, I believed my life had changed. I had spent a little over 5 hours alone with Simón.

I refused José Palacios's offer to accompany me home. "He would want me to accompany you," he insisted somberly.

"I know, but I wish to be alone right now. I thank you."

I mounted my horse and left. My evening clothes and the slow clop of my horse's hooves contrasted with the gray quiet of the city. The hour being quite early, only a few Indian women were up, carrying their red earthen water jugs on their backs, shuffling between bits of debris left from the celebration the night before. I passed the fountain in the square where other women were already drawing water that trickled into pools below. The sky was overcast and the city was very still.

When I passed the spot where I had thrown my wreath at the Liberator, the city itself seemed to be a small room in which I was secure and comfortable because Simón was in it. The moment took on an unexpected intensity. I wanted to retreat into that room and stay there with Simón. The smell of him, and our love, was all about me. I was in love and never wanted to wash his scent away.

I was not blind or simple minded about Bolívar's past. He was 39, and I knew that he had been married at one time and that he had known many, many women. I did not have to be given an account of his "conquests" to know that there had been dozens, and perhaps dozens more. No man could know a woman's body so surely, so intimately, so expertly, without experience. Neither did I have any doubt that, before the wars were over, he would know one or two more. However, I felt I could recognize the difference between sincerity and theatre. I was convinced that a special bond had formed. I believed in his deep affection for me and that we shared a new and blossoming love. It was in a quiet moment, when he need not have said anything, that he reached over to me and said, "I have needed you, Manuelita."

I knew with lucid certainty that morning that he and I were meant for each other. Before the sun climbed above the Andean volcanoes nearby, to warm the others in the city who were not as lucky as I, I felt I had entered a "marriage" deeper than any Catholic priest could make for me. When I fell into my own bed that morning, exhausted with love, I slept as a woman content.

I arose quite late in the morning. Jonotás and Natán had been out to buy me some fruit, and they had already heard the scandal of the Liberator going off with that bastard, "La Sáenz." I smiled at how I could not seem to keep from upsetting the busybodies of Quito. However, for once, I did not take full delight in shocking the citizens of my town. I did not consider *anybody* worthy of discussing my relationship with Simón. Still, I was too happy to care what anyone thought.

I went off to work in the hospital, accompanied by Jonotás and Natán. I knew by the way I was avoided by certain women there that I was the subject of much gossip. I was a little surprised because I had actually made a few friends in the previous days and believed that most of the women there liked me. One woman I enjoyed, from Venezuela, was still very nice to me, but most were aloof.

I could not blame the women who glared at me that day in the hospital. Some were young and beautiful and would no doubt liked to have been with Bolívar the night before. Some were old and dispirited by their aging, and the rapidly changing times, and I was a reminder of the loss of control of their lives. I understood them all. I had been the lucky one.

When I saw the looks in the eyes of some of those around me, it made me consider the future. How vicious would the stories about me be this time? Would they go beyond "Just what you would expect from a bastard"? Would they surpass "Just like that whore, Joaquina"?

Then, I began to worry about my husband. My near indiscretion in Guayaquil recently would have been nothing compared to the dilemma I was about to face. For one thing, my husband was sure to find out. Bolívar was too public a figure for his activities to go unnoticed.

I dreaded the battles to come with my husband. If he had threatened to put me in a convent merely for living unconventionally, what would he attempt when he found out I had a lover, no less a man than The Liberator? Even beyond these facts, I knew I would never be able to give up what I now felt. A more casual affair I might be able to dismiss, but this I would never forsake.

The future seemed bleak at first as I considered my situation. However, later in the day, I began to notice something. Everyone at the hospital deferred to me that day. Everything I asked for, to do my job, was given to me instantly. People knew of my connection to the Liberator, and I was given the same courtesy he might have been given in that situation. Even while I encountered moral disapproval in the eyes of those around me, everyone treated me with deference.

When I realized this, I also realized that James would not be able to make the same kind of trouble for me as he would if my lover had been an ordinary man. Bolívar was too powerful. Perhaps I would never again have to fear being placed in a convent.

That led me to another thought. If the problems with my lawsuit were truly the result of the slow pace of government, then being so close to the man who "was" the government would overcome that difficulty as well. Carlos would no longer be able to interfere with justice, and I at last would prevail. I was walking through the hospital with an armful of bandages when these thoughts struck me, and I laughed out loud, disturbing some sleeping soldiers nearby.

If I had not misjudged the man with whom I had spent the night, I had perhaps achieved all I had been striving for throughout my life. Perhaps I had discovered the means to finally obtain my inheritance promised to me so long ago by my dying mother. True, I did not understand the ways of law, but I could not imagine Bolívar not being able to solve my problems. Also, perhaps I would no longer have to fear punishment for my unconventional style of living. The Liberator would do what I had not been able to do— liberate *me* from the chains of provincial suffocation so that I could be myself at last. I felt like I had won some mythical contest. I felt victorious.

Was it true? Would my relationship with Bolívar allow me to win? I wondered. Yet I knew that no matter whether I won or lost another thing in life, delightful as it was to ponder, this is not what really mattered. If it had all gone away; if I knew I would never have my mother's gift, because I loved Bolívar; if I would have to return to a convent, in order to have him; if I had to suffer ostracism and humiliation beyond what I had known in the past 24 years, I would still have loved Simón, and longed for his companionship. Having met Simón, and loved him, and to have him love me, that was the real victory. That I savored and wanted more than anything.

All day long my mind sifted through these thoughts and I believe I felt every human emotion. Finding it hard to work with so many new thoughts going through my mind, I decided to leave early. When Jonotás and Natán and I were in the street, I said, "Let's go buy some fruit for Doña Larrea and then go home."

My companions agreed and we started for the market. I was silent as I walked the sloping streets to where I liked to shop. Jonotás and Natán tried unsuccessfully to engage me in conversation but I was too caught up in my thoughts. In just a few hours, so many things seemed to have changed. Where would it all end? When would I see Bolívar again? What would my life be like tomorrow? Simón was a part of my life now, beyond any choice I may have had about it. What did my future hold?

I arrived at the market—a long steep section of street with Indian women in bright shawls selling the goods in front of them. We walked through the crowd and I soon found and purchased a few items.

While haggling over the price of some puny limes, I noticed a chaise chair stop at the opposite edge of the market. Antonia stepped out and spoke to one of the bearers, an angry scowl on her face. I quickly gave the vendor the price she was asking, and turned to leave in the opposite direction. I had enough to think about without having to confront Antonia.

Just as I was leaving the market, I saw a familiar face. A face that brought me joy. More muscular than when I last saw him, he was tanned a dark brown like Bolívar and the rest of the patriot soldiers. The handsome man in his late twenties wore his uniform as perfectly as he had that of the King's Guard. I had heard he was in the battle of Pichincha, but I had not expected at that moment to see the handsome smile of Fausto D'Elhuyar.

I felt as though a loved one had returned from the dead. I ran to him and threw my arms around him. "Oh, Fausto. Fausto. It's you," I cried.

He lifted me off my feet while holding me close. He said, almost instantly, his lips close to my ear as he hugged me, "I still love you."

I pulled away. I looked at him blankly, not knowing what to say.

He relieved me of that responsibility. "I suppose things have changed for you."
I was still silent.

"I heard you are married."

The fact that I was married seemed unreal, despite my worry all day about how James would react to my affair with Bolívar. It took me a moment to say, "Yes, for a few years now."

"I went to the Larrea mansion this morning." In response to my questioning look, he said, "I had come to find you when I heard about the ball and who had danced all night with the Liberator. Until then, I had not known you were in Quito." I smiled. "I was just now returning there for the second time to see if you had come home yet."

Just then, I looked over his shoulder and saw Antonia in the middle of the block, glaring at us with more hatred than I had ever seen in her. I must have been making her very angry. The night before, Bolívar; now, Fausto. "Come," I said, taking his hand, "walk me home."

After we had turned the corner, I slowed down. He asked after my health, and I his. However, the conversation was strained. Jonotás and Natán walked several paces behind us.

I said, "I heard that you were here, but I have been here only a week or so. I did not have much success when I asked after you." I was sorry I had not searched harder for him.

Suddenly, he stopped and turned me toward him. I could tell he was not interested in the formalities. He gave me a look that was almost pain. "Is it true that you and the general left together last night?"

I did not respond.

"Manuela, I—"

"Please, Fausto, so many things have changed—"

He turned away, obviously hurt. Then, almost to himself, he said, "Of course, you . . ."

"What, Fausto?"

He smiled and said, "I knew you would surely have new loves and interests by now. But I hoped—" He took a deep breath, "I was hoping that you would dispel my worries. I wanted to be with you—never mind."

"I'm sorry, Fausto."

"I understand. I only want you to know that I still love you—and that I have kept my promise to you." He squeezed my hands.

I did not know what he meant at first. "What promise?"

"I am still your friend."

Tears rushed to my eyes. I pulled him close and held him tightly. I said, "Oh, Fausto, I love you, too. I'm so glad to see you again." I pulled back to look at him. "But you are right—many, many things have changed."

He looked in my eyes. With that old magic and captivating smile, he said softly, "Perhaps, after all, you would like to meet an old friend in the fields tonight?"

Fausto's sudden appearance had dredged up old longings, and he was as compelling as ever. As I looked at his beautiful face, I wanted to agree. I almost did without thinking.

I considered where I would be that night. It was truly clear to me, for the first time, that I did not actually know if I would hear from Simón again or not. That morning, I would have said with absolute certainty that he would call for me. However, he had made no promises. I expected him to contact me, but would he? The fact that he must have had a different woman every night in every town between Quito and Caracas suddenly chilled me. Where *was* I going to spend the night? Was I to be only one more of the Liberator's conquests? I suddenly felt empty inside.

I felt the need to reach out to Fausto, to let his strong embrace comfort me. I needed something to fill my sudden emptiness. I was being offered certain love, from a man for whom I could easily feel love in return. Was I going to pass it up?

The smart action would be to take what is certain. I loved Fausto, and I could have gone anywhere with him he wanted to go, but I did not love him as I did Simón. If I had weighed a doubt against a certainty, I would have gone with Fausto that minute. I looked at his inviting eyes, eyes that spoke to me of love and desire. I almost said, "Yes!" Instead, I weighed my heart against my past, and slowly, weakly, without any determination in the action, shook my head.

Foolish! I felt foolish. I flushed with the embarrassment of making a stupid decision while I made it. Yet, still I shook my head.

I looked at Fausto's handsome smile. I knew the wise thing to do would be to take the glory of having conquered the conqueror and to then continue on with the rest of my life. I had asked for nothing from Simón Bolívar and nothing might be exactly what I would get. I was aware of all these things as I refused Fausto, but I was making the only decision my heart would allow. Neither wisdom nor strategic cleverness was driving my actions. I was moved by my heart, and my heart alone. My decision, at that moment, may have had its effect on history.

As I slowly shook my head in refusal, his beautiful smile vanished.

It seemed he was about to silently walk away. I could not let him go. "Fausto, come home with me and have something to eat, and tell me what has happened to you in the last seven years."

He reluctantly accepted, and three hours later, when he left, I was satiated with stories—my own and Fausto's. As we talked, I was able to bring back his smile. He had fought in many of the major battles for independence since I had seen him last. He was happy with his life, but I could tell he was more than disappointed that he had found me a day late.

When we said good-bye at the door, he put his arms around me and kissed me softly on the lips. "I am asking for a discharge from the army. Then, my brother and I are going to Mexico to take care of our father. He has been ailing." He looked at me longingly and said, softly, "I may never see you again." He smiled, but his face looked sad.

"No, Fausto, we will see each other again," I said to bolster our spirits.

He kissed me lightly again and said, "Good-bye." Then, he walked away.

I stood in the doorway and watched him disappear down the street. Tears fell to my cheeks. Had I been right in turning him away? I did not know when, or if, I would ever see him again. I almost called him back. Instead, I turned and slowly went upstairs.

I asked Jonotás if there had been any word from Bolívar. When she answered, "No, Manuelita," I went to my room and lay down. I was tired, very tired.

I tried to nap, but I could not sleep. I had felt uncertain and foolish for having refused Fausto. I felt even worse now that he was gone, and I still did not know whether I would even see Simón again. True, there were no assurances that he would contact me, but I had truly expected to hear from him by that hour.

Later, as I sat through an evening meal, I became more and more depressed. Despite my fears, I was certain that Simón and I had touched each other, more certain than I had ever been about anything. I could not have given as much of my soul to someone, as I did the night before, and have it be meaningless. Not even if he was the near-God, Bolívar.

I tried to take a walk after dinner, I tried to help Doña Larrea clean up and organize after the party the night before, I tried to read, and I tried to write some letters. I did not do a single one of these things well.

The longer I went without hearing from Simón, the more distracted and upset I became. In addition to such emotions, I was extraordinarily curious about what he was thinking and feeling and whose company he might be sharing. There were so many beautiful women that he could have. So many, like Antonia, who were used to having whatever they wanted.

Antonia. She had been after him the night before. She had powerful friends in Quito. Was Bolívar sitting with her right now? Was she touching him, kissing him? I thought I would go crazy if I thought of it anymore.

I paced up and down for a long time. Jonotás and Natán both tried to calm me, but I would not even talk to them. Finally, Jonotás took it upon her self to have servants bring me bath water.

It annoyed me that she presumed to know what I wanted, but she was right. I prepared to take a long bath and go to bed. As I lowered my naked body into the water. I thought of Simón's caresses. I washed and washed, but I didn't feel that I could adequately rid myself of the scent of our lovemaking. I longed for him, and by the time I dried off I hoped I would never see him again.

I was in a bad humor when I finally climbed into bed. I made Jonotás and Natán sleep on the cotton batting on the floor because I wanted to be alone. I lay there wondering who Simón had in bed with him and why I was so foolish as to care.

You are married, I told myself fiercely. *Longing for Bolívar is foolish, anyway. Stop it!*

After I heard the crier announce midnight, I began to weep. The thought that I had misunderstood him hurt me so deeply I thought I might die. I wanted to know what he had done all day. Who had he been with? Who was he with now?

Later, I knew what happened that day. I found out what Bolívar's days were like.

It was true that Simón Bolívar was a man who had a woman in every city he ever slept in. In one sense, I had been like all the rest. There was probably not a lot special for him the following day, concerning his normal routine. If he had been able to arise when he wished, and to do exactly what he wished, perhaps it might have been different.

However, in Bolívar's schedule, he already had a dozen letters to read, and respond to, before he even got out of bed. I later saw the man in action. When he was working as an administrator (and there was much to administrate in the middle of 1822), he would walk up and down, dictating three letters to three secretaries at once, and invariably they could not keep up with him.

A steady flow of decrees and orders left his offices, and he answered all of his correspondence. He was the president of a new republic and he had to write to his vice president, Francisco de Paula Santander, constantly.

At the time we met, he was working on the education system; he was revising the treasury procedures; he was required to make appointments to judge's seats; he had to write new laws; and he had to assign new names for roadways, provinces and townships. He corresponded with San Martín in Perú, Iturbide in Mexico, James Monroe in the United States, the Prime Minister of England, and other European leaders. He was also making arrangements with Swedish engineers to find out if a canal could be cut across the Isthmus of Panamá. In the middle of all of this, General Sucre and his other officers would come in for meetings and consultations. This kind of activity went on from early morning until late at night.

In all this activity, if something was asked of him, a wounded soldier needing money perhaps, he would spend the time to see that the soldier was paid out of his own pocket. He was the most generous man I ever knew.

On the day after the ball, he was busier and perhaps more tired than usual. Only after he finished working that day—the hour being almost midnight—and a glass of wine was brought to him in order to allow him a moment of relaxation, did he sit down and write a note in his own hand.

The night of Monday, June 17, was quieter than the previous night. The moon was only a sliver in the cold Andean night. Everything was still except for perhaps one or two industrious thieves who may have been "on duty."

However, they would not have attacked the tall Indian, leading two gigantic dogs, making his way through the dark streets. José Palacios, with two mastiffs for protection and a lantern to light the way, carried a note to the back door of the Larrea mansion. He knocked and awoke the servant sleeping on straw inside.

When I heard a knock on my bedroom door, I threw back the covers and prepared to dress to see what was needed. I was sleeping in a thin undergarment, and the coldness brought bumps to my skin when I arose. I quickly threw on my *saya y manto*.

Jonotás was already at the door to our bedroom. She came over to me and said, "There's a messenger for you downstairs."

"Downstairs?"

"Yes. At the back door. Do you want me to go see what it's about?

"No, I'll go." I finished dressing and went downstairs as quietly as I could. When I arrived, I saw Bolívar's servant. Without speaking, he reached into his cape and pulled out the note that had only recently been on Simón's desk. The note was not dated or even signed, but I immediately stepped through the door and followed the silent José Palacios to the center of town.

I knew, at last, that I had not been wrong to trust the man I now loved. I had been full of worry and that had been made foolish by a few simple words on a piece of paper. To me, it is perhaps the most valuable document that the Liberator ever wrote, though it was only six words. Those words set my life in motion after that, changing my future and perhaps history.

When I closed the door and followed José Palacios that evening, I stepped through the last threshold towards finding myself. All my life, I had been divided: Spanish or Creole, Sáenz or Aispuru, wife or revolutionary. Yet, when I consummated my love with Simón Bolívar, there was no turning back. I had gone through many doorways, winding my way through the maze of my life, but I emerged when I met Simón. La Sáenz had taken 24 years to mature, and she had emerged a fighter. As I walked down the street, making my way to a rendezvous with a man some considered the greatest warrior in the world, I looked at the walls that I always felt had excluded me. I had broken those walls as surely as the earthquake that had conceived me. I was at last fully formed, and the course of my life was set.

However, I did not ponder the future as I walked to the Liberator's palace. I thought about the words he had written in his note and how much they meant to me. I could read more than mere words in his message. I could read Simón's fatigue. I could read his need for me. I understood him. I held the words close to my heart as I made my way to him. They were simple words, yet he moved me more deeply than if he had written me a poem of love: "Come. Come to me. Come now."

MANUELA

Part II

Wherein I tell of my years with The Liberator, and beyond

MANUELA

Chapter 1

Having been born illegitimate and having grown up with the revolution, I had always lived with uncertainty and change. I do not mean the rhythmic change of the sun through the heavens, or the change of seasons, but violent upheavals that keep the human heart from rest. In those first days after I met Simón, I thought I had at last found tranquillity.

I imagined I had everything I could hope for and I believed I knew what my future held. Being so deeply in love, I found myself hungering for calm and security. I had grown up learning to fight the world; but for the first time in my life, I no longer wished to do battle. Soldiers were everywhere, and yet I longed to finally be at peace.

In those first sweet days with Simón, I believed I had found the way to peace, at last, after lifelong conflict. After all, the war with the Spanish was nearly over. The last "viceroy," La Serna, who had deposed Pezuela, was still holding much of the highlands outside of Lima, but everyone assumed it was "only a matter of time" before San Martín captured him. Was there any reason to fight anymore?

After our first night together, despite Simón's busy schedule, he sent for me every evening, and I was escorted to the President's offices by José Palacios and Simón's mastiffs. There, Simón would be waiting for me, tired but happy to see me. There, we would share a joy that I had not known before. There, we would escape the world of soldiers to our own private place and know love. I knew that he must surely be as deeply in love with me as I was with him. For three days I enjoyed the bliss that Simón brought to me. Our passion grew stronger each day and I had no thoughts for anyone else.

Yet, ironically, during this time I was on everyone's list to invite to social events—even by those "good" families who had spurned me as a child. They knew that I was Bolívar's lover, and they wanted me to be their friend. I smiled at their insincerity. Some of these women had snubbed me only days before.

I was too happy to care what had happened in the past. Life seemed wonderful. I could foresee the end of the war and the pacific days that I would soon share with the man I loved. Then my dreams would be made real.

I was awakened from my dreams on the third morning that I awoke with Simón. I was not roused by Simón's servant that morning. Instead, I was awakened by an earthquake.

Both of us sat up, the chill morning air enveloping our naked bodies as the bed clothes fell away.

"It's over," said Simón.

"Yes," I said, shivering, as I pulled the blankets up to my bare shoulders.

He leaned over and opened his watch to look at the time.

I saw the empty hammock across the room still swinging in the shadows like an ominous pendulum. It was not yet dawn, but a faint light from the windows gave an eerie aspect to objects in the room, especially the hammock. Bolívar had been in the habit of sleeping in a hammock since the early days of the revolution. It was his favorite bed when sleeping alone. Because of me, it had not been used since José Palacios had hung it up days earlier. I did not like the look of it, swinging as though pushed by an unseen hand.

Simón sat up and kissed me softly on the cheek. When I did not respond as he expected, he said, "Are you all right?"

"Yes," I said, "but I was awakened from a peculiar dream. I feel strange."

He kissed me again and said, "Strange? In what way?" I did not know what to say. He lay down, pulled me into his arms, and whispered, "Tell me about it."

I had the feeling that I should perhaps keep it to myself, but Simón's strong, firm arms gave me courage.

"I was watching La Perricholi in her coach—"

"La Perricholi?"

"Yes. My friend, Micaela Villegas."

"Oh, she was—"

"Yes, Viceroy Amat's lover." I turned over and smiled at him. I touched his lips with my finger. "A viceroy's lover, like me."

He did not respond. I knew when I said it that he did not find it funny.

Before he could deny that he was a viceroy, I said, "I know, I know, Simón. You are the leader of this country though." I gave him a little kiss. "Anyway, she was riding behind white mules, in her infamous coach, and she blew me a kiss."

"What do you mean, 'infamous coach'?"

While having heard of La Perricholi, Simón had not heard the story of Viceroy Amat building her a coach and letting her ride it through the streets of Lima. When I told him about the incident, he smiled and said, "And that was the carriage you saw her in?"

"Yes."

"When did you hear that story?"

"I heard it soon after I met Miquita." A lump came to my throat. I missed my friend. "White mules, and that coach, were leading her funeral procession. That is the only time I saw it. This was the same coach in which she was riding, in my dream."

"In a way, that was the last time you saw her," he offered.

"Yes, that's true. When I saw her in my dream, I wanted to ride with her, but there were people all around. Many were in front of me because the streets were crowded. Everyone was angry at her. Because she was upsetting everyone, I wanted to join her." Simón gave me a look of indulgence. I smiled and went on. "Then I looked around to see if there was anyone else I recognized, but there was not. When I looked back, you were in the coach also."

"Me?"

"Yes, Simón. I tried to get through the crowd, but I couldn't. I felt like I couldn't breathe. Then, without knowing how, I was with both of you. We were riding along together and it felt good to be with the two of you. I was suddenly happy."

"Strange dream. Impossible to decipher." He scowled a little and suppressed a small yawn.

"Everyone around us, who moments before had been angry, grew quiet. Then, they began following us in respectful silence. I looked back, and it seemed like an entire town was walking behind us. Then the street, which before had been flat, smooth, worn earth, suddenly became sand. The coach lurched and shook, and it seemed like many people were with me. I was frightened, but . . ."

Simón waited for me to go on.

". . . the earthquake woke me up."

"Quite interesting. What do you suppose would have happened next?"

"I don't know. I remember I was both happy and sad. If it means anything, I probably dreamed it because I love the two of you so deeply."

A tear came to my eye and Simón noticed. He turned to me and touched my face, lifting my chin, to make me look at him. He gazed at me with sympathy and love. "You are an amazing woman, Manuelita."

"Never mind," I said, wiping my eyes. "Oh, Simón, I want to go away with you. I'm tired of war. I'm tired of fighting. I'm tired of everything. I want something—anything else."

He kissed me softly on the lips and said, "I'm tired, too. But, Manuelita, probably it is only that you are tired. I keep you up too late." He smiled, and I laughed in spite of my self. "Maybe, for the sake of our health, I should not call for you," he suggested slyly.

"Don't you think of it. You are the one thing in my life that does not make me tired." I snuggled close to him and relished his warmth and the sensuality of the moment.

He slowly turned my face to his and pressed his lips to mine. My heart quickened. His hand gently found its way down past my stomach. All the strange feelings, from the dream and the earthquake, began to dissipate. I needed him. I returned his kiss passionately, feeling my body respond to his embrace. I pressed myself to him, feeling secure and alive in his arms. My passion grew.

Without warning, he pulled away, coughing.

He coughed hard. At first he tried to restrain the convulsions, turning to the wall slightly, but soon his coughing was violent.

I was worried. Helpless. All I could do was say, "Simón, are you all right?"

He only shook his hand at me, in a weak gesture meant to convey, "I'm all right," or "Don't worry."

When his fit died down, he lay back on the bed, exhausted. His thin, naked chest rose and fell quickly as he tried to catch his breath. He continued to suppress little coughs.

I reached out and placed my hand on the small tuft of hair in the middle of his chest. Some of the hairs were gray. He sat up and coughed a little more, vainly trying to conceal his agony, and then lay back down.

All at once, I saw his life with frightening clarity. I saw him sleeping uncovered on the *llanos* (plains) of Venezuela. I saw him riding through the ice-covered Andes while half his men expired from exposure. I saw him fighting in swamps and mud, in all sorts of weather, breathing dust, pollen, and miasma. He had fought both nature and oppression in his fight for liberty, shunning doctors, shelter, or food when it did not suit him to pay attention to such necessities. The truth struck me with ferocity and overcame me: the man I loved was ill. I could see clearly that his famous vitality was being eaten away—by consumption.

The thought filled me with terror. I reached for the cover to pull it up over him, but there was a knock at the door. Wrapping another blanket around me, I went over to answer it. Simón coughed again and said, "Don't—" just as I pulled the door open. José Palacios entered, dressed meticulously, as though he never slept.

"Are you all right, Señor?" he asked.

"Fine, José, fine. Is the rest of the palace awake?" He coughed a little.

José gave him a quick look of worry and then said, "Yes Señor, the earthquake woke everyone. No one is hurt."

"Very well." José started to go, but Simón said, "Oh, make arrangements for Manuelita to leave without being bothered. Make sure you escort her home."

"Yes, Señor."

"And I'll take my letters now."

"Yes, Señor." He left and Simón rose and began to put on his clothes. He kept clearing his irritated throat and coughing a little.

"Simón," I said, "it is still early. Why do you not rest some more?" I tried to make my voice sound calm, though I was still inwardly frightened.

"I have too much to do, and I am awake." He coughed. He moved about the room, looking for his clothes. His movements were quick as though activity could drive away his illness. With his back still to me, he said, "You should not have answered the door—under the circumstances. What if it had been someone else, awakened by the quake, coming to find me?"

I considered his question and asked one of my own. "Are you afraid of scandal?"

"It wouldn't do either of us any good."

I let a little pique into my voice. "All your officers must know about the women I'm sure you sleep with in every city." I sat down on the bed and pulled my blanket around me.

He turned around and looked at me with a mixture of amusement and resentment. His face softened and said, "Never before have I spent so much time with one. Perhaps they believe you mean more to me than the others. That would concern some, knowing someone was able to get so close to me—"

I interrupted angrily, "Yes, we would not want anyone to get the wrong idea—that I mean something to you."

He sat down next to me, turned my chin to face him, and kissed me softly. "That is not what I meant. I . . ." He paused and I had the feeling he was about to say, "I love you." Instead he said, "I was speaking of other's thoughts." He looked at his watch. "I must get to work."

Soon I was being escorted out of the palace by José Palacios. However, like the other mornings, we had not gone far when I insisted on walking home alone. I was adamant and made him return.

I liked the solitude, and I wanted to think. I would have liked to walk alone to Simón's palace at night, without waiting for José Palacios, except that he always came for me at a different time. Also, I wanted Simón to ask for me.

This morning, as I began the short walk to the Larrea mansion, there was no solitude. The streets were noisy, much busier than the last three mornings, even though it was earlier. The quake had roused the entire city. Church doors were opening to people already waiting to enter and pray. Despite the commotion, I made my way among the Indians, slaves, shopkeepers, rich *criollos*, and ever present soldiers. I hardly noticed because I was so lost in thought and unsettled.

I kept thinking about Simón. He would not state that I meant something to him. I knew he loved me, but did he love me in the way I believed he did? I was hurt by the idea, but there was an even more troubling thought.

To have him propose that I modify my actions due to the consideration of a possible scandal made me angry. Was he not president? Could he not do what he liked? I did not understand. I thought I had left caring about whether society accepted me or not behind. Surely, I had grown out of that long ago.

However, something even deeper than these problems bothered me. The dream. I had not mentioned it to Simón, but it reminded me of death. La Perricholi's coach, which I had seen only at her funeral, felt like a symbol of death. Then, to see a whole town following me, as it seemed the entire city of Lima followed La Perricholi to her burial, appeared to me to be a prophecy for my own funeral.

It was frightening at first, but in a way there was something comforting about this thought. If the dream were prophecy, it meant that I would be loved and respected when I died, like my friend Miquita. The idea that even though I had been born a bastard, that I would be remembered and honored by an entire city as she had been, softened my fear. The dream even gave me confidence, because somehow I felt everything would turn out all right.

The element of the dream that upset me was seeing Simón join my friend in her coach, as though joining her with his own demise. Then, to have the realization thrust upon me that Simón was ill frightened me to my core. It was not until I was walking home that all this came to me so clearly. I felt danger—and sadness. If the dream truly was prophecy, what could I do?

I had only known my love for three days, yet I felt I had wasted precious time with him by luxuriating in the beautiful feelings he gave me. I knew I could not sit and let pleasure come to me anymore. I was in a race against time.

Even if consumption did not take him, at 39 half of Simón's life was over at least. And these idyllic days surely would not last. True, it seemed the revolution was almost won, but I knew how fast circumstance could change. I should be more aggressive in seeing that we stayed together. I should be much more industrious in trying to help him in his causes.

In June of 1822, Simón Bolívar had already been at war for 12 years. In that time he had conquered three countries, been in exile twice, founded a new republic larger than Europe, subjugated the heights of the Andes and the vast *llanos* of Venezuela, and fought in dozens of major battles. I was awed by the toil, pain, blood, and tears that the patriot soldiers had endured. But, as I knew him, Simón was, above all, a dreamer. I knew that his dreams, conceived long before he met me, and nurtured on battlefields, were not yet finished. I knew it, and as I walked through the crowds that morning, I suddenly felt very tired.

I had done battle all my life. First I fought against the cruelty of other children who called me bastard, then I fought to have the inheritance my mother gave me when my uncle tried to eliminate me from the family. I fought with nuns in the convent who sought to kill my spirit, and with the society of Quito who wanted me to disappear. Though I felt I had to be married in order to avoid a life of poverty, I was forced to live with a husband whom I never loved. Even in Lima, when I had friends such as Rosita Campusano, I fought—this time, for the cause of Liberty. When I was rewarded for my efforts to help the revolution, when I was given membership in General San Martín's Order of the Sun, it was the first time I had ever felt any peace.

Now, my return to Quito had caused me to meet the only man I had ever or would ever love. I had risen, from obscurity to importance, from poverty to wealth, from loneliness to love, all by the force of my will. I refused to drift and I had won everything except a lasting peace it seemed. Must I fight again? Where would the twists of time take me now?

I was being pulled violently in half. Since witnessing the old woman's death a few days before, ultimately caused by soldiers, I had longed for lasting peace. My longing was made more profound when I fell in love. Now, I knew I must take up Bolívar's sword. I did not want to fight anymore. I did not want anything, except to be surrounded by friends, respected, and finally living a life without conflict. I wanted to love Simón, far away from the revolution. I knew what I wanted, and felt grief at the thought that I might never have it.

"Harlot!" I heard the word as someone snatched my *manto* down from behind me.

A horrid countenance pressed close to me, saying, "Jezebel!"

The face was so close I could not make out the features. Lost in my thoughts as I had been, I was frozen momentarily. A putrefying smell, from rotting teeth and encrusted grime, overcame me, and I turned my head away. I sensed that the figure turned around. I looked again and only saw his back. He raised his arms and spoke to the Indians and *cholos* gathering in front of a church to pray. "God has destroyed this city before."

They all looked to the speaker.

"Destroyed, because of sin and sloth . . ." The man's hair was long, dirty, matted, and hanging down over a filthy priest's frock. ". . . and the degradation caused by the loins of women."

The priest spun around, hatred flaming in only one eye. It was the mad priest from my youth, whom I had seen when I entered the city a few days before.

He pointed his finger at me as the gash, where his left eye should have been, tried to flare in anger. "We have forgotten our king; we have let the ungodly claim our city and consort with harlots. Get down on your knees and pray for forgiveness." Before I could stop him, he grabbed me by the arm and forced me to my knees. I tried to push him away, but I was at the wrong angle, and his grip was inhumanly tight.

People gathered from all around. I was infuriated and struggled, yelling, "Let me go!" Feeling stupid and impotent, trying to bite his filthy hand, I continued to struggle with him.

Suddenly, the priest fell face down on the ground beside me. I jumped up, and a young junior officer, whom I recognized, grabbed my arm and pulled me behind him. He had struck the priest with the hilt of his sword, which he now pointed at the filthy frock as the man groggily tried to regain his feet.

I was unable to contain my anger. While he was still on his knees, I stepped in front of the soldier and hit the priest square in the jaw with my fist, sending him sprawling. "Don't ever touch me again, you—"

The man screamed in pain, and scrambled to his feet, while I rubbed my sore knuckles. He hurried off screeching, "Possessed. She is possessed by Satan." He attracted even more attention with his shouting, and new onlookers joined those gathering around the soldier and me.

I turned to my rescuer, and he bowed gallantly. "Antonio de la Guerrera, at your service, Señora."

"Yes, thank you, Señor. I remember. We met a few nights ago at the ball."

"Yes, Señora Thorne, I remember you quite well, but I did not think you would remember me. I hope you were not harmed."

"No, Señor, but I thank you. I was in quite a predicament."

"It seems to me you would not have fared too badly." He looked at my hand, which I was still shaking in pain. "However, I was glad to have been of service."

He turned to the rather large crowd that had gathered around and, raising his arms as though he were shooing away chickens, he said, "Go on now. It's over." He turned back to me and smiled as the curious slowly dispersed. "Now, let me escort you to your destination."

I accepted and thanked him again as I brushed off my clothes. As I turned to walk home, I noticed a tall woman standing behind the scattering crowd. A cape, colored a unique shade of purple, was over her shoulders and a hood was pulled far over her face so that I could not make out her features. Her arms were crossed, and I could tell from her dress that she was wealthy Spanish. She seemed to be watching me. Just then, Jonotás and Natán arrived.

I was surprised they were up so early, because lately they had been meeting at night with other of the city's servants to tell stories and gossip. These sessions often went quite late and kept the two in bed until long after daybreak. This morning, they had been awakened, like everyone else, and had come to find me to make sure I was all right. We started for home. When I looked back, the woman in the cape was gone.

That evening, when Bolívar found out about the incident, he was furious. He called in José Palacios and gave strict orders that he was to accompany me home in the morning. He turned to me and said, "This is not good, Manuela." Then, after admonishing José Palacios, he ordered him to arrange for Señor de la Guerrera to have what was to be the first in a long series of promotions. I believe my friend is General de la Guerrera today and still in the service of my country. It has been years since I have seen him, but he and I became good friends in Quito.

After José Palacios left, Bolívar said, "It is shameless. Whenever there is an earthquake or other catastrophe, the church is there to take advantage of the people's grief. If I could, I would run them off the continent."

I had already heard the story about Simón chasing a priest through the streets of Caracas, who had been damning victims of the earthquake of 1812. There, too, the priests had attributed the calamity to "The Judgment of God!" This was right in the middle of the first attempts at revolution, and the earthquake had been proclaimed punishment by the priest. When Bolívar found him, standing on rubble haranguing the crowd, he had run him down the street, shouting, "If Nature opposes us, we will fight her."

In response to his rhetoric, regarding the removal of the church from the continent, which to my priest-hating sentiments seemed sound, I said, "Why don't you eliminate the church? We would all be better off."

"I would like to do so. They are forever spreading disaffection with the revolution. In practice, if not in actual fact, they are the king's agents. However, it is impossible."

"Why, Simón? You are virtually a dictator here. Why not send them packing?"

"I am the president of a republic, not a dictator. Even so, how long would I be dictator after I had destroyed something so fundamental to the people? There is no such thing as absolute power."

I wanted to drop the subject because he was becoming so agitated. "Anyway," I said, "it was not the church who attacked me. It was one renegade priest."

He snorted his disgust. "He was only more vocal about what most priests would, no doubt, like to have done and said. I have seen the man. He is crazy. Yet, if it is so obvious to me he is crazy, why has he not been defrocked?" He only waited perfunctorily for me to answer. "Because he says what the rest would like to say."

"I know, Simón, but—"

"Don't take it lightly, Manuela. If one zealot calls me or my soldiers ungodly, believe me, in the privacy of confession and from the pulpit, similar epithets are being spread everyday to the lower classes and the pure-blood Spanish who have not yet accepted the fact of our independence.

"With such attacks going on behind our backs, it will spread, and the unity I am seeking will be threatened. Never forget, Manuela, without unity we are lost."

I did not believe the church was any real impediment. "I am sure the revolution will succeed—" I began, but Simón shook his head.

"Revolution is a dangerous thing. It is no more than using force to ensure one's moral right to freedom. Yet using force to ensure morality cannot ever really work."

"What do you mean?"

"All the while, as you plow up the old and try to plant the new, you will find that the people who are supposed to be helping you are there to eat the grain you are trying to plant and are even jealous because you happen to be in front of them in the line of sowers. It is as though a revolutionary sows the seed of his own destruction, along with reform. It makes me weary."

We talked long into the night. For the first time, I truly saw a glimpse of what the war really meant and how hard it was to win and how fleeting might be the victory.

Simón scared me. He foresaw years of fighting ahead. He sounded as though he were less convinced than I about what the future would bring. I felt like I had been fooling myself.

Would I ever find peace? I was more uncertain than ever. It appeared that there were more battles ahead, and I would have to fight with Simón until the fighting was over.

But as he talked to me that night, I understood him more completely. His vision of the future was magnificent, and I became inspired to be a part of it.

As I write my story, my mind is refreshed to that evening so long forgotten. Now I remember his analogy of the tiller of the soil planting seeds of revolutionary change. I dismissed that particular discussion at the time, almost immediately. However, I wish I had written down his words and showed them to him later.

Chapter 2

Those days, the last days of June 1822, were a storm of activity for me. I changed during those two or so weeks.

The most important changes in me were in what I consider my maturity. My lessons were my nightly discussions with Simón. In those romantic moments, feeling the afterglow of our lovemaking as we lay close to each other, we learned each other's secrets. We would talk long into the night of our childhoods, of our likes and dislikes, of our dreams and desires. He told me about the early days of the revolution, about his victories, his defeats, his exiles. "Someday," he said excitedly, "we must go to Jamaica. I enjoyed it there. In fact, I have a friend, Maxwell Hyslop, who helped me when I was in exile there. I would love to have you meet him."

Another time he said, "My estate in Venezuela is beautiful. Someday, you and I will ride away from all this, and live there. We shall ignore the world of war and merely be happy." He smiled a broad smile and I felt tears rush to my eyes.

"What's the matter?"

"Nothing, Simón, it is only that the idea of living with you away from everything is something I long for."

He hugged me and said, "We will do it, I am sure."

We talked about his friends, his foes, and all the people and places in his life. He was the first one who told me about Rodríguez and their historic climb to the top of the Monte Sacro in Rome.

I learned many things from him, not the least of which were a few new lessons about what it took to make a new world. Though I had been a revolutionary all my life, I never really understood what I had been doing, until I met Simón.

Like everything else in my life, my interest in the revolution had always been personal. I wanted change for the sake of change, because so much about society and my own life seemed unfair. Having thus been the victim of injustice, my revolutionary activities were, fundamentally, a striking back. Simón taught me about the revolution anew.

He would talk of his dreams and the plans he had been carrying since the early days in Venezuela. Often he would not be able to contain his feelings or his impulse to action, and he would throw a blanket around himself and pace up and down, his eyes alight with inner fire, while speaking emotionally of his visions of the future: he saw the entire South American continent as one vast country, this same country striving forward as a leader among the countries of the world, a "United States of South America," being an example of liberal ideas embodied in a living government.

"We will begin with this triple republic, with its governing departments of New Granada, Venezuela and The South (Quito). If the people populating the neighboring countries wish it, all will be included. Guayaquil, particularly, we must include in this union."

"Why, Simón? Is it because they are the closest neighbor?"

"No, it is more than that, Manuelita. Guayaquil was once a part of the presidency of Quito, and it has a long tradition of intimate ties with this city."

"Yes, but the interests of the two cities are so different."

He smiled at me. "You have studied the problem, I see."

"No. I merely noticed—"

"You are correct, of course. Their interests are often different. However, there is a more important reason. Quito—that is to say, the Department of the South—and thus Gran Colombia, must have access to the Pacific. It is vital to the future of this country—to the continent."

He made so much sense to me. I was deeply interested in his life and the revolution and I asked him many questions. Each question brought a flood of ideas or stories. I would listen carefully as he answered, far more intently, I'm sure, than the women he had been used to. I was amazed at the scope of his mind.

Unlike most of the revolution's leaders, who saw only the short-term goals, Simón was a true liberal visionary. He chafed at the inertia of the rich Creoles of South

America, who could not see past their own individual estates, who could not envision a society where all men, of whatever race or class, could enjoy the fruits of self rule. "We are not Europeans; we are not Indians; we are but a mixed species of aborigines and Spaniards," he would say as he strode across the room lit only by a single lamp. "We must have unity. The greater portion of the native Indians has been annihilated; Spaniards have mixed with Americans and Africans, and Africans with Indians and Spaniards. We must all realize that we are one people. When we are unified as a country, we will also give birth to a new race—Americans."

I, who had never thought that much about it, had to agree. I naturally treated all people, of whatever color, who treated me with respect, with equal courtesy. But I never considered the fact that in the long run it would be fatal for a new government not to encompass all of its people. No one really seemed to understand that idea as well as Simón. We had to be whole; we had to include all.

I raised the one doubt I had. "Simón, no one has ever created such a government before. Except perhaps the North Americans—"

He interrupted me. "No, Manuela," he said gently as he came over and sat next to me. "When I was in New York, I realized that the people of the United States, as much as I admire their country, and despite their 'all men are created equal,' they still keep African slaves and profit from their work. They have not achieved the ideal of which I am speaking. You are right, no one has ever created such a government. Until now." He smiled self-confidently and threw his own blanket about my naked shoulders. "*I* will do it."

"Yes, Simón, I believe you will."

He went on, softly, but speaking with great intensity. "Manuela. No one has ever seemed to understand me as you do. It is true what you say. Racial equality was not the political dogma of Athens or France, or any other country, nor is it that of North America, but we must exalt it here in order to correct the disparity that apparently exists. And I will free every slave in every place where I have any power. Slavery must be abolished forever."

I realized later, as I was studying the roots of the revolution, that he was paraphrasing himself in his own Angostura address, given three years earlier, in the heart of the *llanos* of Venezuela. On that occasion, his ideas molded the spirit of the new Venezuelan republic, later to become a department in Gran Colombia. He still believed those ideas passionately, as we talked deep into the night in his apartments in the Tuscany-style palace of the deposed *audiencia* of Quito.

Merely being around Simón changed me. I felt like a child in the presence of his studied intellect, and I willed my self to grow. However, there were more personal things for me to know. I not only found a new maturity in those June days, but my life changed in more profound ways. I began to know myself as a woman, really, for the first time.

Never before had my love been given such expression. Prior to knowing Simón, my passion had always been stifled, either because my partner and I, or the times, were not suitable, as with James; or because my relationship with my partner was cut short, as with Fausto; or because I was simply too young and foolish, as with those lovers of mine in Panamá. Simón was the only man who ever made me truly happy in loving, and I cherished him more every day.

The only taint on my perfect happiness was the knowledge that it might end someday. There were many conditions that might tear us apart: the war might intrude again someday, Simón would have to leave to handle affairs of state, or my husband would make trouble. I also worried because I knew Simón did not yet consider me a part of his future. Since his marriage as a very young man, he had never let himself become attached to any woman. These thoughts almost made me deny the love growing in my heart, to protect myself.

One obstacle alone was almost worth bowing to. Every sensible thought told me that my own marriage was the only thing that would give me any acceptance in society. While it is true that Simón's power would preclude a frontal attack by James, it was also true that Simón's power also had obligations to the moral sense of the people. If I was not careful, Simón would ride off to war and my marriage to James would already be damaged beyond repair. What would I do then? If I tried to abandon my marriage, my husband's anger and tenacity would know no limits. Even if I succeeded in escaping my union with James, it was the only thing that had ever allowed me any security. Could I give it all up, if I had to? Could I live for a vague hope that Simón would one day want to live with me, far away from any war? Or, if I had to, could I live for a liberated continent instead of my own happiness?

I battled with myself over this. Knowing real love for the first time had given me a taste of security and true contentment. I never knew how much I had thirsted after these. I had grown up tough and fighting, but having spent only a few days with Simón had made me soft, longing for a peaceful life. What was I going to do? Though the earthquake had revealed the precarious state of my happiness, I clung to my dreams of peace like a drowning swimmer might cling to a branch on the shore.

I did have choices. I could have continued to merely enjoy the time I spent with Simón and ignore the future. I knew that would mean that we would part someday, but what else could a woman contemplate from loving a soldier? Already I had received more time and love than I could reasonably expect.

I could have found Fausto, whom I still loved and who had no dreams larger than his love for me. He might have filled the empty space, if I were to ignore Simón, which I could not.

More realistically, I could have had all the peace and security I desired if I returned to James and feigned love. If only I could pretend to feel something I did not, I would have enough money to buy any material desire of my heart. I could have even persuaded James to take me to Europe, where there was no war. James would have given me anything I wanted, if only I had been willing to deny my true heart and show him unfelt affection.

Not only did honoring my marriage vows offer what I thought I needed, but I knew that very soon I would be hearing from James. He was certain to know of my affair with Bolívar and he would demand my return to him. By then it might be too late for me to make a happy life with my husband. Thorne *was* still my husband, not Bolívar. If I did not obey James, I would have to face his fury and he might very well try to put me in a convent after all, or worse.

I wrestled with these conflicts until early one morning, a few days after the earthquake. When José Palacios escorted me home, I did not go inside. Instead, I found a groom that was awake and had my horse saddled and I rode out of the city.

I rode for a long time, trying to form some idea of what I should do. I rode long enough to tire my horse and then slowed her to a walk and finally let her graze. The usual overcast had turned to fluffy clouds strewn across the sky. The rising sun illuminated the western hills and showed the green of the Andean grasses with splotches of purple here and there. I sat in my saddle and looked across the plain, at the city of my birth, and wondered about my future. By the time the sun was all the way up and the mist had cleared away from the top of Pichincha, I knew what I must do.

I must stop my childish longing for a secure and happy life while Bolívar was still at war. There was no other answer. There could be no security for anyone until the war was over. The war might be nearly won, but it was not over yet. Nor were his dreams.

It was clear that Simón would not be through fighting until the last Spaniard had been defeated, and I knew that I must support him. Even my husband could not get to me if I stayed active in the war effort, nor could he dissuade me from fighting. The revolution was a fact of South American life that transcended all others.

"All right," I said to myself at last, "I am a revolutionary. I've have always been so, and I can continue. It is foolish of me to wish for a peace that is unattainable right now."

I felt stronger as I thought it all through, and knew what I must do. I would have to deny my marriage, regardless of the consequences, but for the honor of the revolution. I would also have to ignore my deep longing to be far away with Simón, living in peace—at least for a while.

After I made my decision, I even felt happy that I was to face the same challenges that confronted Simón and other brave revolutionaries. But I knew I did not want to fight forever. Someday I wanted the rewards of victory, and I made a vow to myself: *I will fight now, but one day La Sáenz will be at peace.*

Chapter 3

I rode back into town that morning feeling powerful and happy for having made my decision. At last, I knew what I must do and I would not be idle any longer. I would help Bolívar achieve his dreams. I would fight until he won.

The first thing I did that morning was to seek out General Sucre, who was still military leader of Quito. After I went home, cleaned up, and had some chocolate, I went searching for him. I found the victor of Pichincha outside the presidential palace just before the noon hour, dressed in his finest uniform.

I hailed him and dismounted. We had not spoken since the ball, but he remembered me.

"Señora, how are you?" he asked effusively.

We exchanged greetings, and then I asked, "What does the cause need today, General?"

His slender, handsome features became more angular as his brows crossed. "One might think that, with having women as brave and as eager for the success of the revolution as you, we have everything we need. However . . . ." He spoke of the soldiers that needed new uniforms, the widows who had not yet received pensions, and artillery that needed of repair. "Money, Señora, money is what moves an army. And money is what we are most in need of now."

Here was something I knew I could do, having raised money in Perú for San Martín. "I have little myself, but I will get you some," I said, enthusiastically. There was only one small reservation I had, which I ignored for the moment.

"You have my gratitude and that of the patriot army—" At that moment a chaise arrived, carried by tall, barefoot, Indians wearing wigs and dressed in pale, green satin.

Inside was the lovely Mariana de Solanda, with whom it was said General Sucre was completely in love. In only a few days, the question of whom she had favored most recently, General Sucre or Colonel Sandes, had become a common subject of gossip. The general's face lit up as she stepped out of the chair.

"Mariana. I am glad you have arrived."

"Good morning, Antonio."

"You remember Señora de Thorne, do you not?"

"Of course. How are you?" We talked for a moment, and I could tell that she was taking pains to be extra polite to me. At one point, she said, "That is a wonderful riding outfit. Where did you get it?"

She was referring to my riding habit. When I told her I made it, she looked a bit shocked. However, she made an effort to cover her initial reaction. She knew about me and Bolívar and did not want to offend me. Instead, she said, "Well, I must have my seamstress make me something like that. I hope you don't mind."

She seemed sincere, and I told her that I did not mind. However, before we could continue our conversation, I could see that she had suddenly become aware that she had lost something.

She turned toward Sucre and said, "Antonio, I seemed to have misplaced my handkerchief. Would you mind seeing if it is in the chaise?"

"Of course, my dear." General Sucre knelt down and looked around for the item while she and I continued to talk.

I sensed a certain capricious immaturity in her character, but I knew she was young and had led a sheltered life. Still, she was quite lovely, and I liked her.

Sucre found the handkerchief at last, and brought it to her. We all talked for a moment longer, and then the two lovers wished me "Good day."

As they walked off arm in arm for a stroll, I had an uneasy feeling. I thought about how she had been able to get the great General Sucre on his knees to do her bidding. Was it good to be too much in love? I shook off the feeling. After all, he had done nothing more than any gallant and ardent lover might do.

When they were gone, I went to find Jonotás and Natán. I did not have time to campaign for funds that day because I had decided to set aside the afternoons for working again in the hospital. I had not done any hospital work at all since the day after the ball. Such work was another way that I knew I could contribute to the cause.

As my companions and I walked through the streets, I was so deep in thought that Jonotás finally asked, "What is wrong, Manuelita?"

"Tomorrow we will campaign for funds—"

"Like we did in Lima?" asked Natán.

"Yes." I expressed the one reservation I had not voiced to Sucre. "But Lima is a different city. There, I was respected; here it will be different."

"What do you mean, Manuelita?" asked Jonotás.

"Before the ball, I still felt ancient hatreds. The history of my two families and my own history here are full of conflict here. However, in those first three days after the victory ball, when I became of interest to Bolívar, Quito was different. Even now, I notice that I have been given whatever I want. Shopkeepers cater to my desires before anyone else's. People stop me in the street to exchange greetings or to ask my opinion about political matters. Most of Bolívar's officers smile and salute. I just talked with Mariana Solanda and, if she is any indication, even nobility is bowing to me. Although I have felt *some* jealousy, most who know of my connection to Bolívar have deferred to me."

"I noticed that too," said Natán.

"I have been invited to every liberal household in the city. I was never invited into the salons of Quito before. In short, my connection to Bolívar has made me powerful. For a few days there, I actually felt safe and able to accomplish anything I wanted. Until—" I frowned.

"Until what, Manuelita?" asked Jonotás.

"In the past few days, I have noticed a subtle change. Women I meet on the street—the same women with whom we worked in the hospital and who were friendly only a week ago—seem more reserved. With the exception of a very few, I have not been invited to the latest liberal gatherings. It seems that I was thought of in high regard for three days, and then . . . it is almost as though it was the earthquake that changed things."

We talked some more, and as we arrived at the hospital we agreed that things were going well until the day of the earthquake; but since then, the society seemed more aloof. We even noticed a difference in the way we were greeted at the hospital that day. There was never anything definite, but a subtle attitude lay under everything that was said to me. We were accepted by the doctors and others as needed workers, but I felt estranged. Nevertheless, we did our work and paid little attention.

However, later that day I saw someone whom I had not seen in the hospital before. As I was passing the door to the street, I noticed a tall woman in a purple cape just leaving. I was sure it was the same woman I had seen the morning of the earthquake—the cape was unique—but I only saw her from the back as she left the hospital and I did not see her face.

Curious, I told Natán, "Go find out who that woman is and what she's doing here."

Natán rushed off, and Jonotás and I continued on to the room where sheets of woven cotton were collected. We began tearing bandages.

Shortly, the woman from Venezuela came in with whom, many days before, I had enjoyed talking while we worked. I opened my mouth to greet her, but as soon as she recognized me, she turned and left, a scowl upon her face.

Natán returned just then and said, "That woman with the cape, she's been workin' here since the earthquake. She started that very day. She works the same as all of us, but she only stays an hour or less. She's been talkin' 'bout you."

"About me? What has she been saying?"

I don't know. I don't think it's good though."

"Who is she?"

"I don't know, Manuelita. The slave I asked didn't know."

For the rest of the afternoon I paid close attention to the way I was treated. I was snubbed, ignored, or spoken to in short sentences by the other women. It was obvious to me that someone had used the time when I had been away from my hospital work to undermine me there. It was, no doubt, the woman in the cape.

That night, while I was bathing, I said to Jonotás, "It is not possible that everyone, all of a sudden, merely started hating me again." I stopped speaking while Jonotás rinsed my back.

She said, "Yes, somethin' got shook up with that earthquake." She giggled.

I laughed at her, but I thought it through and said, "I've lived with hate before, but this is different. That tall woman must be vilifying me to the other women who work in the hospital."

"Yes, Manuelita," said Jonotás, "but I wouldn' be worryin' none—"

I was not paying attention. Almost to myself, I said, "I wonder what people have been saying."

Jonotás leaned down and patted me on my cheek, and said, "I wouldn't be worryin' none about what people are sayin' or doin', but if you want to know, I'll find out for you."

I smiled. I knew that whatever she and Natán discovered would be interesting.

The next day, we began our search for funds. We worked hard, but I was not the only volunteer to the cause. Many patriotic women were doing what they could but none had the audacity that I had when it came to asking for money. In the days that followed, I made sure that I spoke to every important household in the city with whom I had even a passing acquaintance.

However, it was harder than I thought it would be. Certainly it was much harder than it had been in Lima. I knew it would be somewhat difficult, because of my past in Quito, but I had underestimated the trouble I would have. However, I was persistent and ignored the animosity that I felt when approaching certain people.

Whenever I did have someone's attention, I usually found a way to persuade them to give to the cause. If I could not obtain a pledge by appealing to someone's sense of patriotism, I used the tools of feminine wiles, sarcasm, knowledge of ancient Quito secrets, or any other means. I was fairly successful and was able to procure a good deal of jewels, silver plate, and currency for Bolívar's war chest. If we heard that leather was needed, we would find a tanner, and using argumentation about the worthiness and need of the cause, convince him of the wisdom of donating. If we heard that provisions were low, we found someone willing to donate several bushels of sweet potatoes. Realizing that much of the army's expense was simply for new uniforms, I found a few households in which I could help organize women there to sew and mend. My insistence that they help the revolution did little to endear these women to me, but their patriotism moved them once I got them started. I think the only reason I was able to persuade some of these women was because they knew of my relationship with Bolívar.

Nevertheless, I was steadfast in my fundraising. The only people who escaped my campaign were the Aispurus and the families loyal to them. I knew it would be pointless for me to ask for anything from those people.

Several days after these activities began, Simón said, "The treasury has grown in the last few days. It is unexpected and I am quite pleased."

I was happy too, but hoped I could do more. Then, I found the reason for some of the difficulties I was having. After letting Jonotás and Natán practice their inquisitorial arts, I learned what was being discussed about me in the city.

"Did you know that me and Natán are magicians?" Jonotás asked. I turned to her in surprise. She laughed and went on, "Yes, we know secret African magic, or so some of the servants have heard. We been practicin' evil by night." She laughed.

"Shame on you." I smiled and sat down next to her. "What else have you heard?"

"Oh, me and Natán are nothin' compared to you. We've taught you some of this magic. Now you know to compel a man to do whatever you bid."

"Would that it were true," I laughed.

"Yes. And you have Bolívar under your spell."

I rolled my eyes. I found it hard to believe that anyone could be that stupid.

"Oh, and a priest said you are possessed by the devil." That was true, the crazy priest had run through streets shouting this on the day of the earthquake. "And you struck a priest." This, of course, also happened.

"Also, I heard that there is gossip about us bein' unnatural lovers."

"Who?"

"You and me."

I snorted in disgust.

"Oh, and you won't believe this. Some of the more superstitious think the earthquake was caused by the practice of magic which you been doin'"

She went on, telling me even more nonsense. Jonotás could attest that these preposterous lies were believed as possible by a few people of the poorer classes. The more educated were slandering me in ways that were at least realistic. Some believed I was profiting from my charitable work in the hospitals and from gathering money for the cause. Some even held that I was influencing Bolívar in the practice of government. There was, of course, truth in the rumor that I was an adulteress.

"Also, I think this damn gossip has already reached the ears of the general's staff. I think there's talk among them that you're a bad influence on him."

I did not realize how thick was the morass of lies through which I had been working or how fast it was growing. I wondered at my ability to raise any money at all, but I now understood some of the reactions I had received.

"That woman in the cape saw me strike that priest. She is the one, I know it. I wonder who she is."

"I'm sorry, Manuelita, but we couldn't find out."

I would not have minded too much when I heard of these incredible stories, even though they were worse than what I had always experienced. However, Simón had taught me many new ideas in our midnight discussions and I was growing up.

The stupidity and maliciousness put me in a fighting mood, and I wanted to fight them all, or shock them more. But, for the first time, I saw danger in my actions and in being talked about by the people of Quito. I could not now openly defy the attitudes and sentiments of the whole populace without reflecting badly on Simón. I chafed at doing nothing, and yet I risked making Simón look bad if I did anything.

I needed to do something to break out of the mire I found myself in. So, I tried to reopen my lawsuit. The one thing I could do, was fight with the Aispurus. They were fair game, as that conflict was my own and had been going on for years. Also, I reasoned that if I could get my hands on my own money, I would be in a much better position to stay in Quito or to go wherever Simón might go.

I entered the law office early one morning and said, "I have come to renew my case against Carlos Aispuru."

"Señora, I have already told you. With the recent changes in the government, I'm afraid it will be months before you will be able to continue." The clerk with the shifty eyes spoke to me as if he were speaking to an insect from a great height. "And, as I last stated, you will have to start all over when that time comes."

I assumed an even greater altitude and said, "Are you saying that nothing can be done?"

"You must wait until the new administration has been fully established," he sniffed.

I despised that man and enjoyed saying, "The 'new administration' has settled in, and he is taking up residence in the presidential palace. I know." I leaned close and whispered, "I have been there."

The man stopped with his mouth open, while still forming his retort. He cleared his throat nervously.

"I will speak to 'the new government' about the matter personally, if you wish," I said sweetly.

The man took a harder look at me and said, "Just one moment. Please wait here." He walked quickly to the back of the room where other clerks and scriveners were sitting and spoke to one of them. Soon a discussion was ensuing between Shifty Eyes and two other clerks, as they looked in my direction.

The man came back to me and said. "It is Manuela Thorne, is it not?"

"Yes, Señor, as you know," I replied.

"Perhaps we can make some accommodations under the circumstances."

I seemed to have caused something to move, though I distrusted him. I smiled and said, "I'm sure you can."

"Please come back tomorrow," he said. I wanted to press on but did not know what else to say. I am always so confused in legal matters. I left, but I felt something was finally going to happen.

However, when I returned the next morning, the men in the office were not as conciliatory. They almost seemed evasive. As I walked home, I was more unsure than ever. That night, as we discussed Simón's ideas about the revolution, the government, and his aspirations for the future, I ventured, for the first time, to bring up my problems.

"Simón, I know you are president of the entire republic, but do you have any influence on local proceedings?"

He did not understand the question and said, "Which proceedings do you mean?"

"I have a lawsuit which is in an administrative soup. I believe I am being treated unjustly and—"

"What lawsuit, Manuelita?"

Until then he had not known I was suing my uncle and aunts. I explained the whole story, about my rightful claim of a portion of the Aispuru estate and my lack of success in obtaining it. When he heard the whole story, he sympathized with me but he was not encouraging.

"If I were to do things legally," and he was particular about such matters in order not to appear to be abusing his power, "I would have to communicate to Bogotá, and they would have to communicate with the local office." He scratched the stubble on his chin as he pondered the problem. "I doubt that would have much effect." He thought some more. "Also, you are a married woman; and if I were to help you openly, it might make our affair too obvious. The gossip could be bad for both of us. Let me think about it."

I was happy that he seemed to want to help, but I resented that Bolívar, who held so much power, would be stopped by what people would say. Every turn I took seemed to bring me up against a wall. Never before had I paid any mind to what people would say. Now, I had to. Would he be able to help me get my inheritance? It seemed not. Even more unsettling was the realization of how precarious it was to have a relationship with such a powerful man.

I, who had never been subtle, found that subtleties ruled political power. It was true that I had the ear of the one man who represented the government, who could perhaps have greased the wheels of justice and insured that my inheritance would come to me. Still, I realized that many, many things more significant than I, and my problems, occupied that ear and that mind. Even a dictator cannot always snap his fingers and have something be done. And Simón was never a dictator, no matter what his enemies have said. Politics played a role in everything that Simón did from morning to night. Political favors and time were required to accomplish anything that was not strictly military and under his direct control.

After a little more than a week had gone by since I had met Bolívar, I came to an appalling realization. My relationship with Bolívar was not the safe haven that I first imagined it to be. If anything, my relationship with the people of Quito had grown worse because of it. Everyone deferred to me because they knew how powerful he was, but underneath their "respect" was a deep and growing resentment. With the gossip more malicious than ever, it even felt like my situation might be worse now that I was associated with Bolívar. Being close to the President of the Republic, while attractive at first, was in reality quite perilous.

Bolívar's power did not matter to me. I loved Simón, and that is all I really cared about. Yes, it would have been advantageous if he could have helped me, but I knew that was not what I wanted most. What I really wanted was for us to go away together. I wished he could have abandoned his responsibilities so that we could be alone together but I knew it was impossible even as I wished it.

It soon became clear that I would have to keep a lower profile in order not to bring any scandal to my love or attacks on myself. I would proceed with my affairs, but more carefully. My feelings were hardened to public opinion, having grown up abused and maligned by those about me. To be myself was to act without considering what the "good" people of the town might think. I was "La Sáenz," who did not look to others to sanction her actions. Now, I had to force myself to consider what I was doing each moment and how it might reflect on Simón.

However, my decision to be more circumspect did not seem to help. It was obvious to anyone who looked at me that I was content and happy. Everyone knew who was making me happy. For those jealous of Bolívar's power, my adultery and my connection to him were reason enough to try to get at both Simón and me. Yet, however much *I* felt the animosity of those around *me*, I understood that it was really Bolívar, for the simple reason of his being successful and President, whom many wished to tear down. The more power one has, the more dangerous is his position.

Except for Sucre and a few others, I was one of the few people to whom Bolívar could talk and with whom he could trust his confidences. Actually, I was the only feminine, and intimate, ear to whom he could speak at all. I was, in fact, his closest friend. Yet, this too, was a problem.

I was in love with a powerful man, and was therefore more trapped and at risk than ever. I worried about Simón's health. I was eager to share his dreams, yet deep inside I wanted to avoid any kind of fighting. I was married and had found the one man in my life I wanted to love and he was not my husband. Yet, above all these problems, was an even greater one. I slowly discovered an unfortunate truth about Simón. He was a man who had given his full commitment to a woman only once in his lifetime, and was determined never to do so again.

My natural response to a friend is to bond close and quickly. Bolívar, on the other hand, had grown up in a different world. He was a wealthy aristocrat who always had everything he wanted. He did not need money, nor did he think he needed anything, certainly not intimacy. His requirement for love was much broader. What he wanted was the love of the entire continent.

When he married as a youth, he had tried to give his life to a woman, but death had taken her away. Since that time, he had rejected all forms of true intimacy. For twenty years, to protect an aching heart, he had built a wall of self-reliance through which women were allowed only if they promised to be a diversion and nothing more. He divided and ruled the space he controlled, but the space in his heart for love was inviolate. He was determined to never think of a woman in any permanent way.

To make his isolation more complete, he lived in a world of intrigue and violence that did not allow anyone to get too close. He was surrounded by people, yet isolated by rank. He could not consider a settled life—tomorrow there would be more territory to conquer.

For Bolívar, at first, I'm sure our affair had been quite simple. He had met a woman to whom he had directed his charm and she had succumbed. Nothing would have been special or new about that. Even after holding me in his arms, one night after another, he did not see me as significantly different to his life—even though José Palacios told me he had never known Simón to keep one woman so long about him. Simón knew I was different than his previous lovers, and he told me often that I filled a special need for him. Yet he did not believe me to be in any way significant to the rest of his life.

Men do not believe in a woman's strength or power. They believe that they influence women, and that they are invincible in matters of love. Simón was not immune to that kind of blindness. It became clear to me that he thought I had fallen in love with him, as every other woman did, but he had no idea that he was in love with me.

I think it was not until many days after we met that Simón became fully aware of the fact that, not true to form, he had not spoken to another woman since that first night we met at the Larrea mansion. I think he discovered too late that it was he who had succumbed to my charms this time, and it frightened him.

He did not understand how much he needed me. He considered his romantic involvement with me a dalliance compared to his "real work." While I did not question that he loved me, whether he knew it or not, I could see that he felt constrained by his feelings for me. It seemed that more and more, in various ways, I was asking how I could help him and fit into his life, and with each such question, he saw me less as an ally and more as a jailer. I felt his withdrawal deeply. I felt it inside my body.

He never said such, but it was true. It was for this reason that I never again brought up my lawsuit. I could not even discuss news that was important to him without risking his retreating from me and the spectre of permanence which our love had conjured.

Each time I brought him some news that Jonotás and Natán had gleaned from the lower classes of the city, I worried. I even worried when I brought him a personal pledge for money or resources from one of my acquaintances. He accepted these gifts, which I wanted to give him in order to feel I was contributing to his dreams. However, each time he did so, I felt him pull away, as if, by accepting something from me, he was building a dependence, which he resented. He was The Liberator and he thought he did not need anyone at all. He could not afford to depend on anybody.

We both realized that the war might take him away from me someday. I was not concerned about the distance between us; I was concerned that we stay united in purpose—and love. That is why I wanted to become invaluable to his causes. Still, Bolívar gave me the impression that I was drowning him when I offered some news or a suggestion. I wanted to work for him, yet I was impeded both by the city's hatred of me and Simón's reluctance to become dependent on me.

Every day I felt Bolívar look farther into the future, to some new battle that would pull him out of his perceived stagnation. I could not help him, because by doing so, he felt ever more confined. I became more deeply in love with him by night, and more deeply frustrated with him by day.

Thus, I was reluctant to "burden" him with news that I received from Rosita. Her letter was troubled, and I worried for her as I read it.

She wrote, "There is unrest and dissatisfaction with the government, and José is unwilling to step in, yet he believes that a strong hand is needed to keep the state together."

I was not surprised that there would be dissatisfaction in Perú with Monteagudo as head of state. San Martín was still the military leader, but he had put Monteagudo in charge of political affairs, and I was sure that had been a mistake. Monteagudo was cruel, and people hated him. Only the revolution's leaders respected him, and that was because he was a great thinker and understood the elements of a successful revolution. The people knew nothing of such nuances and saw only ruthlessness in his methods.

She went on: "The lack of money and trade, along with the lack of patriotism, have convinced José that a monarchy is the only way to bring order to this country. I do not like the thought, but the intrigues of the *criollos* have convinced me that he may be right."

Monarchy. What we had fought against. Not just the rule of Spain, but the idea that one man alone should rule. I hated the thought myself and wondered what could be done. As I read on, her letter led me to believe that order was only barely being maintained by the Protector's presence. It appeared that if he had not still been in Magdalena, Perú would be in complete anarchy, and soon overrun by La Serna and his Spanish legions.

This idea bothered me, but my attention was caught by what I read next. "José does have plans. What seems most important is the cohesion of the country. He believes he can help solve that problem. He is convinced that he will be able to annex Guayaquil to greater Perú."

I knew that Simón should have this news at once. I was convinced that Simón was right—Guayaquil must be annexed to Gran Colombia.

I walked over to the palace, reading the rest of the letter while I walked. "The interior is still held by the *godos*. Do you remember how we celebrated when José entered Lima? We thought the fighting was done. It now looks like there may be many battles ahead. If the problems with the Spanish were not enough, there is dissension between the Peruvians and the Argentine army."

I was appalled at the state of affairs in Perú. I was sad for Rosita's disappointment and even sadder when I read, "José's affliction is worse and he is taking more opium."

I did not feel good about the situation that Rosita and San Martín were in and wondered what would happen to them. Most of San Martín's military decisions, while effective, were misunderstood because he was not one to charge an enemy and waste lives when waiting might bring the same result. His unwillingness to shed needless blood was too often called incompetent by men who were not fit to black his boots. Rosita, I know, was suffering if he was suffering.

However, in the matter of Guayaquil, I had to fight my sense of loyalty to my old friends because I did not want to hurt him, or her. However, I believed, from my nightly discussions with Simón, that if San Martín were successful in annexing Guayaquil, it would be of little consequence to Perú but disastrous for Gran Colombia.

When I reached the palace, I learned that Simón was north of the city for the afternoon. I went away, and waited for José Palacios to come for me later that night. Then, I was finally able to tell Simón about Rosita's letters.

As we lay in the soft afterglow of our lovemaking, I said, "Simón, I have something I want to tell you."

I felt a slight rigidity creep into his body as I lay with my head on his chest. "What is it?"

"I have some news from Lima. It is about Guayaquil."

He sat up and looked at me. Any reticence I might have felt from him was replaced by intense interest. "What about Guayaquil?"

"I have received a letter from my friend, Rosita Campusano."

Bolívar's expression changed. He thought he was going to hear only gossip. What could a woman know, even if she was a friend of mine?

"Rosita is San Martín's lover, and she says that he is moving to annex Guayaquil—very soon."

Simón's reaction was even stronger than I expected. He sprang out of bed and began pacing, naked, up and down the room. "I knew it. I knew it," he said, as he ran his hand through his hair. "How do you know? What did she say?"

We talked long into the night, and I told him everything I could about the Argentine general and the military scene in Lima.

"No one has told me so much about the Peruvian situation and San Martín before," he said. He laughed and said, "I might as well fire all my spies and listen to you."

After asking me more questions, he said, "We must stop the Protector from annexing Guayaquil. We must take action if San Martín's plans are as serious as you say. Already he has a squadron on the Guayas, and his partisans are working for annexation in the city."

"I know San Martín," I said. "I know he wants the people to decide for themselves."

"Yes, I can see that, after all you've told me of the man. However, you also told me how important it is to him. There are many people in Guayaquil who will follow his slightest suggestion. I have received word that the junta there convened an electoral college to vote on the matter."

"There, you see, it is up to the people."

"Manuela, the date they chose is more than a month away. Why?"

I knew his question was rhetorical, but I said, "Why?"

"It is to be convened on July 28."

I understood. It was Perú's first anniversary of independence.

"After what you've told me, I must move quickly. I must stop him."

Thus, having aided my lover with information and advice in order that I might feel more close to him, I had helped him make up his mind to leave me.

On July 4, a little more than two short weeks after I first met Simón Bolívar, our nightly trysts came to an end. San Martín was on the move to Guayaquil and Simón was to meet him there. San Martín had apparently hurried his plans and was on his way to the port city. If Bolívar left that day, he would arrive first.

I asked Simón if I should go with him, but he would not allow it. It would be unseemly.

"Simón, must you go? Are you not needed here?" I asked the morning he was to leave. I knew the answer, but I was already feeling the emptiness of his absence.

It was dawn, and the sun's nearly horizontal rays illuminated him as he stood before a mirror cleaning his teeth. He was meticulous about this chore, using a small round brush and charcoal. He washed out his mouth and came over to where I was sitting and began putting on his military jacket. "No, Manuelita, I must depart. You know I must. Why do you ask such a question?"

"Because I am afraid I will lose you to the war," I said matter-of-factly.

He turned his dark eyes toward me. The shadows in the room had grown shorter. I had meant I was afraid for his life, but another image came to my mind. I could see it clearly at that moment. Simón was eager to return to battle. All the more eager because of me. Because I, or rather the love he felt for me, had captivated him too well. It was not my desire to trap him, but I admit I wanted to hold him in that place of love, never to move from it. Perhaps I held on too tightly.

Unlike Simón, I never questioned my feelings for an instant. I wanted to be with him from that first moment I saw him ride down the street in triumph, and forever. I knew it with certainty by the day after. If I had captured him, he had more completely captured me. I knew I must be his companion from then on—despite my husband, despite Simón's reticence, despite all.

I thought about all these things as I stood to look into his eyes. "Simón, I know you must go. I do not wish to make you stay. It is only . . ."

"Manuelita," he teased as he buttoned his jacket, "do you want me to write to you?"

"You know very well that I do. You must promise to write to me about everything that happens to you. Write to me every day."

"Of course, Manuelita."

I gave him a blank expression. I was not going to show him any more emotion than he was showing me. "Will you?" I demanded.

"I will."

I looked at him as if to say, *Do you promise?*

"Do not worry. I will be back here—if I can—and we will most likely see each other very soon. And yes, I will write to you while I'm gone."

I kept my gaze steady.

"Manuelita?"

"Yes, Simón."

He pulled me to him, put his arms around me, laughed, and kissed me. "The war will not take me from you, my Manuelita. The war brought us together."

He pulled back and smiled at me, making me know I loved him forever. Then, he kissed me again and again, until I, at last, embraced him, for what I determined would not be the last time.

Chapter 4

Bolívar did not keep his promise. He did not write to me. In the first few days, when I knew he would be busy traveling down the Andes with 1,500 men, I did not anticipate receiving a letter—even though couriers returned to the garrison in Quito every day. I hoped he might write to me from Ambato, or Riobamba, but I did not expect it. I too was busy, working in the hospital, continuing to raise money for the revolutionary coffers, and bothering the men who were supposed to renew the lawsuit against my uncle.

They, at least, wrote me a letter. The day after Bolívar left they notified me that a decision would soon be forthcoming. I went immediately to question them and came away with a distinct impression that the decision would be favorable.

Days later, I was becoming quite upset with Simón. Sufficient time had passed. He should have written. I sought out the couriers for news, and on finding one who had time to talk to me, discovered that Simón was well but dealing with many problems. However, it did not sound to me as if he were too busy to keep his promise to send me a letter.

The first letter I received from Guayaquil was from José María:

> We arrived on July 11. We had expected trouble because there had been reports that San Martín had a squadron on the river and troops in the town, said to be there to protect the right of the *guayaquileños* to choose their own government. When we rode down the Malecón, it seemed that we need not have worried. The citizens of Guayaquil had created triumphal arches over the roadway, and the gunboats on the river had raised the tri-color of Colombia. The general said, 'What, so soon!?' and began happily discussing his plans for the new province with his officers.
>
> We soon discovered that we were deceived. Within minutes, the flags of Colombia came down and the white and blue flags of Guayaquil were raised. Bolívar rode down the street somberly, as the crowd shouted, '¡Viva Guayaquil, independente!'
>
> The next morning he sent his deputies to the city's leaders asking the province to join the Republic of Gran Colombia. They refused. All morning long, we discussed ways to change their minds. 'The

annexation of Guayaquil is of supreme importance,' we heard the Liberator say many times that morning.

In the afternoon, Bolívar sent his officers back to ask again. This time, they temporized, saying that the authority lay in their constituted Assembly. As his men were returning to him with the bad news, they noticed that a few citizens who favored the annexation of Guayaquil to Gran Colombia suffered abuse as they went about their business from those favoring independence. There were fights in the street, and the atmosphere of the city was chaotic.

Bolívar worked late into the night. Then, on the morning of July 13, a small group of citizens came to appeal to the Liberator to include Guayaquil into the Republic of Gran Colombia. My sister, I cannot tell you how that came to be, but the general used the opportunity to send me to the Assembly and O'Leary to the Junta to announce that due to the anarchy that reigned in the city, he had assumed Supreme power and had annexed the province to the Republic of Gran Colombia.

José concluded that the Junta controlling the province promptly resigned and left on the Peruvian gunboats. It was done.

I knew what José María could not tell me. Simón had arranged for the deputation asking for his protection so that he could be seen to be justified in his annexation. Once he had eliminated San Martín's partisans from the city, Bolívar would then be able to persuade the assembly to agree to the annexation.

Bolívar did make it clear that the assembly, which was to convene on the 28th, would still do so. At that time, the people would decide for themselves. However, I knew that Bolívar's powers of persuasion were without equal. No one could deny him.

A few days later San Martín arrived in Guayaquil. I received more letters from José María describing the meeting of the two liberators.

San Martín had already been on his way to Guayaquil in his schooner, the *Macedonia*, when the preceding events took place. José María said that when his ship stopped on the river and he found out about what had transpired, he almost returned to Perú. José María told me that a delegation was sent by Bolívar to entreat him to come ashore, which he did. "There," wrote José María, "the Liberator embraced the Protector of Perú and said, 'Welcome, my General, to the soil of Gran Colombia.' San Martín seemed to grit his teeth in frustration."

There followed an official reception that included a formal dinner, at which San Martín seemed quite uncomfortable. Then, the two liberators met alone. From what José María could glean, they discussed several topics. Distinct in its absence was a discussion of Guayaquil. Instead, the two argued over the fate of Perú.

San Martín said that he was in touch with a princely house in Germany and it was his hope to find a monarch to rule Perú. He was convinced that an interim monarchy was the only way to bring order to the country. Bolívar was violently opposed in spirit to this idea and stated that he would oppose it, but he said that he would abide by the decision of the people.

Then San Martín laid out the military picture in Perú. It was dreadful. The Royalist army was growing larger every day, despite the belief in Quito that they had all but been subdued. At the same time, the patriot troops continued to desert. Along with the uncertain political atmosphere, San Martín did not believe anything but a supreme effort would bring an end to the war. He urgently requested forces from Colombia be sent immediately.

I know Bolívar and why he deferred. He did not wish to be pulled into the political disarray and risk losing everything he had gained so far by possibly losing in Perú. The military circumstances were much worse than he thought, and with San Martín apparently losing his grip on the situation, he knew he must not join his forces with the Protector. Instead, he offered the same number of troops that had been sent to him from Perú. He did this knowing that the whole Colombian army would be needed to bring down La Serna and his legions.

San Martín replied that this would not be sufficient and offered to serve under "The Liberator of the North" if he would bring his presence and his troops to Lima.

Bolívar refused. He told the Protector that he could not accept the offer without violating his mandate from Colombia. He had not the authority to leave the Republic and embark on a "foreign" war. Actually, he could have done anything he wished and no one would have dared stop him, but Simón would not do something that might be deemed illegal or abusive of his power. More importantly, he was not sure yet that he could win such a war.

After the meeting, San Martín went to his room and worked long into the night in order to come up with a way to persuade Bolívar to bring the Colombian army to Perú. I was hurt by what my brother wrote me next. While San Martín worked, Simón joined the party still going on and danced into the night. I never did find out with whom he might have spent the night or even if, after all, he slept alone. However, I had spent a night dancing with Simón and I was jealous.

The next day was disastrous for my friend San Martín. In an afternoon meeting, he presented Bolívar with all his arguments. He practically demanded that Bolívar come to Perú.

San Martín could be nearly as persuasive as Bolívar, and I am sure he might have come away from Guayaquil with the resources he needed. However, that morning Bolívar had received a devastating communication from his partisans in Perú, which he handed over to San Martín.

The hated Monteagudo, the minister San Martín had left in charge, had been seized and placed on a ship bound for Panamá. A provisional government had been installed by the country's leading *criollos*. I could see Torre Tagle's hand in this. San Martín is said to have silently left the room.

That night there was a ball held in honor of the two liberators. Amidst the gaiety, Bolívar danced while San Martín could only go through the motions of enjoying himself. My friend left early, meaning to go directly to the *Macedonia* and depart for Perú, but Bolívar saw him leave. He caught up with him, and the two talked long into the night. In the early hours of morning, San Martín left. I knew the bitterness that was in his heart. I knew he would not stay in Perú much longer and I knew that soon Rosita would be grieving.

Not long afterward, Rosita wrote to me, telling me of San Martín's resignation and his return to his home in Mendoza. The *criollo* "nobility," left over from the days of the viceroy, were now in control of Lima. Rosita's status had been reduced to "once-was upstart."

The sad thing was that her friend, Riva Agüero, one of the principal leaders of the provisional government, was one of the people who ignored her. He and Rosita had been very close, yet his jealousy of San Martín took precedence over their past. "I cannot understand how the friend I thought I knew has become so cruel and cold," she wrote. Not only had the revolution reduced her wealth, but San Martín's abdication had ruined her social standing as well. Rosita never sounded so low, sad, and lifeless.

Over the next weeks and months, I learned of the events that followed in Guayaquil from José María's letters and reports from other of my friends, but I still did not receive even one letter from Simón.

Apart from my anger at Bolívar, I was frustrated that I could not do anything to alter the course of events. Lima is a wonderful city, and my years there allowed me to evolve into the woman I was. I loved that city and the Peruvian people, and I grieved that it was being so unalterably changed. Worse, I realized that what happened to Rosita, who had been the lover of the most powerful man in the country, could happen (perhaps was happening) to me.

To make matter's worse, while waiting for Simón to finally write to me, I received a letter from another man in my life:

Dear Manuela,

I have heard disturbing reports regarding your behavior in Quito. I hope what I have heard is not true; but if it is, you must realize the futility of such indiscretion.

Not only is there a moral danger for your immortal soul, but the scandal would be devastating to you, to me, and to the other party. This is especially true if the other party is who I have heard he is.

I ask you now, if there is truth in rumor, to give up this affair. I would hope that you might choose to return to Lima next month when I will arrive there; but since I know the legal processes in which you are involved will take time, I understand that may not be possible.

I do wish to see you again, and I am sorry for the angry words we had when last we talked. I hope you are well, and I miss you.

However, regardless of whether you stay in Quito or not, do desist from whatever you have been doing which may have caused gossip to have reached all the way to Panamá.

As I say, any affair would be useless. You could never hope to have a permanent relationship with another man because we are Catholics and divorce is impossible; even if I were to grant one, which I would never do. Therefore, the only honorable thing to do is to bring any affair in which you may be involved to an end. I hope you see the infallibility of my arguments.

Do I have your agreement, Madam?

Your husband,
James

It had come at last. Though I had expected such a letter from him, it was distressing nonetheless. I knew I could not hide the knowledge of my affair with Simón forever, but I did not expect to have to fight with James so soon. I could tell that he was in a rage when he wrote this letter. All the pretense of not knowing if it was true, the advice, and the conciliatory tone were a veiled threat.

I considered all of the ramifications and still could not bring myself to deny my feelings for Simón. He angered me, and my reply was short:

Sir:

I interpret your letter thus: "Dear Manuela, You must give up what has meaning for you and return to Lima and the dull life you have with me."
I have only one answer, Sir: No.

Manuela

I had no intention of ever returning to Lima, and certainly none of resuming my life with James. However much, at one time in my life, I may have needed and wanted to live in that city with James, that time was gone. Also, with the political and military situation in Lima as it was, I did not believe it would be safe to return in any foreseeable future. I began to make plans to stay permanently in Quito, and I began to look for a house where Jonotás and Natán and I might stay. However, my life in Quito was not much more promising.

After one day of looking for a place to stay, I knew I had to have a judgment in my lawsuit. I would never have enough money to live in Quito long. I needed to have the favorable decision that Shifty Eyes kept promising me. It had been almost four months since Bolívar had left, and I was more frustrated each day.

Late one afternoon, an Indian boy came to the back door of the Larrea mansion with a message from Shifty Eyes that a decision had been reached. I left the house so fast I did not even alert Jonotás and Natán. I raced down to the office, composed myself to look unworried about anything, and opened the door.

Shifty Eyes walked over to me. He looked like he did not know what to say, but he still had an air of moral superiority. Since I had considered him more of an antagonist in this affair than a clerk, I thought what I was seeing was contrition because I had won.

"I am here to receive the decision," I said, totally unprepared for what I heard next.

"I am sorry, Señora, but the case has been dismissed as spurious."

"What?" I could not believe my ears. "Spurious!? What the hell do you mean, 'Spurious?'" I demanded.

"Really," he began, "profanity is not nec—"

I slammed my hand on a table top. "Answer me, damn you! What do you mean, 'spurious?'"

He looked down his long nose and said stiffly, "There is no *will*, Señora."

"Of course, there's a will. I watched my mother write it."

He did not even pause, but spoke as if he knew something I did not. "If you could provide us with a copy, ..."

I did not hear more. I realized that I did not know where my mother's will was. I had seen her write it. She had told me what was in it. I had heard Father Ramón promise my mother that he would see that I received my inheritance. I had always known what her gift had been. Since my youth, Carlos had fought any attempt I had made to obtain my inheritance, and I had assumed that the will was a matter of public record, that the battle had always been over the legitimacy of the will. I never expected the absence of the will itself would ever be the reason why I was denied. Where was it?

I don't remember leaving the office. I was so devastated by the news, that I did not know what I was doing. I walked for a long time without looking at anyone or anything. It seemed I wandered aimlessly throughout the streets, shaken, unable to believe this turn of events. I was prepared to fight "to the death" for what was mine, but it seemed my whole world was pulled out from beneath my feet. There was no one to fight. There was nothing to do battle over. There was no way to prove my claim. There was no will.

I walked for a long time. When I saw that I was outside the city itself, I came somewhat to my senses. When I looked around, I realized where I was. My wandering had not been so aimless after all. I was only a short distance away from the house where I lived as a child. I could see the neighborhood just ahead. I continued my journey and soon found myself standing in front of what was left of my old home.

It had burned down. I had returned on one or two occasions in those first years when I had been in the convent, but it had been ten years since I had been there. The stone wainscoting and the stone kitchen were all that remained recognizable, but they had been weakened by the fire and had all but fallen, and were completely scorched and black. It looked like little more than a pile of ashes.

I walked through what had been the door. I imagined that I could see underneath the debris. There was the corner where I had played. There is where Father Ramón sat and drank tea. There was my mother's bed. There, my mother had scratched out a will and asked for Father Ramón's help in seeing that I received my inheritance—a will that had vanished.

I looked around in despair. What happened to it? As my eyes swept over the rubble, I noticed a man coming from the city, leading a mule that was limping. Before he was close enough to be recognized, I knew it was my uncle, Carlos.

I walked out to the side of the road. When he was almost there, he recognized me and stopped. We looked at each other a long time. He started walking again, ignoring me.

As he passed, I said, "You'll never get away with it."

He stopped. He turned back to me and spoke, his voice rich with hatred, "Get away with what, Manuela? I am not a whore, like my sister. Nor am I a hellion, like you. I do not 'get away' with anything. I am an honest hard working member of this community. Get away with what?"

"You know what, you ass. You know what. How much money did it cost to pay them off?"

"Way too much, I realize, now that you have confirmed my guess. You don't have a will. All these years, I thought you had one. I wasted so much time, trouble, and money worrying about it." His expression was grim and cruel.

My blood was boiling. "No doubt it was nothing compared to one quarter of your land, which is mine—"

"Never!" He dropped the rope he was holding to lead the mule and came over to me. "You will never have that land. It's been in our family for generations. Do you think I would let an adulterous bastard have it, to squander and waste?" His face was flushed and he was nearly shouting.

"It is mine—"

"No! It is mine. My father left it to me, to all of us, but I was to administer it. I was to protect the family and make it prosper. Go on. Go on up the road and look at it. It is one tenth of its promise."

"Damn you—"

"Your mother, with her scandal, ruined my chances of adding to it. It has been twenty-five years and it still is not what I dreamed it would be."

"Carlos, you know there was a will. I saw you read it. If you were a decent man, you would honor your sister's wishes—" I stopped.

Carlos was saying, "Don't talk to me of decency . . ." and other such things. But I could not listen. I remembered something. I turned around and headed back to the ruins of my mother's little house.

"Stay away from there. That house belongs to me. I will prosecute you for trespassing."

From inside the "house," I turned back to him and said, "What house? This pile of rubble, which you have so carefully kept up. You dragged me from this place before. You tore me away from my mother when she was dying. Just try to get me out of here now." Tears rolled down my cheeks, but they sprang from fury.

He shook with anger and took a step towards me.

"Come then. Come try to drag me out again." I motioned him to come forward.

He stopped.

"That's right, Carlos. I'm no longer a little girl you can degrade and bully."

He stared at me, hatred shrinking his eyes to small black stones. He started to walk away, but then he turned back and said, "Don't think that it will always be thus. Even now, your benefactor is far away. And there are many in Quito who think he may not be coming back, or perhaps he should not. You may be able to hold on for a while, but it won't last." He turned and left.

I watched him walk away. I started to shake with a sobbing that soon overcame me. I wanted to kill him. I think, if my pistols had been with me, I would have put a ball in his back. I was so overcome with frustration and anger and grief that I sank to my knees and sobbed.

I knelt in the center of the debris. I was where Father Ramón and I had lain my mother, on a straw mat, four candles set at each corner of the mat. There she had lain like a pauper with only a soiled sheet for a shroud. Never once was she helped by the Aispurus, one of the wealthiest families in the country. My argument with Carlos had brought it all back to me.

My tears flowed as I sat there, face in my hands, in utter grief. I missed her. I wanted to hold her and be loved by her again. I touched the ground where she had lain and felt my heart break. I sobbed in pain. It seemed like a long time later that I was able to wipe the tears from my eyes and stand. I looked over to the place where her bed had been years before—a bed which Father Ramón and I had dismantled. I looked at the spot where Father Ramón had found something that day.

The sky was getting dark. It felt like rain, and heavy black clouds were covering the sky. Suddenly, I knew what happened to the will. I remembered.

As we dismantled the bed, Father Ramón had found the will where Carlos had thrown it on the floor, crushed and disregarded. There is where the kindly priest had uncrumpled it, read it, folded it, and put it in his frock. I also remembered he said something strange. "Family," then, "You and I are much alike." That I did not understand, but whatever happened to Father Ramón, the will, if it still existed, was with him.

I walked back to town. If I could find my old friend, I could still win. I walked quickly because the sky was black with approaching night.

Chapter 5

Simón did not return to Quito until November. The rainy season had started early and was in full force. Jonotás, dripping rainwater from her matted curls, ran into our room. I was composing an angry letter to Bolívar, full of reproach. I threw it away when I heard the news.

"Manuelita, he's here."

"Who?"

She polished some imaginary medals on her chest.

"Bolívar?!" I stood up. "Here? In Quito?"

"Yes. He rode in just now, with his officers."

I had heard he was returning, but I did not expect him for a few more weeks. A scowl must have crossed my face.

"What is the matter, Manuelita? He is here. Will you stay angry?"

I walked to the window and looked at the gray sky and the shower striking the houses across the street. "I am not angry, I am merely going to wait to see if he neglects me as much in Quito as he did in Guayaquil."

"Oh, Manuelita, you should not—"

"Never mind, Jonotás. Come, I want something to eat."

All day I was difficult to be around. I waited to see if he would remember I existed. By the time night fell, the rain had stopped but there was still no word from him, and I was furious.

It was not until late at night that José Palacios showed up at the back door to the Larrea mansion. When Natán told me he was at the door, I was relieved.

Bolívar was asking for me. He was not with someone else. He wished to see me. However, this alone could not keep me from feeling anger at the way I had been treated. Even though he wanted to see me, I was upset because he seemed to have relegated me to "last" on his mind.

"Go down and tell the Liberator's retainer that Manuela Sáenz is otherwise engaged."

Natán hesitated, afraid to be so rude and bold to Bolívar's servant. Jonotás said, "This should be fun. I'll go."

"Someone go."

Natán watched Jonotás head for the stairs and said, "Are you sure, Manuelita?"

"Yes!"

But I wasn't. I did not know how Bolívar would react and I did long to see him. I decided I would go over to his offices in the morning, scandal or no scandal, and tell him how I felt. Only then would I take up with him again, that is, if he had not chosen someone else for his night's entertainment.

I went back to bed and tried to sleep, but I only lay there, sleepless, while my mind churned. I heard the rain start again. Somewhat later, I heard a tapping at the door. Natán went to see who it was. When she came back to the bed, she said, "It is Jorge," one of Don Larrea's servants, "he says Bolívar's servant is at the back door again."

I should have been happy that Simón was persistent, but I was not. For some reason, I took it to mean that I was just another of Simón's entourage who was expected to do what he wished. I threw on my *saya y manto* and flew downstairs in a rage.

When I arrived, José Palacios smiled at me, a light rain dripping from his red hair. "I am happy to see you again, Señora. The Liberator is most anxious to see you also. Won't you please come with me?"

His aspect was most often dreary, and I was softened by his smile and his obvious affection for me. I pulled the *manto* around my face and followed him through the mud to the center of town.

When I arrived, Simón was still working. He was leaning over a table, which served as a desk, and he was writing intently. His blue uniform jacket was unbuttoned and his hair was tousled. Something about the way he looked worked an indefinable sexual magic on my emotions. Despite my anger, I desired him thoroughly.

As soon as I entered the room, he looked up and smiled. Even though he seemed to be in the middle of a thought, he lay down his pen and came over to me. "Manuelita," he said as he embraced me before I could step away, "I have missed you so very much."

I stepped back, but not before feeling his body press close to mine and feeling my own blood and desire grow. "Missed me? Is that why I have not received one letter. Not one."

"Now, Manuelita—"

"Do not, Señor, pretend endearment when you failed to keep your promise to me. From June to November, five months," I exaggerated since he left on July 4, "five months without so much as a 'wish you were here.'"

"I am sorry—"

"Without even asking one of your couriers to stop and say, 'the Liberator is too busy for you.'"

"You are right, Manuelita—"

"Do not call me that."

"Manuela, I am sorry. Your judgment of me is quite correct." He came to me and looked at me with those beautiful, deep, dark eyes. He put his hands on my arms. "You must believe me. I have been very busy. But I have longed for you. It is surprising how much I have longed for you."

I wanted to throw the rumors I'd heard of his amorous escapades in Guayaquil in his face. The images I could conjure up from such gossip disgusted me. Yet I did not want to believe them. I wanted to believe the man, whom I loved, standing before me. He seemed sincere, and his obvious and ardent desire was to be with me at that moment. I could not hide how much I missed him.

"I do not think it is fair," I said a little petulantly. "You're off doing I don't know what, and I'm here, fighting for my life." I wanted to kick myself as soon as I said it. The last thing I wanted was for him to take pity on me. "Not that I can't handle my own problems, but—"

"What problems?"

I didn't answer at first, but with the situation with my mother's will still pressing on my mind, I told him about my lawsuit and my encounter with Carlos. I kept talking as I paced up and down so that I would not simply fall into his arms and receive his kisses.

"Manuela, if there is something I can do while I am in Quito, I promise I will. I want to help you with this. Truly."

All at once I felt like a great weight had been lifted from my shoulders. He must have seen the softening in my face, and he took me in his arms and kissed me. "Oh, Manuelita, how I have longed to hold you close like this."

I could not keep my anger alive. My hunger for him was too great. I kissed him, over and over. My breasts pressed against him and I felt that deep desire again, desire I have felt with no one else. "Simón," I breathed, and pulled him to me, as though to contain all of him in my arms. "Simón. I am so in love with you," I said between kisses.

"Come," he said pulling away, leading me over to his bed. "Manuela, I have been away too long." He pulled me down onto him and kissed me over and over.

Our lovemaking was like a dam breaking, which had been holding back more than it could restrain for too long. We moved as one, and I again believed in our future together. Our sleep afterwards was complete and comforting. There was only a brief moment, before slumber took me, when a doubt gnawed at my mind.

In the morning, we again tasted the joy of knowing each other's body and soul. When at last we lay spent, embracing, and holding off the intrusion of the day, I was as happy as I have ever been, despite an almost hidden sense that something in our relationship had changed.

As we fell asleep again, in the soft, morning light, I knew that, despite my love for him and his obvious affection for me, our relationship was not perfect. We had reconciled, but I did not believe it would be different in the future. Simón still did not understand what seemed so clear to me: we were for each other, and our relationship must be nurtured and protected. Until he accepted that, I knew I would come to grief if I depended on him.

Later, I awoke as Simón was rising. I watched the sinewy ripples in his back alternately go taut and relax as he pulled on his trousers. I truly admired this man and was glad to have had him again in my arms. I wished he loved me as I did him.

"Simón," I said, as he pulled on his shirt. He turned around and smiled at me. "Do you really think you can help me claim my inheritance?" I asked, seeking some reassurance about his feeling for me.

"I can try. I have so much to do. However . . ." He walked over to the door and called José Palacios. When his servant arrived, he said, "José, Manuelita had a lawsuit that was recently dismissed. Please arrange to have the records sent to me."

José said he would do so and left. Simón turned to me and I smiled broadly, feeling new hope, and said, "Thank you, Simón."

Days later, though we spent each night in passionate lovemaking, he still had not mentioned anything about my lawsuit, and I was too happy to break the mood to mention it myself. I remarked on it to Simón one morning and he said, "Yes, I have been meaning to tell you. I have looked at the records. I am still deciding how to proceed. But I plan to look into it again today."

I was thrilled. That evening, I was going to ask him about it again, but he called for me later than usual. When I finally arrived in his apartments, he looked exhausted. There had been a counterrevolution in Pasto and all day he had been busy with arrangements to quell it. He had already sent General Sucre to the scene with the Colombian lancers and he indicated that he might have to lead the foot soldiers. "I do not have an officer available," he said in a weary tone as he sat down on the bed and unbuttoned his shirt. He sounded like he needed two days' sleep.

"When will you be leaving?" I asked.

"Tomorrow, unless things change," he answered, suppressing a yawn. "I wish this had not happened now."

We were in the habit of undressing each other as we began our lovemaking. This night, I went to him and knelt down and took his boots off. He let me. He was exhausted. The wash bowl was nearby and I poured some water and washed his feet. He said, "You don't need to do that."

"I want to. Here, let me help you with your shirt." I was successful in getting him into bed. I undressed myself and crawled in next to him. "Simón, you're working too hard. Try to sleep now, and sleep late tomorrow."

"Ridiculous. I'm fine. I'm just a little tired tonight." He fell asleep immediately. I awoke early, so I arose, dressed, and found José Palacios and explained how exhausted he was. He knew that if he let Bolívar sleep, he would have to face an angry Liberator, but I was able to persuade him to wait an extra half-hour.

While I was talking to him, I asked about the papers from the courts regarding my lawsuit. "They are most uncooperative, Señora. However, I am to pick up more documents this afternoon. I will see that the general has them today."

I went away happy, knowing that progress was being made on my suit and that Simón had rested for a change. It was with a certain improvement in confidence that I went about my affairs that day. Soon my money problems would be solved. No longer would I have to depend on the Larreas. They had never mentioned that my stay with them was becoming over long, but my own feelings were driving me to find a house of my own in which to live.

That day I received another letter from James, angrily demanding my return to Lima. Even that did not bother me. I felt confident that I would soon have control of my affairs. I merely waited to hear from José Palacios. I waited all day and into the night.

When José Palacios did not come, even to take me to Simón, I went with Jonotás and Natán to the presidential apartments late that night. When I arrived, I learned that Bolívar had taken the infantry to Pasto that afternoon.

He was gone. My frustrations in Quito were a nightmare. I know he had no choice, but Simón had left without even a "Good-bye." No word. No way of knowing when he might return. For all I knew, he would not even come back to Quito. Also, I did not know if anything had been done before he left to settle my lawsuit.

I slept very late the next day and stayed in my room upon rising. I did not even go to the hospital that afternoon. I could see my hopes for the future evaporating like the Andean mist. There was no will.

Father Ramón must have it, but it had only been little more than two weeks since I made that discovery and I did not know where he was. I was plagued with uncertainties. What would I do next? When would I see Simón again? Would I see Simón again? I felt completely stopped.

When I put these questions to Jonotás, more in despair than as real questions, she said, "Manuelita, it seems that if we must find a will, we should look for it."

She was braiding my hair and her response, so logical and sensible, made me turn my head around to look at her. This, of course, caused her to yank on my hair. When I cried out, we both started laughing. She made me feel so much better. I hadn't a clue as to how to find the will, and I wasn't any better off than before my hair was braided, but I at least had a direction.

In the next few weeks, I made inquiries into the whereabouts of Father Ramón. I also made inquiries as to the whereabouts of Simón Bolívar, but no one in the garrison seemed to know anything other than what I knew. He was fighting the *pastusos*.

As my birthday came around, I became depressed because I had made no progress. On the evening of my birthday, which I had not mentioned to anyone, there was an amazing thing waiting for me. A letter. The outside had Simón's own handwriting.

I unfolded it and read:

Dearest Manuelita,

I hope this letter finds you well, at least better than I find myself. I am in a miserable little town called Yucanquer, where the main street is as long as two mud huts, one of which I occupy. It is cold and wet.

I apologize for not having found out anything about your lawsuit. There was still no word when I left, but I intended to send José Palacios over personally that day. There was simply no time. I'm sorry I could not see you before we had to depart. I miss you.

You will be happy to know that we have achieved victory here, but we cannot leave yet. We still have much to do. What do we do? We conjugate the verb "to bore." We have achieved a new level of boredom here.

I wish I was with you. I long to see you again and pray for the resumption of the happy times we have shared. You mean so much to me.

All my love,
Simón

I was thrilled. He had written to me of his own accord—without a promise to do so. I did not take note, at the time, of the fact that he said he was bored. I was grateful to have such a welcome birthday gift and I longed to see him. I missed him more each day.

All the while I kept making inquiries into the whereabouts of Father Ramón. The days wore on without us making any progress in tracking down the kindly priest. Then, one evening about three weeks after I received Simón's letter, I was in my room ready for bed. Jonotás and Natán were out to visit some of their friends, and I was composing a letter to a parish priest in Cartagena who, I was told, might know where Father Ramón could be found. As I was blowing on the ink to dry it, Jonotás and Natán rushed in.

"Manuelita. Manuelita."

"What is the matter, you two? Calm down."

"The Liberator is north of the city."

This was news, as everyone had been told he was still far north, in the Department of New Granada. "How close? When will he arrive?"

"No one knows. They say he is alone and walking his horse."

"Who says? Servants?"

"Yes, Manuelita."

I had gathered enough intelligence from Jonotás and Natán to know that the underground network of slaves and servants could spread news faster than a runner on horseback. I could not understand why he would be walking, but I pulled on my *saya y manto* and raced down to the presidential apartments.

No one was there. No one was even in the building except a few officers assigned to administrative duties playing cards. I asked them if they were expecting the Liberator and they all claimed he was in Pasto or farther north.

I went back outside. Jonotás and Natán ran up the street toward the northern gate, but I decided to wait at the palace. It was not raining that night and the moon was almost full. A few people went by carrying lanterns, but otherwise the street was dead.

My companions came back with nothing to report. I said, "We might as well go. Your friends must have been wrong." Just then, I saw him.

Coming down a side street, leading Pastor, who was limping, came a man I would not have recognized except for the horse he was leading. He was similar, but he wore a dirty poncho over a dirty uniform. He was stooped, and he was coughing every few steps. My heart broke for him and I ran up the street. He smiled when he saw me and waved weakly. I threw my arms around him and said, "Simón, oh, Simón, I'm so glad to see you. Why are you alone?"

"The rest of them are pulling some wagons out of the mire up the road. I could not bear to wait any longer."

"Where is José Palacios?"

"He'll be along soon. Would you come upstairs with me, I feel too weak to—" He started coughing. I gave Pastor to Jonotás and Natán and told them to take him down to the Larrea stables and see that a farrier looked at his leg. Then I walked a very tired soldier upstairs to his bed, where I helped him undress.

The silence in the room was oppressive, except for the ticking of his watch on the table and Bolívar's labored breathing. He was so exhausted that he did not speak to me as I undressed him. When he finally lay back against the pillows I propped up for him, he said, "Come to bed with me. I need you."

I undressed and slid in next to him. His body was cold and his breathing was hard. He said, "Ah, now I might survive the night."

"Of course, you'll survive," I said, and I held him close to me, trying to transfer all my energy to him through my skin. We lay in silence. Shortly before he fell into a restless sleep, he said weakly, "Oh, Manuelita, I'm glad you're here. I am exhausted."

Chapter 6

For the next couple of months, with few exceptions, I was with Bolívar day and night. He was very ill. I stayed with him during his convalescence and forgot about my search to find Father Ramón. His illness frightened me so much, I would not have left his side if the whole Royalist army moved on Quito.

The first two days after his return, he either coughed or lay weakly, half drowsing with a low fever. I fed him, bathed him, and, with the help José Palacios, kept his never ending supply of letters from worrying him. José had a sense of what was important and what was not, and I answered what letters I could for Simón. I also kept his staff at bay. The day after his arrival in Quito, there were immediate demands for Simón's attention. I was somewhat successful in deflecting these requests. He needed his rest and I was determined to see that he got it.

A doctor from the British legion, who had been with the liberating army for years, was called that first day. Doctor Charles Moore was about Simón's age, with dark hair and a soft face that betrayed an ineffectual bewilderment. Unfortunately, this same bewilderment characterized his diagnoses. He was a good man, but I never felt any reassurance when he was treating Simón. I liked him personally, and he was loyal and attentive, but not encouraging. He prescribed rest.

Catching up with him in the hallway as he was leaving, I asked him directly, in English, what Simón's diagnosis was. He reminded me of an animal who was trapped. "The Liberator will recover," he said, uncomfortably.

"Yes. I know. I intend to see that he does. But, Sir, what is the actual nature of his affliction?" I felt I already knew, but I wanted to be wrong.

"Uhm . . . well . . . a doctor and his patient, Madam, I can't—"

"Please, Doctor, I must know. It is consumption, is it not?" I was surprised to find my voice cracking, betraying my determination to be strong and to fight for his health and life.

The doctor looked even more pained.

"Please," I repeated.

His face softened and he took on an air of one who has found a friend with whom he could discuss his troubles. He lowered his voice and said, "Yes, Madam, you are right. He has had it for some time. But you must not tell anyone. He has been known to stay in the saddle sixteen hours at a time. His soldiers call him 'Iron Ass' because of his reputation for being untiring. If he will rest, instead of trying his reputation so often, he might have a long and happy life. Try to make him do so."

"You have my word, Sir. I am your conspirator in this." I reached up and kissed his cheek and went back to attend Simón.

I wished I felt as confident as I sounded. How could I possibly make a man of such vibrant energy rest? It was torture for him. I could either let him kill himself by

312

doing too much, or I could kill him by trying to keep him from doing too much. All it seemed I could really do was to help with his current convalescence.

Within two hours after the doctor said he needed rest, Colonel Fergusson, his red-blonde mustache still dripping from the rain lightly falling outside, knocked at the door and entered. He was followed by José Palacios, looking helpless.

"Sir, the Liberator is suffering from a fever and not receiving visitors," I said in English.

"I know it, Lass, but this here is an urgent document that the General must be readin'." He held up a rolled piece of paper in his hand.

"Nothing is more important that the General's rest," I said, and I turned him around and ushered him toward the door. He actually took a couple of steps before he realized I had him set to exit the room.

He stopped and said, "Lass—"

I raised my voice and said, "I have already ordered out two colonels, a lieutenant, and a diplomat." This was true. "Out you go." I pushed him another two steps.

"Wait, Lass, I must—"

Simón understood a little English. From the bed, he said weakly, "It's all right, Manuela, let me see it."

"Simón—"

"I know, I know, let me see it."

Fergusson walked around me, deferentially, and handed the paper to Bolívar."

He glanced at it and said, "Thank you, Colonel, for bringing this to me right away. Manuela, would you fetch me a pen and paper."

Fergusson saluted smartly and turned to go; we looked into each other's eyes as he passed. I thought I read animosity in them, but before he left the room, he turned and smiled at me and said to Simón, in Spanish, "For a fighter such as yourself, Señor, you should be havin' no other companion. It's the ideal woman for ya she is, part Amazon and part hetaera." He chuckled, and then he realized how insulting that may have sounded to a "proper" woman. He turned to me and said, in English, "No offense meant, Lass. I do like ya."

I smiled at him and said, "I like you, too, you Irish rascal. Now be off and let the Liberator rest."

"Aye, Lass, and it's a rascal I am—through and through it is." He laughed again, and said, "That's me." Then he left and I returned to Bolívar's side.

Most of the officers seemed to accept my authority in controlling the Liberator's offices. They treated me with respect and courtesy, and I did not have much trouble with any of them—except for three.

One was Colonel Córdoba, who clearly resented my "style," being more used to subservient women. I dealt with him but dismissed his attitude. Only later did I learn how very much he resented me.

The one who was most vocal in his resentment at that time was General Jacinto Lara. "Señora, or Señorita, or whatever you are. I do not recognize your authority to impede a General on military business. Now out of my way."

He started to brush past me, but I flashed out at him. "The Liberator needs rest, General. That is the only authority I need."

Simón saved the situation by saying, "Please let him pass, Manuela."

I did not argue but glared at the general who walked around me as though I were dirt.

"Really, General, I wonder at the wisdom of keeping this *woman* here." He made no attempt to hide his feelings and said this openly.

"It is all right, Jacinto, she is an excellent nurse, and I seem to need a nurse. I will be all right in a few days."

"Of course, General," he replied, but he gave me a look of displeasure before informing Bolívar of his news. He stayed about a quarter of an hour and left, sneering at me as he walked by.

Simón looked worn out. He closed his eyes almost immediately. He said, "The general is right, Manuelita, you must show greater respect. You have no official position here. Both he and Córdoba have complained to me. It must not look good to the populace either."

"Ridiculous Simón, I only want to see you well, and you can't be well without rest."

I could see he was not listening. I was sorry I said anything at all. He was so clearly in need of sleep, he started to close his eyes while I spoke. I walked back to his desk and did some paperwork for him. Still, I was annoyed. Clearly, I was the best medicine Simón had. How dare General Lara question my authority, which existed for no other purpose than the life and vitality of the Liberator. However, I could see the truth of it. If I was going to help him, then I would have to make my position in the offices of the president official.

The third person I had trouble with was Simón himself. On the fourth and fifth day of his convalescence, he was fit enough to rage and fume at how he could not get any work done, but not fit enough to do it. So he took it out on me. "Manuela, call for José." "Where's my ink?" "Where in hell are my officers?" (Kept at bay by José Palacios and myself.) It was a very trying couple of days.

I do believe he was showing more than mere irritation at being too tired to get any work done. I brought a great deal of organization to his affairs, and helped him write letters and decrees. Most of his officers or staff who came were asking for approval, or verification, of their duties, which could have been handled at a lower echelon of power than "President of the Republic." It was obvious that he needed me as a personal secretary, yet I believe he resented my overwhelming intrusion into his affairs.

He could not stand the idea of "being controlled" by a woman. Like most men, he thought women were playthings, nothing more. Despite having already proved myself valuable to him, he could not get over an obsessive need for independence. This obsession, of course, was irrational, since I did nothing but free up time for him. "I'm being swallowed up," he raged one day, as I prevented one more useless demand for his attention to get at him.

I began spending part of my days back at the Larrea mansion in order to handle some of my own affairs. However, this was more out of weariness at fighting Simón than anything else. Partly due to this weariness, I was perhaps not energetic enough in dissuading Simón's involvement with a certain visitor who came to visit him about a week or so later.

"There is someone to see you, Simón," I said, as he was reading the latest correspondence from Bogotá.

"Who is it?" he asked perfunctorily.

"It is someone whom I would prefer you not see. In fact, I believe he should not be here at all." He looked up, curiosity showing in his face. "Bernardo Monteagudo."

He stood up and looked for his pants. "Show him in. Show him in."

"Simón, I know the man. If you receive him, you will insult the Peruvians, who have exiled him to Panamá."

"Ridiculous. He is the premier intellectual light of the revolution. Let him in. No! Wait until I am dressed."

"Simón, you do not need to dress for him."

"Manuela, this tires me. He is the head of the Lautaro Lodge. I do not think I need to remind you of this most important intellectual society for us. Do I? Now wait until I dress, and then let him in."

"Simón, I urge you to reconsider. Receive him if you will, but do not let him get too close. He is responsible for the mis-management of Perú under San Martín and he will not be good for you."

"I will decide." He was still buttoning his jacket when he motioned to me to admit him.

"Thank you, Señora Thorne," Monteagudo said in a foppish manner, as he entered. "Pleasant to meet you here in Quito." His manners were as dandified as his dress, which he had carried to new heights since I had seen him in Lima. He wore gold cufflinks with several diamonds encrusted on them and a large diamond pin in his cravat. He reeked of *eue de cologne*, and his hair was oiled down and meticulously in place. I never saw any man's clothes so spotless, clean, and perfectly arranged.

If his manner offended me, his meeting with Bolívar made me sick. Not only did Simón welcome him like a long lost friend, but he acceded instantly to the ousted Liman leader's request that he join Bolívar's staff.

They talked long into the afternoon, like old friends. I heard some of it, but I was too busy to be there the whole time, which was probably fine with Bolívar.

When he left, Simón said, "The man is a genius."

"Simón, I really think—"

"No, Manuela, you're wrong. I need men of such vision. He is the only one with whom I have ever spoken who has understood my desire to unify the continent."

I was annoyed by that remark and did not answer. My silence caused Simón to look at me directly, to see if I had heard him.

When he saw the scowl upon my face, he said, "Except you, of course. But, the point is, he did understand it all. He even said the phrase, 'The United States of South America.' No one has been bold enough to state it such."

"Simón, he was only agreeing with *your* ideas."

"Manuela, he understood it."

We did not go on much longer. It was obvious Simón liked the man and I would have to endure him. What ever else was said that afternoon, Simón and Monteagudo and I did agree on one thing: something had to be done about Perú. Bolívar had to take his army there and defeat the Spanish who were slowly taking back the country. If he did not, they would recapture the entire viceroyalty. Within a year they would threaten Gran Colombia.

So it was, in the early part of 1823, I realized that my desire to help Simón would be fulfilled within the year. A resumption of the war was inevitable; and I, who had longed for peace, realized that I would most likely be a "soldier of the revolution" again very soon.

Chapter 7

Simón recovered, but he did not ask me to stop working for him. As the situation in Perú caused the work to pile up, he gave me even greater responsibility and authority to see to his everyday affairs. I felt I had become an indispensable part of Bolívar's staff and I enjoyed being able to contribute to the cause.

However, General Lara and Colonel Córdoba resented my intrusion into Simón's dealings. As I was about to enter Simón's apartments one day, I overheard them talking to him inside. "General, she is about you all the time," I heard Córdoba say.

Lara said, "Yes, some of the men are talking. After all, she is only a woman—a married woman, I might add. A soldier needs a woman now and then, we all know that, but this one does not belong here. This one is intruding in everything, interfering with a soldier's duty. She is a social climber, nothing more."

I heard the weariness in Simón's voice. "Lara, you are wrong. She admires me and she is an excellent administrator. In fact, I cannot do without her right now."

Córdoba said, "She is a bitch. She orders me about like a schoolboy."

"Easy Córdoba," said Simón, "if that is your opinion of her, keep it to yourself in my presence. She can be rough at times, but she does important work for me these days. Now please, gentlemen, enough."

The conversation stopped for a moment and I entered the room. Simón's two officers both glared at me. I expected a smile from Simón but he looked at me as though he were evaluating me anew. His look chilled me. What was he thinking? What did he feel about me? I gave Simón the letter I had just been handed by José Palacios. Simón and I discussed its contents. Lara and Córdoba left.

I was already upset about some of the men that Simón had around him: Monteagudo, Lara, Córdoba, and a few others. I did not think they were good for him. When I overheard this conversation, it did not help my state of mind concerning one other man in particular: Santander.

Being able to view all of Simón's correspondence, I became impressed with one fact about the government of Gran Colombia. While Bolívar was busy in Quito, he had left Bogotá in the hands of a dangerous man.

I did not like Francisco de Paula Santander from the first time I saw his picture on a patriotic poster. His features were angular, almost handsome except for a look of perversion and cruelty which touched every detail in his aspect: the hair, slick and oily, combed forward on the sides; the eyes, deep and dark, seemed to carry the weight of a great deal of sin; the mouth was small and tight; two small, thin, perfect, black triangles, which were his mustache, covered his upper lip. He appeared to be cold, aloof, and false. Bolívar, on occasion, would vent his frustration with him. "A man of laws," he said sarcastically upon being told of some minor regulation that his vice president had brought up to keep Bolívar from carrying forward with some worthy goal.

When I asked about Santander, during one of our midnight talks, he told me something that proved my suspicions about him. From the few things Bolívar said, I could tell he was depraved and loved the sight of blood letting. This was confirmed when Bolívar said, "He makes it a special point to view public executions. I wonder about him sometimes." Then he changed the subject without seeming to mind that the man was obviously cruel.

Having my intuition about Santander validated, and seeing him, as a "friend" and "advisor," try to stop Bolívar with one excuse after another, I knew I hated him. When news of Bolívar's affair with me got back to Bogotá, Santander began asking about me in his letters. Then, my hatred grew to passion.

I tried to advise Bolívar against trusting this man, but I never really had time to make my thoughts fully known. Those were busy days. Perhaps I should have tried harder, even though I know I would not have been successful. Santander was a "hero" of the revolution and he would become a permanent political figure in the affairs of Gran Colombia.

As the daily news from Lima came in, we all worried about the future. San Martín had earlier asked Bolívar to help, but he had left the country by this time. The Peruvians, on their own, would not ask for assistance. The situation grew worse, until finally, a series of events that began a few months earlier gave us to believe the situation would improve.

Earlier, at the end of 1822, when San Martín had left Lima to return to Mendoza, the Peruvian congress had installed a junta led by General La Mar. The junta was unpopular and ineffective. They could do nothing to stop the general confusion that continued to grow in Perú.

At that time, I knew La Mar was a Peruvian patriot. However, Bolívar did not like the man. He called him a "*godo*," the derogatory name for the Spanish. Though I felt La Mar was loyal, I had never been impressed with the man's intelligence. My view of him turned out to be correct. It was La Mar who was most responsible for neglecting help from Bolívar, believing his own glory would be diminished by Bolívar's presence.

While we worried in Quito, La Mar blundered along. Then, the Royalists attacked and defeated the patriot troops at Moquegua. This setback demoralized Lima. Things looked their worst until we heard of something that made me breathe easier. The junta was asked to resign. My friend Riva Agüero was then installed as President of the Republic, by a vote of the Peruvian congress.

Simón did not know what to make of this turn of events, and he could not gain any information from his spies that would allow him to predict what might occur next. I was able to help him. "Riva Agüero is no fool like La Mar," I told him. "Now that he is running things, matters in Lima will become more sensible."

"I hope you are right, Manuelita," Simón said, as he looked at the courier's messages again."

"Riva Agüero will communicate with you soon," I assured him.

As I predicted, a day or so later, Bolívar received a letter from my friend. He was entirely in control of Perú's affairs, and his letter formally requested assistance from "the Liberator of the North."

However, we discovered from his letter that the situation with the Royalists was worse than we had heard. Only 4,000 soldiers were available to defend Lima whereas the Royalist general, Canterac, a French adventurer, had over 8,000 men at his disposal.

Anybody who read the letter could see that Lima would soon be lost. With Lima gone, the entire continent would again become a place for human blood to flow.

Bolívar dictated a letter to Riva Agüero, saying that he would send 3,000 men immediately. While I was finishing up that letter, I overheard him making arrangements with José Palacios and his staff for his own departure from Quito.

When I was done, I asked him, "Are you leaving?"

"Yes, Manuelita, I am going to Guayaquil tomorrow to supervise the expedition's departure myself."

"I can't be ready by tomorrow," I said, as I straightened up his writing desk. He stopped and looked at me. I said, "Perhaps I can join you in a week or two."

He did not speak.

I looked at him and understood. He did not intend to take me. When I understood his intentions, I was infuriated. It reminded me of the rejection I had known all my life. Manuela, the bastard, would not be included.

He still had not spoken, and I said, "I suppose I'll be too much trouble." I did not bother to keep the vitriol out of my voice.

"Manuelita—"

"I suppose you'll tell me it's too dangerous. Perhaps you'll say I'll be of no value." I lifted a pile of papers and flung them back to the desk, causing them to scatter on the floor. "Perhaps you'll tell me the truth and come right out and say you want to get back to a pretty Señorita in Guayaquil."

"Manuela, calm down. I do not know that I will still be in Guayaquil next week, or the week after. Who can tell what the war will demand of me? Look at what has happened already. I've had to return to Pasto and I may have to return again."

"Admit it. You don't want me."

"That's not true. But I have work to do. There are hundreds of details to see to everyday—"

"I know," I said, pointing to his desk.

"—and I cannot see to logistics, plan a campaign, manage Colombia and, along with everything else, make sure that I have a woman with me."

"A woman!? That's all I am to you, isn't it? Merely a woman that a soldier has picked up on his travels? Someone to relieve the tensions—"

"Manuela! That's not what I meant. I am a soldier, it is true. I need soldiers about me to fight battles, that is all. Besides the danger, I would be distracted."

"I'm sure the work I'm doing today," I motioned to a stack of letters as tall as my quill standing in the inkwell, "is a great distraction."

He looked out the window and said, halfheartedly, "It is simply too dangerous."

I was so angry, I barely knew what I was saying. "I have lived with danger throughout my life. I fear not the danger, and I abhor your desire to protect me from a war that I have fought almost as long as you." I stormed out of the office and went home.

I did not see him the next day, but I received a note, folded only once, from one of his messengers, about the same time he was leaving the city. It said: "I will miss you, Manuelita. My thoughts will be with you. I regret that the war has caused us to part."

I raged for an hour over that note. What I deemed his insincerity infuriated me. Did he think that I would accept the war as an excuse, when I had argued to be with him despite the danger? But it was the finality that grieved me. He was saying good-bye. And it was for good.

I could hardly believe it. I knew, above all things, that Bolívar and I were meant to be together. Yet all the chafing at my control over him during his convalescence, which I had deemed only peevish frustration at his immobility, was in fact resentment—coupled with resentment of my authority by some of his officers. The man did not know who his friends were.

I wanted very much not to have loved him then. I brooded for days and nothing could make me happy. Not even Jonotás's antics, performed especially to rouse me from my mood, were able to improve my outlook. I could not think of a future without him.

I tried to keep abreast of developments in Guayaquil. That was a mistake, because I would rather not have found out what I learned next. Bolívar had arrived safely in Guayaquil and was staying at the Guaraycoa Hacienda. It was a Guaraycoa daughter whom I had heard had been one of Bolívar's dalliances when he was in Guayaquil to meet with San Martín.

It was as though I were a child again, when every person I loved had left me. For days I could not focus on what it was I should do.

People around me noticed my state, and some assumed that I was no longer in the favor, or perhaps even in the disfavor, of the Liberator. I received no invitations to the salons of the city, and there were fewer and fewer people who gave me the kind of respect to which I had become accustomed.

It was Jonotás who healed me. I had not seen her at night for some time. She had found a lover, a servant in one of the wealthier households, and been spending her nights with him for weeks. Natán had to listen to my irritation at her. "I swear I will get rid of her if she does not take on some of her duties around here."

One night, when I was feeling particularly sorry for myself, Jonotás left earlier than usual. I was under the impression that she was tired of my moping around. Natán attended me as I prepared for bed.

"Natán, would you see if Cook has some chocolate?" I asked when she finished braiding my hair.

"I don't know if you should be drinkin' chocolate so late." She looked at me and I'm sure I looked as unhappy as I felt. "I'm gettin' some, Manuelita, but only 'cause I hope you cheer up."

I smiled and she went downstairs to the kitchen. While I turned back the bed covers, the door opened.

"That was quick!" I turned around to find Jonotás standing in the doorway. She closed the door and came over and sat on the bed where I was about to lie down and crossed her legs.

Before I could ask her to move, she said, "I don't like to see you the way you are." I was still forming a reply when she said, "You told me a story, when we rode into Quito, about a nun who threatened to jump from a belfry rather than be dominated by men."

Doña Luisa's words came back to me: *Your need for love is not good for you. It will cause you to make decisions that you will eventually regret, though you may not know it is your need that you are acting on.*

Jonotás reclined in a leisurely fashion and said, "Letting a man make you cry, just because he leaves, seems like powerful domination to me."

I knew she was right. I had determined to win when I heard that story, but what did I really want now? Bolívar was my goal.

I sat next to her and said, halfheartedly, "You're right."

She sat up and took my hand. "It seems to me that you should be looking for your will."

"You are right again," I whispered.

Jonotás had not heard me. "What, my sweet?"

I felt foolish. It did not matter that I could not find the will or Father Ramón. It did not even matter if I never found it. I should be looking for it. It was a promise I had made to my mother. I had determined to have my inheritance long before I met Bolívar. It was mine, and had nothing to do with him or any other man. As long as there was still some chance that I might have my inheritance, I should carry on. Only after being stopped completely should I think again about Simón, since he was not with me.

Jonotás said again, "What did you say?"

I pulled her to me and hugged her so tight she giggled. I kissed her cheek and said, "I said, you are right. What would I ever do without you?"

"Nothin', Ma'am," she said in mock subservience.

"It is just that I miss him."

"Yes, Manuelita, but I know 'bout love, and you will see him again. I know it."

Natán came in just then and said, "What're you two talkin' about?"

"'Bout men," said Jonotás, "what else do women talk about."

I felt better the next morning than I had in days. I felt as if I could determine my future again. We began to make more inquiries into Father Ramón's whereabouts that morning.

I threw myself into my search for the missing will. I did not realize how much damage I had done to my standing by letting my grief—and thus my loss of Bolívar—show. Where I might have expected instant cooperation at monasteries or civic offices, I was given only scant courtesy. Where, at one time, I might have been given access to public documents or the city's archives as a favor, I had to pay bribes to accomplish the same thing.

I found one clerk in the city offices who was quite willing to help; in fact, he even suggested a review of all public records relating to the Aispurus. He would gladly provide me copies, for a fee. I accepted his offer, despite my meager funds. "This had better produce that will," I told my companions as we left the building.

Several days after renewing my search, a regrettable event occurred which nonetheless helped me to gain some prestige again. Not only that, it gave me a direction in my search. The event was a riot.

General Sucre had been recruiting soldiers in the plaza for the expedition to Perú when the violence erupted. Throughout the land, there were few men left who were not already giving their lives as soldiers and most of everything else they had. Sucre had conscripted a few men for the Bogotá battalion that day, but it was more than the people could bear. They started shouting "Who will liberate us from the liberators?"

Jonotás, Natán, and I were on our way to Cotopaxi, where we had learned Father Ramón had ministered to the Indians living on the western slope. The disturbance had just started as we rode down the street toward the square. We saw a crowd ahead, but we stopped our horses as a frail old man walked in front of us. I could tell something was going on and was eager to move ahead, but we had to wait for the man to pass.

When we entered the square, we saw General Sucre mounted and standing in front of the "palace" where Bolívar's apartments had been. He had a few men, mounted next to him, and he was shouting to be heard over a crowd that was quickly growing as citizens rushed into the square from the opposite side. "Citizens of Quito, you must withdraw . . ."

We had come from the direction of the back of the palace and so were somewhat behind the general. The crowd grew as we stood there, and they surged toward the soldiers, shouting and shaking their fists. The women in the crowd were shouting insults, too, keeping pace with the men.

It appeared that the rush of people would come around the general's flank, toward the side where we were standing. I understood what was about to happen and how important it was for Sucre not to lose control of the crowd. If they were to get behind him, he would be surrounded, perhaps losing more than control.

I caused my mare to move sideways towards the rush of angry men and women, so that she blocked most of the street. I might have looked like another soldier, in my green, military-style riding habit. I stopped the advance around the general's flank. Jonotás and Natán moved up behind me, on either side, so that they also helped prevent further advance.

General Sucre took over for me, ordering some of his men to move in front of me. Jonotás, Natán and I backed off and prepared to leave by the way we came. In the confusion, a small group surged around us. The press of people created confusion, and the old man who had been watching from behind us was pushed to the ground and trampled by them.

I pointed the man out to Jonotás and Natán. He was trying to get up, after the crowd came around, but was obviously injured. "He needs help," I shouted over the ever increasing noise.

My companions dismounted. One of them held the reins, while the other helped the old man to stand. I kept the side of my horse against the raging crowd.

With Jonotás and Natán on each side of the man, they walked him back down the street. I dismounted, took the horse's reins from Natán, and followed,. We took the man back to the Larrea mansion, leaving the square only minutes before the real violence started.

When the dust had settled in Quito that day, fifteen people had been killed. The war had to be fought, but it was natural that most people would see only the effects on their own families and fortunes. After nearly fifteen years of war, the continent was tired. Though I raged at Simón for his neglect of me, I worried for him. He must transport his soldiers to Lima soon. The revolution could not continue much longer.

When we brought the old man through the door of the Larrea mansion, he was wheezing and coughing and I feared he would not survive. Doña Larrea came down, saw him, and instantly ordered her servants to take him to an empty room in the house that had a comfortable bed. Don Larrea had heard about the trouble and was off to the Plaza Mayor, but she sent a servant to find him and tell him to bring a doctor. Doña Larrea was quite adept at the healing arts. By the time the doctor had arrived, the patient was already resting comfortably. He had survived a broken rib and a broken arm. He would be all right.

Two days later, Natán informed me that the man wished to see me. I was quite busy writing some letters to public officials and did not want to be bothered just then. "Why?" I asked her, not looking up.

"He's wantin' to thank you for helping him."

"That is not necessary."

"I know, Manuelita, but he's wantin' to express his gratitude."

I shrugged, put down my pen, rubbed my tired eyes, and went to the old man's room. He looked much better than when I had seen him last. There was color in his cheeks and a smile on his lips. He was plastering down his thin, almost non-existent, white hair with water when I entered the room.

"Oh, Señora," he said as he wiped his wet hand on the covers, "I am glad you have come. I wish to thank you for helping me." He handed me the bowl of water and said, "Would you mind?" He indicated the little table next to the bed.

I took the bowl and set it down, saying, "That is quite all right, Señor. I could not leave you there."

"You are most kind."

"Not at all," I said, tiring of the discussion.

"Is there nothing I could do for you, to repay you?"

I almost laughed at him. I looked at his almost toothless smile, the splint on his arm, and his aged hands. He seemed so frail, I found his offer funny. Perfunctorily, I said, "That is not necessary. I hope you will have recovered soon."

"The doctor said my arm would be all right in six weeks or so, but I think I could leave my bed tomorrow." He smiled at me. "I am reluctant to do so, however. The food is so good."

We laughed and I said, "Well, I am sure Doña Larrea will not begrudge you a few more days. In the meantime, I hope you are well." I started to leave the room, but when I was at the door, I had an idea.

The old man said, "Thank you again, Señora."

I went back over to his bed and said, "Perhaps there is something you *might* be able do for me."

"I would be most gratified if I could provide some service."

"Did you ever know a Father Ramón?"

I expected to get the same kind of answer I always had, and was already on my toes to turn and go while saying a "thank you, anyway."

Instead, I heard, "Which one?"

Before I could close my mouth from the shock of having someone answer affirmatively, let alone the fact that there was more than one, the priest said, "Or rather, I should say, 'yes.' I know them both, but which one are you inquiring about, the elder or the younger?"

"The younger . . . uhm . . . I think."

"Oh, Señora, I am sorry, he died five years ago—"

"Wait a minute, Señor, let us make sure we are talking about the same man. Who is the elder?"

His face looked perplexed and a little sad, and he said, "He is the one people call 'crazy'—the one who lost his eye in the great earthquake."

I could not believe my ears. I plopped down in a chair sitting by the bed, my legs seeming to have given out. The old man went on. "Now, of course, he is gone."

"Gone?"

"Yes. Well, no one has seen him since the earthquake last June. I do not know what happened to him. Is that the one you were speaking of, or were you speaking of his son?" If I had not already been sitting down? I think I might have fainted. Instead, I started laughing.

"There were only two in Quito, you are sure?" I said through my giggling.

"Only two that I know of. Why are you laughing, Señora?"

"It is only that I did not know there were two men by the same name, and I have been looking for the younger for many months. He is the older man's son, you say?"

The man answered affirmatively, but still I pressed him. I described the Father Ramón I was looking for and all I knew of him, and there was no question.

When I asked about their relationship, he told me, "The young man was born in 1783." This would have made him the same age as Bolívar. "He was born, illegitimate, of a young Indian maiden. She had been seduced by the elder priest, who was a friend of mine at the time. He was her confessor, and I am sorry to say, he took advantage of her.

"When I found out about it, I upbraided my friend, but his guilt was such that he could not face his own responsibility in the affair. Instead, he claimed that she had seduced him, having been influenced by the "evil one."

"I would have none of his excuses nor would his superiors. He was given penance, but he acted as though he had been treated unjustly. I lost him as a friend. He never had a close relationship with anybody after that.

"Then, when the earthquake of 1797 took his eye, he believed he had been anointed as God's special emissary on earth. 'If your eye be single,' he kept repeating. I know he was in a great deal of pain as his wound became infected, and ever afterward, he acted crazy."

I was totally mesmerized by the old man's story. It explained so many things about the crazy priest and the Father Ramón I knew. "Did he ever acknowledge his son?"

"Yes, barely. The young man's mother died when he was about seven and the elder put him in a monastery. There, he grew and studied hard for the priesthood in an effort to please his father, which he never did. Not only did he fail at gaining his father's admiration, he was totally unsuited to the calling.

"Then, about six or seven years after the great earthquake, a young woman died whom he had befriended and whom he had tried to help. After her death, he seemed to have lost his faith. He left the priesthood and went to Cartagena. He came back a few years later and was living a life as devout as any priest, trying to help the Indians around Quito; but he was no longer of the cloth."

My voice was choked up, but I managed to ask, "What became of him, Señor?"

"He died about five years ago, I'm sorry to say. He was a good man. He had been sick for about a year, and it was at my house that he expired. The poor man was penniless."

I sat there in stunned silence. I could hardly believe what I had been told, even though it did make certain things I had observed about both father and son make sense. At last, I said, "Señor, I believe the young woman you spoke about, who died, was my mother."

He looked at me, first in surprise and then in sympathy, and said, "Oh, I am sorry, Señora."

My throat constricted as my feelings for my mother overcame me. I controlled myself and went on. "She gave her will to young Father Ramón and I am looking for it. Do you know anything about where it would be?"

The old man thought awhile and said, "He did not have anything like that with him when he died, but he left many of the few possessions he had with his father when he became ill. If it still exists, it is his father who has it."

I put my hand on the old man's and said, "Señor, I am so very grateful for all you have told me." We said our good-byes and I left.

I felt somewhat defeated, and yet, at the same time, I felt a certain sense of renewed hope. If the crazy priest had the will, I need only find him. True, once I found him, I did not know how I would obtain the will, or even if he had it, but my first job was to find him. At least he had been seen in the last year.

There was another aspect to this situation that eased my mind. I realized I had been pushing so hard for something, so long that I had become obsessed by it. As I left the old man, I actually believed, for the first time, that the will was lost. I believed I would not be able to go any further. I would try, but I did not believe in the quest anymore. My future had been, in a certain way, released.

Chapter 8

In the following days, I made further inquiries, only this time I asked about the "crazy priest." Unlike when I asked about young Father Ramón, people understood whom I was talking about and I received more answers. It seemed that my presence in the group of soldiers led by General Sucre during the riot had made people believe that I was still close to Bolívar. However, I did not make any real progress in finding the old priest.

In the meantime, the news from Guayaquil was worse than ever. The expedition was very difficult for Simón to put together. The search for recruits and money was arduous, and I heard that Bolívar had not received a single letter from Bogotá in the last few months. He had written to his vice president, Santander, asking for an Enabling Act from Congress to allow him to leave Gran Colombia and fight on foreign soil. It did not come, and when June arrived, there was still no word from Bogotá.

I knew from José María's letters that Bolívar was extraordinarily frustrated. He had come to believe he should be in Perú. His destiny seemed to be crying out to him, and everything was telling him he must depart. Still, the Enabling Act did not come. He sent Sucre to Lima, as his plenipotentiary, but it was he who needed to go. If Santander had done his duty, and seen that the Enabling Act was passed by congress, the progress of war might have been different.

The day before Sucre arrived in Perú, a catastrophe occurred. On June 16, Riva Agüero inadvertently let the Royalists take Lima. The entire government had to retreat to Callao, and Canterac and his men began punishing the rest of the city's inhabitants.

Sucre arrived on the June 17. With the men he brought he was able to hold Callao, but he was entirely hemmed in. He insisted on complete control of the military operations, and soon he and Riva Agüero were quarreling.

Though Sucre was a great warrior, it was Bolívar who had the gift of statesmanship. Riva Agüero also wanted complete control, and a bad situation was made very much worse by his stubbornness. In light of Sucre's reputation and his abilities, Riva Agüero ended up making himself look foolish by not lending his full cooperation to the victor of Pichincha. Sucre was going to do what he knew was militarily correct, whether Riva Agüero wished to go along or not, and my old friend would have been wise to have supported General Sucre in every way. Riva Agüero's actions later, in reaction to this situation, would prolong the war. In the meantime, Simón was stuck in Gran Colombia, knowing nothing of these events as they transpired.

He had other problems. The *pastusos* revolted once again. General Flores, head of the garrison in Pasto, lost control and was completely routed. Bolívar had to leave Guayaquil to put down the revolt.

When he arrived in Pasto, he had to fight hard, but he retook the city. He imprisoned important members of every family, except known patriots, and sent them down to Guayaquil. Pasto never quite submitted to patriot rule, but that was the last time Bolívar had to intervene there personally.

I was not in Quito when Simón rode through on his way to Pasto. While he was away, I had continued to search for the crazy priest and I had met a member of the clergy who knew the old zealot Ramón intimately. Upon questioning him, he told me that Father Ramón, the elder, was in Ibarra. By this time, I had chased down so many blind avenues, searching for the mad cleric, who seemed to have vanished, that I almost did not go. However, I would try this last clue. I would try everything. I rode up there the next day with Jonotás and Natán.

It was not an easy ride, and once in Ibarra, our lodgings were not very comfortable. As we were inquiring about the elder Father Ramón in the *locutorio* of a monastery, Bolívar and his soldiers rode through the streets in full gallop. Men ran up the side streets shouting, "The Liberator! The Liberator! He rides to Pasto." We rushed down to the main street, but not until all that was left was the dust raised by many hundreds of hooves.

Having Simón so close gave me an unexplainable thrill. Yes, he had treated me badly. Yes, I had every reason to be angry with him, but I knew that if we saw each other again, he would want me. I was truly sorry I had missed him. If I had seen him, there would have been a quarrel, as I was still upset with his neglect of me. Still, I longed for him.

We found that the crazy priest had been in Ibarra, but we could learn no more. Some said he had gone to Bogotá, some said to Cartagena, and some said he was still in the environs of Ibarra. I decided I had reached the end of my search. The will was gone. By this time, I had given it up as a lost cause. I was anxious to return to Quito so that I would be where Bolívar could find me on his return to the coast.

I was curious to see if Bolívar had inquired of me when he rode through on his way to Pasto. Though we arrived late at the Larrea mansion, saddle sore and tired, I rushed upstairs. He had indeed sent a note, that lay on my bed. He had been in the city only about two hours, but he took the time to write to me:

Manuelita

I cannot see you now, but I will be in Quito for one day upon my return. I would very much like to see you then. I'm sorry, but I do not know when that will be—when the fighting in Pasto is done.

Love
Simón

I was delighted. I was still angry enough with him to know that we would fight, but I still wanted to see him. If he wanted me he would have to endure my complaints of his neglect for me. However, he escaped my wrath because fate played a trick on me.

About a two weeks later, I received another letter. This one was from Spain, by way of Lima, informing me that my father had died.

To Manuela Sáenz de Thorne:

I regret to inform you that during the night of December 27, 1822, your father woke with chest pains. He had not been well and had complained of pains in his chest for many months.

Upon waking, he asked his servants for a pen and paper. Realizing that his time was short, he made a last will.

Two days later, he departed this life.

In his will, which he left to my care to execute, he was quite generous with his progeny. He left them all his possessions and wealth. To you he left an equal share with his other four children.

However, upon commencing to execute this will, many unknown business debts were discovered. After paying these arrears, it was discovered that your father died nearly penniless. About fifty pesos per child was all that was left. A copy of his accounts is enclosed, along with a letter of credit for fifty pesos.

I was a very close friend of your father, and I send my sincere condolences.

May God keep you many years,
Roberto Moreno

Upon reading the letter that had traveled so far, I walked to my room, closed the shutters on the windows, sat in the gloom, and cried. I stayed in my room for a full day, grieving. I did not want to see anyone.

I loved my father, despite our differences and the fact that I had never been able to spend much time with him. I was sorry he was gone, and I felt the need to be alone. I also felt bad for José María. My father had been good to me, and though I only spent two years with him, he had at last remembered me on my birthday.

As I sat alone in the dark, I realized that I very much wanted to see Bolívar. I saw how short was life, and despite my anger at him, I loved him. Having both my parents gone made me think about my own existence. I had lived a productive life, and I had accomplished much. What if I had found my mother's will? What if I had my inheritance? What would I do?

There was only one answer. I must fight the last of the revolution with Bolívar. It did not matter whether he chose to neglect me or not. I should be fighting the war until it was done. If I were with him, close to him, we would find time to share our love. I should fight the war in whatever way I could. I determined that day that I would see Bolívar when he rode back through Quito, and I would not be angry with him.

The next morning, I was informed that José Palacios had come for me the night before, but he had been turned away by one of Don Larrea's servants because I was "in mourning." Bolívar had returned to Quito and he had tried to see me. When I went to the palace, I found that he had already left early for Guayaquil. However, he did leave me a note expressing his sorrow at my loss.

The fates were cruel. What little time we had to spend together had been taken from us. I determined then, that I must return to Perú. There is where the next battles would be fought. There is where I must be. I began making serious plans to follow him to Guayaquil, and later, when he sailed on to Lima, I would be with him.

As I tried to arrange my affairs in Quito, the news we heard from Lima seemed worse every day. Riva Agüero, still jealous of Sucre's power, had taken his cabinet and retired to Trujillo. He wanted Bolívar's army to be in Perú, but he wanted them under his own control. Since he could not have that, he abandoned Sucre in Lima.

Then we heard, on the 17th of July, that Canterac left Lima. His position in the city was untenable and not of any military significance. However, when he left, he took a great deal of silver. This angered the *criollos* and they blamed Riva Agüero for having let the Royalist general in the city to begin with.

I also heard from José María, who sent me a note of commiseration from Guayaquil. His notification had arrived about the same time as mine had, and he too was feeling the loss of our father. He did not have the luxury of spending any time grieving, however, as had I. He was quite busy.

He mentioned that Simón was becoming angrier by the day. Santander had not yet sent the Enabling Act allowing Bolívar to fight in Perú. Bolívar was writing to Bogotá every day demanding that Santander send the Enabling Act, but it did not come. I knew Simón had to go to Perú. He could delay no longer. I cursed Santander for what I sensed was his determination to stop Bolívar's glory. He might just lose all of South America back to the Royalists in the bargain.

When I heard from José María, I chaffed at my inability to join Simón in Guayaquil. I was having trouble leaving because my funds were so low. I had spent money on everything from living expenses to bribes and I did not think I would be able to afford to pay for passage to Lima. I certainly did not want to arrive in Guayaquil with insufficient money, so that I would be stuck there.

On August 7, Bolívar prepared to board a ship, the *Chimborazo*, and depart for Perú without the necessary blessing from the Colombian Congress. He had to go. He wanted to do things legally, but Santander had made it impossible. However, at the very moment that he stepped off the Malecón onto the ship, a courier from Bogotá rode up on a mud-splattered mule. The Act had come, literally, at the very last second.

By September of 1823, Bolívar was in Lima, and he was the idol of the city, just as he had been when he entered Quito. The mayor had welcomed him in an official ceremony, and, in my misery, I could imagine him in that South American "Paris," a lady on each arm. He would be the demi-god again, and he would have no trouble finding a partner to fill his nights. After all, I was in Quito, in my native country, far away, where he might never see me again.

Despite the glory in which he found himself, he also found a country in ruins— in the middle of a political and military mess. Four distinct republican armies were in Perú: Peruvian, Chilean, Argentinean, and Colombian. All had different commanders. Each had different loyalties that they had brought from their home countries. In addition to the military confusion, there were two rival presidents. One hundred leagues to the north, in Trujillo, Riva Agüero had dissolved the Congress and instituted a new Senate. The ousted lawmakers had returned and elected the Marqués de Torre Tagle president in Lima and they immediately declared Riva Agüero an outlaw. All this time, my old friend continued to issue decrees from Trujillo against the newly elected Congress. The Peruvian lawmakers in Lima asked Bolívar to mediate the dispute and granted him the power to do so.

Simón had a great deal of work to do, and he moved into the old viceroy's summer home in Magdalena. He also took over a house next door to keep the guards. There were daily war councils, and nightly parties in the salons of Lima, or in the Magdalena retreat. "After all, he has to get to know the people of Lima," I said to Jonotás, sarcastically, when she asked me about one of José María's letters.

"Sound's like he's gettin' damn familiar," she said in her comic attitude.

I chuckled at her, but I could imagine him there, so close to where I used to live. I wanted to be there. I worried about returning to my husband's city because I did not know where James was and what would happen when we met. Still, I was determined to go.

However, I was trapped in Quito. My financial situation grew worse every day. I almost asked Don Larrea for a loan, but without a way to pay it back, I did not want to borrow from him. Besides, he had been too generous with me already. I could not think of any honorable means to obtain the money I needed. Then, my bribes paid off.

One evening, when I felt particularly low, the clerk appeared at the Larrea's door, the one who was to make copies of city records for me. "I have come to bring Manuela Thorne some papers," he told Jorge.

When I came outside, he held a large sheaf of documents, and he said, "I have made copies of all of the Aispuru's transactions. I believe I understand your problem, and I do not necessarily offer any encouragement from what I found. However, I have marked those copies wherein I found something that you might find of interest."

"Thank you, Señor," I said, as I tried to take the papers.

He turned a little away, so that I could not reach them, and said, "I really do think you might find certain items in here quite interesting."

I was annoyed, but fetched him a few pesos and took the sheaf from him.

Jonotás and Natán could not help me, because they could not read very well—they could recognize my name and a few words, but that was all. So I had to go through the whole stack of papers myself. Not knowing where to start, I dropped them on the floor and picked them up at random.

Nothing was very interesting until I came to one piece of paper with double underlines under certain words, dutifully marked by the clerk. I find such documents so confusing that I had to ponder it a long time.

It appeared to be a copy of a deed from Carlos Aispuru to Joaquina Aispuru in 1798. The land in question seemed to be quite tiny—only slightly larger than the burned out hut that sat on it—but despite its meager size, it appeared that the land on which I had been raised belonged to me.

Because I am so unable to make sense of legal documents, I took it to Juan Larrea, who said, "An old document, but it unquestionably gives you title to this tiny bit of land."

Happiness flooded in and made me feel lightheaded. Not only could I take something away from Carlos, but perhaps I could sell it. "Would you act as my agent and sell this to someone, please?" I asked my old friend.

Don Larrea smiled at me and said, "I can sell it for you. In fact, I can sell it quite quickly, but you would make more money if you were not so eager."

"Sell it quickly." I said. "I have to leave, and I cannot stay to manage it."

Within ten days, Juan Larrea brought me over a hundred pesos. He said, "I was told that when Carlos Aispuru was informed of the sale, he was apoplectic." We laughed.

I went directly to my room, found Jonotás and Natán, and said, "Let's pack. We're going to Lima."

Chapter 9

Three weeks later, Jonotás, Natán and I rode into Guayaquil. The condition of the city had changed a little since I had seen it last. The long lines of Royalists in chains were gone, and the city looked well worn from months of embarking patriot soldiers and supplies for Perú. The streets were busier than usual: men were loading timber and other products onto trade vessels; patriot soldiers were everywhere embarking or disembarking from ships bound for Perú or Panamá; and there was another breed of person to be found—opportunists.

Every kind of merchant with something to sell was in every place something could be sold. One could buy all manner of goods: *chicha* sold by industrious Indians, sexual favors sold by their daughters, sausages wrapped in plantain leaves cooked by large women over braziers on the street, horse's halters and other equipment that had obviously been stolen, milk ladled out of barrels strapped on mules, flowers carried by pretty *cholas*, patriotic songs printed on presses in the capital, or letters "home" drafted by scriveners sitting in the street. It was worse chaos than in Panamá in 1815. I learned later that the confusion had diminished some since the Liberator had departed, but there was still plenty of activity throughout the city.

We made our way down the Malecón first, to see if we could arrange passage to Lima immediately. I hoped to spend no more than a day or two in Guayaquil. However, it appeared that the chance of finding a place on one of the many ships on the river was not good. All available vessels going to Perú were either already on their way or full or needed for purposes other than transporting civilian passengers. I might have to stay in Guayaquil for weeks.

I did not exactly know what to do about lodging, so I sought out Rosita's relatives. Already hot and tired from our ride across the plain that morning, we made many trips back and forth across the city weaving in amongst the crowds following one man's directions after another. We were exhausted when we reached a rather nice house, by Guayaquil's standards, some distance from the river. When I knocked, I received a big surprise. Rosita opened the door.

"Manuela! Oh Manuela, you're here," she said as she embraced me and we giggled like young girls.

She invited me in, and we sat down in the parlor to talk. She looked worn and troubled, but we had a wonderful reunion. We talked long into the night about everything that had happened since I saw her last. She had recently arrived, having left Lima to escape the political and social confusion. I felt so sorry for her. She had been a devoted revolutionary since I had known her. Now the man she loved had returned to his native country and was said to be going on to Europe. Her inheritance was almost gone, like everything else in South America, because of the war.

Her tales of the war and its effects on Lima were frightening. Daily, La Serna's army grew in numbers, power and wealth. At the same time, the revolutionary government in Lima went from one catastrophe to another. As we talked, I could see that the revolution, far from being almost over as I had thought a year before, was yet to be decided. South American soil would inevitably be stained with more of her people's blood. The mines of Potosí, controlled by the Royalists, gave La Serna enough money to bring any number of men and supplies from Europe. All he needed was time to acquire his army. Everything that had been won so far would eventually be lost.

I was chilled at the thought of Bolívar confronted by such an overwhelming task. Any desire I may have had for peace was obviously a foolish fantasy. Simón and all his troops would soon be in mortal danger. I had to get to Lima, and soon. Sometime in the next year, decisive battles and great struggles for freedom would be fought. I worried that I had wasted my time in Quito. I reproached myself for not following Simón earlier.

"Will you ever return to Lima?" I asked Rosita while she replaced a candle that had burned out.

"No. Never. I feel betrayed and do not have the resources to continue."

"I understand, Rosita."

"I'm going to Europe. I've always wanted to see Paris, and I know that one day, José will be there. I want to see him . . . even though he has returned to his wife . . . I am a fool." She stopped. Tears came to her eyes and she turned away. I could tell she was fighting the sobbing that was overtaking her. I stood and pulled her to me and we rocked back and forth while she cried.

I stayed with her family that night, and in the morning I rode down to the stables to find El Árabe.

"Ah, wait, I know you," said the Arab. "How could I forget one so beautiful as you? You are the woman from Lima, no?"

"Yes, Señor."

"Good, yes. You have returned. Next time, you must not wait a whole year to take up my invitation to have food with me. We will have some now." He gestured to a servant.

I smiled at him. "Thank you, no, Señor. I have only come to see if you would buy back my horses."

He looked disappointed and said, reproachfully, "You are not returning to Lima?"

"Yes I am, Señor."

"It is not safe there."

"I have to go."

"Good, yes. I will give you a good price. I like you."

Thus I sold my horses and mules, which gave me additional resources. I put my arms around Espectra Negra's neck and hugged her tight. I would miss her. I had done so many things on her back, not the least of which was riding triumphantly into Quito after being away for seven years, or kissing Simón for the first time. I said good-bye to El Árabe after declining one more time to have a meal with him. Then Jonotás, Natán and I walked through the city to try again to book passage to Perú.

This second day, prospects looked bleaker, if that is possible, than the day before. I had left Quito and my search for my mother's will because I believed my life could be put to better use than tracking down a document that may have long since been destroyed, and here I was, wasting away in a dirty port town.

Though I enjoyed being with Rosita, I was quite frustrated at being stopped in Guayaquil, and I continued thus for several more days, until I chanced to meet Carlson. I had avoided him, because my last encounter with him had been so unpleasant, but when I saw him on the street I decided to greet him.

We stood and looked at each other for a minute before either of us moved. Finally, he walked up to me, avoiding the people rushing through the street and said, "Good morning, Señorita—"

"Señora," I corrected him.

His fair skin blushed through his beard, he dropped his eyes a little and he said, "Señora. How you are?"

"I am well, Señor."

"You caused me a great deal of embarrassment. Señor Aispuru has much angry at me for giving his mules at you. He still suggests I pay for them."

"He knows he cannot make you." Juan Larrea had examined the documents creating the sale and had told me that they had legally belonged to my uncle. Carlson had only been doing him a favor by finding someone to deliver them. I explained this to him.

"That's what I tell him but he no understand all."

"He 'understand all,'" I said, mocking his accent. "He merely wishes to make somebody else pay."

"Yes. Yes. So I tell him, but—"

"I was very angry with you when you sent that messenger." I said, changing the subject that seemed as though it might not end. "You embarrassed me and might have caused me much trouble. My husband—"

Just then, a loud argument began between a man selling *chicha* from barrels loaded on either side of a mule and an inebriated soldier. Carlson took my arm and moved us farther off. He said, "Please, come to my apartments this night. We talk. You can eat. Where you are staying?"

"No, thank you, Señor," I said emphatically. "Your apartment is not safe for me. I very nearly got into a great deal of trouble the last time I was there."

"I promise you. You are safe. I behave badly last time, I apologize. You come."

"Your feelings for me have changed?"

Again he blushed. "No, Señorita—Señora—I love you, but, as you say, you are married." I did not know if I could trust him. While I considered his invitation, he said, "I will have a friend come to dinner as well—you be safe."

That seemed all right, and I agreed to go. After we settled when I should arrive, he walked away; and Jonotás, Natán and I continued back to Rosita's house.

That evening, I arrived at Carlson's door. I did not want to go alone, despite his assurances, so I took Rosita. I might have taken Jonotás and Natán, but they would have been bored, and Jonotás had met a young English sailor with whom she wished to spend the evening.

As it turned out, I need not have been so cautious. Carlson had indeed brought a friend, an Irish sea captain, who was there when we arrived. It was obvious that he had been there a while and had already consumed a glass or two of drink.

"I hope you do not mind, but I brought a friend of mine. Señor Carlson, this is Rosita Campusano."

"I no mind." To Rosita, he said, "Welcome, most pretty one." Then he said, "Please meet Captain Simpson. Captain, this Manuela Sáenz de Thorne and her friend, Rosita Campusano.

With typical Irish enthusiasm, supported by typical Irish whiskey, he practically bounded over to kiss our hands. "Two such lovely ladies. I am pleased to meet you," he said, in quite good Spanish.

We said our hellos, and Carlson sat us at a table. Servants brought a modest meal, some boiled potatoes and fried sausage, and we began to eat.

"I apologize for food," said Carlson, "the war in Perú she make all things expensive."

"Hell, man," said Captain Simpson, "it all goes to the same place—French wine or *chicha.*" Then he laughed. We all assured our host that the food tasted good, which it did.

Captain Simpson was most jovial and talkative, and we discussed Ireland all evening, while he had a few more glasses of whiskey. He was something of an expert on his drink of choice. Every time he poured himself another, he gave a little speech about the particular qualities of the contents of the bottle. He made all of us try some, and soon we were all in a jocular mood.

"Wait, one moment," he said as we ate some spiced oranges for dessert. "Sáenz? Were you recently in Quito?"

"That is true, Señor," I said, "I was." I giggled a bit at his knowledge of me, feeling my face flush with the effects of the whiskey. "I arrived here a few days ago. Why is it, that you inquire, and how do you know of my travels?"

"I know your brother," he said broadly, smiling a wide smile, which made his wide red face emerge somewhat from his long curly red hair and beard.

"My brother?" I said, as we all laughed at the coincidence.

"Aye," he said in English. Then in Spanish, "I only just returned from Perú. I've been transporting soldiers and supplies there on my ship for the last few months."

I laughed again and said, "Oh, you work for Bolívar. I thought you were an Irish trader."

Captain Simpson sprayed the food in his mouth all over and laughed until he fell off his chair. His guffawing made Rosita and I laugh, and soon we were all lying on the floor, under the table. I think I laughed as hard as I ever have. We would stop for a while and then we would notice that we were all on our backs looking at the underside of the table or notice some other absurdity in our situation. Then we would start again.

Finally, when we had all settled down somewhat, he said, "No, Señora, I am not a trader. I am captain of the brig, *Helena.*"

Despite my merriment, I rolled over on one elbow and said, "You are departing tomorrow for Perú."

"Yes, Señora, I am," he said, wiping tears out of his eyes.

"Oh, my dear captain, do you not have room for me and my slaves?" I pleaded, though I could not get the mirth out of my voice.

The captain was also still in a jocular mood, but he said, "I am sorry, Señora, but there is no room."

I sighed and fell back on the floor.

The captain said, "I know why you are going." Laughter was still in his voice.

"I live there," I said simply.

"Oh no, there is more." He rolled over and smiled slyly. He had enough whiskey to say in a mock whisper, "I believe your journey is one of love. I know of a certain lover, a general it is true, but one who has been smitten with love just like the rest of us are wont to do." He was so funny, I had to laugh.

"You know no generals, Captain," Carlson said as he laughed, "except maybe, the Liberating one." We laughed at his syntax, and he laughed some more. Then he stopped laughing. His expression became serious as he understood that Simpson was alluding to my love for Bolívar.

Captain Simpson went on, "This general I speak of is currently without the one he loves—"

"Sir, you are indiscreet," I said quickly in English.

Carlson understood a little English. When I said that, he understood that I was Bolívar's lover. He rolled out from beneath the table, stood up, looked at me, and walked quickly into his bedroom, slamming the door.

The mirth in the rest of us died, and we slowly stood up. Captain Simpson looked puzzled. Rosita said, "I'll go talk to him."

I said simply, in English, "Mr. Carlson is infatuated with me and believes I will not reciprocate his feelings only because of my marriage. It is not true."

"No?"

"No. I will be honest with you, Sir. It is because of my love for Bolívar." Despite the fact that he knew of our affair, I should not have been so indiscreet. I was feeling unstable from the whiskey, but I was surprised at what happened next. It must have been the exhaustion from the whiskey and all that laughing, but large tears came to my eyes and rolled down my cheeks. I wiped my eyes and sat down.

Captain Simpson sat down next to me and put his arm around my shoulders and said, in English, "Lady, certain officers are to be boardin' me ship *late* mornin'. If you and your companions were to be on board by *early* mornin', I might become confused, thinkin' me ship was full, and depart before the officers would be arrivin' at the dock."

I looked at him with gratitude. His face was gentle and smiling. However, he looked a little worried. I said, "Are you sure?"

He thought a moment and then said, "My Lady," he smiled a broad Irish smile, "if the *generalísimo* asks me why I did not bring the officers, I will tell him that my actions were in service of Eros." He laughed. "Sure and your brother has told me that the Liberator has missed ya." He laughed again, and I knew I had found my way to Perú.

Chapter 10

In late 1823 I arrived again at Callao. Neither Simón nor anyone else knew I was coming. I wanted to keep it that way. Captain Simpson was to return to Guayaquil the next day. As we went ashore, I made him promise not to mention my arrival to Simón until he returned a few weeks later. I did not want Bolívar to know I was in Perú until I was ready to tell him.

Though Simón had called for me when he was last in Quito, I still felt unsure as to his feelings for me. How important was I to him? Was I only a dalliance that he thought he had left in Quito? Perhaps he had forgotten me. Perhaps he thought that once he had left me in my native land our relationship had ended. I did not know what he thought.

Being so uncertain of his feelings for me, I could not foresee what he would do or say when he found me living two blocks away. Captain Simpson believed that he was serving Love itself by bringing me to Simón, but I was not sure how Simón would see it. However, the main reason I did not want anyone, especially Bolívar, to know I was in Lima was because I still had not solved one big problem, which I feared my arrival would create. It was a problem about which I was much concerned—James Thorne. Before I could do anything else in Lima, I had to settle with my husband, and I did not look forward to the battles I was sure I would have to face on that front.

Upon landing, I did not go into Lima. I sent Jonotás into the city to bring our horses while Natán and I waited in Callao, guessing that if James was in Lima, he would be in San Sebastiano and not at our seaside house. My hopes were that I could arrive and settle someplace before James or anyone else knew I was back. I was even worried that someone would see Jonotás and alert him. "Do not go near the San Sebastiano house. You are to fetch our horses and you are to swear Manuel to secrecy. Tell him that I will see him before anyone else." We had left our horses with Manuel Amat.

She said, "I know how to keep a secret, Manuelita," and smiled as she climbed into a *calesa* I hired for her and pulled down the curtains.

"Don't stop. Don't talk to anyone," I yelled after her as the driver kicked the sides of the mule.

Natán and I then made our way to a canteen where we waited for her return.

The sun was high in the sky, and already starting to dip toward the Pacific, when she rode up.

"Did anyone see you?" I asked.

"No, but Manuelita, I did not recognize Lima. It has changed so much."

"Why?" I asked, though I knew the answer.

"The war," she said. "It makes me sad."

I knew, no matter how I tried to imagine it, I would be sad too when I finally saw it. "I know, but let's not talk about it now. How is Manuel?"

"He promised not to say nothin', but he also made me promise to bring you up there tomorrow."

"We'll see. Let's go to Magdalena."

We left our luggage to be picked up later. Then we headed south along the ocean. I hoped I would not see any of my friends from Bolívar's staff when we rode up to the Magdalena house. That is why I had Jonotás return to Callao, and not meet us in Magdalena. If one of Bolívar's staff saw her, she would have been recognized. The viceroy's villa was only a couple of blocks away from my house, but we approached from Callao, not from the busier road to Lima, and we were not seen.

The housekeeper at Magdalena was still there and the house did not seem any different than when I'd left it almost a year and a half before. She told me that James was in Chile, not due to return for many weeks. That was an immense relief, even though it was only a confrontation put off, not avoided.

We unpacked, and I spent that afternoon and the next day cleaning the curtains, dusting the furniture, and digging weeds from the patio. I needed to somehow take ownership of my house again. As evening approached, I finally felt like I was home.

After I relaxed and had a little wine, I looked for James's papers to see if there was any new business that I had to manage right away. Then I remembered that I had taken everything up to the San Sebastiano house before I left for Quito.

Before we retired that evening, I considered sending a note to Simón, to let him know I was in Perú, but I thought, *He left me, and he will think I followed him if I approach him. Better to continue with my life and wait for the day when we should meet.* I did my best to ignore the fact that I missed him.

The next day, dressed in my military style riding habit, my pistols in their holsters slung over Midnight's withers, my companions in their soldier's uniforms at my side, we rode into Lima. We had two missions.

First, we wanted to make arrangements to volunteer at the hospital for Africans, San Bartolomé. Second, we wanted to really look at the city. Jonotás had given me a disturbing description, and I wanted to see for myself. I did not know what to anticipate inside the city, and this is why I had taken my pistols with me.

Whatever I expected, after talking to Jonotás, was nothing compared to what I found. No longer was Lima a "Paris." This grand city had been reduced to a fortified medieval borough more decayed than Guayaquil at its worst. It brought tears to my eyes. The effects of war were everywhere. There were deserted and boarded houses in every neighborhood, from poor to rich. Paint was faded, masonry was chipped, and the streets were filled with rubbish. Eyeless or armless beggars stood on every street corner. Indolent soldiers, drunk on *chicha*, congregated around canteens. Where there were no soldiers, bands of ruffians prowled the streets looking for trouble. The many ransacked houses and public buildings on every street made the city feel deserted. There was very little food or flowers at the market. Nearly everywhere I looked I could see disease or destruction. We rode all over the city, and though it was obvious that many households were low on funds, I did notice that the Torre Tagle mansion had been freshly painted.

After I spent an hour or so at the hospital, I left Jonotás and Natán and went to visit Manuel Amat. He was delighted to see me. While we hugged, he said, "I have missed you."

I smiled at him and said, "I have missed you, too."

"Manuela, Manuela," he said in a teasing tone, "you certainly know how to make your friends long for you. You merely stay away. And then you send Jonotás to tease. Where have you been?"

"In Quito," I said, laughing at his histrionics.

He was still holding my arms and we looked at each other. He smiled, and said, "You were supposed to come see me yesterday." Despite his smile, there seemed to be more anger than teasing in his voice now.

I laughed and gave him a kiss on the cheek.

Before I could say anything, or pull away, he held me tighter and said, "Manuela." Then he looked me in the eyes and said, "I *have* missed you, Manuela." He leaned forward to kiss me on the lips.

I pulled away. "No," I whispered. I walked away and then turned back to face him.

I thought I saw curiosity turn to understanding and then to anger. "Is it true then? You've found a lover? An important one? One who is in this city even now?"

The thought that Simón was nearby made me want to see him. I realized how much I missed my love.

"Is that why you've returned?" Manuel asked. He smiled with false warmth, but his voice had become cold.

I felt attacked and longed for Miquita to be there so that I might talk to her. Instead I sat down quietly, in her chair, and said simply, "I've returned to Lima because I was through with my business in Quito. There is a man in this country I love, but he does not love me."

"You are married, and yet you love another?"

"Yes," I said, without emotion.

"But if, as you say, he does not love you, perhaps—"

"Please, Manuel, have your servants bring me some chocolate." I smiled, and said, "Then let us discuss you and Lima and all that has happened since I left."

He gave me a look of resignation, but I could tell he was not happy. However, he did as I asked and we spent all afternoon together. The tension I felt when I greeted him seemed to go away after a short time, and we had a pleasant conversation. He informed me of everything that I did not already know about what had happened in the military, political, and social spheres in Perú.

Then he began to talk about Bolívar, in resentful tones. He told me how "proud" most of Lima was to have the great Liberator taking control of affairs in Perú. He told me how, every night, Simón had received a different invitation to some party or another, and how often he accepted, and with whom he had danced—some of the most beautiful women in Lima. He almost seemed to take cruel delight in his stories. "He is a busy man," said Manuel, referring to his social affairs, a hint of jealousy in his voice.

I did not want to hear, but I made myself listen. I wanted to see things just as they were. We talked a long time, and I rebuilt my resolve. Despite Bolívar's neglecting me, I was going to fight the revolution again until the war was over, even if it only meant working in hospitals and raising money. I could do that at least, and that was what I was doing in Lima. I was not, as a first business, there to see Simón. Bolívar would fit into my life, or not, but he would have to come second.

I had given Jonotás and Natán leave to visit their friends in the *cofradias* when they were done at the hospital. By the time they rode up in the afternoon, between their knowledge of Lima as seen through the eyes of the city's servants and my knowledge gained from one of Perú's leading aristocrats, we felt we knew everything there was to know about Lima as it stood in late 1823.

When at last we left Manuel, he said, "I hope to see you again, soon, *Señora.*" His voice was hard, almost threatening with its obvious jealousy. The way he pronounced Señora seemed as if he was reminding me that I was married, and therefore an adulterer. The implication was clear. If I was an adulterer and Bolívar was no longer in my life, I should be giving my attention to him.

When we left Manuel that afternoon, I felt bad. Not only had I seemed to have lost Manuel as a friend, but I felt more certain that Bolívar had forgotten me. We rode over to the San Sebastiano house in silence.

This district looked the best of all I had seen, being only slightly faded. The war had not affected this wealthy neighborhood as much as others. When we stopped in front of my house, I was glad to see that it was not much changed. However, by that time I felt so bad about Bolívar and so certain that I had lost him, I could hardly bear to look at anything.

I forced myself to move forward. I had business to attend to that had nothing to do with Bolívar. I dismounted and told Jonotás to tend to the horses, and Natán and I went inside. In the patio, we stopped to discuss the sorry state of the flowers. "Natán, we must spend some time here tomorrow." I did not really want to do so because I did not really care about the condition of the patio, but it gave me something on which to concentrate besides Bolívar.

While we stood discussing what should be done, someone opened the door and entered. We turned, and there, in the doorway, stood a man I had seen two or three times before at parties in this very house. It was one of James's sea captains: Captain Manuel Escobar.

He stopped when he saw us. He was not expecting anyone to be inside.

"Why do you enter unannounced, Señor?" I asked as graciously as I could. My impulse was to let my anger at his bad manners show, but I knew he was friendly with James and I wanted to find out what he was doing.

"I did not know anyone was here, Señora," he replied politely, but I sensed a suppressed animosity.

"Evidently," I said, letting my anger show somewhat.

"Now, Señora, I have leave to enter from Don Jaime."

Up to this point he had not left the door. He became bolder and took a few steps inside. I said, "Please, Señor, stay where you are. You do not have leave from me." He stopped. "What are you doing here?"

"Don Jaime has instructed me to bring his papers to him in Chile."

"Why, Señor?"

"He intends to give me his power of attorney."

My heart froze. I knew what he was doing. This was purely to get at me. "That is not so, Señor," I managed to say without showing the fact that I was somewhat unnerved.

"Yes, Señora, it is. Don Jaime will be some time before returning."

"It is not necessary for you to have his power of attorney, Señor," I said quickly. "I have his power of attorney and I have returned to Lima where I have always handled his affairs, and I will continue to do."

"That is not Don Jaime's wish."

"I say again, Señor. I will handle his affairs. You need not be concerned about Don Jaime's wish. I think I know what my husband wishes."

Escobar's voice became surly. "Señora, it is because he wants to protect his papers from you that I am here to retrieve them."

So, James knew I was in Lima, or was coming. He did not intend to give me any freedom to pursue an affair with Bolívar; not knowing that my affair with Bolívar was over. I understood the situation perfectly, but I put on an aspect of amazement. "What do you mean, Señor?"

"I left Don Jaime ten days ago," he said to me, "'Now that Bolívar is in Lima, I believe my wife will return there.' He said this. He said, 'Please, retrieve all my papers from my San Sebastiano residence. I wish to keep them with me. And you, since you will be in Lima many times before I return there, you will hold my power of attorney.' That is what he said, and I intend to carry out his wishes."

For a moment, I felt trapped. Escobar started towards the stairway. I said, "Do you have a letter giving you permission to remove my husband's papers?"

He stopped, looking lost. "A letter? No."

"It is lucky for James then, that I arrived in Lima in time to stop a thief from robbing him."

"A thief? Now, listen, you little—"

"Shall I scream for help?"

He glared at me a long time. At last, he said calmly, "I believe I can be gone with the papers James requires before your screams can raise any opposition." He started for the stairway again. I took a step towards him, but Natán was already at the stairs and stood blocking his way to the steps.

When Escobar reached her, he said, "Get out of my way."

Natán looked frightened but she did not move.

I could not get over to them fast enough. Despite her resolve, Escobar took her roughly by her shirt and flung her behind him. She fell to the ground and cried out.

Fury rose in me. By the time I reached him, I was nearly blind with rage. "You piece of scum," I said as I grabbed his arm, making it impossible for him to turn up the stairs.

He made a fist and pulled his arm back but thought better of striking James's wife.

Then, from the doorway, we heard, "Do you need these, Ma'am?" I turned to see Jonotás holding my pistols, taken from my horse's withers. Before I could say anything, she said, "I like your pistols. I would like to fire them. May I?" Then, she cocked the one in her right and, swiftly changing her attitude, she turned with her side to Escobar. She looked very much like a dueling aristocrat, or a military marksman. She took "deadly" aim at his head.

"Put that down," said Escobar.

It is Jonotás's skill that she very much gives the exact impression of the character she is pretending to be. When she aimed at Escobar, she made it seem as though she would shoot his head off, even though I know she was only imitating men she had seen shooting. She had never fired a pistol before.

I said, "Please, Jonotás, don't kill him like the others." Her eyes became slits and I almost believed she would kill the man.

Escobar wavered for a half moment and then said loudly, "Very well, I'm leaving." Anger covered his face like a cloud. When he reached the door, he turned, his face quite red, and said, "Someday, Señora, I will make you regret this. I will make you regret this deeply."

He slammed the door as he left. Jonotás, Natán and I let out our breath as one, feeling the tension ease, and then we started laughing until we fell into each other's arms.

I sent Jonotás to hire a *calesa* while Natán and I gathered all of James's papers into some wooden shipping boxes I retrieved from a storage room. When she returned, we loaded the boxes into the *calesa*. Jonotás and Natán climbed in and lowered the gauze, hiding themselves and the boxes. I gave instructions to the driver and they left for Magdalena, their horses tied behind. After I saw to the care of the house, leaving strict instructions with the housekeeper that she was not to let anyone inside, I mounted my horse and left.

I walked my horse slowly as I made my way home to Magdalena. It was all I could do to keep moving forward. I kept telling myself, as though some demon in me kept me from believing, "Bolívar has forgotten me."

Then, something happened to brighten my mood. When I was about halfway there, I met Colonel O'Leary. He rode up, smiling from ear to ear. "I saw you way down the road. 'A white woman on a black horse—could it be?' I asked myself." He dismounted, as did I.

"Oh, Colonel, how good to see you," I said in English.

"Good it is to see you again," he answered. "Sure and the General has missed ya."

I let a scowl cross my brow. "It seems he has not been too lonely."

"Now, I wouldn't be worryin' about what loose tongues can be sayin'. The truth of it is, the general needs ya. Nearly every day, he has said somethin' like, 'O'Leary, I wish Manuelita was here.' 'Send for her,' I reply, and he always says, 'I might. One day soon, I might.'"

I looked at him as though I didn't believe him.

"True it is, but also true it is that he does not believe he should, because . . . ," he looked at the ground as though ashamed of what he had to say.

"Because of my husband. Yes, I know." I said, in Spanish.

He answered in Spanish, "But what am I doing? I have not asked if you have a place to stay."

I laughed. "That is not necessary. I live here."

He did not know that Lima was my true residence. He laughed and said "I will tell the general you are in the country."

I did not know if I wanted him to do that, but I let it pass. We talked for a while, and then I said, "Good-bye." I wondered all day if I should have sworn O'Leary to secrecy.

Later that night, after I had already gone to bed, there was a knock at the door. I heard Jonotás answer it. She came into my room and said, "Manuelita, it is Bolívar's servant."

I rose and dressed, pulling on a peasant shift, which only barely covered me. I had not told O'Leary where I lived, and I was surprised to see José Palacios at my door. Then I realized that the able José could find out anything for his general.

He said, "Good evening, Señora, it is a great pleasure to see you again." He produced a note from his cape.

Manuela-

I am surprised to hear that you are here in Lima. I only, this moment, found out from O'Leary as he left me. However much my surprise, my happiness exceeds it. I want to see you. Won't you come to me? Come now.

Simón

I folded the paper and put it back in his hand. "José, when I heard it was you, I dressed to go with you, but . . ."

The somber Indian said, "His Excellency will be very disappointed if you do not come."

"For what, my friend? For what? He will only leave me again. He has his pick of any woman he wants, and never has he even told me he loves me."

"Señora, I want you to know something." He stopped as though considering just how to say it.

"What, my friend?"

He looked embarrassed, almost in pain, as he tried to say what was on his mind. With great effort, he said, "You are different."

I didn't understand. "How do you mean, José?"

He tore his eyes from me and looked at the floor. It seemed to take a great effort to say what he wanted. At last, he said, "He tells every other woman that he loves her and will never leave her."

I gave a sigh of disgust.

He went on, so quietly, I barely heard him. "They are all the same to him. But never have I seen him act the way he does with you. You remind him of ancient heartbreaks, Señora. But I know him. It is you that he loves."

"José, I . . ." I did not know what to say.

"Please do not tell him I have spoken to you. I feel guilty. His confidences . . ."

"José, I thank you. You have helped me. I will never say a thing."

His eyes grew soft and pleading. "Won't you come? He needs you."

I followed José down the street to the Viceroy's retreat where I had first met San Martín. When we reached the corner of the property, José turned silently and walked in the direction of the back door.

I said, "Let's go this way," and turned toward the front of the house.

I could hear José scurry after me, saying, "But, Señora . . ."

As I passed under the fig trees and approached the wide stairway that led to the entrance doors, a guard stood up to detain me. However, I had seen him in Quito and he recognized me. He saluted smartly and let me pass. I could hear José come running up behind me. I walked right through the front door and felt cold tiles through my slippers as I breathed in the smell of the furniture oil.

Simón's mastiffs were sleeping inside the door and, at first, they rose with a growl. One of them barked. Immediately, however, they were like puppies, glad to see me—all wagging tails and wet muzzles.

Simón entered from the next room just as I turned around. He looked at me as though he could see through to my soul. I felt the nakedness of my bare shoulders and seemed to feel naked all over. His jacket was unbuttoned and his hair was tousled. He had a pen in one hand with ink staining the fingers and piece of paper in the other. He appeared the same way he did the day he arrived back from Guayaquil when he had made me desire him so.

Without speaking, he put down his writing materials, walked through the confusion of dogs at my feet, and took me in his arms.

He kissed me long and hard. José Palacios had entered through the open door, and I sensed him standing there in embarrassed silence.

Simón said, "Come," and led me down the hallway to his room. When he closed the door, he turned and looked me in the eyes. He caressed my cheek and said, "You have brought your beauty to Lima. I did not realize how much I have ached for you."

I was shaking with desire and I threw my arms around his neck, pressing my lips to his. His arms encircled my back. He held me close with the strength that passion brings when it must hold on. We kissed.

Our hungry mouths moved from lips to neck to cheek to ears and then returned deliciously to taste again the lips. I removed his jacket and lifted his shirt over his head, letting my mouth leave his for only a second. He slowly pulled the dress down from my shoulders. He followed the garment with his lips and tongue as it slowly slid down the length of my body.

Then, with a power I could not have resisted, he picked me up and lay me on the viceroy's bed. He kissed my whole body and we were wrapped in love.

Chapter 11

Over the next few weeks, we took up where we left off in Quito—with one difference. It was not clandestine. No longer would I allow Simón to speak of "scandal" or what others might think. Nor did I worry about it much myself. We were reasonably discreet but not extraordinarily careful. We were too much in love, and filled with desire, to think about scandal.

Lima was ours. I accompanied him to the theatre and attended other social affairs with him. It was clear to everyone that it was I who had his attention, and the flirtatious women we met were defeated before we even arrived. We attended these functions as "friends," and we did not openly announce our more intimate involvement, but that was our only concession to discretion.

I probably should not have flaunted my love affair with Bolívar in front of Lima's aristocracy. Even though I visited Simón only at night, everyone knew about it and I did not try to hide my affection for him.

When I met Josefa de Torre Tagle, she made no effort to hide her disgust at my loose morals or those of the Liberator. She did not say anything directly, but she was quite able to express her disdain by her look and her manner. Also, she was quite vocal in her disapproval, in private, to her friends and her husband. Some of the things she said got back to me. I had particularly made sure that Jonotás and Natán re-established their "friendship" with the Torre Tagle servants, and that precaution served me later.

"When a country's leader decides to carry on with that bastard, we are all on the road to ruin," was her favorite remark. "Imagine, a little whore, invited into the salons where viceroys have tread," was another. Or, "Her lack of morality is exceeded only by her lover's ambition." I knew that she could never be trusted, but it was not until later that I realized just how dangerous she was or how accurately she reflected an undercurrent of popular resentment—especially among women.

Despite knowing that I might sometimes be an embarrassment to Bolívar or his friends, I knew I would not stop seeing him. I did wish that my presence in the villa did not compromise him so much. I was prepared to continue despite such compromise, but I still worried about it. Eventually, I found a solution that made me quite happy.

As the weeks wore on, more and more, Simón was relying on my judgments of people and events in Lima. I was still a member of the Order of the Sun, on equal footing with Perú's most distinguished families. My husband's business, which I still managed meticulously for James's betterment, gave me contacts with all of the English merchants, and I could speak English with them. I was thus able to assess the world view of the patriot cause better than most. I kept my eyes and ears open at all times, making sure that I knew, intimately, everyone that Bolívar might want to know about. If I could not get close to someone, I made sure that Jonotás and Natán became friendly with their servants. My dear companions kept me informed of all the talk, rumors, and goings on in the households of Lima through their contacts with slaves and servants throughout the city. They visited the *cofradias* every week and made visits to the slaves in households I particularly wished them to know about. They had no trouble being welcomed. The lower classes all loved Jonotás because she was so irreverent and funny.

In very short order, Bolívar made it clear to me and to others that he trusted the military and political information I gathered and my assessment of it as much as anyone else's, if not more. Every day there was some new decision to be made amid the political mess in which Bolívar found himself. These decisions were most often better informed because of the intelligence I was able to gather, and he was open about asking my advice.

Every few days, he would say, "Manuelita, my sweet spy, you have surpassed yourself." It was not only that the information I brought to him was so valuable, he knew I was loyal to him. He knew that there were very few who could be said to be as loyal as I and that he could depend on me, absolutely. It was clear to everyone that I was a vital necessity to his operations in Lima.

By the end of October, I had been officially added to Bolívar's staff and put in charge of his personal archives. This, despite the objections of General Lara, who, when he heard the order said, "All we need, a woman about."

I worked closely with Bolívar's young secretary, Juan Santana. Far from resenting my presence, he welcomed me as a much needed co-worker. He was about my age, thin and dark, and he became as devoted to me as to Simón.

I more than welcomed my new position. Not only could I bring my skills to the administration of his papers, which were in sore need of my talents, but I could officially be close to Bolívar during the day. I had a Colonel's uniform made for me and I wore it.

The first day I showed up at the villa wearing my new uniform, Bolívar said, "Oh, so that's your rank." But I worked hard, and received the respect of all of his officers. I became absolutely indispensable, and soon it was a fact and very natural that I was a Colonel in the patriot army and on the General's staff.

Nearly all of Bolívar's officers welcomed me. They understood how valuable I was in my position. I made friends with all of the men from Lima who now served Bolívar. One I even nursed back to health after a terrible accident.

He was William Miller, a general, who had burned his face quite badly in a recent explosion as he was preparing Congreve rockets to bomb some Spanish ships in Callao harbor. He was young, slender, blue-eyed, and fair of face until the accident left it badly scarred. He was from the same part of the world as my husband, born in England. Learning to fight in the Napoleonic wars, and after Waterloo, he had come to Argentina to fight with San Martín. Now, he was a most valuable officer, devoted to Bolívar, in charge of the patriot cavalry. His left hand was crippled from an old bullet wound, but he was energetic and forceful and no one dared disobey him.

He was the only man that the *montonera* would follow. This was a band of about five hundred independent guerrilla fighters whose only qualification for joining was that they hated the Spanish and rode well. They were cruel and bloodthirsty, having started out as a group of about three hundred survivors from a Royalist massacre in the town of Reyes, on the shores of Lake Junín, in 1821. Almost the entire town had been wiped out, men, women, and children, including the wives and family members of the few surviving men. They had fought their own war against the Spanish since that time and would obey no one. General Miller had taken his cavalry out to meet them and had earned their respect. He alone could integrate their hatred of the Spanish into the disciplined war effort of the patriot soldiers.

When the general suffered the explosion, he had lain for weeks covered in a plaster cast, with only a silver straw to draw in liquids. He had been blinded, and I sometimes read to him in English. When he could finally see, and thus ride again, he made a special point to thank me. "I don't know what I would have done without you, Ma'am. I am most sincerely grateful."

However, General Miller was not the only officer who befriended me. All of the Irish contingent that I'd known in Quito still loved me, as well as the new officers in Bolívar's entourage. They all knew that Simón needed me.

My one regret about this period is that I did not make what little authority I had greater and more secure. I was indulged as a woman officer because people liked me, and my duties were administrative. However, I should have used my rank of colonel so much that no one would ever question my authority. I was to realize later that I could have done more for Simón and myself.

However, I was glad of the service I did provide, because Perú needed Bolívar. For one thing, he did an amazing amount of good for the country. He personally underwrote a loan of 300,000 pesos to the treasury of Perú. But there were other reasons that Bolívar did not get control of the country any too soon, not the least of which was the discontent among the soldiers.

One of the biggest problems was that the Argentine army composed mostly of African officers and men, in addition to not being paid, were treated very badly by the Peruvian troops. Despite having liberated Lima from Spain, they were resented as interlopers—if not because of the color of their skin. Simón set himself to see that all of the patriot armies worked together, despite such petty differences.

About the same time Simón was working on this problem, it was discovered that there was trouble in Trujillo with my old friend Riva Agüero. Spain had sent an envoy to Argentina to persuade the Argentineans to sue for peace between Spain and Perú. Argentina then sent their own envoys to Perú, to Riva Agüero. He had acceded to the peace proposal because he believed Torre Tagle would be deposed and he would be left to rule Perú. He apparently planned to continue his presidency, thus retaining his power, despite the wishes of the Peruvian Congress. All of this boiled down to a dangerous situation.

Trying to help both situations, Bolívar pulled his Colombian troops out of the Callao fortress and ordered the Argentineans in. There, they would have better lodgings and provisions and would not be subject to any more abuse from the Peruvian contingent. I was happy for them at the time, but I could not see the bloody future that would spring from this situation. Once the Argentinean army was in Callao, Bolívar sent the Colombians to Trujillo to capture Riva Agüero.

When I found out about Riva Agüero's treachery, I was shaken. He blamed Sucre for his troubles, and by extension, Bolívar. All the many times I had sat and listened to Riva Agüero planning the coming revolution in Lima and all the respect I had shown him as a leader stood in bold contrast to affairs as they stood in 1823. The impermanence of life frightened me.

Bolívar followed the main part of the Colombians to Trujillo on November 15. He wanted to scout the area and have first hand knowledge of the terrain. I did not mind Bolívar leaving, as he was only going to Trujillo and back. I had plenty to do and, although the Liman aristocracy's hatred of me—especially that of Josefa de Torre Tagle—grew more profound and vocal with Bolívar absent, I continued with my life and handled the day-to-day problems in Bolívar's offices.

The situation that frustrated me the most when Bolívar left was that Jonotás was never around. She had taken up with a black soldier in the Argentine regiment at Callao. She began spending all of her time with him. I wished she had shown a little more consideration for me, because I could never find her when I needed her. Again and again, I told her when and where I would require her, but she would always be late, if she showed up at all. I became more annoyed with her by the day.

Still, I was able to keep order in the villa in Bolívar's absence. I could even feel that I made some progress in assuring the people of Lima that Bolívar's presence in Perú was helping them. Then, something happened which increased the tensions in Lima. Bernardo Monteagudo returned.

Without exception, everyone in Lima hated him. He had been on a diplomatic mission for Bolívar in Mexico or one of her neighboring countries, and I had hoped he would stay there. When he returned to Lima, he reopened old wounds. The Peruvians had exiled him and there he was in Lima, more dandified than ever, and on Bolívar's staff. It was only Bolívar's power that protected him from being shot as he walked through the Plaza Mayor. As December began, with Bolívar still away, I could feel the tension in Lima growing.

Chapter 12

As the new year approached, so did disaster. I felt it in the air, vague and threatening. At first things seemed to be as they should. By the time Bolívar arrived in Trujillo, his men had already captured Riva Agüero. My old friend was exiled to Europe, and I never saw him again. Bolívar then began scouting the countryside to make plans for offensive operations. His Colombian and the Chilean troops were sent to Patavilca, to prepare for the upcoming conflict.

I wrote to him daily. I explained the problems Monteagudo was creating and kept him otherwise informed of the situation in Lima. He only wrote to me twice. I believe some of my letters may not have ever reached him, as he was on the move continually, never in the same town two days in a row. Some did, which were of benefit to him, but his constant motion kept him from writing.

Meanwhile, the Argentine soldiers in the Callao fortress were clamoring for pay, which was now six months in arrears. I sensed real danger here. I was able to learn that it was largely Torre Tagle who kept the jealous resentment of the Peruvians hot. He stupidly thought that if he were to acknowledge their past service, it would weaken his own power. I knew he was of low intelligence, but I never quite realized how power hungry, or stupid, he was. Of course, when I reflected, it was obvious that the hunger for power was Josefa's and not her husband's.

There was much news I had to share with Bolívar, not the least of which was word from the United States. Just after the new year we heard that President James Monroe had issued a proclamation. No longer would the United States accept interference by Europe in the Western Hemisphere. I believe this was prompted largely by Russian involvement in the area known as Alaska, but it also applied to the freedom of the independent states of South America. When I heard the news, I told one of his guards to prepare to ride to him as a special courier. Then I sat down to write the news in a long letter.

I had barely dipped my quill when a messenger rode up. I heard him gallop to the villa and dismount. I could tell it was a rider with an urgent message and I ran outside.

The man was a Colombian soldier. His horse was lathered and breathing hard. Dust covered the soldier's face and he could barely speak from the exertion of the ride. He said, breathlessly, "The Liberator is dying."

My heart stopped. "What do you mean? Speak."

"He is ill . . ." He took two or three deep breaths and said, ". . . I was told to inform the garrison here."

I learned that Bolívar had been returning to Lima on a ship when a coughing fit came over him. It was so bad that his men feared he might expire. He coughed up blood, and vomited. His officers ordered the ship to put in to Patavilca. There he languished close to death.

For a week, rumors came down the coast that the Liberator was dead. I did not want to believe it. I would not believe it without confirmation from one of his officers. I held on, hoping for better news. If I had not been so worried I would have noticed the disloyalty of the Peruvians then.

It manifested itself in the salons of the city. The traitors spoke more freely thinking that Bolívar was out of the picture, but I paid no attention. Finally, I told Natán we were going to Patavilca.

I sent Natán off to find Jonotás, who was in Callao, and then I walked to my own home and began putting a few clothes together. I was frightened for Simón and could not think to pack properly. Without Jonotás and Natán, I had to do everything myself. I became more frustrated by the minute.

When Jonotás and Natán rode up, I was so worried that I raged at Jonotás. "Where have you been? Every time I want you, you are nowhere to be found." She did not answer. I could tell she was hurt by my tone. I said, "I need you. We have to go to Patavilca. Get ready, and meet me at the villa." I stormed off to retrieve something I left there.

An hour later, we had a trunk tied to the back of a mule and we were in our saddles. Just as we started out, a messenger whom I recognized arrived. "The Liberator lives," he said. He handed me a letter from my friend, Juan Santana:

My Gracious Lady,

At last I have the pleasure to tell you that the Liberator has improved so much from his illness that he is now in a state of convalescence. Nevertheless, I feel I should tell you at the same time that our return to Lima is not to be as soon as I promised it would, or as soon as all of us wish it to be. My friend Medina is the bearer of this note and so he will be able to inform you of all you wish to know, and he will doubtless have much pleasure in doing so.

Here we are like souls carried off by the devil, dead from disgust and bored as we have never been bored before.

Juan Santana

I listened to the messenger tell us in detail about Simón's convalescence and how new intelligence developments had dictated his continuation of his scouting when he recovered. I felt depleted when I heard it all. I was very tired. I went home, took off my uniform, and climbed into bed.

I slept until the next morning. Jonotás brought me some English tea when I awoke, and she sat on the end of the bed while I drank it.

At last she said, "I'm sorry I upset you. I love a man, and I want to be with him, too."

I looked into her brown eyes and I recognized the same emotions I carried in my own heart. "I'm sorry I was angry with you," I said at last. "Who is it that you love?"

Her eyes lit up, and she said, "He is big and very black and very strong. He is called Falucho, and he is from Argentina. He crossed the Andes with San Martín, and he has fought against Spain for years." We talked for some time, and she told me all about the man she loved. "We're thinkin' about gettin' married," she said at one point. A look of disappointment clouded my face. She saw and said, "'Course we're not. Not 'till the war's over. And I wouldn't leave you till then." She smiled.

Then she went on to tell me that the discontent among her lover's fellow soldiers was worse than it had ever been and growing worse by the day. It was certainly far more dangerous than I had imagined or anyone knew.

Finally, I said, "Jonotás, I want you to stay up in Callao. Don't worry about me. Natán and I will manage. But do let me know when and if something changes." She said she would and left a little later. I did not see her for two weeks.

The situation in January 1824 was very bad. The most Bolívar could count on in patriot troops was 9,000, whereas the Royalists had accumulated over 18,000. Then, Natán brought me dreadful news.

She was actually in Torre Tagle's kitchen when he led another man into the house through the back. Natán overheard their conversation and discovered that the man was a Royalist, an aide-de-camp of Canterac. It seemed to her that he was making some kind of deal.

The man's stupidity amazed me. Here he was, president of a republic which Bolívar would soon hand over to him, liberated and organized, if he would only wait. Josefa's ambition must have been without limit.

On the morning of February 4, I walked over to my own home to work on James's affairs. There was some business correspondence that I had been neglecting, as well as a stack of mail that Natán had recently brought down from the San Sebastiano house.

In amongst the other mail were several letters from James. I had not been in Lima for about three weeks and I was surprised at how many I had received from him in that time. I opened a couple and they both had the same tone and message: when he returned he would expect me to take up my wifely duties, my affair with Bolívar was immoral, and so forth.

I put James's letters away and concentrated on taking care of his business affairs. I wanted everything in perfect order for him. I did not want James to accuse me of mismanagement, and the thought of something going wrong while in my care was not acceptable to me. When at last I was confident that his affairs were organized perfectly up to that point, I prepared to walk back to the villa.

Natán had just finished washing my dogs, and I helped her feed them. While we were closing the door to leave, Jonotás rode up.

She was out of breath, but she finally said, "The soldiers have mutinied."

"What soldiers?

"At Callo."

"When?"

"At three this afternoon."

"Your soldier?"

"He's all right. I must return." She turned her horse to head back up the coast.

"Be careful," I called after her. "Oh, Jonotás be careful."

It was a deeply regrettable event, but I was not entirely surprised. Torre Tagle had refused to pay them, and despite being the liberating Army of the Andes, who had freed Lima under San Martín, they were treated like unwelcome beggars. I cursed him.

I rushed down to the villa, wrote a letter to Simón, ordered a soldier to carry it to Patavilca, and then Natán and I saddled our own horses and rode into Lima.

The city had heard the news and there was anger at the Argentineans. Torre Tagle gave a speech, lamenting the fact that the fortress might fall to the Spanish. "The mutineers are demanding thousands of pesos. We cannot pay them. If they give the fortress over to Spanish hands, it will be disastrous for us. We will not be able to hold back the Spanish advances. We will have to capitulate."

I was disgusted. His lack of intelligence and courage was the main reason why things were going so badly. Now he appeared to be simply giving in to the problems he had created. I should have realized there was more to it.

The Congress was in a turmoil and had no idea what to do. Everyone expected the Spanish to take Lima again, and this time they might also have the fortress at Callao. The only choice was to pay the soldiers and regain the fortress, but Torre Tagle said there was not enough cash available. The other action might have been to try negotiating with the Argentineans, but Torre Tagle would not.

Then, the Congress—to avoid taking responsibility themselves—did something that made the situation worse. They voted Bolívar absolute dictator over all military and political affairs. Since Bolívar was not there, he could not help the situation. When the situation grew worse, this made it seem that he was incompetent and could not be trusted. Meanwhile, Torre Tagle fumed and seethed at his loss of power.

Bolívar was already taking what steps he could. He sent couriers down and ordered the city evacuated of all military personnel and machinery and had it sent to Trujillo in case the Spanish took advantage of the situation. He also did something else that made the Peruvians hate him. He ordered a tax on the wealthy and had his soldiers collect it. *We are about to be invaded and all he does is steal our gold,* was the only thing the citizens could think about.

About a week later, I was sleeping in my bed at home, as was my usual choice while Bolívar was away. The other bed was too big and lonely without him, and I did not have my clothes and paints and powders when I arose. In the middle of the night, Jonotás climbed into bed with me.

I was roused from my slumber but was too unconscious to ask what was happening. She said, "Manuelita?"

"Uhm . . . Yes?" I was not yet fully awake.

"Manuelita, I am scared."

I turned over and put my arms around her, fully awake. "What is it?"

"Falucho, he told me things. He left the fortress tonight, to be with me, and he frightened me." She started crying.

"What did he say?"

"He says that the men who led the mutiny—he said their names were . . . Moyano and Oliva—have been talkin' to a Colonel Casariego . . ." She wiped her eyes with her hands.

"Who is he?" I asked impatiently while sitting up.

"He is one of the Spanish officers who is imprisoned in the fortress. Oliva had known him in Chile, and he has convinced Oliva that their situation is desperate and only if they release the Spanish imprisoned in the fortress and embrace the Royalist cause can the men hope to come out of their situation alive."

I fell back onto the bed. Nothing would be more disastrous. "What about your soldier? What is he going to do?"

Her sobbing increased. "That is what frightens me. He will not go along." I sympathized with her. I could see the danger and I put my arms around her and kissed her cheek and said, "We'll think of something to do in the morning."

We fell asleep at last, but we rose early. "You must go back, my sweet," I told her. "You must be my eyes and ears up there. Let me know what happens."

"Yes, Manuelita, I understand."

"And try to get your soldier out of there. Tell him that I will give him a position right here." Jonotás was a brave woman. She understood me, and there were no more tears. "Go now and keep me informed."

I expected and feared the worst. I made sure everything in my own house was in order. I paid particular attention to everything in James's desk. Nothing must be amiss, if I had to leave, and he returned before me. Then I packed a couple of trunks. I dressed in my colonel's uniform and I strapped on my pistols.

"Why are we packin'?" Natán asked. "Are we leavin'?"

"I don't think so. I'm sure everything will be all right. I just want to be prepared." We loaded up some of the garrison's mules with my trunks and took them down to the villa.

There, after we saw that the animals were well fed, we went inside to pack Bolívar's papers. Later, I had to send Natán off to get some more trunks and boxes.

If I had to leave, I might be on the road for some time. Everything had to be packed perfectly and recorded so that I could instantly unpack to find something or to file something. In the middle of my work, with papers scattered everywhere, General Lara came in and asked for a copy of a letter.

"I'm sorry, Señor, but Bolívar's papers are being packed. Besides, I do not have the authority to give out the Liberator's correspondence."

He looked at me angrily and said, "It is to do a job for the Liberator that I need the letter."

"Yes, Señor, but I cannot give it to you."

"And why is everything being packed?" He stood in the doorway and surveyed the room, with papers scattered all over the floor.

"Precautions, Señor."

"A fine thing. So cautious that nothing can be done. Why is it, *Señora*," he said, avoiding using the title of Colonel, "that are you being so careful."

"I have reason to believe that an evacuation might be necessary, *Señor*." I kept right on putting papers in sorted stacks.

"That is the most preposterous nonsense I've ever heard of. I'll search for it myself."

He took a step into the room. I jumped to my feet and pulled a pistol from its holster. Leveling it at his heart, I said, "Do not come in here, Señor. When I see authorization from Bolívar for the removal of some part of his correspondence and when you have given me a receipt for the document you will take, you can have it. In the meantime, I am in charge of these papers; and while I am so sanctioned, no one will violate them."

He stood there a moment with his mouth open. At last, he said, "You will be hanged for pointing a gun at an officer of my rank."

I was not going to debate with him. "Yes, General," was all I said, but I did not move.

He grew red with anger and then left abruptly. I went back to my sorting. Despite the fact that I knew he might be right about the ramifications of what I had just done, I spent only a second worrying about it. Then, I finished packing. When I was done, I waited.

It was a rare day when the sun could be seen through the perpetual blanket of clouds that covers Lima. The sun was hot and beat down on Magdalena and the Villa, bringing a stillness to everything. I waited. I tried to think if there was anything I had forgotten, but I could not think clearly. I sat in the patio and looked off across the sand dunes next to Magdalena and to the ocean beyond.

This beautiful little town meant so much to me. Everything I had ever done or experienced here had been warm and comfortable. The breeze blew across my cheek and the scent of flowers filled the hot afternoon. In this little town, I was always happy.

In mid afternoon, the calm was broken by galloping hooves. Natán and I ran to the front steps and out into the street where Jonotás was climbing off her horse. She looked at me and then sank to her knees, sobbing.

We ran to her and she said, "It happened. The fortress has been given over to the Spanish prisoners."

"No! Damn them!" But I realized that she was not sobbing for the loss of the fortress. "What's happened to your soldier?"

Tears washed down her already wet face. "It was horrible. When they tried to raise the Spanish flag on the tower facin' Lima, before they could tie down the rope, Falucho—" Her sobbing overcame her. We coaxed her to go on. "Falucho ran up, pushed them back, and broke his musket against the flag staff. 'Never will I fight for Spain,' he said. '¡Viva Buenos Aires!' he shouted. And then . . . they shot him. Manuelita, they killed him." She fell to the ground, crying softly but uncontrollably.

We picked her up and walked her toward the steps. I said, more to myself than her, "What's to happen now?"

Through her sobs she said, "I saw a messenger leave the fortress. I'm sure he has gone to notify the *godos*."

"Yes. They will retake Lima, now that the fortress is theirs."

We had to leave.

I told Natán to ride into Lima and find out what was stirring there and what the reaction was. "Find out what the last of the patriot army is doing. And, if they're abandoning the city, where they are going," I called after her as she galloped away. Then I took Jonotás into the villa to comfort her.

On the way, I gave orders to the guards. "Find all those who are off duty, bring them here, and load every rifle you have, and saddle every horse or mule you can find, and prepare for an assault by the Royalists."

The two on duty looked at me in bewilderment. I lashed out at them in anger. "Do it. Do it now, damn it." They snapped into motion and started running to rouse the others.

I was able to pull Jonotás together. She is not one to wallow in her emotions when something must be done. It was not hard for me to make her to see the danger and what we had to do, and soon we both were going through the villa to make sure we had everything that was important or that Simón might want.

Then, we loaded our mules with boxes of papers and trunks of clothes and other necessities. We prepared our horses to ride out—to somewhere—as soon as Natán returned. I wanted to go to Trujillo or Patavilca to find Simón, but I did not want to risk crossing the Rimac at Callao. There, of all places, we might be captured. So I had decided to head south, to Pisco. I did not know how long we could hold out, all alone, with only the villa's few guards, but I would try. What I feared most was allowing Simón's letters and papers to fall into the hands of the *godos*.

Then, just when I thought I had secured everything, I found that there were letters and documents of Bolívar's in his bedroom. In all of the confusion, I had missed these. I moved quickly. We pulled a box off a mule and dragged it back into the house. Then I had Jonotás unload it while I gathered everything up that was still in Simón's room. I would destroy my precious organization unless I repacked. As the two of us worked, we heard a horse.

"Let us hope Natán has no bad news," I said, as we heard her come to a stop. We ran outside.

Natán hadn't been gone more than three hours when she returned, her horse lathered and sweating after running hard in the heat. As she swung to the ground, she said, "With his own hands, that President, that Torre Tagle, he opened the gates of Lima and the Spanish soldiers are runin' through the city."

"The fool," I said under my breath.

"Manuelita, I'm scared. They're lookin' everywhere for republican leaders. They're hangin' them."

Chapter 13

We had to leave. But, I was not done packing. Not only did I have to reorganize, but when I pulled Simón's letters from his bedroom, I discovered a great deal of Simón's silver. I had to hide it among the papers.

In the middle of it all, Natán rushed in saying, "The guards—they took off their uniforms, and they're runnin' away."

I ran out to see the last them running down the street toward Lima. I pulled my pistol but thought it pointless to shoot them.

There were only three guards left. Despite their bravery, they would never be able to protect us. "You are brave soldiers. Prepare to leave."

"We are ready, and will protect you, Colonel," one of them said.

I turned away. If it came to that, we would all die. I thought about dismissing them, but they knew their duty.

I did not have time to think about it any further. I rushed back inside and continued sorting. In a few minutes, I had the new letters sorted with the others and I was just beginning to load them into the box when I heard soldiers ride up. I heard no warning from Jonotás or Natán so I kept at it.

General Miller walked in. "What are you doing, Ma'am?" he said in English.

"I'm saving Bolívar's papers," I said in Spanish as I loaded another handful, properly sorted, in the box.

His voice agitated from hard riding and tension, he said, "Do you not know that the *godos* are in Lima?"

"Yes, Señor." I could not concentrate on speaking in English.

"Do you also know that Manuela Sáenz is one of those they want to swing from the gibbet?"

I stopped and looked at him and smiled. "I always wanted to be popular," I said.

"Madam, please—"

"Assist me," I said, as I loaded another stack into the box. General Miller reached down and handed me the last stack and then helped me to close the box. Together we took it out to the mules and tied it on.

Three hundred Peruvian officials, military machinery, and other personnel, along with Torre Tagle went over to the *godos* that day. While the Spanish were busy arresting patriots in Lima or converting them to the Spanish cause, brave General Miller had led a rough group of soldiers and loyal followers out of the city and down to Magdalena to rescue me and the other soldiers at the villa. As we secured the ropes around the boxes, his evacuees stood all about looking shaken and worried. Monteagudo and General Lara were there, as well as several other officers and republican administrators—the last of Bolívar's government. The remnants of the villa's guards were there also, mounted and ready to ride.

General Miller and I were the only ones still on the ground. I double-checked the fastenings as General Miller mounted and said, "We'll take it slow and cautious. To the south, first."

I climbed on Midnight and followed the band of soldiers as they rode south of Magdalena and into the dunes. General Lara passed me as he rode to the front of the column, but he refused to look at me. He did not want to have to acknowledge that I, a mere woman, had been right. However, he never reported our confrontation to anyone.

After riding south a league or so, General Miller led us east, across the dunes, toward the foothills of the Andes. We headed south a little bit more and then east again. The day turned into night. The nearly full moon rose out of the jagged Andes and into the cloudless skies.

General Miller finally turned north, having come far enough to skirt around Lima. He had to weave us in and out between the dunes and hillocks so that our silhouettes would not be seen. We took a serpentine path, left, right, left, reverse, forward, on and on into the foothills beyond Lima. We crossed the Rimac, and when we were finally north of the city, we picked up our pace.

We drove on to meet with Bolívar. Our one problem was that no one quite knew where he was. He had been scouting the terrain in the northern regions when the events in Callao transpired. He would be difficult to find.

I was uncertain as to what was to become of us, but I forced myself not to be frightened. After all, I was experiencing first-hand what Simón's soldiers had experienced many times over the last 15 years. If I wanted to be a soldier, it was all becoming very real. We rode on, into the night.

We could not head out in a straight bold line for his likely whereabouts. We still had to be very careful not to meet up with any of Canterac's men, and we did not make much progress because we stopped while scouts were sent forward and we backtracked many times. However, after we were many leagues north of the Rimac, we moved more easily.

As we rode into the rugged defiles of the foothills, we had to slow down again to negotiate the rougher terrain. After only an hour of such travel, we came to a sudden stop. Everyone was quiet, sitting in stiff tension. Then I noticed a band of mounted men on a small plateau just ahead of us. They looked ominous and dangerous. I could barely see more than their silhouettes, but I saw moonlight glint off swords, knives, pistols, and rifles.

General Miller urged his mount slowly forward. I was frightened and cocked one of my own pistols.

After a few minutes, he rode back and the strange horsemen turned and rode on ahead of us. General Miller said, quietly, "All right, let's move forward."

Our band followed the men in front of us. He rode back to me, rightfully guessing that I was somewhat worried. "It is the *montoneros*," he said. "They will scout ahead of us."

"That is good," was all I could say.

"Are you and your slaves all right?"

I was saddle sore and my back ached. I could tell that Jonotás and Natán were no better off than myself. Still, they had not made even one complaint. I merely said, "We are well. Thank you, General."

He said, "Good," and rode along beside me in the dark. He traveled with me for a long time, the *montoneros* in front, and the general in back with me and my slow moving mules, watching behind us. We talked, and I was grateful for his company and for the information he gave me about his plans and expectations.

General Miller did not know exactly where Bolívar was. It would have been easier for us to move in the general direction of Trujillo, but the Liberator was more likely east, in the mountains. With Bolívar thus ambulatory, we would have difficulty finding him and he would be without any government or administrative personnel for many days.

We traveled for hours that night, along narrow cliffs, the feet of our horses slipping on the sharp, shifting stones. We climbed, hour after hour, short of breath from exertion and the rareness of the air, making our way into the deep shadows cast by the moon, along crevasses that would have been life-threatening in daylight. As the sky in the east was showing the first, faint signs of light, we found a small plateau which barely held our tiny band of soldiers and the *montoneros*

There, with only our *ponchos* to keep us warm, we slept on the freezing ground for three or four hours. Then we continued our climb into the Andes.

A day or so later, riding thus for eighteen to twenty hours at a time, we reached the cold *puna*. We were nearly a league high, surrounded by ice capped mountains, with almost no vegetation, no animals, completely devoid of anything living except an occasional tiny weed sprouting between rocks. We had to rely on what stores the *montoneros* could provide or that they had brought with them.

In the day time we endured scorching heat, and in the night we suffered freezing cold. On and on we rode, occasionally crossing another range of low mountains or deep canyons. We lost two soldiers, who fell to their deaths, in as many nights, when their horses slipped on the path.

Natán became ill, due to the cold at night, and I was glad when we came one day to the town of Huarás. It is a small town, about halfway to Trujillo from Lima, and we slept in huts with our Indian hosts that night.

Bolívar had been to this little village, protected by high mountains east and west, and had at one time made his headquarters there. However, his whereabouts were unknown. I wanted to stay there and wait for Bolívar to be found. But General Miller explained that we did not know what Bolívar's plans were or how much danger we faced from the Royalists.

So we moved on: north, ever north. We slept on the cold ground more often than not. Natán became worse and I feared she could not take much more of such exposure. She was coughing and wheezing, worse even than Bolívar at times. I worried that her illness would seriously infect her lungs if we did not find some way for her to rest. The fact was, neither Jonotás nor I was much better off.

After many days, Bolívar was found. Wide ranging scouts reported that Bolívar had made headquarters again. He was many leagues to the south, in Huarás. If I had waited, as my intuition had told me, he would have ridden right to me.

General Lara, impatient with our slow progress, in part due to my mules, announced to General Miller that he was tired of "women." He looked both at me and at Monteagudo, whose perfume and effeminate ways disgusted the general even more than his distaste for me. He rode off to Huarás on his own.

I wanted to ride down to Trujillo, which was relatively close by, to rest, but General Miller again explained about our precarious position. The Royalists knew about the activities in Trujillo, and it was certainly a military target. Instead, he took a few soldiers and led me and my two companions a short distance to the north. There he arranged a hut for us in the tiny village of Huamachucho.

"This, for now, will be in the sphere of the Liberator's operations. He will keep moving, but you can stay here and rest. You will be safe here." He looked at the cordillera to the east. Its cold peaks seemed to personally blow down the icy wind that was whistling through the broken tile on the roof. He thought for a moment. "If something changes, we will move you again."

I looked inside at the dirt floor, the one table, the small dirty bed filled with straw. I did not relish being left alone here, but neither did I wish to continue our cold trek among the Andes. "General, I am grateful to you for saving me and my companions."

He smiled, and said, "The pleasure of doing so is more than reward for an action which is nothing more than my duty. Do take care of yourself." He turned and mounted his horse in a single leap.

"Give my love to Simón," I said simply.

He smiled and said, "I will do so, Madam." He saluted, turned with his small band of men, and rode towards the *sierra*.

I watched him ride away and fully realized that the battles were upon us. Many would die over the next many months. I could feel death in the glacial air around me. Already, I had tasted, but only barely, the hardships that we would all have to face. If our trials were to be much worse than what we had already experienced in the past many days, death might be preferable to some. Little did I know that so far, we had only lived through the best of it.

Chapter 14

After I was left alone in Huamachucho, I had time to reflect on the events of the past several weeks. The loss of Lima was a catastrophe. Both the capital and the fortress at Callao were now held by the *godos*. The patriots controlled only the tiniest amount of territory in northern Perú—a small buffer to keep the Royalists from invading Gran Colombia.

To make matters worse, the land we held was not able to support a large number of troops. The only food available was the scarcest amount of potatoes or barley to sustain the Indians that lived there. There certainly was nothing in the way of cloth for uniforms, leather for the horses' gear, or other supplies an army might need. Everything the patriot army needed would have to be brought up from Trujillo. If control of the port at Trujillo was lost, the revolution in Perú would also be lost. Fortunately, the Pacific was still held by the patriots. I pondered this bleak situation along with the knowledge that the Royalists outnumbered us more than two to one.

My own situation was difficult enough. It was only by Herculean efforts that Jonotás, Natán, and I were able to keep warm at night. We would have to build the largest possible fire in our stone stove, and all sleep together under two blankets and all our ponchos. The walls were made of earth, covered with *tapia*, but the coverings on the two windows and the door were old and inadequate, and the roof needed repair. While I lay shivering with my friends, I knew that I was in a palace compared to where Bolívar might be sleeping. He might not be lucky enough, with his traveling about, to even be sleeping in a shelter.

I thought of his nearly dying in Patavilca only two months before. Images of him coughing uncontrollably seared my mind. I fought with my fear for his safety every day.

My one happiness in those first dreadful, lonely days in Huamachucho was a visit from José María. He was on his way to Trujillo, on a mission for Bolívar, and he detoured somewhat to see me. It had been months since we had seen each other, and I almost cried with happiness when I came outside as he dismounted from a muddy horse. I ran to him, threw my arms around him, and said, "José, you are here. You are safe."

"Quite safe," he replied, wearily. "And you, my sister, how are you? You look thin."

"I am fine," I lied. "I did not want him to know that since we had left Lima, we had not eaten anything but a little *charqui* and potatoes. Nor did I wish him to know that I was afraid I was catching whatever Natán had, and I felt quite ill.

We walked into the house. José greeted Jonotás and then said, "Natán, are you all right?"

"I'm fine, Señor," she answered, bravely, although she had eaten less than Jonotás or me, and was feverish.

José sat wearily at our little table. I sat across from him and asked, "How go the preparations?"

"They go well. All of Bolívar's officers are worried, but I watch the general. He is confident."

"How is he, José?" I asked. I know he saw concern in my eyes.

"He is well, Manuela. You need not worry."

I smiled. "And you say he is confident?"

"Yes." Jonotás sat the last of our *maté* on the tiny table in front of him. He thanked her, blew a little on the cup to cool it, and went on. "He works, day and night, of course, writing orders, reading dispatches. Or he is scouting. He is tireless and does not seem to ponder our situation or worry. He merely works."

"Does he know where I am?" I asked.

He smiled. "Oh, yes. When General Lara arrived, he informed Bolívar and then started complaining about you."

"About me?" I said, though I was not surprised.

"Yes. You should have heard him. He said, 'I am glad to be here, instead of riding with those "women,"' José laughed and went on. "Bolívar only looked at him. The general continued, saying, 'Here we are, on the eve of perhaps our most glorious campaign, and Your Excellency has brought "Colonel Manuelita" with him, and that Monteagudo.'"

"What did Simón say?"

"'They run the risks of the campaign like everyone else.' He said this with a little annoyance in his voice. He respects Lara, but he does not like to hear complaining."

I laughed and said, "I've seen that in him. I can imagine what he looked like."

"Then, the elder general made a mistake. He said, 'The truth is, Your Excellency, that someone will kill that little Monteagudo.' The Liberator rose, slamming down his paper, and he shouted, 'Just let them touch a hair of his head . . . .' That put an end to Lara's complaining. Bolívar sat back down and asked about your location and well-being."

"The general is right. I don't know why Bolívar insists on keeping that hated man on his staff. Monteagudo is not a good man to have about you. Some one *will* kill him."

"I suspect not before the war is over, and that is what we should have on our minds."

"You are right, my brother." I looked at his handsome face, hardened by war. "I worry for you," I said.

"Please do not. I have fought these many years and I can last a few more months."

The finality of his statement stunned me. I saw so clearly what José María had already deduced. These would be the final battles for us.

If the *godos* won the contests that were to come, he and I and Bolívar and all the other brave soldiers in Peru would certainly be killed in battle, or we would hang. Many more years of war would follow as they reclaimed the continent. Without the leadership of men like San Martín and Bolívar, South America would eventually be lost. We had to win, and yet I could not see the means. The battles to come would decide the fate of us all, and though the odds seemed impossible we could do nothing but face them.

I could not hide the uncertainty I felt and asked him directly, "José, what do think will happen?"

His face grew somber. "I will be honest with you, my sister. I do not see how we can win. I can only look to the Liberator for encouragement."

"And what does he say? Honestly."

"Honestly? He is more confident than he has a right to be. When Lara, upon being briefed, saw the situation, he said, 'Your Excellency, we do not have Lima anymore. We do not have the treasury. We do not have any means of obtaining money. We have no means to attack and are encircled by an enemy outnumbering us by nearly 10,000. What will you do now, my General?'"

"What did he say?"

José María chuckled. "Bolívar looked at Lara as though he wondered why the general could not understand, and said, 'I? I? Why, I will triumph.'"

We both stared at each other, contemplating Simón's words, and then, as one, we burst out laughing. I could imagine Bolívar saying exactly that, and it was so much fun to see him thus, in my mind's eye.

I spent a wonderful morning with José María, in which time we walked around the little town of Huamachucho and found a better place to stay. José María helped me "appropriate" it. It was a little larger and in better repair, so it would be warmer. Finally, after a noon time snack, José left for Trujillo.

A day or so later, we had moved into our new dwelling. A courier almost did not find me to deliver a letter from Simón.

Dearest Manuela—

You have escaped the circumstances in Lima. I cannot tell you how glad I am that you are safe. Please stay in the north in the next few months. The *godos* are a constant threat and I am ever on the move. I want to know where to find you.

I will see you soon. I yearn to see you. My memory of your enchanting nature visits me often and makes me long for you.

Keep yourself well,
Simón

That letter allowed me to make it through the next few weeks, with its awful boredom and privation. I worried about Simón every day, but I kept an image of him, which I knew reflected his true nature: confident, capable in soldiering, and determined to win.

Perhaps the tension of never knowing what was happening, and the feeling of being trapped, is what made me dream so often of Miquita in those weeks of troubled sleep. It was not truly Miquita I dreamed of, but rather of the days of La Perricholi, the days of the viceroys, the days of wealth and grandeur in Lima, the days that were already dying by the time I first arrived in Peru.

I saw visions of aristocratic men and women walking, or riding fine horses, from the Calle de Correro to the Calle de Bodegones. The men, as they bought flowers in the Plaza Mayor, were dressed in the elegant garments of their age: head or neck wrapped in a scarf of silk set off with Chinese ribbons, wide brimmed hats covered their faces and touched a cape of blue Carcassonne cloth, black velvet jackets with gold buttons, knee length velvet breeches, stockings made from Philippine silk, shoes of Cordovan leather, chains dangling from embroidered pockets adorned with emeralds, gold or diamonds. The aristocratic men in my dreams would take their flowers, purchased from beautiful *cholas*, and present them to fine ladies, dressed as elegantly as the men: Flanders lace on their hems, their undergarments, their doublets; pearls, gold, or precious stones adorning their wrists and fingers; pendulant earrings of cascading iridescent stones; and stockings of the finest lace.

I could see these magnificent men and women from the past, making their way to the Coliseo de Comedias, to enjoy the theatricals that would last into the night: ballets, skits, music, and the plays of Calderón or Vales de Guevara or Añorbe.

As I saw these images, I smelled the ladies perfumes, the cigar smoke, the *puchero* cooking in the cafés. I saw the colors, heard the music, felt the people jostle against me in the market. Most of all, I saw a world that was gone. A world of opulence that would never return. A world that I was surprised I longed for—until I realized that it was also a world of peace that I was so afraid I would never see again.

Thus did I spend those first weeks in Huamachucho. The sinister mystery of not knowing what was happening with the war wore away at my nerves. Out of sheer frustration, I made myself get busy and do what I have always done. I gathered information.

I made sure that all the couriers who happened to go through the town were given a meal, befriended, and enlisted as a source of intelligence. I made Jonotás and Natán become friendly with as many Indians as they could. They were not enthusiastic at first, but when they began to produce little bits of information for me, as they can do so well, it improved their spirits.

The Indians moved about the Andes like they were no more than the dunes outside Magdalena. Thus did we hear the news from traders who came up from the coast, and to a lesser degree, the Indians traveling from the south.

Thus, despite our lethargy from rare air, inadequate food, and illness—I was still fighting off a fever—we were able to become part of the war. I almost wish I had not been so thorough. One of the things I found out was that Bolívar, upon passing through a village called San Ildefonso, bedded a young woman by the name of Manuelita Madroño. She was only eighteen and said to be of surpassing beauty.

That bit of news nearly killed me. I felt stupid and betrayed. While I sat in a cold village, with nothing more exciting to do than watch the wind blow the Andean dust in my eyes, fulfilling my duty to do the task of protecting the Liberator's papers, he availed himself of the bounty of the land.

I became feverish that very evening and had to spend many days in bed, shivering in wretched grief. I wrote to my friend Juan Santana telling him that I might die, as I no longer wished to live. I almost meant it.

Jonotás and Natán nursed me back to health, and when my body was better, I felt better as a person. I refused to cry, throughout. I would not let this matter to me. When I saw him again, when the war was over, then I would perhaps have revenge, or at least make a new decision about Bolívar. While the war was on, I was a soldier with a duty, and I would see it through to the end. But my days seemed so much gloomier after that.

One evening, Jonotás, Natán, and I were finishing a meager dinner. It was a Quechua dish of red peppers, onions, and bits of beef, similar to the *picantes* sold in the Indian shops in Lima. We ate as the natives would—without forks.

Just as we were wiping our hands we heard horses outside. I rose and finished cleaning my hands by washing them in a shallow pan close to the table. When I turned around, the door was already open and Simón was standing silhouetted against the gray evening sky.

We all stood in silence for a moment. Then, Jonotás and Natán curtsied—a strange sight because they were both wearing soldiers uniforms—and said, "Good evening, Your Excellency."

Bolívar smiled and said, "Good evening."

Jonotás and Natán excused themselves and left the house.

Bolívar looked tired. He coughed a little and came inside, closing the door behind him. He smiled, and said, "What's the matter, Manuelita?" He started to come over to me, but I walked to the opposite side of the table.

"Sit down, Señor," I said, coldly.

"Are you all right?"

"I am fine, Señor. Sit down, please."

He sat down, giving a look of distaste at the contents of bowl still on the table. "This is an unexpected reception," he said and started to remove his boots. He looked puzzled. "Are you all right?"

"I am well, Your Excellency."

"I insist that you call me Simón," he said, smiling, recalling our first moment together at the victory ball in Quito—was it two years ago. He pulled off one boot and put it on the floor.

"I am to call you Simón? Am I not to be a soldier then?" I stood rigid and stern. He looked up at me in bewilderment. Then, my voice became shrill. "Am I to be another one of your conquests as you ride through the Andes?" The men outside must have heard me. I could hear their low voices become silent.

I came around the table and flew at him, my fists hammering down on his shoulders and chest. He stood up, overturning the chair. As he backed up, I heard the wood in the chair crack as he stepped on a rung with his remaining boot. "Stop. Stop it, Manuela," he was saying, as he defended himself.

All the while I went on. "You couldn't betray me in Lima. You had to wait until I came to the end of the world to be with you. How dare you?"

Finally, he grabbed my wrists and stopped me. He shouted at the top of his lungs, "Enough."

"How dare you?" I repeated, breathlessly, as I tried to pull my hands away.

Anger flashed across his face. He held me firm, and said angrily, "I do not see how you can claim I have been unfaithful to you."

"Do you not, Señor?"

"Have I ever once promised you I would?"

"Yes!" I screamed. I pulled my hands away. "Yes, damn you. Yes. You have. With every kiss. With every caress. You have. You will not say it with words; you save that for your whores, but you say it, damn you."

We stood there, our breath coming in short gasps, staring at each other like two animals, out for the other's blood.

I heard the men outside move discreetly off. As they did, Simón started to cough. In his anger, he tried to suppress it at first, but it was unstoppable. He sat down on the bed behind him.

I cursed my love for him as I sat down next to him and held him while the fit subsided. At last, I said, "Is it worse?"

"No. I shouldn't have yelled at you. It's been a long ride, and I'm tired."

I got down on my knees and pulled his other boot off. Quietly, I said, "You should not have done it, Simón. You nearly killed me."

"I care only for you."

"Then why—"

"Manuela, believe me, I have missed you terribly. I know that life here has not been easy for you. Nor has it been for me. But you are married, and so arguments about fidelity—" He saw the anger cross my face. Then he said softly, almost to himself, "Sometimes, I long not to long for you."

I shook my head, more to shake off the tears I felt building in me.

At long last, he said softly, "Manuela, I do love you so."

The tears came.

"What?" he whispered.

"Simón, you said it." My anger faded completely. I did not want to fight with him anymore. I felt that feeling, that only he could give me. We were alone, in a world of our own. "Simón, I love you."

He looked at me tenderly. I could tell he was weary. Never have I seen someone so weary. His eyes drifted down from my face. I looked down and saw that in the struggle, my uniform had come open. I was not wearing anything underneath my jacket, and the curves of my breasts were plainly visible. He gazed at me with desire, and I felt as though he had caressed me there.

His eyes burned with fever and my breath became short with the desire I felt. He held out his hand, and I took it. I kissed his fingers. I moved his hand to my cheek, my neck, and to my waiting breasts. I wanted him to feel me, to feel the fullness of my hunger. I pulled myself up and placed my lips against his. I had needed him, wanted him so. He pressed me to him and kissed me hard. In that inhospitable terrain, surrounded by enemies, we had no other choice but to love one another with all the passion in our souls.

Chapter 15

We spent almost a whole day together. We stayed in bed. We only arose to eat or handle other necessities. We loved, feverishly, hungrily, for hours. We were tender. We were rough. We laughed. We talked as much as we loved. The desolate land had gripped us. There was so little color or life in those high Andean plateaus that it seemed we tried to grace it with our own creative energies. It was as though our passion for each other could reach out and recreate the world anew.

The following afternoon, almost a whole day after Simón had arrived, we had another disagreement. I lay with my head on his chest, his hand rubbing the small of my back, my thick hair nearly covering my face. We had been quiet for some time, drinking in the peace we had brought to that place and that time. I broke the silence by saying, "Simón, I'm going with you."

"No, Manuela," he said, tenderly. "I am too mobile these days. It is tough on my men, let alone three women—even if they are Amazons." He smiled, but then his face became serious. "Many times I do not find a village before night falls and have to sleep without shelter—from either the elements or the enemy."

"I want to be with you, Simón. That's why I'm here. I want to be there when you need me. I want to do my duty, as a soldier, by your side. Or as close as I can be."

Exasperation took over, and he said, "Manuela, you will not be able to keep up with me."

"I know that, Simón. I will merely follow you. You go where you must, and I will follow. I will move from one village to the next."

"Does this have to do with—"

"No, Simón, but I am still angry with you about that."

"Manuela—"

"Never mind, this has nothing to do with it. I simply cannot stand to wait here. I would rather suffer in privation than sit here. If my job is to protect your personal papers and your government's files, I should not be where I can be found while we are at war. Many travelers have passed through here, and some know who I am. If this information fell into the wrong hands, your government would be forfeit, as well as my life. My whereabouts should be unknown to all but you, and to you I should be immediately accessible, not a two- or three-day ride away."

Simón agreed with that point, but never fully agreed that I should follow him all over the Andes. However, when we emerged from the house a short while later, he assigned a half dozen lancers who were with him to be my personal guard. I don't know what happened to Jonotás and Natán while Simón and I kept to ourselves, but they were there when we came out. Simón and I said a brief good-bye and then he was gone.

It took us until the next day to pack and prepare for the constant traveling that was to come. Natán was still not feeling as well as she might, but neither she nor Jonotás complained about what was ahead. We set out to follow Bolívar to Trujillo as the sun reached its zenith.

Before this campaign, I had never been in the third most important city in Peru—the first and second being Lima and Cuzco. It was here, where the entire army prepared, and waited, while Bolívar scouted the Andes. Trujillo does not actually sit on the ocean, but is inland like Lima. There is a collection of small houses called Moche right on the shore, but you must travel a league or so to reach the city. When I arrived in Trujillo itself, I was amazed at the activity. Even though it was not, strictly speaking, a port city, it was as alive as Panamá or Guayaquil.

Forging together the remains of the Argentine and Chilean troops with the Peruvians, Colombians, and what could be conscripted from the land, Bolívar had created a unified liberating army. He had designed a new uniform, blue with red cuffs. However, since money was so short, there was every kind of uniform imaginable that had been shipped over from Europe. I saw long coats that had been used by the French in the Russian campaign, leftover rags from Waterloo, patent leather bicorn hats on some officers, shakos on others, and a mixture of styles on the infantry. Yet, I did think they looked fine.

The soldiers for whom I felt sorriest were those who wore *jatas* (sandals) on their feet—which was most of the soldiers. Having just come from the mountains, I knew how cold it could be. Some were lucky enough to have boots, but not many. Later, each company was issued a bullock's skin from which several men could carve out, and fashion, their own boots.

Not only were soldiers being amassed in Trujillo; there were hundreds of other items needed by the army: rifles, artillery, wagons, and food. I also noticed, and wondered about, a large amount of lumber being packed into the mountains.

Lack of money was the biggest problem the army faced. Troops were on one-quarter remuneration. Surprisingly, there were few desertions, despite the enforced conscriptions and poor pay. Bolívar made sure that his soldiers at least received the little money that was coming to them, and he made sure they ate well. He saw that a steer was allotted to each mess group daily along with *chicha* and dried corn. But there were other difficulties caused by lack of funds. Bolívar was forced to take silver from church treasuries, cattle and clothing from Indians, and anything else that was needed. This caused disaffection with him that lasted for years.

As we left Trujillo, I shook my head. I saw that the entire area had once been an ancient Indian city. There were ruins everywhere, and I could see that new houses had been built right on top of them. I wondered how many treasures and secrets were being buried by the present inhabitants, never again to be found.

It had been Simón's intention to ride down the coast to Chimbote and then up the river to Huarás. As I had promised, I followed where he went—across the desert that lies along the coast of Perú and back into the Andes.

Sometimes we had to stop longer than I wished, in Trujillo, for example, to let Natán rest—the coastal warmth did her good and by the time we reached the sierra again she was mostly recovered. I wanted to follow Bolívar as closely as possible, but, as he had warned me, he moved too fast. Sometimes we were slow because we were simply too tired, or we wished to stop and wash our clothes—which were becoming rags—or ourselves. Simón and I corresponded, and I received regular visits from couriers with orders, or letters to file, but I never caught up to him.

Weeks later, when we came into the valley of Huarás, Bolívar's plan was evident. He intended to cross the Andean passes, as he had done in Colombia, and drive south to meet the enemy where they controlled the center of Perú.

As I rode up to his headquarters, I learned the reason for so much lumber being brought up from the coast. It was to build shelters along the intended route in order to keep the loss of life, from the elements, to a minimum. General Sucre also had Indians cutting *champas* (native peat) for fuel; and hidden caves along the route, revealed by the local Indians, were being filled with jerked llama meat, rice, tobacco, salt, and sacks of the stimulating coca leaf. Once the Indians who helped hide these provisions were done with their jobs, they were taken to Trujillo and held there lest they reveal the secrets to the *godos*.

Though Simón was many leagues ahead, in the freezing Andean passes scouting marching routes, I decided to stay in Huarás for a while. We needed to make new uniforms and I wanted Natán to rest.

After I was there for a day or so, I saw General Sucre and Colonel Sandes get into an argument. "Do you accuse me of dishonesty, Señor?" said Sandes at one point. I saw him turn toward the door where he had set his sword.

We were in one of the largest houses in Huarás. I sat in the large wooden floored room, that served as communal dining area and war room, writing some letters. Sucre and Sandes had both arrived at the same time looking for some ink. They each discovered that the other was writing to Mariana Solanda and they began to have words. When I saw Sandes reach for his sword, I said, "Gentlemen, gentlemen, we do the cause no good when we argue amongst ourselves."

At that moment, O'Conner, who shared a room with Sucre, entered saying, "Ah, there you are, Sucre. This just arrived." He handed over a letter, and I could tell that Sandes presumed it was a letter from Mariana. He flung open the door and stormed outside.

Sucre raced after him, saying, "Sandes, it's from Trujillo. You need to know this."

The door was still open, and Sandes, upon hearing it was military business and not business of the heart, turned back and let Sucre show him the letter. I watched them through the door. They discussed the letter awhile, but then it appeared that the argument started again.

O'Conner said, "Those two are friends. I know they are rivals for the same girl, but that is not what the problem is."

I saw Sandes turn away angrily. Sucre walked off in the opposite direction, obviously disgusted. "What is the problem?" I asked.

O'Conner was another of the Irish soldiers so valuable to the patriot cause. His hair was very blonde and he was quite handsome. He looked out the door. "The war," he said. "All this waiting. Day in, day out, we prepare, we drill, we plan, we make ready again. It is getting on everyone's nerves." He went to the open door and looked out, saying, almost to himself, "And no women." Then, sheepishly, he turned to me and said, "That is . . . I mean—"

"That is all right." He gave me an idea. Sowerby had attacked a supply train the day before and had just returned with cattle and wine that had been meant for the viceroy's table. "And you are correct," I said. "We should do something about it."

O'Conner looked at me as if to inquire into my meaning.

I said, "Tonight we will have meat. Let us all have a party. We will dress as though we were in Lima, and give a lie to this place." I smirked. "My companions and I will have to serve for women. But we all have to make do."

He laughed, and said, "That is a magnificent idea, Señora. I will tell all the officers." He left.

I finished my letter, and then I found Jonotás and Natán. We prepared all afternoon for the evening's festivities. I enjoyed putting on my dress that evening. It had been many weeks since I had worn one, and I realized I had been missing a sense of femininity as much as the men. I only had some verbena to provide a scent to my skin, but I splashed it on liberally.

Often the infantrymen might be followed by their wives, but none of the officers had women with them. For noble ladies, the hardships of a campaign would be unbearable and unthinkable. Jonotás, Natán, and I were the only women in Huarás at that time who were not Indians.

Jonotás said, "You are cruel to wear such a dress to a party where the men have been so long from their women." She laughed and looked at my bosom, which was much revealed by the dress I had chosen.

I laughed and said, "It would be cruel to *me* if I were wear anything else. I feel light, and this is the first time I have felt so good since Lima."

"I know, Manuelita," she said sympathetically, as she twisted my hair to pile it high on my head.

She had done a wonderful job of braiding my hair, and, when I looked in a glass, I felt I had defeated the rigors of military life somewhat. I was still able to be beautiful, despite the time and the place.

When the officers arrived for dinner that night, each looked especially handsome. They all wore clean uniforms, with their medals in place, their boots polished, and their hair slicked down. After eating, we pushed the tables against the wall. The rough timber would have to serve as a dance floor.

Late in the afternoon, Captain Simpson, who had brought me to Lima in the *Helena*, arrived with a case of Irish whiskey. Fergusson had sampled much of it by the time we started dancing. "Simpson," he could be heard to say many times that evening, "it is a true patriot that ya are. You supply the army out of your own reserves," and then he would laugh. Simpson would always laugh along and then join him as he emptied his glass.

Only Jonotás, Natán, and I represented the "fairer sex," but we danced with everyone. I told my companions especially they must wear dresses. Jonotás did, but Natán, reticent as always to expose her beauty, wore her uniform. Nevertheless, men danced with her and flirted with all of us. Everyone provided music by either playing a guitar, singing, or simply clapping their hands.

The handsome Captain Sowerby was particularly attentive to Natán that evening, and I thought perhaps she might at last allow a man to show her some affection.

When I danced with him, in an attempt to do a little matchmaking, I said, "She is a pretty woman, is she not?" He looked over at Natán, who was smiling at us. He said, "Aye, Ma'am, that she is. If I had not already made up me mind to return to Ireland, she might almost make me want to stay."

"Are you going back to Ireland? When, Sir?" I know I did not hide my disappointment.

He laughed and said, "Not until this war is over." He was only twenty-nine, but he seemed even younger. It was often hard to believe that he had fought all over Europe in the Napoleonic wars and was as hardened a veteran as any of them. "But me mother and father are old. I wish to see them again, as much as I wish to see me home." The singing stopped—some patriotic song to which we had waltzed—and we walked over to where Natán was sitting.

His eyes twinkled with delight and a lock of his blond hair fell onto his forehead. The viceroy's wine had overcome me a bit. I laughed and said, "You are a handsome rogue, you are."

The three of us laughed and he said, as I had heard him say so many times before, "Aye, but only because of me luck. I have fought all the wars of the old world, and the new, and I have never received a scratch." It was true.

Just then, everyone started singing a lively tune, and Fergusson grabbed me and danced me around the floor. Everyone laughed and clapped their hands in time. "Ah,

Lass, it is good to dance again." He slurred his words, but he was amazingly accurate with his feet.

I laughed and said, "Yes, it is wonderful to dance." So it was, all evening, as I danced with one man after another.

Later, Fergusson was the first to dance alone. There was a lull, and he said, "Come, gentlemen . . . and ladies." He was slurring his words, but he gave a gallant bow to Jonotás, Natán and me. We all laughed. "The night is still young," he went on, and with that he did as fine an Irish jig as I had ever seen any of the Irish officers do. He could hardly talk, but he danced superlatively. His countrymen took up immediately singing an Irish melody to accompany him. Some joined him.

Not to be outdone, I took the floor while he was being congratulated and teased—he nearly fell over on the last step. I walked to the center of the room and signaled to Jonotás and Natán. They began humming the music while Jonotás tapped the time, and I did the *hondu*, a bolero that was popular in Lima.

When I was done, everyone applauded, and then one of them, who had seen me dance it at the victory ball in Quito said, "*ñapanga.*" Everyone took up the chant, but I quieted them down and said, "I am tired, gentlemen. Anyway, Jonotás does it better than I."

They did not have to urge her much before she was in the center of the room, her dress held high, often showing that she wore nothing else but her dress, dancing the most sensual South American dance I know. She was too good at it. If the men had not been so drunk, I think they might have left the Andes for the cities, where young women might be found, despite their duties.

After Jonotás's dance, the room became a riot, everyone danced, men arguing with each other as to who would lead, all to the tune of the songs we sang. We danced thus for some time before we all sat down, exhausted, drunk, and happy.

It was time to go to our beds. The party had been a grand one, and we were all tired.

Then I noticed that Sucre and Sandes, who had mostly avoided each other all evening, were sitting next to each other. The room became quiet. All eyes were on them as it became apparent that they wanted to speak to each other, but neither quite knew what to say.

Presently, Sucre said, "Don Arturo, I know you seek the hand of the young, beautiful daughter of the Marqués de Solanda. I also desire her for my own." He was smiling, letting the wine have its effect.

Sandes turned sharply toward Sucre, saying, "Don Antonio, there is no man I like better than you. But this is love, and I will have her." He too, through the wine, was smiling.

"Perhaps, but if you will permit me, I have a suggestion." The rest of the room was quiet. All ears waited to see what would come of this. "Let us try our luck to see who is to be her suitor."

Sandes looked stern and said, "Your suggestion, Señor?"

"Let us toss a peso. If you lose, I will send my offer of marriage by proxy this very hour."

Sandes kept his eyes on Sucre for a long time and slowly his face gave forth with a smile. "It is good for friends to find solutions to their problems. If you lose, it is *I* who will send an offer this hour." He looked around and said, soberly, "Who knows that we might not both be killed in this bloody war, and it won't make any difference anyway."

Someone produced a peso and passed it around the room, from hand to hand. I took a look at it when it came to me: the likeness of the King of Spain on one side and the arms of Castile and Leon on the reverse—a small metal disk that would decide the future somewhat of two men and perhaps a young girl. I passed it along.

O'Conner was sitting next to the two and stood up with it. Sandes said, "You may choose." Both the suitors nodded their assent and O'Conner threw the coin high in the air. Sucre said, "The king." The coin fell and it rolled across the rough boards for a short distance and spun to a stop.

It was the king. Mariana was to be Sucre's, who jumped to his feet and said, "You must all excuse me," and left.

Sandes looked morose, but we all, with some success, endeavored to cheer him up before we said goodnight.

That morning, we all went to our beds, tired but happy. It was a rare instance for me and my companions. It was Jonotás and I who went to our beds alone, and it was Natán who had found a lover for the night.

The next day, as Jonotás, Natán and I took a meal, and Jonotás teased Natán about Sowerby, Natán finally said, "He is a good man, but he is white. If he thinks about taking me to his family, he will not want to see me again. Even so, I would not be with him any more, even if he was born in Africa."

Both Jonotás and I let out cries of surprise. "Why?" we asked her.

She said simply, "He will be dead soon."

Jonotás and I stopped talking and looked at her. She drank some more broth. "What do you mean? How can you be sure?" I said, at last.

"I don't know. I only mean the war makes it all uncertain and he may be, he might as well be."

I thought about the night before and how so much of our lives is decided by nothing more meaningful than which side of a coin will come up on a toss. In Sucre's case, it altered his life, as I was to find out.

Each of the men I had been with the night before might, or might not, come out of the next few months alive. They were facing the crossing of hazardous mountains—as dangerous a trek as any in history. Their adversaries were men as seasoned as themselves—better equipped, clothed, and financed—from one of the mightiest powers of Europe. How many of them would slip into an abyss, or turn the wrong way in battle, and fall with as much finality as a fallen coin?

Sowerby was young, handsome, and a prize for any woman. He had never been hurt in any battle, had more experience than most, and was considered a competent soldier. Yet, as I let the warm broth strengthen me, I considered all this and decided that Natán was right not to let her heart become entangled, as I had let mine, with a man who might never return.

Chapter 16

Bolívar's entire army had assembled in the valley of Huarás by the end of June. Winter was approaching and it had grown colder by the week. They had to march.

Simón returned to Huarás the night before the army was to begin its arduous trek. We had one night of love before he was to lead his men into the cold limits of the Andes. I could not shake the thought that this night together might be our last.

"I love you," he said, as we lay in the dark after our lovemaking. "I will always love you."

I pulled myself closer to him and put my head on his chest. "You know I love *you*, Simón."

"I will leave tomorrow," he said, after a while. I felt him about to say something else, but he stopped.

I lifted my head, and tried to read his expression in the darkness. "Is something wrong?"

"No. It is only that the future is so uncertain. I wish I could do something for you—"

I did not want him to worry. "Don't, Simón," I said, softly. "Everyone in this valley faces the same uncertainty."

"Yes." His voice was hard.

After a moment, I said, "Tomorrow you will ride out to find and defeat the *godos*. You will succeed, and it will be your greatest triumph—the end of Spanish dominion in the Americas."

His answer seemed small and lonely in the dark. "We must not fail."

He ran his hand up along my back, a tender caress that made me wish there would be no tomorrow. I made myself not think about the possibility that we might never see each other again as we talked into the night. I worried about the lateness of the hour just before I drifted off. Simón must ride hard on the morrow, and he needed his sleep.

I need not have worried. The next day he was a picture of himself as he must have been in the early part of the war: the young general subduing Venezuela, conquering New Granada, and founding a new republic. He was dressed simply, a heavy poncho thrown over a plain uniform and a wide brimmed hat that darkened his eyes, eyes that seemed to see everything. Yet his ordinary uniform did nothing to diminish his authority, and it seemed like he personally moved the entire army into position.

Pastor pranced with impatience, as though he wished to be leading the columns into the passes himself. With his nostrils flaring, and the cold air showing his breath, he looked like some great mythological steed.

Bolívar sat in the saddle, vibrant and energetic, barking orders to his officers who rode back and forth mustering their men into marching columns. "No, Sucre, take your men further down the valley." "Córdoba, have the cattle moved far to the rear." "Why are the trumpeters not in position?"

Each command or question energized those around him, and the there was flurry of activity wherever he rode. Putting the plan into motion that Bolívar had conceived so many months before had given him new life. The only word to describe him that day was "magnificent."

The sun was barely up when the trumpets sounded. Bolívar's soldiers, assembled into perfect lines, began their march. The exodus was in three columns so that the enemy could not ambush the entire army as they moved through the defiles. Each column followed part of the *montonera,* who rode ahead and guarded the passes. Behind each column walked men with food—driving 6,000 head of cattle. Trumpets wailed at every hour, as signals rang back and forth between the passes.

I watched them begin their awful trek, splendid and proud. I dismissed the thought that I might be watching men march to slaughter. I sat on my horse and saluted as they passed. The fighting would be deadly, but the march itself would be deadly, too.

When the trumpet calls died down, the last of the army far up the trails, I turned toward the hut I shared with Jonotás and Natán. I was to wait a day or so, finish some business, and then follow.

In Huarás I was safe, but hardship for the army began that very day. Every league the army walked took them higher into the meager atmosphere. There, many suffered from the *soroche,* the mountain sickness. Once, I had seen the effects of rare atmosphere. A group of men rode up a hill and, one by one, they dropped off their horses when they reached the crest from lack of air rich enough to fill the lungs. It was this illness from lack of breath that affected Bolívar's soldiers first.

If the *soroche* did not drag them down, the treacherous rocks and caverns of the mountain trails exacted their payment in human blood. Comrades of those who fell heard the scream and a dull thud as bone met rock far below. Those who were not lucky enough to reach one of the shelters at night risked dying while they stood sleeping on the narrow passes in the frozen night. For every league of progress, a man died.

These hardships were communicated to me by Juan Santana, who sent back, not only letters, but dispatches to file, every day. Bolívar, who ordinarily could not keep enough scriveners busy, was too busy himself to write anything. I noticed that once the campaign began, not only did I not hear anything from him, but the people with whom he always corresponded, such as Santander, ceased to hear from him as well. Santana and I communicated with each other in code, and thus I was kept aware of Simón's activities. We would refer to Bolívar as the Colonel in our letters, so that his location would not be given away should our letters be captured by Royalist agents.

I did not want to be too far behind the army. I would be hanged, if I were not shot immediately, should the *godos* find me. However, my duties kept me in Huarás much longer than I hoped. My half dozen lancers were still with me for my protection, but this gave me little comfort when I thought of being caught alone by a platoon of Royalists. I waited almost three weeks in Huarás to receive certain dispatches from Trujillo. In that time, Simón received two letters from his vice president.

Santander's letters always raised my ire to the point that I was blind with rage. To every useful, logical, and decent request of Bolívar's he replied with nothing but ways to stop him. "I rule Colombia, not Perú," he would write as an excuse to avoid his responsibilities to his President. "Either there are laws, or there are none. If there are, they must be kept and obeyed," he would say as a reason why he would not send money, or men, or even paperwork. I could see, as plainly as if he were standing in front of me, that he had no intention of ever supporting Bolívar. Nor did he intend to ever let Bolívar succeed if he, at a thousand leagues distance, could stop him. I thought that Bolívar's army was heading in the wrong direction. The real enemy was in Bogotá. Yet, I comforted myself with the fact that Santander was far away in Colombia, whereas Bolívar was marching steadily towards his triumph.

My companions, my escort, and I finally started out at the end of July. We took it slow at first, so as not to climb too high, too quickly. The ride over the passes was cold, gruesome, and treacherous, nevertheless. Not only was it extraordinarily difficult to ride the trails without letting our mounts stumble, but we had to witness dead soldiers, horses, mules, and cattle, literally scattered along the passes and the canyons below. Often we would come over a rise to see a soldier who had not yet begun to deteriorate because of the cold, eyes frozen open, staring at us through a mask of death. On and on we rode, losing one of our six soldiers and two of our four steers. It is a wonder that Jonotás, Natán, and I, and our mules with all of Bolívar's papers, survived.

When we reached the plateau, we rested. We were able to find lodgings in a small group of Indian huts, not even a town. We all slept in the same little house.

During the night I heard the animals move around outside, as though agitated. I looked out the window, and the moon was bright enough to reveal two or three forms moving in amongst the horses and cattle. I could not tell who it was, but I was sure they were stealing our animals.

I woke the soldiers and informed them quietly of what was happening. We all pulled on our boots and readied ourselves. I put one of my pistols in my belt. We all agreed, when the door was open, they would first rush outside and retrieve their lances, which were leaning against the outside wall of the hut. Then we would confront the thieves.

The door on this hut swung out. One of the soldiers carefully pushed it open.

It was not silent. We heard whispers and the sound of men mounting their horses. By the time we were outside, we saw several figures riding off across the plateau.

There was a silver sheen on everything from the light of the moon. It was as cold as death, and none of us had on our ponchos. Jonotás brought a candle and gave it to one of the soldiers. I told her to go back inside, and then quickly looked at the animals. There was an extra horse.

I examined it and found it was the horse of a Royalist soldier—part of a scouting party or a deserter. While I continued to examine it, my soldiers secured our horses and cattle to the other side of the house where they would be easier to hear.

Just then, someone grabbed me from behind and pulled me around. It was a soldier. His Royalist uniform was tattered but recognizable. He had been hiding behind the house, not having been able to escape with the others. His fist was pulled back to strike me, but when he saw I was a woman, he hesitated. I dropped the candle and ducked under the horse's belly, pulling my pistol from my belt. I screamed, "Lancers!"

They ran toward us. The Royalist mounted and pulled a pistol of his own from his belt. The lancers were running up to him, not aware of what I could see—that he was taking deadly aim at them. I pointed my own weapon at him and said, "Don't shoot!"

He looked at me, pointed his gun in my face, and I fired. The ball ripped through his shoulder. The smell of gunpowder stung my nostrils. His mount reared and twisted around, and he toppled backward onto the lance of one of my men. His horse galloped off across the plain.

Jonotás and Natán ran out, crying, "Manuelita! Are you all right?"

I could hear the soldier struggling, but by the time we picked up the candles and lit them again, the Royalist was dead. We stretched him out so that he would not freeze at an awkward angle and let him lie there until morning.

When the sun rose, we could see that he was a few years younger than I, about twenty-two. We buried him, with little more than a thin covering of earth, and rode on.

We continued on our way to find the patriot army, but we were much more cautious. Though we were fearful, and took more precautions, we hurried. We were too far behind the army for safety. It was a deadly game we were involved in. Life or death hinged on every decision.

In the meantime, I received word from Santana that Bolívar was in Huriaca. We hurried to meet him, but he had already taken his army farther south, to the Lake of Junín, which is the source of some of the water that flows into the Amazon, and it was there he prepared to meet the enemy.

I was glad that I learned of the events that followed after they occurred. If I had watched as it happened, without being a participant, I would have collapsed from fear.

Bolívar led his men toward the plains surrounding the lake. The infantry was ready—composed not only of conscripts but of veterans from Quito, Lima, Chile, Venezuela, and Colombia. Also, Bolívar had foreign veterans of the Rhine, Moscow and Paris. The cavalry, commanded by General Miller, not only included the *montoneros*, but *gauchos* from the Argentine pampas, Venezuelan *llaneros*, and the *gausos* of Chile—all masters of the horse unequaled in history as horse soldiers.

Bolívar had been able to bring these men to a battlefield he had chosen despite the enormous odds against him. On August 6, the Royalists were taken off guard, thinking only that a division of patriots was coming over the passes.

They rushed to meet them, but when they found out they faced the whole of the Liberator's army, they ordered a retreat. Bolívar sent the cavalry around the lake to cut them off while the rest of his troops followed the Royalists.

In the afternoon, the cavalry saw the *godos* on the plains below. With their twelve-foot lances in hand, they charged.

The Royalists, stronger in numbers, saw them coming and formed themselves into a line. They also charged.

The two armies collided at tremendous speed. Miller's horsemen bore down on Royalists with such fury that their lances went right through human flesh and impaled their targets to other of the enemy or their horses.

The Royalist line was broken. Swords were drawn and a mêlée of confusion and blood overtook the dusk creeping across the valley floor.

The patriots retreated. They rallied. A reserve of Peruvian cavalry came into the fray, causing the *godos* to flee. With Miller's men following, the Royalists were in full retreat.

In little more than an hour, Bolívar's army had defeated the best soldiers that Europe had ever assembled in the New World. Hundreds of dead lay on the field.

While Bolívar and his staff gathered in a small hut nearby, Indians came down from the hills and stripped the fallen Royalists. In the meantime, men looked for their comrades. However, the wounded who were not found at once, died from the cold.

The officers assessed their victory. The first time the hosts of Spain had met Bolívar's army, they had gone down in defeat. The effect would devastate the Royalist cause. Bolívar told his men that they would commence, on the morrow, to follow and harass the enemy, and to find a place to have a decisive battle. If they could keep the edge they had won that day, they would be victorious.

Then, they went over the losses. The casualties were light. Sucre read the report. "Less than a hundred wounded, fifty soldiers dead, and only seven officers slain."

A cheer went up from everyone in the room except Sowerby, who stood against the wall. When the noise had subsided, he said, "The numbers are wrong." Everyone turned to look at him.

"Which numbers?" someone asked.

"The number of officers slain," he replied. "It is eight." Then he slid to the floor, leaving a trail of blood on the wall.

Miller rushed to him. He gently lifted the handsome soldier, his face still untouched, and held him while he struggled to speak. Sowerby's throat was full of blood and he could barely make himself be heard. "I received two lance wounds early in the day, but I thought them superficial."

Miller said, "You fool. You fought all day while you lost your blood."

"We have fought side by side. You are my closest friend. Write to my mother and father and tell them I fell in a glorious cause." The blood slowly collecting in his lungs bubbled up to his lips and the last of the day's casualties expired.

Chapter 17

I arrived on the battlefield the next day. I tended to the wounded, and I buried Sowerby. Natán would not attend to anything on that battlefield. She stayed with one of the *montoneros* in his reclaimed house in Reyes, waiting for us to leave. "I will not go to the battlefield," was all she said, and rode off to Reyes.

I was many days behind the army when I left Junín. I knew that the area into which they traveled was the most dangerous yet invaded. I also knew that a decisive battle, which would determine the fate of South America for generations, would soon be fought. I thought it best to find some place to wait. Besides, it was August and that meant the spring rain would soon fall. We rode to the village of Jauja, at one time used by the *godos* as their headquarters. I dismissed my men so that they might join the vanguard, and we waited.

The rains came. Jonotás, Natán and I paced our tiny hut while we waited for news. We heard nothing for days and then a letter, swiftly written, would arrive from Santana. Then we would wait again, impatient, worried, fearful, and bored. I had followed my love over the most severe landscape on earth, riding hundreds of leagues, and yet my activity had been reduced to waiting and worrying.

I tried to read. I read Belisario and Tacitus, but I spent many hours with an old favorite, *Don Quixote*, Simón's own copy that he kept among his papers. However, I could never really concentrate. I was always afraid. What was happening to Simón and the other brave men of the patriot army?

Bolívar's troops were in enemy territory, so they must have suffered the worst, but neither the climate nor the land nor the situation allowed either side to rest. Both were moving, advancing, fighting skirmishes, retreating, trying for the best position. I could not get any closer to Simón. Nor could I ever really be sure that he was all right.

On the first of November, after three months of waiting, while it rained, my companions and I were out of sorts with each other. We arose that morning to the ever-present downpour and did not have any *maté*. We exchanged harsh words over matters that were not important and continued to do so all that day; trapped in a tiny dwelling, nearly crazy with the confinement.

Near mid afternoon, the rain had stopped and I sent Jonotás and Natán out to see if they could find us a bigger place to stay. There were only a few huts in the whole area, and the prospects were not good.

After they left, I started to climb back into bed to keep warm while I read a passage from *Don Quixote*. Before I had my shoes off, there was a knock on the door. It was a messenger who handed me a letter and gave a quick salute.

He turned to leave but I made him come in and warmed some leftover sweet potato for him. While he ate, I read the letter from Santana.

It was brief. "The war goes well. The Colonel will arrive where you are very soon."

I questioned the soldier, but he was not very informative. However I did learn that Simón was mostly victorious, and he, Sucre, Miller and other of my friends were all alive and well. "However, we can never let up, and everyone is tired."

I looked at the letter again. It was from Huncayo, dated October 24. This meant I should see Simón within a day or so. I gave the soldier some water to wash down his food, and then I tidied up the little house. A few moments later, I sat down to write Santana a response.

Just then, we heard horses outside. I went to the door, and saw a very tired Simón climbing down from a very muddy Pastor.

My heart leapt for joy to see him again, alive, not ill, victorious, soon to be in my arms. I ran to him. We embraced and kissed eagerly.

He said a few words to José Palacios, who was taking Simón's mastiffs out of the two enormous baskets where they rode on the back of a mule. Another soldier took Pastor away.

While this was happening, the messenger came out of the house and greeted his comrades. I indicated the soldier and said, "Santana's letter, telling me that you were coming, only just now arrived."

They discussed which road the messenger had taken, trying to learn how they had missed each other. Then, Simón dismissed everyone and put his arm around me.

He held me close and said, "Manuelita, I am so very happy to see you." His words were bright and effusive but his face was grim, not what I expected with him having just come from his victories.

Then, I wondered why he was there. Surly, the military situation was too tense for him to leave the fighting merely to visit me.

We went inside and closed the door behind us. Before I could say anything, he said, "I have missed you, Manuela." He put his arms around me roughly and kissed me. The hunger I felt for him was matched by his own unstoppable desire. Without another word we undressed and kissed our way into bed.

He filled such an emptiness in me that day. I had not realized how very much I had kept my desire for him hidden, even from myself. I had traveled so far, so that I might be with him between battles, and here was my reward.

Later, we lay quietly. I marveled at how he always brought me this rare satisfaction that I could not seem to enjoy except with him. I felt him slip into slumber and lay there, listening to his heart beat in its own peculiar, restless rhythm. It was like music to me in my happiness. It spoke of nobility, valor, victory, and love. It beat with his familiar urgency to be in action. I smiled as I remembered how irascible he was when convalescing under my care in Quito. Yet, here he was, in my arms. Soon, I happily fell asleep too.

I awoke before Simón. Jonotás and Natán were quietly preparing some *maté* that they had found. Their resourcefulness was a constant amazement to me.

They motioned to me, so as not to wake Simón, asking if I wanted them to warm some cold *quinua* cakes that we had stored. I shook my head. Did I want them cold? Yes.

When the *maté* infusion was prepared, Simón woke up. "Hello, Jonotás. Natán." I could tell he was still weary.

They brought him the *maté* and he thanked them. They brought some for me and said, "We found a house. The owner is goin' to the coast today, for a month or so. We can stay in it while he's gone. It's bigger than this."

In response to Bolívar's questioning look, I said, "We thought this house too small, so they looked for one that was bigger."

"If you want, we'll go there now and return tomorrow to fix your breakfast," said Jonotás.

I agreed, and they left. I climbed out of bed, thankful that they had come and built up the fire. The evening rain had started, and I could tell it was cold and windy outside. I picked up the griddle cakes and brought them over for us to eat in bed.

"Thank you, Manuela," he said. "I have not eaten since last night." The cakes were cold and I intended them only as quick snack, but he ate them all hungrily.

It was while I watched him eat that I noticed how silent he was. Ordinarily, after we made love, we talked. He calls me Manuelita, and there are hundreds of things he has to say. Something was different. I waited until he was finished eating to see if he would talk to me, but he merely finished off the cakes and sat back, staring at the wall.

"How goes the war?" I asked at last.

"It goes well. There will soon be a battle that will decide it all." Silence again, while he continued to gaze at the wall.

"When will that be?"

"I am tired, Manuela; let's talk later." Silence.

We sat there. Finally, I said, "How are Sucre, O'Leary, and—"

"Fine."

I let my irritation show. "Talk to me."

"Not now, Manuela. I don't want to talk. I don't want to do anything." He raised his voice beyond what was needed.

That upset me, and I said, "Why are you speaking to me that way?"

"Because, I want to be left alone."

I was angry. I wanted to ask him to leave, if that was how he felt. Instead, I controlled my anger and forced myself to see that Simón was not himself. Something had happened. Perhaps he had fought a decisive battle and lost after all. Why then would he tell me it was yet to be fought? Perhaps because he was trying to convince himself that it might still happen. Where were his officers, then? How many had died? The idea of the loss of my friends and fear of the unknown filled me with dread.

"Simón, what has happened?" I could not disguise the fear in my voice.

"Nothing important."

"Then something *has* happened."

"No! Nothing important. The battle will very likely be within the month. It will very likely be near an ancient city called Ayacucho. It will be decisive. Sucre will win. There is nothing more to say." With each short sentence, he grew more irritable.

I sat in stunned silence for a moment. He stared at the wall. At last, incredulous, I asked, "*Sucre* will win?"

"Yes. Sucre." He turned to me at last.

"Why?"

He got up, pulling a blanket around his thin frame. He paced. He would stop, as though he was ready to say something, and then he would pace again. For minutes this went on. It was all I could do not to jump up and demand he talk to me. At last he said, "Sucre will finish. This is for political reasons."

I'm sure I looked as confused as I felt. "What reasons? What do you mean."

"It is best for Colombia."

"What? Why?"

"If I were to lose the coming battle, I would have my political position weakened. Thus the Colombian Congress would be weakened."

"But Simón, you won't lose."

He stopped. His shoulders seemed to slump a bit. "Manuela," he said, failing to hide his frustration, "Santander has convinced the Congress to revoke my Enabling Act."

It took a moment before I was able to piece it all together. When I understood, I was stunned. Santander, whose letters never ceased to infuriate me, who had never really supported the liberation of Perú, had seen the possibility that Bolívar would win after all. His failure to produce funds or to send recruits and supplies in a timely fashion, even his many months of silence when Bolívar had been demanding the Enabling Act from Congress, all amounted to treason, in my eyes.

That day, I saw it clearly. He had sent the Enabling Act—reluctantly and after many weeks—because he had imagined that Bolívar would come to Perú, be mired down in a political mess, fail, and thus tarnish his reputation. Now, that he was on the eve of the supreme and final victory over an enemy he had fought all his life, he would come back to Colombia in even greater glory than when he left—so great it would be unequaled in South America. He might even be seen to be the greatest conqueror in history.

When I understood it all, I controlled my anger and spoke very slowly: "You must not accept it!"

He walked back over to the bed and sat down wearily. "What do you mean, Manuela?"

"Ignore whatever news you have heard. Fight without the Enabling Act."

"Manuela, I cannot."

"Yes, you can! You have raised an army out of nothing. You have scaled the mightiest mountains in the world. You have defeated the flower of European military strength. You do not need to listen to any reasons why you should not reach out and take the victory that is in your grasp." My eyes flooded with tears of frustration and anger.

He shook his head a little.

"You, of all people, deserve to have the fruits of the liberation of Perú. The Peruvians themselves, if not outright traitors like Torre Tagle, are your most lackluster soldiers. Santander, or the politicians he so easily and obviously manipulates, have no say. None whatsoever. You must ignore—"

"No, Manuela," he said, softly, but uncertainly.

"Yes! You know I'm right. It is not the men in Colombia who know what is at stake here. It is you. It may even be immoral to turn over command to Sucre at this point. Your lack of presence may mean the difference—"

"No, he can win. Sucre can win."

"Regardless, it is still not right. You must disregard whatever communication you received from Bogotá."

"I cannot."

"Yes, you can. Not only that, but you should send back orders to have Santander shot as a traitor."

"Manuela, I *cannot*. There is already too much talk of me abusing my power. I will rule by law or not at all."

"But, Simón—"

"Now listen, Manuela. If I disregard Congress now, no matter that all might call me justified, I would ruin any chance of ruling them later. The coming battle is not the last I will fight. It may be the last military battle, but the real prize is a united American continent."

I shook my head slightly, unable to believe he would give in, no matter what his principles told him.

He looked at the floor a long time and finally he said, "Sucre and the other officers are coming here tomorrow. I will inform them of the decision of Congress and I need you to support me." I didn't know if I could do it. It was so unjust. Before I could respond, he said, quietly and almost to himself, "I only wish I knew what I should do with myself."

I thought I heard tears in his voice. I moved next to him and put my arms around his neck. "If the real prize is a united American continent, then you must work on that."

"Yes," he said quietly, "yes, you are right."

Thus did the Bolívar I knew finally emerge. He began talking of his plans. He would invite the leaders of Chile and Perú to join him in Panamá for a congress of American republics. No, the coming battle must be fought first. He would return to Lima. All military strength was in the mountains; he would retake the capital, if possible. No, he would not go directly to Lima. He would make a circular route and recruit for Sucre on the way. Soon he was walking up and down as he had done so many times in Quito, or in the villa in Magdalena, his blanket wrapped around his shoulders, planning, talking, dreaming. I listened. I helped him. I made suggestions. I was happy to see him happy.

It was with the greatest of effort, however, that I engaged in so enthusiastic a conversation. My heart was seething with rage. My deep thoughts were on Santander, and my wishes were that he might soon come to some violent end.

Chapter 18

The next morning, Sucre, O'Leary, La Mar, Córdoba, Lara, Miller, my brother, and several junior officers arrived in Jauja. The day was cold, windy, and overcast. Simón and I had been up early, riding around the area. He had decided that headquarters should be moved there, and we were examining the remains of the Royalist encampment. We were still on horseback when his officers rode in.

He faced them in the middle of the several dilapidated houses that was the town. It was there, as soon as they arrived, that Simón informed them of the decision of the Colombian Congress.

Shock, disbelief, and anger followed. Their reaction was as deeply felt and angry as had been mine. Bolívar was able to calm them and then he passed command to General Sucre.

Miller said, "No man would refuse to fight for Sucre, but it galls me that, but for a whim of a few 'civil servants'"—he said this last with great rancor—"over a thousand leagues away, it is not *you* who will lead us to victory."

Many shouted agreement in response. Sucre, his voice cracking from the effort to control his tears, said, "Your Excellency, I refuse the honor you have given me. It is for you to lead us, and it is for you to reap the rewards of all the battles you have fought."

"Yes," said the others. "We will resign." "It is unjust." The shouting was loud and passionate. Bolívar and I were moved deeply at their loyalty and affection.

"Gentlemen, I beseech you, do as I ask of you. Your loyalty is most gratifying, but there are even more important battles than the one we are soon to face." Only then did we dismount. They gathered in the house, and Bolívar gave his final orders.

While this meeting took place, I found Jonotás and Natán, and we prepared to leave. As Simón had said, he would travel through the country with only a small corps of cavalry as his escort. He would recruit for Sucre and the coming battle. I would ride directly to the capital. If, as he said, there was not a significant military force in Lima, and with all eyes on what was to transpire in the Andes, I had no doubt that I would be able to arrive back in Magdalena and prepare the way for him.

Simón and I made love that night—with only a stove to light the room with an orange glow—as though we might never see each other again. Our urgent need for each other was irrational. If anything, we had an even greater chance of being together soon. But it was Simón's loss of command that made us so feverish for each other. Though we both bravely accepted it and had moved forward, inside there was a hurt that was deep and personal.

I left the next morning. Simón and I had discussed it, and we both agreed that I had a much better chance of riding unaccosted into Magdalena if I did not have any soldiers with me. So it was only Jonotás, Natán, and I who rode out that morning, leading the mules that carried the Liberator's papers.

We headed west, over passes slippery with fresh mud from the daily rain. At least once a day one of us was thrown to the ground from our mounts loosing their footing. Our descent to the lowlands was not very dangerous, but we were caked with mud—every day, all day. A week or so later, we found the headwaters of the Rimac. Because of its swollen condition, we had to take many detours, but we followed it down into the foothills behind Lima.

By the time we reached the desert, we had not bathed in two weeks. We stank from accumulated mud, filthy clothes, and our own bodies. The rain had stopped, but that only made our dirty condition harder to bear.

We had skirted Lima, never seeing a single Royalist soldier. As we made our way across the dunes, following somewhat the same path we had taken when we escaped, we were starving. Our rations of *charqui* had run out two days before.

When we arrived at a position south of Magdalena, we waited two or three hours for the sun to drop into the ocean. Then, using the cover of darkness, we approached the town.

When we rode past the villa, I was surprised to see that it was deserted. It became apparent that General Rodil, who was in command of Lima, had not bothered with the Magdalena retreat. This was welcome news, because that meant we could stay in my house and be relatively safe until Bolívar arrived.

We rode up to my own house, as tired, hungry, and dirty as I have ever been in my life. The housekeeper was not yet in bed and she shrieked when she opened the door to three dark apparitions unrecognizable through the mud as human beings.

We dragged the trunks and boxes inside where they would be safe. Then, sweet Jonotás helped me take a bath before she took one herself. Natán attended to the horses and mules.

Once I was clean, I put more hot water in the tub and personally washed first Jonotás and then Natán. An hour later we were all asleep, together, in my bed. I did not wake up until noon the next day.

A week or so later, on December 6, Jonotás and Natán brought word of agitation in Lima. I had kept away, but I had asked my companions to dress as slaves might and spend some time in the city every day.

"Bolívar is approachin'," said Natán.

"Everyone is carryin' on like it's the end of the world," laughed Jonotás.

"It is—for some of them," I said with a smile.

We walked into the city as *tapadas* and I saw the fear in the faces of those who had put their faith in the *godos*. The well armed Royalist soldiers, of all the people in Lima, seemed most alarmed. However, the towns inhabitants who had capitulated with the Spanish were also afraid.

There was a general effort to move everything into the fortress. Carts full of furniture, boxes, horses, mules, and the people themselves were all heading down the avenue towards Callao. I saw General Rodil ride through the Plaza Mayor looking very worried.

The next day, there was no one to stop Bolívar as he rode through the city gates. Without so much as a doubled fist, he had retaken the capital. Later that night we reunited in Magdalena while his few troops watched the only place where there might be danger, the gates to the fortress of Callao.

I was so happy to have him back home. While we waited for news from Sucre, I anticipated many happy days ahead. We would be clean, well fed, and able to satisfy our passion for each other. The war, still undecided, raged in the mountains, but I was glad for the time we had together. We did not know if the patriot army would win or lose and until we knew, we could enjoy each other. If they lost, these might be the last days of tranquillity we might ever enjoy in each other's arms.

It turned out to not be as happy a time as I had hoped. After the lights went out, Simón was an ardent lover who filled me with happiness, but during the day, he was irritable and almost abusive.

"Where in hell is the courier?" you could hear him bellow almost hourly. When a soldier arrived breathless, dirty, and tired, Bolívar upbraided him for being shiftless and slow. If he didn't arrive at all, it was my fault, or he blamed Juan Santana or José Palacios. He even took it out on Jonotás and Natán.

"Why do you have to speak thus to Jonotás?" I asked him one day when he had been particularly rude.

"Because she's in my way. And can't she wear a dress?"

"Yes, I suppose she can, but she would have looked awfully silly had she been wearing a dress while she followed you around the Andes. Also, I might remind you that I am not wearing a dress."

"We're not in the Andes now. Furthermore, Jonotás is not a soldier—you are. And I wish you *would* wear a dress."

"Sometimes a dress is a good—"

"You should write them letters of manumission and get rid of them," he said, as he paced over and looked out the window. "It is too late in history to keep slaves."

"You know they are more than that. I love them."

"You should free them then."

"To do what? There is no place for a poor woman to go in this world, especially if her skin is dark."

"Give them money then." He collapsed into a chair.

"Even if I had any—" Just then I saw them come through the door. I turned to them and said, "You both know you can go at any time."

They looked confused, maybe even hurt.

"Simón thinks I should not keep slaves. You know you are free, do you not?"

Jonotás said, "Yes, Manuelita, but with you, life is full. Why leave a banquet to go look for food?" She laughed, Natán smiled, and they walked through the room.

Bolívar snorted in disgust. He could not see that with me they had a position far more mobile and purposeful than they ever would as women alone. Still, Bolívar complained about them.

The next day it was, "Do you have to smoke? I can't walk through here without suffocating. Is that all you have to do?" This he said while Santana and I sat behind a stack of paperwork that practically hid us. So it would go, with each day there was a new reason to complain.

He drank more wine in the evening than I had ever seen, before or since. He even began having José pour him a glass in the afternoon. He was in such foul humor one night while I tried to read to him that I stormed out of the villa and walked back to my own house. Soon, José Palacios was at the door, with a note apologizing and begging me to return. Of course, I went.

I understood his anger. All of this misdirected energy was because he knew that the battle that would finally decide the future of the world was forming high in the Andes, and he was not there. His concern worried me, and I wondered about the actual military situation. He told me everything, but even he did not know exactly what the circumstances were. Somewhere, far away, at the top of the world, important battles were being waged. Sucre was a brave and competent warrior, but he was not Bolívar. What was happening?

All I really knew for sure was that I loved and respected the men who were far away fighting for liberty. If they were to lose, the consequences would be unthinkable. The rest of our lives, our fortunes, and the future of the entire continent were to be decided, within the month, and all we could do was wait and snap at each other.

So it was, day after day. He would pace, I would try to do paperwork, he would rage at the couriers, I would try to placate him, he would have coughing fits and demand a poultice or a special tea—always it was some new remedy. Either José Palacios or I would try to satisfy his needs, but we were not enough. Finally, in the late afternoon, when it was too late to expect a courier to arrive, he would sit down to work. For the rest of the day, he would write and pace some more.

When he had it worded just the way he wanted it, he sent a letter off to each of the patriot leaders of the former Spanish colonies. In the letter, he called for a meeting six months hence on the Isthmus of Panamá for the purpose of binding the new republics together in solidarity. He worked on the speeches and documents that he wished to deliver to the assembly, and with this he found some happiness.

In the evening, we would read. He liked it when I read to him. "I find your voice, your equatorial accent, most comforting," he would say.

On December 17, he was feeling quite ill. Ever since he had returned, he had appeared to be getting sicker and sicker. That day, he had coughed all day long. When night came, I had to find him another of his cambric handkerchiefs as he had worn out the one he had used all afternoon. He was so exhausted that when it was time to read he said, "Read to me here."

I did not think it a good idea because I knew he might fall asleep in the chair and then he would not sleep well. However, I pulled a brass brazier up to warm his feet and I threw a blanket over him. Then I sat down and opened *Don Quixote*.

I had spoken only two or three sentences when we heard noises outside. Santana ran in. He was dressed for bed, with only his trousers quickly thrown on, and he said, "There has been a battle."

Bolívar stood up, strong and vibrant, as though he had not coughed in weeks. "Where? What is the outcome? Where's the messenger?"

A Captain Alarcón entered behind Santana. He was filthy from his ride, and he looked exhausted. He handed Bolívar a note and said breathlessly, "I left the battlefield at Ayacucho, eight days ago."

Bolívar quickly opened the dispatch and read. I saw his features change from questioning to amazement and then to delirious happiness. As though he were drunk, he ran around the room, jumping over furniture, leaping onto the table, waving the letter, and shouting, "Victory! Victory! Victory!"

Chapter 19

Victory! It had finally come, and with it, I presumed, peace at long last. We rejoiced that evening, and later we loved. A new happiness had filled our hearts—a happiness that could only be born out of peace.

That night, and many times over the next several months, my lovemaking was accompanied by fantasies that we were conceiving a child. Peace had made me want a daughter or a son, with the man I loved. I knew I could not conceive, and it was doubtful that Simón could either. He would have had offspring all over the continent, if he could. Nevertheless, irrational desires for children filled my mind during our lovemaking. I was still too young to see that peace would bring us more insidious problems than war.

My first awareness that victory did not necessarily mean an end to hostility was when terms were offered to General Rodil. He was still holding the fortress of Callao, with about 4,000 soldiers, and citizens, who had escaped when they heard that Bolívar was entering the Lima. Among them was the traitorous former president, the Marqués de Torre Tagle, and his wife Josefa.

Two days after our hearing the news about the victory at Ayacucho, I sat at Bolívar's desk, writing out the generous terms that he dictated and would send to General Rodil. After he had finished, and I had given the paper to him for his signature, Simón then briefed a young soldier who was to be the courier. The boy, younger than I by four or five years, was a relatively recent recruit that Simón had added to his personal command when he had made his way back to Lima. "Should he question you, you are to make sure that the General understands that we will repatriate all soldiers who wish to return to Spain; the garrison, including the general, will be given all the honors of war; and the civilians, except for those who have been traitorous to our cause, will be given full amnesty. Do you understand?"

"Yes, Señor," said the young soldier.

He folded the paper and handed it over, saying, "Leave immediately."

The young man saluted smartly, saying, "Yes, Señor," and left. Shortly, we heard him gallop away.

It was about three hours later that another soldier came in saying, "General, there is trouble."

"What is it?"

"Your emissary . . . you must see."

We went outside to see the young soldier thrown over his horse. The note I had so recently written had been pinned to his back with a long knife. Blood poured from the knife wound and the soldier's mouth to the dust in the street.

Bolívar was furious. It was hours before he was calm enough to write a very restrained letter, advising the general of his improper diplomatic conduct and asking him to reconsider his decision and his behavior.

This letter was sent off the next morning. The second messenger had orders not to enter the fortress. An hour or so later, we learned that he had been taken inside by the fortress guards. That afternoon, we were informed that the man had been thrown into the harbor from the fortress wall.

Simón, in addition to being as angry as I'd ever seen him, was disappointed. He very much wanted to bring the war to full completion, and to start implementing his plans for rebuilding Perú and for uniting the American states.

It was a busy period, and he continued to work on his upcoming Panamá meeting. Monteagudo, who had already served as his Ambassador in Mexico and Guatemala, when Simón was in Guayaquil, was with Simón every day—planning, writing, or being briefed on such preparations. Already, the soldiers and some of the officers, the victors of Ayacucho, were arriving, bringing with them long lines of Royalists. Ships were being readied to return to Spain with those who wished to go—about half—and plans were being made to assimilate the rest into whatever republic they considered home. Everything would have been just as it should have been, except for General Rodil, and the fact that Bolívar felt he must besiege the fortress of Callao.

Surrounded by the ocean on all sides, with only one drawbridge for an entrance, it was obvious that it would be impossible to take the citadel by force. Simón determined that no food would reach them and he started a daily cannonade. The cannonade turned out to be a mistake and, in the long run, worked against Bolívar.

In the meantime, I was to learn that, for me, "peace" on my continent meant "war" in my home. When Bolívar arrived in Lima, I had finally felt safe enough to enter my San Sebastiano house in Lima again. I discovered piles of letters.

James had been writing to me throughout the period when I had been in the Andes, almost a year. There were enough letters waiting for me at the house for him to have written almost every day. Before the victory at Ayacucho, with Simón acting the way he was, I did not have time to pay much attention to them. Once there was "peace," I brought them all down to Magdalena and read them.

James had talked to Escobar. He was angry about how he had been treated. He had heard more talk of me and Bolívar. He was furious about it. He was coming home. He would stay away. No, he would come. He demanded that I be there waiting for him. He decided to stay in Chile. Each letter was different from the one before. He was abusive, threatening, demanding, pleading—first one and then another as though each day brought a different emotion.

Then I received a fateful announcement. A servant brought down a letter that had arrived that morning. It was short. "I will return in April. When I arrive, I will demand, and have, my marital prerogatives." There was only one other paragraph in which he made it clear that he would never allow me to be honorably happy with Simón. This meant he would not agree to a divorce (even if the church did), and that he would never restrain from harassing us.

"Manuela, this is not good," Bolívar said when I told him of Thorne's return and about the letters he had written to me. "We will have to bow to your husband's wishes."

"Never. I will never bow to any wishes he may have, or to anyone else's, unless they coincide with my own. In this case, they do not."

"But, Manuela, we cannot continue. I love you. I want to have you, but we will be ruined if he makes a scandal."

I looked at him, competence showing in every sinew and every movement of his eyes. "No one will ruin you."

"You underestimate the power of opinion. Anyone, at any time, can drag me down by merely shouting your name in a crowd."

"No one would ever try."

"Manuela—"

"Why must you give in! I defy you to find a married man in Lima who does not also have a lover. Why are you different. For that matter why should I not have the same privileges."

"But they are discreet. Do you not see? They are men, not women. Their wives do not object. This husband will object loudly."

"Simón, I care not. No one can hurt you. If a man can have a lover, then so can a woman."

"Men do not display their 'sin' for all of society to see, as you seem to want to do."

"Yes, I do. You and I have the real marriage, despite any vows taken in some parish church."

"No one will ever take our side. No one will agree with that sentiment—no matter how logical you deem it to be—if your husband does not agree."

I was infuriated. He was probably right, but I was sickened to see him, the worlds greatest warrior, giving in without a fight.

"There must be some way . . . damn it, Simón, I have not followed you over half the continent, through the most dangerous territory in the world, just so I can return quietly to my husband."

He shook his head. I could tell he understood but saw no other way.

"Simón, just because I was foolish seven years ago, not much more than a child, am I to be kept from my bond with you which surpasses all else? You and I are for each other. Nothing will ever change that."

He only shook his head again in resignation.

I could not induce him to take a confrontational position. I, myself, was thus forced to wait until James arrived, to see what would happen.

While I waited, the situation in Lima grew worse. The guns firing at Callao fortress continued, hour after hour, day after day. They announced the rising of the sun when the firing commenced and everyone knew the sun was setting when they ceased. Even at two leagues distance, in either Magdalena or Lima, the sound of cannon fire jarred everyone throughout the day. It was as though someone, in another part of whatever house one was in, was slamming a door over and over. Chickens stopped laying, people snapped at each other or—like the case of a night watchman found naked in the fountain one morning—simply lost control.

To escape the cannons and the reminder of war, a victory ball was given in Bolívar's honor, which I looked forward to attending. We rode into Lima together, and Simón talked about his Panamá Congress of American Nations while we rode. "Monteagudo will leave as my emissary for Chile, on our first official visit there, to invite their participation."

I thought, *Good!* I couldn't wait for him to be gone. I always thought Bolívar's affairs ran smoother when he was away.

We rode up to the palace and I let Bolívar make a triumphal entrance into the Hall of Viceroys before I entered. I drank wine and talked with Fergusson, O'Leary, José María, and the other officers while I waited for Simón to play the part of hero that was expected of him—though he enjoyed it. Sucre was still in the Andes.

I was having a great time. My friends had brought a mustache for me, made from the hair of a fallen Royalist soldier. We played and laughed for three hours or so until Bolívar finally asked me to dance.

I loved to dance with Simón. I was enjoying myself, but the music had barely started on the second waltz when we were interrupted by a Liman official. "Excuse me, Manuelita," he said, kissing my hand, after hearing what the man whispered to him, "but I must attend to something." He looked very serious.

"What is it, Simón?" I asked. I was worried.

It appeared he wanted to tell me, but he looked around. Then, he shook his head and said, "Later." He left, calling O'Leary after him.

I followed him. I was too curious to stay. They walked down several streets to where a crowd was gathering.

When I pushed through the people who were standing about, Bolívar was already saying, "They will pay!" His stentorian voice chilled even me. The rest of the populace and officials who were there were also stunned at the unusual vehemence of the Liberator.

I looked at the ground. There, lying in blood that was still soaking into the dust, was Monteagudo. Knife wounds covered his expensive silk ruffles. I knew he had a lover in this neighborhood, and he must have been coming from or going to the ball at the time he was stabbed, because he was dressed as foppishly and as elegantly as I have ever seen: a golden nugget on the end of his gold watch chain, diamond studs for buttons, and jewels on the rings on his fingers. He was a fool to be out alone wearing a treasury.

I heard Bolívar giving orders. Several names, the first of many, were spoken as he ordered them brought in for questioning. Each had either shown signs of Royalist sympathies in the past or had spoken openly against Monteagudo. Everyone—absolutely everyone—had spoken against Monteagudo, because he was so hated. Not everyone had spoken loudly.

When Simón returned to the villa later that night, I tried to get him to see reason. "Monteagudo's murderer could have been anyone: relatives of the victims of the terror he administered to control the populace while governing Perú, or simply a robber wanting the gold and diamonds he wore."

Bolívar was adamant. "If it was thievery, why was he not robbed? No, Manuela, he was most valuable to me. Not only was he the only one who really understood my vision for a united America, but I needed him as Ambassador. Everyone knows this. It is a conspiracy, and it is directed at me."

All through the first part of February, while the cannon sounded at Callao, Bolívar investigated to find a conspiracy. I seethed with frustration. He was finally using his dictatorial powers to find a conspiracy that probably did not exist, and yet he would not move a finger, just two months before, to bring down Santander. In the meantime, my husband was on his way. Simón and I did not have much time, and his attentions were turned to what I deemed to be a useless investigation.

The siege at Callao went on and on. It was known that the Spanish gold and silver taken into the fortress by Rodil was paying for smuggled food. Still, people began dying in the fortress from disease or starvation—sometimes as many as a hundred a day. At night the bodies were lowered into the sea. They would wash up on the shores leaving families and friends, sick with grief, to find them. Those that were not found soon enough rotted and fouled the beaches. One of the men found on the beach one morning was the Marqués de Torre Tagle. Josefa was found a few days later.

The days dragged out. On went the cannonade, on went the investigation, and daily James Thorne drew nearer. When my husband arrived, Bolívar would put me away. He felt he had to. I would have to come to terms with my husband before I could continue to be with the man I loved.

Finally, the police found a couple of thieves who confessed to murdering Monteagudo. The police had the testimony of a witness who disturbed them before they could rob him. When the evidence was presented to Bolívar, he called off his investigation.

Even though he acted immediately, when he knew the truth, it was too late. He had arrested most of the aristocracy and leaders of opinion. His investigators had subjected them to humiliation and hardship. Thus, Bolívar's reputation was severely tarnished—I could tell from the stories Jonotás and Natán brought to me—and all for seeking the killer of a man everyone hated.

Bolívar was troubled by the affair, which troubled me to see him engage in self-doubt. To make matters worse, the distance between us grew more each day. I noticed it creep gradually into our relationship, but I could not stop it.

It was his conscience. He knew James Thorne was approaching and he would have to give me up. I was a reminder of some kind of guilt or failing, and everything I did bothered him. Jonotás and Natán annoyed him. My smoking got on his nerves, already agitated by his own endless cannon fire. No one had ever been allowed to smoke in his presence except me. Suddenly he found it "immensely irritating."

After we made love at night, our discussions always turned to our parting. Time sped forward, leaving us behind.

Chapter 20

One night in early March, I said, "Simón, I am going back to my house to sleep tonight."

"Why, Manuelita?" He had, only minutes before, made a sarcastic comment about some trivial failing of mine.

"Because I cannot be here tonight."

"Why?"

"How can you ask me? You rage at me all day long, and then you want me to come quietly to bed—"

"Manuelita, you are correct. I apologize."

"I'm sick of it. You will not fight for me. You are ready to hand me back over to my husband—"

"We cannot—"

"Yes, we can. You won't. I'm sorry I did not give you more warning so you could find someone to replace me." I walked out, and slept at my own house. José Palacios did not come to my door with a note asking me to return.

In the morning, I was not so angry with him. He, while angry at my leaving the night before, had softened too.

"What are we to do, Simón?" I asked that night, as we lay in the dark before sleep.

We talked long into the night, but Simón could only imagine one answer: I would have to return to my husband.

I urged him to fight for me. Though inwardly I knew there was nothing anyone could do, I stubbornly held on to the idea that my marriage should not be an impediment to our loving each other.

"I do not see why we need to accept this. What does it matter if my husband returns? What can he possibly do to interfere with our love for each other?"

"He can damage our reputation. He can make us hated. He can ruin my effectiveness in my efforts to unify this continent—"

"Simon—"

"Manuela, I love you. I love you deeply. But there is nothing for us to do. You must try to solve your problems with your husband." I rolled over, withdrawing into my anger. "You must return to him. It is the only decent thing to do."

I turned over and lifted myself up on one arm and shifted my position so that my shadow would not cover his face. Candlelight illuminated the room, and gave soft sadness to everything. I said, "Simón, Gran Colombia and all of Perú are at your command. No one man, since Alexander, has ever ruled so much territory. Why can you not use some of that power to make a way for us to stay together? Simply order what you wish to happen, and it will. With the army behind you, no one will—"

"What you suggest is criminal. How can you think such thoughts? What possesses you?"

"Perhaps my suggestions are criminal. What does it matter? Are not Santander's actions criminal? Yet you—"

"No, they are not. His actions are within the law however much we may abhor the results or his motives. I will not break the law. The love of the people—"

"The love of the people," I scoffed. "I know about society's love." I stood up, wrapped a blanket around me and sat in a chair across the room. "When I was young, I wanted the love of the people around me. I wanted to be accepted. I wanted to fit into society. I wanted it desperately." I took a breath to calm myself. "I wanted to contribute to it. I wanted to be a part of it. Yet, no matter what I did, I was called bastard and base. So I learned not to care what people think—not to care about the rules. That is why I think and feel as I do. I even made a vow at one time, to ignore all forms of human decency if it would interfere with what I desired."

He gave me a look that told me he didn't believe I was capable of that.

"You are right. I could not keep that vow. I could not bear to hurt innocent people anymore. But I did make such a vow, because I believed there was no order or justice except that which I made myself." Simón opened his mouth to speak but I went right on, my emotions building with each word. "My husband was one of the innocent victims of my determination to have what I wanted at others' expense. What I did to him was not right, and he deserves something better than the marriage I have given him."

Simón looked speechless.

"I deserve better, too. Simón, I was young and foolish when I married. Why should I be punished for being young, for wanting something better for my life."

"Even though you were young—"

"But I have grown since I married. I learned to love people despite their rejection of me. I understand things I did not fully understand then. I also understand the value of a covenant promise. But I cannot simply leave your bed and return to my husband's."

He let out his breath in exasperation and weariness. He and rolled onto his back, and said, "I am guilty, too."

"Guilt is unimportant. It is done. You and I belong together." He looked at me. "Tell me I'm wrong. Tell me that we should never have met."

He slowly turned his face and stared at the ceiling.

"Simón, I ask you, either use your power to allow us to live together in the open, or let us retire to Venezuela, or Europe, or wherever you want to go where we may live in peace away from all this political chaos. I will not go back to an immoral marriage, merely because society will not honor my true love."

After a long time, he said, "I cannot do either of those things, Manuela."

"Why? Why can you not?"

"Manuela, what have we been fighting for?" He stood up, a blanket about his shoulders, and paced. "Freedom! That's what has fueled this conflagration of suffering we call the revolution. Freedom from Spanish rule. And we have nearly achieved it. Rodil cannot hold Callao fortress forever. We have won."

"Yes."

"Very good, success! Bravo! Now what?" He looked at me a long time collecting his thoughts. "Now that we are free, what do we do? We can do anything. What do we do? Do we act like animals? Throw away thousands of years of civilization and fight among ourselves, fornicate wherever we wish, grab anything we want? We are free, yes. Free to be brutes. That is the truth of it." He came to me and knelt down so he could face me. He looked at me with his dark, beautiful eyes. "Do you not see, Manuela. That is why you must honor your marriage vows."

"*You* say that to me?"

"I know. I am as much an adulterer as you. I am worse. My morals could never stand real scrutiny. But I am not talking about morality right now. I am speaking of conventions, agreements, social contracts . . . . These are what will keep us together until we can forge a liberated and united South America. That is why my work is not done." He stood and paced again. "Yes, I have freed the countries of this hemisphere from Spain. Now, unless we work very hard, we will be at each other's throats in no time. We will fight among ourselves until any country in the world can walk in and pick up the pieces. What is worse, countries more united than ours will simply buy our land and resources." He walked over and sat on the edge of the bed. "The Andean Confederation I envision will unite Gran Colombia and Perú. First I may split Perú into two provinces, but all will eventually be departments in one vast country—strong and unassailable."

He paused and held out his hand to me. I went to him and sat beside him. He put his arm around me and held me a moment. "I love you, Manuela, but if I rest one week from my efforts in these crucial times, this continent will descend into anarchy. I cannot stop my work. I cannot do anything about the reverence the people hold for marriage. It is not what I selfishly wish for, but . . ."

I turned away, not wanting to hear.

". . . you must return to your husband."

After a while I said, "Very well. I do not claim to have as much foresight as you. But I believe you, and even think I understand." I looked at him, and thought I saw his eyes wet with tears. "I will try, Simón, that is all I can promise," but I knew I would never be able to do it.

As soon as I spoke, he seemed to crumble. His aspect did not change but his energy seemed to recede into nothingness. He lay back and said, "I am sad already. I swore, when María Theresa died, that I would never remarry. Most of the women I have slept with since then are a blur—images which at one time kept away the loneliness. But you— Manuela, I love you deeply. I want you to know that, and that I will *always* love you." A tear fell down my cheek. His voice cracked when he spoke next. "We must be strong. We will have honor on our side—" He could not speak because of the lump in his throat.

I held him close. I cried, though I knew in my heart that even if Thorne returned, I would soon be back in bed with Simón, one way or another.

Simón, however, believed his fantasy, and a few days later I thought I saw his eyes roam to other female distractions. He denied ever doing so, but I knew what was happening. That ancient suffering from the loss of his bride could not allow him to feel our separation. He felt a primitive loneliness and needed to know there were other ways he could intimately connect with someone.

Despite my understanding of what he felt, I was roused to rage about it. "I will never—do you hear me—never, allow you to replace me." I realized I was shaking my fist at him. We had just entered the villa, having come from Lima.

He turned toward me, and lifted his hands as if to illustrate a thought. "Manuela—"

I would not listen. "I have fought with you, cared for you, loved you, and I will always do so. You have lived a cavalier life, but you love *me* now, and I do not believe you will ever love another. I have agreed to return to my husband, but that is for the sake of convention. What is real is *you* and *me*."

His voice grew very quiet, and he sat down wearily in a chair. "Manuela, I love you, truly. I do not want to replace you, but . . . you are married—"

"I do not care."

He lay his head back and closed his eyes. "Well, I do. Everyone does. It will matter. It will always matter. I see nothing but a black void in our future."

I felt a chill pass through me. I had nothing to answer, because I was completely disarmed by his argument. I could do nothing to convince him that we could or would be together in the future. I felt loneliness, too. "I will sleep alone tonight," I said, and I left.

The next night I was with him, but then I returned and slept in my own house on the following night. So it continued. We were never at peace. Both of us were convinced that our love for each other would be crushed. We frantically tried to defend our emotions from the sadness that would come.

One night, as he and I lay together, naked, kissing each other in our passion, I rolled over onto something. I said, "Wait." I reached behind me, and pulled up a large and beautiful diamond earring—not mine.

I only looked at it a second and said, "Damn you!"

"I don't know—"

"How dare you . . ." I became blind with rage, threw the earring across the room and grabbed at his face with my nails. At that moment, I felt as though they were knives and I wanted to wound him like prey.

He fought me, saying, "Stop it. Stop it."

I would not stop. I was in a rage. It was only with supreme male strength that he was able to pin my arms down. I was furious—and frustrated. "Don't let me go, if you value your eyes," I hissed at him.

At that moment, blood fell from his eyelid onto my cheek. It stunned me enough that I stopped fighting. "You're bleeding!"

"Of course, I'm bleeding. I've been attacked my a vixen." His voice was subdued and hurt. I jumped up and grabbed a cloth, ran to the wash bowl and wet it. Then I returned to the damage I'd done.

Both sides of his face were bleeding, but the cut on his brow was profuse in the blood it produced. He lay on his back, complaining, while I tried to make it stop. His face had so many cuts that he had to stay in his room "with the grippe" for over a week. He never admitted knowing how that earring might have been in his bed.

Fortunately, he was "cured" in time to report on his activities to the Peruvian Congress, as had already been arranged. He spoke of how he had come to the country when the enemy had surrounded the city and how he had vanquished them. Then, saying that his work was completed in Perú, he resigned all power.

There were many who had been clamoring for that very thing, but the country was not yet ready to be left to their own devices. His resignation so shocked the Congress, knowing they would be left to solve their own problems, that they immediately voted to reinstate him until democratic order prevailed. He was also voted a million pesos, which he declined, as well as a statue made to honor "The Liberator."

About that time, some wonderful news came. The United States of America, in January, had officially recognized the new South American republics. In March, the frigate *United States* arrived in the harbor and Commodore Hull invited Bolívar and his staff aboard for a dinner. I was not allowed to attend because it was a matter of state.

I found out that Commodore Hull's sister-in-law, about my age and very beautiful, had intrigued Bolívar. I found out because, being in Bolívar's secretarial staff, I saw a poetic letter of admiration sent to him and heard about a poetic response from him. I was infuriated.

Later, when a ball on land was given for the officers of the *United States*, I was there. The more I watched this woman, whose name was Jeanette Hart, the more I could tell she was very much in love with Simón. Finally, I would have it no longer. When she was by herself, I walked up to her and said, in English, "How long do you intend to be here?"

The woman looked confused and said, "I don't know."

"It would be better if you departed soon—and meanwhile much better if you associated with your own countrymen, or with the English."

She was taken aback and angry, and she said, "And who are you, to give me such advice without having been asked?"

"I?" I replied. "I am La Sáenz." I gave her a look, which if it communicated what I intended, must have frozen her heart.

I stared at her until she said, "Such rudeness," and walked away. I kept my eye on her and saw her make some inquiries of me to others at the ball. I also noticed that she kept her distance from Simón for the rest of the evening.

Later that night, after the candles were out, Simón, whose voice was quite weary, said sleepily, "You needn't have bothered, Manuela."

"What?"

"I saw you talking to Jeanette Hart, and how she avoided me the rest of the evening." I was not amused. He should never have made it necessary for me to talk to her in the first place. Now, it seemed, he was teasing me. "I will be gone in a few days anyway."

I was not prepared for that. "Where are you going?"

"To Upper Perú. I still believe we should form a separate republic there. I will leave for Arequipa on the first of the month." I was silent at first, and he went on before I could say anything. "You must not go."

I saw what it would mean. He would be conveniently gone when James finally arrived, thus making it easier on everyone. Simón would not be put in the position of becoming directly involved in any scandal. James would not be put in the position of having to fight for his marriage while its major impediment still lived in the city. I would not be tempted to simply disregard my marital obligations.

At last, as though my thoughts had been spoken, I said, "And this is what you truly want, to have me finally and completely returned to my husband?"

"No. I want . . ." He was silent a long time. "I wish many things were different. But there is no solution."

After a moment, I said, "I don't know what to do either, but I am a soldier and my place is with you."

"That may be so." After a long pause, he said, "You will have to return to your husband, but perhaps you might accompany me . . . I don't know."

We did not resolve the issue that night, but I overheard a conversation he had with General Lara a day or so later which made me decide to stay. I was writing a letter when I heard Bolívar say that perhaps I should be included in his trip to Upper Perú. I know, in his heart, he wanted to have me along.

General Lara was firm. "Manuela must not go, Señor. In this critical period of your career, with the future of Perú and Colombia in the balance, with everything that you and thousands of others have sacrificed, you cannot allow a scandal right now. Do you realize what people are saying; that you have ordered Thorne from Perú, not to return?"

"Yes, Lara, I know. I know," he replied, wearily.

Lara's arguments hit me hard. He was right. If I went with him, I would only delay the inevitable confrontation with James and make matters worse for Simón. There could only be scandal and it could possibly mean political destruction for Bolívar when we returned. I could not do that to him.

It was painful for both of us, but I knew at last that we must end it. We loved when there was no husband to intrude; we loved while the war raged and in all the confusion that followed. It seemed that our love was not meant for peace. It was over.

When we rose on the morning that Simón was to leave, we made love as though we would never see each other again.

"I do love you so, Manuela. I love you more than I have ever loved," he told me.

I answered him, with tears staining my cheeks, "And I will always love *you*, Simón."

We lay there, looking at each other as though we might take away something with our eyes that would last us through the days, weeks, maybe years ahead. When would I see him again? Never, perhaps. That inner, gnawing dread of the future ate away at our hearts as we lay together, wrapped in each other's arms.

Later, after preparations had been made, when everyone was ready to mount their horses, Juan Santana promised tearfully, as he embraced me, to keep me informed. I kissed Simón good-bye one last time. He mounted his horse and rode away.

Soon, they would be in the mountains, and Simón would throw himself into his work. Every night, for weeks, I reached out for Simón in the dark and then I would cry when he was not there.

A few days after he left, I received my first letter from Santana telling me they were a day and half away from Pisco. I did not take joy in Santana's letters as I did when he was writing about "the Colonel," when I knew it was only war that was keeping Simón apart from me.

Three days after Santana's letter came, my husband arrived.

Chapter 21

Late in the afternoon I hired a *calesa* and went to meet James at Callao. Our meeting was awkward, and we said very little. The siege cannons punctuated our silence as we stood regarding each other for a moment. Finally, James said, "Let's go, shall we?"

To be honest, he looked better than he had ever looked. His dress was not as staid as when I had last seen him. He was wearing the latest English-style, high-collared, frock coat made fashionable by Beau Brummell. He looked even more opulent than before our parting.

His wartime activities, no doubt doing business with both sides, had obviously done him well. Now his ships were carrying materials for reconstruction, and his wealth was compounding. He was almost 50 years old, not much older than Bolívar, and a little thinner than he used to be, quite good looking. However, his aspect could not hide a look of suppressed anger.

I had moved all of his papers to Lima earlier that day when I heard that his ship had arrived and would not pass through customs until afternoon. I hoped he would not want to live in Magdalena. I knew he would be happier in the San Sebastiano house, and my Magdalena home was a retreat I hoped to keep for myself. I was glad when he ordered the driver toward Lima.

When we entered the house, while the servants were in the street unloading the *calesa*, he kissed me. A mixture of sadness and rejection were the only emotions it aroused in me. I did not respond; and when he finished, I could only look at him and wait for the sense of danger I felt to go away.

We looked at each other for a moment and finally, through an attitude of stoic rigidity, I said, "This is very difficult—for both of us. I cannot simply change all of my feelings in a day."

"Madam," he said softly, in English so we would not be overheard by the servants moving past us in the patio, "I understand. I am prepared to be patient."

I could never have been so restrained, had I been in his situation. We were so unlike each other. At last, I said, "I have prepared the main bedroom for you, Sir, but I hope you understand that . . . for now . . . I will sleep down the hall."

His face flushed with hostility. He might have become belligerent but I think he was prepared to do anything to win me back, including holding his tongue for a while. "Very well, Madam," he said patiently, "we will discuss our circumstances later."

He went upstairs to freshen up, leaving me to supervise the unloading and unpacking of his belongings. The cannons in Callao were particularly annoying to me as I went about my work that afternoon.

Jonotás and Natán showed up an hour or so later from Magdalena. I knew that James hated them, and I did not want to make the situation worse by having them around when we met. When they arrived, we spent the rest of the day putting order into the house. While we worked, James went to the center of town. By the time he returned, I had closed myself in my room with Jonotás and Natán.

The situation in which I found myself was more than difficult. I loved Simón, and nothing James could do would ever change my feelings. Yet I had to live with, work with, and be with a man I must call husband. Bolívar was gone, and in *his* mind it was for good. Both James and Simón expected me to start my life anew as Señora Thorne. They both wished me to live as a dutiful wife. I knew I could never live up to such an ideal, and yet, I would have to try—if only to show to both of them how it could not be. Still, I feared I might never see Simón again.

At breakfast the next morning, James said, rather sternly, "Captain Escobar told me you would not permit him to have access to my papers as I directed."

"I would not allow someone, having no more authority than his own claim, to walk in and take your papers. No, Sir."

He looked frustrated. "I suppose you are correct in that."

I walked to the door and opened it so that we might have some air.

After I sat down, he was silent for some time. The atmosphere became rigid with tension. At last, he said, "I examined my affairs last night, and I must say everything is in perfect order. In fact, I admit there were one or two problems I had worried about, in which your administration exceeded my expectations."

I did not want to talk, but I forced myself to say, "Thank you, Sir."

"Well done, yes. Thank you," he said graciously.

"James, you need not thank me. I will always look out for your interests to the best of my abilities. I am your friend."

"Yes, you are here now." He looked at me as though to satisfy himself that it was true. "All is well."

He did not understand. This last meant: you have decided to leave your lover and take up your marital responsibilities.

He came over to me and put his hands on my shoulders. "You are here," he said.

Again, I could only be silent. I tried not to respond to his touch, since all I felt was aversion. I did not move. Yet, though I sat still and in silence, it felt as if I was pulling away. Only the siege cannons could be heard for a long time.

After a moment, with no response from me, he pulled back his hands sharply. He sat back down and stared into space, his face dark and ominous. To him, my silence was not consent, but defiance. I could see it took all of his will to keep from speaking his thoughts.

At last, I said, "I am going to the market." I stood and turned to leave.

"Manuela!"

"Yes, Sir," I said, as I came back into the room.

His face was red with frustration and suppressed rage. A cannon fired in Callao while I waited for him to speak.

I knew why he called me back. He could not stand for me to act independent of his dictates. In his mind, my ability and determination to come and go as I pleased was the most serious threat to his manhood, and his marriage, of all the things I did.

"Nothing," he said at last, his eyes smoldering with fury.

I left.

Late that afternoon, I sat in the salon alone, smoking. James walked in and paced up and down slowly while the cannons sounded in Callao. He had been drinking wine all day and when he stopped to fill his glass, he said, "Manuela, I know you have experienced much in the last three years." He resumed his pacing and drinking. "Much has changed for both of us. I know . . . that is, you have . . ."

"Sir, let us be honest with each other. I have had a love affair these last three years, in your absence."

He stopped dead still.

"I have, perhaps, wronged you in this, but I do not feel I have. I do at least owe you an explanation."

Slowly, he set his glass down. He turned to me. He asked, carefully, as though it were a great effort to control his emotions, "Why do you not feel you have wronged me?"

"Because, Sir, I love him."

I could see him force the tightening sinews in his face to relax. At last, he said, "This man you love—"

"Let us name him, Sir. It is Simón Bolívar."

"Yes, of course, let us name him." He raised his voice, almost losing control. "You have given yourself to him, in conjugal relations, without the sanctity of marriage. You have cuckolded me. You have endangered my position in society. You have endangered my ability to do business. You have betrayed vows you made to *me*, vows made years before you met this 'revolutionary general.'" He was shouting and he spoke his last words with icy scorn. "And you do not see how you have *wronged me?*" he shouted.

I stifled my own anger at his disdain of Bolívar. "Yes, I did all those things. You are justified in feeling wronged. However, our marriage was a mistake. *We* are wrong for each other—"

"That is not the point, Madam."

"Yes, Sir, it is the point." I put out my cigar and stood up. "You have bullied me, you have tried to enslave me, to restrict me, to make me a plaything. For that I could not love you. If I wronged you, it was in marrying you to begin with, and for that I am truly sorry. If it *were* you that I loved, it is *you* who would have my loyalty and affection. But it is not."

He was breathing hard. I saw him take a deep breath. Slowly, he walked over to me. He put his arms around me and said tenderly, almost a plea, "Manuela. I love you. I love you so very much. Can you not see it in your heart to love *me?*"

I pulled back and looked at him, as if I could study the problem away. Tears welled up in my eyes. "James, I . . . ." I didn't know what to say.

"Manuela, please let us look at it rationally. We are married. Even if it was possible, I love you too much to grant a divorce. There is no honorable way for you and

Bolívar to ever be together. Do you not think it would be more logical to concentrate your affections, and your energies, on our marriage?"

How little he knew of me, or of women. "In the end, Sir," I said through tears I tried to ignore, "the situation is not about logic. It is about love."

"But, Manuela—"

"The love I feel, I cannot deny. Neither can I think affection into existence for you or anyone else."

He turned away in disgust.

"It *is* rational, as you say, but—"

"I want you to consider something else. Consider what I am about to say as a statement of the world as it is; a statement such as 'The sun will rise tomorrow.' Do not take it as a threat."

"What, Sir?"

"Consider that I also have the power to punish you, despite your assertion that you have not wronged me. Others will think you have wronged me, and I would be justified to place you in a convent. Or I could strip you of all livelihood, as is my right. I do not want to do this. Not at all. I merely want *you*. I want you very badly. I want all of you."

I had stiffened at the thought of being placed in a convent. I held myself very still, so that I might try to listen.

James did not notice my rigidity and went on, "However despite such prerogatives I might have, I will forget them. I will also forget the past. I do not care about what has happened in the last three years. What is done, is done." He took a deep breath. "You are here now, and I am willing to forget it all. I will give you everything you desire. And I will be just what you want me to be. I only ask that you let me forget." He closed his eyes, as though to wipe out an unpleasant thought. "This I can do, if you will forget about Bolívar. Completely. Forget him, never mention him again."

I could not do that. I could not betray him. When I finally answered, I tried to be as gentle as possible and said, "Sir, you must know by now that I cannot dissemble. Have you ever seen me do anything half-way? Have you ever seen me pretend. I do not understand how to compromise, Sir. I love him—"

"*NO!*" His anger was violent, jealous, and immediate. "No, damn you. No! You cannot."

We stared at each other. At last, I said, "If you will give me time, Sir, I will make the best effort I know how." It was all I could promise.

I could see it was with difficulty that he kept himself from saying or doing anymore. "Very well, Madam," was all he could manage, and then he walked slowly out of the room.

So it began, the unhappiest period I ever spent in Lima. Day after day James would bring me flowers, abuse me, beg forgiveness, cajole me, buy me presents, threaten me, apologize, promise me happiness, and try to make love to me. Weeks rolled on as he wore away at my sanity and my own sense of self. All the while, the siege at Callao went on and on.

The only thing that kept me going was my work. I continued my duties at Bolívar's villa, managing correspondence from all over the continent. Thorne was particularly incensed at my spending my days away from him. "It is my duty," I told him, and I went.

Most of the time James and I were civil to one another, despite an undercurrent of tension and conflict. I made an effort to be with him on social occasions, despite knowing that people who knew about Bolívar and me were making judgments even while I spoke to them. I suppressed my anger at their looks and innuendoes. I tried to fulfill all aspects of James's life with as much marital happiness as I could. However, I would not sleep with him, and this undid every other effort I made.

I wondered about Bolívar. Deep in my heart, I believed that he could not live without me, any more than I could live without him. Yet, everything about my life in that period told me otherwise.

Then, a letter arrived for me. When I recognized Bolívar's hand, my heart flew to the heavens. The cannons in Callao pounded many times before I opened it. It was the first moment of true happiness I had known since his departure. When at last I broke the seal, I did indeed find a love letter. However, it had a tragic character that broke my heart.

My Beautiful and Adorable Manuela,

Each moment, I think of you and the fate that has touched you. I see that nothing can unite us under the auspices of innocence and honor. I see well, and deplore, the horrible situation for you. You must be reconciled with one you do not love and I must be separated from one I adore. Yes, I adore you, today more than ever before. Tearing myself from you and your love has multiplied in me all the sentiments that bound me to your heart, your soul and heart, that heart without equal.

When you were mine, I loved you more for your enchanting nature than for the delicious attraction of your body. Now it seems to me that an eternity separates us. In the future you will be only at the side of your husband; I will be alone in the midst of the world. Only the glory of having conquered ourselves will be our consolation.

My love always,
Simón

I wept the most profound tears of my life thus far. Such a beautiful expression of love. Yet, in the same letter, he declared his complete surrender to a fate that was so wrong for both of us.

I wrote him back. I told him I did not believe in the future he painted. I would see him again, one day. However, he never received it. He, or my letter, were swallowed up by the Andes.

About that time, we had a remarkable visitor, who bolstered my spirits immensely. I was arranging flowers in my San Sebastiano home when Jonotás came in with a note from Colonel O'Leary. It said only, "Samuel Robinson has arrived."

Simón Rodríguez, Bolívar's tutor, still going by the name Robinson, had been in Europe for the last 20 years. Simón wanted his mentor to take over the public education system. I knew that Simón had written to him and asked for him to come back to his home continent, but I did not know he had left Europe.

I threw on my uniform, saddled Midnight, and raced down to Magdalena. There, pulling saddlebags from of a tired mule, was a stooped man who looked like he was almost 70 years old; but I knew he was only about 50. He was almost completely bald, except for strands of white hair flying here and there. His clothes were the latest English fashion. They were brand new, but they were wrinkled, ill-fitting, and dirty. I knew at once who it was.

"Rodríguez," I cried as I dismounted.

He looked around, and, of course, he did not recognize me. He looked perplexed as he peered over the rims of his spectacles at me. He pulled on his chin, as though it had more growth than a day or two of stubble. "You must have mistaken me, Señora," he said, his voice high and nasal, but pleasant and intelligent.

I threw my arms around him, stifling a reaction to the odor of his filthy clothes, and I said, "No. I could not mistake you. Bolívar has told me all about you."

He was so surprised at my effusiveness that he didn't know what to say. "Oh . . . uhm . . . well then, if you are a . . . friend of Simón's, then you are a friend of mine." He looked at my uniform and said, "I take it you are more to him than one of his officers." He smiled a crooked smile.

"Come, my friend—for I feel you are my friend already—let us talk about your student."

We went inside the villa, and Rodríguez, who insisted that I call him Robinson, and I got to know each other. He was funny, brilliant, and seemed to know something about every important event and person in the world. He told me a much more romantic and improbable version of his and Simón's climb up the Monte Sacro than any I had heard before. We laughed and talked for a long time. We made a friendship that day that has lasted for almost 30 years. I loved him. I know by his actions that he adored me. However, I could not enjoy him for long. When he learned that Bolívar was in Upper Perú and would be there for some time, he left to find him.

It was with a sad heart that I made my way from Magdalena to Lima the next afternoon after watching Rodríguez head down the coast for Ica. The cannon fire from Callao, aided by the overcast that covers Perú most of the year, sealed the gloom I felt in my heart.

Because Rodríguez represented Simón, I had a brief glimpse of my true love. Yet, his leaving made my future seem more futile than ever. There was little to which I could look forward. Bolívar was lost in the Andes, braced by his romantic martyrdom: *"Only the glory of having conquered ourselves will be our consolation."*

My soldier's duties seemed to have so little meaning for me, without Bolívar there, and yet I needed something to keep me going. I could not count on my husband to bring me any joy. The most I could expect from James would be persistent demands that I give myself to him completely.

Perhaps, there was no other way. If Bolívar was not coming back, perhaps I should make an effort to fortify my marriage.

I wept as I rode back to Lima. I could not help it. Every time I thought of truly reinvesting my marriage with my full commitment, I had to cry.

The overcast sky oppressed me as I dismounted in Lima. The cannon fire could be heard in the distance. When I went inside and asked Jonotás where James could be found, she said, "He was just ridin' off to Magdalena a little while ago."

"Magdalena?" I must have missed him in the streets of Lima. "Why was he going there?"

"I don't know, but he was swearin' and angry."

An hour or so later, he rode back on Natán's horse. He had apparently taken it in order to hurry to Magdalena and back. He had been riding hard, but I was unprepared when he thundered into the house, yelling, "I have had it! I can never find you. You are always 'off' somewhere. Your slaves either don't know where you are, or they are with you. I have had enough, Madam." He was pacing up and down in as foul a mood as I had ever seen him.

I tried to get through his tirade. "Why are you shouting, Sir? Tell me why." All the while he slammed the furniture about and paced. Natán came into the room, but joined Jonotás in the corner, away from his anger.

"Madam," he said, at last, "I will not have it any more. I insist that you fulfill your duties to me as a wife and stop play acting at soldiering."

If, by looking at James, I could have killed him, he would have been dead instantly. "How dare you? How dare you speak to me that way?" I came across the room at him in fury.

"Stop right there, Manuela. You will mind your manners and show me respect."

"You go to hell. You will not speak to me that way."

"Damn it. You are my wife." He grabbed me in order to stop me from moving. He looked in my eyes and then tried to kiss me. I fought, but his left hand held me by the neck. He thrust his right hand between my legs.

"Stop it! Stop it!" I shouted. I turned around and escaped his grasp. I did not expect what happened next. When I turned back to face him, he slapped me.

The shock of having been struck stunned me for a second, but it seemed like minutes. I tried to look through a red blindness that took over my vision. Dimly, I saw a look of horror filling his eyes.

I wanted to destroy him. Before his arm recoiled from the slap, I attacked. I wanted to gouge my nails into his flesh and rip out his eyes.

I did not touch his face. He reacted by bringing his arms up, and when we collided, we both fell over a table and crashed to the floor. "You filthy dog," I cried as we fell. "Don't you ever strike me. Don't you ever," I said, as we scrambled for our footing. My fists were doubled, and I was striking out but my blows did not connect.

By the time we climbed to our feet, Jonotás and Natán were in between us. "Leave her alone," they were saying.

We stood there a minute staring at each other. I in fury. He in confusion.

He turned and walked out the door.

I did not see James for the rest of the day. He was gone for only a minute when I started packing. In two hours, everything I cared about in the San Sebastiano home was in a *calesa* and on its way to Magdalena. I followed.

James showed up at our seaside residence later that night. I could tell he was drunk as he pounded for admittance, slurring his words as he yelled, "Open up. Let me in. I'm sorry Manuela."

When I opened the door, he looked awful. He swayed so much he could barely stand, his clothes looked like he had slept in the street, and his face was dirty.

As he took a step to walk in, he tripped and fell. He lay there unmoving. When I knelt down to see if he was hurt, I heard him sobbing. He spoke softly in English, "I'm sorry, Manuela. I must have you. I must. Don't you see? I'm so sorry," he kept repeating this over and over.

"Never mind, James," I said, "Let's talk about it tomorrow." I sent Jonotás off to find a guard at the Magdalena villa. When they arrived at the house a few moments later, I had the guard help James onto Natán's horse. Then I gave Jonotás's horse to the soldier and told him to take my husband home. All the while, he kept repeating, "I didn't mean it, Manuela. I'm sorry."

My anger at being struck was over. I felt sorry for him. I went to bed that night in utter confusion. I did not know what I was going to do.

The next day, I sent a letter to Arequipa. I told Simón what had happened: "As you say, I have no honorable way to love you and be with you. Now, after his striking me, I have no honorable way to stay with Thorne. I am lost."

James came over that day, completely contrite. He apologized again and again. He pleaded with me to give him a second chance.

"I can do no more than ask you for time," I told him.

"Yes, Madam, I understand," he said, and went back to Lima.

I could hear the siege at Callao. I felt sorry for General Rodil, loyal to an Empire that was no more, holding on to a tiny bit of land surrounded by crumbling fortifications, resisting the constant pounding of cannons determined to tear down the walls.

Day in and day out, James wrote to me. I received two or three letters a day. He sent me presents. He came to see me. He brought me flowers. He, or a messenger, would come up to me on the street, in my office at the villa, at home, wherever I was, bringing me letters or gifts. Always, he wanted to "talk."

I became more unsettled as each day passed. What was I to do? His arguments made sense. I had no future but to be his wife. I was chained to him like a prisoner, with invisible bonds that were tighter than iron. I could not allow myself to be trapped thus and yet I could not escape.

During this period, Jonotás and Natán told me that Señora Orué had invited him over to console him when her husband was out of town. The irony of it almost made me cry.

At my wedding, when I realized that the wife of James's friend Domingo Orué desired my husband, I had felt threatened. When I heard that he had gone to her house, I hoped that she would distract him from his unrelenting interest in me. However, Jonotás told me that he only stayed a short time and though she invited him again the next day, he did not go.

A day or so later, with James still pestering me every day, I received a letter from Simón. It was the first of many that would arrive from him in the next few months:

Manuela, My Love:

I am in bed with a cold and have read your letter. I do not know which surprises me most: the bad treatment you have received because of me, or the force of your sentiments which I at once admire and applaud. If you wish to fly from the things you fear, come to Arequipa, where I have friends who will protect you.

I am desperate to return to Lima. If I do not do anything else, then I think constantly throughout the day and the entire night of your loveliness and of my love for you—and about my return—and what you will do—and what I shall do when we see each other again.

All my love,
Simón

It was like breathing fresh air. We would see each other again, after all. I did not know when or how, but we would. I wrote back immediately.

Later that day, however, James came to me and said, "I apologize for my actions recently. You will not find a breach in my gentlemanly behavior in the future. However, I have decided that it is far too painful for both of us here. I am going to take you to London."

London. I longed to go there. I believed I would have trouble living the life of a proper English wife, but I longed to see the famous city and the rest of Europe. If only he had taken me when we were first married. I could not go. His words chilled me.

What if he made me leave? All of his problems would be solved, and my future would be irrevocably altered. He would have me permanently away from Bolívar and I would never see my love again. It would take some time for James to wrap up his affairs in Lima, but he had made his decision and we would leave in a month or so.

I wrote to Simón, and told him of my predicament. He wrote back and asked me if I was going. My return letter informed him that I did not know what to do. His reply finally told me what I had believed all along.

Darling, My Adored One:

Your answer is not clear about that terrible trip to London. Is this possible, my darling? Don't give me mysterious riddles to solve. Tell the truth, that you don't want to go anywhere. Answer what I recently asked you, so that I know your intentions definitely and surely. You want to see me again with your own eyes. Well, I want to see you again, to touch you, feel you, taste you, join myself with you in every sense. Don't go away, even with God himself.

One who loves you deeply,
Simón

At last he had said, without equivocation, that he wished me to stay and be with him. We would once again be united—somehow. In the months that followed, our letters were no longer filled with indecision about the future. He wrote often, beautiful letters that I cherished. The letters I wrote to him were the same as his—full of passion and certainty that we would see each other again.

I told James that I would not accompany him to London.

"What do you mean? I am going. Therefore, you are going."

"James, I cannot. It would kill me, and it would probably kill you too, for I would be so unhappy as to make you wish you had never left."

"But, Manuela—"

"James, I know you have done well in the last few years. If you leave, you will be throwing away your money and your business which has taken you years to build."

"I don't care—"

"And it would not change anything. It will not make me love you more; in fact, I will die so much inside that my indifference will be like a sword in your heart." He started to retort, but I said, "Wait. I am not threatening you. I am asking you to understand."

"Very well, Manuela, we will not go to London, but please come back to me. Please."

"I cannot." I said the words softly, but I had to keep from screaming the words in frustration. I reached out my hand and touched his arm. Softly, quietly, I said, "I am sorry my friend, but I *will* see Bolívar again. I must be truthful and tell you that my only regret is that it will hurt you."

He did not look at me. After a moment, he walked away. I did not see him for three days, and thought perhaps he had given me up.

After the third day, he began to write to me again. I received two or three letters a day, for almost a week. All this while Señora Orué kept after him, and he continued to reject her. I believe James liked her but he did not wish to betray his friend, Domingo. Thus he concentrated all of his attention on me.

Fortunately, my sense of myself had returned. I knew who I was and what I would do in the future. I was alive again. I ignored his letters and threw myself into my work.

I went to the San Sebastiano house one afternoon to pick up some material. I found the heavy cotton bolts I was looking for in the second bedroom—I intended to make another uniform. I had just spread it out on the bed to examine the quality when James walked in. I did not expect him home for an hour or more.

I stopped, waiting to see what he would say. He was quiet for a moment and then he said, "Manuela, I cannot continue this way." He walked toward me. He stood on the other side of the bed and said, "Please, I beg of you, for the sake of righteousness and honor, return to me and our marriage."

I shook my head, slowly. "It will not work—"

"No, you're wrong. It can work." He reminded of one who was grasping, grasping at anything—fearful and hopeful. "We can work anything out." He came around to the end of the bed. "I know you're angry at me because I struck you. I am truly sorry. It won't happen again. Honor is the only—"

I threw my hands to my ears. "No, no, no more, man, for God's sake say no more!" He stopped—as though he was surprised he had been talking. I looked at him, and said quietly, "Why do you try to force me to change my resolution?"

"Manuela, I know we can—"

"A thousand times—no!" I shook my head and paced up and down alongside the bed. I stopped and took a breath. My exasperation had the better of me.

James looked hurt and angry.

I went to him. I spoke to him in English. "Sir, you are excellent, you are inimitable. But, my friend, it is no small matter that I leave you for Simón Bolívar. To leave a husband without your qualities would be nothing."

His jaw set. He struggled to control his emotions.

"Do you think for a moment that, after being beloved of this man for years, and with the security that I possessed his heart, I would choose to be the wife even of the Father, Son, or the Holy Ghost, or of all three?"

He turned away in disgust. "That is exactly the problem," he said, with his back to me as he walked to a chair. "We could resume our marriage, but you choose to blaspheme our religion." He turned and pointed a finger at me. "God will never honor your affair with this man."

I was not listening. My head was lowered. I shook it and said, "I know very well that I cannot be united with him under the laws of honor, as you call them, but do you believe that I feel less or more honored because he is my lover and not my husband?"

"That is shameful!" he shouted. "You simply refuse to live as everyone else."

"Sir, I do not live for the prejudices of society. I gave that up years before I met you."

"That is exactly what I mean—" His anger was out of control .

I shouted louder than he. "Society's rules were invented only that we poor humans might torture each other. I must live for myself, for what *I* believe, not according to some set of rules made thousands of years ago."

He sat down. He looked at the floor, and said softly, "I love you, Manuela."

I walked over to him, and said, "Let me be, my dear Englishman. Just, let me go. We will both be happier."

"It is not right!" His voice was soft but full of emotion.

I knew this discussion would get us no farther than any other we had. I was tired of it. I walked around the bed, and continued to fold the material I had come after. James jumped up and began to pace up and down. "It is not right!" he repeated loudly.

I went on folding the material and said, "Oh, James. Come man." I let out a nervous chuckle. I could not continue on in such a serious vein. "Let us do something else, my friend," I said, after a minute. "Let us marry when we get to heaven."

"Now you make jokes." He looked at me with disgust

"I do not think so. In heaven we can be married, that is something that I can promise you. But on this earth—no."

He sat back down in his chair, his face set in anger.

I put one square of the smooth green cloth on the bed, and picked up another piece. I did not look at him, but went on folding. "Do you think this arrangement is bad? In our heavenly home we shall lead entirely spiritual lives. There everything will be quite British—monotony is reserved for your nation (in love, that is, for they are much more avid in business)." I laughed at my own sarcasm.

"Do you pretend superiority of race," he said with a sneer.

"Oh, no." I laughed, setting another neat square on top the other in perfect organization. "It is only that you love without pleasure, you converse without grace, you walk unhurried, you sit down with caution—you do not even laugh at your own jokes. These are divine attributes, to be sure, but I, miserable mortal who can laugh at myself, laugh at you too, with all this English seriousness."

He stood and paced back and forth.

"How I shall suffer in heaven! Quite as much as though I were to go and live in England, I'm sure."

He ignored me and said, "Is there nothing that I can say—"

"No, Sir! You do not understand. You are violent, controlling, and more jealous than a Portuguese. That is why I do not love you."

He looked at me in disgust.

"Ah, I see that I am in bad taste?"

"Quite droll, Manuela. We are on the crossroads of our lives, of our souls, and you . . ." He threw up his hands.

I walked over to him and stood in front of him. He stopped pacing, looked at me, and then looked out the window. I said as quietly, and with as much meaning as I could muster, "Very well, enough of jesting. Seriously and without levity and with all the conscientiousness, truth, and purity of an Englishwoman, I say this: I can never return to our marriage again."

Slowly, he moved his eyes to me   I saw something different in them. For the first time, he saw that it was so.

"You are a Catholic, I am an atheist, and this is our greatest religious obstacle; that I am in love with someone else is a greater and still stronger reason."

He did not speak. I saw resignation take over his face and he looked older. My husband turned slowly and walked out of the room.

Chapter 22

In January of 1826, it had been almost a year since the siege at Callao had begun, a year of hearing the distant cannons pound away at the fortress. It had been almost as long, nine months, since Bolívar had left and Thorne had arrived. Like the rest of Lima, I was worn down by the siege.

After my last discussion with James, he stopped coming to see me as often. I rarely saw him anymore and could tell that he felt he had lost, even though his manner was belligerent when I did see him. Nevertheless, he had not stated that our battle of wills was over. I waited to see what he would do next.

Three events occurred in the month of January that greatly simplified my life. First, General Rodil finally surrendered. He and his troops were granted the honors of war, but they were a sorry sight when they finally left the fortress: diseased, famished, and dirty. I felt sorry for them, but I was so very, very glad that the siege had ended.

The second event was more welcome even than the first. I knew something had changed when James arrived, early one evening, at the villa. He had never been inside before and was out of place in Bolívar's residence. I almost did not recognize him.

"Manuela," he said simply, "I would like to speak to you."

It was the first time he had spoken to me respectfully, in weeks. "Yes, Sir," I said, "let us take a walk."

We passed through the orchard and walked across the dunes toward the ocean. I waited for him to speak while we walked in silence. The sun was setting and the water was bathed in golden light.

When we arrived at the water's edge, we both looked at the horizon for a long time. The waves rolled against the sand, and I waited.

At last, he said, "I have decided to move to Panamá." That was the last thing I expected him to say. Before I could respond, he continued without animosity, "You have chosen to dishonor me, and I cannot stay. I will manage my business from there."

"You know it was not my intention to dishonor you—"

"Nevertheless—"

"Nor do I consider that you have been dishonored. You are the same person, and my actions should not reflect on you or your accomplishments."

"Nevertheless, I am dishonored."

I shook my head while James stared at the horizon. After a moment he said, "I am leaving. Soon. There is too much temptation for me here." I knew he was speaking about Señora Orué. "And too much shame."

"Are you saying that we will divorce—"

He raised his voice. "NO! No divorce. Ever. I am leaving, that is all. I would as soon never see you again. But there will be no divorce."

Despite everything that happened, this hurt me. I knew he would not divorce me, even before I asked, but that he wished to cut all ties with me was painful. "James, I—"

"I would under normal circumstances avoid you forever, but my business interests in Lima . . ." He looked confused but finally found the right words. "Perhaps you can help me."

"You know I will. You know I would do anything for the least of my friends, and you, Sir, are a most important friend. You—"

I could tell he did not want to hear anything from me. He rushed on, saying, "I feel I must leave tomorrow. However, I have a great deal of business to be done in Lima over the next several weeks. Captain Escobar will not be back in the area for months." He turned to look at me. "You have always handled my affairs in a superlative manner. I do not want to admit it, but I do trust you to administer . . ." He looked out at the water and it appeared as though he was fighting with himself to speak to me. He cleared his throat. ". . . perhaps you could . . . handle a few of my concerns after I leave." It was so typical of him. He allowed himself to speak to me because there was an important business reason.

I said, "Of course." I wanted to say that I would do anything for him and somehow reconcile further.

Before I could think of the right thing to add, he said, "Thank you. I will send you the work."

He turned and looked into my eyes. His expression was deeply sad. He whispered, "Good-bye," and walked away.

I watched him disappear behind the houses. I never saw him again.

The next day, a courier brought me documents for the various transactions he wished me to administrate. One of them was the sale of the house in Lima. Another was a lease in my name, for the Magdalena residence. It was at a very good price, for three years, at which time it was to be sold.

It was my home, and I determined then that I would have the money to buy it myself when the time came. However, I was grateful that he had seen to my needs and that he had avoided rancor in our parting.

I set to work, but no sooner had James left Perú than the third event occurred which brought me a few months of ecstatic happiness. Simón arrived in Magdalena.

He had come home to a country at peace, having indeed formed a new republic out of Upper Perú. Sucre was still there, settled in to be its first president. The new country's name filled me with joy the first time I heard it: Bolivia. Named after the Liberator himself, it was to be a model of Bolívar's political ideals. At last, after so much hardship and bloodshed: peace at last.

I did not know that Simón was on his way to Lima because it had been some time since I had heard from him. It was about two weeks after James set sail for Panamá that I went to bed one night feeling quite lonely. As I was dropping into slumber, my dogs barked.

Opening my eyes and listening carefully, I heard a faint tapping at the door to the street. I threw on a *saya y manto* and arrived at the door before Jonotás and Natán. There, silhouetted in the light from the windows of the houses down the street, was José Palacios.

I held up my candle and illuminated a man somewhat different than I had known. His customary short, black cape and impeccably clean, starched shirt were both wrinkled and dirty. He said softly, "We have ridden hard all day in order to arrive tonight." He pulled a slip of paper out of his cape and handed it to me.

For three hundred leagues I have seen your face before me. I could not wait to see you again. I long to hold you. Come to me. Come now.

He was home. Happiness rushed through me so quickly that I almost cried. I think I said, "Thank you, José." I know I swept past him leaving the door open behind me. An instant later, I ran past soldiers still lifting saddles from the backs of tired horses and up the steps of the villa. I opened the door and ran down the hall to Simón's room.

He was in civilian clothes instead of a uniform, and they were in the same rumpled condition as José's clothes had been. He had just set a candle on the ornately carved table beside the viceroy's bed. As he turned toward me I ran into his arms. His mouth found mine and I drank in the feel and taste and smell of the man I loved. We kissed long, searching kisses, and I heard José closing the door behind us.

Simón pulled my *manto* down over my shoulders and let it fall. He took hold of my *saya* and pulled it to my ankles. I stood before him naked and then he took me and parted my lips with his.

I wanted to feel his skin pressed against mine. I tore open his shirt, scattering buttons on the tiles. He brought his lips to my neck and my shoulders and then lifted me in his arms and laid me down on the viceroy's bed. His lips covered me while he whispered, "I love you." Through breathless kisses he said, "I thought I would never see you again. I love you."

I dug my fingers into the cloth of his jacket as if I could hold onto him the tighter by doing so. I whispered between kisses and tears, "I love you, Simón. Never leave me again. I was so afraid I'd lost you."

He smothered me with love. It seemed hours before we satiated ourselves with the passion that washed over us like an ocean. We loved as though we had thirsted for each other for centuries instead of months, and we filled each other. We were one.

Simón fell asleep almost immediately, but I lay with my head on his chest, listening to his heart beat softly as he slept. I savored the idea that we had finally arrived. The war was over. The last Spanish general had surrendered. My husband had abandoned his battle to posses my soul. Simón had formed governments that represented his ideals in all the countries he had freed. We would have peace.

Four years earlier, I had sat on my horse and resigned myself to battle. *I will fight now, but one day La Sáenz will be at peace,* I had told myself. At last it had come. What would happen now? I drifted into sleep.

He woke me as dawn crept through the windows. I felt him kissing my lips before I opened my eyes. His passion had returned and we loved again. This time it was not uncontrollable forces that moved us, but sweet, pure, delicious love. Our rhythm was slow as we savored every movement, every touch, and the powerful feeling of the love that we shared.

Then we talked. The first thing he said, after we huddled close to each other to ward of the morning chill, was, "I wish I could tell you how much you have filled my thoughts since I left you."

"I have thought about nothing but you, Simón."

He touched my face and said, "I am sorry I did not take you with me."

"You are my life, Simón. I could not go back to him."

"I know. I thought it was for the best, but I have not looked at another woman since I left. I must have *you*." He leaned close, and I looked into eyes that were full of emotion. "You are my wife, Manuela."

A sweet feeling of belonging, of being in the right place at the right time, came over me. "And you, Simón, only you are my husband."

We held each other close. After a time, he said, "What do you say to this idea?" He smiled happily. "The hard work is almost over. It is almost time that we can go to Venezuela. I have not seen my estates since—how long has it been?—six years? Seven years? Oh, you will love it there, Manuela. The fields go on forever, and around the buildings the flower gardens produce every color imaginable in the spring."

"Yes, Simón, yes. Oh, you know I want to go—tomorrow."

He smiled and kissed me. "Tomorrow, no. But soon."

"When? When can we go? The Liberator has freed an entire continent. Surely, his work is done." I smiled at him.

"The Liberator's work is perhaps done. However, my duties as founder, and statesman, and protector—"

"Founder?"

"Of these Republics. That work is not done. I have created—" I was shaking my head. "Manuela, surely you must realize that three states are weaker than a large country that is unified. We must bring them together. We must create a coalition that unifies them. *The United Republics*, perhaps." He stood, threw a blanket around his shoulders, and paced up and down. "Perhaps we can invite Chile, and Argentina, or the Northern provinces to join. A strong central government coordinating the interaction between these countries will insure their cooperation and strength. Unity. Unity is and must be our goal— What's the matter, Manuela? You look—taken aback."

"I am. Only moments ago, we spoke of retiring to your estates—"

"I said, 'When we have the time . . .'"

"Yes, but what you are speaking about will take years."

"Oh, I don't think so." He sat on the bed close to me and held my hand. Slowly, he brought my fingers to his lips and he kissed them. A surge of emotion went through me at the feeling he was able to communicate in that one tender kiss. "As I have said, the hard work is almost done."

"Simón, your dream sounds wonderful. I am behind you. It seems impossible to me, yet I believe that you could do it. But honestly, how long will it take.

"A year, maybe two—" I slowly withdrew my hand. "Manuela?"

"That cannot be."

"Certainly—" I lay down and turned my back to him. As I pulled the covers up he leaned over and put his hand on my shoulder. "Manuela?"

I looked over my shoulder and said, "Perhaps *you* could do it in a year. But only if everyone of importance was behind you." A frown crossed his face. I sat up and said, "But people will not see your dream. They will only see one powerful man trying to make one vast big country—"

"Yes, of course, that is what I am trying to do." He threw up his hands in exasperation, as if wondering why I could not grasp the obvious, and turned to put his feet on the floor.

I touched his back, and said, "Tell me something. Was not Napoleon interested in unity?"

He snapped his head around said, "I am not Napoleon. I am not like him. I am talking about the future of the continent. Why did you ask that?"

"Because, people will not believe in or see unity. They will believe you do all this for yourself, for your own power."

"That is ridiculous."

"Yet, that is what they will believe. They will fight you."

"I don't believe any rational man can oppose my ideas of a strong central government controlling a large powerful nation."

I was suddenly overcome with a feeling of loss and fear. Fear for his life. Why? Why did I feel this? Was I too sensitive to people's hatred? Was my past preventing me from seeing the future he envisioned? I put my arms around him from behind and put my cheek against his neck and held him as though I could keep him forever with me that way. "Simón, maybe you are right. But, I don't want to wait that long. I don't want to wait even two weeks, to say nothing of years."

"Manuela, I—"

"Yet, even if I was willing to wait, I do not believe you. It cannot be accomplished in so short a time. Leave it to your officers and friends. Let us go to Venezuela now."

"Please, my beautiful darling, who breathes life into my soul, let us not quarrel. I cannot leave things as they are. You must see that. I need to give these three republics the strength to survive. If I do not do so, or if I fail, they will splinter and war with each other. Instead of three republics, or one strong one, we will have six or more."

"But Simón, are you not tired?"

"Yes. Very tired. I wish the job were over, but it is not." He turned to me and held my hands. "Help me. Help me for two more years, no longer than three, and then we will retire. I swear it."

"What if it takes longer than three?

"Then . . . but it will not."

I looked into his eyes and knew I must follow him where his dreams must lead. I was only interested in us. Yet, he was working for the future prosperity of an entire continent. "Yes. We can do it. But, two years, maybe three, but no more." I forced a smile.

He smiled back and kissed me. That very day he wrote to the leaders of the other American states promoting his idea of a congress of the continent's leaders in Panamá. He also wrote to his vice president, stressing his ideas for a strong central government.

As he wrote to Santander, a twinge of fear went through me. If Bolívar's plans were to fail, it would very likely be because they would be dashed against Santander's treachery. I sensed somehow, that he was the danger. However, I said nothing.

For many more months, it was almost as I had hoped. Simón loved me, he was happy to be with me again, and he made no excuses when he brought me with him to affairs of state and less formal social gatherings.

For a while, it appeared he could do no wrong. Despite rumors of moral outrage, we lived together openly. He commissioned a painting of me, showered me with gifts, and acted as though I were his wife. We enjoyed our days together; and when we were alone at the villa, after Simón's meetings and other work was done, he was all mine and nothing could stop our passion.

For the first time in 15 years, the Liberator, who had done all he had promised he would do, could take his ease. He did not ask for, or even desire, the gifts that came from the Congress and the citizens of Perú: a jewel-studded sword covered with diamonds and emeralds, a gold service for his table, the viceroy's carriage redone with Bolívar's arms painted on the side, and a dress uniform so ostentatious that Simón would not wear it.

The one gift he truly cherished came from the United States of America. George Washington's family sent a letter of admiration and the golden medal that had been struck for him after the Battle of Yorktown. Simón was deeply moved by the gesture and wore that medal, and no other, from then on.

I urged him to accept all that was given him. He deserved it. I enjoyed the gifts, but I would not have cared if—in fact I wished that—we had been completely ignored. But it was not to be. Bolívar was the man of the moment. Poets wrote epics to their Liberator. Prayers in the churches began, "O Lord! All good things from thee. Thou has given us Bolívar . . ."

Not that there was no complaining. We heard that our political enemies railed against us and we heard some of the complaints. The upper classes did most of the complaining. Though we knew it was happening, we did not realize how deeply Simón's success upset them. We believed the dissatisfaction was very small, and so we had a sense of peace in those months.

Because I am sensitive to the mood of society, I was more aware of the rancor that was building against Simón than he was. He always believed people loved him more than they did. Still, I kept quiet, ignored the rumors, and enjoyed our peaceful life together. I was pleased that Simón took the rewards he deserved, and even more pleased that he was taking some well-earned leisure.

Chapter 23

Though the first few months of 1826 were unhurried and peaceful, Simón did not stop working altogether. He worked very hard on the constitution that the people of Bolivia had asked him to write. He also continued his work on a Pan-American Congress and the many needed political reforms in Perú.

In the meantime, I had my hands full trying to take care of the business that Thorne, no longer in Lima, had left to my care. I wrote to him constantly, informing him of each negotiation or event, and he returned short, businesslike notes, advising me of his wishes. I followed his dictates; and when called upon to exercise my own judgment in his absence, I often made him a little more money than he had told me he was expecting.

The only transaction in which I lost money, and his trust, was in the sale of the San Sebastiano house. At first, I believed I might make a good deal more than James expected. I had a government official from Arequipa and a Chilean sea captain from a noble family both interested and willing to pay more than the other in order to have it. James advised me to sell to the highest bidder. "Make as much as you can. It does not matter who buys it," he wrote to me.

However, that afternoon, Jonotás came in and said, "There's a nun wantin' to see you."

I looked up from my writing. "A nun?"

"Yes. She's there at the door, makin' it holy, sure as can be."

I heard the soft roar of the waves striking the shore in the distance while I wiped the ink from my fingers. I was incredulous. *What could a nun want?* I looked down at my work. I was quite busy; and had it not been so unexpected, I would have asked Jonotás to send the visitor away. "A nun you say?" I asked as I walked to the door.

When I arrived, I found a young nun waiting for me patiently. She wore a coarse purple habit and a rope around her neck signifying her as a woman of the Convent of Las Nazarenas. She said gloomily, "I am here to deliver a message from the Abbess Doña Augustina de San Joaquín." She handed me a letter written on fine paper in an even finer hand, signed by the abbess herself.

It has come to my attention that you are to sell a house in the neighborhood of our Convent. For some time now it has been our desire and dream to open a house for the rescue and education of the poor women of Perú. We wish it to become self-sustaining and not part of this convent, however we must advise and support it in its formative period. Thus, we need a house close by in order to begin our project.

We have waited to begin this venture until we were sure of the peace, but we feel now is the time. Our funds are limited, but we hope to make a suitable transaction for all concerned.

Would you please come to my office so that we might discuss the sale of your property.

I handed it back and said, "I am sorry, but I will not go into a convent, not even the *locutorios*. Tell the abbess that she will have to come to me. However, I already have two bids, both for a considerable price."

The nun took the letter, maintaining a somber expression, and left. I assumed that someone as self important and powerful as an abbess would not come to see me at all. She had said that she did not have much money, so why bother. I was surprised that very evening.

I was in the sitting room when a sharp knock sounded at the door. Natán opened it and there were two nuns this time. The older one said, "I am Augustina de San Joaquín. I am here to see Señora Thorne."

I walked over to the door and looked at the tall woman who stood on my doorstep. "I am Manuela Thorne." I was unsettled to see her there, but I managed to say, "Please come in."

She entered but told the other nun to wait outside. We sat down and Natán brought us some refreshment. The abbess came right to her business. "I am here to persuade you to sell your property to us. Now that peace is secure, we feel we can spend the money we have budgeted for our project. It is important to us that we have a place very close to our convent. As you know, the neighborhood is wealthy and there is not often a chance to buy there."

"Señora," I interrupted, "I do not mind selling the house to you, but can you meet my price? As I told your messenger, I already have two very good offers."

"Yes, and I know what they are."

"Really? How?"

She smiled and said, "Our convent is much loved. Often, helpful *limeños* will give me information which is believed to be of benefit. However, that is not the point. I am here to persuade you to sell me the land for a little less."

I am sure I could not hide a look of surprise at her audacious manner. For a convent renowned for its spiritual austerity, she was showing a great deal of material business sense and confidence. I set down my cup and looked at her more carefully.

She had sharp eyes that were a rich chocolate. Her mouth had a sensuous shape and was the only feature on her patrician face that did not announce a keen intelligence touched with penitent suffering. Her feet were bare, of course, and scabbed. She had walked the two leagues to my house in order to persuade me. There was a tiny new cut on her right foot. I had heard that the nuns of Las Nazarenas wore a crown of thorns under their veils to make their mortification more complete.

Yet, there she was, boldly asking for what she desired. I suddenly admired her. I was inclined to indulge an offer from her—I would insist that she match the other offers in the end, of course—but I thought I might test her.

"Is there any reason in the world I would sell property for less than it is worth?" I asked sternly.

She was not affected by either my tone or my question. Without the slightest pause, she said, "Yes. I can think of one or two." She smiled a very friendly smile.

I wanted to smile back, but instead I asked sharply, "What would those reasons be?"

"One might be that you have sympathy for the good work we will do. Our home will help the poor, underprivileged girls of our city. These girls will be orphans, or perhaps abandoned. At any rate they will have no home or position with which to educate themselves, and no dowry to marry. Such girls, grown to women, will either have to marry for money alone, often into an unhappy union, or live a life of prostitution, or worse. Do you not see a need for such a charity?"

I was beginning to like this woman very much. She reminded me of unhappy times in my life, but she was presenting herself as someone I would have been desperate to know then. "Why do you not take them into the nunnery? Why a secular home?" I asked.

"Let me ask you something, Señora. Why did you refuse to come to the convent to see me?"

"Because I spent ten years in a convent when I was a girl—a girl very much like the ones you describe—and I chafed at how my life was controlled by convent rules."

"Now you have an answer to your question."

I smiled at her.

"But it is deeper than that," she went on. "Our convent has rules which are quite severe. In one of the *conventos grandes*, a girl would be able to go to the convent school and still take a secular life when she matured. Our little convent is too demanding for such an arrangement, and yet we desire to help such girls."

She was saying everything that I wanted to hear. I became suspicious. "You said that you are often given valuable information. What have you heard about me?"

She looked genuinely surprised. "Nothing, except that you have a house for sale. Why?"

"No reason." I looked up at Natán, who had been listening to us. She was smiling. She liked this woman as much as I did, which was enough endorsement in itself. However, I decided to test her one more time. "Usually, white girls do not need such help."

"Oh, I do not expect there to be many white girls. It will be open to girls of all races, but I especially hope that I can help the Indians and the Africans."

And thus she convinced me of the worthiness of her project. I wanted to help her, but I worried at selling James's house for less than it was worth. "How much are you willing to pay?"

"I can pay an amount equal to 500 pesos below your highest bid."

James would not be pleased. I did not have the money readily available to make up the difference. If I did not sell to the highest bidder, as I had been instructed, it would violate my sense of pride in the work I was doing for James. If I did not grant this lady's request, I would violate my sense of justice, for I believed that the poor, lower class women of South America were desperately in need of help such as this woman promised.

She waited patiently for my answer. After a long time, the little girl inside me, from whom I grew, won out over the businesslike woman I had become. At last, I said, "Very well, I will have the papers drawn up, but I must ask for 100 pesos more. I cannot in good conscience sell it for less." I asked for this because I knew that such an amount, plus 100 pesos of my own sparse funds, was more than James had originally expected before he received word of the higher offers.

The abbess knit her brows and thought a moment. At last, she said, "I believe I may persuade one or two of our patrons to make up the difference."

When the abbess left that evening, I felt I had made another friend. "You must inform me if I can help you further," I said as she was leaving.

"You have a good heart, Señora. Even if I had not persuaded you, I would have been glad to meet you." This from a nun. Never did a statement of admiration have quite the same meaning for me.

James, on the other hand, was not so gracious. When he was informed about the contract I had made, he wrote, "How dare you make a transaction to gratify your own feelings of benevolence—with my money. When Captain Escobar arrives in Panamá, he will be handling my affairs in the future. You are to send me all of my papers at once."

I tried to convince him of the good he was doing, but he would not consider my arguments. I offered to pay him the difference later, but he was through with me. I doubt if he even read my letters. It was inevitable now; I would lose all connection to James Thorne.

It would have happened one day, no matter what, but I was sorry he could not be mollified. While I worked for James, I could take a small draw for expenses and for my services. That little bit of income would be gone. It would be a few more months, but soon Escobar, who had sworn vengeance on me for having evicted him from my house 3 years earlier, would have full control of James's affairs in Lima.

Despite the unhappy aspect of my loss of James's trust, the house was sold to the Convent of the Nazarenas and I took satisfaction in the good I had helped accomplish. In the meantime, Simón and I were as happy as ever.

However, the Congress of the new republics in Panamá did not come off as well as Bolívar had hoped. He had sent José María Pando, who reported that many of the delegates did not arrive. One of the delegates from the United States, coming as invited observers, died of a tropical disease on the way.

Simón was disappointed, but he began to make plans for another congress. It was at this same time that he received some very good news. Bolivia had adopted his constitution.

He was jubilant, but I could not share his joy. That very morning, Jonotás and Natán brought me more news of discontent among the ruling class of Lima. Publicly, there was nothing but adulation for Bolívar. He was showered with wealth and opulent gifts—most of which he refused—from the Peruvian Congress. However, underneath was a growing resentment at both of us for living a life of luxury and power despite the fact that Bolívar lived more modestly than any aristocrat. Yet that was not the impression we gave. I believe that those who were jealous of us saw us as wolves devouring all wealth and power in Perú.

I had my companions spend more and more time in the city in order to determine the depth of such feelings. The more attention I put on the matter, the worse it appeared.

One evening Jonotás said, "They's plannin' somethin', Manuelita."

"Who?"

"The people who're complain' 'bout the general. People're sayin' he's too powerful. I think some men are plannin' to capture him and his officers and banish them, like they did to that Monteagudo. I don't know who they is, though."

I could not believe my ears. Surely, no one could be so ungrateful. I went to see Manuel Amat, to see if he knew anything about it.

I found him bleary-eyed when I arrived at his house unannounced one cold morning. He looked like he was feeling the effects of too much wine from the night before. I was overcome by the smell of spirits on his breath and the garish perfume of a bawdyhouse on his shirt. He looked like he did when we first met, after his mother died, only older. Worse, he was not happy to see me and was not at all gracious.

"You presume a great deal, Señora, coming to see me so early."

"You used to welcome me anytime."

"Yes, but I have been up all night . . ." He staggered. "Besides, then, you were a different person. You have changed."

"How have I changed?"

"When I first knew you, you were a revolutionary, and exciting. Now you are an 'aristocrat,' a common born 'vicequeen.'"

"I have not changed. It is you who have changed. Why do you treat me thus?"

Anger flared in his eyes. "I am the son of a viceroy, and I have never eaten off of golden plates. The new regime is more wasteful of public money than the viceroys ever were."

"You are not bothered by public waste. You are jealous that it is not you whom I take to my bed."

He looked at me angrily. I knew I had hit the mark. He almost crumbled, but in a split second found something to retort. "I wouldn't have a whore who takes herself so seriously, and who puts on such airs."

"How dare you talk to me that way? Obviously you don't know anything about—"

"I know enough to know that Perú is being used by a power hungry dictator who is wasting our wealth."

"Stop it. You talk to me of waste. You have wasted more personal talent and opportunity in your life than most of the rest of us poor commoners ever had." I motioned to his appearance. "You've gone back—not achieved, but returned—to debauchery."

"Yes, Señora, I have." His lips quivered and his voice rose and his words became more slurred. "This revolution you have made has elevated the rabble and ruined three hundred years of peace and prosperity. I'm through with it. No viceroy ever had as much power as the man with whom you commit adultery every night."

I slapped him.

He convulsed. He was about to be sick. Suppressing the wine in him from coming up, he started to leave the room. Before he left, he turned and said, "Yes, I have returned to my old ways. I will gamble every bit of my money away and sleep with every girl in Lima before I embrace respectability as defined by 'the revolution.'" He ran from the room.

I left. He was irrational, angry, jealous, and still drunk. However, I came away knowing that the peace I longed for, the revolution I had fought for, and the man I adored were not universally loved, even by those that benefited from them. The apparent loss of Manuel's friendship upset me deeply.

In the next few weeks, I kept my "spies" busy. I learned that, as much as he had accomplished for Perú, resentment for Bolívar was growing daily. There were many indications that Santander was writing to the disaffected of Perú and actively sowing dissension, yet I could never prove it.

Whoever was behind the trouble, it was an irony that people resented Bolívar because he had too much power. This, the same power he refrained from using. I tried to advise him of these affairs. I urged him to be more active in assuaging some of the bitterness I knew the populace was feeling. It did no good. He was so determined not to be seen as a despot that he would not use the authority he had to bring down evil men like Santander, or even to force the Peruvian government to compensate his troops, whose pay was in arrears.

Most of the resentment, and jealousy directed towards the Colombians, seemed to be coming from the leaders of the Peruvian army. As more and more reports came to me, and as I passed them along, Bolívar began to pay attention. When I finally convinced Simón of the plot to depose him, his anger overcame his judgment. He arrested eighty people, including the mutinous officers.

I wish he had let his own Colombian officers handle the matter. Bolívar handled the matter personally and, as a result, he came from the affair tainted even more surely in people's mind with the aspect of "tyrant."

It marked the beginning of the end of our "peace." We would never recover it.

While he was still upset about the near mutiny, Simón received a message from Santander. Páez in Venezuela, who had ridden with his band out of the *llanos* of Venezuela to help Bolívar achieve victory when the revolution was still young, had threatened to separate Venezuela from Gran Colombia. There was also news about civil strife in Bogotá. "The country is falling apart," he yelled, when he received the letter. I knew what would happen next.

First, Bolívar sent O'Leary to Venezuela so that he might have fresh intelligence of the situation there. Then, he made plans to depart himself.

I was asked to stay in Lima. "We will be traveling at such a pace that you and your slaves will not be able to keep up." He was dressing. As he moved about the room, I was reminded of his departure from Quito, 4 years earlier. However, this time there was not as much energy in his movements. He was growing tired.

"I will follow you as I did in the Andes."

"That is not a good idea this time."

"Simón, I do not trust you to take care of yourself."

"I will be fine, but I must go alone."

"Why? Why must you?"

He looked at me with sadness. He came to me and placed his hands on my cheeks and said, "I love you. I love you, dearly. I do not want to leave you, but I must not have . . . a mistress with me, when I arrive in the capital. Bogotá is a hard city, with a strongly religious history. Not like Lima."

I put on my stoic face. I did not speak.

"Manuela, I have many problems to solve, but it will not take forever. Then I will . . . I long to take you to my estates in Venezuela. I promise you. It will happen. Soon, very soon."

"How soon?"

"In less time than you think; we will share a simple country life together. No more politics, no more war. Please. Wait for me here. I will send for you, and then we will go home."

His words echoed my deepest desires. I wanted to say, "Yes!" Instead, I said, "Very well, Simón. But do not make me wait too long." My voice cracked, betraying the sadness I felt. "Is it to be months or years?"

"Months, no more than six months—I swear—and we shall be together again. Then, no more than a year to bring about my coalition of these governments. Then, I will retire."

"That soon? Do you promise?"

"Yes, Manuela, yes."

I threw my arms around him and we held each other close.

"I love you," he whispered softly.

"I will always love you, Simón, no matter how far apart we are. But I need to be with you, to hold you like this. Keep your promise. Months, not years."

"Yes. Months." And he kissed me.

It was only with an act of will that we pulled ourselves away from each other so that he could finish dressing. As he buttoned his jacket, I had worried about the future.

I did not speak to him of my anxiety about what I knew would happen after he was gone. It would appear to the people of Lima as though I were a cast-off mistress. I knew the women of Lima would spurn a woman who had neither wealth nor a man of importance. Especially if they already had reason to be jealous of her.

I believe Bolívar was not blind to my future. A day or so later, he made arrangements for my well being while he was gone. He left me plenty of money, and particular orders with his minister of war, Tomás de Heres, to watch out for my safety.

My brother—now General Sáenz—would accompany Simón. He was to join the garrison at Quito, as the senior officer. He wished to return to his home city and settle down. As much as I wanted José María to stay, I knew that he would be happier in Quito.

I understood that Simón had to go. The distances were too vast in the countries he created, and it seemed that only Bolívar's personality could make things right.

The Congress of Perú, felt the same. Once they realized he would not be there to protect the country from civil unrest they begged him to stay. He declined. He could not be in all places at once, and Gran Colombia was the cornerstone of all South American peace.

Bolívar departed on September 2, 1826. When he left, I was immediately ostracized by Liman society.

Like Rosita before me, I no longer had any social standing, except among my closest friends. Jonotás and Natán continued to bring rumors to me, and it was obvious that the women of Perú were turning more vicious by the day. The jealousy of other women was always something I could count on, but in Lima it reached new heights. I was on the lips of Lima's female population on rising, and I was gossiped about until dusk.

One very unsettling rumor emerged that was not about me. It seemed that Santander had sent agents to Perú to help persuade the disaffected to remove the Colombian army from the country, not as victors, but as usurpers. I could not gain any definitive information about it, so I waited to write to Simón about it until I could get more information. This delay may have been a mistake.

While I waited, I suffered in my loneliness and social isolation. The one bright light in that period was the letter that Simón sent me from Ibarra.

My Charming Manuela,

Your letter delighted me. Everything in you is love. I, too, am suffering from this searing fever, which consumes us like two children. In my old age I suffer from a sickness I should have long since forgotten. Only you keep me in this condition. You beg me to tell you that I love *no one else but you*. The shrine which is yours will never be desecrated by another idol or image, unless it be God himself. Believe me—I love you, and shall love only you, and nobody else but you. Live for me and for yourself. Live to console the unfortunate ones, and your lover who longs for you.

I am so tired with all this travel and with all the troubles of your country that I shall not have time to write you long accounts as you wish me to do. But day and night I think of your charms, and when we shall see each other, and what I shall do when I see you again. No more! Do not write.

All my love,
Simón

Though I continued to write to him, I did not receive any replies.

I know he was busy keeping Gran Colombia unified and constantly working for the greater unification of the continent. As his letter proved, even in Quito he had been forced to personally intervene to bring order out of chaos. He was good at that, but he had not even reached Bogotá yet. It was likely that he would have to travel all the way to Caracas before his work was done. How could it only be six months? What would happen to his health in that time?

Even after he quelled the current disturbances, and brought order wherever he was, only then would he begin working on his coalition of all the republics. All this while, the populace questioned his ambition. I knew the question in everyone's mind, *Is it really unity that Bolívar wants? Does he really want a coalition of free republics? Or is it an empire?*

Chapter 24

In Lima, the anti-Bolívar Peruvian factions grew stronger every day. Santander seemed to be the mind behind it all, but I could never prove it. It is one thing for Jonotás and Natán to bring me gossip and bits they overheard, but they could not search offices for the letters I'm sure Santander was writing to Peruvian military officers. Nevertheless, every indication was that dissatisfaction in Perú was being actively sown by Santander.

I knew why. He was determined to tarnish Bolívar's glory so that his return to Bogotá would be weak and politically ineffective. The rumors I heard led me to believe that something was about to happen, but I could not tell what it was.

This affected me emotionally more than it should have because I no longer had Bolívar's administrative work to do. Without my daily activities at the villa, I was adrift. I decided to return to my hospital work in San Bartolomé, but my heart was not in anything. I missed Simón. My life seemed empty. I longed to follow him, but I could not.

The weeks wore on. Then, on the 25th of January, 1827, it happened. A traitor by the name of José Bustamente, a colonel of the Colombian troops, struck a blow to his own countrymen, according to Santander's plan.

At a prearranged time, while it was still dark, Jacinto Lara, Arthur Sandes, José María Córdoba, and five other officers of the Colombian corps were arrested. Tomás de Heres, who was to protect me, was the only important officer who escaped. He took a canoe out to a French warship lying in the harbor and, shortly thereafter, left Perú. When I awoke on the morning of the 26th, I found I was the only one, still loyal to Bolívar, who was free.

It had finally happened. Bolívar's vice-president, determined to embarrass the Liberator and break his hold on the Colombian legions in Perú, had set his scheme in motion. He knew that if Bolívar returned while still in control of Perú, there would be no stopping him politically, in Bogotá. Santander had found the right man in Bustamente, who played his part well without ever considering that when it came time to shoot traitors Santander would "know nothing about it."

Bustamente censored all mail out of the city. I knew that Bolívar was on his way to Caracas and that he would not find out what had happened for months. By then, it would be too late.

La Mar, the Peruvian general whom Bolívar had trusted despite his first impressions, took what had been offered to him by the traitorous Bustamente. He took over the government and severed ties with Colombia. Bolívar, the man who had won Perú's freedom, had his power cut in half by the ungrateful Peruvians. I could see Bolívar's dreams of unity evaporate into the air.

After days of sitting and waiting for something to be done to punish the mutineers, I could take it no more. I put on my colonel's uniform, strapped on my pistols and a sword, and rode to the Colombian barracks. The men knew me from the war, and liked me. They gave me a salute when I entered the building.

I said, "There has been a mutiny. I've come to find those loyal to the Liberator so that we might restore order. We must free the officers and re-establish the Liberator's plan."

There were no volunteers. I spent an hour, walking up and down, trying to persuade them to take action. I could tell that they felt it would be useless and dangerous. Finally, I said, "I will return tomorrow and some of you will at last achieve the honor of patriot, and will join me in putting down the usurper."

I walked outside, where Jonotás and Natán, in their uniforms, were holding my horse. I mounted quickly and we rode back to Magdalena. I learned later that I narrowly avoided a squad of Bustamente's men. He had heard I was causing trouble in the barracks and had sent them to arrest me.

I wish I had encountered them, because I would have been alerted to how threatening I was to him. He heard I was in the barracks, one lone woman with two slaves, and had sent a whole squad of men to stop me. If I had understood his fear of me, I might have escaped the events that ensued.

As it was, all the way home I kept thinking, *I'm the only one, in all of Perú, who is standing against Bustamente. No one shares my feelings.* I felt insignificant. The entire military character of Perú had changed, and I considered myself nothing but a tiny speck in the wind that was blowing down all that Bolívar had built. Thinking thus, I did not prepare myself for what happened next.

That night, February 4, exactly thirty years since the big earthquake of 1797, another event occurred, nearly as devastating to my soul as the earthquake had been to Quito. Intruders broke in my door. With it, they shattered my life in Lima and all I had achieved there.

When I heard the wood splinter at the front of the house, I rose in terror. Wearing only a thin muslin shift, I ran across the room and fumbled for the sword I had carried earlier that day. Jonotás and Natán were down the hall. Their screams terrified me. I found my sword and turned around.

Just then, men broke through the door to my room. The space was so small that I could not defend myself. One of them grabbed my arm; another grabbed my hair. They forced me down onto my bed, their hands all over me, as they bent my wrist in an agonizing angle. I screamed at them, "You do not know who you are attacking. I order you to desist." The sword clattered to the floor.

Just then, a figure came through the door carrying a lantern. It was Bustamente. Tall, aristocratic, light skinned with fine features. He smiled, but his expression was cruel.

"Breaking into a home in the middle of the night. You must be proud. Not only a traitor to your country, but a common criminal as well."

He ignored me and said, "Bring her along. Bring her slaves too. The black ones. Let the others go."

He turned to leave the room; but before he left, he said, "Do not take your eyes off her. Get her dressed—and not in that." He pointed to my uniform thrown on the foot of the bed. "Then, bring her outside."

While three soldiers leered at me, I put on a dress and some shoes. The men pushed me out into the dark, dusty street. Jonotás and Natán were already there, shivering in their own dresses. Fear was in their eyes, but neither made a sound. I was proud of them.

They ordered us to mount waiting horses and then our hands were bound behind us. Our feet were spurless. "Where are you taking me?" I hissed at Bustamente.

"Where all women of loose moral character belong—a convent."

My heart stopped. After all I had gone through, it had come to this. I reacted violently. I jumped down, hands still bound, and ran back towards the house. I screamed, "No you won't, you traitor. NO!"

Three of the men grabbed me and threw me to the ground. While I continued to scream, my mouth was gagged. They tried to tie my feet together, but I continued to fight and squirm in the dust.

Then I saw Bustamente pull a pistol from his belt. He walked over to Natán and pulled her off her horse. Grabbing her by her hair, he walked her over to me. "I am not going to have this much trouble. I'm going to have to shoot you all 'trying to escape.' Starting with this one."

I stopped fighting. I tried to speak through the rag in my mouth. He motioned one of them to untie the gag.

I spit out the dust in my mouth and said, "Let her alone. I'll go with you." Natán, shaking with fear, dropped to her knees and started shaking when he let her go.

When he saw that I would cause no trouble, he put blindfolds on each of us. The soldiers helped Natán and me to mount. I could hear the sound of the ocean receding into the distance as we rode toward Lima.

It seemed like hours before we stopped. I was still blindfolded. I heard a soldier knock on a door. The *portera* of a convent answered, "You cannot enter at this hour."

The abbess was summoned. Orders were given. We were forced to dismount. They pushed us into the nunnery, the cool monastic tiles chilling my feet through my slippers. It seemed that I had gone back in time.

I heard Bustamente say, "Señora Abbess, she is to be kept in seclusion. Only her slaves are to be with her. She is to communicate to no one, and she is particularly forbidden to have either pen or paper."

A voice I recognized said, "I know my responsibilities, Colonel."

I was in a convent, in prison. There is nothing they could have done so easily that would have done more damage to my soul. My heart raced as I listened to Bustamente turn and walk outside. I heard the door slam shut, the reverberations mixing with the sound of the bar being drawn. I felt like I was dying.

I tried to pull at my bonds as I heard Bustamente and his men ride off. Our hands were finally untied and our blindfolds removed. I looked around. Except for one friendly face, I was in hell.

Chapter 25

I was lucky. Bustamente had chosen the most rigorous convent he could find. I am sure he was hoping to torment me as much as he was hoping to ensure my confinement. Yet, of all the nunneries in which I could have been placed, I was in the very best. Abbess Doña Augustina de San Joaquín said, "I am sorry, Señora, that I must keep you and your women. Truly."

I could not say anything. I was exhausted.

She went on, "However, I am not bound to any other stipulation. You may have what you wish that I can provide. I will try to make you as comfortable as possible. But please, for my sake, do not try to leave."

"Thank you, Señora," was all I could manage to say, and then she had someone lead us to our cell. It was small—it was too small for the three of us—not far from the *locutorios*. It had a familiar smell of must and candle wax.

As Jonotás, Natán and I stood in the dark that first night, the life drained out of me. I was so weak I could barely stand. I sat on the bed. Jonotás and Natán sat next to me, and we did not speak. We sat close to each other and shivered in the cold, waiting for the approaching dawn to bring light.

As I sat there, I relived the time of my mother's death. Dragged to a convent by a brutal, uncompassionate man, giving up fighting in order to save someone I loved, being placed in a small dark room to shiver in my isolation—all these remembrances filled my mind. An incredible turbulence of sadness and anger fell on my spirit like a violent storm.

My friend, the abbess, tried to do all she could for me. The next day, I was not denied when I went to the library and asked for paper and pen. I would not be kept silent, no matter if there were a hundred Bustamentes censoring me. I wanted to write to Bolívar, but such mail would not leave the country. I began my campaign by writing a letter to the Colombian Consul, Cristóbal Amuero.

> I was taken to the Convent of the Nazarenas as a prisoner of war or as a criminal; as I am not truly the latter, I do know for what reason I should be considered the former. Permit me to remind you that as a representative of the Republic of Gran Colombia, it is your duty to demand my release, and you should do so with all the energy befitting a representative of Simón Bolívar.

Once the letter was written, I realized that delivering it would be another problem. I looked out the window and saw soldiers guarding the door. I would never be allowed to leave.

Though both she and I knew the danger, I sent Jonotás to deliver the message. Together, we found a way for her to "jump the wall" and she left. She wore the simple dress of a slave, with the letter wrapped in her turban, and she was not detected as she walked down the street toward the Plaza Mayor. Despite the fact that she seemed safe enough, I was glad to see her back, unmolested and secure, that evening.

I waited for a day or two and found that only a tiny protest had been made by Señor Amuero. I knew he was ineffective when I first met him years earlier. Yet it was most important that he make a loud protest.

I wrote more letters. I wrote to soldiers, friends in government, tradesmen. The word that Jonotás brought back was that I had started a tiny groundswell of dissatisfaction with the way the Colombian officers and I were being treated—not enough to make a difference yet, but a start.

I did not like my indefensible situation in the convent. I was sure there would be reprisals from Bustamente. Surely, some of the letters I had written had reached him because I noticed more guards posted around the convent. It was harder for Jonotás to get out and get back safely.

Then one evening, I watched from a high window as Jonotás crossed the street on her way with two of my latest missives. A soldier stopped her, questioned her, and then spoke to the officer in charge. They removed her turban and found the letters. She tried to run back inside but was tripped by another soldier, and I saw her go sprawling in the street. I screamed, "No! No! Leave her alone!" I ran downstairs. By the time I arrived, she was out of sight, taken away.

I was beside myself. I tried to leave, to follow her, and was thrown back inside. I asked where she was going. "In the name of God, tell me what you are doing with her," I pleaded.

The officer in charge said, "None of your business,"—he pushed me back through the door—"now stay inside."

The next morning, Doña San Joaquín entered my cell. "I told you, Señora, that I was duty bound to keep you here—you and your women."

"What's happened to Jonotás!?" I had spent the night in terror for her.

"She has been taken to Casa Matas."

Natán and I looked at each other. Casa Matas was a woman's prison known for the degradation of its inmates. No one ever came out of it unscathed "Without a trial?" I asked.

"As I understand it, yes."

"I have to get her out of there," I cried. It was a demand and a plea for help.

The Abbess looked at me a long time. She said, "I cannot let you leave."

She turned to go. Before she closed the door behind her, she stepped back inside and said, "I'm sure your other slave will have much better luck, if she has a habit. I will have some one bring you one." She smiled.

"Thank you, Señora." I stood to go to her.

She put up her hand and said, "Be careful," and left. I was so grateful to that woman.

I wrote more letters. This time I sent Natán out, dressed as a nun, to deliver them. She did not have any difficulty, and after a few days, I could tell that the government's position in keeping us was starting to crack.

Then, I learned that Córdoba had been let out. At last, someone loyal to Bolívar, who had some power, was free. I expected some action, but my intelligence told me that he was let out only because he promised no trouble. I was infuriated at his inaction.

A few days later, I was told by one of Bustamente's men that things were returning to normal. However, if I wanted to stay in Perú, I must stay in the convent, permanently.

Natán and I lived and slept together, day and night, but I could not shake my feeling of isolation and loneliness, despite her welcome companionship. Her illness, caught while in the high Andes, had returned. I nursed her, but the rigid and ascetic lifestyle of the convent overwhelmed my strength.

It was not like Santa Catalina, which had a loose moral character and no discipline at all in contrast. We rose early, before dawn, and were in bed late because I stayed up writing letters. The nuns went about their work carrying small but heavy crosses on their shoulders, and every day gave a new reason to abstain from this or that little pleasure.

I was crushed by the depths to which I felt I had fallen and from what height. From my scandalous birth, I had risen to the top of South American "aristocracy," as powerful as any woman had ever been in the New World. In a matter of weeks, I had descended to the lowest echelon I could have imagined. In that couple of months, I could easily have embraced death, had it come. The only thing that kept me going was my fury. I kept trying, from inside my little nun's cell, to foment a revolt.

On April 27, I was called to the *locutorios*. When I arrived, Bustamente was there. "What do you want, you traitor?" was the first thing out of my mouth.

"You are finished in Perú. I am here officially to tell you that you have until tomorrow to leave the country—"

"Why? Am I too much of a threat to you, one woman locked in a convent? I'd rather stay and see you hanged."

"It is you who may hang, as an enemy to the people of Perú. You and Amuero have never once ceased your efforts to seduce the loyalties of the people. I have proof of your correspondence." He pulled some papers out of his jacket and shook them at me. "Therefore, if you are not out of the country by 4 o'clock tomorrow afternoon, you will be taken to Casa Matas and all of your property will be forfeit."

"It is forfeit anyway, is it not?"

"You may have whatever you can take with you—that is yours." I started to ask him about Jonotás, but an idea came to me. He went on, "It is all laid out in this order of exile. But you must leave." He handed me the paper and left, ordering the nuns to release me.

Natán and I walked immediately to Magdalena. I searched through my papers and found the one document I needed. Then, Natán and I found our horses and rode— Jonotás's horse in tow—to Casa Matas. I left Natán in the street holding our mounts and banged on the iron door. When a pock marked and whiskered face peered through the opening, I demanded to see the warden.

The custodian of Casa Matas looked like he should be in prison himself. He was fat, his face was dirty, his clothes were wrinkled, and his eyes reminded me of cesspools. I sat in a small office that might have had fresh paint on the walls at one time. Now, it seemed to be covered only with soot from lanterns and candles that had lit the dark room through the years. The blackness of the building weighed down on me as I made my demands. On the other side of the door, down the halls, I could hear women screaming at each other, howling in pain or crying out in grief.

The warden said, "You cannot just walk in here and demand the release of a prisoner without due process." He belched, and his eyes shifted to my bosom as he spoke.

"Due process? She was not put in here with 'due process.' There was no trial. Let her go."

"No!" He sniffed and looked at me as though I were naked and ready to serve him. "There is no reason for me to let her go."

"There is a reason, damn it."

He changed his look and took his eyes off my body. He realized that I was not a potential victim. I could tell he wanted me to leave, right away. He stood and went to the door. "I don't have to listen to this. You get out of here."

"Yes, you do, by order of Bustamente." He looked confused. I put two papers in his dirty hands: the original bill of sale for the purchase of Jonotás and Natán, and Bustamente's order of exile. I said, "I am to be allowed to have all of my property that I can take with me. I demand that you release my slave."

He looked at the papers for a long time. He walked back to his desk and sat down. Every once in a while he would say, "But without due process . . ." Finally, while grumbling about "bureaucrats," he yelled to someone on the other side of the door and ordered her release. A jailer put his head in the door to confirm the order and the warden repeated his command and gave a wave of his hand in dismissal.

I looked back at the warden and noticed that he was still looking over the documents as though he were trying to find a way to keep her.

I walked over to him, unnoticed in his reverie, and snatched the papers out of his hand. "Thank you, Señor Warden. Now if you don't mind, I'll fetch my slave and leave." I turned and walked out of his office. As I left, I heard him say, "I do not think this can be considered due process . . ."

I hurried down the hall after the jailer. To our right were large rooms with dozens of women in each one. The stink of urine and vomit and mildew assaulted me. I held my breath and peered through the bars. A few of the dominant prisoners sat around a fire in each large cell while others stayed against the dark corners. I saw a fist fight in one, with all the women in the cell encouraging the brawlers. In another cell, I saw women standing at the bars yelling loudly with others crying softly to themselves in the corner. Some of the women were naked, or barely clothed. All were filthy and scabbed. Most looked diseased if not actually dying.

When the jailer unlocked a cell that was darker than the others and went in, I felt afraid for Jonotás. He took a torch in and looked for her. When he brought her out, her face was swollen. If her skin had not been so dark, I'm sure I would have seen large bruises around her eyes and cheeks.

"Jonotás," I cried, "what have they done to you?"

"Jus' some folks in there who don' like my sense of humor," she whispered.

I could not contain myself. I flung my arms around her and hugged her. I whispered, "I thought I had lost you."

"Not me," she whispered back. She smiled through her distended face.

"Come on, let's go," I said, and began leading her to the door by her wrist.

"I won' argue, Ma'am," she said, in mock subservience.

When we arrived at the entrance, the *portero* unlocked the door and we left. I looked back over my shoulder to see the warden coming down the hall toward us. I hurried us to our horses and we climbed on.

Natán cried, "Jonotás, what happened to you?" Tears came to her eyes.

I said, "Never mind. We have to leave." I motioned to the door where the warden had just come out and stood blinking in the light. We spurred our horses and galloped down to Magdalena.

I was so glad I had not listened to Bolívar when he complained that I still owned slaves. If it was well known that I had freed them, they would not have any protection I could offer. Because of my intuition, my friend had been saved.

By the time we left the prison, it was dark. We rode back to Magdalena and spent the night packing. I could not take everything, but we managed to load a great deal into three trunks. I gave the housekeeper a good deal of money and dismissed her.

The next morning, I searched Lima until I found an Indian I felt I could trust to deliver our horses, and two trunks of Bolívar's papers that were still in my care, across the Andes to Quito, where I hoped to be soon. I would like to have taken them myself, but I had to leave by ship in order to be out of the country in time.

Later, at the villa, I briefly saw some of the other officers that had also been held these two months. They were also leaving that day. There was Lara, Sandes, and Córdoba, among a few others. General Lara was nicer to me than I'd ever known him to be. Córdoba was cold and appeared to snarl when he looked at me. I was furious at what I considered his complicity with the traitors, but I was too busy to think about him. Sandes had always been a good friend and was very helpful that afternoon.

I looked for a long time before I found people to look after my dogs, cats, and birds. It was late in the day when we made our way up to Callao with our three trunks—the only things I would be allowed to take from Peru.

We had to wait until a boat came back from taking some officers out to the *Bluecher*, a brig that looked too small to sail an ocean, rocking in the swells of the harbor. A cold wind blew across the water as we waited on the sands of Callao. I felt beaten, having been up all night, as I slowly walked back and forth in impatience.

Not only was the four o'clock hour approaching, but every minute I stayed there I was reminded of all the things that had happened to me in Perú and that I had made happen. I had helped to bring about a revolution, and yet here I was, more outcast than I had ever been. I thought of all of the travail Bolívar and I and his men had endured in Perú. Now, to be brushed off so rudely was cruel fortune.

Across the water, black clouds covered a gray-blue and uninviting sea. As I watched the sky, like a pall covering my future, three of Bustamente's men rode up—I recognized them as the same men who had abducted us from my home—and demanded to search my belongings. It was almost four o'clock, and the boat to ferry us to the ship was just landing at shore. "We must go," I said.

"Your belongings will have to be searched. No letters or documents are to leave the country without review by the censor." They dismounted and began going through my trunks, throwing dresses and slips, books and mementos, on the ground.

"Why are you doing this?" I protested. "Bustamente said I might take anything I owned with me."

"And so you might. Our job is to look for papers which are to be censored and to take you to Casa Matas if you are not gone by four o'clock." I saw a look of fear cross Jonotás's eyes. I did not know exactly what time it was, but it was only minutes to four.

"May I take this?" I asked, picking up a dress I loved. The soldier nodded. "And this?" picking up something else. So it went. I finally had to rush to the boat with the three of us each carrying only a handful of our belongings: mostly dresses, my uniform, my pistols, and a few other personal items. We left everything else lying on the shore.

I was so infuriated by the time we reached the ship, that I was beyond reason. The other officers were watching as we pulled alongside. The look on Córdoba's face matched the blackness of the sky. As I stepped onto the deck, he said, "We don't have enough misery, so the Peruvians have sent a harpy to eat at us."

I flew at him like a bullet. "You! You traitorous shit pile. Why didn't you take a firmer stand against the usurpers? You were even let out of confinement, and you did *nothing!*"

"Don't talk to me that way, you opportunistic—"

"Your disloyalty is a disgrace, you craven coward."

He came at me. Both Lara and Sandes held him back. He recovered himself and said, "I won't waste any more breath on a low-born exhibitionist. Stay out of my way." He walked off.

I yelled after him. "Don't worry, you miserable scum. I don't want to contaminate myself with your filthy dishonor."

I stormed off, by myself, towards the bow. I shook with anger, standing there until we were far past the island of San Lorenzo.

Arthur Sandes came to me and said, "It is no use berating Córdoba. All he understands is war. If someone attacks him, it only makes things worse. He never has shown any sense when it comes to politics, or even social affairs."

"I am sorry, Arthur," I said in English, "but I need to be alone right now. I thank you for trying to make things better."

Sandes left me and shortly Jonotás and Natán came up. They had found our cabin and set the few things we recovered in it. Natán said, "Manuelita, come—lie down—we will find you food." Despite their kindness, I sent them away. I was angry and lost and I wanted to be alone.

Several leagues out to sea, rain started falling from a black sky. Of all the things that could have happened to me, imprisonment and expulsion shook me to my core; and I had experienced both of them in a matter of a few months. Six months had passed, and no word had come from Bolívar. Either he had so much work to do it would be impossible for us to be together or he had forgotten me.

I was in despair. This world that the revolution had made was not the Elysium we had believed it to be. What had we started out to do? Now we were free, but free for what? It seemed that only the rapacious and plundering were free. "Free to be brutes," Bolívar had said. There appeared to be only one thing men could think to do with their independence, destroy the liberty that had been so newly sown.

As I looked over my life, I was no better off than when I had been expelled from Santa Catalina twelve years before. I was without property, title, income, or friends. I was being forced where I did not wish to go. I could still not look forward to any self-determination outside the "protection" of a paternalistic world set on its own self-destruction.

I decided then that I would no longer believe in any "revolution" or future happiness that I could not see a way to claim by myself. No matter the cause, if one did not have control of the outcome, the forces at work might go in any direction. Believing in one's government or country or "the cause," without being willing to take responsibility for what might really happen was foolish.

The rain soaked my dress, and I shivered in the approaching dusk. Making my way to my cabin, I determined to be alone with my two companions—even from Bolívar, if I had to—rather than depend on any person or government again.

Though the cabin was small—no more than two narrow bunks against the wall—I stayed there for most of the trip. Jonotás and Natán traded sleeping with each other or with me. The two beds were too small to make a permanent arrangement for three people.

One of the few times I did go on deck I ran into Córdoba, who was not finished berating me. As I walked around several sailors braiding rope together, I came upon him. I overheard him giving his opinion of me to the other officers. When he saw me, he turned and glared in my direction.

I took a step forward and said, "What is it you are saying about me—as if you had the right?"

His face turned ugly, and he said, "You may as well hear. I said that it was you and your opulent living, your disrespect for the elders of society, and the flaunting of your immorality that were to blame for the Peruvian's treatment of us."

The first was unfair, as my living was no more opulent than Bolívar's and existed because of the lavish gifts pushed on him by the Peruvians. As to the rest, I had heard all that before. Nevertheless, I was angry that he, little more than a traitor, even dare discuss me. "At least *I* am a *loyal* member of Bolívar's staff—"

"You are nothing but a cheap harlot in expensive clothes," he said, "And now you are bringing your shame back to Colombia to embarrass The Liberator again—"

"You have no right to talk. You never raised a finger to stop the insurgency."

"Because I—"

"You're a spineless dog, Córdoba," I said, as though I had spit the words at him.

"Why you—"

"What is it, General?" I looked at his trousers. "One testicle short or do you just *enjoy* being disloyal to Bolívar?"

He turned purple with rage and he let out a howl. He pulled a pistol from his belt and put it to my head and cocked it. His lips quivered and his hand shook. I backed up in confusion and he followed. "I'll kill you. I'll kill you," he said, becoming more out of control.

I recovered somewhat, flailed my arms and pushed the gun out of the way. Just then, the other men caught up to him and pulled his arm up in the air, and a loud report sounded as the ball went through a sail. Anger surged through me like pain.

Just then, I stumbled on the rope lying about and sprawled on the deck. I found a piece of thin rope in my hand, about the length of my arm, braided at one end so that it was heavy. Infuriated, I stood up and began whipping Córdoba, and the men trying to hold him back, with the rope. "You filthy piss bucket! How dare you threaten me!? How dare you!" The sailors behind me grabbed hold of my arms and took the rope out of my hands.

"If you ever pull a pistol on me again, I will kill *you*," I hissed at him through clenched teeth.

"If you were not a woman, you would be dead already. Stay away from me."

Jonotás and Natán came up just then and took me back to my cabin. I stayed there for most of the rest of the trip, but my mind worked over and over with anger and thoughts of revenge.

When we arrived in Guayaquil, Córdoba, Lara, and the other officers headed off immediately toward Quito. Only Sandes made gallant enough to say, "Shall we make the journey together?"

My companions and I were tired and dirty, but he wanted to leave immediately, so we left. It rained off and on throughout the journey; and when we finally saw the church spires of the city of my birth in the distance, I was exhausted. I had made this journey before, but never on foot. We had trodden through mud, rain, and wind, day after day, with very little to eat, and even less rest. I never thought I would be glad to see Quito, but even my exhaustion was not on my mind as we walked across the plain towards the city. It had been almost 8 months since I had seen or heard from Simón. *Where was he? What was he doing? Would I ever see him again?* My confidence had been shaken. Maybe Córdoba was right. Maybe I *was* to blame for the Peruvians hating us. *What would happen next?* I trusted in nothing. I believed in no one. Still, I wondered, *Where was Bolívar?*

Chapter 26

I found out where my brother lived—near the Plaza of San Francisco—after only a few inquiries. We made our way quickly across town.

I was sorrowful at the look of the city. Every now and then, I would see "Down with Bolívar" scribbled on the sides of buildings. It looked like there was very little business being done, and the people walked through the streets dejected and apathetic. Little did I know that it foretold the times to come.

José María was happy to see me, and I was never so glad to see him. He knew I was coming because Lara and Córdoba had told him as they passed through.

His house was almost as comfortable as the one I had left in Magdalena; and soon we were all bathed, fed, and rested. José María found Sandes a horse, and my friend left when he awoke the next morning.

"Take care of yourself," he said to me.

"Thank you, Arthur. I don't know what I would have done without you. You will let Simón know where I am, won't you, and give him this?" I put a letter into his hand that told Simón of my whereabouts and all that had happened in Perú.

"Of course."

José María said, "The others stayed here a few days. If you hurry, you can probably catch them in Ibarra."

"Thank you, José. Good luck." He mounted, and I watched him start the long ride to Bogotá.

When José María and I finally sat down to talk, we discussed the condition of Quito. "There is no money," he said, when I asked him what was wrong. "The interruption of trade, after all of the resources that have poured into the war . . . the people are worse off right now than at any time under the rule of Spain. It's no wonder they hate Bolívar." He could see me react, and said, "It is true, Manuela. You know I'm right. No one is more loyal to their comrades than I, and I venerate Bolívar, but the people see only their own plight."

"It is not Bolívar," I said angrily. "It's Santander."

"I hate Santander as much as anyone, but he is not to blame. It was the war. Then, when the financial crisis in London hit almost a year ago, there was no way for us to recover. The whole world is suffering because of the crisis, but we are worse off than anywhere—"

"No, José! It is Santander. This country would not be half so bad, if it were not for him. Everywhere that Bolívar tries to plant peace or prosperity or new laws or any other element of a new republic, Santander is there to sow chaos." I rose from my chair, and paced back and forth.

He watched me thoughtfully for a moment and said, "It is true. I have no doubts about Bolívar; it is the men around him."

"Whatever the rest of them do, it is Santander who is the enemy."

He looked at me sideways, as though deciding on what he should say. He was thoughtful for a moment, and then said, "You may be right. Bolívar has broken all ties with him."

"What? How do you know? Tell me, José? We have heard nothing since January."

He had received letters from O'Leary and others, and had followed Simón's travels and troubles. He told me that when Bolívar left Perú, he was headed for Caracas to handle Páez. However, he had to stop when he passed through Quito in order to bring his charm to bear to avert civil disorder. Then he had gone on to Bogotá.

Congress was about to vote for president, and Santander was openly opposing him. There had been dissatisfaction and unseen treachery there, but the problem with Páez was becoming worse and he had to push on. When he left Bogotá for Caracas, he was quite ill.

When he found Páez, despite the fact that his friend from the early days of the revolution had been traitorous in threatening to secede from Gran Colombia, he made peace with him and ratified his having supreme command of Venezuela. While in Venezuela, there had been more disturbing reports of political intrigue from Colombia. When he heard about the revolt in Perú, seemingly influenced by Santander, he broke all ties with him. He sent him a letter saying, "Do not write to me again, because I do not wish to answer you or call you friend." Then, he sent a letter to the congress in Bogotá renouncing his presidency.

The country was without a president. However, José María told me that Bogotá had rejected his renunciation and was sending word that he should return to Bogotá to take the oath of office.

José María said, "They say his health is not good," when he finished his story.

I shook my head. Why had I let him go without me? The times were hard to understand and harder to live through. It was the most miserable period South America ever endured. It would have caused strong men and women grief enough, after fifteen years of bloody revolution, to make new and prospering republics; but with men such as Santander in power, who create nothing but trouble around them and seem to enjoy the suffering of the people, it could only mean an ignominious end to a revolution once glorious.

I retired early that evening. I expected a better day on the morrow after having been rested and fed. I hoped that when he arrived back in Bogotá, Bolívar would send for me. I told myself that all would be well, now that I had escaped Perú. However, the next day brought me more misery.

Late in the morning, Jonotás and Natán and I walked over to see the Larreas. When we arrived, I could hardly believe the condition of their house. Once one of the finest in the city, it was in disrepair like the rest of Quito, only worse.

Their ancient Indian servant answered the door, a man I had known since my childhood. His eyes were lifeless and sad. "Hello, Señorita," he said, failing to notice that I had long since ceased to be a maiden.

"Hello, Jorge, are Don and Doña Larrea inside?" I asked, fearing the worst.

"Doña Larrea is upstairs . . . she is ill . . . Don Larrea is . . ." His eyes became wet and he looked like he could not speak anymore.

I rushed past him and found Doña Larrea in bed, ashen faced and feverish. She looked so bad when I saw her that I cried.

"Oh, Manuelita, I am so happy to see you. It is all gone," she said, her voice so weak I could barely make out the words.

"What is, Señora?"

"My life. Everything in my life is gone." Tears ran down her face. "Everything has changed so much. My husband is . . . gone."

I felt like I had fallen apart. I cried the tears of a little girl, hiding my face in the blankets she clutched in her withered hands. Don Larrea had died of some indefinable illness only weeks before. The friend I had known and loved all my life ceased to exist.

I left Doña Larrea when she became tired. I went back that evening. When we arrived, she was quite apathetic. It was clear that she had already given up. The thought of that lovely old woman dying was too much to bear.

That night I missed the Larreas so much, I thought the whole world would fade into oblivion. Jonotás, who could always make me laugh, could not comfort me—though I suspected she was also wrapped in grief and did not try very hard. She hardly knew them and she missed them. I missed them terribly. I missed my mother. I missed the people that I had seen lose their lives in this world of strife I had been born into. I missed Simón. I sobbed myself to sleep that night.

The following day, my lifelong friend joined her husband. Her last words to me, as I watched her die, were, "My husband is gone."

That big-hearted woman had lived for her husband. When he passed away, she had no reason to go on. It is no wonder that she should die so soon after his death. In the city in which she had lived all her life, she found herself alone, almost as though she were a stranger in a desert.

In my grief, I was able to realize that I was feeling something very similar. So much of what I'd done in the past few years had revolved around Bolívar that he had become all there was to my life. Not having heard from him in months and not knowing if there ever would be a future for us together, I too was feeling as though everything was gone.

Bolívar was no longer riding through the Andes; he was in the capital of Venezuela. Why did he not write to me?

Doubts filled my mind. His last letter had said, "Do not write." Was it to keep me out of his life? By now, he knew of the revolt in Perú. Did he not care?

Of course, I had no way of judging whether he had tried to communicate with me or not, with the mail censored in Lima. His six-month promise had already passed, and I would have to wait a few months to see what the future would be. I tried not to think about it. Doubts grew in my mind every day. I had given up husband, and position, because I dreamed of some far off Venezuelan estate where Simón and I would happily spend our lives together. Yet nowhere in my world was there any promise even of the man, let alone the happy days in Venezuela. Would I ever see him again?

After many days and nights, pondering these very ideas, I knew that I had do something on my own, something that did not depend on a future happiness I could not make happen. I had to act as though my future was my own.

I would live in Quito. No more would I travel. I would find some way of surviving whatever might become of my country, and I would be alone.

During this period, General Flores was coming to José María's house nearly every day. They were good friends, and I too came to like the stocky veteran of the revolution whom people called "The Strong Man." The garrison in Guayaquil had mutinied and it was Flores who had brought back the rule of law. He and his men were keeping order in the whole area called the Department of the South of Gran Colombia that used to be the Presidency of Quito. When I discussed what I might do in Quito to live, it was Flores who suggested that I follow in my father's footsteps and be a trader.

"You have told me of your work in Panamá and of all the people you know through your husband," he said to convince me.

"Yes, Manuela," said my brother, "I remember father's praise of your abilities in his letters."

"You do not have to convince me further; I think it is a wonderful idea," I said, laughing. We all smiled at each other. I cherished the comradeship that my brother, the general, and I enjoyed. Even though I had always felt alone there, perhaps I could make a home in Quito at last.

Chapter 27

General Flores was right. With the many acquaintances whom I had met through James—sea captains and merchants throughout the hemisphere—I realized that I could probably own a botica and make more money than the merchants who had been in Quito all their lives. They could not know as well as I the best places to buy their goods or how to get the best prices.

I did not have much money, but José María said he would lend me some, and I had him make some inquiries for me about a place to have a shop. A few days later, he brought word that there was a man across town whose shop, according to rumor, was soon to close.

On my way through the streets to talk to the man, I noticed the way people looked at me. I knew it was not only Jonotás and Natán with their bright turbans and large earrings that caused people to stop and whisper. I was back in town, and I could almost hear the words "bastard" and "La Sáenz" drift through the air.

I had been in town less than two weeks and already the clacking of tongues had started. It was for this reason that I did not do any hospital work. The soldiers were not in such need as the last time I had been there, and I saw no reason to endure the abuse. I already knew, from my experience in Lima, that it would be much worse this time. I was little more than a cast-off mistress. In the eyes of the world, Bolívar had used me and moved on.

I found the shop and spoke to the proprietor. He was a small man, about ten years older than I, with a thick shock of hair that fell in his eyes and a tiny mustache. He was pleasant, but I did not like his eyes—they were fearful.

His shop was small, in the middle of the block, but it would do. I looked at some of the jars on tables next to the wall. The usual: lizard excrement, bezoar stones, snake skin, mercury, and other dangerous concoctions. The first thing I would do is eliminate most of those. I had enough experience with nursing to know how deadly some could be.

While I discussed my proposal to him, Jonotás and Natán waited outside. He seemed open to the idea of selling and I was so involved in my negotiations that I did not notice another customer enter behind me. We agreed on a price and payments and I left, happy that I had found what I wanted.

Once on the street, Jonotás and Natán said, "Did you see her?"

"Who?"

"The woman who entered behind you," said Jonotás, indicating a chaise waiting in the street with well-dressed Indian porters standing about. "She came 'round the corner after you entered, got out and went inside. Didn't you see her?"

"I didn't pay any attention."

"She was tall, and she wore that cape, the purple one."

So, the woman I was sure had spread lies about me to the women of the hospital, the last time I had been in Quito, had been in the shop with me. She had been listening to my conversation, and I hadn't even noticed. All I need do was wait until she came out of the shop, and I would find out what she looked like. I waited quite a while.

The door opened. I saw the woman's form in the entrance as she turned back to say something to the owner, a small package in her hand. She turned around, came out, and gave a little start when she saw me. Then, she said, "Welcome back, Manuela."

The sound of her voice was bitter and weak; she seemed to have lost the sardonic intensity I expected from Antonia. She had never forgiven me for not succumbing to her abuse when I was a student at the convent. Her height still gave her a stately appearance, but her face was thin and pale. She did not seem as strong as I remembered her.

"So it was you. I might have known."

"Might have known what, Manuela?" she said, attempting a sugary tone.

"When I was in Quito last, it was you who worked so hard at sabotaging my reputation."

"Oh, I think you have it wrong, Manuela." She sat down in the chaise chair, saying, "Nothing could make that any worse. Of course, it behooves decent people like my husband and I to let those who don't know about you, know the truth . . ."

So, she had been married in the last five years. It was then that I noticed for the first time, as she reclined in the chair, that she was pregnant. Her skirts hid her condition quite well, but as she sat down, I could see. A flash of jealousy ran through me. She was to have children—something that I would never have. She was, no doubt, living in peace and tranquillity, with everything in life that people held dear.

She smiled at me and went on, ". . . such as this shopkeeper." I already knew, when I saw her coming out of the shop, that she had sabotaged me to the owner. "It is fortunate that I needed some medicine today." She motioned to her servants, who picked up the chaise and went down the street. "Good-bye, Manuela," I heard her say as the chaise moved down the street.

When I went back inside the shop, I found what I had expected. The owner had "made a different decision."

In the days that followed, the social climate for me became much worse. Not only was I pilloried from the top of society to the bottom, but I was not able to find a single business situation. As I came upon one wall after another, it ate away at me. There were so few people in Quito with whom I could even have a conversation that was not riddled with stares, or animosity. The isolation I felt, so well remembered from my youth, killed me a little each day.

I became lonelier and lonelier as the gray Quito days turned into months. Despite my resolve to forget him, I missed Bolívar. I had waited a reasonable amount of time, for Sandes to arrive in Bogotá and for him to send my letter on to Simón. He had not answered, and I was aching from the hurt. He knew I was in Quito, he knew what I had suffered in Perú, he knew he had promised me a tranquil life in Venezuela, yet he did not write. Perhaps he was not still in Venezuela. Where was he? What was he doing? Did he ever think of me?

As an act of survival, I looked to see if there might be some other man to whom I might turn my attentions. There was one officer in the garrison that was very flirtatious. Although he never made any advance that an outside observer could positively deem improper, his solicitous behavior would have been enough to provoke a duel from a jealous lover, had I had one.

His name was Colonel Charles Demarquet. He was French, very handsome, and quite charming. He was a perfect specimen of masculinity for a man of his age, except for three missing fingers on his left hand, lost in the service of Napoleon. However, I could not participate in his flirtatious play. Whenever I considered it, I simply could not engage myself.

The reason was simple. I loved Bolívar.

It seemed that Demarquet's advances had worked a reverse charm on me. My inability to respond to him frightened me. What was wrong? Simón had all but abandoned me. There was no actual reason to think that we would ever see each other again. I believed we would, but I did not know for sure. I longed to see him, but I longed, even more deeply, to forget. What had I meant to him? How much did he really love me? Was there no one in his life whom he could love? I still had two strongboxes with his papers, on their way from Lima, which I must return to him. Yet, every day of loneliness made me believe there was no future I might have with Simón Bolívar. Yet, I could not make myself look at another man that way.

Jonotás, Natán, and José María all complained because I looked thin and lifeless. All encouraged me to eat, thinking food would matter when my heart, my whole life, was ailing.

Then one day, I met an old friend. For one brief moment, I believed he might brighten my life—a man whom I was sure could light the fires in my heart again.

He was coming through the door of a seamstress shop just as I walked by. The sun was out, and I was so happy to see him I let out a cry of delight. I threw my arms around him and held him as though I could not stop.

"Fausto, Fausto, oh, my darling, what are you doing here?" The last I knew, he was on his way to Mexico with his brother.

He held onto me, and said, "Manuela, it is so good to see you again. I did not know you were in Quito."

We did not let each other go. We held on fast. I noticed that the old fires he ignited in me had cooled only a little. I loved seeing him, and holding him. I felt alive, as a woman.

I needed the excitement his body promised to give, though he was no longer a dashing young man. Even though he was only a little over thirty, he looked like he had worked or worried himself into old age already. However, he was still handsome, and I think under different circumstances I might have been as completely taken with him as I was in my youth. Yet, I knew, even as I stood there, that Simón's memories were already intruding on our reunion. I promised myself, with my arms still around him, that this time I would not put him off for Bolívar, though as I thought it, I felt irrationally guilty.

I boldly said, "Do come around to visit me, won't you? Perhaps this evening would be a good time." The smile I gave him was meant to entice.

His own smile fell into a frown and he froze.

"What, Fausto? What's wrong?"

"Manuela . . . I . . . I'm married and my wife . . . is going to have a baby." He pulled his arms back, as though he had been told he had no right to touch me. "Almost five years now."

As he took a step back, I saw for the first time what he had been carrying out of the seamstress's shop: a heavy velvet cape, colored a unique shade of purple.

Almost silently, I said, "Antonia." I felt unable to breathe. I turned and looked at my surroundings. The buildings seemed to be falling all around me.

"Yes, you must have known her, she was at the convent of Santa Catalina." He was speaking from a great distance.

I have since come to realize how often we build our dreams, aspirations, and future on illusions. Such foundations will suddenly vanish one day, and you find your life changed and your world crumbling. It is as though you lose yourself. You become adrift, not knowing who you are.

For several moments, I was lost. I had held Fausto in my mind as the handsome soldier in the King's Guard. I never even considered that he would change, even though he had changed each time I had seen him since I was seventeen. Even though I expected him to marry, and I had married, and I had even found another lover whom I could not abandon, I did not expect this. The realization that he had married Antonia—who represented all that had ever threatened me—changed everything.

"Manuela . . ." I heard Fausto's voice calling from far off. "Manuela, please . . ."

"I am sorry, Fausto, I was shocked to find out you were married." He looked quite sad. "I hope you will be very happy."

If it was possible, his expression became sadder still.

"Fausto, I must go, but perhaps we will see each other again sometime," I said, distractedly.

He looked at me as though he wanted to stop me from leaving, but did not know what to say.

"Good-bye," I said, at last, and turned to walk away.

He called after me, "Manuela!"

"Yes," I said, turning back again.

"I am still your friend."

It was too much for me. I almost ran back home, barely seeing the buildings and people around me. My eyes were drowned in tears.

The weeks wore on. José María had news from Bogotá now and then. Finally he came to me with the news I had been waiting for. "Bolívar is in Bogotá." He went on to tell me that he was quite ill when he arrived and that there were a great many political problems awaiting him.

"What happened when he met Santander?"

He looked at me, unsure of how I would react. "He embraced him."

"Embraced him?" I was incredulous. "Why did he not shoot him?"

José María sighed and said, "It is not totally clear, from the news I received from the couriers. However, I believe he is afraid of splitting the country in to Santanderists and Bolivarists."

There was something final about José María's words and I stopped and studied his face. I could see the truth of it. Bolívar was fighting for unity, yet he could not eliminate his main rival without making an entire faction of the country an enemy.

José María saw the look of resignation on my face and said, "Such is the character of our times."

I said, "I hope that while The Liberator immerses himself in the politics of Colombia, that he does not forget to see Santander for what he is."

"Yes," said José María, thoughtfully.

"And I hope it is worth it."

"Yes, it is a dangerous game. Because of the trouble in the capital, he has had to assume dictatorial powers to hold the country together. This only fuels the Santanderists in their cries of 'oppression' and 'tyranny.'"

I shook my head in apathy, seeing the irony of this. Especially since I knew he would never do such a thing unless it was to repair a country already made chaotic by his vice-president.

What really worried me was hearing that Simón was ill. I worried about the lack of care he must be giving his body and wondered how long he had to live. I cursed myself, for longing for him so much.

Why should I be reduced to such longing. Yet, at that time, there appeared to be little else in my life or my future except that longing. My life seemed to be reduced to one question: Would I ever hear from Simón again? Perhaps there were other questions. Would he ever call me to come to his side? Did he need me at all? Did he love me? Did he ever love me? If he called, would I go?

I hated my predicament. For the first time in my life since I had met him, I was willing to live without him and I was willing to stay in Quito, despite the hatred and disappointment all around me. Yet, I was stopped. Everything I wanted to do there was closed to me. Even if I had wanted to move on, I seemed to have no where else to go. I was determined that Bolívar would not be the question in my life, but rather I—I must be the only question. I had no friends outside my household, no way to earn money for myself, no future. Yet, I knew I had to find something to do.

Who was I? I had to admit that what I had always been was a revolutionary. Yet, the revolution no longer seemed to need me. I could see its demise every day as I passed words in the streets that read: "Down with Bolívar."

As I thought it through, it became clear that there was only one job for me. Simón may have abandoned me as a lover, but I was still his colonel, and I owed him allegiance, even if only because my country was part of Gran Colombia.

The question still plagued my mind, "Would I ever see Simón again?" I overcame it with the only weapon I ever had: robust activity. I knew, once I began working, on anything, no matter what I did, that I would find some way to get control of my life in Quito.

I began writing placards and bills, and posting them at night all over the city. *Quiteños* found the words, "Down with Bolívar" painted out when they rose each morning and replaced by the words, "Long live The Liberator!"

Ordinarily, my companions accompanied me as I made my midnight rounds. But one night, Natán, who never really recovered from her illness during the Peruvian campaign, was feeling quite ill. Jonotás stayed to care for her, and I went out alone, over their objections. I did not let José María see me, as he would have stopped me. He admired what I was doing, but he would not have thought a woman out alone at night would be safe.

As I left the house, I sensed someone following me. The sky was clear and the moon was quite bright. I ducked into doorways and around corners. I peered back, trying to see who it might be, but I could never be sure I was not alone. The blue moonlight reflecting off the shiny stones in the street pronounced every detail except who might be behind me.

I was heading for a certain portion of the city walls where I knew there were ample anti-Bolívar slogans to deal with. I had a large stack of bills, secretly printed on the garrison press, and I hurried on, despite my worry that I was being followed.

As I was walking under a wide balcony, where the shadows were deep, I heard footsteps. They were quick and coming fast. Someone was running up behind me. I spun around just as a dark form was upon me. I dropped the bills and involuntarily started to let out a scream.

My pursuer's hand clasped over my mouth and he said quietly, "Don't cry out, Manuela." I tried to focus through my fear. "It's Fausto."

I shook his hand off my mouth. I took a breath and said, "Fausto, what are you—"

"I had to see you, Manuela. I had to see you alone."

"Why?"

His face looked stricken with pain. "I still love you," he said and pulled me to him and kissed me full on the lips.

He made me want him. I had been too long without a man's love. My whole body responded to him with aching desire. I threw my arms around him and pulled him closer. But something in me made me doubt what I was doing. After a moment, I slowly pushed him away.

"Don't stop me. I need you," he said and he kissed me again, backing me up against the wall behind me, deeper into the shadows.

I felt waves of passionate pleasure run up and down my body. I was too surprised and too overwhelmed by the feelings to stop him. He kissed me, long passionate kisses. My hands were at his chest as if to defend myself, but I was too weak of spirit.

"Come away with me," he said, as he began to kiss my neck. His hands pulled my skirts up. "I want you to come with me," he said as he kissed my breasts.

"No, stop," I said, as I pushed him away again, breathless. "What are you saying?" I could not let this moment overwhelm me. I felt dizzy with desire, but I knew it was not right. I could barely breathe.

He started to embrace me again, but I put my arm out. He turned around and paced up and down a little and said, "I am sorry, Manuela. I am leaving. I want you to come with me."

"What about your wife—and child?"

"The child I would stay for, but I cannot stay with Antonia. She is cruel, to everyone, for no reason: the servants, shopkeepers, old women in her circle . . . . I was a fool to have married her. It seemed to happen before I knew it." He paused as if he was trying to figure out how he happened to be married to her. He went on, "To make matters worse, her family did not approve, and they hate me."

I did not know what to say. Why did he marry her? How did she get married without her father's consent? While I formed these questions, he answered them.

"They try to control—no, they do control—her life. She, in turn, must have her way in everything with me, with everyone, or there is no peace. When the baby comes, it will be so much worse, since her parents consider that the child belongs to them. They said so. She cannot resist them openly, but if she can find a way to thwart them, in anything, she will.

"Oh, Fausto . . ."

He paced up and down. "Manuela, I want you to know everything. Our marriage was arranged secretly, just so we would not be stopped by her parents. She married me, knowing they would disapprove—I believe because she *knew* they would disapprove. Now that she is with child, it is worse. They will not leave her alone. Her father and mother are the most domineering people I've ever seen. They tell her what to do, how to think, everything—in every part of her life. She has stopped eating, and I think it is to punish them. Naturally she does not feel well, and so she takes 'medicines.' I fear for the baby."

For the first time in over 20 years, I understood her. If Antonia was smothered as much by her parents as Fausto's words made me believe, it fit with the things I saw her do. I saw that her life, in her own way, had been a rebellion. I knew her family's reputation. They were the most aristocratically aloof of any in the city. Unlike me, she never felt she won, and if what Fausto said was true, she was still fighting them.

In the silence, he looked into my eyes. "Why don't you come with me?" he asked.

I reached out and put my arms around him. I pulled him to me and held him close. My eyes became teary. I made myself stop crying and said, "No. I cannot. I won't be a party to you leaving your wife and child. Besides, I am in a time of my life when I must be alone, Fausto."

"Why, Manuela? I need you to come with me," he whispered.

"I did love you, Fausto, but I cannot revive it this way."

"It's Bolívar, isn't it?" he whispered.

"Perhaps it is. But since he is not here, it is irrelevant."

"Why are you not with him?"

"I don't know."

"He has abandoned you, hasn't he?"

Tears fell from my eyes.

"Oh, Manuela, I hate to see you hurt. You should not love him so much that it hurts."

I shook my head, not knowing whether I was denying what he said or what I felt in my heart.

"Manuela, why will you not come with me? There is no reason to love him so completely."

"Fausto, the reasons why I should or should not love him do not matter. I do. That is all."

He looked hurt. "So, for him, you will not come away with me."

"It is not Bolívar which is stopping me."

"Then?"

"It is my heart, which is not wholly with you, that must decide for me. In a way, it would be an opportunity for me to escape my problems here . . ."

"Well, then—"

I thought about it for a moment and said, "Which is why I won't go. I would only be running away from my loneliness, and I believe I would end up hating you for it."

"Manuela, I want you to come with me." The urgency and need in his voice touched me. "I will miss you. I need to see you like this, in the moonlight, as I've known you before. I need to hear you laugh." He reached out and caressed my cheek, wiping away a tear.

He touched my heart with his caress. We were reliving that night, so many years before, when we loved for the first time. At that moment, I longed to go with him, but I knew I could not. I could not take him away from his baby, and I could not run away from my need to deal with my loneliness.

As Fausto left me, unhappy and resigned to staying, I felt I had won a victory in my own life. I did not run. I stayed; I accepted my aloneness. I was stronger as the days went forward.

Fausto did not seek me out again, nor did I seek him, but I heard that he had not left and was still with Antonia. I continued to do the only thing I could do, which was to try to increase Bolívar's power and influence in Quito.

My horses, mules, and Simón's strongboxes with his papers finally arrived, and I set myself to bringing a higher degree of order to them. I longed to see him. Every morning when I climbed into bed after posting bills the night before, I thought about him. Still, he did not write to me. Still, I longed for him. I felt lost because I did not know what my future held. I had long since given up riding off to his estates in Venezuela. Still, I longed for him.

Then, in the first week in November, Arthur Sandes showed up at José María's house. I was in bed with a terrible cold. Jonotás was nursing both Natán and me. When I heard who was in José María's parlor, I dressed and went to meet him.

He was muddy and tired. However, even before we exchanged greetings, he said, "I have an urgent letter from Bolívar, who gave me strict orders that I was to deliver this directly into the hands of 'Manuelita.'" He laid the paper, no longer crisply folded, in my hands.

At last, he had written. With Arthur Sandes himself having been given the task of delivering it over the vast distance from Bogotá, I half expected it to be some urgent military matter. I slowly opened it, afraid of what it might say. It was dated September 11; it had taken almost two months to arrive. Then, I read the most beautiful letter he ever wrote. It was only one paragraph:

The memory of your enchantments dissolves the frost of my years. Your love revives a life that is expiring. I cannot live without you. I can see you always even though I am far away from you. Come. Come to me. Come now.

Chapter 28

As thrilled as I was at the prospect of finally joining the man I loved, his neglect of me had cut deeply into my heart. In my abandonment, I had found a kind of integrity, which I was not going to throw away on the basis of only one letter, no matter how much it moved me.

I asked to speak to Sandes alone, and I questioned him about Bolívar and the situation in Bogotá. "He misses you, Ma'am. In fact, he needs you. You should go—for your country, if for no other reason."

"What do you mean, Arthur?"

"Santander wants him to fall. He could win, too, and the entire country would be in ruins if the Liberator were not there. Only his presence in the capital is keeping order in the whole country."

"Yes, he is a very able statesman," I said absent-mindedly. I was thinking about how Bolívar had once said he was like a plowman, sowing liberty, while all around him were others ready to undo his work.

"I don't think you understand me," he said, interrupting my reverie. "Yes, he is a very able statesman, but that is not what I meant. It is not his abilities; it is his being there which is keeping the country together."

I looked at him in puzzlement.

"It is because he is there, as much as what he is doing. It is his incredible presence which may be his most valuable tool in statesmanship. To give you an example: One time, before he was about to have a meeting with the Liberator, I overheard Santander say, 'I will tell Bolívar that the Federal system, and not his Bolivian Constitution, is the only way our people can unite.' However, when he went into the meeting, all he did was agree with everything the General said. Neither Santander, nor anyone else can thwart the Liberator when finally confronted with him."

"Yes. I have seen that happen to other men."

"It is impossible to defy the Liberator," Sandes continued, scratching his face, which had not been shaved for several days. "In fact, Santander said it best himself."

"Santander?"

"Yes, when he heard that the general was on his way back to Bogotá from Venezuela, he told Congress, 'He must not come! His influence and his secret power are so great that even I have yielded to him again and again, full of shame and admiration, when I saw and heard him. No man can so beguile others by his personal presence as General Bolívar. Woe to the man who feels his charm. In a moment he is as wax in his hands.'"

I smiled.

"He merely has to arrive in the city, and the disquieting elements are kept down," Sandes mused. For a moment the thought gave me comfort until Sandes, after a long silence, said, "In a way, that is his flaw."

"Whose?"

"The Liberator's."

"What do you mean? Why?"

"Because he believes only he can solve every problem—if he can get to it. If he can arrive, everything will be all right—or so he believes. However, he cannot be everywhere at once, and at some point men will have to behave themselves for the sake of virtue and not because Bolívar is there."

We were both silent for a long time.

"That's why I'm glad he has sent for you. He needs help. He cannot go on forever, keeping entire republics in control, all alone."

"I will go to Bogotá, as soon as Natán has recovered a bit."

He smiled and, after a moment, he said, "I must return to Bogotá, now."

"Must you go so soon? Can you not ride back with me?"

He looked uncomfortable.

"What is it, Arthur?" I asked, in English.

He answered in English, as well, "I am ordered to return right away. I could stay a little while, but I am uncomfortable here."

"Why?"

"Mariana. She has written to me that she is returning from Bolivia. She says that there is a great deal of unrest there, but I felt there was too much invitation in her letter. She will be here soon, and for the sake of Sucre, I do not want to be in Quito when she arrives."

I did not like this. Sucre was having as much trouble in Bolivia as Bolívar was in Colombia. Not only was she abandoning him when he needed her most, but she was apparently unwilling to keep her marriage vows.

He went on, "I wish to return right away. Bolívar needs me, and . . . I still love her." He looked at me and smiled, "I am afraid I would only get into trouble if I stayed here."

After my discussion with Sandes, if I had any doubts about going to Bogotá, they were gone. I began to make plans for the journey, but I wrote to Simón and sent the letter with Sandes when he returned:

> I am very angry, and very ill. How true it is that long absences kill little loves and increase great passions. You had a little love for me, and the long separation killed it. But I, I who had a great passion for you, kept it to preserve my peace and happiness. And this love endures and will endure so long as Manuela lives.
>
> I am leaving for Bogotá the first of December—and I come because you call me to you. However, once I am there, do not afterward suggest that I return to Quito; better that I should die than to be taken for some shameless trull.

As I was preparing to leave, a few days before the end of November, Jonotás brought home some news that almost made me change my mind and stay.

"Manuelita," she said, as she rushed in, dripping from a light rain that was falling. "I just heard somethin'." She stopped to catch her breath. "I just heard that Carlos Aispuru is dead."

I had been so withdrawn from any sort of public life that I had not heard about it. When Jonotás told me, it had been almost a week since he had died—of food poisoning. I pressed her for details. All she knew was that it was said he died weeping, saying, "Papa, forgive me, I have failed you." Apparently, still feeling shame because he believed he had failed to manage the estate as well as he could. No wonder he blamed my mother. He was so wracked with guilt, even weeping on his death bed, that he would have to have someone to blame.

I had our horses saddled and we rode directly out to the Aispuru home. I intended to see if my aunts would be more reasonable about honoring my mother's request that I inherit a portion of the property.

I did not even make it to the door. Apparently, we had been recognized as we rode up. An old man, whom I recognized as one of Carlos's retainers, met us as we dismounted. "Get back on your horses. You are not welcome here."

"I am Manuela Sáenz and I am here to see my aunts—"

"We know who you are," his quavering old voice announced. "We do not want you here."

"What do you mean 'we?'"

"They do not." He gestured excitedly toward the house. "The mistresses. They do not want you here."

I looked at him as he stood there, angrily staring at me, his head shaking with a kind of palsy. "This is ridiculous," I said. "I'm going to announce myself."

I pushed past him, as he said, "They won't answer the door."

I turned back to regard him, that I might know by his aspect if he told the truth. I looked back at the house and I knew he was right. They would cower in the house, and nothing would happen. I became quite sad, for which I inwardly chastised myself. Why should I care about these women, whom I had barely even seen? Slowly, I mounted my horse and rode back to Quito.

When we came to the spot of land where my house had been, I stopped for a moment. Everything had been removed and it was part of a larger fenced-in area where mules were grazing. I knew I would never see the place again.

It was becoming dark. Somewhere behind the overcast vault of the sky, the sun was slipping behind the Andes. A light rain grew stronger as I sat there. I felt quite immobile, and I might have sat there a long time if Jonotás and Natán had not urged me onward. Slowly we rode back to Quito.

By the time we reached the city walls, it was raining quite hard. Being on the equator, the transition from day to night is quick—not like Lima or Panamá, where the dusk and dawn seem to linger, or closer to the poles, where I've heard the dusk will go on for months. To me, that evening, the fall of night seemed like a curtain drawn on my past. Never would I think of the Aispurus again, I told myself. It was over.

The rain seemed to pour out of the sky as we entered the city. Our ponchos were soaked, and we urged our horses faster. It was a little dangerous riding so swiftly through the barely visible streets, hidden by rain and darkness, but we wanted to return to the comfort of José María's house where we could dry out.

When we were a block or so away from the center of town, I saw a man running through the streets up ahead. In the gloom, it was difficult to see him, but his whole manner seemed distraught. He was barefoot, and he would run a short distance, look around as though searching frantically for something, run some more, then stop again. When we reached him, he ran up to us, grabbed the my horse's halter, and shouted over the rain, "Help me!"

Then I saw who it was. "Fausto?"

"Manuela, it's you! Help me! The baby."

"Come on," I said. As though he was still a member of the King's Guards, he sprang up behind me and directed me to his house. We were there in seconds.

"Go find a doctor," I yelled at Jonotás, over the downpour as I dismounted. She turned her horse in the other direction. Natán and I followed Fausto inside.

Antonia looked terrible. She was in bed, sweating and shivering, as white as the lace on her pillows. "What are you doing here?" she said so weakly that it sounded like she was far away.

"I'm here to help," I said, matter of factly.

"I'm cold," she said, and her eyes closed.

I pulled back the heavy blanket she was clutching around her neck. Droplets of blood flew across the room from the underside of the blanket, and the smell of gore pervaded the air. She was lying in a puddle of blood as large as the mattress.

I looked around, but Natán already had her turban off. She quickly refolded it and pressed it tightly between Antonia's legs.

Fausto said, "She wouldn't let me call anyone to help."

"Get us some clean cloth."

"I'm cold," Antonia said quietly. Natán and I flipped the bed cover around, so the dry side was down, and covered her up.

Fausto came back with a stack of clean kitchen towels. Natán and I pulled the cover up from her feet and began sopping up the blood. As I worked, objects in the room seemed to loom larger and take over my thoughts.

I would have killed for the things she had in that room at another time in my life. The furniture was of the richest European manufacture. The bedclothes were of the finest linen, lace, and silk. The tiles on the floor were polished to perfection. When I looked at Fausto, I was reminded how much I had once loved him. I wished at that moment that I could have borne children. I wished I had been his wife and we had lived in this house.

I also noticed "medicines" beside her bed: purgatives, emetics, strychnine and other vials of dubious medicinal value. Most would make you vomit, or urinate. I also knew that they could be poisonous. I feared for the baby.

Jonotás and a doctor arrived. His face was grim as he looked at the sight. He pulled back the covers and placed a small funnel shaped object to her belly. After putting his ear to the small end of the object, he listened for the baby's heart.

Antonia's hand reached out to me and she pulled me close to her. Her voice was very weak, and hoarse, almost a whisper. "I'm frightened."

"Just rest now," I said. Despite all that had happened between us, I felt so sorry for her.

She pulled me closer and said, "I was jealous of you because you were free . . . I'm sorry, Manuela." I felt her lose her grip on life as she let go of my hand.

The doctor worked furiously. Soon, a fine baby girl was placed in Fausto's arms. He held onto her as though she was the entire world.

When I left that night, it was still raining. I walked my horse slowly, despite the downpour. The last thing I expected was to be sitting at the deathbed of one of my enemies, wishing for her life. It wasn't only that I wanted the baby to live for Fausto's sake. It was Antonia herself who I hoped would recover, even as I felt her expire.

If hoping for her life was unexpected, what she said was almost beyond believing. I—who had resented Antonia for all that she had, all that I had been deprived of—never expected her to say that she was jealous of *me*.

The realization that someone I had fought all my life was made of straw, astounded me. No, I learned that night that she, who had always been my enemy, was made of the same stuff as I.

If I had understood her, I would have loved her. If she had understood me, or had been raised in a home of understanding instead of class hatred and abuse, she might have loved me. My tears fell on clothes and harness already drenched by rain that seemed determined not to end.

I was sad for the next few days as I prepared to depart for Bogotá. Fausto came to see me the day I left. I was ready to mount my horse, when he walked up. His eyes, and his unshaven face, gave evidence of the tears he had shed in the last few days. "I am going to Guayaquil today—my daughter and I, and her wet nurse."

"Why, Fausto?"

"We are going to Mexico, to be with my father and brother. I want to leave before Antonia is buried." We were standing under an overhang, outside of José María's house. Rain was still falling, and it was cold. "Before her parents take my daughter away."

"Can they do that?"

"*They* can do anything they want." He shivered.

"Are you feeling well?" I asked.

"Yes. At least I will be, once I am away from here."

I put my arms around him. "I won't forget you. Of all people, I will remember and love you."

"You know it is the same for me." He appeared to be crying, even though there were no tears. We said our farewells and he walked away, but the look on his face stayed with me.

I never heard from him again. Whenever it rains, or when new life comes into the world, I still see his sad face in my mind, just as it was the day we parted in Quito.

Chapter 29

I left the city of my birth on December 1, 1827, to begin a journey of over three hundred leagues, escorted by Colonel Demarquet and a squadron of Lancers. It was raining when I left, and it rained until we arrived in Ibarra. There, we rested and dried out for a day. Ibarra is at a slightly lower altitude than Quito or the passes we came through, so it was a bit warmer and it provided a welcome rest.

A little after noon, the day we arrived, Jonotás brought word that she had heard something from one of the Indians in the market. The old, crazy priest, whom I had given up as lost, had, in fact, been in Ibarra the last few years. She said that he slept in the deep gorge next to the city, no one knew where.

"Did she say *anything* about where he might be found?"

"He's spendin' most of his time in somethin' she called *Caranqui*."

Neither of us understood what that was. When I inquired, I found that it was close by, the ruins of an Incan temple of the sun and a convent of vestals. This was where Atahualpa, the Incan king who was murdered by Pizarro, was born.

We saddled our horses and rode out to the ruins. We rode across the plain of Hatun-Taqui (the "Great Drum") where the Inca, Huayna-Capac, fought the battle in which he overcame the Caranqui Indians. In the vicinity is Yaguar-Cocha (the "Lake of Blood"), where the victor butchered thousands of the defeated. Legends say the number was as many as forty thousand and their blood dyed the lake crimson, though it was nearly a league across. As we rode to the ruins, we saw hundreds of *tolas* (sepulchral mounds) on the plain which treasure seekers had long since stripped of their history.

There was not much to see at the ruins, and certainly nothing of the crazy priest. I was of mixed feelings as we rode back to Ibarra. In one way, I had a glimmer of hope that my mother's will might still be found. In another way, I wished that such hope had not been given new life, if it was to die so swiftly.

We could not confirm what Jonotás's informant had said and we were to depart for Tulcan, the border town between the departments of the South and New Granada, the next morning. I told Jonotás and Natán to see if they could find out any more about the mad priest before we left.

When they returned, late in the afternoon, they had indeed received independent reports that the crazy priest was in the environs, but no one seemed to know where he could be found. As the last light of the day slipped behind the northern slope of the dark volcano of Imbaburra that dominated the town, I noticed storm clouds rolling in. It looked as though our departure, in the morning, would be attended by more rain. I did not enjoy the thought of traveling in such bad weather, even though the next day we would be traveling down into green Andean valleys. I went to Demarquet to ask him to wait a day or so while I searched for the priest.

"But I cannot. The general, he will be angry with me. I am to bring you to him very hastily." His soft patois was animated with disapproval.

I was about to argue with him, but I realized that even if I found the old priest, it did not necessarily mean I would find my mother's will. In the meantime, Simón needed me. In an instant I decided my own fate. I smiled, and said, "Very well, Colonel. But get me there quickly."

We left the next morning, in a downpour, leaving the mystery of the priest and my mother's will behind. As we made our way down the trail by the edge of the Mira River, I realized and accepted that I was leaving the last chance I had to find the will. I was making a conscious decision about what was to be important in my life, though I still felt that in a small way I was betraying my mother. By the time we turned and headed upward into the mountain passes again, beginning our climb to Bogotá, I was too busy keeping my horse from falling to think about it anymore.

We rode day after day in the rain until we reached Pasto. It was a hard ride, up narrow, muddy trails, along jagged edges, sometimes through rain and mist so thick that we could not see the horse in front of us. The passage from the Department of South to the Department of New Granada had been marked only by the few miserable huts of Tulcan.

The reception for the once proud lancers escorting us was less and less enthusiastic as we went from one town to the next. Indians and whites alike came to their doors and looked at us with eyes of misery and resentment. Every bit of hope had been bled from their lives. We were a reminder of years of war, and there was no cause for celebration. *Down with Bolívar* was scribbled somewhere in every group of houses along the way.

In Pasto, it was even worse. These defiant *criollos* had fought the hardest of all the northern Andean Royalists. When I arrived there, I understood why. One would have to be stubborn indeed to live in the cold, rocky reaches that the *pastusos* called home. There, it was not only words on the walls but voices beyond the veil of rain calling us the hated name, the name that meant oppressor: *godos*!

I was incredulous. They called us, who had bled and cried, and nearly died in the battles for liberation the name of the hated enemy we had fought so hard to vanquish. Colonel Demarquet did his best to keep my spirits up, but even his charm froze in the icy rain and the even more chilling stares from the inhabitants of New Granada.

I could see, as I rode through *pueblo* after *pueblo*, how difficult it would be to forge these diverse peoples into a unified country. Each clutch of huts or a town or a community we came upon was separated from the others by vast, irregular and violent chasms, or walls of high volcanoes made of frozen stone and ice. There was no sense of communication between any two places except the little inadequate trail on which we rode. Each little pocket of humanity had its own little leader, its ways and customs slightly different than its neighbors, and a unique identity.

Yet Bolívar believed he could do it. Could he not see, he who had ridden all over South America, that these people would never be unified? The more I looked at the country, from which he was trying to create a united and modern republic, the more I believed he was wrong. If he could truly be in all places at once, all would be well, but he could not.

He did unify when his commanding presence entered the stage, but he always had to be in the center of the scene to pull off the trick. This, of course, left room for no one else. Sooner or later, someone would want some of the attention. Since men could not seem to compete with him directly, they would follow any other actor willing to challenge him—even if that actor was the cruel "man of laws," Santander.

The weather and the low state of commerce made food scarce. Not once, not even on Christmas, did we feel rested or well fed or warm or clean. Natán, who seemed ever more susceptible to extreme conditions since her illness during the Peruvian campaign, was weak and ill. She never complained, though I knew she was miserable. As 1827 closed its doors on yesterday, we rode on and on through mud, chilling weather, and hatred from the local inhabitants.

Forty days after we left Quito, feeling like we had suffered an even greater deluge than the biblical Noah, we arrived in Cuarto Esquinas outside of Bogotá. Here at last was a road, paved with stones, that could almost be said to be in repair. Here, the mountain passage almost deserved its name of King's Highway, and here the rain gave way to oppressive, dark, late afternoon clouds.

Colonel Demarquet ordered his lancers to straighten their jaguar-skin shakos, lift their lances on high, and raise the Colombian gonfalons for their entrance into the capital.

It was of no avail. The populace came out of their doors in meager numbers, gave us sullen or hateful looks, and returned inside.

The wind blew cold as we rode down the Calle de Florian to the Plazuela de San Carlos. Lima was also a city of overcast skies. Most of the year there were gray clouds covering the capital of Perú, but they were not dark, ominous, cold, and without joy as those above Bogotá. The streets were narrow and somber as were the few faces that turned toward us when we passed. Mostly the streets were empty.

I knew why Bogotá was as it was. This is what a city governed by a man like Santander would look like. This "man of laws" had found every way to wring out the happiness and prosperity from an already conservative and religious community. I knew, when I saw it, that I would not do well in Bogotá. I resolved at that moment, despite what might come, that I would not lose my dignity. I would, by force of will, impress my personality on this joyless place, and I would do everything I could to see that Bolívar achieved what he was after.

I had hoped to be able to clean up before going to Simón, but Colonel Demarquet had strict orders. I was to be to taken to him immediately because "The general is most anxious for your arrival."

I knew it was true. All along the route, his officers had been ordered to stay alert for our passage. There were even letters of encouragement for me along the way. In his own hand, he had written, "Hurry to me. I long to see you."

Colonel Demarquet sent a soldier to the Palace of San Carlos to see if Bolívar was there. The man returned quickly, saying, "A recent earthquake has caused him to move permanently to the Quinta." We turned our horses and mules and headed north through the plaza.

The grayness of the evening was quickly becoming black. There was indeed earthquake damage to the spires of the ancient cathedral, and there were cracks in many of the other buildings—most of which looked the same. Except for a few two-story buildings on the Plazuela, they were all one story, all white. This, for the capital of the most powerful country in South America, was quite wrong. There were only about 20,000 people in the city and the environs. The white walls of the simple, austere buildings were dirty and squalid by comparison to Lima.

We moved through the dim light of evening, past the edge of the city toward the Rio San Agustín, no more than a stream that carries away the city's waste. There we crossed the Carmen Bridge, made of stone, not far above the slow moving river. As I looked below, even in the near darkness I could see, and smell, black mud and sewage lining the viscid banks of the tiny river. By the time we approached the Quinta, the last of the light had left the sky.

It had been almost two years since I had seen Simón. True, he had called for me, but I became nervous as we rounded a curve in the road and started a short ascent. The Quinta was set amongst a grove of cedars, oaks, and cypresses at the foot of a mountain. Fog enveloped the villa, a fog that glowed from the fires and candles within. Laughter and the tinkling of glasses escaped the closed windows that were ablaze with the lights inside.

As we made our way through the trees, from out of the night came a voice: "Halt!" Suddenly, we heard rifles cock and boots crunch on the fallen leaves all around us. From out of a sentry house a lantern came, held by a captain of the guard.

"Who lives?" said the voice behind the bayonets.

"The Liberator!" cried Demarquet.

The captain came forward and peered at us. He saw my uniform, my jackboots, my pistols, on a feminine form, with my earrings of coral dangling at my neck and he came closer. He did not understand at first, until Demarquet said, "This, Señor Captain, is La Sáenz."

There was instant recognition and murmurs among the soldiers standing around us as I heard them uncock their rifles. The captain said, "Ah, Señora, please come this way."

Demarquet and I dismounted and followed the captain to the doorway. My military-cut pelisse brushed against war mementos along the path: cannons, mortars, broken caissons. The sound of my jingling spurs was drowned out by a roar of laughter from within. Who was inside? Was it a state dinner where I would have to meet my enemy—Santander? Or was it a simple meeting of friends?

We walked through glass doors that allowed access to the foyer. To the right was a small, dimly lit salon, filled with mahogany and sofas covered in red damask. Red and gold covered the walls. We walked through the salon and through the French doors that led into the library. There, amid a blaze of lights and a roaring fire, were my friends: Fergusson, O'Leary, Doctor Moore, Santana and others.

There were also some new faces I was to come to know. One was General Urdaneta, mature and handsome, with a reputation for bravery and loyalty—a Venezuelan like many of the revolution's heroes. Also, another man who was to become a good friend of mine was José "Pepé" Paris, a civilian, slight of stature, with a big heart. He operated one of Colombia's emerald mines and was Simón's financial advisor, having done business all over the world. There was also a new, young, handsome face in the room. His name was Lieutenant Andrés Ibarra, the latest addition to Bolívar's staff. He was Simón's youngest aide and fiercely loyal. He had a patrician face, which seemed to state that here was a brave soul. "Very capable," Bolívar would remark on several occasions.

I could see that I had interrupted a meeting—later I was to discover that it was the strategy meeting for the upcoming congress of Ocaña—but the men rose from their chairs and came to greet me. Everyone in the room—except General Córdoba, who glowered at me from his place next to the window—treated me as though I was Simón's wife. Fergusson handed me a glass of Irish whiskey. "Good it is to see ya, Lass!" he said, in English, and laughed with merriment. They all gathered round to inquire about my trip and to make me feel welcome.

Then there was Simón. He held back at first as old friends came to give me a hug, smiling with delight. Then, he gently pushed his way through until those around him, sensing his desire to come to me, stepped aside. He kissed me quickly on the lips and gave me a hug, amid a scene of confusion and happiness.

"Gentlemen, please," he said, to quiet the room. "Manuelita has had a long trip, and if you will excuse me, I will see to her comfort."

We went through the library, amid promises from the men in the room that we would talk later, through Simón's study, which I could see was in need of my touch, and into Simón's bedroom. José Palacios was there. His somber face formed what was, for him, a big smile, and said, "Welcome, Señora."

"Oh, José, how I have missed you." I still had Fergusson's whiskey in my hand. I took a long drink and Simón said something funny. We began to laugh, and the next thing I knew, José was gone and I was in bed with the man I had ridden across half a continent to see. He kissed me, again and again.

The long hard journey had been worth it.

Chapter 30

I was deliciously happy for the next few weeks. By taking over the administration of Simón's affairs, I became the mistress of the Quinta. Though it only had a few rooms—a library, a bedroom, a study, a salon, and a dining room—the grounds were large and beautiful. Many kinds of trees had been planted along with bougainvillea, honeysuckle, and fuchsias. There was even a small pool for swimming (more like a very large bath really). To me it was an island of beauty in a depressing country.

It was not the house, however, that really needed my care, but Simón himself. He raged once or twice at my insistence that he eat something healthy, or wear something warm, or get some sleep, but I could see that he was glad I was there. Mostly, he let me guide him in those first weeks.

We had nights of passion. Not every one, but they made me feel like the nights we had known in Quito. Remembering those early days, it became clear to me that his once famous vitality had at last been sapped by the demands of his roles as liberator and statesman, and by tuberculosis, from which he suffered increasingly. Often he would have long fits of coughing, sometimes coughing up blood. In addition to his poor health, I noticed the signs of age; his step was weaker, our evenings of love were not so often, and his thin frame was, if possible, even thinner. He also wore his hair cut too short and slicked back, which revealed a thinning hairline that seemed to become more pronounced each day.

On the other hand, I was in the prime of my life. My own vigor, and my voluptuousness, were cause for the clacking of tongues to begin. The gossip said that Simón, like Samson, had been stripped of his vitality by a witch.

Jonotás and Natán brought back the gossip every day. Not even in my young days in Quito was there as much animosity toward me as there was in Santa Fe de Bogotá—especially from the women. This was a city built by religionists, where fatalistic sorrow and moral righteousness pervaded the air. Anyone who did not think and act as they did were devils. My refusal to accept societal constraints on my behavior only proved my evil to citizens of Bogotá. Daily, the reports from the streets came to me through Jonotás and Natán of the vile invectives and profound hatred directed at me.

I know that some of Bolívar's friends would have preferred that I stay in the villa and make myself invisible so that such associations would not surround the President of the Republic. Of course, I would never do this. On the contrary, I lived my own life as fully and unapologetically as I could. Bolívar often invited me to ride in his open landau (there were no others in Bogotá) and I did, even though I knew that it made the small minded of Bogotá angry to see their President-Liberator riding so openly with his mistress. The city's sense of propriety was as rigid as cured oak, and the citizens mistrusted everyone who did not do things exactly according to their own religious ideas.

Despite the political and social climate of the city, Bolívar and I loved each other, and we loved each other with new fervor. Simón looked the other way when I rode through town in my hussar's uniform. He ignored my smoking, which no woman in Bogotá did. He did not remark on Jonotás and Natán, whose often disheveled appearance and manner irritated him.

Mostly he kept busily to himself. He would stay in his study, writing his newly proposed Constitution for the Congress of Ocaña, while guests gathered in his salon. He paid no attention to what was happening while he wrote: the music or the spirited discussions or the laughter when Jonotás made fun of a Bogotá matron. Jonotás always chose to mimic whoever had been heard to criticize me, and her victim would invariably be one of Bogotá's most important women.

What happened in the salon, in Bolívar's Quinta, I soon discovered, would next day be known all over Bogotá. Everything that was said, even what we had for dinner, seemed to be known by the most common beggar. Everybody seemed to know everything, always, and it was impossible to keep a secret.

Jonotás tried, and failed, with one important secret. She had fallen in love with an Irishman, a colonel in the British Legion. He reminded me very much of Fergusson, but he was much more rash and sometimes acted foolishly. His name was Richard Crofston; very handsome and he seemed to adore Jonotás.

At first they tried to remain discreet, but the news of it reached the streets of Bogotá. It was a scandal because of their races. Jonotás's reputation for mimicking the "best people" of Bogotá's society did not help mitigate the scandal. But whether it was Jonotás and Crofston, or a risqué joke I told, all of Bogotá heard about it the next day.

Some of Bolívar's friends were so shocked by my behavior that their friendship turned to bitterness. Jonotás and Natán were in the Plazuela one day when I rode through toward the Palace of San Carlos, which was being repaired for Bolívar's return. I did as I always did. I rode fast, wearing my bright red uniform with skin tight trousers, astride (not side-saddle) on my black mare.

José María Restrepo, one of Bolívar's trusted advisors, who was writing a history of Colombia, was walking along at the time. He was from one of New Granada's oldest families, and Jonotás said that both he and his wife turned red with rage. This happened before I realized the extent of the effect my actions would have on such a conservative city. However, at that time of my life, I am not sure I could have done anything other than be fully who I was. Jonotás overheard Restrepo say, "I swear to you, my wife, that no history of Colombia will ever mention the name of Bolívar's greatest shame: Manuela." This was to foreshadow things to come.

The animosity of the ladies of Bogotá was more than I expected, but only slightly. However, the severity of reactions such as Restrepo's were far beyond what I anticipated. Before I knew it, the Santanderists had been able to increase their influence, merely by talking about *me*. It hurt to think that I might be hurting Simón. Still, since I knew it was not for malicious acts but because of the narrowness of their minds and Santander's lust for power that they hated me, I did not see what could be done. Should I, could I, suddenly not be "La Sáenz?"

Bogotá was divided into two camps: Bolivarists and Santanderists. The city had been divided before my arrival and whether I was in Bogotá or not, it was obvious to me that the battle would rage until one of them was in exile or dead. My actions and my presence were only the latest excuse for the widening split between the two sides. I was not the cause. I knew that the texture of my personality was essential to Bolívar's love for me, and I knew that he was far stronger, and more able to fight, after I arrived. Thus, I continued to support all of Bolívar's friends in every way I could, and I fought his enemies with as much vigor. I was not careful about who might be stepped on.

I knew why some of the women of Bogotá hated me. They were jealous. Some of them, at one time or another, had been in Bolívar's bed. They did not like it one bit that I, "a foreigner," as they called me despite the fact that Quito was now part of Colombia, had won him.

One of these women, Bernardina, a rejected lover of Bolívar's from the early days of the revolution, was particularly incensed by my presence. She had her husband, Florentino González, who owned a printing press, publish damaging stories about me and Bolívar in a *papelucha* (a scandal sheet) called the *Incombustible*. He was not the only publisher to use his power against us. Daily there were broadsides on the walls, or stories in other such "newspapers," mentioning the hated "foreign" woman who lived with the President, alongside the stories about the hated president himself. The only publisher in Bogotá who was consistently supportive of Bolívar was a man named Bruno Espinosa. Unfortunately, he was not a very effective writer.

Vicente Azuero was another of Bolívar's enemies who had a printing press. He was a close friend of González, and together they would feed on each other's animosity. Azuero was even more vitriolic than González in his attacks on me. Some of the stories were written by the vice-president himself, although he was not bold enough to use his real name.

I saw Santander only once during that first couple of months. He made no attempt to call on Bolívar but relied on the safety of his writing desk to communicate with his President and to manipulate his nefarious schemes. The fact that he was not around was perhaps fortunate, because if I had seen him when I had my pistols, I might have put a ball in his malicious head. I had found out from my friends that Santander had been diligent in seeing that my reputation—adulterer, harpy, meddler—had preceded me. That was one reason there was so much hatred directed at me so quickly.

However, despite all, Simón and I were happy together up until he had to leave for Ocaña. Though I would miss him, I was anxious for Bolívar to go, since he would be able to institute his new constitution. Simón was already hard at work on solving the problems of an empty treasury, stagnant agriculture, slaves not yet free, soldier's welfare, and many other problems under which the populace suffered. It surprised me, when I saw him work so hard, how little people understood what he did for the country. *Soon*, I thought, *Simón will have this country under control. Then we will be free of these endless hatreds.* He must go to Ocaña. He would win, the republic would be on sound footing, and Santander and his ilk would have lost.

In March of 1828, he rode to the Congress—convened far from the political atmosphere of Bogotá—in Ocaña. Despite coughing frequently in preceding days, I watched him ride away happy and confident that he would return with the government established as he wanted it. I stayed to mind things at the Quinta and to look after the rest of Bolívar's interests in Bogotá.

The first time I knew that things had gone wrong was when I received my first letter from Simón, about two weeks later.

I am in Bucaramanga. Why am I not in Ocaña, you ask? It is because I cannot move. When I arrived here, a little over a week ago, I was told that, as I feared might happen and as I have warned everyone about, our disunity has caused Spain to consider an invasion. A fleet is said to be in the Pacific waters looking for a place to land. These reports I could not confirm, but I stopped here to send dispatches to prepare for a resistance force. The next day, I heard that an officer by the name of Padilla, in Cartagena, was preparing to revolt "against tyranny." I was angry, and began gathering information there in order to quell the insurgency. I was trapped. If I went North, I would lose the South. If I went South, the North would revolt. I have no other choice but to stay here, and wait.

I sent O'Leary and the rest of the delegates ahead. In the meantime I wait. And while I wait, I think of you, and what we will do when I return.

Padilla, a Santanderist, was an admiral in Colombia's navy. He continued to foment trouble the entire time the Congress was meeting.

Meanwhile, in the fertile valleys of Ocaña, Congress was not enjoying the scenery. Simón and I wrote many letters to each other—love letters to be sure, but he also told me of the congress. The Bolivarists and Santanderists were disputing every point, and the first part of the Congress went badly for Bolívar's delegates because he was not there. One part after another of his constitution was voted down.

The life or death of the republic was at hand, and whether or not the new constitution was adopted, one or the other, either President Bolívar or Vice President Santander, would end up in control of the country. The opposition, convinced that Bolívar wished to be dictator, was redirecting the proceedings in order to establish enough power to vote him out of office.

"Those wretched creatures," Bolívar raged, "even the air they breathe, they owe to me." Despite Santander's best efforts, Bolívar's delegates worked hard and at last were able to generate enough votes to win adoption of his constitution after all—albeit watered down. Then, Padilla revolted.

When the news reached me, knowing that Padilla was a Santanderist, their scheme became clear. Even I, miles away from events as they unfolded, could see that the plan was to threaten revolt, keep Cartagena agitated, and if the congress went badly, to revolt in earnest. Fortunately, Bolívar had not left his strategic position in Bucaramanga and the threat of the Spanish seemed to have evaporated. When word came to Padilla that Bolívar was close and moving towards Cartagena, the traitor fled to Ocaña to meet with Santander. When news of these events reached Bogotá, the disaffection between the two sides grew more ugly. The Santanderists could be heard shouting "Down with Bolívar," every day.

About that time, Fergusson, his hair grown long in the last two months, came to Bogotá on business for Simón.

"How is it?" I asked him in English as I poured him some whiskey.

He frowned, took the glass, and said, "Ah, Lass, you would not want to be hearing it."

"You know me better, Colonel. Tell me." We walked into the garden, but the sweet fragrance of honeysuckle did little to alleviate my mood when I heard his story. We sat on a bench and he drank his whiskey in one gulp. I poured him another.

"Lass, you know how to make a soldier feel rewarded." He smiled and then said, "Only two weeks ago, I had it in a letter from O'Leary that there was a movement afoot to take His Excellency's life."

I was not surprised by the news, but a surge of fear and anger went through me, "By whom?"

"At least some of the delegates of Santander were involved, Lass."

I know I must have looked infuriated, because he said, "Angered I was, as well. I made sure, from then on, that His Excellency was in me sight. The general noticed me watchfulness and he said: 'You are guarding me as though you suspect a plot upon my life. Tell me frankly, has someone written to you from the convention?'

"I pulled out the letter from O'Leary and gave it to him. He read it and then reached into his desk and pulled out a report from another source. He showed it to me and said, 'I did not show this to anyone or speak about it, but as I know of the same incidents of which O'Leary speaks, all the officers here should be informed. O'Leary's fears are justified.'"

Fergusson finished the last of his second glass of whiskey and I sat silently, fuming at the news I had just heard. "If I may," he said in Spanish, indicating the bottle. I handed it to him absently. He poured another drink and finished it off before I moved.

"Come on," I said. I grabbed his hand and led him to the stables.

"Where is it you're leading me, Lass?"

I had my horse saddled and told Fergusson to get on his. We rode into the city.

We had no trouble finding the latest *papeluchas* and broadsides that spoke of Bolívar as a tyrant. Fergusson, strengthened by whiskey, was livid as we read one libelous attack after another of our beloved Bolívar.

When we came upon González just coming out of his shop, Fergusson yelled at him, in English, "It's poison you have in your ink."

González didn't understand, but he recognized Fergusson as one of Bolívar's officers and he could not mistake the tone. He yelled back, "Death to the tyrant."

Before I could stop him, Fergusson yelled, in Spanish, "You son of a whore, I'll teach you . . . ." He jumped down and threw a punch at the printer's jaw, causing the man to fall in a heap on his doorstep. Fergusson turned around and smiled at me.

González recovered, jumped up, grabbed a chair sitting against the wall outside the door to his shop, and just as I was saying, "Look out!" he shattered it on Fergusson's head.

Fergusson was not hurt. On the contrary, he proceeded for the next quarter of an hour to beat the man senseless. When some neighbors tried to intervene, I pulled one of my pistols and cocked it, saying, "Don't interfere."

When Fergusson had finished with the man, he then proceeded to take apart the man's shop, his printing press, and all the furniture in the little room.

At that moment, Vicente Azuero ran over from across the street. He saw González on the ground and heard the noise in the shop. "You bitch," he said to me, and before I could threaten him with my pistol, he turned as though to run inside the shop to stop Fergusson. He was too late. Fergusson was already finished. He came out of the shop, smiling broadly, just as Azuero reached the door.

"You filthy tyrant's dog," said Azuero.

"Who are you?" asked Fergusson, staggering a bit.

I moved my horse sideways, into Azuero's back so that he was thrown to the ground. "Señor Azuero," I said, "you should not interfere. An Irishman and Irish whiskey are too much for any man." Fergusson started laughing hysterically and tried to sit on the chair with a recently broken leg. He fell to the ground and laughed even harder.

Azuero was not humored by these events. On the contrary, he was livid with rage. His face turned bright red, and he picked up a broken board and came at me. I moved my horse sideways again while the board was raised over his head and I brought my pistol barrel across his forehead, sending him spinning dizzily away.

At that moment, General Córdoba came up. I could tell from the direction he came that he had been to see Fanny Henderson, the daughter of the British Consul in Bogotá, with whom reports said he was madly in love. He pulled a sword and came at me, so that I had to back up my horse to keep her from being cut.

"You've gone too far now, you vicious harpy," he yelled at me.

Fergusson, aware that something was happening, stood up and spun the general around, and only at the last moment before he landed a blow in Córdoba's face, recognized him. "Oh, I'm sorry, sir," he said, "I didn't realize it was you," and giggled.

Córdoba was fuming. He sent my Irish friend to his quarters. "You are to stay there until your court martial," he yelled after him. Then he turned to me and said, "I am writing to Bolívar this very hour. You have not been wise. You *will* be punished for this."

The town was in an uproar. The next day, the opposition demanded that Fergusson be taken to civilian court. Some demanded he be hanged without trial. They sent an angry messenger to Bucaramanga with demands that Bolívar do something about the affair.

He did. Still undecided about what to do about the talk of assassination, this last was too much and made up his mind. He recalled his delegates from the convention and had them announce that the decisions of the meeting were to be set aside—"without a quorum there is no more Congress." He also had Padilla chased down and arrested. Other soldiers were sent to Bogotá to declare, in his name and by his order, that the office of vice president no longer existed, thus removing Santander from the government.

"Now that the bull is out, we shall see who has the guts to take it by the tail," he said to his officers. Then, Bolívar mounted his horse and, taking the rest of his troops, he moved on the capital.

By July he was standing in the plaza in front of the cathedral. The people of Bogotá looked on while he took an oath of office. When he finished, he had assumed full dictatorial powers for the three departments of Gran Colombia.

Chapter 31

The good of the Republic does not consist in hateful dictatorship. Dictatorship is glorious only when it seals the abyss of revolution, but woe to a people that accustoms itself to live under dictatorial rule.

Thus Bolívar spoke to the people before he left the square. It was never Bolívar's desire to turn his republic into what it had become. He tried to tell the populace so that day. If his words were not enough, his actions in the ensuing weeks should have been. He meant to end the chaos by working on what he considered to be the main problem: the poor economic situation of the country.

He moved back into the Palace of San Carlos. I did not like such arrangements because it required me to travel back and forth to see him. I knew it would be for only a short time, until he had restored the country to order, so I did not make any comment. What I mostly did not like was that too often he became so busy that he failed to send for me.

Nevertheless, we continued to work together and were happy. However, he did chastise me for my involvement in Fergusson's spree. "With you there, it can only reflect badly on me and the entire government," he said soon after he arrived back in the capital.

I scoffed at the idea. "How could I affect—"

"Manuela, please listen to me. I am treading, very delicately, through the sentiments of the people. The country is split. Santander and many people who revere him, with their federalist ideals, believe that only he can save the country. If he wins, we will not survive. Reversing his influence will take time."

"How much time?"

"It is a slow process."

"But, Simón—"

"Public demonstrations, such as your and Fergusson's escapade, set back the process by months, maybe years."

"I don't believe you. Besides, it is so unfair. You wish to bind me, yet you leave him free to 'set back the process' by decades."

He gave me an exasperated look. "What would you have me do?"

"Have him imprisoned. It is obvious that Padilla was taking orders from him."

He shook his head. "You simply do not understand."

I understood. With Napoleon's example so fresh in the eyes of the world, he would do anything to avoid looking like a despot. He did not believe, as I did, that he would be called such no matter what he did. He believed in the love of the people. So, instead of bringing Santander to justice, he selected his adversary to be the first minister to the United States of America. "To get him out of the country," Bolívar said.

"That is not enough," I raged in frustration. "Has he not caused enough trouble here, without sending him off to a neighboring republic to speak ill of you there?"

"And what is your suggestion?" he asked, his mouth black with charcoal as he cleaned his teeth.

"He ought to be shot," I retorted angrily.

"Whatever you think of me, I am not a murderer," he snapped back.

"Execute him then. Try him and execute him."

"There is no evidence," he said in exasperation.

"That cannot be," I retorted.

"Besides, it would do more harm than good. The country is nearly torn asunder. For me to use my power to bring down a hero of the revolution, and he is revered as that, would only rouse his supporters. The times require delicacy, not more slaughter."

And so he continued. To this day I believe he was too lax in dealing with that man. If, in the beginning, he had simply eliminated him by one means or another, our fortunes and the entire fortunes of the South American republics might have been different. Hundreds, perhaps thousands, of lives might have been saved. But Bolívar was determined not to be seen as a tyrant. I believe such concerns, in the long run, did more harm to his posthumous reputation, and the Republic, than any despotic act he might ever have committed.

Still, I was to blame too. I should have taken it into my own hands and paid some assassin to solve Bolívar's problem. I didn't and I regret it, especially considering the useless and destructive act I did perform.

It started one morning, after a delicious night of love. When we arose I said, "On July 24 it will be your birthday. I want to have a celebration at the Quinta—"

"Manuela, please don't. I am too busy, and besides, I do not want to leave the city right now."

"Come, Simón, why not?"

"I've told you before. In order to unite the two factions of the country, it will require diligence and delicacy. I work all day long—"

"I know you do. You always work hard. Oh, Simón," I said, teasing, "you know, if you don't come, everyone will be there but you—all of your friends anyway." He scowled at me, stood, and began to dress. "Simón, I want to have a party, and I want you to be there. Please, try to come, even if only for a few minutes."

"Perhaps," he said, absently.

"Good!"

He smiled and said, "Ah, my lovable madwoman, I should probably come, if only to keep an eye on you." He leaned over and kissed me.

When the 24th came—it was a Thursday—everyone who could possibly be considered a friend of Bolívar's was at the Quinta. His officers were there, members of the government, men of business, and even foreign luminaries such as the visiting, French scientist, Jean Louis Boussingault, and his countrymen. Barrels of *chicha* were rolled out for the common soldiers, who enjoyed themselves outside. Inside the villa, we drank wine.

It was a grand party until someone mentioned the name of Santander. At once, everyone in the room seemed to compete with each other as to who could find the vilest phrases to describe him. This would have been fine, but someone suggested following the old Spanish custom of shooting him in effigy.

I admit that the wine I had been drinking was part of what prompted me to carry out that suggestion. However, most of my motivation was my extreme frustration at Santander's never having come to justice. I was delighted with the suggestion and said, "Yes!"

Jonotás and Natán found a sack and stuffed it with old clothes. We dressed it in a uniform and I drew a fairly good likeness of the vice president on the sack. Someone painted a sign that said, *Francisco de Paula Santander—Killed for Treason* and hung it on the figure. A group of soldiers, now drunk on *chicha*, marched "Santander" to a wall. I persuaded the Dean of the Cathedral to give last rites. Then, Richard Crofston, also a little drunk and urged on by Jonotás, ordered the soldiers to fire. "Santander" was blown to bits.

Almost everyone at the party loved it. A few didn't and one of these was General Córdoba. He wrote a letter to Simón, in which my slaves and I were nearly the only active participants in the execution of the effigy. This I could abide. I could even have taken a censure from Simón. I was not prepared for what did occur.

Simón called me to him the day after the party, after he had been given Córdoba's account. He paced up and down, refusing to look at me. I sat at his desk waiting. At last, he spoke, and his words hit me like a thunderbolt.

"You must leave the country."

I could not believe my ears. I sat there, unable to speak, unable to believe he could say such a thing to me. He continued his pacing, only more slowly, as though he were walking through mud.

At last he said, "Or go wherever you might."

I did not speak. The fire of my anger was burning me inside.

"At least for a while."

I exploded at him. "How dare you? Is your memory so short that you do not recall my letter to you? The one I sent from Quito, before I left to come to your side?"

He looked at me.

"I will remind you of it. It said, 'Once I am here, do not ask me to leave.'"

His stern countenance softened, and he said, "Manuela, you make it impossible—"

"No! You make it impossible, for yourself, for everyone, by not doing in reality what I did in effigy. I told you that villain should be shot. I said it to you years ago, in Perú—"

"This is a republic," he said, throwing up his hands in anger, "not some lawless band of rogues sitting on a mountain. I cannot simply shoot someone because I don't like him."

"But you can let him make a mockery of your laws, pervert your efforts so that people are hurt, destroy—"

"Manuela, I am not a despot. Do you want the people to think I am no better than Napoleon? I am the president of a republic—"

"But, Santander is—"

"We are not here to discuss Santander," he shouted. His face flushed red, and the veins stood out in his forehead. "We are discussing you, and Crofston, and how your irresponsible acts have destroyed the peace and unification I am working so hard to achieve."

"Crofston? What has Crofston to do with it?"

"Reports say that he was a principal player. I will be posting him in Venezuela so that he might be removed from public view. Just as you must be."

Jonotás loved him dearly, and I was determined that Simón would not do this. I said, "Why must he be removed from public view? Why?"

"Because he is an embarrassment to me."

"He is not. His loyalty is a tribute to you. He has broken no laws. You cannot punish him."

"I can punish him if I wish," he shouted.

"You yourself just said this was a country of laws, damn you." I stood up and flung my arms in the air in exasperation. "You infuriate me. You rage at me for being who I am. For feeling and acting. And yet you yourself, because you are embarrassed, propose to punish someone who has broken no laws, who is your friend." He started to speak but stopped. I went on, "And yet you will not eliminate a dangerous foe who can only mean your death."

We stood there, staring at each other, flushed with anger. At last he said, "Santander has already been stopped. That is enough."

"How can you be so foolish? You know so much about fighting, yet you leave your enemy unvanquished."

"Regardless, my villa has been used to embarrass a hero of this republic. Already, word is on the street that I was involved—"

"He must be stopped, do you not see?"

"In matters of statesmanship—"

"Simón," I pleaded, "please see the future. Even a child can see that Santander, if left unchecked, will kill you."

He looked at me in puzzlement, as though he were trying to understand how I could say such a thing. He looked at me as though I were a child, or crazy. His expression changed to disdain and said, "No he won't, and besides, I have virtually exiled him. Why can you not let it be?"

"You haven't exiled him. He's not even gone. He's still sitting at his lawyer's desk, writing sedition."

"He will be—"

"There will be no peace, no unification, as long as he lives."

In fury, he came at me, saying, "You are not directing the affairs of this country. I am."

"Fine," I flung back at him. "You do that. But you will not ask me to leave, and I will not go, in any case." We stood staring at each other for what seemed like a long time. My anger began to dissipate, and not wanting to let my emotions disintegrate into weeping, I turned to leave. Before I left the room, I turned and said, "What is to happen?"

He came to me and took me in his arms, tenderly, so tenderly. "I cannot, of my own will, make you leave me. I love you too much." He pulled me to him and pressed me against his heart. He held me there a long time. "I don't want you to go; it is only that—"

"I know, Simón. I will take the blame. Leave Crofston out of it. Please. For me."

He looked in my eyes and seemed as sad as I have ever seen him. "Can you not, at least, *modify* your behavior?"

I had to fight back tears that seemed to rush to my eyes. "You said you love me, Simón?"

"You know I do."

"I do not know. Tell me why you love me."

He put his hands on my shoulders and then buried them in my hair as he gently touched my neck. "I love you for . . ." The look of adoration and passion that I knew so well, and that made me love him so much, came to his eyes.

"Say it. You love our passionate nights together." Tears spilled onto my cheeks.

"Yes, and . . ."

"And the friendship we have in the morning."

"Yes . . ."

"Passion and loyalty, that is who I am, Simón. It has always been so. It is from inside me that my behavior springs." He seemed suddenly to have lost all his vitality. He walked slowly over to his chair, sat down, and stared at the floor.

My face was wet with weeping. "I will not change myself," I said, "I cannot. Not even for you whom I love with all my soul . . ." My voice cracked so that I could not speak. " . . . and that is what you have just asked me to change." He looked at me. He looked trapped. Neither of us had anything else to say.

Chapter 32

I went to Pepé Paris that day, explained the situation, and asked him to find me a place to live. "It must be close to the palace, and it must be easily accessible," I said with a voice filled with grief.

"I am sorry for you, Señora. I understand the general, but he is a stubborn man. Nevertheless, you should be close by, so that you might help him. He is so burdened these days."

Two days later, for 32 pesos, Pepé found me a large apartment overlooking the Plazuela de San Carlos. It was in the center of Bogotá where I could watch the commerce, the comings and goings of officials, and the life of the street. When I stood on my balcony, I could feel the pulse of the city. It could not have been more perfect for gathering information. Both the palace and the Calle de Comercio were in plain view. The church of *La Compañia*, of San Ignacio, was directly across the street where all the wealthy and prominent went to mass. The balcony was wide and long, and it overlooked the little park in the Plazuela with its fountains where Indians gathered water, horses slaked their thirst, and lovers met.

The lock on the door was heavy and solid, requiring a large iron key to enter. Outside the door, a narrow stairway descended to the street. I particularly liked the building's history. It was on a secret printing press, in the room beneath my apartment, that Antonio Nariño printed his translation of *The Rights of Man,* from which the revolution sprang.

I settled in, but during the days that followed I did not see Simón. I heard that he heartily disapproved of the location of my new lodgings. Like Pepé Paris, most of Bolívar's friends agreed with my sense of what had to been done, and they sympathized with me. Many came to visit me in those first few days bringing gifts for the new place. Many gave me money to buy furnishings or simply bought it for me. Wealthy Pepé was most generous, and I was surprised at how quickly the apartment became elegantly furnished.

One unexpected donor of a little cash was General Jacinto Lara. "We have had our differences," he said, looking older than usual, "but I know you want the best for his Excellency. Here." He handed me several pesos. "For your new dwellings. Because, I wish to reward your loyalty."

I was moved. "I thank you, Señor," I said, as I kissed his cheek. "You, too, are a great friend to the Liberator."

Not only were my furnishings provided, but bountiful food and sundries were brought by my friends. Fergusson came by, quite regularly, with meats and vegetables. After the first evening when I invited him and my other friends from the British legion for a *tertulia,* and we were short of wine and whiskey, they kept me supplied.

All of the animals I had adopted since arriving in Bogotá were there too. Natán insisted on taking care of them. She cleaned up after them, fed them, and never complained. Everything I needed was in that apartment, and I was happy except for my anger at Santander and my disappointment with Simón.

Actually, except for those moments, Jonotás, Natán and I lived quite comfortably. This was the first place I had that was all mine. It reminded me of the only thing I enjoyed during my convent days: women, living together, apart from men, and managing our own affairs. It was most refreshing.

But, ultimately, my affairs concerned the world of men. The *tertulias* I held were not merely entertainment or diversion for me. I was building a network of spies that would empower Simón with intelligence of all that was happening that he could not directly see. Jonotás and Natán went to market in the morning and gleaned the mood of the populace. At night, I turned my large sitting room into a salon and everyone from the visiting French scientists, to army officers, to merchants, to political figures, all came to drink wine and talk. In short order, I knew something about everything that happened in Bogotá. Even in Lima I had not been so well informed.

However, it was not only information that I desired. I was able to influence these people, and to have them influence others. With my many connections to important people, I may have been the most influential person in Colombia. I was able to keep Simón ever before his constituency as liberator, protector, and benefactor.

He did not realize all that I did for him, but there was never any question in my mind of my loyalty to him. In Bogotá, I had many occasions to take up with someone else, but I did not.

When everyone else, having had their fill of wine and conversation, made their way to home, a lone man might be left in my apartment. If he was not one of my old friends, he would make advances and then complain when I rebuffed him that my "charms" were irresistible.

I could not love another. I loved only one man, and I would visit him once or twice a week. Often, José Palacios came to me with Simón's old mastiffs in attendance. Sometimes, I would go of my own accord. Simón did not approve, but I went anyway.

These visits, however, did not always mean a night of passion—for which I seemed to be quite hungry in those days. Bolívar's age, infirmity, or the pressures of the times would keep him from accomplishing all he wished that day. Often, he would be depressed and need care or spiritual sustenance from me more than carnal pleasure. Actually, it seemed that he called for me most often when he had not accomplished all he wished, as though I might be able to give him back the sense of energy, vitality, and accomplishment that had eluded him that day. On such occasions, I would often read to him or merely discuss his troubles, and then we would fall asleep, close and secure and at peace in our own little world.

Thus did I begin my stay in the apartment above the Plazuela, and in the first weeks of August, I felt busy and happy. That is until I learned enough information about the Santanderists that there was no longer any doubt. There was a conspiracy brewing, deadly and determined, to assassinate Simón Bolívar, "the tyrant."

I tried to warn him, but Simón did not believe he was in any real danger. Thus, he did not listen to my urgings to investigate Santander. I begged him not to leave the palace without an escort. He would not agree. I asked his officers to sue for authority to find and imprison the conspirators. They did, but he would not let them. "There has been too much dictatorship. My problem is to end it, not make it endless," he would fume at me and his other advisors. The most he would agree to do was to alert the palace guard and to encourage us to report any new information to him.

By this time, I was in the habit of making my way to the palace at any time of the day or night with this or that bit of information. Unfortunately, nothing was definitive enough for him to take the plot seriously. Sometimes I would stay and sleep with him; sometimes I would go back home. One time, he said, "It is unseemly for you come and go here. The Quinta is my home, but this is a government building."

"Do you want me to just wait around for you to call for me?" I asked.

He gave me a look like he wanted to say "yes" but thought better of it. At any rate, I did not alter my habits. I continued to try to ferret out the names of the conspirators and some solid evidence. Though I found very little, I took any new information to him immediately.

I learned a little more each day, but the conspiracy was not yet fully formed. Everything pointed to the conspirators striking in the next few months, but that is nearly all I really knew. Santander was at the center of all indications, and in my mind he was the conspiracy..

One day, I found out a bit of news that I thought proved Santander's implication in the plot. I went to the palace and found Simón in his office. He was writing something, and I saw that I was interrupting his thoughts, but I told him the information I had just heard.

He looked at me impassively.

"Don't you see?" I said, trying to rouse him to action. "Santander must be implicated in the conspiracy."

"Perhaps he is. It doesn't matter. He will have left for his post in the United States, and it won't matter."

"You should arrest him."

"On what charge?"

"Sedition. Suspicion of treason. Anything."

"I will not. There is no evidence, and it would only make matters worse."

"Simón, you are letting your murderer walk about free. He was ordered to leave months ago and he is still here. You have the power. Do something."

"You do not understand what it means to live in a republic. We must have laws, fairness, due process—"

"Oh, Simón, what difference will all that make if you are dead."

He scoffed and looked at me as though I were a child. He was right. I did not understand the intricacies of governing as he did. I only saw danger and worried about it, and tried to stop the oncoming disaster. I had tried that afternoon, but all he did was decree that Santander must assume his duties as United States ambassador. "General Santander will leave the country by September 5."

I breathed a little easier for a few days until I learned that this had only hurried the conspirators' plans. I soon found out that they were now planning to strike at the masked ball, toward the end of August.

I reported this to Bolívar, but this was during a period when he was feeling energetic and in control. I barged into a meeting wherein some local judges were briefing him on the trial of Padilla, who was still in the Bogotá prison. "Not enough energy is being exerted to keep him silenced, your Excellency," one was saying as I entered. I felt the man spoke truly. Every few days we heard another anti-Bolívar pronouncement of the traitorous Admiral.

I realized I had interrupted something when I entered the room. I excused myself and waited outside. Simón came out a moment later. He was angry. In the hallway, he said, "Manuela, this is too much. You cannot—"

"Yes, Simón, I am sorry, but I just found out the conspirators are going to strike during the masked ball. You must not attend."

"How can they be so bold as to strike at a ball. Manuela, every day you bring me another report, but it does not all hang together. Now you barge into meetings to report something your slaves received from a servant of the gardener of someone who is married to the sister of the owner of the local *botica*."

His sarcasm did not hurt as badly as the look on his face. I knew he was a stubborn man—how can someone who has won as many military victories as he be otherwise—but his lack of faith in me was too much. "Damn it, Simón. I wouldn't be here if I wasn't sure. Yes, my intuition plays a part in what I say, but has my intuition ever been wrong? I warned you about Santander in Perú. I was right then, and I'm right now."

"That's enough, Manuela!" His face softened and he said, "I love you, but I cannot take these stories too seriously. If you find some solid evidence that does not rely on your admittedly accurate intuition, let me know. Otherwise, make an appointment." He turned and went back into his meeting.

I was miffed and stayed away from him. As the ball drew nearer, I knew he had not taken any precautions and was still planning to make an appearance. He felt he had to, for political reasons, but I wrote him two letters to warn him of the ball. I even went to him late at night once without his calling for me and begged him not to attend.

However, the more I spoke about it, the more he rejected the idea—and my presence. In the meantime, despite my anger at him, I was feeling terrified about the prospect that he might die soon at the hands of assassins.

On the night of the ball, it was cold and windy. It had been overcast all day, promising to rain. Wearing my colonel's uniform, I walked down to the Coliseo Teatro, across from the Palace of San Carlos. Jonotás accompanied me and wore a domino, in enjoyment of the festive atmosphere, even though she would not be going inside. I was too worried about Simón to partake in the festivities. I only went to try to protect him.

Jonotás waited outside, while I went through the dark foyer and glanced into the auditorium. Since the floor was to be used for dancing, it was empty. The chairs usually brought by those attending a performance were not in the room, except for a few lining the walls. It was early in the evening, but already there were couples doing a *contredanse*. Bolívar was not there, that I could see.

Instead of going in, I decided to walk up to one of the boxes, where I might have a better view. The foyer was still dark, lit only by lanterns from the street and the doors to the auditorium. I climbed the stairs at the side of foyer. When I was about halfway up, I overheard two men, in masks and costumes, talking as they came out from below the stairs.

One, who had a sun painted on his costume, said, "Within a half hour—death to the tyrant." He opened his doublet and let the other see a knife. It was so dark that at first I did not realize what it was. When I saw the blade catch the light from the street, a surge of fear ran through me.

"We will not fail. We are twelve," said the other, who wore only a courtier's costume and a domino. "Quiet now," he cautioned, and they walked away.

I let them get a few feet ahead of the stairs and then I followed, staying in the shadows so I would not be seen. When they turned and went boldly into the auditorium, I hurried after them. I still did not know for sure if Bolívar was in the theatre.

"Just a minute," a voice said as I stood peering at the dancers inside, who were doing the sinuous *cachucha* now. The voice belonged to the mayor, Don Ventura, a short round man with a large mustache. "You cannot go in," he said, in an official manner. He had been standing in the doorway, talking with some members of the group that now served as the "*cabildo*."

"What?" I said, distracted, while trying to look over the heads of those in front of me.

"You cannot go in there," he said, louder than before, as though he were making an official announcement to the town elders.

"Why not?" I turned to him, angry at his interference.

"Because of how you are dressed."

"What? I am Manuela Sáenz."

"I don't care who you are. You can't enter dressed in men's clothing." His rotund shape shifted so that he might face me directly.

"This is a costume ball," I said, incredulously.

"Nevertheless, it is an offense to public morals and I will not allow it."

"Listen, you damned hypocrite," knowing that he liked to visit prostitutes, "I am a Colonel in Bolívar's army, and I am here on official business." I pushed past him.

He reached out a sweaty hand and grabbed the sleeve of my jacket, causing me to turn back to face him. "As I have already said, I don't care who you are—"

"Stop that! You filthy whore monger," I shouted, pulling my arm loose. Then, over his shoulder, I saw Bolívar standing in the street, looking at Jonotás, who was performing some risqué mime for the Indians standing around outside. He was shaking his head and speaking to Fergusson and Córdoba. I could tell he was disgusted. Then he turned to come inside.

I started to push past the mayor, to warn Simón of the danger. Perhaps I could get Fergusson's help in arresting the conspirators in the auditorium. Señor Ventura, infuriated at my accurate insult, grabbed both of my arms and said, his mustache shaking sweat to and fro while he spoke, "You cannot speak to me that way." He grew purple. It appeared to be all he could do to keep from hitting me.

Violently, I shook my arms free and yelled, "Don't touch me again, damn you!" I was loud enough to stop the dancers close by and I caused everyone in the foyer to look at us.

Over the mayor's shoulder I saw Bolívar. He had just entered the foyer. He still had a look of disgust on his face from what he had seen outside. When he saw me making a disturbance, he threw up his hands and left. Outside, he stopped and spoke to Córdoba, pushed Jonotás out of his way, and walked off.

I rushed past the mayor and ran into the street. He was gone. "What happened?" I asked Jonotás.

"When he come out he said, 'This is really the slave of Manuela?' 'Yes, my General,' said one of his men. 'This is insufferable,' he said. I heard him and knew somethin' was wrong so I turned 'round just as he pushed me aside. I'm sorry, Manuelita."

"That's all right, Jonotás. Where did he go? Did you see?"

"No, just off that way. The one man, in the blue cape"—Córdoba—"ran after him and said, 'You are going, my General?' 'Yes,' he said and walked down there. He said, 'I go away very disgusted. Accompany me.' Señor Fergusson ran after them." She had pointed in a direction away from the palace. I assumed he wished to walk.

Jonotás and I followed, but we did not find him. After we had gone several blocks, we returned to the Plazuela. I was afraid that he might return to the ball. When we arrived, I saw Bolívar just heading into the Palace. At least he did not go to the theatre.

I called out to him. He turned and saw me. Then, he went inside the Palace. Fergusson looked sad and apologetic. Córdoba looked satisfied.

A light rain started to fall. Jonotás and I went home, very sad. When I arrived, Natán brought me some wine and I wrote Simón a letter:

Señor:

    I know you are vexed with me, but it was not my fault. With the pain of this displeasure upon me, I can scarcely sleep. However, this much remains certain. I will not come to you again, until you ask for me, or want to see me.

Manuela

I did not see Bolívar again for three weeks, and he made no attempt to communicate with me. Not even to meet his nephew who arrived a few days after the ball. Young Fernando was the son of his favorite sister, María Antonia, and Simón had been educating him in Philadelphia.

Fergusson introduced me to the young man outside the palace, and I liked him very much. He had the same slender appearance as Simón, and he bubbled over with youthful enthusiasm and pride in his famous uncle. "I am so happy to be here where important events are unfolding. I will make my mark and make my uncle proud of me," he told me that day.

He was already aware of the great esteem in which the world held Simón Bolívar. On a visit to the United States, the Marquis de La Fayette had made a special request to meet the nephew of the Liberator. Fernando had even been offered an appointment at West Point because of his relationship to Simón.

Now Bolívar had called him home. His arrival helped me feel better in one way. I could see that Simón wished to have blood relations around him so that he might feel more secure. At least his refusal to accept my advice did not mean that he did not entirely disbelieve my warnings. Fernando moved in with Lieutenant Ibarra, in the room down the hall from Bolívar.

Though he was a young man, the "green" young Fernando fit right in with the hardened veterans of the revolution. He took an instant liking to Fergusson, who joked with him about his youth and inexperience. I could tell that a deep and lasting friendship was being made.

Fernando also liked me. Like Fergusson and other members of the British Legion, I could speak English with him, which he knew almost better than Spanish. "Sure and he looks like an image of the general," Fergusson said to me. I laughed at how true it was, and Fernando grinned from ear to ear.

Those were happy days in Bogotá just after Fernando arrived. Fernando particularly was happy. He and Fergusson were always together and he loved the knavish Irishman. However, no matter how happy I was in those few days, I could not shake my unease. The reports of discord and treason I received, almost daily, from the streets of Bogotá weighed on me with impending doom. Something was about to happen.

If my worry over affairs in Colombia was not enough, we learned that Sucre had been deposed in Bolivia and was on his way to Quito. His wife, Mariana, fearing there would be trouble had returned to her home about the time I left there. The victor of Pichincha, wounded in the arm during the fray, was riding to meet her and to retire in the city of my birth.

The Bolivians had resented the fact that he was Venezuelan. This same resentment was part of the rancor that was directed toward Bolívar. It always amazed me. Brothers in the fight for liberty, having fought a common enemy, could become so nationalistic about their own small area of the continent that they would resent a great leader merely because he came from another small area of the continent. However, this irrational individualism is the nature of South America's people and is the same trait that would produce the *caudillos* (petty political bosses of districts and provinces).

About three weeks into September, I was beside myself with worry. I became more nervous with every passing day. Finally, I got wind that the conspirators had set a date. They would strike on October 28. Bolívar, Urdaneta, a few others, and I were all to be hit at once.

As far as I could tell, Santander was not directly involved with the men who had decided to strike; he only sat back and encouraged them. They were depending on him to pick up the government when it was broken with Bolívar's death, and to pull it together. The one thing they hoped to accomplish in the next month was to remedy one deficiency left in their plan. They had no important man in the army on their side. I wrote Bolívar all I knew, but he still refused to communicate with me. I could do little else.

Chapter 33

On September 25, it had rained quite heavily all day. Natán was feeling ill and so I decided that I would not entertain that evening. I stayed home all afternoon and nursed Natán, who was coughing and feverish. I did send Jonotás out to the homes or offices of people I expected that evening, to ask them to come the following night.

In the late afternoon, Jonotás returned with some news I found disturbing. She said that an officer named Captain Triana, drunk on *chicha*, had staggered into the barracks and talked sedition. He had actually drawn his sword and shouted, "The time has come to drown the tyranny of Bolívar in oceans of blood."

"Let me write to Simón," I said, as I looked for a pen.

"He knows, Manuelita," she said. "The man was jailed, and news was taken to the general."

Since Simón already knew about the incident, I decided to ignore the matter. It did bother me that someone should be so bold, even if he was as drunk as Jonotás had said.

Little did I know that the turncoats, which the conspirators had been looking for in the army, had already been found. One of these was a Major Pedro Carujo. Short, surly, red-haired, and Spanish born, he had at one time fought loyally for Spain. When the patriots were victorious, he suddenly became a loyal republican. I never liked him. When the news of Triana's drunken outburst reached Bolívar's staff, another traitor, Ramón Guerrera searched out Carujo and told him what happened. He did not realize that I, along with a few others, already knew a great deal about the conspiracy, so Carujo assumed that it was now exposed.

The bellicose little Carujo rashly called all of the conspirators together in the home of Luis Vargas Tejada, in the parish of Santa Barbara. Santander was not there, although messengers went back and forth all afternoon carrying reports to the vice president and returning with his advices.

Bolívar, even though he had Triana jailed, still assumed the threat to be small and considered the whole affair an opportunity to catch a few malcontent conspirators. He did not take any precautions whatsoever.

The thirty or so men on the other side of the city, plotting his death, decided to strike that night. There would be three groups. One, led by the traitor Carujo, would attack the palace and kill Bolívar. Guerrera would attack the Vargas battalion, from whom the only military resistance to them could come, and his men would also release Padilla. The third group would hold itself in reserve. By the time the sun had gone down, they had decided what they would do.

Later that evening, someone tapped at my door—someone I did not expect. When I heard the knock, I thought it was one of my usual visitors, even though it was quite late. I went to the door myself and opened it. It was José Palacios, and Simón's two enormous dogs. It had been a long time since Simón had sent for me in such a fashion. I read the message with interest: "I am suffering with a terrible headache. Please come to me now."

He made me angry. I hadn't heard from him in nearly a month, and here he was ordering me to come to him like one of his aides. I said, "Tell His Excellency that I am more ill than he is and that I should not come." I could not help slamming the door a little too hard when I closed it.

From my balcony, I watched Simón's faithful servant walk back through the puddles to the palace. Within minutes, José was back. "He says it is urgent, and won't you please come."

I put a pair of large double-soled rubber boots over my satin slippers and put a scarf around my neck. I was wearing a dress that evening. Together, Bolívar's retainer, his dogs, and his mistress, walked to the Palace of San Carlos. I walked between the guards at the outer door and climbed the stairs. When I entered his room, he was in a bath.

"I am very happy you have come," he said.

"No doubt," I said, "whenever you snap your fingers, some will of yours is carried out. That must make you very happy."

"Manuela, I am truly happy to see you."

I snorted in disgust.

Then he told me what he knew would catch my interest and why he had really sent for me. "There is to be a revolution."

"I know that. I am happy that you received notice of it in good time. Someone in your orbit must love you and be giving you good information."

He ignored my sarcasm. "I am speaking about something that happened today."

"Do you mean Captain Triana speaking treason in the barracks?"

He gave me a look of admiration. "Yes."

He stood and I handed him a blanket. Servants were called to remove the tub. He sat on the bed as I closed the door behind them.

He said, "There is no doubt about the conspiracy now. With it out in the open, they must strike soon."

"I know that already. You never believe my information, no matter how many times it has proven to be of value to you. You always receive my suggestions unfavorably."

"Something *may* happen tonight."

"Why? Why do you say that?"

"Too many suspicious men are not to be found."

A swift wave of fear went through me. "What have you done to prepare?"

I helped him dry off, while he explained that all he had done was to double the guard and put his most trusted officers on duty at the barracks.

"Is that all?" I threw up my hands, letting the blanket fall.

He picked it up and said, "What would you have me do?" He threw the blanket on the end of the bed and pulled a night shirt over his bony frame.

"Where is Santander?" I asked at last.

"At home."

I did not know what else to suggest. I knew if I gave my only other suggestion, arrest Santander, he would reject it.

While I formed a reply, he said, "I also have these." He smiled as he pointed to a sword and pistol sitting next to his watch on a table beside his bed.

I smiled, too, in spite of myself. He was beginning to convince me that I need not be so troubled.

"Don't worry, Manuelita. If anything happens, and I don't think it will, it will be a small unorganized effort. This will only serve to simplify the problem of arresting the traitors."

I was not so sure. "I don't know, Simón. But, perhaps you are right."

He climbed into bed and said, "I am tired. Please read to me."

I took off my rubber-soled boots, sat next to him on the bed, and opened his copy of *Don Quixote*.

Soon he was asleep. Before getting up to blow out the candle and get undressed I lay there holding him, thinking how much I loved this man—and how frightened I was of his death. It had been so, ever since the day of the earthquake in Quito back in 1822. I could hear his watch ticking quietly, steadily, next to the bed. I imagined that each tick moved us in the dark somehow, through time toward his demise.

My fear built as I lay there in the quiet. I told myself to be calm. I tried to convince myself that all would be well. *Simón knows about the conspiracy now. Everything will be fine.*

I lay there a long time and was about to drift into sleep, still wearing my clothes, when I thought I heard movement down in the street. At first I dismissed the noise, but my anxiety would not let me rest.

I stood up quietly, so as not to wake Simón, and went to the window. When I opened it I remembered a remark that Pepé Paris had made one day: "This window is too close to the ground. One man standing on another's shoulders could climb in before you know it."

Suddenly, everything, especially the window, seemed unsafe. I looked out. Nothing. Darkness. Quiet. The street was empty. I breathed more easily and started to close the window.

Then, I heard something again. Footsteps.

From the front of the palace I heard, "Who lives?"

I expected to hear the usual response, "The Liberator." Instead, someone shouted, "Liberty."

Fear went through me like lightning. I heard a scuffle. By the time I was back at the bed, I heard a thud at the main doors.

"Wake up. Wake up!" I said softly to Bolívar.

He awoke, heard the noise, the shouting back and forth, and the sounds of men slamming against the doors. Jumping out of bed, not yet fully aware, he looked around. He had presence of mind enough to grab his weapons.

The doors downstairs gave way with a splintering crash. It sounded like hundreds of men were pouring into the palace. I heard them search one room after another. Dogs barked, boots mounted the steps, and doors opened down the hall. We stood facing the door.

I laughed, in spite of the situation, to see Simón standing in his night shirt, rapier in hand. "Don Quixote in person. Put on some trousers," I said, taking his pistol so that I might watch the door.

He laughed, too, fully awake now. He pulled on his uniform, came back to me, took the pistol, and stood facing the door. "Bravo! I am dressed. What do we do now?" The shouts and door slamming were coming closer. Gunshots were fired. Terror raced through me. It seemed that one guard after another was cut down.

"Simón, you have to get out of here." I ran to the window.

From other parts of the palace, I heard, "Where is he?" "Where is the tyrant?" "Long live Liberty!" Closer they came. "Death to Bolívar!"

No one was in the street. I flung a cape over Simón's shoulders and brought him my double-soled rubber boots. "Here. Put these on," I said, taking his pistol.

"Why?" He began pulling on the boots.

"There's no one below. Escape. I'll delay them."

"I'm not going to leave you to them."

"They're not looking for me." I had never told him that many officers loyal to him, including me, had been marked for death.

He ran to the window and looked out.

"Jump!" I said. "Hurry!"

He put one foot out and then turned back around, embraced me, kissed me quickly, and said, "I love you, Manuela." Then he jumped to the street, pistol in hand, and ran toward the Quinta.

The men outside had reached his door. They tried the lock. They threw their shoulders against it. Its hinges tore at the door frame. I picked up the sword. Metal cut against metal. The wood splintered at the lock, and the door flew open. Carujo and several others crushed into the room.

"Where is Bolívar?"

"In the council room."

He stepped around the others, back outside the room, and looked over the railing into the foyer below. "Have you looked in the council room?" he called down. One of the men who was still in the room walked to the window and said, "Why is the window open? Has he escaped?"

"No, he is in the council room. I opened the window to see what the commotion was about."

Carujo had not overheard this and, from the railing, said, "Come on. Let us see. Bring her along."

Two men came at me. I put my sword out, but the man behind me at the window knocked it out of my hand. A searing pain went through my wrist. They seized me and dragged me down the steps. I yelled, in the direction of the council room, "Run, Simón, run!"

When we reached the foyer, I was horrified at the number of dead that lay about. Then I saw Lieutenant Ibarra. He lay in a pool of blood at the bottom of the stairs.

I broke free and ran to him. I kneeled down, lifted my skirts, and ripped my petticoat for bandages to stanch the blood gushing from his arm.

The two men who had hold of me followed. "Leave me alone. Let me help him," I shouted at them.

Carujo said, "Leave her. We'll check the council room." One man stayed to watch me while I tended to Ibarra's wound, a huge gash that ran the length of his arm. There was another in his side. He was still alive but unconscious.

José Palacios, sad and worried, knelt down to help me. In a whisper, I said, "He's gone to the Quinta. Go after him." The next thing I knew, Simón's faithful retainer was gone.

I watched as they checked the council room, the salon, the kitchen. Each moment they wasted made it more certain that Simón had made the hills and was out of danger. Their curses of frustration were intermingled with sounds from the barracks: shots, a cannon being fired, and the cries of soldiers in battle.

Carujo and the others came back to the stairs, they conferred, they searched the rooms again, they searched outside, becoming angrier every moment.

Ibarra woke up, his pale face the picture of death, and asked weakly, "Is the Liberator dead?"

"No, Ibarra, he is alive." I whispered, but too loudly. Carujo was in earshot. He came over, grabbed my hair, and dragged me to my feet.

"Where is he, you damned bitch? Where is he?" The rest of the men crowded around me, anger contorting their faces. "Where is he?" he said again and slapped me so hard I spun around and fell to my knees.

As I started to get up, one of the men hit my head from behind with the hilt of his sword, almost knocking me out. When I fell to the floor, another kicked me in the side. I rolled over holding my ribs. When I looked up, their knives were raised to strike. It was over.

"Go on, kill me, kill me, you miserable cowards," I screamed at them in fury.

A Frenchman who was in the group pushed them aside. He stood over me and said, "Stop! We are not here to murder women."

Carujo said, "This is no woman," and kicked my head so hard it blacked me out for a moment. I felt blood trickle into my hair. From a great distance I heard him say, "Put her in Bolívar's room. Search every room again and search outside."

I was still only half-conscious. I felt myself being carried upstairs and I regained my ability to think just as I was thrown onto Bolívar's bed. Groggily, I stood up and went to the door, its lock broken, but staying shut because the hinges were sprung and it was wedged against the jam. When I pulled it open, the guard shoved me back inside. "Stay in there," he snarled and pushed me back. I fell to the floor, and he closed the door.

Jumping up, I ran to the window just as Fergusson came running up. "Where is he, Lass. Is he dead?" His saber was drawn but he had no shirt on, only boots and trousers.

I did not want anyone to hear him, and I was afraid the man on the other side of the door would come in and he would be discovered. I put a finger to my lips to caution silence. Just then, blood from my forehead drained into my right eye. I wiped it away as I heard a commotion in the front of the building. Fergusson noticed the blood and said, "Stay there, Lass," and ran toward the front door.

I called after him. "Don't come in. They will kill you," but he ran out of sight. A moment later I heard the loud report of a pistol.

While all this was happening, the conspirators had succeeded in freeing Padilla and had attacked the barracks where the Vargas battalion was billeted. Colonel Charles Whittle, despite rifle fire and artillery at close range, kept his men calm and was able to decimate the attackers with sniper fire. It was largely due to him that the conspiracy failed.

Barely ten minutes had passed when I heard the men leaving the palace. I opened the door cautiously, and when I saw I was no longer being watched, I ran downstairs. Ibarra was on his feet, still ashen and wobbly. Other members of the palace household were coming out of hiding, and through the door I saw Bolívar's officers running across the square toward us.

I went to the door. Jonotás and Natán ran up just then, saying, "Manuelita. Manuelita. Are you all right? Oh, my God, you're bleeding." I looked down and saw my chest and the entire front of my dress were drenched in Ibarra's blood. The cuts on my forehead, my lip, and my hand were flowing freely and adding to the impression that I might be mortally wounded.

Then to my left I saw a horrible sight. Fernando Bolívar was on his knees holding Fergusson's body, shaking and sobbing hysterically, covered in blood. Where the Irishman's smile should have been, there was but a mass of gore. The head was gone. I turned away in horror.

Doctor Moore came up to me just then, saying, "Sit down. Come. You're bleeding." He took me inside and led me to the stairs to sit down. Jonotás and Natán helped carry Fergusson's body inside. I started shaking a little. Ibarra came over and sank to his knees. I said, "See to Ibarra, Doctor. He is bad."

Bolívar's officers began asking, "Where is the general?"

"He has escaped. He ran toward the river."

Exclamations of relief from everyone. All but a few went to look for him.

Poor Simón. The thought of him that night still fills me with sadness. José Palacios had found him before he reached the river. They were about to cross the bridge when they heard the artillery from the melee at the Vargas battalion. They ran under the bridge and stood, knee deep, in the smelly swamp that carries the sewage of Bogotá down the mountain. They stood there for almost two hours, wondering what had happened, who had won, and were the calls they heard saying "General, where are you?" friend or foe.

The men who had gone to look for him came back alone. They questioned me and took off again. In the meantime, the little plaza was filling up with manacled, dispirited suspects who had been hunted down by the army. I was happy to walk out among them to identify some of the traitors. But I was sick with worry, wondering what happened to Simón.

Meanwhile, Bolívar came out of hiding when he heard his men ride by a second time shouting "Long live the Liberator."

"How is Manuela?" he asked.

"She is alive."

They had his horse, and he rode immediately to the barracks. After inspecting the damage, he changed into a clean uniform. Then, he rode back to the square.

The most wonderful music I ever heard was the cheer raised by the faithful when Simón rode into the square. He waved at them. He smiled. He put on a show of victory, but in his eyes I saw something I had never seen before: defeat.

He had shivered, while standing in a cesspool, to avoid assassin's knives—hunted, hated, and watching his dreams of a unified continent seep into the muck in which he stood. It must have broken his heart to think that the blade that might have found his heart that night would have been wielded by a man he had set free.

He quieted the crowd with a motion of his hand. Then, with his voice sounding more hollow than I ever heard it, he said, "Citizens of the Republic, I thank you for your loyalty. I commend your bravery. And I praise the spirit of liberty you carry in your breast which has saved us from this dreadful night of anarchy."

One by one his Generals rode up and saluted him. When they were almost passed, he noticed me standing by the door.

"Manuela," he cried over the cheering and noise as the last officer passed. He dismounted and walked toward me. The crowd, carrying candles and lanterns, parted to let him through. Before he took two steps, the snake, Santander stepped out, extended his hand and said, "Congratulations, General."

Bolívar stopped, for only a brief moment. As it grew quiet he said, "You have no right to even be in my presence," and walked on.

¡Viva El Libertador! ¡Viva El Libertador!

He walked right up to me and took me in his arms, saying "Manuela, oh, my Manuela." He held me a long time while the crowed cheered, "Long live the Liberator."

Turning to the throng, still holding my waist, he shouted, "Long live the Liberatress of the Liberator." Then he looked into my eyes.

I could not cry; I had to hold on. I saw the strain the night had put on Simón. I led him inside as the crowd cheered, and took him back to his room.

He had to know all. He made me tell him everything, though he said many times, "I don't want to hear any more." Then, he would ask me more questions. The sun had already risen far over a new day before we fell asleep. We had won. For that we were glad.

However, the country staggered under the blow. In the next few days, we were to see how to kill a country. Bolívar *was* Gran Colombia, and if he had died, so would the country have died that night. From then on, the country's health exactly matched Simón's.

One other effect of the night of September 25 was entirely personal. It is nothing I would have asked for, but it made me feel that my efforts to save Bolívar and what I had endured to do so were understood and admired. From the night of September 25, 1828, until this day, I have been called "La Libertadora."

Chapter 34

Simón insisted on taking personal depositions from every conspirator. For two days he listened to them, and each day he came home sicker and sicker.

He moved back to the villa, and his cough had returned. More and more he could be seen with specks of blood on his lips or with a linen handkerchief stained with red.

Though I liked him, old Doctor More seemed more ineffectual every day. I called a new doctor, who had just arrived from Scotland, to attend him. Doctor Cheyne was young and vigorous, and his advices were much more practical. His treatment seemed to alleviate some of Bolívar's suffering. Yet, he could not seem to heal a broken heart. The vigorous soldier, known as the Liberator, seemed more distant and sad each day.

At first, Simón thought the conspiracy had been only a few foolish men who were being used by the Santanderists to gain political control of the country. When he saw how pervasive was the sentiment against him; when he took depositions from university professors, young men brought up in good families, businessmen, and even a member of his own staff, he was struck a blow more deadly than the knives that might have pierced his heart that night.

"I have been wrong. I must have been wrong. It is not Santander and a few malcontents. It is the people themselves who hate me."

I tried to get him to see that it did not matter who hated or loved him: he must stick to his vision.

"But they think I'm a tyrant, merely because I wish us to be unified. They think I want power."

"I know, Simón."

"If we choose unity now, we will have a longer and more glorious future," he said, as though *I* needed to be convinced.

To his mind, someone, somewhere needed to be convinced that he had given everything to the people. Yet, he did not see that with all he gave, he gave everyone a way to kill him. All they had to do was not love him. He was collapsing before my eyes.

"It is the people themselves who have planned my death," he announced on the third day, "thus I will proclaim a general amnesty."

"Simón, you can't be serious. That would be like legitimizing the insurrection."

He wasn't listening. "Then I will resign my offices and go into exile."

"No! You cannot do this."

He began coughing and I helped him into bed. As soon as I had a moment, I sent Jonotás to find General Urdaneta. This was a man whom everyone respected. Simón respected him enough that he, in fact, was the leader of Gran Colombia during this period. Bolívar delegated all of his duties to him.

When the refined and handsome general arrived, I told him what Bolívar had said. Then I went to Bolívar and told him that Urdaneta wished to see him.

Simón said, "Very well, I will come right out."

I went back to talk to Urdaneta, assuming that Bolívar wished to get dressed. But Simon arrived immediately, and I saw him as his visitor must have seen him, old and infirm. He had not dressed but wore only his night shirt. His hair was tousled and he coughed as he shuffled into the salon, thin blue legs sticking out from beneath his shirt.

"My General, Manuela has told me what you are planning to do. You cannot do it."

"Oh, Rafael, I am too weak to continue anyway."

"But, my General, you must not. If we do not deal strongly with this conspiracy now, it will mean the death of the Republic. You cannot resign."

Simón looked at him. Then he said, "It is what the people want."

"This is not true!" Urdaneta stood and approached him. "If you leave, you will say to Santander, 'Your calumny and malice are worthy of reward.' You will say to your soldiers, those who are loyal to you, those who have fought and will continue to fight to the death for you, 'You are not worthy of my constancy.' And you will abandon the people of this republic—whom you love—to chaos. It will be generations before there is peace again."

Simón began coughing. When his fit had died down, he said, "Rafael, I understand and respect you, but I cannot, in good conscience, continue. Right now, I can talk no more. Please excuse me." He walked back to bed.

I accompanied him and would have spoken to him myself, but at the moment I did not know what to say. Urdaneta had said, most eloquently, all that was true. Simón was coughing so hard, anyway, by the time we reached his room, that I did not even try.

The next morning, he was troubled by Urdaneta's pleading, wondering what to do. All of his officers and advisors arrived. All made pleas. He appeared to consider what they said, but again excused himself and went back to bed.

By the time everyone had gone, I was angry. I knew what he was considering was wrong. It would mean the end of everything, absolutely. After only a few minutes, letting my thoughts churn inside, I stormed into his room. He was at the wash basin, putting some water on his hair to comb it.

"Simón. I love you. You know I love you. But you are wrong, and I will not let you betray me, your men, or the people of this Republic."

He looked at me, and he seemed very tired. "Manuela, please—"

"You cannot do this. You cannot abandon your men, or the people who love you."

"Who loves me?" he shouted. "What people?"

"Many more than you think, that is clear. If it were not for those who maliciously confuse them and turn them away from knowing and understanding you—"

"Santander cannot have this much influence; it must be me."

"Of course, he can. When you stay away for years at a time. When your visions see farther than the people understand. And when he uses every opportunity to sway the people with his pronouncements, without your presence—"

"But they believed him."

"That does not matter. If I tell you a lie, and you believe me, does that make me any less despicable? You knew about him. You were the first to tell *me* about him."

"He is a hero of the Republic. We fought together—"

"Damn him. Damn him to hell," I shouted. I took a second to calm down a little, and then said, "He is evil. Everyone— I mean everyone but you, it seems—knows the depth of his ambition. Why are you not willing to see it as it is?"

"I see it," he said wearily. He walked to a chair and sat down.

"I told you years ago that he was a problem. I told you, when he had the Enabling Act rescinded that he should be shot as a traitor. Now you see what he has brought the country to. If you back out now, you are compounding your own sin of not dealing with him earlier."

"How can I, after having been wrong—"

"You will only have been wrong if you fail. You must deal with him. Do you think, just because this attempt on your life did not meet with success, that there will not be more attacks on you?"

"Then I will go into exile."

I had been pacing up and down, as though caught up in an intricate dance. I went to him. I kneeled in front of him and grabbed his sleeves so hard I felt my nails dig into my palms through the cloth. "Exile? Simón, you know that will not protect you."

He looked at me a long time. At last he said, "What's to be done then?"

I stood up. "When things come this far, the conspirators have to die. Better that ten should die, that millions be saved."

He lifted his eyes to me and said, "Did you not tell me about the Spanish, in Quito in 1810, doing the very same thing? Have you not resented them your whole life, and have not the scenes you witnessed then fired your revolutionary spirit all these years?"

I kneeled again, to look him more directly in the eyes. "Yes, Simón. You are right. But there is a difference." He waited for me to go on. "In 1810, it had been three hundred years of abuses by the monarchy. The 'conspirators' in 1810 did not attempt assassination of the only man who could save the country from anarchy; they merely made the Count Ruíz stay at home. Montúfar, when he rode into Quito as victor, had received orders from the then governing body of Spain itself. Later, when he received orders to lay down his arms, he acted like a gentleman and did so. The *godos* walked in, tortured him, and beheaded him."

He sighed and looked off into space.

"You, obviously, will do all you can to be fair, but you will have to punish the conspirators—for attempted assassination, not to move forward your political ends. Then you will bring forth a strong and prosperous republic, not merely exploit the one that already exists. There is a great difference. You must see that. And you must do it."

"Perhaps you are right, Manuela." He sat there a long time and then went to his desk and wrote a decree. General Urdaneta was to assemble four officers and four judges. They were to hear the case of every conspirator they could find. They were to take any further depositions and try any other men who were found in the course of the trials. There was to be no appeal from the judgments given, except to Bolívar himself.

On September 30, Santander was arrested.

On October 2, the first executions began. They were to be public. By eleven o'clock the square was filled with the citizens of Gran Colombia, to witness justice.

The first men to be executed were two of the worst traitors. One was Guerrera, the officer in Bolívar's staff who had sparked off the night of September 25th by warning Carujo. The second was Padilla, who had been the leader of the revolt in Cartagena.

They were marched to the gallows and, after they ascended the steps, General Urdaneta stripped the medals off Guerrera's uniform. The man stood, head hung, until it was over.

Not so Padilla. This strong, stocky, dark-skinned, officer began to wrestle with his bonds, causing soldiers to have to come up and restrain him. He shouted, "These medals were given to me by the Republic, not by Bolívar."

He continued to shout until a hood was slipped over his head. Likewise, Guerrera was hooded. The condemned were then shoved onto the execution stools. A noose was tightened around each man's neck and the stools were kicked out from under their feet.

Guerrera died instantly. The drop was not long enough to kill the huge Padilla, however. He began to squirm and his hands pulled free from their bonds. He fought with the rope at his neck. Urdaneta could see a certain amount of admiration in the eyes of the crowd. He wanted no heroics here and he ordered several soldiers to fire at him. Padilla's body was filled with bullets and he stopped his dance in the air.

Carujo, the man who kicked me and left a wound on my forehead that had still not healed, should have been there that day. However, he made a deal with his executioners. He was allowed perpetual exile, instead of dancing on the gallows, if he would give evidence against Santander. He did so. However, in his desire to save himself from hanging, he became quite creative with his testimony. Some of what he told the council about Santander was not true, as if Santander were not guilty enough. Because he did this, he changed history.

The council's case against Santander was weak. True, he had known about the conspiracy, and they had found him treasonably remiss in his duties to report it, but other elements of the evidence against him were strained. In the meantime, foreign emissaries had arrived in Bogotá from the United States and other neighboring nations. They were avidly interested in what would happen to a co-founder of the Republic. Then, Carujo's lies were discovered. The council advised leniency.

When I heard this, I was outraged. "Santander should die," I told them. For three days I argued the case that he should not be let off. "It was failure to be resolute in dealing with him, to begin with. This inflamed the country and brought us to this state of affairs. It matters not that he has hid his crimes so well. He is guilty of treason already, and we all know he is guilty of far more."

Santander languished in jail the whole time, knowing that his fate might very well lie in my persuasiveness. At last the council listened to me and recommended death. But my efforts had been in vain. By that time, Bolívar had heard about Carujo's lies, and he commuted the sentence to exile.

I longed to plead with him to commute it back, but I knew he would not do it. Besides, although I did not think justice was being served by letting Santander and Carujo escape execution, I took comfort in knowing that they both would be removed from the country forever. They made the trip to Cartagena and were imprisoned in the dungeon there until passage could be booked to Cuba or another of the Caribbean islands. Santander, at last, was as I longed to see him: without power.

Chapter 35

By the end of October, the gibbet had been taken down. The conspirators were all dead, or awaiting exile. The seditious who had not partaken in the conspiracy, such as Vicente Azuero, were also in jail. The country looked brighter to me for having had so much evil removed, and Bolívar's health had returned, thanks to the care of Doctor Cheyne.

I now lived with Simón as his wife. There was no pretense whatsoever as to the nature of our relationship. Despite Simón's fears, most of Bogotá loved Simón. They believed that I had saved his life and honored me. The people of Bogotá no longer called me a "foreigner" but greeted me with respect. "Good morning, Señora Sáenz." Or, "A pleasant day, Liberatress."

I had hope for the future. However, on Bolívar's Saint's day, October 28, there was a ball in honor of The Liberator. I was on his arm as we entered the theatre. Many visitors from Europe and the rest of the Americas were in the hall that night.

We stayed only long enough for Bolívar to satisfy the "obligations" of one in his position, and we left. I wish I had stayed, because later that night a fight broke out between one of the foreign emissaries and an army officer. It was said to have been sparked off by a comment made by the foreigner about me, and it ended in a duel the next morning. The foreigner was killed, and the officer was hunted down by the military police.

That event opened my eyes and was a signal of things to come. We had eliminated the conspirators, but the seeds of chaos they had planted were growing. My hope for the future had been an illusion.

I began to gather information again. Soon it was clear that Santander had completely infected the country with disunity. The illness had permeated to the core. The attempt on Simón's life had brought deeper consequences. It had, in short, devastated his vitality and his control of the country.

There had only been a few days of peace between the last conspirator's death on the gallows and the night of the ball. From that night on, Colombia withered in agony.

It was only a matter of days before we heard word from Venezuela. The illiterate Páez, who only weeks before had publicly proclaimed his never ending loyalty to Bolívar, once again threatened secession from Gran Colombia.

He had ruled Venezuela for Bolívar for years, but he had always been jealous of the Liberator's power. Often there were reports that he was threatening secession, but whenever Bolívar arrived, the Venezuelan leader always took on a puppy-like submission in his presence. He had been the reason that Simón had left Perú. If only Simón had punished him, or removed him from power when he arrived in Venezuela in 1827. Instead he forgave him. Thus, Páez (unable to learn a lesson about friendship or power) threatened the unity of Colombia again.

At the same time we were receiving reports from Venezuela, we received reports from Quito that General Flores was also in favor of separating the southern realm from Colombia. The country was breaking up.

My brother wrote to me:

> There are many here who agree with Flores. I have spoken loudly,
> and at length, in favor of Bolívar and unity. I do not believe we should
> separate from Colombia after all we have fought for. I am convinced
> that if Flores were not my friend I would be struck down by his faction.
> I believe it is only our friendship that keeps him from doing something
> rash.

Then, as if the internal pressures the country was feeling were not enough, Perú invaded the South to reclaim Guayaquil. Simón was infuriated, and so was I. On January 1, 1829, Simón took to horse, to ride south and fight once more. He sent letters ahead to Sucre, to form troops together, and then he followed.

I argued with Bolívar not to go. "You are too ill," I told him, but he insisted.

"I have to go. If Perú wins, the entire continent will fall into anarchy." Perhaps he was right. It always seemed to require him being there in order for his will to manifest. Still, I felt so sorry for him as I saw him ride off, old and in pain, to fight for the Republic once more.

I moved back to my apartment, where I could watch the city in his absence. It seemed that I almost ruled Bogotá now, while Bolívar was gone.

Though Simón had made it clear, and I had agreed, that I would stay out of governmental affairs while he was gone, Urdaneta, who was most able and needed no help from me, occasionally asked me what Bolívar would want in a given situation. There were some other members of government with whom I would have long discussions as well. People fought to be invited to my nightly *tertulias*, and Bolívar's officers listened when I spoke my opinion. When I put on my hussar's uniform and rode with my two companions through the city, there were waves and smiles of admiration from many people, which would never have happened only a few months before.

Though I had many visitors at my apartment, Doctor Cheyne came to see me every day. It was clear that he was infatuated with me, and it was all he could do to keep from making some romantic advance. Some of Bolívar's friends thought it was improper how much time the attractive young doctor spent with me. His visits fired gossip about me among my enemies. However, I spent no more time with Doctor Cheyne in that period than I did with any number of other important members of Bogotá's intellectual circle. For example, Lolo Boussingault, one of the French scientists invited to Colombia to survey the country's natural resources was also often at my apartment.

During the first part of 1829, I was able to keep Bolívar and his aims and ideals in front of those who mattered, in my nightly *tertulias*. I also kept Simón's papers and correspondence carefully organized. I was happy for a while, considering that Simón was far away in my own country fighting the Peruvians. He and I exchanged letters almost daily—long letters full of love, passion, and longing. He also wrote about the war.

My days were busy as I kept an eye on the capital for Simón, and my nights were enjoyable as I gave the latest news of Simón's activities to his friends before we drank wine or danced. Sometimes, Jonotás would give a performance. However, no matter how well things seemed to be going, I was never left completely alone by those who hated me.

I kept my intelligence network alive; and it was clear that the Santanderists were silenced, but not defeated. More upsetting than the activities of Santander's supporters was evidence that there was also some dissension among Bolívar's own officers. I tried to learn more, but my efforts were obscured by news from the South.

The Peruvians had made their way to the highlands south of Quito. Sucre, leader of the Colombian forces, was to meet the Peruvians, led by La Mar, at Tarqui. It was sad that these two, who had fought side by side defeating the last of the Spaniards at Ayacucho, should be in deadly conflict against each other.

In late March, we heard that the battle was decisive for the Colombians, thanks to new rifles with sighting devices on them. Until that time, bullets went where they may. Now, each shot could be deadly. These rifles helped the Colombian forces, but I was acutely aware that such an invention made war much more deadly.

I was filled with hope and anticipation by the thought that Simón would soon return. I wish he had come back then, but he spent the next 10 months in the southern provinces repairing the damage done by the war. We wrote constantly, and I urged him to come home, but to no avail. I knew he was not heeding his health and I worried about him. I now wish I had made greater efforts to make him return. Perhaps if he had returned immediately, some of the ensuing events might have turned out differently, or not have happened at all.

Chapter 36

Soon after we heard the news about the battle of Tarqui, a representative arrived from the United States. His name was William Henry Harrison and he was an opinionated old soldier with a long face who did not understand the slightest thing about the country he was visiting. He insisted on wearing clothes suitable for the climate from which he had come, stating, "They were good enough for me back home." Consequently, on his trip up from the coast—exhausting under the best of conditions—he caught an infection in his lungs. I understand that it bothered him for as long as he lived. A dozen or so years later he was elected president of the United States and, still suffering from the infection, he died within the month.

At a banquet, on the anniversary of the Battle of Boyacá, he said something rash. A gentleman made a toast to the two American liberators: Bolívar and Washington. Harrison, feeling the wine a little too much, angrily stood and avowed, "Washington dead is worth more than Bolívar alive." This infuriated me, and I kept a close watch on him after that.

By observing him and the members of his party, I learned something important about the United States. He was not alone among his countrymen in his animosity towards the Liberator. They all saw the dictatorial powers that he was obliged to exercise as threats to their ideal of liberty as practiced in North America.

They could not see that this country was different. This country, divided so roughly by the land itself, gave an automatic individualism to all who lived on its ragged mountains and vast plains. Without the monarchy of Spain, leading and directing trade, only anarchy of the most brutal kind could reign in such a land: unless a strong leader can show the way until there is educational and economic parity among the many states and departments. That is why Bolívar pressed so hard for unity at all costs. In the meantime, I could see that the international winds were not blowing in his favor.

Whatever his mistakes, real or imagined, the Liberator was seen as an impediment to liberty by anyone who did not have the insight to understand what Bolívar was trying to do. "He has too much power!" was the phrase on everyone's lips. Never did the speaker actually discuss the tangible uses Bolívar made of the power he had and how beneficial his actions had always been for the country. Nor did they seem to remember that a new Congress was scheduled. When Bolívar returned, they would decide who was to rule and under what form—the people would decide, not Bolívar. However, while Bolívar was absent, the Santanderists were able to spread the idea that the country was oppressed.

Ironically, Bolívar's own officers saw in that same power the seeds of eventual disaster from a different direction. "If Bolívar—close to death so recently—were to die, anarchy will follow as surely as the seasons follow each other," one brash young officer bellowed at one of my nightly parties. Anarchy is what Bolívar's officers feared most. "If real anarchy begins," said another, "the republic would fall into a hundred pieces."

Thus, when a French delegation arrived and spoke of possibly returning the country to a rule by monarchy, they listened. When it was proposed that Bolívar be monarch for life and then have the crown passed to Louis Philippe, Duc d'Orléans, some of Bolívar's supporter's seriously entertained the idea. "Who else can hold the country together when Bolívar is gone?" they asked.

Urdaneta, who held authority while Simón was absent, did nothing to inhibit such talk. He was actually heard to say, "If Gran Colombia cannot survive under the present republican form, then it should have its permanence under the aegis of monarchy."

I was upset by this, as I knew Bolívar would never agree, but it was too late. The months wore on, and still Bolívar stayed busy in the South: establishing townships, building roads, and wringing the chaos out of my country that had seeped in during the Peruvian war.

He kept in touch with me, and I know he often wrote to Urdaneta and Pepé Paris about my welfare. I continued to invite all of his officers to my place—except Córdoba, who could find no way for peace with me, nor I with him—and I kept them all informed of Bolívar's plans. I tried to quell their talk of monarchy and to keep Bolívar's ideals of a republic alive. Without his presence in the capital I could feel the country's disintegration as though it were a sharp wind cutting through my clothes.

I now regret not having kept a better eye on Córdoba. I did not interpret his activities correctly, because of my antipathy for him. I should have been more careful, because his great popularity—almost matching the Liberator himself—made this hero of the revolution able to exact strict obedience from those in his command. I never considered what would happen if he decided to use that power.

Often in my *tertulias*, I heard that his fiancée was ambitious. Both she and her father urged him to take more power. "Poor Córdoba," one of the British officers would say as he filled his glass, "all he knows is war, and that woman is urging him to run for office." Everyone in the room would laugh. "The man has no head for politics, or even for people."

It was true. Córdoba had never been appointed to any government post because he was so bellicose. He could only be a warrior and did not have the slightest idea of political necessities. We found the idea of him in office amusing, but we should have seen how dangerous Córdoba would be when filled with desire for power, urged on by Fanny Henderson.

We knew that it was her idea, not his, that he be opposed to the idea of monarchy. All the British were against monarchy, since it appeared to mean an alliance with France. But there was something else, much more dangerous, going on in his mind. Fanny and Consul Henderson had made him come to believe that he should be the one to put a stop to talk of monarchy. He should be the one to take over the country.

By the end of July, it became clear that Córdoba's ambition got the better of his simplistic reason. His men were ready for revolt, as he had made them, and he let the fact be known. He all but threatened it. Urdaneta tried to bring Córdoba into the cabinet, to appease him, but too little was being offered, and too late. Córdoba refused.

What followed happened quickly. His men took over the barracks in Medallín. General O'Leary, knowing he had to quell the rebellion quickly, marched immediately. A month or so later, the fighting was over; and my old enemy, Córdoba, was killed in the battle.

General Harrison from the United States along with Córdoba's intended father-in-law, British Consul Henderson, were found to be instigators in Córdoba's hunger for power and his revolt. They were asked to leave the country. Harrison defied the order, saying, "I will leave my post, only by force." Eventually, their governments recalled them, but Simón felt that his ministers had mismanaged the affair, and insulted important foreign powers whose friendship was needed.

Simón, on his way back to Bogotá, had heard the reports and was most unhappy about events that had transpired in his absence. Urdaneta told me, "The Liberator will be making changes when he returns."

"What do you mean, Rafael?"

He pulled a letter out his jacket and handed it to me. The tone of the letter was quite angry. Urdaneta was correct. If his mood did not change by the time he arrived, heads would roll.

I was glad he was returning. I missed him, and it was becoming more difficult to keep the political wind blowing in the proper direction. Córdoba's death had shaken the Republic. Even though he was a traitor and would have been executed anyway, the country took the death of their hero hard. Before O'Leary's men had sheathed their swords, broadsides were on the walls of the city saying, "Down with Bolívar Down with the Tyrant!"

Chapter 37

Simón rode into the capital on January 15, 1830. He was greeted by cheers as he rode through the streets, and I watched him from my balcony. There were no wreaths for me to throw at his feet that day, and the cheers were distant and false, prompted more by Urdaneta's urging than love for the Liberator. Unlike his entrance into Quito, the day that I met him back in 1822—had it been only 8 years before?—his entrance into Bogotá was more chilling than glorious. He looked old, tired, and ill. Before he had crossed the square, tears obliterated my vision.

I went inside, sat down, and sobbed. Jonotás knelt down in front of me. "Manuelita, what's the matter?" She stroked my cheek with her long fingers.

"I have let 8 years go by. Every day I have yearned for time to be with him, to love him, and to be loved by him. It is all gone."

"Manuelita, he is here now." Her voice was full of sympathy and encouragement, but I derived neither.

"Yes, but how soon before he rides off again?" I raised my voice, a deep anger overtaking me, "When will the endless conflict finally end? I want peace."

She looked at me sadly and shook her head.

I knew he would be upset about the events that had transpired in Colombia since his departure and that he would be busy at the palace all day handling these affairs. I went to the villa and waited until he came home.

In the early evening, he arrived, coughing and feverish. He looked even worse up close. He was thinner than when he left and his lips had a blue cast to them. "Oh, Manuela, here you are. You are the one vision today that uplifts me." He reached out to embrace me but started coughing.

I took his arm and walked him to his room. "Oh, Simón, why, oh why, do you not take care of yourself?"

"They have killed me. Their knives have found my heart." He sat down on the bed and looked at the floor.

I was worried. "What is the matter, Simón?"

Just then, I heard a commotion outside. I went out to find General Urdaneta dismounting. "Don't come in now. He is very tired."

"But, Manuela, the entire government has resigned today—together—at once."

"What?"

"The Liberator was so infuriated, and berated them so badly, that they left the council room in a group." Urdaneta told me the details about the afternoon. He told of how Simón had upbraided his ministers for not handling Córdoba better, for bungling the political climate, for even allowing the idea of monarchy to enter into political discussions when they should have known that he would be violently opposed to it. By the end of the afternoon, they had resigned. Urdaneta then asked again to see Bolívar, because he wanted to plan a reconciliation. I persuaded him to wait until morning.

I walked back to Simón and saw that he had collapsed in his clothes. He was too tired to rise when I entered. There was not enough energy in him, and there was too much fear of the future in me, for a passionate kiss. I helped him undress while he lay there, and then I undressed and climbed in next to him.

After lying still, silent, for a while, he said, "I am angry at the idiocy of my ministers."

"Urdaneta told me," I said, still distraught over this turn of affairs. Such a situation could only make things worse for him, and for everyone. I tried to point out to him the ramifications of such a bad set of circumstances, but he seemed indifferent to everything.

I was only able to bring peace to my heart, and interest to his mind, by discussing irrelevancies concerning his absence, such as the scenery or the weather. I persuaded him to tell me a few stories about the last year. Soon, he fell asleep, exhausted, before we could love one another.

The next morning, I called Doctor Cheyne. He was not optimistic about Simón's future. "He needs rest," the young doctor said, shaking his head as we walked under the fuchsias. I knew then that Simón's condition was beyond Doctor Cheyne's arts. He would either recover his vitality, or he would not, and it was in the hand of providence and Bolívar.

Simón coughed all that day. He only got up once, long enough to write to General Sucre, requesting the victor of Ayacucho to come and represent him in the new Congress.

For weeks he was doubled over in fits of coughing. I would wipe blood from his lips several times a day. Unlike his other convelescences, he made no complaints when I pushed his visitors back outside without allowing them to even see him. He gave me no arguments when I made him stay in bed and take the medicines brought by Doctor Cheyne. At 47 years, the man I loved had grown old.

He would have spells wherein his familiar courage and impulse to action would break through, but his plans at such times were impractical and frightening because they were so loosely connected to reality. Worse, his designs rarely included me or the dream I had of simply riding away to his estates in Venezuela and living out our lives. "I will return to France, and damn the Republic!" he would rage. Or, "I will not hold any office. I will simply stay here and unify the Republic by my presence." Or, when it appeared that Páez would cause trouble again, "I will go to Venezuela." He could barely walk, let alone ride.

He had these momentary plans, yet he would not listen to any reports. Daily, the situation became more frightening. The country was disintegrating into anarchy, and was held together only by the fact that he was still President. Bolívar was blind and deaf to the chaos.

I read to him, I nursed him, but I did not discuss politics with him, or argue. He needed peace from such misery, and I knew that he would not listen in any case. When he recovered, then he could listen and take action.

When Sucre arrived, Simón was well enough to meet him. They embraced, even though Sucre was still favoring his arm from the wound he'd received when he was deposed in Bolivia. They talked for some time and then Simón, feeling the exertion of just being up, excused himself and returned to his room to nap.

"He looks so ill," said Sucre, sadly.

"He is," I said, looking in the direction Simón had gone. "But he is recovering."

"That is good," said my friend quietly. He contemplated the port in his glass that I had just poured for him.

"How is your wife?" I asked innocently, and immediately his face clouded with pain and sadness, "and your little girl?" I added.

He brightened again, and said, "Never have I known such happiness as that which is given to me by Teresa. She is the joy I once—" His eyes clouded with tears. He froze, fighting for composure before he finished. "She is my joy," he said, simply, at last.

When I pressed him to tell me about his wife, I found that they were irretrievably estranged. "She is having an affair with a general on my own staff, named Barriga." He seemed to sink into his wine. He said, so softly that I could hardly hear him, "I loved her more than anything. If it were not for my daughter, I could die. I would die."

I felt sorry for him, and did all I could to comfort him with words and reassurances. I was glad that my old friend was with us again in Bogotá. I missed Sucre while he had been away, but his arrival was the worst thing that could have happened. The day after Sucre arrived Bolívar resigned the presidency.

With the upcoming Congress, he felt that Sucre could handle everything, so he simply quit. I did not have time to try to stop him. He wrote the notice:

> Today I have ceased to rule. Listen to my last words. At the
> moment when my political career comes to an end, I implore, I demand
> in the name of Gran Colombia, that you remain united.

He sent it to the Congress before I saw it. Thus he precipitated the very thing he had warned against. He assured the disintegration of the country.

"Why did you do this?" I demanded, tears in my eyes.

"Because Sucre is here, and I am tired. They will know that I am not hungry for power." He had told the congress that Sucre was the "worthiest of Generals." Despite the truth of the phrase, this infuriated Urdaneta, who had been in Bogotá ably managing Simón's affairs for the last several years. "Sucre will be elected when a new Congress is formed, and through him my vision of a united republic will be realized."

"I don't see how that will happen."

"Do not worry, Manuelita, it will all work out."

I did not argue with him further, but he was wrong. The very next day, I began hearing the reports I feared. Every one of the *caudillos* (petty dictators) throughout the country began scrambling for power and control of their own areas. In the capital, it was the same. Every political official wanted to rule, and each began making a play for power. Worse yet, no one, not even his friends, believed Bolívar should take over leadership again. "He will only cause the country to divide," they would say as they shook their heads.

Then it happened. What was happening with the *caudillos* happened on a continental scale. Páez, not having to report to Bolívar anymore, did what he had been longing to do for years. He broke Venezuela away from Gran Colombia.

The entire country was upset and fearful, unsure of what would happen next. Simón was roused to anger, and he roared, "I will pull this country together, by my own will." He dressed in his best uniform, and summoned Colombia's ministers to the villa. These were the same men who had resigned in his presence three months before and who now controlled the country. Yet they politely complied with Bolívar summons.

When they arrived, he vented his fury at Páez and ended with a simple demand. "Restore me to office, and give me the power to take an expedition and make war on Venezuela." His denouncement of Páez was moving, and his resolve was firm, but it was too late.

The ministers left without answering him directly. "Yes, well said, Your Excellency." "Yes, by all means, we will certainly take the prospect into consideration." "Yes, a fine idea, we will notify you very soon." They left. A few hours later, a letter arrived from that same body. They had made a decision that finished us all.

In the letter they spoke of Simón's many deeds in service of his country. They spoke of the many problems surrounding the Republic. They were grateful for his past service, but they stated clearly that a war with Venezuela would be unpopular and they could not sanction it. Unwritten, but stated quite clearly, was the declaration, "We have lost confidence in you."

Urdaneta delivered the letter. He was still angry at seeming to be ignored in favor of Sucre and his resentment could not be hidden. When Simón expressed his disbelief at the council's response, the general said coldly, "If you had executed Páez when he revolted three years ago, instead of merely trying to mollify him, we would not be in the trouble we are in now." He was right, but I hated him for the way the words struck Simón.

Less than a week later, Urdaneta brought him the final blow. This time there was no rancor when he delivered the news, "Your Excellency, I am most sorry for the news I bring you. Truly."

"What is it Rafael?"

I could tell he was trying to be as kind and gentle as he could, perhaps feeling sorry for his remarks a few days earlier. His affection for the Liberator became evident as he struggled with what he had to say. At last, finding no better way to say it, he said, "Most of the government has agreed that the presence of Simón Bolívar in the Republic of Gran Colombia will no longer be in the best interests of the general good."

Simón did not react.

"They are weak, my General, and they are looking for a way to rule without you."

Simón nodded slowly and said, "They do not know."

"I hate to say this, but you should not stay here."

"Exile?"

"Or you will certainly be the target of assassins again."

"I will go. I knew on the night of September 25 that the people no longer loved me."

Thus, in late April of 1830, without benefit of law or even decree, merely by general agreement, Simón Bolívar was exiled—exiled from the country that he had created.

Chapter 38

Once again, Simón was to leave. Once again, I was to stay behind.
I argued, I pleaded, I raged, I demanded, but his simple logic prevailed. "I do not know where I am going."
"But, Simón—"
"Let me settle someplace first."
"Simón, all the future I have is with you, and it will always be so. My love for you gives me no other choice. There is no place in this world for me anymore if it is not by your side. Your well-being, your health—"
"I know." His eyes grew wetter. At last, he said, "I long to have you with me." He looked out at the flowers in the garden and drew a deep breath. "It will only be a short while before I send for you. Right now, I do not even have enough money to leave the country. In the meantime, with my enemies everywhere and no secure place to stop, it will truly be too dangerous. Besides, I need you here to inform me of what is happening and to care for the belongings I leave behind. Please, let me go. I *will* send for you." He took me in his arms and we held each other for a long time.
He was right about one thing. He was poor. Suddenly, the once richest man in South America had no more than the money he could get for the silver plate I had salvaged when escaping Magdalena and that I had carried with me all these years. He had some resources from which he could draw, but they were very few.
In the last days of Simón's residence in Bogotá, I nearly killed myself with work. So much had to be done. During the day I kept order and peace for Simón. I kept the unruly or venomous visitors away, and I wrote or visited his friends. I was up most of the night, every night.
I would read to him until quite late. It seemed to be the one pleasure he could derive out of life. After he fell asleep, I answered the correspondence that he was too ill to care about. Every night, I heard alerts from the guards outside while sitting at his writing desk.
There were still rumors that his life was in danger. All of this activity should not have been so trying. True, I was not as young as I used to be—I was 32—but I had seen worse. What was killing me was the desperation. Every day, it seemed, I was writing to, or visiting someone, anyone, who might be able to change what seemed inevitable. All to no avail. Simón would have to leave the country. After all we had gone through, after all the work that Simón had done, it had come to this.
Exile. The very word chilled me. It reminded me of other words I had heard so much in my life: *outcast; sinful; a spurious child; shamed our family; stay away; you are not wanted here; just what you would expect from a bastard.*
These words rang in my ears throughout the day, seeming to have new meaning. Terrified about the future, my anxiety, would not leave me, day or night. I could not rest and I could not properly do the work I felt I had to do. When I looked into the future, I

could see nothing—nothing but misery, loneliness, and pain. I could not accompany Bolívar—and even if I could, to where? He would be traveling towards Cartagena, but he would be stopping along the way, traveling with a squadron to protect him. There would be no privacy, nothing to accommodate three extra women, and money was so short.

In my mind I could understand all this, but two enormous fears ate away at me and would give me no rest. The first I had faced before, but the finality of Simón's exile made me question my ability to fight again the slander I would face from the community, especially the women, after Simón was gone. I would be, once again, a cast-off lover—not of a still powerful man, but this time of a fallen leader in exile. Women had always been the most cruel to me. I would be fair game, and without resources. I did not know how I was to live, or what I would do.

I did not want to go back to Quito. Already we had heard that General Flores had followed Páez's example and had broken my own country away from the Republic. Even though the General was a friend of my brother's, he had a rival by the name of Rocafuerte, in Guayaquil, who had denounced me. I sensed danger in Quito. Not only did I feel danger for myself, but for my brother as well.

Besides, I needed to stay in Bogotá in case the political winds began blowing again in Simón's favor. I had to be his eyes and ears in the capital. I had to stay. I would have to submit to the coming public vilification of me.

Yet this, as much as I wanted to avoid it, was not the worst. If I was not with Simón, what would happen if he became really ill. My deepest terror is that he might die before I could help him. These are the thoughts that plagued me. They wore me out. "You are so drawn and pale, Manuelita," Jonotás would say. "You must eat and sleep," Natán warned me. But I could neither eat nor sleep. I could only work.

The seventh of May was the last night I spent with Simón. As had been my habit, I read to him. I opened *Don Quixote* at random and began reading at the beginning of the chapter:

> "Ah!" cried Sancho. "Now I have you! This is what I have longed
> to know with all my heart and soul. Come, Señor, can you deny what
> everyone says in these parts when someone is feeling low: 'I don't
> know what's the matter with him; he doesn't eat, nor drink, nor sleep,
> nor answer when you ask him a question; surely he must be
> enchanted—

Simón interrupted me. "Read the last chapter, Manuelita." He sounded very tired.

I did not want to read the last chapter. I did not want to be reminded of death. "But, Simón, this is funny—"

"Please," he said, softly.

I slowly turned to the proper page and began reading. Don Quixote reclaimed his lucidity. He squared everything with Sancho. He dictated his will. He died. When I read the lines:

> Here lies the noble fearless knight,
> Whose valor rose to such a height;
> When Death at last did strike him down,
> His was the victory and renown.

Faint and hoarse, Simón said, "Will it be so?"

I looked at him and saw that his eyes were closed. I did not answer. I waited to see if he was sleeping. He did not open his eyes, and his breath was slow and rhythmic. I blew out the candle, leaving only the faint glow of a brazier in the corner.

I took off my clothes and climbed slowly into bed with him. My naked skin slid across the linen until my breasts pressed against his nightshirt. My arm reached gently across his chest and I held him close to me. I felt the tears I had held back all day slowly brim in my eyes and fall softly into the darkness.

I would not go with him tomorrow. He and José Palacios would walk outside to the men, his followers, who would be waiting to accompany him. He would climb onto his horse and he would ride with them. They would turn away from the fresh smell of flowers in the gardens of the Quinta, and they would ride through Bogotá. The streets would be filled with people, but there would be silence—only the clacking of hooves on cobblestones. Once or twice they would hear "Down with the tyrant!" Once or twice, little girls would run into the street to hand the Liberator a flower. Simón would ride on, silently, towards the road to Honda, to catch a ferry down the river. All this would happen while I stayed in his bedroom. I would wait all day if I had to, but I would not watch him ride into exile.

As I lay next to the man I loved, I decided that he would return. How that would happen, I did not know, but it would happen. I would wait for him, and I would do what I could to make it so.

I tried to imagine what else might occur, but his return was the only future on which I could fix my mind. I must make it happen. Then, at last, he would bring order and sanity to the men who ruled Colombia. He would realize, finally, his dream of a united republic. Then, we would be free.

No, I would not accompany him tomorrow. Nor would I watch him go; I could not. I would stay the night with him and comfort him in his last hours before his ride into exile—but I would not watch him go. I would wait for him to return. I would make it happen.

In the dark, he said softly, "There have been three great fools in history: Jesus Christ, Don Quixote, and myself."

I sobbed. I could not help myself. I sobbed like a child.

"Do not cry, Manuela."

"Oh, Simón, what's to happen to us?"

"I care not for myself—"

"You must not say that."

"I am not giving up. It is not what you think. No." He lay still a moment and then said, "I am in a state of restfulness, but I am not sleeping. I am experiencing the world as it exists for me at this moment. The smells of the charcoal, the candle that has been recently snuffed out, your hair, your delicious odor exciting my senses. I hear the guard outside walking on the fallen leaves; I hear you breathing; I hear you crying."

"Simón, I—"

"Manuela. I love you. I have never loved anyone as I love you. I am grateful to you for your steadfast loyalty. I am thankful for all of your abilities that have helped me so much over the years. Words are not enough to tell you of my love and gratitude."

I pressed my cheek against his chest and held him tighter.

"I am also sorry."

"Why, Simón?"

"I am sorry you have had to live through these trials with me, and I have not repaid you."

I wiped away my tears. "You do not need to think that way. You know I love you, and to have done anything differently would have been to have deprived me of my own life."

"Still. I feel like Don Quixote, who must say to Sancho, 'forgive me for making you seem as mad as I was myself, and for drawing you into my errors—'"

"Stop it, please," I said softly. "I love you. I love you passionately, with all my heart. I loved you from the first day I saw you, and I have never stopped loving you. If there is a way to feel love for you after death, I will do so. You did nothing to persuade me to have taken the road I have taken. On the contrary, you have done much to dissuade me."

After a moment, he said, "I know. But I am sorry for you."

I reached up and put my mouth to his. When our lips touched, he pulled me to him, strong, passionate, full of desire. I kissed him. I kissed him deeply. I moved on top of him, our lips still trying to find any part of each other that we still did not know. Slowly. Tenderly. I moved up and down, loving him, trying to find every point of intimacy we shared. He filled me. He filled my soul. Softly, slowly, sweetly. We loved.

We stayed as one for a long time, and I cried as we lay close in the night.

"Thank you for loving me all these years," he said softly. "I have needed you so; how I have needed you."

"Stop. We will be together again. You will send a message: 'Come now.'" We both laughed softly. "And I will go."

"Yes. And we will live together. You and I. No more will I be on any quest. You will be there. All the happiness I need." He was speaking slowly, drowsily, almost asleep.

"Yes," I said. I waited. I listened. I felt his heart beat. He was asleep. Yet, despite my exhaustion, I could not find slumber. I kept a vigil that night, our last night together. I listened to him breathe and felt every move he made in the night.

As the silent hours wore on, I would return to his last words as though they were a puzzle. Towards dawn, I realized what it was that kept me thinking about them.

I was not some idealized woman or a foolish quest of some Don Quixote. I was Bolívar's partner. I rode with him in war and peace. I kept him safe and cared for his very life. I was not Dulcinea, illusory lover. If I was anything, I was Sancho, loyal friend.

Chapter 39

I sat in his bed as he prepared himself, his thin frame giving evidence of the illness that had withered him. I had pulled on his nightshirt, to defeat the chill in the room, and I watched him, unable to keep from crying. He methodically shaved, cleaned his teeth, his nails, and dressed in simple civilian clothes.

"Eat something, Simón," I said quietly, though I knew he would not. He declined, and when he was ready to go, he came to me. He took my hands and pulled me to my feet. We looked in each other's eyes. Slowly, he put his arms around me and kissed me. My lips pressed against his and I held him close. He looked in my eyes again and said, "Good-bye, my love." Our eyes said everything else there was to say. He walked out the door.

I stayed in his room for over an hour, until I was sure he had left the city. Then I slowly made my way home.

I did not go out for the next day or so, and I paid little attention to the news that Jonotás and Natán brought back to me from the streets. What little I heard was no more or less than I expected. Both Bolívar and I were being reviled. The only news that was not about either Simón or me was that General Flores had proclaimed himself President of the new state he had broken off from Colombia. It was called Ecuador. I wondered how my brother was.

A week later, La Sáenz recovered enough to take some action. First, I needed information. I asked Jonotás and Natán to tell me again all that had occurred in the last few days. As I knew would happen, the attacks on me were growing. I was being vilified in every public place, in every way that people could communicate to each other. Now that Simón was gone, I was a target for all manner of public revenge.

If my enemies thought I would succumb because Simón was gone, they were mistaken. I would fight. Once again, I would fight. But I would not fight only for myself. I would fight the reality of Simón's absence. I would bring him back.

I spent the next few days making plans as to how I would do so. However, it was a *papelucha* that Natán brought back to me that solidified my plans. In this shameless paper, I was described as a threat to public morals. This was printed along with a most unflattering caricature.

The next day, I took a document of my own to Bruno Espinosa, whom I knew had a printing press and was an avid supporter of Bolívar's. He printed a simple newspaper that did not have any readership to speak of because its stories never had any controversy. Consequently, he was quite poor.

Señor Espinosa was a small man. An untrimmed mustache covered a small mouth and his eyes darted about, as if he were expecting danger to well up from the corners of the room.

"I want you to print something for me," I said, as I handed him what I had written. It said *Long Live Bolívar, Founder of the Republic* and then there were a few paragraphs listing his accomplishments. Espinosa's eyes doubled their efforts when he looked at it. I wondered how he could read when his eyes were constantly roving all over the room. "I would like the first words in a large type," I said.

"Señora, I . . . that is, I . . ."

"You don't have to distribute them. Just print a few, when your press is not busy, and I will put them up."

"Well, I . . ."

"Thank you, Señor. The Liberator would be happy. I have very little money, now that—" Suddenly, a lump came to my throat. This had happened to me alone, since Bolívar's absence, but not when I was with someone, not even with Jonotás and Natán. It was uncontrollable and I had to stop speaking for a moment. I suppressed my sadness, but he noticed.

His eyes darted about the room again and he said, "I . . . I will help you, Señora, but please do not let anyone know who did the printing."

"No, Señor. Tell me when you are ready to print, and I will come help you."

He thought a minute, his eyes doing their dance, and he said, "Very well. Come back in two nights."

As I was leaving, I saw a stack of blank paper by the door. "Might I have several sheets of this paper?" I asked.

"I . . . that is . . . you see, this paper . . . you see . . . and all of this," he pointed to a stack along one wall, "is already prepared with my name on the bottom. He showed me where, in tiny print, it said, *Printed by Bruno Espinosa.* "Please take some of this other, which is completely blank." He pointed to a few stacks of paper on the other side of the room. "This is the paper we must use when printing your bills."

"As you say. Thank you, Señor. You are a true patriot." He smiled, as though my compliment meant something deep to him, and I left with my paper.

I went home. On the clean white paper he had given me, I painted *Long Live Bolívar, Founder of the Republic* or *Long Live The Liberator* in large letters. That night, Jonotás, Natán, and I put them up on the walls of Bogotá. Having had experience with this kind of activity in Lima, ten years earlier, and in Quito, was it only three years ago, we were not seen.

The next morning I heard something that infuriated me. The coalition government, set up only temporarily to appoint a new congress and elect new leaders, had taken it upon themselves to release Bolívar's political enemies. Among them was the vitriolic Vicente Azuero, who had attacked Simón and me in the press so violently before. I knew I could expect the *papeluchas* to double their attacks on me.

What was worse was that Vicente Azuero had received a position in the Cabinet of this shameful excuse for a government. This, I knew, was because he was a friend of the new president, Joaquín Mosquera, a man chosen only because he was from a well-known family in Popayán, and he was a good orator. He had no capacity whatsoever for leadership.

I paced around in fury when I heard the news. As I walked out onto the balcony, I was there only for a moment when I saw this same man, Vicente Azuero, walk into the plaza. He was smiling broadly and had every appearance of satisfaction in his manner and walk. I was disgusted and about to go back inside when I saw him notice one of the bills I had posted the night before.

He stopped, walked over to it, and then tore it off the wall as though he were trying to kill it. He crumpled it and threw it in the street while he looked around the square. He noticed another one and ran over to it. The glue on this one held better and he worked hard, but only pulled the edges down.

When he turned around this time, he looked up to my balcony, as though the thought had just come to him as to who put these posters up. When he saw me smiling at him, he knew I was the one. His face became red and was full of undisguised hatred.

The next day I put on my uniform and went riding with my companions. However, I noticed that the number of Indians in the streets selling *papeluchas* was four or five times what there had been the day before. There were also broadsides on the walls attacking Bolívar and me, in far greater numbers than I had ever seen.

In the place where we kept our horses, I had accumulated three or four lances. We rode back, picked them up, and rode back into the streets to fight those who warred on Bolívar and me.

The first man I saw selling *papeluchas* was right around the corner. He walked down the street lazily in front of us yelling to passers-by, "Learn the truth. Come buy one."

I rode down on him and stabbed him in the rear of his trousers. He screamed and threw his hands behind his back, throwing all of his papers in the air. I urged my horse forward and trampled them where they fell in to the street until they were shreds. A small crowd gathered. I shouted to him and those standing around, "Anybody who defiles my name will regret it, but not so much as if they defile the name of the founder of the Republic, Simón Bolívar."

My companions and I continued through the town, tearing paper off the walls and destroying all the *papeluchas* we could find by trampling reams of them under the hooves of our horses. In a few hours, it seemed we had done a great deal of damage to the opposition.

I felt much better, as though there was something that could be done about the evil that was infecting the land after all. However, despite how confident I felt that morning, in the evening I received some bad news.

I had invited General Sucre to dinner. I was enjoying my meal with the Field Marshal of Ayacucho, the only man who could succeed Bolívar, when he gave me regretful information. "I will be returning to Quito."

I suspected that he would, but the reality of it, and what it would mean, made me want to try to dissuade him. "Antonio, you should not leave. The Liberator will need you here."

"Like the Liberator, I have given my life to the revolution. Like him, I am tired. His many accomplishments go unappreciated and I, after my experience in Bolivia, am not confident that I could do any better. If he returns and he needs me, I will come back."

"Do you not see how indispensable you are to the rest of us, who love Simón? Do you not see how much the State needs you?" I said.

"I do not refuse to serve the State, but I wish to know the system and the aim," he said, his training as a scientist and his experience as a soldier showing through the words. "For a long time we have been without both, and I am too tired and too ill to work at hazard."

"Your leaving will be felt most deeply."

He looked at me, his thin handsome features reminding me of the victories we had shared. "I will miss you as well, you perhaps most of all, who has been so close to my friend. But I also miss my daughter and I am tired. I thank you for your many kindnesses."

"When are you leaving?"

"Tomorrow or the next day."

"But Antonio . . . Does Urdaneta know you are leaving. Has he prepared a squadron for your escort. What with the men who are with Bolívar, there are very few who can go with you when—"

Sucre interrupted, "It is not necessary. Urdaneta knows I am leaving, but did not offer an escort. However, I do not need one. I will go alone."

I tried to persuade him against such foolishness. "You are as much a target as Bolívar," I said.

"I do not think so. When they see that all I want to do is go home and play with my daughter, they will be more than happy to let me be."

"My friend, it may be your presence alone that is keeping the entire country from coming apart. Your past victories make you important to the country as well as an enemy to those who wish to steal power from Bolívar. It is not safe for you to ride without an escort."

He laughed and called me a "worrier." I knew I was not worrying idly. I urged Sucre to be careful.

The next day, he left for Quito. I gave him a little doll I had sewn from some scrap cloth to give to his daughter. He thanked me, smiling from ear to ear. Then he mounted his horse and rode hurriedly away, eager to see his beloved Teresa.

I regretted his departure. I felt as though the fight I had in front of me would be a hundred times harder after he left. He was the one who could take over if Bolívar could not—as he had done so often before.

Later that night I went to Señor Espinosa and helped him print my bills while Jonotás and Natán tore down some more broadsides we found on the way. The printing took a couple of hours, but I was happy how it looked. The first day I had only been able to put up a slogan, but this contained my ideas concerning the frailty of the government without Bolívar and enumerated his many accomplishments.

My companions and I placed the entire run around the city. I heard the next morning that Azuero and other members of the cabinet were livid. I began composing another.

A day or so later, I received a letter from Simón:

Guaduas
May 11, 1830

My Love,

I am glad to tell you that I feel well, but I am filled with your grief
and my own over our separation. I love you very much and I shall love
you much more, if you will now be more reasonable than ever before.
Be careful what you do, or you may ruin yourself, and that means ruin
to both of us.

I am always
your devoted lover,
Bolívar

Though he did not know exactly what I was doing, he knew my nature. He feared for me. Still, despite his warnings, I persisted in tearing down bills, and suppressing the attacks on the man I loved, as fast as I could find them. Methodically, I replaced the evil on the walls of the city with my own ideas. I was set on my course.

At least I was no longer crying over Simón's absence. My sadness had been converted to anger. Only late at night did I weep, hoping for the day when the violence and strife I had known all my life would cease. I longed to be far away from any city, peacefully living my life. I knew it would be years before such a dream could come true. First, I had to bring Simón back. First, I had to do battle.

So did I continue, each lonely night moving me closer to the day when Simón would arrive back in Bogotá. I fought a war of words and I kept close contact with

Urdaneta and others of Bolívar's friends still in the capital. I also made sure the Callao regiment, who were loyal to Bolívar, was on my list of people to befriend and visit often, in case some military force might be required when he came back. I was determined that the man I love would return.

Chapter 40

All through May, I kept Bolívar's name and his deeds in front of the people. Bolívar's absence had rocked the country to its core, and the government was slowly disintegrating. Every day there was yet another desperate measure by those in power to keep order and maintain their positions. One of these measures concerned me in particular.

One afternoon, I received a notice from Azuero. It was very official, and it had the customary flowery language. Though its rhetoric was in the most noble terms, it amounted to nothing more than a demand that I turn over any papers in my possession that belonged to Bolívar's archives, saying "such instruments are the property of Gran Colombia."

I did indeed still have three strongboxes that contained Bolívar's papers—in among them were the many letters that we had written to each other, over the years. I would die before I gave any of it up.

Late that night, Jonotás and I carried them downstairs and loaded them onto some mules I had waiting. Then we climbed on our horses and led the mules quietly through the dark and empty streets, out to Bolívar's Quinta.

Simón had given his villa—which had been presented to him by the Republic years before—to one of his closest friends, Pepé Paris. He, in turn, had given it to his daughter, Manuelita. She had been moving in that same day and planned to sleep there that very night. I had sent Natán ahead to tell her I was coming.

She and I had been on friendly terms, but I expressed my fears to Jonotás as we rode through the dark streets: "Let us hope that I have assessed her character correctly and that she will not decline to help us . . . or betray us."

Jonotás thought for a moment and said, "Don't worry, Manuelita. Natán believes she is our friend."

When we arrived, it was strange, because it was the first time I had ever ridden up to the villa without soldiers on guard outside. At this time of night it was usually ablaze with lights and activity. Instead there was only one faint candle glowing in the window of the library. Inside I could see Manuelita Paris and Natán looking outside, waiting for us. When they heard us ride up, the light moved towards the door. Manuelita came out, dressed in night clothes, her hair under a sleeping cap.

She was small, almost a head shorter than I, and very pretty, with delicate sensitive features. She and I liked each other, although she had been embarrassed when I tried to arrange a marriage between her and Jean Baptiste Boussingault. They had both been embarrassed. He fled my apartment one night when he learned of my designs, fearing he would be trapped into a sudden marriage. But I knew he loved her, and he did call on her after that. She later expressed her gratitude to me. They might have married, but she had told him that she did not want to live in France, so he stopped courting her.

I dismounted and walked past the sweet smelling flowers. "I am most sorry to have disturbed you so late," I said, as I walked up to the door, "but I need your help."

"Yes, of course, come inside. What do you need?"

"No, please, I can't." Again, that traitorous lump in my throat appeared, betraying my sadness. I could not enter that house again. A tear rolled down my cheek.

She saw, and she handed her candle to Natán and put her arms around me.

I explained that I needed to hide Simón's papers and told here where I thought they would be well hidden and out of the way. She agreed. While we talked, I told her of my troubles and of my vilification in the city. She already knew most of it and sympathized.

"Why do you provoke them?" she asked.

"I am not trying to merely make them angry."

"What then? Why do you do these things? What *are* you trying to do?"

"I am trying—I will—bring about the fall of the government." She looked at me, incredulous. I went on. "The country is breaking up and the signs of impending anarchy are clear. Soon, the populace will beg for Bolívar's return."

"Ah, so it is for the man you love that you do these things."

"Yes." I made myself not feel the sadness again. "That seems to be the reason women do most things."

"Yes. It is our plight, and I understand. I will help you."

When we had safely secured Bolívar's papers, Jonotás, Natán, and I rode back to our apartment. Though it was late at night, I wrote the Cabinet a letter so that it could be delivered at first light:

> To your demands, may I say that I have nothing, absolutely
> nothing, in my possession that belongs to the government. These
> private papers belong to His Excellency, the Liberator. I will surrender
> neither these papers nor his books.
> And can you show me the legislation which has outlawed General
> Bolívar and sent him into exile?

There was little response. I heard from my friends that Azuero had railed against me. There were one or two other written demands, but I ignored them. They let me know they were not finished with me, but they had their hands too full of political problems to continue. I left the papers in hiding.

It had been a little over a month since Bolívar had made his way to the coast. The celebration of Corpus Christi was about to begin. The government was most enthusiastic in supporting the festival, in hopes that the populace would be distracted from their failures at leadership.

One morning, I had word from Bolívar's camp that Simón was being more irascible than ever, and that his fits of coughing were more frequent. I tried to calm my fear, that I would not have enough time to do all I wished to do and see Simón again. As I was folding the letter to put it away, Jonotás and Natán came into the room wearing dresses for a change.

"Where are you going?

"To the fair." I looked out the window at the vendors selling sausages and religious mementos, and I was irritated that they would be running off when I needed them. However, I said nothing to dissuade them. After they left, I set to work to write another attack on the government.

When I was done, I took it to Señor Espinosa, along with a little money. I did not have much, but I felt guilty making him pay all the material cost for my "war" on the government.

Towards mid-afternoon, as I was making my own tea and wondering where Jonotás and Natán had put my favorite cup, they returned.

Before I noticed their excitement, I said, "There you are. I can't find—"

"Manuelita, they are goin' to burn the Liberator and you in effigy."

"What? Who is?"

"There is a platform of bamboo bein' made," said Jonotás.

"Yes, for fireworks," said Natán. "Straw figures are on it."

When they explained everything, I learned that in a plaza a few blocks distant, Vicente Azuero, as a representative of the government, had ordered the building of a platform on which were two caricatures of straw. One was a male, in uniform, with a sign that said "Despotism and Bolívar"; the other was a female with the face of a harpy and a sign that said "Manuela Sáenz and Tyranny." "They've been loadin' fireworks inside the figures and around the platform," said Jonotás.

I stood up and started to put on my uniform.

My companions followed my example, taking off their dresses and pulling on trousers. They asked, "What are we goin' to do?"

"I am going to put a stop to it," I said, simply.

"But, Manuelita," said Natán, "there are soldiers with bayonets guardin' the platform."

"I don't care." I strapped on my pistols and headed for the door.

They followed me. As we mounted our horses, I had Jonotás and Natán each grab a lance and some rope. Then we rode down the streets to the square, fast, three Amazons scattering the people who did not want to be run over.

We did not stop when we came to the square, but rode down on the hussars guarding the platform so fast that they did not have time to pick up their rifles sitting in pyramid-shaped stacks. Running in all directions, they left the platform temporarily to my comrades and me.

The leader of the platoon immediately drew his sword and came back at us. I pulled out a pistol and directed my aim at his head. He stopped and motioned for his men to stay still. The rest of the soldiers gathered behind him.

"You bitch," said the captain, "I order you to desist."

I did not respond and, while a crowd gathered, Jonotás and Natán destroyed the two figures with their lances. When the figures were no more than shreds, they threw the rope to the top of the platform and pulled the whole affair into a bigger pile of bamboo, fireworks, cloth, and straw. My comrades mounted their horses.

I yelled out, "Long live Bolívar!" and then I turned and fired a ball into the heap and set off the fireworks.

The sound was like a cannonade and our horses recoiled, nearly causing all three of us to lose our balance. The crowd ran, escaping the rockets firing in all directions.

The soldiers scattered as well, except for the captain, who came at us and sliced at Jonotás's horse, causing a superficial wound. I spurred my own mount and knocked down the captain, and the three of us galloped out of the square.

The next morning, the *papelucha* sellers were out in force. Azuero had personally recruited the sellers, and had written several articles himself.

> We understand that the Municipal Corporation prepared a castle of fireworks ornamented with figures which were created to excite patriotism in the hearts of the people and persuade them to hatred of tyranny. But a petulant woman, who was always in the van of General Bolívar and who goes about dressed in the daytime in male clothing, came out with her creatures similarly clothed in a style which insulted all moral laws. This woman extended her insolence toward the whole city. Dressed as a hussar she went to the plaza with two or three of her servants, assaulted the guards, set off the fireworks with a pistol she carried, and then declaimed against the government, against liberty, and against the people.

Public outcries for my arrest were in print by sundown. The denunciations were more vicious than ever before. The furor went on for days. I had Espinosa print a letter, which I sent to all government officials and the newspapers. I also pasted it all over the walls of the city.

> Because of the opinions held by those who attack me, I am obliged to speak out to the people, lest my silence make me a criminal.
>
> I have offended no one in high office. What I have done is not dishonorable. Those who calumniate me do so because they are unable to persecute me legally; this is my vindication, since everyone knows how I have been insulted, slandered, and vilified.
>
> I confess that I am not tolerant, but my serenity rests on the knowledge of the rightness of the cause of His Excellency, the Liberator. I shall never, never retreat a single step in that respect, from the friendship and gratitude I hold toward General Bolívar; and if anyone believes that to be a crime—it demonstrates the poverty of his soul.

It did no good. The city became filled with *papeluchas*, which seemed to drop like snow from the sky. My detractors heaped every kind of insult on me, from the moral to the political. Soldiers put bills on their lances. People received one while going into church and another when coming out. When I went out into the streets, in the daytime, the clamor that followed me was appalling. Boos and hisses attended me everywhere. I was called a whore, a shrew, a harpy, a vixen, a bitch, and a number of other things that were positively filthy and vulgar.

I took my pistols everywhere. I had to pull them out in order to counterattack for my honor, or to defend myself, on more than one occasion. Whenever I confronted my enemies I made sure the words, "Long live, Bolívar," were the last thing they heard from me.

I was so busy fighting with nearly every man in the capital that I did not notice something. At least one faction of the city was on my side, a faction I would never have conceived as my friends: women.

Women had always hated me. I was unconventional, and women set conventions. Throughout the centuries, women have grown to believe in their mission, imposed on them by men, that they must be like the Virgin. Thus have men enslaved them all, by making them feel guilty for their own desires. Women, if they agree with such constraints, reduce their own humanity. Few human roles are left for them: virginal wife for their husbands, nighttime whore for their lovers, or moral magistrate for society. Thus, they are livid when another woman chooses to live a different kind of life.

My mother was ruined by hypocritical morality, and I have never liked women who have pretended to lofty sentiments. It was for this reason that the women at the center of society always hated me: in Quito, in Lima, and most definitely in Bogotá.

I never expected support from women as a class—and certainly never from the women of Bogotá, who were the most prudish I had ever encountered. They hated me deeply from the first day I arrived. When I realized that these same women were on my side, I was astonished.

I learned that a letter had been sent to the government from a group that called itself "Liberal Women." One day, when I sat in my room, wondering if I would ever know a time of tranquillity and peace, there was a knock on the door. Natán brought Manuelita Paris into the room. She said, "My friend, I have something to show you. A duplicate of this letter was sent to all of our country's officials today. This one is for you." She handed me a copy:

> It is urged by many that Señora Manuela Sáenz should be sent to prison or into exile. But the government should remember that when she had, as is well known, a tremendous influence—she used it for the public good, before and after that famous night of the 25th of September. We, the women of Bogotá, protest against the inflammatory libels which appear against this lady on the walls of the streets.
>
> We honor, although we may disagree with, the sentiments that have been manifested by one of our sex. Señora Sáenz is no delinquent. Insulted and provoked in various ways by people she has not offended—these insults have caused great irritation and she has been exasperated into imprudence. But imprudence is not a crime. Manuela Sáenz has violated no laws; she has attacked the rights of no citizen.
>
> And if Señora Sáenz has written or shouted, "Long live Bolívar," where is the law which prohibits this?
>
> The persecution of this lady has its origin in base and ignoble passions. Alone, without family in this city, she should be an object of commiseration and esteem rather than the victim of persecution. What heroism she has shown! What magnanimity! We hope that the heavens will treasure sentiments as noble as those which have been uttered by Manuela Sáenz and that they will serve as an example for all of us.

I wish I could explain how that letter made me feel. My sisters, at last, had understood me. They understood and admired that I was fighting for my integrity and for the man I loved. After a lifetime of knowing hatred and jealousy from those of my own sex, I had come to a moment in time when I finally felt the admiration and acceptance of other women. This admiration, so freely given, may have been the most profound glory I have ever known.

Chapter 41

I think the support of the women of Bogotá might have made an enormous difference. How powerful we might be if we could put away our jealousies. However, news of an event that had happened almost a month earlier changed everything.

In the first week of July, we received word from the south. On June 4, General Antonio José de Sucre, traveling home to see his beloved daughter, had been shot dead while riding through the Berruecos Mountains. The victor of Pichincha and Ayacucho died before he hit the ground. A hole in his forehead spilled the blood of one of South America's greatest heroes.

Later, when Bolívar heard the news, he said, most accurately, "My God, they have shed the blood of Abel. It is impossible to live in a country where the most famous generals are cruelly and barbarously murdered, the very men to whom America owes its freedom. I believe the purpose of the crime was to deprive the fatherland of my successor." I agreed with him. This most certainly had been the reason Sucre had died.

The foolish men who had him killed were thinking that the present government's hold on power was now more certain. The opposite was true. The petty dictators of small individual regions (*caudillos*), all over the country, trying to carve out their own sphere of power, no longer feared anyone. In days, the government had lost all control, except in the capital itself. There, they only barely maintained their power. Anarchy ran rampant, trade stopped, and people were feeling the effects—less food, little money, and thievery or violence on every street corner.

I spent nine days in mourning for my friend, whom I would miss dearly. Then, I published an anonymous pamphlet. The ideas had been in my mind for some time, and I hoped my writing would help push a desperate government over the edge. Señor Espinosa and I worked hard, it being several pages, and the sun was starting to light the sky over the mountains by the time we finished.

Tired, almost unable to see, I left for home. On the way, I left my pamphlet on important doorsteps and in small stacks around the city. It was called *The Tower of Babel*, and it was my most vicious attack on the government thus far. I did not expect the trouble it caused me.

There was no author listed on my little book. Unfortunately, in our haste to print it, Señor Espinosa and I used the wrong paper, with his name imprinted on the bottom, on one of the pages. Knowing who the printer was, they simply arrested Bruno Espinosa. Under threat of torture he told them what they wanted to know: "Who is the author?"

Later that day, Natán came home and said, "Manuelita, the alderman, Señor Duran, is comin' here to arrest you."

"Why?"

"I don't know."

"How soon?"

Her voice became a little shrill with worry. "He is comin' down the street now. He has large men with him. They're armed with pikes and he himself is carryin' a big sword."

We peeked out the door and saw men lining up at the bottom of the stairs. There was no time.

"When they knock, answer the door," I told Natán, "and offer no resistance. Let only the alderman in. Do not let him state his business. Instead, invite him into my bedroom."

"Your bedroom?"

"Do as I say. Jonotás, come with me." We went to my room, and I lay on my bed with a rag on my forehead. I opened my jacket so the roundness of my breasts could be seen. When Natán brought Señor Duran in, Jonotás was stroking my brow. She even made a tear fall down her cheek.

He was so rotund that he had trouble making it through the door with his oversized sword strapped to his waist. He looked like a sow at a tea party, and I almost started laughing. He held out the warrant.

"What is it?" I asked, weakly.

He looked nervous and said, "It . . . uhm . . . is a . . . uhm . . . warrant for your arrest, Señora." He set it down, seeming to be afraid to come further into the room.

"Señor, you would not be so ungallant as to arrest me when I am so ill, would you?"

"Well, Señora, that is . . . uhm . . . well, you see . . . uhm . . . well, no, of course not . . . it's only—"

"Perhaps you could come back later," I said. Natán stepped back as though expecting him to leave.

He looked confused and said, "Yes . . . uhm . . . perhaps later. I am sorry, Señora." He bowed a little, getting his sword caught against the wall, as he tried to back out. With great difficulty, he got himself turned around in the hallway and made his way downstairs.

I quickly read the warrant he had left and found out that it was about my pamphlet—"inflammatory and seditious acts." At least I now knew what kind of stand to take. I sat down and began composing my response to the charges. I was infuriated that I might be arrested for merely writing my thoughts.

It was not long before there was another knock on the door. I grabbed a saber, unsheathed it and flung the door open. The point of my sword was a few inches away from Señor Duran's large belly, and behind him, on the stairs, were two or three bailiffs. He was sweating and panting, and I smelled, even at the length of a sword, the rum on his breath with which he had braced himself since his last visit.

"Manuela Sáenz," he said as soon as I opened the door, panting as though he were running a race, "the fact that you are ill is no reason . . ." He looked down at the sword and his eyes opened wide. He looked back and forth between me and the point of my saber. With what he considered to be bold determination, he took a step up and said, a little louder, a little more formal, "Manuela Sáenz, the fact—"

"Señor Alderman," I interrupted, calmly but firmly, "if you set one more foot above the other, I will run you through and make a widow of Señora Duran."

He went white, and began backing up. He stepped on one of the bailiffs, who yelled out in pain. They all stumbled back down the stairs, nearly falling, which would have been disastrous for those underneath Señor Duran.

I locked the door and had Jonotás load my pistols and put them on the table while I continued to compose my answer to the charges. About a half an hour later, I heard feet on the stairs. There was a knock and a call from Señor Duran outside saying, "Open up . . . uhm . . . I have with me the Lord Mayor, the judge who issued the warrant, ten soldiers, and eight convicts who have been granted leave to capture you." Jonotás looked out the window and said, "Manuelita, there is a large crowd formin'"

I laughed. "It must be quite embarrassing having all those people see all those men come to capture one woman."

There was a knock again. "You do not have my permission to enter my house," I called out.

Another knock; followed by the sound of voices arguing. Another knock. Louder angrier arguments. Finally, I heard the alderman throw his considerable weight against the door, followed by his distinctive panting. The lock held. It sounded as though others joined him from behind. After a few minutes, the door flew open and the alderman's round form pushed through the door followed by two or three others. I picked up my pistols, stood, and faced them. They stopped dead still.

Señor Duran was far enough in the room that the Lord Mayor and a judge were able to stand behind him. The stairs were crowded with confused men, wondering why they just didn't finish the business at hand.

No one spoke for a moment. They were afraid to come forward. Then, there followed a long outburst from the three of them, full of demands, pleas to reason, and threats. They stopped when I lifted my thumbs and cocked the pistols. I took one step forward, and they all took a half step back.

We stood that way for a long time. I said, "You are invading my property, and I will kill you if you do not retreat."

They pleaded with me. They argued amongst themselves. Señor Duran looked like he wanted to go, but the men behind him would have been in his way. They threatened. They demanded. They swore at each other and argued among themselves. I don't know how it would have turned out if Pepé Paris had not seen the crowd outside and pushed his way up the stairs. Everyone respected him, and he was able to negotiate a compromise.

I went to jail, but only long enough to be arraigned, so that the government would not lose face. I was back home within two hours. As it had been agreed, the charges were dropped.

Jonotás and Natán told me how scared they were that the government would not keep its word and that I would stay in prison. I was not as worried as they, because I truly expected the government to fall within days.

As it was, the administration lasted a little over a month. Finally, it happened, marked by President Mosquera's returning to his home in Popayán. It was unclear whether he still claimed to be the rightful president, but General Urdaneta took over the government on a provisional basis until Bolívar returned.

Chapter 42

At last! The chance that all of Simón's friends had waited for had come. Simón could return and bring order out of chaos again. In Bogotá, Cartagena, and other cities throughout Colombia, there were demonstrations in favor of The Liberator returning to power.

We waited, and started to worry. By that time his forty-seventh birthday had passed, and we had not received word from him in almost two months. We had heard from others that he was ill and that he was prepared to depart for Jamaica so that he might convalesce there. Rumors said that he had already written to his friend, Maxwell Hyslop, who had helped him in exile back in 1814, and that he would sail at any time.

Everyone wrote to him, but we only received back one letter, in October, stating to Urdaneta why he would not return. He saw no reason when Mosquera could still possibly lay claim to the office of president. He would only return as president if a national vote elected him. My hands shook as I held the paper when Urdaneta showed it to me. I read between the lines and knew that he was tired, probably very ill. "Rafael, what are we to do."

"Hold on, Señora, hold on."

I was losing my hold on courage. I needed to hear from him directly and I worried until I became ill myself. It had been difficult for me to write to him directly since his departure. The mail couriers were ordered not to carry correspondence from me to Bolívar. Consequently, I had to slip my letters in with Urdaneta's and I was never sure what he received and what he didn't. He only seemed to write to me when he could say that he felt well and I had received no letters recently.

We waited, throughout October. When the November rain began to fall, we heard bad news. Simón had decided to sail to Jamaica. The ship had only made it a few miles down the coast from Cartagena when he became so ill that they put to shore at a small town called Santa Marta. Bolívar had to be carried ashore. There, an aged Royalist, Don Joaquín de Mier, hearing of his illness, offered Bolívar his hacienda in which to recuperate.

By this time, Urdaneta and I prevailed on an old friend, Péroux de Lacroix, to ride to Santa Marta and bring back some word of his condition. On November 29, he left on the fastest horse we could find. But I was consumed with worry. Every minute that I stayed in Bogotá without news was like torture.

I fretted for almost two weeks, and finally I told Jonotás and Natán that we were going to Santa Marta. "I can wait no longer," I announced to Urdaneta. I packed as quickly as I could and headed off for the coast.

The trip was difficult. It rained nearly every day on the slope down into the valley. A week after we left, we were in Honda; tired, miserable, and impatient.

We tried to get a steam ferry, but the captains would not allow me passage. The steamers were owned by German businessmen who were angry at Bolívar for taking away their exclusive rights to ferry the river two years earlier—and I was a well-known Bolívar supporter. Finally, we hired an Indian crew of eight, and we loaded our supplies into dugout canoes.

I was about to step into a canoe for the journey north, when a muddy rider galloped up. "I am looking for Manuela Sáenz," he said, breathlessly.

"You have found her, Señor. I am whom you seek."

"I have been asked to deliver this letter to you." He rode up, handed me the letter, and then was gone.

I expected it to be from Bogotá or from Simón and I unfolded it while the Indian crew and my companions stood waiting. It was from Lacroix.

I read the last line and sank to my knees.

The letter dropped to the ground, and the wind blew it away. I sat there in a daze, without thinking, or seeing—I don't know for how long. Later, I was aware that I walked to the nearby stable, found my horse, saddled her, and started up the trail for Bogotá.

Bolívar was gone.

I knew it. I expected it. But I was overwhelmed by the shock. The man I had loved, and would always love, would no longer hold me in his arms.

Soldiers. Soldiers lived to die, or to watch their friends die. To win is the object. To make the enemy die is the object, but it taints your soul. The soldier himself dies. I had lived the life of a soldier, and I had now lived to see the man I love depart from this life. A part of *me* left this earth that day.

I could not see anything as I rode up the trail toward Bogotá. I rode all day, tears covering my eyes, before I realized that Jonotás and Natán had not caught up with me. I waited, watching the heartless landscape that demands so much of the humans who walk upon it. About an hour later, they rode up, tired and sad. They were so far behind me because they had taken the time to collect our things. "I saved the letter, Manuelita," said Jonotás, and handed it to me.

Many days later I had the courage to read it.

My Respected and Sorrowful Lady,

I promised to write to you and speak only the truth. Now I have finished your charge, and I shall bring you the most fated of notices.

I arrived at Santa Marta on December 12 and left at once for the hacienda where I saw the Liberator. His Excellency was already in a terrible state and fatally ill. I stayed in San Pedro until the 16th, when I left. His Excellency was then in the last state of agony—all his friends surrounding him, including myself, were reduced to tears. About him were Generals Montilla, Silva, Portocarrero, Infante; Colonels Oruz, Paredes, Wilson; Captain Ibarra, Lieutenant Fernando Bolívar and some other friends.

Yes, my sorrowful lady; when I left, this great man was ready to quit this ungrateful earth and pass on to the mansions of the dead, there to take his seat in posterity and immortality, side by side with the heroes who have figured most on this miserable earth. I repeat to you, with a sentiment made more deep by my enlivening pain and with a heart filled with wounded bitterness, that I left the Liberator, on the

16th, in tranquil agony, but in which he cannot long endure. I am waiting any moment now for the fated notice. Meanwhile I am filled with agitation, with sadness, with tears for the father of our country, the unhappy and great Bolívar, killed by the perversity, the ingratitude of all of those who were his debtors and who received from him so many proofs of generosity. This then is the sad and dire notice of what I myself saw, and it is now my duty to send it to you. I hope that the heavens, which contain more justice than displayed by men, will look down on poor Colombia.

Allow me, gracious lady, to mingle my tears with yours over your immense loss.

Chapter 43

On December 17, 1830, Simón Bolívar said his last words. Very few people were there: a doctor, the man who had offered him a place to convalesce, and a soldier. Outside, José Palacios could be heard cutting down the hammock that Bolívar had ordered him to hang days before because he knew he would get well. But he said the swaying of the empty hammock in the wind annoyed him and he had ordered his servant to take it down. The brig *Manuel*, on which he had started for Jamaica, still lay in the harbor of Santa Marta, as it had for the three weeks in which he languished.

As he put his affairs in order he spoke of the hopelessness of fighting a revolution. Toward the end, through labored breathing, he said the words that he believed summed up his life: "I have plowed the sea."

Then, The Liberator died.

On that same day, some of the world's greatness died. On that day, the sand in the hourglass that marked the time when Simón Bolívar and Manuela Sáenz loved on this earth ran out. On that same day, it seemed that everything that I was and had been, died too. Never before had I been so tired—tired of fighting.

I did not talk to my companions as we rode back to Bogotá. I could not talk at all. Time stopped.

What was I to do? What could possibly make me strive for a future? I did not want to fight anymore. Even if I tried, what good would it do?

As we rode through the rain, I stared ahead, seeing nothing. My horse found her way home, and by the time I rode into the capital I wondered if I should no longer live.

When we arrived at my apartment, I ordered Jonotás and Natán to find a fer-de-lance, one of the deadliest serpents in America, and bring it to me. They began to cry.

"No, Manuelita, no," Jonotás murmured.

I lay in the dark, in my bed, motionless. "Do as I ask you."

They protested at length. I only repeated my demand, and in the end they complied, bringing a small snake in a cloth sack. I told them to leave the room and I could hear them wail outside my door.

I sat on the edge of my bed and, through the sack, I felt for the serpent's head. Taking hold of it, I slowly opened the sack with the other hand. Its mouth was open, trying to reach behind its own head to attack me. Despite its quick movements, I was able to grab it with the other hand so that the sack fell away. Holding its head and its body with two hands, to keep its thrashing about from breaking my grip, I looked at its fangs. They were weapons. Weapons for killing. I was acutely aware of how close I was to death.

What would my death bring? Would it be a timeless state, such as I felt in these last hours of my life? Would I feel the same weariness, the same longing for something, as I felt at that moment? Would the state in which I left this world continue for eternity?

Suddenly I knew what I hungered for. I had been fighting the world around me since my birth. I had won and lost, but mostly I had won over those that held me down. I wanted to return home. After more than 30 years of fighting, I wanted to live in Quito in peace. At that moment, I felt the most profound longing of my life, a longing for tranquillity.

I would not take my life. *Bolívar may be gone, but his dreams still live,* I thought. Then, my companion's sobbing in the next room made me realize that I could not leave them. I loved my friends too much. I could certainly never leave anyone who depended on me. I wanted to live among friends, family and community in peace.

I called out to them. When they entered my bedroom, I said, "Here, take it away."

They cried out in happiness and came over to take the viper away. However, as I was putting it in the sack that Natán held up, we lost control of the serpent and it bit my shoulder.

Since I had decided to live, I became very frightened.

Natán ran for Doctor Cheyne. He came immediately, bringing Jean Baptiste Boussingault as well.

When they arrived, my arm had swelled to twice its size. Their remedy was that used by the Indians and consists of rum and other medicines. People have died despite the remedy, but apparently the snake my companions found was too young. I believe this was no accident.

And so I lived. I have not regretted my decision to live on past the death of my beloved, but in those first weeks I was without purpose. I was terribly lonely for Simón and most days I was grief stricken and did not know what to do with myself. The new year came and went, and I remained alone with my two companions, rarely seeing any of Simón's old friends. A few months later, before 1831 was half over, the most vicious snake of all returned to Bogotá.

The government held by Urdaneta had lost its strength when news of Bolívar's death reached the capital. When the Santanderists took over, they recalled my old enemy from exile.

As I look back now, with the perspective of time on my side, I am ashamed of my behavior then. I am ashamed I did not fight harder against his return, but my will had been almost shattered. I did not want to fight anymore. I also believed I was too weak to fight for Bolívar's dreams while still grieving over his death. I would wait awhile.

It was because I was not the old La Sáenz that I gave in to my friends' urgings. I left the city and moved to a small village, far enough away from Bogotá that I should have been no threat to the new government. Once there, I began to make plans to move back to Quito, where my brother had invited me. I wanted to be home, among family and friends, at peace.

José María and I exchanged many letters but a year later I was still in New Granada. For one thing, I did not have enough money to leave. Also, I had moved out of my apartment so swiftly that I left most of my possessions behind in Bogotá. I had sold my jewels for only a thousand pesos in order to move and to have something to live on. Yet, my medals, papers, glassware, fine China from England, weapons (souvenirs from the war), and little gifts given to me by soldiers and admirers over the years were all left behind. The landlord took these items for his own, but I had Manuelita Paris try to reclaim them. It became a legal battle and eventually most of it was delivered to her at Bolívar's villa, but not until much time had passed.

In the meantime, Santander solidified his power. Gran Colombia, no longer holding Venezuela or the old Presidency of Quito, changed its name to The United States of New Granada. Santander then declared war on the new state of Ecuador in a dispute over the border. When the war started, I could no longer travel south to Quito.

I desperately wanted to return to José, because my brother's letters were full of rancor at General Flores. He did not approve of the secession from Colombia to begin with, and the thought that Ecuadorians would now be fighting Colombians ate away at him.

I was afraid José would get into political trouble, and I wanted to be there to help him or to keep him out of trouble. He wrote that he was in no danger.

> It is a constant battle between Flores in Quito and Rocafuerte in
> Guayaquil. Each wants to rule, and I want to rejoin Colombia. Even
> though Flores and I disagree, he is a friend and will not harm me no
> matter what actions I am forced to take because of my principles.
> Rocafuerte is a different matter, but he should not rule in any case, even
> if we stay separate from Colombia.

Meanwhile, I was still stuck in a New Granada that was ruled by the cruel Santander. Not only were his executions and stupid political moves too much to bear, but his first act when back in office was to order Bolívar's name stricken from all public documents.

This was not the worst. Santander also spilt the blood of Colombians, in order to solidify his power. I could never persuade Simón to practice Santander's arts, despite the fact that a few men, such as the new president of the Republic, deserved to die. However, Santander was not so sensitive and far-seeing as Bolívar. He had no moral compunctions against killing anyone he did not like. Terror spread across the land, and blood flowed from every village wherein might reside an active Bolívarist. I heard that he attended every execution that he could, watching with icy lust.

As 1834 approached, it became clear that I, who was completely silent politically, was a target for Santander's terror. I longed for the war with Ecuador to be over so that I could leave. I had not heard from José María in some time. Every week my friends brought me stories of more and more ridiculous accusations against me. I could not travel to Quito, and it was becoming clear that I could not stay in New Granada. I felt trapped.

When I was summoned to Bogotá to answer "certain charges," I wrote back:

> They say that my house, where I live on the savanna, is a rendezvous of all the malcontents. When my friends visit me, must I first ask them if they are content or discontent?
> Santander gives me an unimaginable valor, saying that I have the capacity for the most monstrous of deceptions.
> What I really am is a woman who is a friend of my friends, enemy of my enemies; I have nothing in common with this miserable Santander.

Despite my will to hold on, my pen could not keep me out of prison; on the contrary, my writing always inflamed my enemies. On January 1, 1834, Santander signed an order that I was to leave the country. I was given three days.

Maybe I could have been in Ecuador within three days and on my way to Quito, but it would have been very difficult. There was no guarantee that I could slip through the armies stationed on the border roads, and I had nowhere else to go. I sent a letter stating that the decree was illegal and that I was not a threat to the republic, and thus I would stay.

Though I half expected it to happen, I was not prepared for the number of soldiers who came to arrest me, assisted by convicts released temporarily for the purpose. I barricaded the door, but they broke into my house, tied us, gagged us, and placed us on mules. We rode for hours before they ungagged us, but they kept our hands tied all day. I no longer had any choice as to what I would or would not do. Soon, we were in Honda, and my future looked bleak and desolate as we prepared to journey down the Magdalena River.

We waited in Honda a day because the soldiers did not want to use steamships. We finally departed on barges. I was glad to leave the place where I had learned of Simón's death. Our progress was slow, and we stopped many times on the river trek. Jonotás, Natán, and I slept together in improvised quarters each night. During the day we suffered either fierce rain from oppressive clouds or unbearable heat from an unremitting sun. Thus did we drift down the river accompanied by ungallant men.

My friends could see that I was in an uncharacteristic apathy. They tried their best to comfort me, but I was difficult to console. "Don't be so sad, Manuelita," Jonotás whispered to me as we lay huddled together on the floor of an abandoned building by the shore of the river somewhere. Natán was outside cooking some purgative tea on the soldiers' fire because she felt her old illness coming on. I was feeling particularly low that night when Jonotás lay down next to me. "We will win this battle, too—like all the others," she said, when I did not answer her.

I was sniffing and so she knew I was crying, though we were lying in near darkness. "I am not so sure this time," I said at last. I could not tell her that I no longer wished battle. I was afraid she would think me craven. Instead, I said, "I don't have the will I once did. I am 36 years old. I am tired, and I have not much left to live for." I could tell she was having trouble knowing what to say. "And I'm worried about the two of you."

"Us? Why?"

"Oh, my Jonotás, how can you ask? This is the second time I have been responsible for your going to prison." We had been told that we were being taken to the Cartagena dungeon.

"But, Manuelita, we will not be there long. Only until they find us passage to Jamaica, yes?"

"Yes, but—"

"And I'm happy to be goin'. I've not seen Jamaica since I was a little child."

"It is only that—" I had to stop to wipe my eyes. "I cannot stand to be imprisoned, even for a little. And when I think of you and Natán, arrested, humiliated, and shut up because of me, I . . ." I began to sob.

She held my head against her breasts, and I cried like a little child. Jonotás kept saying, "There, there, my love. Don't be sad."

She made me feel better; and when I calmed down a little, Jonotás said, "I have spent my life as a slave. I know somethin' 'bout imprisonment and freedom. I've had to cook, clean, wipe up after people, cut sugar cane, and in the years before I met you, I never spent no time behind any bars. Yet that was not freedom.

"Since I met you, I've done things, seen things, been places I never would've known. I've even seen the inside of a prison. Yet in all that time, I been free."

I let out a sigh, and said, "Oh, Jonotás . . ."

She said, "So I don't want no cryin' 'bout me bein' in prison."

"But I do feel bad. You loved Crofston. It was because of me that you haven't seen him much in these past few years. Now we may never come back."

"Yes, I miss him." She was silent for a moment. "But he's goin' back to England and I would not see him anyway."

We were quiet for a while.

"I'll tell you somethin' else," she said next. "I love you, Manuelita." I could hear her start to choke up. "I was 'bout 24 when I met you and now I'm over 40. Yet I'd have spent that whole time in prison if I could be with you. I would have left any man I've known in these past years to be with you." Now she was crying.

Natán came in and said, "What're you two doing?"

Jonotás cried harder, and I started to cry again. I motioned toward Natán, and she sat down her tea. As she came to us she lost her balance and fell. Jonotás and I were practically crushed and we started laughing—laughing harder than we were crying. A weight seemed to lift from me. That night, I released some of the sadness I'd been feeling since Simón's death. I felt a little better as we finished the journey.

When we arrived in Cartagena, we were taken to the 16th century prison that sits out on a narrow strip of land, a place from which there has never been an escape. We were marched up to the gates and turned over to guards who escorted us into the bowels of the fortress.

We seemed to walk through dark stone hallways for a long time. At last, we were brought into a large bare room, with only two high, barred windows. Shafts of sunlight entered the room through the windows at sharp angles. The room was much brighter than the hallways.

We waited to be given over to the warden. Finally, he entered, a slim, oily man whose face was covered with pox scars and who kept yawning. He paced up and down while he read over the letters and documents in his hand. The three of us stood, hands bound, waiting for him to speak. He yawned twice, as though it was too much for him to stay awake. The two soldiers who had escorted us in stood against the door, either leering at us, or looking at the floor in boredom.

"It seems we won't be keeping you long," he said at last. "However, while you're here, you will be treated like any other prisoner. President Santander, in his letter, has asked that you be assigned a specific cell. I believe that was the cell he occupied when he was on his way to Jamaica." He smiled and looked at me, to see if I would react, but I kept a stoic face. He went on, "However, it is in use and you may be gone in a day or so. It is too much trouble, and . . ." he yawned, ". . . I don't want to do the paperwork." He looked at me and smiled, "You won't tell, will you?"

I said nothing.

"Well, then, I am done here. Is there someone in Jamaica with whom you will stay when you arrive? I will notify them for you."

I shook my head at first, but then I remembered Maxwell Hyslop, with whom Bolívar took refuge 20 years before. I gave him the name.

He said, "Fine. I am done. My trustees do most of the work here." He smiled conspiratorially and said, "I like my leisure, eh?" When I did not react to this attempt at affability, he said, "Anyway, they will be here in a while to unbind you and take you to your cell."

While yawning, long and hard, he was able to enunciate, "I'm putting you all together." He waited until he stopped yawning. "It will be crowded, but you'll be gone soon. Otherwise, it is just too much trouble." Turning slowly, he walked to the door. He yawned while he waited for the soldiers to open it, and then he was gone.

We sat down clumsily on the floor with our hands still tied behind our backs. Jonotás sat very close to me. I felt as if she had put her arms around me, yet they were still tied. She whispered, "This jail makes me nervous, Manuelita. I don' know if I can stay here."

I knew she was thinking of Casa Matas and I said, "We should only be here a short while. Then we're going to Jamaica. Remember?"

"Yes, but maybe we should find other lodgin's for our stay in Cartagena," she joked, mirthlessly.

Despite her words several nights before, she was deeply upset at being in prison again. I ran my cheek across her hair in an effort to comfort her. We were tired from the journey, and we did not speak after that.

We sat and waited a long time, comforting each other with our closeness. Natán was on my left, her head against the wall. Jonotás was on my right, her head on my shoulder. I think I dozed off.

I was startled when I heard a key turning in the lock and an oddly familiar voice. "Go in and untie the prisoners, and wait for me. I have to check next door."

The door opened. Two men came in and smirked at us, leaving the door ajar. They looked dirty and I assumed that they were prisoners entrusted with special duties. The familiar voice called out, "Lock the door behind you, you fools."

One of them went back and locked the door. "Stand up," barked the other and pulled us roughly to our feet. When we were standing, they untied us.

From outside the door I heard. "Is it really you?" Then I heard the lock turn hurriedly. I looked over to see a familiar man walk in reading a piece of paper.

He was so near sighted that the paper was practically touching his nose. He locked the door behind him while he peered in our direction.

I could not place the short, stocky man at first. His hair and beard were completely gray, thick and curly. It was the hair that finally identified him, falling in tight coils from under a kind of skull cap. He still wore a knife in his belt, though it had obviously been manufactured from found materials. It was Juan Guzmán from Panamá.

He walked right up to me, put his face very close to mine and scrutinized what he saw. I could feel Jonotás shaking next to me. I stepped a little between them.

My hair was out of place; down and fallen over my cheeks. Reaching out a filthy hand, he whipped my hair over my shoulders. He grinned, exposing decaying teeth. His face was uglier and more sinister looking than it was 17 years before. He squinted at me and moved his face closer. He had trouble making out my features unless he was very close. Then, he reached behind my neck, grabbed my hair, and jerked it back and up so that it resembled the way I wore my hair in Panamá. His smile grew broad.

"Well, well, well. The white bitch who was too good for me. The one who thought it fun to tell lies about me."

I felt as though I had withdrawn into myself and was looking at him through a long tunnel. I forced myself to say something. "Señor Guzmán—"

He ignored me and touched my hairline, next to my ear, and ran his finger down my cheek, along my jaw line, down my neck, and across my left breast. I pulled back.

"Still too good for me, are you?" He smiled and turned to his men, who stood grinning stupidly, and said, "Boys, I think we'll have fun with these." He turned and looked back at us. Walking up close, he peered at Jonotás and then at Natán. His eyes lingered on Natán. "What kind of goodies have you brought with you, Señorita Sáenz?"

"Señor Guzmán," I said, "whatever argument you had was with me. Take your revenge on me."

"Revenge? I have no cause for revenge. Why should I want revenge? I've learned my place here among the other 'animals,' even though I was sent here by lies and jealousy. No my interest in your friend here," he stepped close to Natán, "is derived from the love she has inspired in me."

He reached out his finger and ran it across Natán's face as he did mine. Natán recoiled. "So pretty. Such beautiful skin. You're mixed blood like me, aren't you." He looked her up and down. "But you should not dress in so unfeminine a fashion," he said to Natán, as he fingered the buttons of her soldier's uniform. He turned to one of his men and said, "Go stand in front of the door." The man went and stood with his head covering the small barred opening in the door. Then Guzmán started to unbutton Natán's jacket, saying, "Let us get you out of this uncomfortable—"

Natán stepped back—terrified.

Fear surged through me, and I said, "Don't!" He looked at me in anger. "Please!" I implored.

He grabbed my own uniform, pulled me to him, and snarled, "I remember now. You like to interfere." He pushed me away from him, into the hands of the other man and gave him a nod. The man tied my hands behind me.

Guzmán turned around, placed his hand on the flap at Natán's top button. Slowly, he slipped his fingers inside. Then, with one ferocious yank, he tore open her jacket. The buttons flew in all directions, bouncing on the stones. Immediately, he grabbed at her underslip and tore it down, revealing her breasts. I screamed at him, "Stop it. Stop it."

Natán backed against the wall, saying, "Please, Señor . . ."

Then Jonotás did an amazing thing. She walked over to them and slapped Guzmán on the shoulder.

He swung around, saying, "What the hell are you doing?"

Jonotás already had her eyes on the floor. Then she stamped on something invisible and kicked it away with her foot. "It was about to sting you."

"What was?" said Guzmán suspiciously.

"That insect."

Guzmán peered at the floor but did not want to admit that he didn't see anything.

Then, Jonotás put her hand on his face and said, "Why do you want that skinny girl who doesn't want you?" She seemed to have completely lost her fear and moved up next to him and brought her hand down to his neck. "I want you," she said seductively, "I want you bad."

She pressed against him as he put his arms around her. She moved her hands down to his chest. She said, "You're so beautiful—and strong." In his eyes I could see the violence that he had directed at Natán, only moments before, turn to lust for Jonotás.

She moved her hands farther down his chest. Her left hand dipped lower and slid down to his private parts. Guzmán smiled a wicked smile, obviously enjoying the attention.

Then I saw Guzmán's knife in Jonotás's right hand raised high in the air. It seemed to hang there like some static pendulum that had stopped time. Then, she drove it into his neck.

Blood spurted like a fountain as she backed away. She ran toward us as Guzmán dropped to his knees. The other two men were so stunned for a moment they could not move before they ran toward the fallen Guzmán. The three of us rushed into the corner. Natán untied my hands and Jonotás wiped the blood from her face saying, "What have I done, Manuelita. What have I done."

"It's all right," I said, and urged them along the wall towards the door.

The two men stood looking stupidly at Guzmán as he fought with the knife, unable to breathe or talk. His body convulsed as he tried to cough up the blood that was filling his lungs. He thrashed on the floor for a moment and then it was over. Then, his men looked at us in disbelief. We froze.

They stood there in simpleminded contemplation for a moment, and then they lunged for Jonotás. Natán and I fought with them, but they called for help. Guards rushed in and they finally had Jonotás's arms tied behind her back. One man held Natán to the floor as she cried out for Jonotás. Two others had me pushed against the wall, immobile. As she was dragged out of the door I screamed, "No, don't take her. It's not her fault. It's mine."

"Don't worry, Manuelita. I love you," I heard her cry as she was taken down the hall. Her voice was filled with terror.

Shortly, other soldiers came in. They examined Guzmán for a moment and then took Natán and me roughly down another hall. We pleaded, "Where is Jonotás? Where is my friend? What have you done to her?" There was no reply.

After descending lower into the prison, we were all but thrown into a cell. They locked the door and left.

Natán and I sat together for days, not speaking, not crying, not moving. We feared for Jonotás, while we languished there, but there was no word. When I thought of the future, I could only imagine emptiness. What could I latch onto that could make me move forward in time?

The cell was dirty, and there was no light except for a flambeau. A day or so later, Natán, who had looked weak and felt ill all the way down the river, began shivering and coughing. It was difficult to tell time in the dungeon, except by noting the slop they called gruel brought to us every morning, but I know she stayed that way for days. I begged my jailers to get her a doctor and I begged for word of Jonotás, but we received neither.

While I held onto Natán and cried for Jonotás, I had time to reflect on my life. I had been at war with life since I was born. I was born into a world of violence, and I had fought with the world. Most of the time I won, a few times I lost, but what had it all been worth? I doubted everything I had ever done. In Perú I had vowed to regard myself as my friend, and to give myself the same love, or more, that I gave to all my friends. As I lay holding Natán, shivering close to me, I could see myself as an enemy, and I began to loathe myself as I would any other foe.

After several days the cell was opened, and Natán and I were led through the fortress, out to the town, and down to a ship ready to sail to Jamaica. Natán was shaking and coughing, and we were both soiled and unpresentable. I begged for news of Jonotás from every soldier we met. One of them said she was about to stand trial. I knew then she would die.

"But it was my fault," I told him in despair. I grabbed him and said, "Don't you understand, it was my fault," as though he had anything at all to do with it.

I wanted to stay and save her somehow. Instead I was forced to board the ship that was to take me into exile.

Chapter 44

Maxwell Hyslop met us when the ship landed in Kingston. He was a well-dressed English gentleman with snow white hair, very soft spoken and kind. He greeted me in Spanish, and I greeted him in English. He was surprised, but pleased, and said, "I am so very happy to receive a friend of Simón Bolívar's. I received word from the warden in Cartagena, but I was already watching for your arrival."

"Why, Sir?" I asked, holding my hand over my eyes to shade the bright sunlight.

He smiled and said, "Word of the exile of the woman known as *La Libertadora* had already come to me."

"You are most kind, Sir. I cannot tell you how happy I am to see a friendly face."

"You are welcome to stay with me as long as you are in Jamaica."

Our host took us to his home in the center of town. Natán and I were introduced to his wife and family, and we were offered tea, but Mr. Hyslop noticed that Natán was not feeling well. "Come, you must be tired," he said, when introductions were over and led us upstairs.

He opened the door to a small room and I looked around the place I must now call home. It had two beds and it was very clean. The smallness did not bother me. The room was no smaller than my life had become. Could I be at peace here?

Our host said, "Bolívar had a room down the street when he was in Jamaica— was it 20 years ago?"

A lump came to my throat and I made myself breathe slower.

He did not notice and went on, "He was having trouble with his landlady and sometimes he would stay in this room. Once he stayed here to let a recently arrived friend sleep in his hammock. An assassin, sent by the Spanish, came into his room that night and killed his friend."

I knew the story and I was reminded of the night of September 25. Tears filled my eyes.

Mr. Hyslop looked at the street through the window and said, distantly as though lost in his memories, "It was in this very room that the *Jamaica Letter,* was written."

I fought off tears and thought to myself, *Simón knew, even then, what had to be done to make a strong new country.* I went over his words from the famous document in my mind. *"I shall tell you with what we must provide ourselves in order to expel the Spaniards and to found a free government. It is union . . ."* He spent his life trying to achieve this impossible goal, and 20 years later he was no longer there to make it happen. If he had achieved it, he would have created the mightiest and wealthiest nation on earth. Instead, the South American people were splintered beyond hope of any future cohesion. I feared I would weep.

Mr. Hyslop noticed my distress and said, hurriedly, "I have been inconsiderate of your feelings. I am sorry. If there is there anything I can do for you, Madam, please ask." He began to leave.

"No, thank you, Sir," I managed. Natán sat down wearily on one of the beds.

"Very, well," he said, as he started to close the door.

"No, wait. There is one thing. Would you be so kind as to send for word about our friend who was kept in Cartagena."

I explained what happened to Jonotás and he said, "I will send a letter on a departing ship this afternoon." Then, he left us.

I sat down next to Natán. She put her head on my shoulder and cried. The tension of the last several weeks drained out of us both.

In the days that followed, Natán was so very worried about Jonotás that I could not get her to take an interest in anything. Her condition had not improved at all since leaving Cartagena, not even in the fresh air on the ship. I had hoped that healthy food in Jamaica would be medicine for her, but days later she was still lethargic and mildly feverish. Then she became sicker and began coughing up a viscous, yellow-brown sputum. I watched her constantly, day in and day out, for two weeks.

At last, she began to improve. I had barely left our room in that whole time, so Mr. Hyslop insisted that I go out for a ride with his family.

Jamaica was not unpleasant, but it was not home. I never felt comfortable there. It was too flat, and the food always seemed foreign. Mr. Hyslop was a most gracious host, and he showed me around the town and the outlying area that afternoon. The countryside was beautiful, but the populated areas were not a pretty sight. Houses and shops were in disrepair, and the streets were filed with dispirited looking blacks, on business for their masters.

"We have recently received word from England that has changed us. A new law, The Imperial Abolition act of 1833, requires all slaves to be freed."

I looked around. These looked like slaves, not free men and women.

Mr. Hyslop went on. "In a way, it is worse for the Africans."

"Why is that, Sir?"

"The emancipation law requires that the former slaves undergo an apprenticeship—six years of labor at 40 and ½ hours a week for plantation workers, without pay. The household servants must serve four years with no limit to the number of hours they must work each week, also without pay. Thus, the Africans know they are free, yet they are still virtually slaves. Sugar production is down, and the country is feeling the effects of little money. The plantation owners are angry and take it out on the blacks—and the blacks are resentful.

He shook his head, as an old African approached the coach for charity. "Some, such as myself, have long since freed their slaves completely, but there is little work for them to do. My own household has not relied on slaves, or sugar, since the early days of your revolution. After Bolívar's visit with me, I followed his example when he began freeing slaves upon returning to his country. My servants have been paid workers for years. However, most of the rest of this country has not been so modern in their thinking." He looked away, a sad look in his eyes. "Now the country is degenerating."

When I contemplated the changes that Jamaica would have to endure, I was overwhelmed at the idea of what lay ahead. "What can be done to assimilate the Africans into the citizenry?" I asked, almost to myself.

"I cannot say. There are those who resist these changes and there has been violence against the Africans. I am afraid we will suffer for some time as we learn to live in a modern world without slavery. If only the United States could be as enlightened. Their continued use of slaves only confuses the issue for her neighbors."

I had to agree with him. I was glad to see the slaves freed, but I could see that they suffered and that it might take generations for true freedom to come. In the meantime, I could see there would be much misery. It made me feel sad for them, and it reminded me of the turmoil in my own country—centuries of abuse from Spain, years of war, finally free, and we fight among ourselves. Always strife, never peace. There was no end to suffering.

I did not spend much time with Mr. Hyslop or in trying to get to know the land I might have to call home permanently, because I wished to stay with Natán. I could not even think of what I would do or where I would go from Jamaica. I only thought of my friend. I nursed her, day and night, until she improved enough to get out of bed.

In a month or so she was on her feet again, but she did not ever fully recover. She continued to cough and was constantly weak. She could not make it through the day without napping.

In the meantime, I forced myself to think about my future, despite the fact that all I could imagine was emptiness. One evening, as we were about to lie down for the night, I said to Natán, "I think we should not stay in Jamaica. It feels so foreign to me. Do you have any desire as to where you would like to live?"

She did not answer.

"Is there no place you would like to go?" I prompted.

Still she did not answer and continued to turn back her covers.

I climbed into bed and said, "We cannot return to New Granada."

"Until Jonotás arrives, we cannot go anywhere, Manuelita," Natán said, as she blew out the candle and lay down in her bed.

I did not have the heart to say what I feared she had already refused to accept. In all probability Jonotás would be executed for killing Guzmán. Instead, I spoke into the darkness and said, "No, of course not. But when she arrives, we can go somewhere. We can leave here if you wish." I thought for a moment, and said, "Or we can stay here. Of course, I'll need to have some money . . ." My voice trailed off, because I did not know how we were to live except on the charity of Mr. Hyslop.

"I would love to return to Panamá," she said.

My thinking about my lack of funds distracted me and I did not answer. I realized fully, at that moment, that my only immediate source of income was to have some of my friends in Bogotá sell my personal property.

"I miss Panamá," she said, drowsily.

"Yes, Natán, that is a possibility. Certainly, if we return to Ecuador or Perú, we will pass through. Perhaps we will stay there a while." I was hardly thinking about what I was saying because I was so worried about our future. As I listened to Natán's rhythmic breathing, I lay there and wondered what would happen to us.

The next morning, I wrote to Manuelita Paris to have her claim as many of my possessions, as she could. I wrote, "I am most hopeful that you will be able to recover all I left behind and sell it. Much of it is of great value, my horses particularly. You have my gratitude if, through these endeavors, you are able to send me any money. Thank you, my dear friend."

I worried about money every day. While I know Mr. Hyslop would have provided everything I needed, I did not ask him for anything beside the food and shelter he gave us. Thus, I only spent the little money I had, that I had carried with me from New Granada, on medicines.

A few weeks after our arrival, Mr. Hyslop rented a small house for us, close to his. He moved Natán and me there, thus giving him back his own household. He also knew he was providing us some privacy and freedom from the pressure to be social. It was a most welcome respite, and the quiet did us a great deal of good.

He also acquired a servant for me from one of the neighboring islands, who spoke only Spanish. She was a large black woman named Juana Rosa. He told me he would pay her way until I could afford to do it.

She was large and tough looking but with a heart like a lamb. She took instant pity on Natán and did everything she could for her. Later, she even invited Natán to the evening "church" meetings that she had begun attending, though she did not understand what was being spoken.

When I questioned one of the leaders of the church about their religion, I did not understand it all. It was nothing like the Masses I had attended as a child. I gathered that while professing to be Christian, the religion was an amalgam of Christianity and African sorcery called *Myal*. When they went to the church, where only Africans attended, they were admitted to the meeting by a leader called a "daddy." Once inside, there was a great deal of wailing and dancing. I thought it all sounded silly, but it seemed to help Natán.

Over the next couple of months, Manuelita Paris regularly sent me funds, along with encouraging letters that contained the news of events in Bogotá. I often wondered how much of the money she sent me was actually proceeds of the sale of my goods, and how much was charity. However, I was able to maintain my household on what she sent to me.

When I wrote back to her, I found it difficult to respond with more than gratitude for her efforts. I could not discuss politics with her. I found it hard to even read her letters because I did not want to know about Santander's cruelty or the degradation of Bolívar's country. I, who had always written to my friends, had to force myself to write letters to them. It was an effort to keep these letters from being pitiful. I wrote because I wanted to maintain my connections, but every page brought me grief.

Some of my correspondence was answered; some was not. José María did not answer at all, and I worried about him a great deal. The last that I knew, the war between Ecuador and New Granada still raged on. José María, ever loyal, was against the war and the separation, but I did not know which side he would choose or how he fit into the political events in my country.

In the first week of April, Mr. Hyslop knocked on my door. He had a new beaver hat in his hand, and he was dressed in his finest black suit of clothes. He looked uncomfortable. I thought I knew what he was about to say.

"I have some bad news." At that moment, Natán came up behind me. "I have received word from Cartagena . . ." He noticed the tears already falling down my cheeks. I was frozen and could not move. "Your slave—"

"*Friend*, Mr. Hyslop," I said softly.

"Yes, of course. Your . . . friend . . . was hanged . . . that is, executed . . . last month." A cry of anguish came from Natán. I turned to look at her. Her chin was quivering and her eyes were flooded with tears. I too cried out as I took her in my arms.

"I am sorry," our benefactor said kindly. "If there is anything Mrs. Hyslop or I can do . . . well, I am very sorry."

He must have left. I do not remember. I do not remember closing the door. I held Natán in my arms. "I loved her, Manuelita," she said. Her voice was full grief. I could not stand up anymore. We sank to the floor. "I loved her so much."

"I know. I loved her, too." I held her in my arms and rocked her back and forth. "I loved her, too."

"Oh, Manuelita, what are we going to do?"

I did not know. Evening became night. Juana Rosa found us and urged us to go to bed. "Please, Señora, please—rest now," I heard her saying from a great distance as she tried to help us rise.

Natán and I walked into my bedroom, and we lay down in our clothes. We held each other tightly as though to assure ourselves that there was still life in the world. We fell asleep and slept a long time, holding onto one another as though we could not let go.

The next day was one of the most difficult I have ever had. I was still grieving, even after three years, for Simón. I missed him every day and often wanted to join him. The death of Jonotás—even though I knew it would be thus—tore out what I thought was the last of my soul. Also, Natán relapsed the next morning. She looked worse than I'd ever seen her, and she had a high fever.

I threw all of my attention and resources into her recovery. She would not eat. She frightened me. Juana Rosa brought herbs and medicines from African matriarchs throughout the city, and Mr. Hyslop hired a doctor to look at her. Nothing seemed to make her any better.

When Mr. Hyslop brought the doctor, I pulled him aside. "Please, Mr. Hyslop, where was Jonotás buried?"

He looked at the floor and said softly. "It is my understanding that she was buried in a common grave for the poor."

I cried out. When I thought of her being thrown into a pit, on top of rotting corpses, with a few scoops of lime for a shroud, the horror of having her die was felt again, doubly hard. She was my friend—the best friend that anyone could ever have. She deserved the finest monument, the most beautiful crypt, the most glorious parade through the most magnificent city—not a common grave. It was too much for me to bear.

I held my chest and bent over, almost unable to walk. Mr. Hyslop said, "Are you all right? Please, are you all right" He helped me to sit down. It must have looked like I was dying, and I was. It seemed my spirit was leaving me.

I did not believe anything else could happen to me. There was nothing in my future. I felt I had surely lost my ability to feel any more. It was not so. There was more of my heart yet to break.

A month later, Natán died in my arms. She begged me to return to Panamá, and I promised her we would, but she never got out of bed. Her illness had weakened her so. Without the food she had refused, her heart failed. She died of that which I knew might also happen to me: a broken heart.

I had loved my two friends more than myself. I had loved them as much as I had loved Simón. I had spent more time and more hardships and more triumphs with them than with anyone. Together we had done so many things, things that few men have done, let alone three women.

I believed then that my life was finally over. After giving Natán the best burial I could, I walked home with Mr. Hyslop; and I intended to die as Natán had done. I would no longer eat. There was nothing left for me anyway. I was alone and there was no more use for me anymore.

When we were about a block from my house, I gave some instructions to Juana Rosa in Spanish. Just then, a little black girl came up to me and said, in Spanish, "Please, Señora, my sister and I are hungry."

I looked down at her and Mr. Hyslop said, "What did she say?"

"She said, she and her sister are hungry."

She was terribly thin, her voice was weak, and her expression was a mixture of exhaustion and urgency. Feeling as sad as I did, I might have ignored a beggar; but this little girl was emaciated, and she spoke my language. I took instant pity on her.

"Where is your sister?" I asked.

She pointed in an indefinable direction.

"Take me to her," I said.

She took my hand and led me around the corner, between two buildings, where another little girl sat. She was younger by a year or so, huddled against a large box, looking too weak to stand.

"What is your name?" I asked the older one.

"Dominga," she said.

"And what is your sister's name," I asked.

"Mendoza."

"Where are your mother and father?"

"Dead," she said stoically.

"Can your sister walk?"

"Yes, Señora."

"Then come with me. I will feed you."

The children were about 11 and 12, about the right age for children of mine if Simón and I could have fulfilled my wish to have children together. They were so small and thin they looked several years younger.

They did not understand all that had happened to cause them to be in Jamaica. When I questioned them, I did not understand at first. Eventually, I deduced that they had escaped the cholera epidemic that had been raging in Cuba for almost a year, with the help of some kindly missionaries from the United States. However, by the time their ship reached Jamaica, the missionaries themselves had died of the disease. The young girls had been lost in the confusion upon landing—alone and unable to speak the language—and had been without shelter or food for almost a week.

I fed them and cared for them. They were lovely, fascinating little girls. I did not even try to find someone to take them off my hands. For the next month or so, they gave me something to live for. I still lived day to day, but they kept me alive.

These sweet little girls gave me a future. I loved them more than I thought my heart could bear. I still did not know what the future would hold, and I still had not yet fully reclaimed my desire to survive. But I had something that kept me alive. Then, I met someone that brought me completely back from the grave.

Chapter 45

One morning I went shopping for special herbs to make a tea to strengthen my orphans. Juana Rosa had said, "You find these herbs Señora—you buy them where I always go. The girls will be strong soon." Then she directed me to a part of town to which I had not been before.

When I arrived, the street was crowded, full of women with bundles on their heads, going from one shop to another. These "shops" were little more than cane shacks by the side of the street. As I passed one of these, a big white man, unshaven and obese pushed a pretty *mulatta*, about seventeen or eighteen years old, out of the door. "You go on now. I gave you a fair price."

"No, you damn didn't, you damn buckra!" the woman yelled back.

The man's face grew dark and red. "Get out of here and don't come back!" He walked inside, and she let go some English words that I guessed to be curses. Then she walked down the street in my direction. As she passed, I heard her muttering to herself, "Damn white ass. They always be cheatin'." Just as the few curious onlookers turned away, she yelled back at the shop, "You're a damn thief," and continued walking.

I thought I recognized her, but then I knew it could not be. I was so curious that I overlooked the woman's mood. I said, "Excuse me—" just as she passed.

She turned on me violently, her voice full of hatred. "I don' have nothin' to say to no damn white woman."

"But—"

She hissed, "You damn buckra," using the insult the blacks used for whites, meaning "back raw" which whites had the ability to make the blacks suffer, "you leave me alone." Then, she walked on.

"Wait," I said, and grabbed her arm.

She shook her arm away and looked at me in fury. "Don't you touch me. I be free now. I ain't no slave. You can make me work for nothin' you bitch, but I don' have to talk to you." She turned away again.

Other blacks around us looked at her in shock, and then at me to see how I would react. I worried for her, if a white man had heard her talk to me that way, he could have and would have made her suffer.

I said, "Carmen?"

She stopped and turned back. She looked at me more closely and saw my interest in her was innocent and meant no harm. She said, suspiciously, "My name be Manuela. Dat be my mama's name."

I started to laugh with delight. This woman looked almost exactly like my friend from the convent, almost 20 years ago. She was a little darker, but otherwise exactly like my Carmen. I knew it was Carmen's daughter. I let out an expression of surprise, in Spanish. The woman peered at me in curiosity. I said, in English, "I'm a friend of your mama's."

"My mama's?"

"I've not seen her in years. Oh, where is she? I must see her."

"Where you know my mama from?" she asked suspiciously.

"From Quito, many years ago."

Her face softened. "I'm sorry," she said, "I was angry—"

"I know. It's all right. Where is she?"

"She be workin'"

"I would be most pleased if you tell her, Manuela Sáenz would love to see her."

Her eyes lit up. "Are you who I was named after? Manuela, from the convent in Quito?"

I smiled and admitted that I must be that Manuela, and she hugged me. She was all smiles now and said she would tell Carmen right away. My old friend was working as a maid that day, but would be off the day after next. I gave her daughter my address.

That very afternoon, Carmen knocked on my door. The years had been hard on her, but there were many reminders left of her youthful vigor and beauty. She was a little heavier, and her hair had whitened considerably. She was about 45, yet there was something still uniquely sensual, beautiful, and young about her. After all the years, I had found my friend again.

"Manuela, Manuela," she said, as we fell into each other's arms.

"Oh, Sister," I cried as she held me.

"My daughter was so happy to have met you. I heard, a year or two ago, about *La Libertadora*, and who she was. When I told my daughter, she was very pleased."

"Why?"

"She admires the revolutionaries of the continent."

It seemed so strange to see my old friend standing there in a fine English dress—not expensive, but very nice—when we both might have been in servant's habits. "Surely, I was nothing when she was born. Why did you name her Manuela?"

"You were never nothin' to me. I loved you then, and I love you now."

513

I smiled at her and said, "I love you, too, my friend." I reached out and took her hand. We looked at each other for a moment and then I said, "She seems like her own person, who should be given a name all her own. Why was she so pleased to find out I was her namesake?"

"When she was young, and we were still workin' on the plantation, I passed along all the stories my mama told me and I sang her the African songs that my gran'mama taught to me. I gave her pride in her African ancestors, but I also seem to have instilled a rebellious hatred of whites."

"I felt some of that hatred," I said, smiling.

"Hatred was never my intent, but the abuse she—we all—suffered at hands of the cane overseers . . ." Her eyes grew wet. "She lost her father to their cruelty." She composed herself and smiled as she put her sad thoughts behind her. "Anyway, she thinks highly of the revolution. In a way, you are a heroine for her."

I laughed at the idea. We talked a long time, mostly in Spanish with bits of English scattered throughout. Life had been hard on Carmen, but she was very much alive and happy. She told me of how she had persuaded the man she was seeing in Quito to steal her away. They set out for England, where slavery was no longer legal, but the man changed his mind and left her in Jamaica. She had been treated as a runaway slave, and was auctioned off to a plantation owner.

There, she had met the man she was to marry. "I loved him more than anyone I ever knew," she said. Later, their daughter was born. When Manuela was 5, Carmen's husband was beaten to death by an overseer. The man was tried for the crime, but he was acquitted. She and her daughter continued to work in the cane fields until the emancipation.

It had grown dark in the room and Juana Rosa came in with some lamps. This reminded Carmen of the hour, and she departed shortly after that. When she left that evening, I felt better than I had in months.

Her work days were long, but she came over every day after that. She always brought little treats for Dominga and Mendoza from the kitchen of the household where she worked. Sometimes she could stop for only a few minutes on her way to market or on some other errand. But often, she would come over for dinner or long talks in the evening. Her daughter came with her on occasion and I got to know her.

Carmen helped me recover from the loss and grief that pervaded my life. My spirit began to return under the influence of our renewed friendship. However, sometimes I cried over the loss of Simón and Jonotás and Natán. Sometimes when Carmen came over, she found me already in bed, where I had gone without an evening meal, because I had to escape the sorrow that weighed down on me.

She would rouse me, make me eat the dinner Juana Rosa had kept warm, and we would talk. She loved me, and she loved Dominga and Mendoza, who were like daughters to me. Slowly, over the months, I was able to regain some belief in life again. I've never stopped missing Jonotás and Natán, but in those later months of 1834 I began, once again, to live.

With renewed life, I wrote more often to my friends. I wanted them to know that I still lived, and I made myself ask about what was happening on the continent.

Occasionally, I received loving answers from my friends, but never from José María. I heard that he was alive and active in the politics of Ecuador, but I wanted more than news. I wanted to hear from him. The longer I was without word from his own pen, the more I longed to see him.

My financial situation was poor, so I could only hope that he would write. Then, something made me think that I might be able to travel to Quito. I was able to make a little extra money.

Knowing something about importing, being able to speak Spanish, and being my father's daughter—and in my frustration at the quality of tobacco in Jamaica—I was able to arrange to buy cigars from a Cuban merchant and resell them. I did fairly well.

When it looked as though I could pay for my household and myself, and still save a little money, I began to think seriously about returning to Quito. By that time, I had not heard from José María himself in almost two years. When I heard news from Rafael Urdaneta, in the one of the few letters I received from the continent, that José was actively opposing the president, our old friend, Juan Flores, I was determined to go "home."

Twice I tried to obtain a passport to enter Ecuador, but I was denied. So, I decided to communicate directly to Flores.

I thought a long time about what I would say. I had written to him from Bogotá, but he had not answered. I needed to make sure that I would at last be heard.

In May of 1835, I wrote President Flores:

> I wait for this to arrive in your hands from this island. I wrote to you often from Bogotá, yet without the smallest of answers.
>
> But now times are hard. There exists in my hands your intimate correspondence with the Liberator, and I am going to make full use of it. Much effort did it cost me to save these papers in the year 1830—and these papers remain my property—very much mine. You know my rules of conduct. You know the rules by which I govern my life, and this is the way I shall go until I leave for the grave. Time will justify me.
>
> No one writes me now. And you see me alone on this island, abandoned by my family. I always remember with pleasure our old friendship, and in its name I beg that you aid me.

I knew he did not want to be associated with Bolívar in the political times that were upon us and that he would help me in order to keep me quiet. It was two months before I received an answer; but finally I received a letter welcoming me back to the *patria*. He sent a passport for my servants and me. He also sent a letter of safe-conduct. The tone of his letter was effusive and open.

I made plans to leave immediately. I thanked Maxwell Hyslop for his generosity and made arrangements to sail by the end of August.

Two weeks before we left, although I was eager to leave, I began to feel nervous. I had been promised safe-conduct from Flores himself, but I did not know what I would find in Quito. The more I thought about it, the more I was dragged, by my own emotions, back into the pit of despair and grief from which I had so recently climbed. I wanted to live a new life with my brother but I did not want to enter the political, military, and social arena again, except as a spectator. *Must I always fight?* I asked myself when I thought of returning to South America.

One evening, when Carmen stopped by to see me, I was already in bed, crying. I heard her in the next room and thought about getting up, but I could not bear to see anyone. However, instead of leaving, she opened my door.

"Manuela, you'll be gone soon. I can't let us waste even a day."

"I know," I said, apathetically, "but I need to be alone right now."

She did not speak for a moment, and then she sat on my bed. She leaned over and wrapped me in her arms and said, "Manuela, I love you. I can't bear to let you go like this."

Tears came to my eyes, and I cried. I sobbed long and hard. Soon, my grief became contagious and Carmen wept. We both lay there, holding onto each other as though each meant life itself to the other. It seemed as if we stayed together like that for a long time and then we fell asleep. Just before dawn, I awoke with Carmen standing above me. She had slept in her clothes and she was trying to smooth out the wrinkles.

"Thank you for comforting me," I said, hoarsely.

"I can't bear to see you sad." She came over and knelt by my bed. "You have lived a rich life. So many things you have done, and so many things you have seen. Most women go from father to husband to son to grave—workin' hard until the end. Workin' for others that they might live and be and do. You have been completely you own, for your entire life."

She smiled at me. Then she reached over and ever so softly placed her lips on mine. She made my blood rush as she had that night in Quito so long ago. It made me think of physical love, that had been so long absent from my life. I thought of Simón, who was the only one who ever allowed me to express my true physical feelings, the only one who ever satisfied me. I missed him so at that moment.

She pulled away and looked in my eyes. She said, "I love you." Before I could respond, she said, "Good-bye. I will see you tonight," and left, leaving me lonely.

But the words she said made a difference. Yes, I was lonely. Yes, I had lost my loved ones. But so had hundreds of other women in the last quarter of a century—so had many millions of women in the history of man.

Women especially are victims of armed conflict. Dying could not be as hard as losing father, brother, sister, son, or daughter to man's need to destroy his kind in the organized system of waste and devastation called war.

When I was young, eager to fight the *godos*, I thought that I would be helping to eradicate injustice and evil. Over the years, I gradually changed my point of view. I had been utterly wrong. Neither the *godos* nor any other group carries any more of the malice of the human heart than any other.

Bolívar had spent his life "freeing" his fellow man. For what? Yes, self-determined government and free, prosperous trade are worth fighting for. Yes, the freedom of the individual human mind to think and act without political constraint is worth fighting for. But to throw away all beauty, social significance, traditional order, and the lives of thousands or millions to achieve it, prevents the scales from finding balance.

When I finally boarded a ship for Panamá on my way to Guayaquil, I left a friend in Jamaica who loved me. Her tears upon my departure almost made me want to stay, to keep company with her. I do not know what would have happened to me if Carmen had not been there when I needed her, just as she had promised so long ago. She restored my life and spirit. I did not want to leave her, but I knew I had to find and help my brother.

I loved Mr. Hyslop and his family as well. When I said good-bye to them, he too made me want to stay. He was a decent man—a good friend—who was in some small way a connection to Simón. But Jamaica was not and never would be "home." To me, Jamaica was only a stopping off place in my many travels. When would I be at rest?

As I watched Kingston diminish over the horizon, I thought about the long, hard roads I had traveled. As my thoughts ran over the years, I grew weary. I was weary of travel and strife. I missed Quito and José. When I arrived there, I would stop my journeying at last.

Later that night, Dominga, Mendoza, and I came up on deck for some fresh air, and the captain and other sailors stood looking at the sky.

"What is happening?" I asked one of the sailors.

"The captain says that the Vatican observatory has sighted the comet. He told an officer about it today, and we have bets. I say there's no such thing."

"There is," said another. "It was last seen in 1759."

"We'll see," said the first, and turned his eyes back to the sky.

A third one said, "The captain said we may not see it. That doesn't mean it isn't there."

I had heard that we might see a comet that season, but I had been too busy to think about it. I assumed that they would not settle their bets that night. It might not even be visible in that part of the world or it might take an observatory to see it.

At that point, Mendoza, pulled on my sleeve and asked, "What's a comet?"

I didn't know how to explain it, and I sat down next to her and pointed at the sky. "Do you see between those clouds over there—and over there?" She nodded. "Do you see the stars? You know what stars are, don't you?" She nodded again. "Well, those stars have families. Each star has other stars close by, and these families are called constellations. Each night, the stars move across the sky and they disappear beyond the horizon, just like the sun in the daytime. But even though they are moving, they are always with their fellow stars, so they are happy, just like us."

She smiled broadly and gave me a hug. I held her close. After a moment, she looked up at me and said, "But what's a comet, Manuela?"

I laughed. She was right, I hadn't answered her question. "Oh, yes. A comet is a different kind of star. A comet is sadder because a comet has no family. It circles the heavens looking for a home. It goes away for years and years, and then it tries to come back and join the other stars, but it never can. It's a wanderer that can never return."

"I'm glad we're like the stars who have families," said Mendoza.

"So am I," I said, and held her close to me as I watched heavens. While we looked at the sky, I began to feel whole. In that moment I found the strength to finally recover from all I had suffered since Simón's death. I knew I would survive. I pressed my lips to my little girl's head and whispered into her tight black curls, "Yes, my love. So am I."

Chapter 46

I regretted, as I always do, the leaving of friends. Leaving Jamaica was no different. Yet on this journey, I had brought new friends, whom I already loved deeply. Juana Rosa asked to come with me. My "daughters," Dominga and Mendoza, were a new joy in my life. I delighted in the idea that soon we would be settled in Quito. My brother would be close by, and we would live together in peace.

We arrived in Panamá and began our ride across the isthmus. When we rode our burros through Puerto Bello, I was reminded of the soldier I saw die there. I had been so afraid for José María that day, and yet if he had not left to be a warrior, my own life would have lacked so much. He was there, or nearby, in nearly every important event in the wars that followed. It was partly because of him that Lima fell so quickly to San Martín, saving so many lives from violent death.

When we came to the city of Panamá, I took the time to go to the warehouse where I had lived. It changed very little, but it was run down and not in use. There was not much for me in Panamá, and I was glad when we could depart for Ecuador.

In October, we landed in Guayaquil. The streets were quieter than I had ever seen them, even along the Malecón. There seemed to be fewer people, and they moved with a slow, apathetic step. I was anxious to begin the trek to Quito, so I did not pause to consider how bad off my country had become.

I had sewn a riding habit—all black—on the trip, but I was unsure if I could or should spend my money on a horse and mules. We could walk, but that meant we would have to leave our baggage, and send for it later. I had an idea. I made my way—Juana Rosa, Dominga, and Mendoza in tow—across town to see El Árabe.

His corral was still there and he said, "I know this woman. Wait, good, yes. You are the young lady from Lima."

"Yes, Señor, how good of you to remember me."

"Good, yes. But why do you wait so long to return? Look at these gray hairs." He pulled his hair out from his temple. "This is what happens when you wait so long."

"You are right, Señor. I have been remiss." I smiled at him. "Now after all this, I have come to ask a favor."

"Anything for the Señorita."

I need to borrow one horse and as many mules as you can spare, up to four. I must travel to Quito, and . . ." I did not want him to see I was that bad off, but I had no other way to say it. "I have very little money."

He rubbed his chin and frowned.

"I will send them back immediately. You should see them again in less than three weeks."

He looked at me a long time and scowled. He looked at Juana Rosa, Dominga, and Mendoza. I was sure he was going to refuse. "These are not the same black women you traveled with before."

Tears filled my eyes. "No, Señor," I said, my voice harsh from fighting a sudden constriction in my throat.

"I can see the Señorita has had hard times since last we spoke."

"Yes, Señor," I said, trying not to look pathetic.

"You may borrow what you wish, if, as you say, my property will be returned in three weeks. No charge."

"I thank you, Señor."

"Perhaps, at last, after almost 15 years, the Señorita and her slaves—"

"Friends."

He smiled. "Good, yes. *Friends.* Perhaps you are hungry and will take food with me."

I laughed out loud. "We are starved."

"Good, yes." He had a man bring us out some *tortillas*, beans, and *chicha*, that we all ate standing up. It might possibly have been the best meal I ever had.

El Árabe looked at me when I mounted a black mare in my black riding outfit and said, "I think you need something else." He walked inside his hut and brought out a black, silver-handled riding whip. "You may return this as well." He held his head back to look at me. "The picture is not quite complete without it."

I smiled at him. "Thank you, Señor."

He gave me a broad smile and said, "The Señorita is very pretty."

We said our good-byes. Then, my companions and I began the long ride to Quito.

As we rode onto the savanna, I thought about the times I had made this trip before. I was only seventeen, taking my first steps as an adult, when I descended the Andes for the first time. Later, I had been wealthy, successful, and important on returning to the city of my birth from Lima. There I met the man who changed my life and took my heart forever. It was for him that I came down the slopes of these mountains a year later. Then, one more time, eight years before in exile from Perú, I climbed these same slopes. My return to Guayaquil had been circuitous, but this time I was climbing the Andes to go home.

I would not come down again. I would find my brother and live in my own country. I would import products, as my father had done—with my brother's help—and live the life that La Perricholi had lived. At last I would be an important member of Quito society. I would make lots of money and I would donate it to public works and hospitals. None of this would I do for the "fame." I longed, at last, to live in peace, and to be part of a community. I was through fighting the world or striving to influence other's opinions of me. I would give, out of love, all that I could to the city of my birth. Instead of fighting it, I would at last embrace it.

The next couple of days were hard after so long without riding or even getting any exercise. I was saddle sore the first day. Later, when we began climbing, my companions were tired, never having breathed thin air.

The slopes rising off the plains are the most slippery and difficult of the entire trip, and there is always a fierce wind along those trails. Yet we had no accidents. On the afternoon of October 9, we reached Guaranda. I was in a mood to spend the night in a comfortable bed and so I rode up to the beautiful house I had admired on my journey down the mountain when I was 17. It was quite run down but was still elegant enough to have clearly once been the home of the local *corregidor*.

I did not know who lived in it, but I hoped it was the same man, Don Gaspar Morales. He had told me that if I came that way again I was to sleep in one of his comfortable rooms for guests.

I knocked and a servant answered. Behind her, in a stained Royalist uniform, a man came out of the darkness. He was fat and his appearance was messy. I barely recognized him.

"Don Morales?"

"Yes. Who is it?"

"I am a friend of Don Carlson's," I said.

"What do you want?" He stepped into the doorway, and I noticed that he did not look at me.

"I am a traveler, on my way to the interior. Long ago, you offered me a room in your house. If your offer is still good, I would most appreciate—"

Mendoza came up to me and said, "Manuela?"

"Not now, darling," I said, turning to her.

"Who else is with her?" he said to his servant.

She said, "Two black girls and a black woman."

I realized then that he was blind. To simplify, I said, "These are my servants, Don Morales."

"When were you here before?"

"Almost twenty years ago. I was being escorted down the mountain by Don Carlson, and you invited me to stay with you."

"I do not remember." He paused and then said, "However, nothing interesting happens here. You may stay."

I was relieved. His servant gave us rooms and a pleasant, light meal. I observed, with irony, that the meal was maize cakes—the same poor meal I had eaten with servants in the back twenty years before. I did put on some of the salt from Tomabela and enjoyed them.

The conversation was a strain, but he did give me some interesting news. Flores had, for a short period, in an act of political appeasement, given over the presidency to Rocafuerte. "He will not have it long," said my host. "I have heard that Flores is fed up and will soon take the government back by force."

This news was of interest. If Rocafuerte was in power, it could invalidate both my passport and my letter of safe-conduct from General Flores. However, I saw no cause for alarm. In a few days, I would be in Quito, safe in my brother's house. If I left politics alone, I was sure I would not be bothered.

I might have stayed up and talked, but our host was vociferous in his criticism of the revolution. In my earlier days, the discussion would have been a time for me to attack. But I understood him. He was, in a very human fashion, lamenting the lost past; that was all. I was tired anyway, and so I soon went to bed, as did my companions.

A few hours later, I was awakened by a harsh pounding at the main entrance. I heard Don Morales bellow from down the hall, "Who the hell is knocking?"

Midnight disturbances were upsetting to me. I rose and dressed quickly.

By the time I was finished, Don Morales's servant was at my door. "Please, Señora," she said, "men wish to see you."

"Me?"

"Yes, Señora."

I was frightened, but I walked to the front door, where an officer stood with another soldier, who held a lantern. Behind him, other soldiers stood, with bayonets fixed. "Antonio Robelli, Señora," he said, giving a swift salute. "I am glad to have found you. I am ordered to arrest your journey to Quito. You must return to Guayaquil, and I am ordered to see that you do so, by force if necessary."

"Why?"

He handed me a paper. I unfolded it and read:

To Señora Manuela Sáenz:

> The President understands that the Señora has returned from Jamaica to Guayaquil and is taking the road for cities of the interior. He also understands that she is spreading seditious talk in favor of her late brother, General Sáenz, who died in 1834 fighting against this Government. I am disturbed about the effect on public tranquillity— therefore you are ordered to return to Guayaquil and leave this country as soon as possible.

President Rocafuerte

I don't remember the next few minutes. I know I let out a howl, I know I flung myself at Robelli, and my desire was to kill. I heard shouting and felt hands on me. We struggled in the doorway. Time stood still. I found myself on the floor, sobbing. "José María," I cried through my agony and tears. "José María!" I shouted again as though he might be able to hear me. "I didn't know. I didn't know. José. José."

Since I could not be comforted and I could not be reached by reason, they placed me under house arrest "until she comes to her senses," Robelli told Don Morales.

My emotions swept from violence to despair and back again. At times, I could not fathom the truth and raged around the house in confusion and near delirium. At times, I was so angry I could have killed. I argued with Robelli. "This decree must have been written by a drunk and an imbecile. You must let me pass."

He was young and not without compassion. "I did not realize that you did not know about your brother's death. I am sorry to have been the one to deliver the news so rudely. However, I have orders. There is nothing that either of us can do."

"I will go to Quito, and no one will stop me." I was wrong. Robelli stopped me with his next sentence.

"Why do you want to go?"

"Because . . ." I had no answer.

"You must return to the coast, Señora," he said, compassionately. Then, he saluted and left the doorway.

The next day, I said, "You are right. I will not stay here any longer, since I cannot get my hands on Rocafuerte."

Thus, did my companions and I return under guard. I never saw Quito again.

Tears and despair blinded me all the way down the mountain. I was almost crazy when we reached Guayaquil. When I returned my horses and told my tale to El Árabe, he said, "I am sad for the Señorita. I know she will fine, but I feel sorry for her."

I found it hard to be kind, though he had always been kind to me. I said simply, "I thank you for everything," and left.

I went to the customs house, and asked, "When is the next ship leaving?"

"Where do you want to go?"

I was infuriated beyond all reason. I said, "Have you been drinking ink?" I threw his ink pot across the room, its contents splattering the wall and several desks. "I don't *want* to go anywhere. I asked you a question: 'When is the next ship leaving?'"

An argument ensued. I apologized perfunctorily and found that a cargo ship was leaving in two hours.

"Don't you want to know where it is going?" he called after me as I walked out the door toward the moorage.

"I don't care," I shouted back.

I marched to the ship and spoke to the captain, "I am ordered to leave the country." I showed him Rocafuerte's letter. "I have little money. Will you please take me to the first stop, wherever it is, that is not in Ecuador."

Thus did my companions and I set sail. Thus did we find and disembark in the town where I now live. Here have I stayed for the last twenty years.

Chapter 47

I do not know how the town of Paita came to be. It is difficult to understand why men would build houses on an ocean bound desert, with no water or trees. There is nothing but sand and rock and saltwater in Paita. The only value it could possibly have is that it sits on the edge of a wide and slightly protected bay about half-way between Guayaquil and Lima.

I looked at the several one- and two-storied houses of wood standing in front of crumbling gray cliffs. The captain said, "Either I will leave you here or you will have to pay more to continue down the coast."

"I will stay," I said, as I wondered where the wood came from to build the houses. Any wood that was used must have washed up on the beach or been shipped in from Guayaquil.

Although it looked like the end of the world, or perhaps the first outpost of hell, I did not mind. Its desolation, loneliness, and lack of color matched my frame of mind, and it seemed like a perfect place from which to start life in exile. Juana Rosa, Dominga, Mendoza, and I were deposited on the sand, with our little bit of baggage. The ship that brought us lifted its anchor and set sail.

I looked down the street that held apart two rows of houses. There was also a modest church, a small customs house, and a dilapidated wharf. I felt the firmness of the earth beneath my feet. The sun was not hidden behind the usual Peruvian overcast that day and it felt hot and comfortable as it pressed down on my skin and hair. The rhythmic crashing of the surf and the hot stillness made me feel something. Having been on the move for months, and before that, having done nothing but fight and travel, I suddenly felt at a new emotion: tranquillity.

On the way down the coast, I had spoken to the captain of the ship about the place. "It is a port for ships to pick up barrels of water and food, both of which have to be brought overland by mules." He barked an order to one his men and continued, "Ships stop. Sailors satisfy their thirst for rum or their other appetites. They leave. That is all. It is nothing but a few falling down houses on the beach."

I looked over at my "family," sitting quietly in the sand, and I could see that they were exhausted. They were enjoying their rest in this little town as much as I. We had not felt so content in weeks. I did not make a firm decision at that moment, but I dimly saw that I could stay here awhile. Perhaps I could write to my friends and arrange to sell cigars and sundry items to the sailors.

That afternoon, we found a shabby two-story house. It had more windows than most of the others. The purchase price was incredibly low compared to what a house in Lima, Quito, or Bogotá would cost. This was due not only to the remote location of Paita but the sorry condition of the house itself. I convinced the seller that I would be able to pay him. When I mentioned some of my friends, he was very impressed. He agreed to sell me the house on credit.

We moved in, and I found a great deal of satisfaction being away from the rest of the world in my own place. The houses I owned before really belonged to James. This one was all mine. The four of us began the immense task of repairing walls, doors, and windows and of moving out what seemed like piles of dust and sand. By late that night, with the stars shining overhead and the moon full, we had made ourselves places to sleep and eat.

I was poor when I was dropped off in Paita, but I sent a draft to Mr. Hyslop in Jamaica and I had him write to those in Cuba from whom I had bought tobacco. A few weeks later, I hung out a shingle that read, in hand-painted letters:

TOBACCO
ENGLISH SPOKEN
MANUELA SÁENZ

The wood was rotten, so my sign never stayed up. Every few months I would have to go out and nail it again, but it would inevitably sag.

Despite the unevenness of my "store front," sailors from the ships that let down anchor in the bay to victual there would come and buy cigars or chewing tobacco or sweets that Juana Rosa made or candles or items I crocheted or whatever else I could find to sell. When Dominga and Mendoza were a little older, they washed clothes for the sailors. That was how my household stayed alive. We did what we could, but we never had enough money. We lived from one shipment of tobacco or sundries to the next. Occasionally, I would be able to earn a peso or two by translating or by writing a letter. This was my poor life for many years.

At times I considered moving back to Lima. The main reason I did not go was because I knew that I would only become involved in political affairs again. I heard, from time to time, of this leader's mistakes or that leader's excesses and it would anger me. Then, I would return my thoughts to the ocean, the sand, and the peaceful life I was leading. I knew I could not go back to any big city, not even if the theatre, the food, the music, or the delicious excitement of city living called to me. I could not be so close to the fools who were governing the republics and trade centers of South America. I would be drawn back into the life I had left behind.

Thus, in October of 1837, when I received a letter from President Flores with an offer of repatriation, I refused. He had taken back power in Ecuador and had taken the time to write to me:

I regret that you were prevented from returning to Quito, as I promised. You have my word that you will not be denied in your repatriation again. I invite you to come home.

I did not have to think about it, and I have not regretted the decision I made. I answered him, resisting my impulse to reproach him for the death of my brother. I did not know if it was he or Rocafuerte who was responsible, and I did not want to know. I wanted peace. I said so in my reply:

What terrible anathema of hell had been communicated to me when the government ordered me from my *patria*.

But my decision now is definite; I will not return to the soil of my country. It is, as you well understand, my friend, easier to destroy than to make anew. This order for my repatriation cannot now revive my deep affection for my country and for my friends Now it is no longer possible.

But one thing is certain. Paita or Lima, Manuela will always be to you the Manuela whom you knew in 1822. Nothing gives me greater peace than the tranquillity of my country, and nothing gives me greater joy than tranquillity.

A few months later, I heard of de Lacroix's death. After writing me the letter, which both told of Simón's death and foreshadowed my own downfall, he had returned to Paris. Destitute upon arriving, he suffered for years and then committed suicide.

Shortly after hearing about Lacroix, Manuelita Paris wrote to me to tell me of her father's death. Pepé had injured his arm in a mining accident and gangrene had set in. It was amputated, but too late.

One by one, I heard of the deaths of people who made up my life. I grieved for them, of course, and yet my life in Paita—detached geographically—symbolized my spirit. I lived and grieved from afar. I went on, day by day, and that was all.

When my friend Cayetano Freyre wrote to me from Lima that my husband was involved in a scandal, I did not respond to the temptation he offered. It seemed that James was the executor of the estate of his late friend General Domingo Orué and had somehow gotten hold of the deceased man's sugar hacienda and Señora Orué and my husband had become close. I knew that she liked him when I met her after my wedding. The scandal began in earnest when the man's widow bore children that were English in appearance. "Do you wish to assert your rights in this matter? You have legal cause, and I could oversee the legal process here in Lima for you."

I wrote him back, saying, "I have no interest in my husband's affairs." I had no interest in anything that might draw me back into the battles of life.

In the next few years, the whaling ships out of New Bedford began to fill the bay of Paita. It became the last port of call before they made their way into the vastness of the ocean. If I had been able to acquire enough tobacco in a timely fashion, we would have done better. However, for a while we had enough to eat and enough of the other niceties of life.

In 1839, my friend Alexander Ruden Jr. of Cincinnati came to Paita. He was the consul from the United States, there to look after the interests of the whaling ships who claimed that they were being overcharged for goods and services in Paita. If it was true, I certainly never saw any exorbitant amounts of money pass through my hands. However, I was happy he had arrived, because I could speak English with him and he was well educated. We had long talks in the evenings. I also helped him, as a translator, in dealing with the Peruvian authorities.

The only thing that tormented me in those years was knowing that Bolívar was being lied about, if he was being spoken of at all. I heard of the lies concerning Bolívar (and me) told by the Santanderists, but even more frightening was hearing reports of the systematic suppression of his memory.

Not one book or pamphlet written about the revolution in that period mentioned him as anything more than another soldier. Here was the greatest military leader and statesman in the history of the continent, perhaps the world, and yet he was being treated as if he were nothing.

Time passed. In 1841 I met the North American author Herman Melville. I remember one incident in particular, involving Mr. Melville. I was helping the authorities take depositions from the sailors on his ship regarding some dispute, by translating the English into Spanish. While Mr. Melville was giving his deposition, a fight erupted right outside the door. Mr. Ruden and the official who were in attendance, went outside to help quell it. While we waited, Mr. Melville began to tell me stories.

It was almost a half hour later when Mr. Ruden returned. The air was filled with smoke from my cigar—keeping the flying insects clustered around the one inadequate oil lamp. He told us a story about the capture of a large whale. Mr. Ruden sat down and listened to the frightening tale, and we thoroughly enjoyed it.

That was the first time I ever heard such stories about whales. He told us an account of the sinking of the whaler *Essex*, by an infuriated whale apparently seeking vengeance for the killing of his fellows. That was hard for me to believe, but apparently true. Then he told a tale, which apparently all sailors know, of a dangerous great white leviathan that has caused many sailors to lose their lives. Years later, when his novel *Moby Dick* was published—obviously inspired by such yarns and experiences as he revealed to us that day—I was compelled to read it.

That was almost 15 years ago now, when he was only a sailor on a whaling ship. After he left, I forgot him quickly because I was so busy writing letters to public officials throughout the continent. What I was concerned about in those days was reversing the suppression of Bolívar's memory. I also wrote to my friends to try to get *them* to pressure local officials to acknowledge Bolívar for the hero of the revolution that he was.

When Simón Bolívar died in 1830, there began a terrible silence about him. Santander ordering his name removed from public documents was the least of it. He and other Santanderists wanted Bolívar silenced permanently. His memory—still powerful, even in death—was capable of influencing the hearts of our people, and they knew it.

In the years between 1830 and 1842, I had suffered humiliation, poverty, exile, and the loss of those I loved. My suffering was turned more bitter by the realization that Simón Bolívar, the man I had adored so deeply, was being vilified in death through a campaign of silence and lies by those who never had the manliness or power to do so in life. Nearly all of our leaders at that time tried to rob Simón Bolívar of his glory in order to achieve their own. The only exceptions were a few of his friends who truly loved him. Much has been written or pronounced from the pulpit or spoken over drink about the Liberator since his death. Those who wished to climb to positions of power themselves trampled on his memory for their own purposes, proclaiming him a power hungry despot whose kind we must not allow among us again. He was never that. He was a visionary who saw farther into the future than his brothers, for which they hated him.

It was not enough for those who sought his blood that The Liberator should die penniless and in exile. His enemies also sought to deprive him of his place in history.

I knew they could not succeed. Bolívar's glory would last for thousands of years, and would not be obliterated, even in death, by a handful of small-minded, petty politicians. Yet it still hurt.

Then, in 1842, what I had longed for happened. Bolívar was at last given the posthumous honors he deserved. Since his death, Bolívar's sisters had begged to be allowed to bring his body from Santa Marta to his boyhood home to be buried. Other people supported their endeavors and pressured the governments of New Granada and Venezuela to honor his sisters' request.

The cowardly officials refused for 12 years. At last, the will of the people prevailed, and their petition was granted. No doubt the politicians thought it would be a quiet affair after so much time had passed. They were wrong. There was a great vent of public emotion, and Simón Bolívar's funeral became an international event.

It gave me comfort and peace at last, after years of suffering and lies, to see that he was again being remembered and honored in the hearts of the South American people. If it had not been for the persistence of his sisters, he would still be lying in a virtually unmarked grave—in the vaults of the church of Santa Marta.

Though many who feared his memory tried to deprive Simón Bolívar of the posthumous glory he deserved, they could not erase the love of the people for the man who had liberated them. As his body passed along the road to Caracas, one demonstration after another spontaneously erupted. The populace was able to express their true feelings—their love for the Liberator—at last. When it became clear that Bolívar would live forever in the hearts of the people, despite efforts to eliminate him from history, those who defamed him during his lifetime were finally forced to honor him in death.

They owed their lives and liberty to Simón Bolívar, and never understood it. Who knows if time may not one day prove Bolívar's vision, he who sought to build a country as wide as a continent—a United States of South America. It may not happen in these days, when we have leaders such as we have, whose interests lie in their own power before the well-being of their country. At the very least, I feel that the countries in this hemisphere will one day follow through on Bolívar's plan to form organizations (as he tried to do in Panamá in 1824) for their mutual protection against European intervention and for future prosperity. I also envision Bolívar's dream one day coming to pass of the Isthmus of Panamá becoming a center for world trade, with a canal cut from ocean to ocean. Someday the rest of the world will follow Bolívar's example and end slavery forever. I knew Bolívar's dreams. There were many that have come to be and a few that I know are yet to come. Be these things as they will be, at least the people remember their hero.

After 1842, when I thought that the lies were over, new falsehoods began. This time, the lies were there to embellish and magnify Bolívar's glory to allow his enemies to align themselves with him. Statues were erected and history was again re-written; this time in glowing, idealized, romantic, and false terms.

When this happened, no one quite knew how to deal with our love affair. Surely, so great a hero could not have been an adulterer, could not have loved a lowly bastard, could not have allowed a woman to ride with him on the road to battle—as an officer. No, this was not the romantic Bolívar with whom they wished to align themselves. So, it was *I* who was then written out of history.

My enemies were still able to strike at me, by eliminating me from published accounts of the revolution. I thought about returning to Lima or Quito and taking up the fight for truth. I had been formidable once. I could be so again. However, this was not to be my destiny.

I, who had traveled all over the Andes, sailed the oceans, and lived through fifteen years of desolating revolution, was finally injured. Not by participation in any heroic deed, but by merely climbing the stairs. The lowly termite brought me down.

A step broke and I fell over the edge of the stairs and shattered my hip. I was carried upstairs by neighbors, and here have I stayed. I am close to the window so I can see the vastness of the Pacific, but I have not walked since then.

The years passed. I heard of the death of General Urdaneta and grieved. Santander and the traitor La Mar also finally left this life. I had given their names to my dogs, and when I heard of their individual deaths I gave each an extra portion of food.

In 1847, my husband was murdered and mutilated. He was walking with his mistress, a woman named Ventura Concha, who was also slain. He had apparently recently left the widow Orué, and it was whispered that she had hired the assassins.

Poor James. I believe he was not unfaithful to me before I met Bolívar and he never would have left the sanctity of our marriage if it were not for my own disregard of our marriage vows. Yet there was never a choice for me. I had to do what my heart led me to do; and after I met Simón, there was no turning back. My actions changed James's life, but who knows how things might have turned out.

I was very distressed about my husband's death. He had always done his best by me; and because I considered all men or women either friends or enemies, I had to consider him a friend. I never wanted to see him harmed, and it hurt me to know that he had died so cruelly.

James left me only 8,000 pesos, the amount my father had given him as a dowry, plus fair interest for thirty years. It was not anywhere near what he was worth but would have been almost untold wealth to me in my situation. Cayetano Freyre took it upon himself to see that I had it expeditiously. What with my own household and the charity I gave to members of the town, I was in need of money. I waited in vain for it to arrive.

It was at this juncture that the reality of how the world was treating my memory, and what it would mean to my future, became brilliantly clear.

James's executor was Captain Manuel Escobar, whom I had chased out of my house that day when I had first returned to Lima. He had sworn to see me ruined. When Cayetano Freyre asked for my inheritance, he reported that Escobar had said, "She'll die before she sees any of Thorne's money."

Escobar had gathered my enemies to his cause. They successfully saw to it that my character was assassinated in official eyes. "A public woman, as everyone knows." was one of the many accusations brought before the judges. Escobar would have his way, and like my mother's inheritance, I knew I would never see any of my husband's. With my inability to work, what little I had seemed to be evaporating like water in the Peruvian desert.

Chapter 48

As the years passed, with the whaling industry tapering off in Paita, I could barely sustain my household. We did our best, but there was less money every season. The poverty and hardship my family felt did not prevent us from enjoying life, but once in a while I had spells of worry.

Then, one afternoon, I received a welcome letter. The next day, I received an even more welcome visitor.

The letter had brought me happy tidings, and I still had it with me the next morning when I sat at my window crocheting. I stopped my work at one point and read the letter again and then looked out the window while musing over memories of the writer. While I sat there, I saw sailors disembark from the ship I had seen arriving earlier. An old man was among them. When he reached the end of the wharf, he looked around and then slowly made his way toward the town. I thought he looked familiar.

Dominga and Mendoza came in just then. My inactive life had added weight to my frame, and I shifted uncomfortably to look at them.

"Manuelita, Manuelita," they cried excitedly.

They had already flowered into womanhood, but they were small. Also, perhaps because of the lack of food in our household, they were quite thin. However, food may not have been the reason. Both Juana Rosa and I had added heaviness in the intervening years, but the girls remained small and thin, almost as if they refused to grow despite the urgings of nature.

They were quiet, watchful, young women that rarely gave me trouble. I wish they had. It seemed that their obedience stemmed more out of never having recovered fully from the hardships of the early part of their lives, than mature sound judgment. They almost always had a serious look on their faces. On this occasion, they were happy and excited.

"Yes, my loves."

Dominga, who always seemed to speak for the two of them, said, "Manuelita, we wish to go to Amotaje." This was a small village inland several leagues.

"Why, what is in Amotaje?"

"Nothin', we just wish to go."

"Tell her," said Mendoza, "she wants to see a boy."

I smiled. When Mendoza spoke, she was always blunt. "How are you going to get there?"

"We've arranged to borrow a mule," said Dominga, after pushing her sister in retribution for exposing the truth.

"Very well, but be home by nightfall."

"We will."

They left, and I was happy to see some exuberance in them. I returned to reading the letter and forming a response in my mind. I called down to Juana Rosa to bring me some paper and a quill.

When she arrived at the top of the stairs, which emerged directly into my room, I heard a shout from below. "Does the Liberatress live her?"

"Enter," I shouted back, without thinking. Then, intensely curious as to who would refer to me in this way, I called out, "Who wishes to speak with the Liberatress?"

"A friend," came the answer.

I motioned to Juana Rosa to go down and greet the visitor. Soon, at the top of the stairs, there appeared a bald head, spectacles, stooped shoulders, and tattered clothes. When the figure turned toward me, I recognized an aged Simón Rodríguez.

I was very happy to see him. "Oh, Simón," I said happily, though my eyes had become wet, "have you come to commiserate with one who misses our dear friend?"

"Yes," he said. He saw that I could not move from my chair, and he came over and kissed my hand. "We may be the only two people left who knew him as he really was."

"No, my friend," I said, indicating a chair for him to sit, "there is at least one other." I smiled, waiting for him to ask.

He lowered himself into the chair with difficulty. He appeared quite old, and my best guess was that he was in his middle seventies. "Who is it?" he asked. "Who knows him as well as we?"

"One who has spent more time with him than perhaps you and I together. One who rode all over this continent with him."

"I did not know his officers."

"Surely you remember O'Leary—"

"Oh, yes, but he is in England."

"No, he is in Bogotá. He is the Consul General for Great Britain." I could not contain my excitement.

I showed him the letter and said, "He intends to write a history of the revolution. It will be published in South America and later in England. Then, no one will be able to deny the truth." I was positively gleeful. "As you can see there, he has asked me for my remembrance of the night of September 25th and if I have any papers and documents to help with his research."

"This is good, Manuela. Do you have any papers?"

"Yes. They are hidden away in Bogotá, and I was about to write to him to reveal their hiding place. But, my friend, how are you? Tell me about yourself."

He told a long tale while Juana Rosa served us some weak tea. We could not afford chocolate, which I often wished I had. While we sipped from the cracked rims of the cups I had collected, Simón told me of his recent years.

He told of publishing, at his own expense, the pamphlet, *Defense of Simón Bolívar*, for which he had been asked to leave Perú. From there, he went to Quito and was able to convince the government that he should be taken on to teach his new system of education. When he was not paid for this, he moved to Ibarra, where he opened a candle factory. However, imprudent affairs with other men's wives caused him to leave, but he was already going bankrupt at the time. Later, in Latacunga, he opened a powder factory; but before he sold anything, an explosion caused him to lose all he had.

"I was so poor, I had to move in with a parish priest who took pity on me. I have never gotten along too well with priests, but he was a kind and friendly man."

I chuckled, thinking of the conversations a priest and this ancient revolutionary might have had.

Simón went on. "That first evening, while we had a bit of soup, I told him some stories such as I have just told you. I also told him some tales of my travels in Europe." Rodríguez smiled, showing a couple of gaps where he had lost some teeth. "And then a wonderful thing happened. The priest asked, 'Do you mean that you knew the man known as The Liberator?' I told him that I knew him well and that I had been his tutor. The priest said, 'Did you also know a woman named Manuela Sáenz, whom I am told was close to him?'"

My mouth flew open. "How in the world would a priest in Latacunga know my name?" I asked, though I knew he was about to tell me.

"When I answered that I did indeed know you, he asked, 'Do you know where she is?' I said, that I did, having kept in correspondence with some of the same people to whom you have written over the years. He said, 'Then I have something that belongs to her. Perhaps you could see that she receives it.' And he handed me this."

Rodríguez pulled a folded, crumpled, yellowed piece of paper from a pocket in his rags. I opened it and read:

> I, Joaquina Aispuru, being of sound mind, bequeath to my only
> daughter, Manuela Sáenz . . . .

Images of the death of my mother flooded through my mind and I wept. I could hardly believe it. After all these years, the will my mother had written that stormy day in Quito, almost 50 years before, had been found.

When Rodríguez tried to comfort me and to find out why I wept so profusely, I said, "This is my mother's will, which I had given up for lost. I have searched for it for many years. I cry in happiness at having finally found it, and in sadness, for the memory of my mother. Perhaps now I will be able to force the Aispuru family to give me my share of their estate." I briefly told him the story. "How is it that a parish priest in Latacunga had it?"

"When I was in Ibarra, I heard of a crazy one-eyed priest who lived there. I even saw him a couple of times. He was quite mad, dirty, and thin. He died, six or seven years ago. His belongings were given to the priest in Latacunga, who had been his friend, there being no relatives. This was in amongst some other papers."

"But why did he save it and how—"

"The priest in Latacunga recognized your name from your notoriety, but did not know how to contact you. When he gave me your mother's will, my decision was made as to where I would go. I too have questions. How did the one-eyed priest come to have your mother's will?"

"That, my friend, is a very long story—that I will tell you soon. I thank you from the bottom of my soul for finding it and bringing it to me."

"I'm glad I came in any case. I am glad to see you."

"What will you do now?" I asked.

"I don't know. I need a place to live and some way to support myself."

We talked all day. We were only interrupted once by a neighbor who needed some blankets for a sick child. Juana Rosa took over some blankets, and Simón followed her and gave the woman some medical advice from his considerable experience.

Toward the end of the day, we had the last of some soup left over from the day before. I said, "It has occurred to me that I no longer have a way to offer you comfort in your stay with me. I gave away my only blankets."

"I will sleep in the sand," he said, brightly.

A little later, Dominga and Mendoza came home. After I introduced them, Simón and I had another discussion about his future.

"What can you do around here?" I mused.

Dominga overheard us. "Can you read and write?" she asked.

I laughed at the thought of Simón Rodríguez, educator, not being able to read and write. Simón smiled and said, "A little."

"We heard in Amotaje that someone was lookin' to pay someone to write a letter."

A little later, Simón borrowed a mule, with the help of Dominga and Mendoza, and rode off to Amotaje. He found a place to stay there and decided to live there, earning a modest income writing letters and such. My friend came and visited me almost every week after that.

His companionship made me happy, but one day when he came to see me, he remarked on my mood. "You are not yourself, Manuela. You have something on your mind."

"I am fine," I lied. I saw Rodríguez so little that I did not want to burden him.

"Come, come. I know you. Tell me." He lowered his thin and aging frame into a chair.

"Very well, my friend, I will tell you. I have sent a copy of my will to Quito, and I have reopened the case against the Aispurus." I had several papers in my hand, including the will itself. I handed them to him so that he could understand and perhaps help me with it.

"This is what you wish, is it not?" he said, as he flipped the pages over.

"Yes, but as you see, they have sent me back a letter asking for information. This information I have long since given them. I owe it to my mother to carry out her last wish; and I want what is rightfully mine, but the thought of going over this same ground again makes me quite sad. Pictures of my life in Lima, and in Quito with Bolívar, come to my mind. I am reminded of the hostility and suffering I have been through, and I feel as though I were reopening a wound."

"Ah, this is the will." he said, reading the last of the papers.

"Yes. The real problem is that I have found some measure of peace here and, in truth, I do not wish to fight anymore. But I feel as though I am giving up. I feel like I am failing my mother." I could not help it—two large tears rolled down my cheeks.

"You say you feel like you are failing your mother?"

"Yes." I wiped my eyes.

"But, Manuela," he said, "you have not failed her."

"What do you mean?"

He showed me the will, and he reached over and pointed to the first sentence, which I had read several times since he gave it to me. This time, I grasped its meaning:

I, Joaquina Aispuru, being of sound mind, bequeath to my only
daughter, Manuela Sáenz, so that she might have a full and rich life . . .

.

It was like the room was suddenly filled with light. I saw her face, damp and feverish. I heard again her words: "Shhh, my child, listen to me. I won't be around to make it happen. Your aunts and uncle will try to take my gift from you. I cannot go back to my home. There is nothing for me there. But you, *you will own a house some day.* You will sell what you receive from me and buy a house of your own. *You will sleep in a fine bed. If I could know that you would have all that, I would be happy as I die.*"

All this she had said when she wrote her will. Thus had she set me on my course, unable to be at peace until I made her happy.

I remembered the little hut and the bed we shared, and I remembered that I was happy there. I had not wanted anything more. Then, she had died. I had lived on. During my life I had helped in the freeing of a continent. I had experienced so much. For myself, I had achieved all that she said would make her happy. I had slept in a viceroy's bed. I had achieved, before I was even twenty, all that she wanted for me. I knew in that moment, that I did not have to fight anymore.

I saw so many things differently after that day. I was able to examine my life, and I was truly set free.

From then on, I could see my objectives clearly. I did not stop living. I lived each moment more completely. I could see what I really wanted from my lawsuit in Quito: justice.

However, I was not concerned that it might never come. At my age, I know that justice is not static. Justice comes from doing what is right. My motivation was entirely different. It was enjoyable now to try to learn about the law, which I never understood. My feelings were no longer adversarial. They were creative.

The officials in Quito, as I write this, still have not granted my mother's last request, but they certainly must do so. I am in no hurry. I do what is right, and that is enough. There has only been one other thing that has made me unhappy since then. This concerned the letter I received when Rodríguez had arrived.

I had written to O'Leary and answered his request for documents that he might use in writing his history. I told him to get in touch with Manuelita Paris because she knew where I had hidden Bolívar's papers so many years before in Bogotá.

"My friend," I wrote to O'Leary, "I do hope you finish your work. You may rely on me for anything that I can provide to help you. Those who are writing history now have betrayed the cause of honesty and virtue. I know that I, in particular, am being lied about if not neglected completely. You, I know, will write the truth. No one will be able to deny what you have seen and done."

About a year later he sent me what he recovered from hiding. All of my possessions had been sold and the money had been used by me over the years to live on. The most valuable possession I owned was all that was left—and O'Leary sent it to me.

What he sent wasn't much by the standards of monetary wealth, but when I opened the large box, recently arrived by special courier, it was like opening a treasure— stacks of letters: mine to Bolívar and Bolívar's to me. In among the letters were papers, bills of sale, medals, flowers pressed in small books, mementos, and other tokens of remembrance of our love affair.

I spent months going over them. I could do very little else because of pain in the joints of my hands that had settled there. I could no longer crochet, and so I read my letters, one after another, until I read them all. I cried. I laughed. I remembered things forgotten. I thought about my life and the love that had been mine.

I wanted to keep these things forever. I organized them. I put them where they would be safe from soils and accidents. I still have them in my house, and I have told Dominga and Mendoza that they will be responsible for safeguarding them if I die.

O'Leary also sent me news that many volumes of historical data had been collected by the nation's best scholars in the early 1830s. He assured me that in these volumes were accurate representations of my life among the soldiers of the revolution and the ensuing political events. "I found Volume 56, entitled *Correspondence and Documents Relating to Señora Manuela Sáenz, which Demonstrated the Esteem in which Various People of Note Held Her and the Part She Played in Political Affairs*, to have a great deal of information in it. It is accurate to the best of my knowledge and places you among the heroes of the revolution," he wrote to me.

I was happy. At least in one place, some of the things I knew to be true were recorded and available for viewing.

He went on to say, "I am gratified for you, because there are men here who are doing everything they can to keep you out of any new book of history about Bolívar. Even I have been threatened if I write about you. I will, of course, but it is good to know that the truth exists."

I agreed with that idea so very much. However, my satisfaction did not last long. About two years ago, in early 1854, I heard that O'Leary had finished his history. It was to be published in twenty-nine volumes: twelve were of Bolívar's correspondence, fourteen of documents, two of narration, and the final volume would accurately discuss, among other things, my role in Bolívar's life. At least in O'Leary's writing, the truth would be told. However, a few months later, my friend Daniel O'Leary died of an illness. This was at the time his books were to be published. I had not yet begun to recover from that blow when Rodríguez died. These two events immobilized me emotionally, and I also could not attend Rodríguez's simple funeral due to my physical immobility.

I still wept for the loss of my friends, a month or so later. Then I learned that the last volume of O'Leary's history, particularly because it contained the truth about me, had been suppressed by the government of New Granada. With O'Leary no longer alive, to protect his writing, all copies had been burned.

My friend Alexander Ruden did his best to comfort me, but the turn of events was too much. Almost frantic with a need to know, I wrote to Manuelita Paris. I asked her about the folio in the central library concerning me. "Please give me a listing of volumes to be found in the nation's records, particularly of Volume 56."

Her reply dismayed me deeply. The volume of which O'Leary spoke, Volume 56, had been stolen. "The librarians assume it was taken by your political enemies," she wrote. "They say there is now nothing of you in the country's archives."

The anger I felt and my helplessness to do anything about it turned into a kind of despair and apathy. I could not keep from brooding about it. I had been, at last, forced back into the oblivion from which I had come.

In the next month or so, I thought a great deal about my mother and about how hard I had fought those who tried to keep me in the obscurity of "bastard." If I had believed in a god, I would have thought the deity had driven me purposefully back to my former trials because I had not been punished enough. I no longer seemed to have the will to fight.

It was not until Mr. Ruden pointed out that I had produced nothing in the month prior, and my household was living off the charity of the people of the town, that I tried to see what I could do. It was he who gave me the idea of writing the truth myself.

This I have done. I have written this story of my life.

The act of writing my history has strengthened me. I know it will be published one day, and I have learned much in the writing of it. Most important of all, I can say at last that I am truly at peace.

Chapter 49

Men are creatures of space, women of time. Men spend their lives capturing territory; women give birth to life and hope to make it last. Bolívar failed to make the unified continent he hoped for. He died still trying. I, on the other hand, have survived. I lived on, and came to know a time when I was not at war. I have written this history of my life, and the last of my trials are over.

I hold in my hand an English poem, written by one who met Simón in Paris and is said to have named his boat *Bolívar*. When I consider the heroic men I have known, who have died in circumstances beneath what they deserved, I think of the truth of these lines, written while I was living in Lima:

> To do good to Mankind is the chivalrous plan,
> And is always nobly requited;
> Then battle for Freedom wherever you can,
> And, if not shot or hanged, you'll get knighted.
> (from STANZAS To Thomas Moore, by Lord Byron)

The fate of the emancipators of South America is a tragedy played on a stage far more vast than any Greek amphitheater. My friends Manuel Morales, Señor Quiroga, Carlos Montúfar of Quito, and the other early revolutionists in distant parts of the continent died no sooner than the sparks of liberty were ignited. Miranda, the precursor, was given over to his enemies to die alone and naked in a dungeon. Moreno, the priest of the Argentine revolution, found a grave in the ocean. Hidalgo, the first popular leader of Mexico, was executed as a criminal. Belgrano, the first champion of Argentine independence, who saved the revolution at Tucuman and Salta, died obscurely while civil war raged around him. O'Higgins, the hero of Chile, died in exile, as Carrera his rival had done before him. Iturbide, the real liberator of Mexico, fell a victim to his own ambition, causing him to be executed when he tried to return from abdication and exile. Sucre, the conqueror of Pichincha and Ayacucho, was murdered by his own people on a lonely road. San Martín died in self-imposed exile. Simón Bolívar, the greatest of them all, the liberator of half a continent, once the richest man in South America, died in exile, so poor that he had to be buried in a borrowed nightshirt.

Conceived by an earthquake, suckled on misery, and reared in an era when the entire world was at war, I have had to fight, throughout my life: for love, acceptance, freedom, and respect. All of these things I have both won and lost and won again in my life. A great deal of blood has been spilled on the soil of this continent, and my friends, my relatives, my companions, and my great love, one by one, have all died. Despite my lifelong suffering, I have managed to wage war against my enemies and nurture my friends. And now, at last, I have found serenity.

At one time, I felt I might end up like the old Indian woman who died with the word "soldiers" on her lips. Unlike, her, I refused to drift through life. I fought life. In most things, I achieved what I was after. Yet, when I felt her die in my arms, I feared that I too might die a lonely woman.

I had spent my life as a "soldier" and thought I might die at the hands of soldiers. Yet I have survived. I am loved by the people of this small community in which I live, and I love them. In truth, it is their generosity that has kept me fed these last years. I also have a "family" now that nurtures me, as I try to nurture them. Dominga and Mendoza have married, and they live in Amotaje. They are poor, but they will raise children who will know from where they came. Things are, after all, as they should be.

My fear that the old woman's death was an omen of what my future held was wrong. Even my wish that when I die I will be followed through town by all its inhabitants in a great funeral procession like La Perricholi, will not come to pass. My seemingly prophetic dream in Quito will turn out not to be prophecy. I know now, when my time comes, it will be a quiet affair, but I will be loved and friends will be nearby.

However, I intend to live many more years and I will enjoy the turmoil when the truths and revelations in this book come to the attention of our "leaders." While I no longer hold the hatred I had for my detractors, I will still enjoy seeing the petty minded, who make others suffer, brought down.

There was a time in my life when I would have relished seeing the evil or greedy come to justice because of my hatred for them. Now, I no longer hate—not even my enemies. I will enjoy justice being served because I love justice. I have lived long enough to understand my enemies, and, though I am determined to have them be seen for what they are, I refuse to set myself against other human beings in hatred.

We are all subject to the same weaknesses. Any hatred I hold will only keep me from fulfilling my destiny as a human being: to share this world with my brethren, a world we have all made, and to make it richer and more meaningful for everyone.

The one thing that I have longed for, from my early days and through all my trials, has always eluded me: peace. My life has been that of a soldier, but I was a warrior who could never seem to achieve the real fruit of victory. Yet now I have it, and I will not give it up in order to hate my enemies. I will love instead. I will most certainly love my friends—including all those I have lost to this life—even more.

I have been a lucky woman. Simón and I shared a great love and that made everything else worth the cost. I love him still, and, if it is possible, I will be with him one day.

The only other thing left for me to desire is to be remembered. Will I be remembered as a woman who lived through these hard times and who made a difference to the world in which she found herself? That, dear reader, is up to you.

My Story Ends

MANUELA

December 5, 1856
Paita, Perú

Dear Mr. Ruden,

My name is Antonio de la Guerrera, and I know that you do not know me, but I write at the request of a mutual friend: Manuela Sáenz. I fear it may take me some time to find a suitable address where I might send this letter to you. I beg your forgiveness if excessive time has passed between this sad moment and the time of your reading.

I have known this fine lady since that busy period after the battle of Quito. Now I must bring you sad news about her death. She has died of the "*bobbio*" that has ravaged the entire town of Paita.

I had heard that the Liberatress was living in poverty here. I was on my way back from Lima, on a mission for President Flores, and I made up my mind to see her when my ship stopped for water in this little seaport.

I found her as gracious and delightfully witty as the first time I met her back in 1822. Even though she could not move from the chair in which she sat, she remained a perfect hostess. Due to her inactivity, she had grown more corpulent than when I last knew her, but she still seemed to have all of the life, fire, and beauty she ever had. The one remarkable change I found in her was that she seemed not so volatile. She seemed to have found an inner harmony that I did not ever think she could possess.

I stayed with her a few days. When I finally decided to obtain passage on a ship, to continue my mission, I was told by the authorities that no ships would stop. While my friend and I had talked and reminisced those few days, a sailor, from another ship, had come ashore with a fever. People of the town feared he was contagious because two other men had contracted the same symptoms.

I went to explain my predicament to Manuela. She immediately sent her servant Juana Rosa out to gather more information. I sat and talked with Manuela for a half an hour or so and then Juana Rosa returned. The sailor had died, the two others were worse, and two more people had been reported with the same symptoms.

The manner of the sailor's death was appalling. His body temperature became very hot and his throat filled with a viscous phlegm on which he finally strangled. Each person who died did so in the same manner: choking, unable to breathe.

I was caught in the epidemic. Within days, many people had died and many had taken off over the desert to escape the contagion. As worried as I was for myself, I felt sorriest for Manuela, who could not move.

Those were days of true horror. Hourly there would be a funeral procession slowly moving down the street. By the end of November, there was no time for the delicacy of individual burials. A committee of masked sanitary workers came to the houses where death had struck and loaded the dead onto carts with other bodies. They were then taken to a common grave at the foot of the cliffs. Behind them there followed another worker who carried all of the victim's possessions into the street, which he summarily burned. There wasn't a day when the skies were not covered with thick black smoke and a pall of grief.

Manuela's old retainer, Juana Rosa, died. Manuela cried bitterly at her loss. What was worse, when I saw Juana Rosa being carried out to the cart I knew that Manuela had caught the disease.

When Manuela knew she would die, she told me that she had written a story of her life that she had entrusted to you to try to have published. Through coughs and the listlessness produced by the fever, she asked me to write to you and urge you, if you had not done so already, to please press for the publication of her story.

Four days later, on the twenty-third of November, the indomitable Manuela lived no more.

I tried to keep the authorities from treating this heroine of the revolution as they did the others, but to no avail. She was carried out to a cart and thrown on with the others who died that day. I followed behind, in a crowd of mourners also grieving for their loved ones, as the cart made its slow way to the communal grave. It seemed that the crowd was bigger that day, almost as if all of the inhabitants left in the entire plague-ridden town were following that little wobbly cart in a macabre funeral procession.

I said a silent prayer for her at the edge of the pit into which she was thrown and then hurried back to reclaim her possessions. I was too late.

Everything she owned from that rickety old house: furniture, bedclothes, pictures, books, papers, medals, and all of her mementos from bygone days were burning in a roaring fire. I could see the pages of books curl into blackness. I made out the title of *Don Quixote* on one. I watched as one of Manuela's embroidered handkerchiefs, with a blue M on it, turned to cinders. The very sand of the street seemed to be on fire. The atmosphere filled with black smoke. I was painfully aware and could see that burned to ashes, in amongst her effects, were the love letters that Manuela had accumulated since the battle of Quito—letters written by her and Simón Bolívar in their eight short years together.

I watched the fire burn down to gray ash. As the smoke dispersed, I could see one piece of paper, which had been partially burned, carried by the wind to some distance away from the fire. It finally rested in the sandy street.

I went over and picked it up. It was from Bolívar. I recognized the hand even though it was charred and I could barely make out the writing. I have enclosed it as a token of remembrance.

I could not contain my tears upon reading the lines and only now feel strong enough to communicate about this event. I have written to my wife today and now to you. I am sorry if you had other friends in Paita, as I cannot impart any news to you on their account. Now I must embark on a ship and leave this place. I will mail my letter to you in Ecuador.

May the lord keep you many years,

Antonio de la Guerrera

Mr. Melville:

I have kept that scrap of paper sent to me by General de la Guerrera. He was most kind to send it to me. I cherish it as an object connecting me to my friend, Manuela Sáenz. A copy of what is written on the paper is attached, translated to the best of my abilities.

Alexander Ruden

MANUELA

The memory of your enchantments dissolves the frost of my years. Your love revives a life that is expiring. I cannot live without you. I can see you always even though I am far away from you. Come. Come to me. Come now.

Notes

Truth is stranger than fiction, but it is because Fiction is obliged to stick to possibilities; Truth isn't.

Mark Twain

MANUELA is a novel. There are no anachronisms in my story, but still, it is not a history lesson or even a completely correct biography. Although I attempt historical accuracy, the purpose of my story is drama, not veracity.

Yet, if one can see past my particular slant on the rich character of Manuela Sáenz and the times in which she lived, one will find both history and biography. My story is quite accurate as to her whereabouts at the stated times and her involvement in historical events mentioned. She did live where I have said she did at the various times of her life depicted here. She also encountered all of the historical figures mentioned in my story and the dynamics of each relationship are as precise as my research can confirm. In many ways there is more truth than fiction in my tale, and what may seem like fantasy, because it seems too strange, is most likely truth after all.

For example: Manuela did meet Herman Melville in Paita because of the strife between the men and Captain Pease of the whaler *Acushnet*. She was also a friend to the American Consul to Peru, Alexander Ruden. When she was in Paita, the rest of South America did try to write her out of history, even though she was still remembered by those who loved her as "The Liberatress." The accounts I tell about the suppression of her memory by the theft of documents from Colombia's archives and the suppression of O'Leary's writings about Simón Bolívar are true.

Earlier in Manuela's life, men such as Morales, Quiroga, and Montúfar did exist. All the events connected with them and the abortive revolution of 1809 in Quito as recounted in my story, actually happened—except some particular scenes involving Manuela. We do know that it was the failed revolution that somehow precipitated Simón Sáenz leaving for Panamá. The fact that he was thought to be a revolutionary because of association with Morales and Quiroga is my invention. The story of Manuela being the one to steal the damaging papers that freed the conspirators from jail is also a product of my imagination. It is true that the papers were lost, but Manuela was surely not involved. However, it is said to be true about Manuela passing a flower to Montúfar while he stood waiting to be executed—but there was no Antonia there.

Manuela's parents were who I have said they were, but how they met is uncertain. One of the world's most destructive earthquakes did kill 40,000 people in Quito on February 4, 1797, the year of Manuela's birth. Also uncertain is who Joaquina

Aispuru's siblings were, what they were like, and why they opposed Manuela's gaining her inheritance so steadfastly. How and when Manuela's mother died is also uncertain.

Manuela did spend 10 years in the Convent of Santa Catalina in Quito. Santa Catalina is not quite as large as I have portrayed it. I have taken liberties and invested Santa Catalina with the attributes of some of the conventos grandes in Lima where convent life was much like I describe. However, the story that Doña Luisa tells Manuela about the convent riot at Santa Catalina is one that actually happened.

The role the Larreas played in Manuela's life is unsure. All that is known is that she was on their balcony when she threw a wreath that hit the Liberator in the forehead when he rode triumphantly into Quito. Also, the Larreas did host the victory ball where Manuela Sáenz met Simón Bolívar.

Manuela can occasionally be found in history books that are written about the man known as The Liberator. Often such accounts are no more than a paragraph or two. This, for perhaps the most significant relationship in the life of the great South American hero, is far too little. Usually she is said to be the wife of an English doctor. James Thorne was not a doctor, but as I have described him: a merchant who did business with the elite of Peruvian society and all over South America.

While in Lima, Manuela became friends with San Martín, his mistress Rosita Campusano, José de la Riva Agüero, members of Lautaro Lodge, and the other revolutionaries of the time. She acquired guns, money, uniforms, and other items for the cause. However, her most important contribution to South American liberty was in persuading the Numancia Battalion to change sides. She was able to accomplish this most significant feat because her beloved half-brother, José María, was in the battalion.

This transformation of the military situation very likely shifted the war decisively to the patriots in the fighting to liberate Lima. Such an important contribution to history is most often downplayed in narratives of the time or not credited to Manuela at all. This is, no doubt, because it was not performed by some important, military *man*.

How she accomplished this deed is unknown. It might have been as simple as asking her brother to speak to his officers over tea, or there might have been great danger involved, as I have written. No one really knows. Nevertheless, we do know that it was Manuela who seriously endeavored to change the affiliations of the Numancia Battalion. It was for this contribution to the cause of liberty that San Martín included her in his attempt at revolutionary "nobility": The Order of the Sun. If it had not been for Manuela, if in no other single act, history would have been different.

That she knew Manuel Amat, son of a former viceroy, is probable. Whether she had any relationship with him beyond acquaintance is entirely speculative. We do know that she was close to his mother, the woman known as La Perricholi, Micaela (Miquita) Villegas. This woman existed in Liman society until just before the fall of Lima and represented all that was life under the rule of the Viceroys. She is fictionalized in *The Bridge of San Luis Rey* and has appeared in other writings. However, I believe I have given the most accurate picture of her as any you will find.

Other facets of Liman society that I have included in my story, which were facts for Manuela when she lived, were the layout of the city and its landmarks (many of which have been destroyed by earthquakes since then) and other elements such as the existence of the *tapadas* and the *cofradias*. The *cofradias*, (slave organizations) did exist in Lima when Manuela lived there as did Mamma Rosa, "Queen of the Mandingos."

Some characters are entirely fictional, as are the events surrounding them. They are Juanita (both Joaquina's friend and Manuela's nurse), the "crazy priest," Father

Ramón, the Aispuru servants, Antonia, Doña Esclara, Beatríz, Carmen and her daughter, the old Indian and his wife, Carlson, El Árabe, the sailor with the scar (Manuela never went to the Galápagos), the Captain (there must have been some master on the ship to Panamá but nothing is known about him), Paulo (the worker in Panamá), Juan Romero in Panamá, Juan Guzmán, Captain Valdéz (who escorted her to Quito in 1822, although lancers did escort her on that journey), Jorge (the Larrea servant), and the old man wounded in the riot in Quito.

The following characters are true but have been embellished to my purpose:

Señor Quiroga did have a wife and two children. We know nothing about them except that his children died in front of him before he too was killed in the massacre in Quito.

Jonotás and Natán joined Manuela in Panamá and were lost somehow by the time she reached Ecuador on her return from Jamaica. Jonotás was more likely from Barbados than Jamaica, and it is not known where Natán grew up. Their personalities and abilities are accurate to the best of my research. How they died is uncertain. All that is known is that they were loyal friends who adored Manuela. They remained with her, and helped her in everything she did, from Panamá until she left Colombia in exile.

There was a man in the Callao fortress, named Falucho, who refused to fight for Spain and was killed. Jonotás did have a lover in Callao at the same time. There is no indication they were the same man. Another of Jonotás's lovers, Crofston, in Colombia, is real. In fact, all of the events written about Bogotá happened very nearly as I described them thanks to the memoirs of Jean Baptiste Boussingault. Jonotás always gained notoriety wherever Manuela went because of her outrageous character and her abilities as a mime.

Manuela did live with a woman named Juana Rosa and a pair of homeless waifs, named Dominga and Mendoza, after leaving Colombia. We know nothing of how they came to be together.

Rodríguez, Bolívar's tutor, who truly walked the Monte Sacro with him, is a real character. He spent many happy hours with Manuela towards the end of their lives.

Fausto D'Elhuyar was truly the son (and nephew) of the scientists who invented tungsten. However, all the events after Manuela left Quito at 17 are fictional.

Manuela died of diphtheria in Paita and was buried in a mass grave as I have described. All of her belongings were burned, including the love letters between her and Bolívar. This was reported in a letter by Antonio De La Guerrera, to his wife, but not to Alexander Ruden.

All other characters and events, as fantastic as they may sometimes seem, were part of the life of the woman who was the lover and companion of Simón Bolívar—a brave, beautiful, capable, South American heroine. The world does not often see her mettle in man or woman.

Gregory Kauffman began his writing career by winning a national poetry contest while still in school. After earning a Master's Degree in Theatre, he worked as a theatre educator. He has spent most of his career as a theatre director working with playwrights in developing new scripts.

Of his own work, he has had three original plays produced. His produced film and television writing includes two television commercials and four short films. In addition to having written science fiction short stories, he has done many film reviews and film essays for local newspapers in Seattle, where he lives.

After finishing a draft for a screenplay about Manuela Sáenz, he began research to novelize the story. Years of meticulous research into life in the Spanish colonies have gone into the creation of a historically accurate novel about one of South America's most intriguing heroines.